GOTREK & MALENETH
— THE OMNIBUS —

WARHAMMER
AGE OF SIGMAR

Other great stories from Warhammer Age of Sigmar

GOTREK & MALENETH
— THE OMNIBUS —
Darius Hinks & Robbie MacNiven

BLACK LIBRARY

A BLACK LIBRARY PUBLICATION

The Bone Desert first published in 2018.
'The Neverspike' first published in
Black Library Events Anthology 2018/19 in 2018.
Ghoulslayer first published in 2019.
'The Dead Hours' and 'Death on the Road to Svardheim' first
published digitally in 2020.
Gitslayer first published in 2021.
'The Crown of Karak-Khazhar' first published digitally in 2023.
Soulslayer first published in 2022.
This edition published in Great Britain in 2025 by
Black Library, Games Workshop Ltd., Willow Road,
Nottingham, NG7 2WS, UK.

Represented by: Games Workshop Limited – Irish branch,
Unit 3, Lower Liffey Street, Dublin 1,
D01 K199, Ireland.

10 9 8 7 6 5 4 3 2 1

Produced by Games Workshop in Nottingham.
Cover illustration by Saeed Ramez.

A CIP record for this book is available from the British Library.

ISBN 13: 978-1-80407-966-9

See Black Library on the internet at

blacklibrary.com

Find out more about Games Workshop
and the worlds of Warhammer at

warhammer.com

Printed and bound in the UK.

The Mortal Realms have been despoiled. Ravaged by the followers of the Chaos Gods, they stand on the brink of utter destruction.

The fortress-cities of Sigmar are islands of light in a sea of darkness. Constantly besieged, their walls are assailed by maniacal hordes and monstrous beasts. The bones of good men are littered thick outside the gates. These bulwarks of Order are embattled within as well as without, for the lure of Chaos beguiles the citizens with promises of power.

Still the champions of Order fight on. At the break of dawn, the Crusader's Bell rings and a new expedition departs. Storm-forged knights march shoulder to shoulder with resolute militia, stoic duardin and slender aelves. Bedecked in the splendour of war, the Dawnbringer Crusades venture out to found civilisations anew. These grim pioneers take with them the fires of hope. Yet they go forth into a hellish wasteland.

Out in the wilds, hardy trailblazers restore order to a crumbling world. Haunted eyes scan the horizon for tyrannical reavers as they build upon the bones of ancient empires, eking out a meagre existence from cursed soil and ice-cold seas. By their valour, the fate of the Mortal Realms will be decided.

The ravening terrors that prey upon these settlers take a thousand forms. Cannibal barbarians and deranged murderers crawl from hidden lairs. Martial hosts clad in black steel march from skull-strewn castles. The savage hordes of Destruction batter the frontier towns until no stone stands atop another. In the dead of night come howling throngs of the undead, hungry to feast upon the living.

Against such foes, courage is the truest defence and the most effective weapon. It is something that Sigmar's chosen do not lack. But they are not always strong enough to prevail, and even in victory, each new battle saps their souls a little more.

This is the time of turmoil. This is the era of war.

This is the Age of Sigmar.

CONTENTS

THE BONE DESERT

ROBBIE MacNIVEN

PROLOGUE

Hazim's Parlour was closing early. Hazim himself, rarely seen in the *hasham* den, emerged not long after nightfall with two of his burly Karami bodyguards. They started ushering the patrons out, regardless of how delirious or inebriated they were. Those who tried to resist were forcibly ejected. The regulars went quietly. Even affected by the den's opiates, they weren't going to argue with Hazim. Not tonight. Not when the normally unflappable hasham seller was so obviously afraid.

The parlour's front doors and windows were boarded, but business continued unseen. The rear rooms had been commandeered, bought for a price that Hazim hoped he was never offered again. He withdrew to his private chambers without dismissing the two Karami, and barricaded the door for the rest of the night.

His new clients were not the sort of people he wished to spend the nighttime hours with.

'Barkash?' asked one of them. The parlour's rear room was supposed to be kept for only the wealthiest of clients, but the new edicts by the city's ruling council had brought hard times on downtown business. The chamber was now mostly given over to storage space, the walls stacked with sacks of unfiltered hasham leaf and the various other contraband goods Hazim's criminal network had acquired over the years – silk from Merport, counterfeit coins forged by renegades from the Jelali banker guild, grain stock being held for merchants wishing to avoid the city's market tithes. The air, lit by a single tallow candle set on a small table at the room's centre, was dark and heavy with dust.

'Yes,' came the answer to the question. 'The target is expected to arrive there within the next three days. How long they will stay, I do not know, but I doubt they will wish to linger.'

'And beyond Barkash?' the original speaker asked. He was a Kharadron, clad in the bulky silver armour plates and rubbery sky-suit worn by the airborne duardin reivers, his face obscured by a grim, gold-etched ancestor mask. There was another of his kin beside him, a heavy blunderbuss slung casually over one shoulder.

'Now, that, I do not know,' answered the voice, lost in the shadows at the far end of the room. 'But it is likely Khaled-Tush, and from there the Eight Pillars, or the Temple of the Lightning.'

A murmur ran through the assembled group. Besides the Kharadrons there were four others present in the back room. Two were human females, dark-haired and black-eyed, clad in the shimmering, multi-hued silkweave and pearl strings of traditional tribal dancers of the Alharab. The third stood apart from the others, wearing a heavy cloak, its species and gender unknowable behind cowl and veil.

'And you wish the target dead?' one of the two Alharabi dancers asked. 'Not taken?'

'Dead,' the voice hissed. 'Plus proof of its demise, by whatever means you can procure.'

Silence followed, disturbed only by the clawing and scratching sounds of the rats that seemed to infest the hasham den.

'Full payment only to the group that makes the kill?' the Kharadron asked eventually.

'That is correct, duardin.'

'Then what are we waiting for?' the duardin growled, nodding his kinsman towards the door.

The assassins left, the Kharadrons first, followed by the Alharabi. The cloaked figure went next, saying nothing. Only after they were all long gone did the being in the shadows stir and depart, melding instantly with the refuse-stinking darkness in the crumbling alleyways outside.

It was a long time before Hazim dared check the back room and bar its open door.

CHAPTER ONE

'How much further?'

Gotrek's growl ended the last hope Maleneth had of sleeping. She opened one eye to look at her companion, but the sunburned duardin hadn't been speaking to her. He'd been addressing their guide.

'A half-day's journey yet, *sellah*,' Aziz replied, glancing back nervously from his perch atop the front of the wagon. The scrawny young merchant had chattered incessantly when their journey had first begun, his words clearly driven by the anxiety he felt at being in the presence of the cantankerous red-crested duardin warrior. Gotrek's surliness had quickly drained him of words, though.

'You spat those lies half a day ago, manling,' Gotrek snarled. Aziz cringed, and Maleneth grimaced. The duardin's perpetual ill mood was becoming infectious.

'The temple inscriptions have been there for the better part of an age, Gotrek Gurnisson,' Maleneth responded over Aziz's stammered apologies. 'I doubt one turning of day to night will alter that.'

She closed her eyes again, trying to ignore the incessant rocking motion of the wagon, the sack of meal grinding her back, the infernal heat cooking her tight-bound leathers. She tried to ignore existence itself, but to no avail. Silently, she cursed everything – the heat, the journey, the sleeplessness. Most of all, she cursed Gotrek Gurnisson, the greatest monster-slayer of a dead age and the being – some said demigod – that Maleneth was murder-sworn to protect.

As though the mad red-crested Doomseeker needed protecting.

'Will there be any dwarfs at our destination?' she heard him ask. She could tell from the pained silence which followed that Aziz was struggling with the question.

'Will there be... *duardin*, at the outpost,' Gotrek rephrased, pronouncing the name of his own race with painful hesitancy.

'Duardin at Khaled-Tush, why yes, sellah!' Aziz said eagerly, grasping on to any perceived good news he could offer his ill-tempered companion. 'It is the beginning of the Golden Season, when the master smiths of the Great Karagi will ply their wares to the tribes up and down the trails. Some of their retainers will likely already be setting up at Khaled-Tush.'

Gotrek spat on the golden sand. The gobbet sizzled. 'Then when we arrive, you be sure to keep me and my axe away from them,' Gotrek said. Aziz lapsed back into silence, clearly unwilling to enquire what dark deed had left the lone duardin estranged from his kindred. Maleneth knew well enough – in the months since Gotrek had hammered the Master Rune into his flesh and bonded with its power, his name had surged from one duardin hold to another. Some warriors of the Fyreslayer lodges believed him Grimnir reforged, their shattered god made whole once again. It hadn't been long before Gotrek had found the genuflecting too much to bear. He'd sent them all away, made them swear oaths not to follow him. All except Maleneth.

That had surprised her. She had been preparing for the day when Gotrek would demand they part company, rehearsing her own arguments. Speaking in terms that a duardin would understand, she was oathsworn to protect the Master Rune, even if it was currently hammered into a mad Doomseeker's heart. She could not leave an item so precious to the Order of the Azyr unguarded, and thus she could not leave Gotrek.

But God of Murder, she wished she could.

Focus, Witchblade, whispered the voice of Maleneth's former mistress, bound to the blood vial she wore around her neck. *Now is not the time to let the heat take you.*

She opened both eyes to regard the Slayer and the rune on his breast. Forged in the grim likeness of the god Grimnir, it blazed with a deep golden lustre, as though drinking in the heat of the desert. The same could not be said for the rest of Gotrek's body. His exposed arms and torso were burned red raw from Hysh's unyielding light, his swirling tattoos almost lost amidst the flaking skin. Yet he showed no discomfort in the heat, even though she was certain she could see blisters forming on his inflamed skin. She had told him to at least don a cloak, had even offered her own, but he'd ignored her. According to the Slayer, fancy cloaks and clothing were for *umgi*, not dwarfs.

The duardin shifted. He had noticed Maleneth's attention. His single eye moved from the fyrestorm greataxe slung across his lap, and she found herself dropping her gaze before it met her own. That was a feeling she had rarely experienced since leaving the Murder Temples. There was something about his one remaining eye – more than grim resolve, more than stony determination, a fire that seemed able to burn bare the very thoughts of those it touched. It was the eye of a being that had witnessed a great deal more than it should have. The eye that, for all the private scorn she held for such a view, could well have belonged to a deity not of the Mortal Realms.

'Drink, aelf.'

It was a statement, not a question. Maleneth realised Gotrek was holding out a water skin. She reached over the meal sacks that separated them in the back of the wagon, and took it.

She hadn't realised how thirsty she was. Dehydration was just one of the desert's thousand dangers. To live in such places was to defy the odds. Here in the Bone Desert especially, nothing lived beyond the wagon's flank, bar the shaven tusker that was dragging it. All was a sea of undulating, bleached yellow dunes, punctuated only by the skeletal remains of vast beasts. Some said those carcasses were what gave the desert its name. Others claimed the sand itself was bone-dust, blown fine as powder from the realm of the slaughter-god on a burning furnace wind.

It didn't do well to ponder such things. Maleneth had begun the journey with just one hope – that they would use the opportunity to stop at the outpost maintained by the Order of the Azyr deep in the desert's heart, close to the monument city known as the Eight Pillars. Gotrek had already brushed the suggestion off. His destination was the Pillars themselves, driven by the rumoured presence of an inscription detailing the location of the Axe of Grimnir within the ancient ruins. An axe the duardin claimed was once his while the dead world lived.

'Finish it,' she said, tossing the half-empty water skin back to Gotrek. The Slayer let it land in his lap without catching it. Maleneth fought the urge to snap at him.

Aziz had sworn to take them as far as Khaled-Tush, the oasis settlement a day's journey from the Pillars. They had found him in the market at Barkash, a young tusker pack driver and teamster who shifted trade stock along the desert trails for one of the local merchant cartels. A single gold coin from Gotrek had been more than enough to allay his reservations. Now, three and a half days since Barkash's fertile river basin had given way to the desolation of the endless sand dunes, Maleneth was beginning to consider riding ahead once they reached Khaled-Tush and bringing the servants of the Order of the Azyr directly to Gotrek. The Master Rune had to be examined and Gotrek's true abilities assessed. If even half the rumours already spawned about him were true, he was too valuable and too dangerous simply to be wandering the Mortal Realms.

She didn't relish the thought of telling him that.

You are afraid of the duardin, hissed Maleneth's mistress, the disembodied echo-voice slipping into her thoughts. *No true child of Khaine would hesitate because of that brutish race.*

'I would like nothing more than to see if this Khainite could rip out your heart, mistress,' she muttered darkly. 'If only you still had one.'

There was no response from the blood vial around her neck, and she tried to put her mind elsewhere. The wagon lurched uncomfortably. Anywhere that wasn't coarse and burning hot. The lurch came again, and the tusker hauling the wagon let out a bellow.

'What is happening?' she demanded, pulling back her hood and rising onto her knees to look ahead. They had entered a shallow depression between two dunes, following the line of Hysh-bleached wooden stakes that marked out the route in the event of a sandstorm. They trailed away over the next rise directly ahead, but the tusker seemed to be struggling.

'*Esha, esha!*' Aziz was snapping at the beast, poking its stubbly rear with his goad. '*Maliki esha!*'

'It's trapped in the sand,' Maleneth said as the tusker let out another fearful bellow. 'We are sinking.'

'But the posts,' Aziz said. 'We are still on the correct route, sellah. This cannot be the dragging sands!'

'Well, clearly this route is the wrong one,' Maleneth snapped. 'Gotrek, get up. We must abandon this wagon. Now.'

The duardin had strapped his axe across his back and was leaning over his side of the wagon, peering at the sand around them. The wheels were already half-submerged, and the tusker was now floundering visibly.

'The dunes must be stable,' Maleneth said. 'Grab the water skins, and jump.'

'We cannot leave the produce!' Aziz said, scrambling into the back of the wagon with Maleneth and Gotrek and trying to heft the meal sacks. 'I cannot lose them! They will beat me if I fail to bring them even one less than I am signed for!'

'You'll be delivering them straight to Shyish and the God of Death himself if you stay,' Gotrek snapped, grabbing a pack and the two nearest water skins and tying them around his waist. Even now, it still sounded strange to hear him trying to pronounce the names of the Eight Realms.

'Gotrek, the boy first,' Maleneth said.

'Hold still, manling,' Gotrek grunted, and grabbed Aziz around his skinny waist. The pack driver struggled, then let out a terrified wail as Gotrek braced himself on the wagon's side, and flung him. Aziz thumped into the sand on the bottom of the dune to the right of the trail, rolled with surprising dexterity and stared back at the wagon. He didn't sink.

'Go, you oaf,' Maleneth said to Gotrek. The timber around them was beginning to creak and groan at the pressure exerted on it, and the tusker was going wild, lowing and goring the yielding ground beneath it. Gotrek scowled at Maleneth for a moment, then mounted the wagon's side and, with a bellow of exertion, flung himself. The rune on his chest burned brighter than ever, and he cleared far more ground than Maleneth had expected. He slammed into the sand half a dozen feet short of Aziz.

And began to sink.

'Khaine's bloodied blades,' Maleneth swore. She leapt. Lithe as a feline, she landed in a crouch next to Aziz. Without missing a breath, she turned and slid the belt from around her waist. Gotrek was already half-gone, sinking like a lodestone. He let out a roar that eclipsed even that of the tusker, clawing in vain for firm ground, seemingly more angry than panicked. Maleneth darted forward until she felt the yielding sand begin to drag at her feet. She knelt a pace back, and flung the belt out towards the duardin.

'Is that all you have?' Gotrek bellowed as the strip of aelf-cured hide reached him.

Maleneth smiled. 'Take it or drown. It matters not to me. I can always recover your corpse and dig the Master Rune from you cold flesh.'

Gotrek snatched the end. Maleneth stood, dug her feet into the sand as best she could, wrapped the belt's end around both fists and began to pull. It was like trying to drag a Khainite sacrificial slab single-handedly.

You should leave him, her mistress hissed. *He is a mad fool.*

'Help me,' Maleneth snarled at Aziz, then realised he was no longer at her side. The teamster was sprinting along the bottom of the dune, headed away from them.

'I will seek help!' he yelled back at her.

'There's no time, you fool,' Maleneth barked after him, but to no avail. He kept going.

She cursed the boy's cowardice, every muscle straining as she leaned back. The belt was taut and quivering, but she was certain it would hold. She had strangled the life from enough people with it to be sure.

Gotrek's downward motion was arrested and, with agonising slowness, reversed. He began to rise up out of the dragging sands and, with a last roar of effort, dug his fists into the edge of the firm ground and hauled himself from the mire like some primordial earth-god returning to the Mortal Realms. Maleneth collapsed backwards, panting.

Behind them, the tusker was gone. The two stood and watched in silence as the rear of the wagon, upended now, was dragged under inch by slow, creaking inch. Eventually there was a final sucking sound and the whole thing was gone. The sand lay silent and undisturbed, as though the wagon and its tusker had never existed.

'We must leave, Gotrek, son of Gurni,' Maleneth said. 'If we wish to reach Khaled-Tush before nightfall.'

'What happened to the beardling?'

'He ran,' Maleneth replied. 'He probably thought you were going to eat him for leading you astray.'

'Better than stabbing him in the back, aelf.'

'Only in your deranged imagination am I forever murdering those who are trying to help me, Gotrek.'

Gotrek levelled an axe at her. 'I saw enough of your kind's treachery in the world before.'

'The world before is dead,' Maleneth hissed, rounding on him. 'And it pains me that you did not die with it.'

He didn't offer a retort, and she assumed he was struggling to master his anger at having to be saved from so ignominious an end as the dragging sands. When she caught his gaze, though, she realised his focus was elsewhere.

There was a figure atop the dune behind them. It was little more than a silhouette, dark against the cloudless blue of the heavens. She saw it only for a second before it disappeared back beyond the rise, clearly sensing their attention.

'What was that?' she asked.

'I know not, aelf. But they have been following us since we left the city.'

'Since Barkash?' Maleneth snarled. 'Why didn't you say something, you foolish dolt? Do you not think it's even slightly relevant that there is someone hunting us?'

Gotrek shrugged. 'They were keeping well back – we couldn't have caught them unless we laid up some sort of ambush, and I'm in no mind to linger in this place when I have my axe to find. Besides, they were mounted, meaning they weren't the Grey Lord's vermin.'

'They are not skaven, so you do not think they are relevant?' Maleneth demanded. 'And just what if they are being recompensed by him?'

Her words were only an attempt to mask her anger. She hadn't seen the figure before, and she had never known a duardin to be more attentive to his surroundings than her. Then again, she had never known a duardin like Gotrek Gurnisson.

'Let us move, as the day is wearing thin,' she said, then realised Gotrek had already begun to stomp off. She rolled her eyes, bound her belt around her waist and followed.

CHAPTER TWO

They walked. The heat raged against them like a physical force, a beast that sought to bear them down into the shifting sands. They followed the tops of the dunes running parallel with the trail markers. Maleneth didn't trust them not to end in the dragging sands once more, but they were the only apparent clear route to Khaled-Tush.

They hadn't gone far before they stumbled across the last thing Maleneth had expected to find in the desert – water. In a cleft between two dunes they discovered a timber trough, its bottom full. Next to it was what looked like a hitching post, the rope tied around it lying abandoned in the sand.

'A waypoint for message riders?' she wondered out loud. Gotrek said nothing. They filled up the water skins and carried on, the shadows cast by the dunes starting to stretch.

They reached Khaled-Tush just as the bone-chill of deep night was beginning to creep over them. Chamon and Ghyran were ascendant overhead, soaring half-lit spheres amidst the constellations spread across the ink-spill of the aetheric void. The lights above were mirrored by the lights below, a thousand campfires creating a flickering firmament surrounding the mirror sheen of the great oasis of the Khaled.

The trading post's veiled guards intercepted them as they approached the outer wagons, peering at the strange travellers by the light of raised torches. One of Gotrek's coins saw them safely through.

Ahead, Khaled-Tush sprawled, a great encampment of desert traders, tribespeople and travellers. What had once been little more than a watering hole for those moving between the cities of Barkash, Hedina and Merport had become a settlement in its own right. Ranks of wagons, carts and covered caravans surrounded wooden structures constructed from the trees that clustered around the banks of the oasis – counting houses and taverns, brothels and guard posts, the heart of an ever-expanding trade hub on a route made rich by the astute ruling councils of the Triumvirate Cities, and the wares of the duardin known by the desert peoples as the Great Karagi.

'I didn't think I could find a more miserable *kruk* of a place than the Unbak lodge,' Gotrek grumbled as they halted on the edge of an opening between the circled wagons. 'But it seems this mannish age knows how to disappoint.'

Ahead of them lay a dirt square formed between the idle caravans and a row of ramshackle buildings. Despite the lateness of the hour, it was bustling with trader stalls, haggling booths and merchants selling wares from the backs of their carts. The cool night air was thick with the aromas of spices and perfumes, and lit by the light of braziers and firepits.

'We trek for half a day through blistering desert, with no food and little water, yet the sight of this place dulls your spirits?' Maleneth demanded. 'Hysh must have cooked whatever remains of your addled brains, duardin.'

'I'd wager they'd still be more filling than whatever this place has to offer,' Gotrek muttered.

'We require fresh food and water,' Maleneth said, forcing herself to ignore the Slayer's retort. 'And a place to rest. Tomorrow we can start looking for someone to give us passage to the Eight Pillars.'

'*Thagi*,' Gotrek spat. Maleneth assumed the duardin insult had been directed at her, and was instinctively forming a Khainite curse back when she noticed Gotrek was moving off into the crowd. She started after him, realising what he had seen.

Aziz tried to run. The crowd around him hemmed him in though, and he squealed with terror as Gotrek snatched him with one scarred fist.

'Thought you'd seen the last of us, beardless *thaggaz*,' the duardin barked.

'Please no, sellah,' Aziz wailed, cringing back. 'I went to get help, I swear!'

'Then where was it?' Maleneth demanded, reaching Gotrek's side.

'There were riders,' Aziz insisted, eyes darting between the aelf and the duardin. 'Three riders, I told them you would pay them well if they could reach you.'

'Liar,' Gotrek snarled, and for a second Maleneth though he was going to strike the youth.

'I can still help you,' Aziz yelped. 'Please, sellah, I know many traders here at Khaled-Tush!'

'We need food,' Gotrek growled. 'And shelter for the night, then transport to the Eight Pillars.'

'I can bring you all of those things, sellah,' Aziz insisted. 'My uncle, Fazeel, is a moonfin trader posted here. He will not turn me away.'

'You are thinking about running,' Maleneth said, her voice lower and altogether more chilling than Gotrek's. 'I know your kind, desert rat. Do not do it. Go to your uncle, and when everything is arranged, return here and find us. Or I will find you and I will skin you, slowly, using these.'

She tapped the long fyresteel knives in her belt. 'Do you doubt me?'

'N-no,' Aziz stammered, tears in his eyes. Gotrek released him, and he stumbled away into the press.

Gotrek harrumphed. 'We will never see him again,' the duardin grumbled.

'We will,' Maleneth replied. 'He is but a boy. He is terrified we will use our mystical powers, or blades, to hunt him down.'

'Aelf nonsense,' Gotrek said. 'You don't know the first thing about mystical. The gods themselves have tried to betray me, slay me even. I have broken daemons and fought deranged wizards and slain beasts and monsters that would tear apart legions of your gold-armoured champions. I have fallen from the skies amidst fire and battled through the depths of the earth for days at a time. I have been flung into an ocean of madness and filth and then clawed my way back out. The boy knows nothing of fear, because these realms know nothing of it. I spit on your idea of fear.'

Maleneth leant against the wheel of the nearest wagon. Exhaustion was trying to drag her down. The pack on her back felt like a lodestone. A part of her just wanted to curl up beneath the closest cart and sleep.

It took her a few seconds to realise that Gotrek was no longer beside her.

'Duardin,' she snapped as he headed off deeper into the square. He didn't stop or turn. Cursing, she followed him.

'Do your kind never rest?' she demanded as she caught up.

'Rest is something for people without anything to do,' Gotrek said, not looking at her. 'Rest comes when you find your doom. I have never known rest. Sometimes I wonder whether I ever will.'

The marketplace embraced them. They passed a row of stalls selling Hedina silks, the traders calling for their attention, then had to brush aside the advances of a Hilathi tribal spice-seller offering samples. The aroma of cooking meat drifted over them as they passed a half-tusker being slow-roasted in one of the firepits, and Maleneth's aching stomach lurched. A little further on they had to move aside for a sect of white-veiled Shez-pah priests swinging sweet-smelling censers. None spared either of them a glance. At Khaled-Tush, a weary aelf and a sunburned duardin were hardly the strangest sights on show.

They moved on, deeper into the busy menagerie, the market and its inhabitants pressing in on every side. Maleneth found herself fingering the hilt of one of her daggers, the compulsive motion concealed by her cloak. She didn't like crowds.

Gotrek seemed unperturbed. She didn't demand he tell her what he was looking for. She knew he'd give no clear answer. In the months since they had first met, she had grown accustomed to his sudden bouts of melancholy, to his distant gaze and to the unexplained interludes where he would stomp off on his own. Sometimes she left him to do so, trusting he would always return, but occasionally she would follow him. It always seemed as though he were looking for something or someone, though exactly what or who she was never quite sure.

She felt something bump into her shoulder, the pressure a little more than the mere passing of bodies in the teeming space. Her fyresteel knives were out in a flash, faster than the eye could follow, every one of her aelf senses poised to kill before conscious thought had even engaged.

She found herself looking into a pair of dark eyes. To her surprise, there was neither fear nor anger in them, only a reserved, knowing amusement.

'*Shemali, sellah,*' said the woman, taking her hand off Maleneth's shoulder. She was human, young but almost as tall as the aelf, dusky-skinned and clad in gossamer folds of pink and purple silk. Maleneth realised she was smiling. She took the knife away from her throat.

'My apologies, travellers,' she went on, offering a curtsey. 'I have been sent by the mistress of my troupe.'

Her eyes travelled from Maleneth to Gotrek. The duardin had stopped his progress through the market, and one scarred fist was clenched firmly around the haft of his fyrestorm greataxe.

'The Fyreslayer with only one rune hammered into his flesh,' the woman said, her smile dissipating as she addressed him. 'We possess something of great value to you, Runetamer. A man who has seen the words you seek.'

'Who are you?' Gotrek growled. 'You look too much like another damned aelf to me!'

'We are dancers of the Alharab,' the woman said, giving the duardin an elegant bow and producing a slip of paper between two fingers with a flourish. 'We see much, and hear even more, especially in a place like this. The man my troupe has made contact with is not the only one to have gazed upon the riddle of the Eight Pillars. My mistress, Shaldeen, awaits your pleasure at the black top.'

'And why would we trust you, or your mistress?' Gotrek demanded. He reached for the paper, but Maleneth snatched it first.

'I am only a messenger,' the woman said, beginning to move away through the crowd. 'That is not for me to say.'

'Not much of a message, is it,' Gotrek growled after her, but she was gone. Maleneth laid a hand on his shoulder. She had glanced down at the parchment – it was an invitation in native Alharabi script, inviting weary travellers to the night-time performance of the Seventeen Blades. Maleneth tensed. The Seventeen Blades was a traditional aelf dance, still popular among the Murder Temples. She had rarely heard of a human troupe performing it.

You remember the last time you saw it danced, don't you, Witchblade?

'What is it?' Gotrek demanded.

'Nothing,' Maleneth said, shrugging off the voice of her former mistress. 'We should not follow her. It is some sort of trap.'

'If it is, then it's about time. Almost a day has passed since the last one,' Gotrek rumbled, shrugging off Maleneth's hand. 'I want answers, and I'll have them whether they want me dead or not.'

'If only you held your own life as dearly as the Order of the Azyr does,' Maleneth snapped.

'I lost it a long time ago, aelf. If this is another plot by the Grey Lord, I will slaughter his verminous *griks*. I always do. More so than any fool or coward in the World-that-Was, the rat Thanquol was determined to fulfil my doom oath. I should have known he'd follow me into a new reality.'

'If you don't care about your own life then at least consider the rune,' Maleneth said, struggling to keep her exhaustion-stoked temper in check. 'More than anyone else, you must be aware of its power. It cannot be allowed to fall into the hands of servants of disorder and darkness. Or do you think I have been following you merely for your good company?'

'It'll be hard for the rats to get their hands on it as long as it's here,' Gotrek replied, thumping a fist against the Master Rune on his chest.

'For one moment, stop to consider the consequences of your actions,' Maleneth raged, her anger finally getting the better of her. 'At least one unknown being is tracking us, presumably the same one who shifted the trail markers and nearly succeeded in drowning us in dragging sand. That is not to speak of the ratmen assassins that have been hunting you, three in the last month alone. Whatever these dancers have for us, it is almost certainly a trap.'

Gotrek glared at her, and she noticed the grim-faced rune stamped into his skin glow a little more brightly.

'I told you, dark aelf, the vermin have been trying to stab me in the back for as long as I can remember,' the duardin replied, pointedly ignoring her last words. 'If you don't like rats, you should stop following me. The mad one, Thanquol, will never stop hunting me. From what I've seen of these accursed realms, he'll probably return even after I've put an axe through his horned skull.'

'You think because you have lived this long that you are immortal,' Maleneth said, taking a step towards the duardin and pointing down at him. 'You think you are a god–'

'Do not insult me more than you already have, wretch,' Gotrek barked. 'You know nothing of the gods. I have seen foolishness and craven treachery among mortals, but none to match that of the divine. I have met many thousands of dwarfs worthier and more honourable than Grimnir alone!'

'Regardless, you will not live forever, Gotrek of the World-that-Was. I serve a true god, the Bloody-Handed one, Khaine, Prince of Murder, and if there is one thing my devotion has taught me it is that all beings die. Even gods. Guard your own life, duardin, for there are many eager to steal it from you.'

The commotion of the market around her had stilled.

You are attracting attention, Witchblade, hissed her mistress' voice. *Sometimes I wonder whether you were ever my student.*

'I knew your god in that long-dead age,' Gotrek growled, his eye flaring like the stoked embers of a forge pit. 'His servants there were just as weak and pathetic as they are here. I fear nothing, dark aelf, least of all your threats.'

Before she could reply, Maleneth felt a presence intruding from her left. She half turned, lightning fast, barely resisting the murderous urge to lash out with her blades.

Aziz cringed back and yelped with fear. He had returned.

'I've been looking for you, sellah,' he stammered. 'My uncle, he has agreed to let you stay under his roof tonight. But...'

He trailed off, and Maleneth realised he was looking at the writing on the slip of paper she still held in one hand.

'The dancers of the Alharab,' she said, holding the note before his eyes. 'You know of them?' Aziz hesitated before responding.

'Yes, sellah. You will not find many here who have not. They perform for the councils and guilder lords of the Triumvirate Cities. I have never heard of their troupe visiting a place like Khaled-Tush to dance before.'

'And?'

Aziz shook his head, clearly reluctant to continue. 'They say that the daughters of the Alharab are spies, that they buy and sell knowledge to those who pay for their performances. Their dances are not merely for the entertainment of onlookers.'

'See!' Maleneth snapped, turning back to Gotrek. 'It's a trap.' But the duardin was already pushing away through the market once more.

'I'm going to watch the dancing,' he barked back over his shoulder. 'Don't you aelves love that kind of thing?'

Maleneth closed her eyes and bit her lip, forcing herself not to spit a string of Khainite curses in the Slayer's wake.

'My uncle,' Aziz said slowly, edging away from the aelf. 'He is expecting us. It would be a disgrace to turn away his hospitality now. Please, sellah, bring the angry duardin back. The Alharabi will surely not have anything that he needs. They sell only lies and secrets.'

'Go back to your uncle,' Maleneth ordered. 'Apologise for us, and try to save us some food. We will return as soon as we are able.'

Before Aziz could protest, she picked one of Gotrek's coins from the pouch around her waist and pressed it into his palm. Then she was gone, slipping through the crowds after the Slayer.

CHAPTER THREE

The black top was a tented pavilion sited on the banks of the great oasis, beneath the shade of spreading palms and poplar trees. The oasis itself was unlike any Maleneth had seen in the Bone Desert – its water was not bound by the dry earth, but floated gently in a thousand liquid spheres ranging from a few feet or so off the ground to nearly a hundred yards overhead, far above the tops of the surrounding trees. Occasionally one of the slowly swirling globes would break apart and come pattering down in a shower of water, drenching the moist oasis bed, while others would slowly come together amidst a fresh spray.

The black top's flanks were glistening from such collisions. The great tent was removed from much of the rest of Khaled-Tush, and Maleneth felt her senses becoming increasingly on edge as Gotrek's route led them away from the braziers and torches and ceaseless activity of the caravan market and into the darkness. The night was still, the lapping of the oasis spheres against one another and the rustle of the trees overhead providing a disconcerting change to the bustle they had left behind.

As Maleneth drew closer to the pavilion the sounds of the night faded, overtaken once more by the hubbub of activity. Her attuned hearing picked out voices, laughter, shouts and, underlying it all, the thumping rhythm of drumbeats. Light glimmered from the entrance of the pavilion ahead, silhouetting two veiled guards. She saw Gotrek entering, the flames flickering across the surface of the Master Rune and the greataxe slung across his back. She quickened her pace, one hand on the blade of her dagger. The two men watching the entrance looked at her, but neither moved to intercept the aelf. She passed between them and in through the entrance flap.

The pavilion was packed. Candle stands illuminated hundreds of figures pressed in beneath the black canvas arching high overhead, their attention fixed on a wooden stage that had been erected across from the main entrance. They looked for the most part like merchants, tribal leaders and better-off travellers, clad in the white or deep red robes, silks, headscarves and veils of the Triumvirate Cities' wealthy guilds. They applauded the stage or chattered and laughed amongst themselves, creating a clamour that made Maleneth grimace.

Be on your guard, child, murmured her mistress' voice in her head. She clutched her pendant in one hand, the blood vial a cold reassurance.

Gotrek was just ahead, pushing his way unceremoniously through the crowd towards the stage. The complaints died rapidly when those he forced aside saw the scarred duardin's dour expression, or the broad blades of his axe.

Maleneth darted after him. The air in the pavilion was stifling, heavy with the stink of sweat and the sickly sweet cloy of perfume. The whole place vibrated to the primal drumbeats coming from the stage. It was making her feel light-headed. She caught Gotrek just as he forced his way to the front of the audience.

'Changed your mind, I see,' he said over the noise of the crowd.

'You should try it some time,' she snapped back.

'I would, if I wasn't always right.'

Maleneth's response died in her throat as she saw clearly what was happening on the stage for the first time.

Four female dancers were spinning around one another, their darting motions dictated by the rhythm of a pair of hide drums being palm-beaten by two more women sat with legs crossed behind them. The performers were scantily clad in the same pearls and pink-and-purple silks worn by the messenger that had first invited Maleneth and Gotrek to the pavilion. Their black hair was unbound, and it whipped about as they wove and pivoted. Their dark, toned flesh was glistening with sweat.

You have seen this before.

'I have,' Maleneth murmured, her eyes not leaving the performance.

Each dancer carried a knife in both hands, and as they spun close to one another the wicked blades would kiss the clothing of the others with immaculate precision, slicing silk and turning the garments into long, flowing strands that further accentuated their fluid movements. With every slashing sound the crowd would let out a gasp or a cheer of appreciation, the whole mass swaying in time with the beat.

It was not the presence of the dancers themselves that had made Maleneth pause, nor even the knives in their hands. It was their motions. It was the Seventeen Blades. She had performed the dance a hundred times, had long ago memorised every step and pivot, every duck and flick and twist. It was the dance she herself had watched on the night that her life had changed forever, when her father had ripped her from the aelf she was to marry and had cast her into the temple's bloodthirsty sisterhood.

She had never seen the dance performed by humans before, and she could never have imagined that they would do so with such precision. They could not match the speed or grace of an aelf, but every step and motion was assured and practised, and every knife-kiss precisely made. Though together, the four women represented a hail of razor blows and bared flesh, not a single one had been cut by the sharp steel.

She closed her eyes, willing away the memories the scene had brought on. Her four younger sisters, dancing the Seventeen Blades, their faces lit with joy. Jakari's hand in her own, her half-smile – always so wicked – as she teased her about which noble house they were going to be married off to. The slam of doors, the rush of feet, the screams. The pain of cold, spiked gauntlets gripping her arms. The greater pain of Jakari's hand being ripped from her own. The utter indifference in her father's eyes.

The dance had stopped. Raucous applause dragged her back to the present. Despite the tent's stifling heat, she felt cold.

Gotrek was still watching the stage, arms crossed over his broad chest, seemingly unimpressed. Those behind him were roaring for an encore, a cry that was quickly taken up by the rest of the crowd. The four dancers, their garments in tatters, offered a bow before parting with fluid grace, admitting a fifth woman to the centre of the stage. A rapid tattoo of drumbeats announced her arrival.

She was older than the dancers, and more formally attired, her hair bound up in a patterned tribal headscarf. Maleneth realised she was probably the troupe's mistress, the one the dancer in the market had called Shaldeen. She raised her arms, a knowing smile on her lips. The drums came to an abrupt stop, and a hush settled over the crowd.

'Shemali, sellah, friends and companions,' Shaldeen said. 'I hope our performances this night have brought pleasure and delight to one and all!'

A cheer greeted her words, and applause spread like a ripple. She held her hands up once more until silence returned.

'It pleases me to say that our performance is not yet quite done. You have just borne witness to the Seventeen Blades, that famous old aelf dance, the signature of the dreaded and murderous temples of Khaine!'

The words were delivered with dramatic relish, and the audience responded with gasps and hisses.

'We Alharabi have performed it to the best of our abilities, and we pray to that dreaded god that we have done his dance justice. I do not deny, however, that the best of our efforts would surely pale in comparison to the mastery of the aelves themselves.'

The crowd let out cries of denial, but the mistress waved them away, her smile fixed.

'But we are blessed this night, friends and companies,' she continued. 'Blessed perhaps by that terrible power whom this dance venerates. For we have a servant of Khaine here among us, this very moment!'

A shocked silence fell over the spectators. Maleneth froze. The troupe mistress looked directly at her and extended one hand, the smile never wavering.

'You honour us with your own presence, child of the Bloody-Handed. Now, will you help us honour your god as well, one more time?'

The whole tent had gone deathly silent, and those in the crowd closest to Maleneth had edged away from her. She glanced at Gotrek. The Slayer's expression was stoic, but he nodded, once. Her own mistress remained silent.

Maleneth tensed, and leapt, clearing the edge of the stage easily. The lithe motion caused the crowd to gasp and exclaim in their native tongues. She landed lightly on both feet. A part of her, buried deep inside, quailed at the realisation that she was standing being watched by hundreds. She was an assassin, not an entertainer. A fire-lit stage was the last place she wanted to be.

But the memories had come on, too strong, too overpowering to be denied. She unclasped her cloak, letting it fall to more gasps. Her leathers were a far cry from the light silks of the Alharabi, and what little of her body that was bared – only her forearms – was a pale contrast to their dark complexions. Her raven hair and eyes, however, matched those of the dancers perfectly.

Two of the previous performers had backed off to the rear of the stage, leaving their two other dancing partners alongside Shaldeen and Maleneth. The shocked quiet was replaced by cheering and applause as the drums began to beat out a rhythm once more, slower this time. She mirrored the bow offered to the audience by the dancers. They were all still smiling. Heartbeat rising, Maleneth slipped her fyresteel knives free.

Remember the steps, child.

The dance began. Maleneth forced herself to stop thinking, to stop worrying, and obey the rhythm being set by the drums. The pavilion faded into the background as she let the motions sweep over and through her, the memories resurging stronger than ever. Jakari was opposite her once again, dancing the same dance, laughing freely, hair unbound and the slender blades in her hands glittering. Maleneth's heart surged, and she almost misstepped. She recovered with a speed and precision no human could have matched, and drew another gasp from the crowd.

It was not Jakari opposite her. It was the troupe mistress, Shaldeen. Her mastery of the dance's complex weave of steps and motions was as complete as Maleneth had ever seen. She moved with a fluid, controlled passion, channelling an energy that didn't concern itself with anything beyond the next step, and the next, and the next. Maleneth slid past and around her, their bodies inches apart, the Alharabi silk flowing. The cloying perfume was thick in her nostrils.

The blades glinted in the firelight. A razor kiss, accentuated by another acceleration in the drumming. Gasps from the crowd intruded on the flow of Maleneth's thoughts as she slid one of her blades up and along the troupe mistress' spine, the tip just missing her perfect, dark skin, feathering open a section of her silken garment. She felt the same connection along her own back, sliding down her leathers. It failed to penetrate, and there was no cloth to cut open, but that was not the point – the garments were merely accessories. The power of the dance lay in the caress of death, the aching closeness of being an inch away from Khaine's red touch. The sensation of her own knife darting along someone's back, and another at her own, almost made the breath catch in Maleneth's throat.

You're enjoying this too much, Witchblade. Focus!

Maleneth ignored the cold voice. The dance moved on, another slash, this one to the shoulder, hers alone to make. She knew even as she spun away that the knife of another of the dancers would be coming for her, a low, precise cut that grazed across the clothing on her hip. Another touched her own shoulder at the exact moment that she cut more of the silk cladding the troupe mistress, the blades making a slitting noise as they slashed air and cloth, just audible over the rising frenzy of the drums and the raucous awe of the crowd.

Then came the pain. She'd become so absorbed that she almost didn't notice it at first. The sudden jab in her side was lost in the web of movement, no room in her mind for anything beyond the dance. Then it registered and she stumbled, unable to correct herself this time.

To be cut in the Seventeen Blades was not uncommon. She had seen aelves of the temple far more experienced than her slashed in half a dozen places, white flesh streaked red. Such injuries showed the favour of Khaine, for it was by his will that sharpened steel had first pierced mortal flesh.

It had been so long since Maleneth had last performed, however, that the sensation of actually being cut interrupted her rhythm. It also saved her life. Had she carried on then the next step, a downward lunge angling towards her right, would have carried a misplaced knife into her bare throat. It came at her anyway, and she was forced to change her footing to avoid the jab.

The blade hadn't been misplaced at all.

More lunges, from left and right, Shaldeen and her three dancers breaking step to stab and slash in perfect synchronisation. A human would have been dead in only a few seconds, heart and throat pierced. But for all the speed and suddenness of the attack, Maleneth was quicker.

She danced out of reach. The drums had stopped, and from the shouts and screams behind her it seemed as though the crowd were unsure whether they were still watching a staged production or a murder attempt. Maleneth ignored them all – her blood still sang with the rhythm of the Seventeen Blades, and the tempo of her movements continued to accelerate. There was no time to think about what the Alharabi were doing or why – Khaine demanded the dance go on.

Kill them all, Witchblade.

They were fast, there was no denying it. Shaldeen came at her head on, and steel rang against steel as Maleneth flicked each knife stroke aside. It was only a distraction, however. The other two dancers, along with the pair who had stepped aside and both of the drummers, came leaping at her from either side, a blur of stabbing blades. Maleneth gave ground with desperate, focused speed, moving towards the edge of the stage, knowing that if even one of them managed to slip behind her the dance would be finished. She ducked, twisted one way then another, too busy parrying and weaving to even consider going on the attack.

And through it all, they were still smiling.

Behind her the black top had descended into pandemonium. Some in the crowd were pushing and shoving to get out; others were trying to reach the stage, the whole mob overcome with hysteria. Insomuch as Maleneth was aware of any of it, a single thought broke the tempo of her thoughts.

Gotrek.

Move right.

Maleneth had never questioned her mistress' advice, and she wasn't about to start. She twisted right, almost throwing herself into the two Alharabi assassins coming at her from that direction. For a moment, her back was completely exposed. She felt the boards of the stage shuddering, and flinched away from the killing blow she expected between her shoulder blades, even as she turned aside the weapons of those in front of her.

A roar broke the moment to pieces, accompanied by a sickening crunch of bone. Gotrek had leapt onto the stage, Master Rune blazing, and now came thundering to Maleneth's aid. His greataxe was ignited, the fyreforge brazier between the twin heads blazing with a light almost as hot and furious as the one that burned in the Slayer's single eye. He slammed into the two assassins trying to slip in behind to Maleneth's left, his shoulder-charge sending both flying across the stage. Bones cracked and split, but they belonged to the lucky ones. A third was caught as she attempted to sidestep the raging duardin. Gotrek moved with a speed that belied his muscled bulk, the axe inscribing a white-hot line as it cleaved into the Alharabi's midriff and cut her effortlessly in half, blood and viscera bursting from the horrific killing blow.

'If anyone's killing the aelf, it's me,' the Slayer snarled.

As blood pattered down onto the stage and smeared beneath Maleneth's feet, Shaldeen and her three remaining dancers broke off, darting back out of reach of both the Slayer and the aelf. Neither of the two pitched over by Gotrek's charge were moving. The duardin was snorting like an enraged beast, the Master Rune glowing with a deep lustrous power.

'Get on my left side, dark aelf,' he snapped. He nodded his head to his left shoulder, guarded by his lion-headed pauldron. 'If we're going to do this together, I'm more used to having someone on my left.'

Maleneth didn't question him, but moved around behind him just as the Alharabi came at them again.

She met them equally this time, blade-for-blade. She felt her hatred surge. They'd been lured here, tricked into exposing themselves. Exactly why, she did not know, though in the months she had spent with Gotrek she'd rapidly grown accustomed to attempts on their lives. The list of those who coveted the Master Rune was long, and grew by the day as rumours of the strange Fyreslayer spread through the Mortal Realms.

Whoever the Alharabi really were, or whoever they worked for, they were not going to be the ones to take either the duardin or the rune, not while Maleneth drew breath. She knocked aside a knife and lunged into the woman's guard, too fast even for the well-trained human to counter. In a single rapid heartbeat Maleneth's knife was in her throat, and the aelf felt the Alharabi's arms clutch around her impotently as she tried to pull herself off the cold steel. The death grip trembled against the tall aelf before Maleneth ripped her blade free in a gout of blood.

'Hold still, damned thaggaz,' she heard Gotrek bellowing.

He had met Shaldeen. Fast as the duardin was, the dancer swept past his guard, blades darting across his scarred flesh. Maleneth realised that the expressions of the Alharabi had finally changed – gone were the smiles, replaced now with looks of pure, concentrated hatred. The realisation brought a strange relief. They were not as preternatural as they first appeared. During the dance and in the desperate seconds when it had turned to combat, Maleneth had found herself doubting the teachings of the Temple of Khaine, even the abilities of her own race. Now, however, as steel rang against steel and sliced through flesh, certainty returned once more.

No one hated, and no one killed, quite like a servant of Khaine.

She moved right as Gotrek was forced to turn after the troupe mistress, covering his back. The other Alharabi had seen the opening created by their leader, but Maleneth stopped them from exploiting it, despite their numbers. In a few seconds she'd taken half a dozen furious blows, but her armour, light though it was, ensured they only grazed her. She heard Gotrek grunt behind her, and could feel the burning heat of his axe as it swept and spun, keeping Shaldeen at bay.

They could only sustain this defence for so long. They were still outnumbered, and no one in Khaled-Tush was going to come to the aid of a duardin and an aelf in a knife fight with the Alharabi. For all Maleneth's own abilities, there was only so much she could do while pinned defending another's back. She'd already taken two shallow cuts across her right arm, and the first stab she'd received in her side was still throbbing. She could feel blood running down her thigh.

The tempo of the dancers' blows picked up as they sensed their victim's uncertainty. She heard Gotrek snarl with frustration, a sure sign that he was still unable to lay a blow on the troupe mistress. Another knife blade struck and twisted into Maleneth's hip, making her hiss and slash her own steel over the attacker's arm.

To die here will bring eternal dishonour to the temple.

'Be silent, mistress!' Maleneth snapped, her back now physically pressed up against Gotrek's, as one of the veiled dancers made a series of jabs towards her face and eyes, forcing her to give ground.

A tremor shuddered through the stage. It was not a pounding tattoo like Gotrek's initial charge, but something altogether deeper. The Alharabi sensed it too. Their attacks faltered.

Maleneth didn't get a chance to attack. A blast wave hit the black top. The screaming of the crowd intensified as the black canvas ripped, and the whole structure buckled. Maleneth saw a jagged line torn across the ceiling directly above her, a section of the pavilion plucked away to reveal the night beyond.

It was riven with fire.

Another explosion shuddered through the air, intensifying the screaming of the spectators. They had begun to stampede, some for the pavilion's entrance, others for the hole ripped in its flanks. Maleneth realised that fire had caught and was kindling on a section of the canvas near the ground to her right, whether from the flames spreading outside or from the overturned candle stands it was impossible to tell.

The black top was about to become a furnace.

Get out.

'We must flee,' Maleneth said to Gotrek, still at her back.

'Tell that to your treacherous dance partners,' the duardin snarled. 'Dwarfs don't flee, especially not Gotrek Gurnisson!'

Despite the conflagration taking hold around them, the Alharabi came at them once more, more furious than ever. Maleneth met them in a low fighting crouch, blades held tip-down to either side, one wet with the blood running down her wounded arm.

Their attackers' blows never landed. Flames burst from the rear of the stage, searing heat blazing over Maleneth and making her flinch and choke. The clothing of one of the assassins ignited, and she shrieked as the fire took her.

Maleneth felt the stage begin to tilt under her. More flames were licking at the support beams, and there was a crack as one blackened length of timber gave way. The dancers maintained their balance, but the distraction was enough. Maleneth gritted her teeth and thrust herself back against Gotrek with all her strength. She felt the Slayer going over, carried by the movement of the collapsing stage past the troupe master and the platform's edge.

Maleneth's stomach lurched as she tumbled into freefall. Her foot connected with the side of one of the collapsing beams, and she was able to use the brief buttress to turn herself round in mid-air. She landed next to Gotrek on all fours, knives thumping into the pavilion floor either side of her. A second later there was a splitting crash as the rest of the stage behind them gave way, the flames leaping up to gorge on the splitting timbers.

The crowd at the front of the stage had long since fled, packing into the mass now struggling to fight their way through the ripping canvas walls. The flames were still spreading, their heat overwhelming. Some onlookers had caught fire, their horrific screaming only adding to the panic and confusion. Black smoke was starting to fill the claustrophobic space. Maleneth knew they had seconds before the greater part of the pavilion's roof gave way and descended on them all in a smothering blanket of burning cloth.

'Rise,' she snapped at Gotrek, retrieving her two blades as she did so. The Slayer grunted and picked up his axe. Its fires had gone out, an irony given the flames that were now engulfing everything else.

'Damned piece of dross,' the Slayer snarled at the weapon. 'Why is everything in this new reality so worthless?'

Maleneth heard a shriek just as she found her feet. She spun in time to see Shaldeen leaping at them through the flames consuming the stage. Her silken clothing was alight, and she looked like a daemonic fury as she flung herself at the aelf and the duardin, her face a terrible rictus of pain and rage.

Down.

Maleneth dropped into a crouch as the troupe mistress flew at her, screaming. She felt something heavy pass overhead, and realised that she'd reflexively screwed her eyes shut. There was a sickening thump, and the scream was cut off abruptly. Something hot and wet splattered her. She opened her eyes to find herself covered in blood. The two halves of the troupe mistress lay either side of her, bisected by Gotrek's overhead swing, the flames quickly eating up the gory remains.

'Dance around that,' Gotrek said.

'We've got to get out,' Maleneth repeated. She pointed towards the nearest opening in the pavilion's flank. Fire had seared it away, its edges licked by flames. The heat was keeping people at bay. Maleneth reached down, sheathed her knives and snatched a heavily embroidered desert trader's cape from the ground.

'Stay behind and stay close,' she ordered Gotrek.

'Don't worry,' Gotrek panted. 'If you go first, I'll get to see you burn to death before I do. Maybe I'll even get out, and then I can find the inscription in peace. Go ahead, aelfling.'

Maleneth charged the gap. The smoke was making her eyes sting and choking her throat, and the heat had slicked her with sweat. She stumbled but kept going, the cape held up before her like a shield. She could hear the heavy thumping of Gotrek's footfalls at her back.

She flung herself against the fire-eaten hole in the canvas, feeling the intense, blistering heat wash over her. Something scorched her hands, and she dropped the cape reflexively. Initially, she could neither breathe nor see, her eyes forced shut by the smoke, the ash making her gag and retch. Then she was through – the heat was gone, a memory at her back, and she could breathe again. She stumbled, but turned the fall into a roll, finally coming to a stop on her back amidst rough oasis grass, staring up at the sky, panting.

Gotrek had come to a halt beside her, hands on his knees as he gulped down air untainted by the pavilion's fiery demise. He muttered something, but Maleneth wasn't listening. Her eyes were still on the sky. It was almost wholly engulfed by smoke billowing from the burning caravans, the market and the black top, but she had caught something amidst the swirling ash and red embers. It took her a moment to recognise its outline.

She was watching a duardin skyship, an arkanaut frigate most commonly used by the piratical Kharadron Overlords. Its bulk resembled the iron hull of a seagoing vessel, but instead of watery waves it traversed the clouds of the aether thanks to the arcane power of three spherical endrins suspended by cables and copper wiring above the ship's structure.

Maleneth thought at first that the ship had been moored somewhere amidst the caravans of Khaled-Tush, and was making its escape as the fires leapt and spread throughout the outpost. As she watched though, she realised that its course must have brought it in over the oasis, and that it was holding station rather than pulling away.

Something dropped from the airship's flank. She followed it as it plummeted through the smoke and ash, a black sphere, seemingly innocuous amidst the devastation surrounding it. She lost it as it disappeared among the remains of the burning marketplace. Fire flared, silhouetting the intervening wagons, and the thunderclap of another detonation rolled out across the desert, bringing realisation with it.

The arkanaut frigate was attacking Khaled-Tush. They were dropping incendiary grudge-bombs over the side, onto the helpless caravans below. It was their fire that had first ignited the black top, and toppled the stage. Now the entire outpost was ablaze.

Maleneth's view of the Kharadron skyship was obscured by a shadow. She blinked, and realised that Gotrek was standing over her. It took her a moment to realise that he was offering her his hand. She took it, her slender fingers encased by the duardin's scarred, stone-hard fist. She allowed herself to be drawn up onto her feet, and glanced back at the pavilion. It had almost wholly collapsed into the flames consuming it, and the space around it was a heaving mass of people, trying to push and shove their way out of the reach of the fires as they spread to the nearby trees and the under-growth that carpeted the banks of the oasis. It was chaos, and amidst it all no one seemed to have noticed the skyship. It was turning, banking around through the smoke and heading back in their direction.

'Dwarfs?' Gotrek said, following Maleneth's gaze.

'Not as you know them.'

'Apparently not,' Gotrek growled. 'The only *dawi* that take to the sky are brain-addled. Just like everything else in this place.'

The skyship was losing altitude. Some of those on the edge of the crowd, stricken with fear and confusion, had started to flock towards it, not real-ising that it was responsible for the devastation reigning around them.

She pulled her knives from her belt once more.

'I pray the idea of kinslaying does not disturb you, duardin,' she said darkly.

Gotrek's expression, usually stony, hardened further in the flickering firelight.

'Not any more, aelf. Not for a long time.'

CHAPTER FOUR

Durbarak's steel-shod boots hit the earth with a satisfying thump. He let go of the grav-ladder's rappel line, steadying himself. Around him, his crew were clustering, the fires of destruction unleashed by their skyship gleaming from armour plates, cutlasses, ancestor masks and pistols. He paused to assess the two dozen Kharadron reivers, and the inferno taking hold around them.

Khaled-Tush was no more. The incendiary grudge-bombs dropped by the arkanaut frigate and the heated shot of its cannons had set fire to the trading post's few permanent structures, and to hundreds of the wagons and carts that had been clustered around the oasis. They now presented a wall of flame, against which were silhouetted hundreds of individual figures – those who had survived the aerial bombardment and were now attempting to flee out into the desert night with whatever they'd been able to snatch before the flames took hold.

The crew would need to be quick, before their quarry escaped with them. Assuming, of course, that the inferno hadn't taken the target already. The thought of so many perishing in the flames brought a grim smile to Durbarak's lips. Sometimes, he doubted his life choices. He doubted breaking the Kharadron code, and turning his holdings to nothing but reiving and murder. But at times like these, all those doubts were burned away. Even the fear of losing the incredible bounty the Slayer represented could not penetrate the thrill of witnessing unchecked devastation on a scale such as this.

'Throm, Dregg, take six and scout towards the marketplace. Borin, another three and circle east – cut off anyone fleeing down the main trail. Set more fires if you need to. The rest of you, with me.'

The Kharadrons moved off into the fire-lit darkness, weapons drawn. Durbarak led his group towards the waters of the oasis, shimmering through the flames and heat haze. He could see hundreds of people spilling from a large tent, its burning canvas almost wholly consumed by the skyship's ponderous bombing run. Some were throwing themselves into the oasis itself, others were stumbling towards the fires consuming the marketplace, overcome by confusion and the black smoke hanging heavy over the outpost. Like the rest of the Kharadrons, Durbarak had bound a wetted rag around his mouth and nose before donning his ancestor mask, knowing he would need it to breathe amidst the inferno their attack had ignited. He could feel the heat even through the rubberised insulation of his sky-suit, slicking his body with sweat and making every movement chafing and uncomfortable.

'Please, sellah, help us,' shouted a man in a torn headscarf, stumbling from the direction of the burning pavilion. Durbarak shot him, relishing the brute kick of his aetherlock pistol. The heavy ball flung the man down as though he'd been poleaxed, a chunk of his torso blown away. The Kharadrons continued over the corpse. More gunshots rang through the night as they fired indiscriminately into the fleeing crowd. Few seemed to have realised that the fires were no accident, and that the outpost was under attack.

'Keep a clear watch,' Durbarak bellowed, gesturing at his landing party to spread out further. When they'd first passed over the outpost, the ship's navigator, Zeggi, had been monitoring it with half a dozen enhanced vision scopes, linked to various parts of the frigate's underbelly. He'd been unable to discern their quarry amidst the sudden blossoms of flame or the panicked crowds, however, so they were doing it the old fashioned way – a ground raid, pistols and cutlasses drawn. In truth, Durbarak wasn't complaining. It always did him good to see the carnage they sowed up close.

'Watch the starboard side,' growled his midshipman, Threg. A trio of men came running from the crowd, scimitars raised, the nearby conflagration reflecting like liquid fire from the curved steel. Durbarak raised his second pistol, but before he could fire, the duardin nearest the attackers – Lorik, Stromm and Gurbad – had already put them down with a hail of shots.

'Keep going,' Durbarak ordered. He heard more firing coming from the direction of the caravans as the other Kharadron landing parties began to move in among the survivors there. Those directly ahead had finally realised that the duardin had not come with friendly intentions. They were screaming and pushing at one another, forced forward by the pressure of those behind still desperate to get away from the burning pavilion. More went down to the renegade Kharadron's gunfire.

For a moment, Durbarak entertained the fear that their quarry had already escaped. He doubted it though. From what he had heard, running away from innocents while they were being cut down by ruthless attackers was the opposite of what the target would do. He was counting on it.

The remains of the pavilion collapsed, fire and sparks billowing into the air. The last of the crowd ahead of them were beginning to disintegrate and scatter. There was a noise like a thunderclap from behind Durbarak, and he realised the skeleton crew left aboard the frigate, the *Draz Karr*, had probably fired one of the cannons to keep those fleeing the fires from mobbing the landing area.

They were running out of time.

Perhaps the one they sought was already dead. Perhaps the target's bones were currently snapping and crackling in the white heat at the heart of the settlement, or in the remains of the pavilion ahead. Perhaps the job he'd been hired to do had already been done. He hoped not. Despite orders, he had no intention of killing the target, or its accomplices.

'I can see something up there,' Stromm shouted. For a moment Durbarak had no idea what the ship's mate was talking about. Then he caught it, through the dark figures milling about before the pavilion's flames, trapped between the fire and the advancing Kharadrons.

It was a light. Not, as he first thought, a torch. The little flicker of fire, almost swallowed up by the greater conflagration behind it, was being reflected back from two broad axe heads, set either side of it. After a moment he realised what he was looking at – rune-etched fyresteel, a greataxe of one of the Slayer clans, a brazier of forge-flame burning in its heart.

The light illuminated the being carrying it. From a distance, it looked like a particularly large Fyreslayer, complete with red crest and beard. As it drew nearer, however, Durbarak could pick out distinguishing features. The duardin's bare torso and arms were covered in thick knots of blue tattoos, and his wrists were encased by battered vambraces hung with loops of broken chain. Most noticeable of all was his chest – a single rune glowed there, its lustre immediately making Durbarak feel sick with envy.

Despite himself, he grinned. He knew taking this contract had been a good idea. It had led him right to Gotrek Gurnisson.

'*Draz Karr*, on me!' he shouted, summoning his crew. 'And remember, don't shoot him! If we're going to ransom them on, we need them each in at least two pieces!'

'You did this?' the approaching duardin bellowed, gesturing with his free hand at the bodies scattered before the Kharadrons. 'Does my old eye deceive me? Are you the pitiful creatures that dare claim to bear the legacy of the dawi in this mad world?'

The fury was now visible in his burning gaze, and Durbarak felt his spirit quail, as though he were a beardling whose misdeeds had been discovered by an elder. He thrust the feeling aside.

He'd heard the rumours. They all had. That only made Gotrek Gurnisson all the more valuable. Damned if he was going to kill so much potential profit, regardless of the orders of the one who'd hired him.

'The aelf,' Stromm snarled, spitting before pointing his pistol over the oncoming Slayer's shoulder. A shape had materialised behind the duardin, tall and slender, wrapped in shadow.

'This is perfect,' Durbarak growled. 'Both of them, for the highest bidder. Threg, Krazak, take them.'

The two shipmates stepped forward, ratcheting up their net launchers.

'Surrender if you want to live!' Durbarak shouted at the duardin and the aelf.

But they didn't surrender. Instead the Slayer roared, and charged.

CHAPTER FIVE

It was not often that Maleneth found herself approving of Gotrek Gurnisson's more rash moments. Just then, however, with the fires of Khaled-Tush at her back and the screams of the burned and the dying ringing in her ears, Maleneth understood the Slayer's fury perfectly.

The Kharadrons opposite him fired. The motions seemed half in haste as they started back from the charging Slayer, and though their faces were inscrutable behind their ancestor masks Maleneth didn't doubt that the sight of Gotrek unleashed had more than intimidated them. As he broke into a run the Master Rune surged with light, and bright energy seemed to suffuse the duardin's body, blazing in his eye and making his hair bristle, the red dye shot through with gold.

Maleneth had seen it only a few times in all the months they had spent together, and every time it burned away any doubts she had about the power of Gotrek Gurnisson.

The net launchers carried by two of the Kharadrons failed to fire properly, one entangling its own muzzle while the second simply thumped into the dirt at Gotrek's feet. Maleneth heard one Kharadron screaming at the others to reload as the Slayer closed the ground between them with a thunderous charge, the fire wreathing his greataxe blazing.

Maleneth raced after him, knives out. Her anger boiled no less hot than the Slayer's, a murder-curse on her lips. If the Overlords thought Gotrek was fearsome, they had never seen a servant of Khaine raised to ire.

Gotrek hit them first, while the ones with net launchers were struggling to reload. In a panic the nearest Kharadron tried to shoot his pistol at the Slayer. The point-blank discharge simply grazed Gotrek's flank, and he burst through the smoke with a furious two-handed overhead swing of his axe. The mighty weapon struck the Kharadron clean on the skull, and parted helmet, head and sky-suit with ease, shearing the duardin in half in a shower of blood that hissed where it pattered against the glowing steel of the heated axe blades.

'Oath-breaking *grobkaz*,' Gotrek roared, his voice booming like a thunderclap. He shouldered his way through the bloody remains of the first Overlord and swung for the second, cleaving his head from his shoulders and sending it hurtling like a catapult stone away into the night. More weapons discharged, only adding to the confusion as Maleneth leapt in among the melee. One of the Overlords had managed to look away from Gotrek long enough to see her coming, and he brought his cutlass up in time to knock away a stab towards his heart. He went back, cursing, and Maleneth kept going, jabbing at the unarmoured parts of his rubbery sky-suit, keeping her body in perpetual motion. It was like the Seventeen Blades all over again.

No, she corrected herself as she slipped around a desperate slash of the cutlass and back into the duardin's guard. The Seventeen Blades was like murder.

'Stand firm, you *wannazi!*' one of the Kharadrons was bellowing, and Maleneth realised that more were rushing towards the fight from the direction of the burning caravans. She was hopelessly outnumbered. They should never have confronted them, even after realising the skyfaring duardin were responsible for the firestorm. She couldn't have stopped Gotrek though, not after he'd seen the way they were cutting down those who escaped the flames.

A feint to the right, and the dagger in her left hand slipped in under the chin of the Overlord she was fighting, plunging up behind his ancestor mask. A single line of blood ran from the mouth slit down the mask's stylised silver beard, and he made a wet gargling sound as Maleneth twisted the knife and dragged it free.

Something slammed into her from behind as she did so. She tried to spin away, but it grappled with her, fighting to find a purchase on her light leather armour. She felt something crack into her leg, making her gasp with pain. The stink of rubbery sky-suits and filthy duardin sweat invaded her senses, overpowering the reek of burning.

She managed to twist and writhe her way out of the grip, spinning with one blade outstretched as she turned. It jarred off a Kharadron's helmet, and as she tried to dance further back to give herself more room she felt her leg give. One of the new attackers rushing to the scene had hit her calf with the swipe of a hammer, and the limb couldn't properly support her weight any more. She buckled, spitting a blood curse at the Kharadrons as they rushed at her.

'Alive, I said alive!' she could hear one of the duardin shouting in his grating language. She slid around the thrust of a sky pike and knocked aside another swinging cutlass, but as she tried to repost her leg gave way entirely and she went down on one knee. Another Kharadron tackled her from the side, bearing her down onto the ground, and she felt her grip go on one of her knives. She wrapped her arms around the struggling bulk of the one on top of her and slammed her remaining blade into the small of his back, trying to work it through his thick sky-suit. He cursed, then headbutted her.

Stars burst before her eyes as the ancestor mask slammed down. She tried to turn her head away, gasping at the pain in her skull, and through her blurred vision saw Gotrek, splattered with blood, being ensnared by another volley from the net launchers.

She tried to reach out to him, tried to shout, but the Kharadron's helm cracked into her jaw again, and she knew no more.

CHAPTER SIX

'Move,' Durbarak urged, throwing a glance back over his shoulder at Khaled-Tush. The flames had spread to the greenery clustered on the banks of the oasis, and now the once-bustling outpost was wholly consumed, the constellations overhead lost in a thick bank of smoke and ash.

'Hurry,' Durbarak reiterated, smacking his leather gauntlet on Throm's back for emphasis. The *Draz Karr* lay ahead, the throbbing of its idling endrins a welcome sensation in the ash-choked air. He glanced at Stromm, Elki and Borin, all three of them struggling to keep up. He'd ordered the *Draz Karr's* stoutest crewmen to drag the Slayer prisoner, and even between them they were sweat-drenched and panting, half divested of their sky-suit cowling and armour plates.

The prisoner himself was unconscious, as was the aelf. It had taken considerably more effort to knock the former out than the latter. Even just looking back at the duardin, wrapped in thick strands of skywhale gut netting, Durbarak found himself at once afraid and fascinated by the Slayer and the infamous rune gleaming in his flesh. He wanted to get him back and clapped up in the *Draz Karr's* brig before he stirred.

Gotrek Gurnisson was going to make them all rich, that much he was sure of.

'Hook him up,' Durbarak shouted up at the skyship's main deck. He saw a figure – probably Skeg – appear briefly at the deck's railings, and seconds later a pair of long cargo hooks, attached to winch lines, whickered down over the side of the hull and thumped into the dirt in front of Durbarak. He motioned at the Kharadrons around him. With practised speed, the duardin who had been hauling Gotrek attached the hooks to his netting.

There was a clattering noise as one of the frigate's cargo winches began hoisting the Slayer skywards. 'The axe,' Durbarak said, motioning to Krazak. The crewmate had taken custody of Gotrek's huge Fyreslayer weapon – from the beginning, Durbarak had been clear about the importance of not just taking Gotrek alive. The Slayer's equipment and his companions were also vital. Capturing the infamous Slayer in his entirety would magnify his value, and Durbarak wasn't going to miss out on individual payments in exchange for an easy life. That wasn't how the Kharadrons functioned.

Krazak handed the Fyreslayer axe to Durbarak, who strapped it over his back. Grav-ladders were being lowered from the *Draz Karr's* flank now, and the pitch of the endrins was rising as they prepared for a full lift-off. The second prisoner, the unconscious aelf, was being carried over Throm's shoulder. The big duardin mounted the ladders first, followed by the rest of the landing party. Durbarak waited until the end, as was customary for the captain of the sky reivers, casting his gaze back at Khaled-Tush. The outpost was now little more than a sheet of flame. The formerly cool night air of the desert was thick with the stink of charred wood and burned flesh, and hung heavy with black smoke and grey ash. The oasis had been transformed into a furnace. The sights and smells filled Durbarak with a deep grim happiness, and it took an effort to turn away and climb back aboard his ship.

As delightful as such devastation was, thoughts of the bounty he would collect with the Slayer and the aelf as his prisoners proved even more tantalising. The amount he had been offered to kill them was trifling by comparison.

The visions of wealth lasted only a few moments. Durbarak's boots had barely thumped down on the *Draz Karr*'s decking plates before he realised something was out of order. Both the Slayer and the aelf had been safely deposited, but they were not the only beings brought on board by the crew. A human, young and scrawny, was being held in Skeg's steel gauntlet, shivering and wailing in some garbled desert language.

'Who's this?' Durbarak demanded, uncoupling himself from the grav-ladder and stomping across the deck to Skeg.

'I caught the umgi hiding under the hull after we lowered the endrins,' Skeg growled, shaking the terrified manling roughly.

'So? Why is he still alive?'

'He started babbling about the Slayer. I think he knows him, and you said that anything related to Gotrek Gurnisson is valuable.'

'Sellah!' the human wailed. Gotrek had been dragged along the deck to the open brig by a brace of boarding grapnels and now lay slumped, still netted and unconscious.

'Sellah, sellah, please,' the human shouted, making a pathetic attempt to get free from Skeg's steel grasp. 'You must wake up, sellah!'

'Bind him too,' Durbarak snapped. 'Throw them all in the brig and let's get under way. We've lingered here long enough.'

His orders were disturbed by a shriek. He turned, reaching for his pistols. The aelf was awake. She had slipped out of Throm's grip and had almost flung him over the frigate's side. The two closest crewmates, Lorik and Stromm, rushed at her, grabbing her arms and trying to grapple her to the deck. She twisted and broke free again like a frenzied felid, punching Lorik in his prodigious gut. There was blood from a graze across her scalp running down the side of her slender face, and her dark hair was whipping around her, her black eyes wide and wild. They fixed on the human prisoner still being held by Skeg.

'Mistress, help,' the human pleaded piteously. She hesitated for the briefest second, and Durbarak knew she was sizing up remaining with her captive companions or leaping over the side.

In the end, the decision was made for her. Stromm, barely a foot to the aelf's left, had cocked his aetherlock.

'Move and die, witch,' the duardin growled.

'We haven't come here to kill you,' Durbarak added. 'Grimnir knows, I wouldn't mind if we did, but you're more valuable alive. Consider that before you throw yourself over the side.'

The doubt seemed to do enough. He sensed the aelf become a fraction less tense as she accepted the situation. Durbarak made a terse motion to Lorik and Throm, and they began to edge back towards the aelf. Her expression had changed from one of wild desperation to haughty, reserved acceptance.

'Release him,' she said in the local human tongue. She pointed at Gotrek's sprawled form.

'If you have any respect for your kindred or the survival of the Mortal Realms, you won't deliver him to whoever is paying you.'

'I don't have any respect for either,' Durbarak answered in the same language, making the rest of the crew laugh.

The aelf made to answer, but Lorik slammed the butt of his aetherlock into her stomach, doubling her over, then delivered another blow to the side of her head.

'Grungni's golden balls, that felt satisfying,' he said as the aelf hit the deck.

'Get them all below,' Durbarak snapped, turning towards the helm wheel and gear block on the skyship's bridge. 'And get us aetherward. Now, before any of the others catch up with us.'

CHAPTER SEVEN

The vibrating of the arkanaut frigate's buoyancy endrins woke Maleneth. She sat up, and immediately regretted doing so. Pain split through her stomach and skull like a sunburst, making her flinch. She slumped back.

She groaned, and let her aching head come to terms with her new surroundings. Her hands were bound, looped with coils of duardin cabling. That was the first thing she noticed. The second was that Gotrek and Aziz were beside her. Both were awake, and both tied like her. Gotrek was glowering into the middle distance. Aziz just looked terrified.

The third realisation was that the wind was in her hair, and that they were skyborne. She looked around, tentatively, wary of the pain in her scalp resurfacing.

They were tied up in the brig-pit of a Kharadron skyship. Its hold was open, but there was no way to climb the pipe-ribbed walls to its edge. Above them the metallic orbs of two buoyancy endrins throbbed, their brass-and-steel shells gleaming brilliantly in the unfiltered dawn light. Their arcane power competed with the thudding of the rotor blades that adorned the skycraft's sleek flanks. Beyond was nothing but the azure.

'How long was I unconscious?' Maleneth asked, having to swallow before speaking. Her throat was parched.

'Since you were captured,' Gotrek said, without a hint of humour.

'And how long ago was that?' she snapped, anger flaring up from the pain suffusing her body.

'Last night. You new aelves are just the same as the old ones. One hit and you crumple.'

'Would that I had the strength and fortitude of the great Gotrek. He would never have allowed himself to succumb to a pack of sky pirates,' Maleneth hissed. 'Unless that was you, laid out and netted on their deck when I last saw you...'

Gotrek rounded on her, and she thought he was going to lunge at her before she saw his bonds – heavy metal clamps, rather than the cords that bit into her own wrists. Clearly their captors were well aware of the Slayer's deadly potential.

'Have you tried to negotiate?'

'And why would I do that?' the Slayer growled. 'The only thing I would negotiate is whether their blood feeds my axe's thirst now or later.'

'They're duardin, for Khaine's spite. They've not killed us, so they must want something. They're not just assassins, or if they were they've disobeyed their directives. So negotiate with them.'

'I-I think I heard something about a ransom, sellah,' Aziz stammered. 'These sky dogs, sometimes they take people from the trails, usually wealthy traders. They do not follow their kindred's code.'

'Then why did they take you too?' Maleneth demanded.

'They think he's with us,' Gotrek said, looking up and frowning at the endrin orbs above. 'I told them he wasn't. Told them they should just throw him over the side of… whatever this thing is.'

'It is a skyship,' Aziz said, wringing his tied hands together.

'Not like any skyship I've been on before. And I've known one or two.'

A tremor ran through the cold decking plates surrounding them. A moment later a figure loomed at the edge of the brig's entrance, followed by two more. Maleneth looked up into the grim, unyielding ancestor masks of their captors. One was pointing the gleaming barrels of an aethermatic volley gun down at them. She remembered waking up on the skyship just as it had been about to pull away from the inferno that had once been Khaled-Tush. The duardin had spoken about taking them alive. In the hands of the Kharadron Overlords, that wasn't necessarily a good thing.

One of the captors pointed at Maleneth. He had Gotrek's axe slung over his back.

'Bring her.'

One of his companions tossed a grav-ladder down from the edge of the hold. Covered by the volley gun, he swung in and snatched Maleneth, gauntlet clamping around her arm. She didn't try to resist. Now was not the time. Aziz whimpered but Gotrek remained unmoving, his eye still on the endrins overhead, as though oblivious to what was happening around him.

The duardin holding Maleneth pushed her up the grav-ladder. It was difficult negotiating it with her hands tied, but near the top the Kharadron above snatched her beneath the arms and hauled her up. The wind hit her properly, making her flinch, and her feet touched the main deck just as another tremor ran through the ribbed metal. She was sure she heard one of the endrins skip a beat.

'This way, aelf,' the duardin snarled, a hand in the flat of her back pushing her towards the skyship's external railing. She staggered, her stomach lurching as she became aware of just how high up they were. The Bone Desert stretched out in every direction, like a Hysh-bleached sheet, each of the thousands of tiny ripples spreading away below her one of the great dunes that covered the desolate expanse.

'Who is that?' the duardin demanded, pointing down past the rear endrin latched to the skyship's stern. Maleneth frowned against the wind, unable to discern anything amidst the distant haze.

'I do not see anyone.'

'You're not using my spyglass, murder-aelf,' the duardin snarled. 'You'll throw it overboard. Put that famous eyesight to use, or we'll see how long you enjoy being dangled by your toes over the side.'

The Kharadron pointed again and Maleneth gripped the skyship's railing, staring down into the endless desert. Eventually she began to discern a shape, dark against the pale ochre, a distant spec that seemed to be following in the frigate's wake.

'A rider,' she said, having to shout over the wind and the endrin's throb.

'Who?' the Kharadron demanded.

'I don't know! I have no companions besides the duardin and the boy!'

'Then you won't mind if we give him a Kharadron salutation. Skori, prime the skycannon and bring us about.'

Before the duardin's orders could be obeyed there was a metallic pinging noise, followed by a shriek of escaping steam. Maleneth looked up to see the rivets had burst around one of the rubberised pipes leading to the endrin domes. Steam was now jetting from the opening, and a thick, oily substance was drooling from cracks further up the metal orb.

'Dregg, get aloft!' the Kharadron gripping Maleneth shouted, gesturing towards an endrinrigger emerging from the ship's forecabin, lugging a half-welder and a cog-toothed hammer.

'Another one's about to go!' shouted a second Kharadron, pointing towards another of the endrin's valves. The entire sphere was beginning to visibly buckle and deform under some sort of internal pressure, as though a vast, invisible fist had closed around it and was crushing the metal shell.

'Grungsson's oath,' the Kharadron beside Maleneth managed to swear, before the whole ship lurched.

The motion threw the entire crew, Maleneth included, hard to the right. She banged against some rigging cables, her natural poise undone by the cords pinning her wrists together. She spat a curse of her own as the ship lurched back violently in the opposite direction, banging her off the railings protecting the edge. Her duardin captor grunted as he held his own balance, the spikes on his boots helping him dig into the deck.

'Check the endrin readings!' he barked. Since the first rupture the tone of the orbs keeping the skyship aloft had changed noticeably. Gone were the steady vibrations, replaced by an ugly sputtering, clattering sound. The noise seemed to grow even more harsh and irregular as Maleneth listened to it, and a note of panic had entered the voices of the duardin around her as they hurried to sign in from their stations. She couldn't decipher all of the gruff reports, but none sounded positive.

The skyship shook again. This time it wasn't with sudden fury, but with an even more terrible, slow sense of slipping. Maleneth, attuned as she was to her surroundings, was the first to sense the slight change in the slope of the deck. She was able to hook her bonds over the railings along the edge of the hull as the angle continued to shift, and the duardin finally noticed.

'Throm, the stabiliser gauge!' the duardin next to Maleneth bellowed. 'She's going to capsize!'

The two remaining endrins were vibrating, their agony audible as an ear-piercing scream. The metal all around Maleneth was juddering violently, steam pouring from the skyship's ports and hatches, wreathing the stricken frigate as it continued its slow, inexorable roll.

'The hatch!' Maleneth heard another voice, rising above the barks of the duardin and the shriek of their crumpling ship. It was Aziz.

The cart driver and Gotrek were both still in the brig. Even more importantly, the brig had a hatch.

The duardin appeared to have forgotten her. Several had flung grapnels to the far side of the hull and were using them to scale the tipping deck with surprising dexterity. Others were using cutlasses, daggers and boarding pikes to anchor themselves to the ship, trying to claw their way back to the tiller and the gauge that appeared responsible for the craft's aerial buoyancy. One lost his grip on the rigging and plummeted back, slamming into the railing running along the edge of the ship with a grunt.

The railing. Maleneth stopped trying to fight the tipping sensation, and instead allowed herself to drop to the metal rungs. For a moment they were the only things between her and a plummeting drop, the desert laid out at a dizzying, stomach-turning angle. She forced herself not to look down, but planted two feet on one of the rungs and, from a crouch, leapt for the edge of the brig hatch.

She almost cleared it. Her hands, still bound together, clamped over the edges, the impact of her body against the unyielding metal of the hull almost driving the wind from her lungs.

'The hatch!' she heard Aziz still screaming. The angle of the ship was such that it had almost tipped him and Gotrek out into the open air.

'I am trying, you fool,' she hissed back. The brig's hatch lever was set into the deck just to her right, but reaching it would be impossible with her hands bound, at least if she wanted to avoid losing her grip.

She grimaced. When had a servant of Khaine ever had doubts when playing these games of life and death?

She flung herself to the side, letting out a yell of effort as she did so. As her grip left the hatch and her stomach lurched at the void opening out beneath her, it seemed as though she'd thrown herself to her death. Time slowed as she arched her back and thrust her arms out towards the lever. She saw the bonds slide up and over it as her jump reached its apex and, as it seemed her momentum would drag her back down over the side of the tipping deck, the cords caught and snagged.

They held her weight only for a second before snapping around the lever, but by then she had her hands around it. She thumped into the deck again as her fall was arrested once more, the weight dragging the lever down with a heavy click. She was left dangling again, her arms straining. But it was done. The locking mechanism had engaged.

She heard a crack and something smacked off the deck next to her head. She realised one of the duardin, anchored below her by a grappling hook, had fired an aetherlock up at her. Above, the brig had started to clatter as the hatch rattled shut over the hold.

She had a couple of seconds at best before she was locked outside.

Muscles burning with the unrelenting strain, she hauled herself up onto the lever block. The cords had bitten deep into her wrists, but with her hands free she suddenly felt more confident. Perched like a feline on the narrow block of metal, she gave herself a split second to gather her strength and focus, ignoring the horrifying angle of the ship as its flank approached ninety degrees to the desert floor far below.

She leapt, shrieking as she did so, though she barely realised it. The hatch yawned before her, its grate sliding shut, just a few yards left before the whole brig was locked off.

She was trapping herself in the bowels of an arkanaut frigate that was plummeting towards the desert. But it was that, or tumble from the open deck when it finally tipped all the way upside down.

She dropped in through the hatch, a hair's breadth from the grate's locking spikes, not even hitting the deck below before she heard it clang fully shut. She slammed into the metal beneath with a grunt and was then almost immediately thrown to one side. What had once been the bottom of the brig was now one of the sides, and the wall they had previously been lying against was now the floor. The hatch, now barred, was to her right. Through it the desert was swinging ponderously into view, the horizon stretching dizzyingly away.

The realisation of just what was happening caught up with Maleneth.

'Hag's spite see me safe, that I might claim more lives for the Bloody-Handed,' she intoned.

'Hold on to the bars!' Aziz was screaming, barely audible over the death-shrieks of the crumpling, rupturing endrins. The teamster had managed to work his way free of his own bonds, and had braced himself up against the corner of the hold.

The skyship turned over on its axis. Maleneth was thumped against the bars of the hold, now the floor. Beneath them was nothing but the desert. She clung to the grate, her stomach turning. A duardin hurtled past, his grip on the ship's deck gone, his scream whipped away by the wind and the earache of the endrins. She could see others dangling by grapnels and sky pikes, hooked to the rigging or railings. The dunes below were rushing up to greet them.

'Hope you don't get air-sick, aelf,' she heard Gotrek say. He was balanced against the grate, arms braced against one of the corners. It sounded as though he was enjoying himself.

She screwed her eyes shut and tried to drive out the juddering fall of the skyship with words of spite and murder, an old lullaby of the Hidden Temples. She was going to die, a part of her had already accepted as much. Her only hope was that it would be Khaine who claimed her soul, and not some other cruel deity.

The sound of the endrins' torture reached fever pitch, driving out all conscious thought, reducing anyone still on board the falling frigate to base, primal terror. Maleneth found herself opening her eyes again, and saw a dune directly ahead, caught for a second in perfect clarity, serenely still in the burning heat.

The world seemed to calm around Maleneth. The gut-wrenching shuddering and the plummeting sensation went, along with the pain of the endrins. All she could hear was the rapid tattoo of her own heart, the blood in her ears, the breath rasping in her lungs.

'*Khaela mensha adrathi Khaina*,' she said, reciting her temple's last rites. The skyship struck.

CHAPTER EIGHT

She remembered being told by a human warrior, Bayzor, a fellow member of the Order of the Azyr, that whenever he awoke after being struck unconscious, it was the pain that let him know he was still living. Apparently in whatever afterlife he believed in, there was no pain, so its presence indicated that he was not yet dead.

Maleneth had no such certainties. The temples of the Black Courts and the Shadow Covens preached little other than pain, and the cold murder that eased it. As she woke, acutely aware of the spikes of agony in her side and throbbing in her skull, her sluggish thoughts wondered whether she was about to face her final trials before the Bloody-Handed, and perhaps reckon one last time with her old mistress.

A part of her, distant and icy as a Shyish morning, hoped Jakari had already crossed over, and was waiting for her.

The God of Murder would permit no such mercies. Maleneth's eyes fluttered open, and she found herself looking once more at Gotrek's scarred, blunt face. She started, trying to push herself away from the duardin and realising when she did so that she was sitting up with her back to the skyship's hull. A section of copper pipes, ruptured, had been digging into her side, slicing her leathers. She groaned as her movements teased the dozen cuts and bruises she had gained over the previous day.

Gotrek stood, turning away from her. He had recovered his axe from somewhere, and she thought she caught a rare hint of amusement in his eye. She tested her throbbing head, touching it tentatively. Neither the lump on her scalp nor the bruises from the pipework seemed dangerous, but being flung around the hold seemed to have opened up the wound in her side given to her by the Alharabi dancers. She noticed as Gotrek moved away that his arm was injured too. Something had cut his right bicep to the bone, and the wound was still pulsing fresh blood, leaving his arm a sheet of glistening crimson.

She reached out one hand, grasping a metal strut that was broken out beyond the ribbing of what she took to be the skyship's hull. As she stood she realised that the ground underfoot was shifting and hot – gone were the decking plates, replaced by sand.

They had landed, and they had survived. She saw that she was still in the hold, or what remained of it. The ship appeared to have grazed the top of the dune they had been plunging towards and settled on its flank in the valley between the first rise and the second. Wreckage littered the sand beyond the broken and twisted remains of the hold.

She tried to speak, but the sound came out as a dry croak, and descended into coughing. Gotrek turned back to her and undid something from his belt, tossing it down beside her. It was a flask, engraved with Kharadron markings. She put it to her lips, and was relieved to taste water rather than a burning duardin ale.

She'd barely started to drink when her stomach heaved, and she was forced to double up by a bout of retching. She was sick, the bile leaving her gasping and choking on all fours, its stink in her nostrils and its foul acid aftertaste thick in her throat. She slumped back into a sitting position, panting, wiping sweat-slick hair out of her face. She realised that she was shaking.

'I'm almost impressed. I'd have thought such a crash would have ended a weakling, runty aelf,' Gotrek said, standing over her.

The words made her laugh weakly, though she didn't know why.

'Drink more,' he told her, turning his back again. She spat out the sickly aftertaste, and tentatively took another sip of what remained in the flask.

'You are wounded,' she said. The words came out raw sounding. He grunted, not turning back to face her.

'Had worse.'

'Not while I've been with you.'

'You've not been with me very long, dark aelf.'

She somehow found the strength to roll her eyes. 'You need to clean and bind that wound, before you lose any more blood.'

'I'd rather clean and bind your incessantly jabbering mouth.'

Gotrek moved out of the hull's shadow and into the burning light of the desert. Taking a moment to compose herself, Maleneth found her feet and followed him, shielding her eyes from the glare. Side by side, they surveyed the wreckage of the downed Kharadron skyship.

It had taken a section of the dune behind them with it during its first collision, ploughing a deep furrow down into the valley floor. Most of the ship's broken hull was intact, but two of the three endrins had come apart completely, their twisted metal strewn all over the sand. There were bodies too, Maleneth realised. Kharadron corpses, scattered indiscriminately amidst the ruination of their frigate.

'I've never known duardin-crafted machinery to fail like that,' she said, looking at the crumpled remains of the only remaining semi-intact endrin, buried in the dune a hundred yards off to her right.

'Malakai's would not have,' Gotrek grumbled.

'Whose?'

'The only dwarf I would trust to fly a damned skyship. He was an inventor, the likes of which you won't find in these dull realms. The manling says we are not far from the Eight Pillars. They are that way.' He gestured over the next dune.

'The manling...' Maleneth began, then spotted movement among the skyship's remains. A figure was crawling from the shattered portholes of what had been the frigate's main cabin section. As he wormed his way out into the sand, Maleneth recognised Aziz. The teamster got to his feet and, noticing her, waved cheerfully. Miraculously, he seemed completely unharmed.

'They had supplies,' Gotrek said by way of explanation as Aziz jogged over. He had tied half a dozen more Kharadron flasks around his waist, and they clattered with every step he took. There was a sack over his back as well.

'You are awake, sellah,' he exclaimed as he reached Maleneth. She grimaced.

'I feel like I would rather not be.'

Aziz's cheerful demeanour withered before Maleneth's icy response. She forced herself to acknowledge him properly, against her better instincts.

'Had you not told me to close the hatch, I would likely be standing in judgement before Khaine right now. For that, you have my thanks, Aziz.'

The teamster's smile returned, infectious. He reached back into the sack and drew out two lengths of blood-encrusted silver – Maleneth's knives.

'Anything for you, sellah,' he said, handing each blade to her in turn.

'They were in the cabin,' Gotrek said.

'They wanted to sell us on with all of our possessions,' Maleneth said, appreciating having the two weapons in her hands, before sliding them into her belt. 'Many thanks once more, Aziz.'

'The Eight Pillars,' Gotrek said to the human. 'You're sure of the way?'

'Sure as Hysh rises over the Sea of Mer, sellah,' Aziz said, gesturing up at the burning orb dominating the cloudless sky. He dropped his arm to point over the nearest dune. 'Though upon my word I do not know how far it will be.'

'We can't go back,' Maleneth said. 'Khaled-Tush will be nothing but ash now. Besides, your wound must be seen to.'

She reached out to touch Gotrek's injured arm, but the Slayer drew back with a scowl.

'Do not treat me like some newborn beardling, aelf. I see through your scheming. You will advise me to go to that temple of yours. You want to make me their prisoner.'

'There are healers at the Temple of the Lightning,' Maleneth said, trying to mask her exasperation. 'A learned human chirurgeon, loyal to the Order of the Azyr. If you do not have it properly cleaned it will become infected. How well will a demigod deal with amputation?'

'I have fought through this world and the last without losing any part of me I hold dear,' the Slayer grunted. 'I'm not going to start now.'

Maleneth looked to Aziz, but the human wouldn't meet her eye, clearly not wanting to be drawn into an argument between his unlikely companions. She sighed.

'I am going to the Eight Pillars,' Gotrek said. 'The location of the Axe of Grimnir will be revealed to me. Where you go is your own choice.'

The Slayer trailed off as Maleneth moved suddenly to her right, her face contorting with anger.

She'd seen one of the Kharadron bodies littering the desert stirring. She had assumed they were all dead, pulverised by their fall or broken by the frigate's impact. She realised now that she was wrong.

She recognised the duardin – it was the only one with a golden ancestor mask, rather than silver, the same one that had dragged her out of the brig. She felt her spite surge and, without thinking, dropped to her knees in the sand and pressed her knife against the Kharadron's gorget seal.

A fist clamped like a vice around her wrist before she could push the tip home. She looked up at Gotrek, face contorted with anger.

'What are you doing?' she asked.

'Call it habit,' Gotrek said. 'But it wouldn't sit right to watch an aelf slit a dwarf's throat in his sleep.'

'They're pirates,' Maleneth said incredulously. 'They killed hundreds of innocent people at Khaled-Tush. They were going to sell all of us to the hag only knows who!'

'And they've collected their rewards,' Gotrek answered, pointing with his free, bloody hand at the wrecked skyship and the bodies scattered around it.

'If any more of them have survived they'll follow us!'

'You think they'll go far?' Gotrek replied. 'We've taken all their water. If you want them dead, you'll only have to wait. Anyway, we don't have the time to go through the wreckage and follow its trail to find every last injured one. I want to get to that damned inscription.'

The son of Gurni is correct, Witchblade. They're as good as dead. Stop wasting time.

'He is a fool,' Maleneth growled back, but moved her blade away from the Kharadron's throat. Gotrek released her arm.

'Let us make haste then,' she said, standing. 'Or we could wait until he's fully awake. Will you let me kill him then?'

Gotrek said nothing, but motioned to Aziz, standing uncertainly nearby.

'The Eight Pillars, manling. Lead on.'

CHAPTER NINE

Durbarak's arm was broken. He had cracked it back into place and formed a makeshift sling from a length of endrin cord. The pain was a dull, constant throb, a distant second to the anger that burned through him.

The *Draz Karr* had been wrecked beyond repair. The hull was buckled and split and the endrins shattered. Twisted wreckage littered the Bone Desert.

Bodies littered it too, crewmates who had failed to tie themselves to the deck before the skyship had capsized. Not all those who had done so had survived either. He'd already found Stromm and Borin, both crushed by one of the endrins when the remains of the crumpled orb had come down after the frigate had ploughed into the desert.

Durbarak's livelihood was in ruins and his crewmates were dead. Someone would pay. He'd already checked the hold, but the *Draz Karr*'s collision with the desert had ruptured the hull and left a tear in the brig's flank. There were three sets of prints leading from the downed skyship, three sets headed east, over the dunes. Durbarak had pulled off his ancestor mask and was staring after them, cradling his broken arm and trying to stop himself shaking with anger.

They'd taken the water with them too. He'd managed to find a single flask, half-empty, in the brig's remains, but that was all. He would have to go, and soon. A part of him simply wished to remain with his frigate's wreckage.

He heard a sound carried to him by the whispers of the desert wind. At first he thought it was the low groan of the skyship's remains settling, then he realised it was a voice, a voice that he recognised. He turned and moved back in amongst the hold, struggling in the sand that had been ploughed up by the *Draz Karr*'s impact.

He found Throm lying in the shade of one of the broken endrins, its misshapen sphere half buried in the sand. The Kharadron's legs were broken – bone and cartilage were protruding from his dusty sky-suit, and the sand was speckled with blood, a trail marking where he had dragged himself from the shattered decking plates nearby. Scraps of armour and his ancestor mask lay scattered around him, discarded in the infernal heat. He was only half conscious.

Durbarak trudged to his side, unhooking the water flask from his belt as he went. Throm's eyes flickered, and he blinked up at his crewmate.

'Captain?' His voice was a dry, deathly croak.

'Easy, lad,' Durbarak said, kneeling beside him and pressing the flask to his lips with his good hand. Rather than drinking, Throm turned his head away.

'You'll need it more than me, captain. I'm done.'

'I'm going to find the one who did this,' Durbarak said. 'Some oath-breaking *thaggoraki* has betrayed us.'

'The ship,' Throm murmured. 'The ship would never have gone down like that. Someone... someone had uncoupled the valve lines.'

Durbarak's response was interrupted by the sound of a horse's neigh. He froze. Throm had heard it too, his expression becoming clearer.

'Was that–' he began to say.

'Stay here,' Durbarak growled. He left the flask in Throm's lap and, after checking one of his pistols was still loaded and wedged in his belt, started to move towards the main section of the *Draz Karr*'s wreckage. The sound had come from the other side of the skyship's carcass.

He trudged around it warily, eyes creased against the glare of the sun and the streamers of sand being carried from the baking hull by the wind. He rounded a broken propeller that had lodged itself upright in the dirt, and found himself staring at a horse.

Even to a duardin it was a fine-looking beast, white and ill-tempered, tugging at reins that had been tied around the propeller's broken spoke. Durbarak drew his aetherlock, expecting the rider to be nearby, but there was no sign of anyone close to the beast. It snorted at him angrily and let out another shrill neigh. Only then did he notice the saddle on its back, and the device on its cloth. He turned and started to run back to Throm, stumbling and cursing as he went.

He heard a cracking sound – the discharge of another pistol, echoing back from the *Draz Karr*'s remains. Cursing more loudly, he reached the broken endrin once more, his shattered arm in agony.

He was too late. Throm slumped on his side in the dirt, gagging and choking, beard and hands slippery with his own blood as he tried in vain to hold shut his slit throat. A figure stepped away from the dying Kharadron, the wind snapping at its cloak. It sensed Durbarak and spun as he brought his pistol up.

'You,' the former captain of the *Draz Karr* snarled. The assassin didn't respond, reaching into its cloak instead.

Durbarak fired, but by the time he had squeezed the trigger a throwing star had thudded in between his eyes, killing him instantly. His shot went wide and he fell straight back, spread-eagled in the sand, eyes staring sightlessly into Hysh's fiery glare.

The assassin retrieved the throwing star and then crouched next to Throm, watching with apparent fascination as the last surviving crew member of the arkanaut frigate slowly bled to death. When his eyes had finally glazed over, the killer made one last circuit of the wreckage site, ensuring every last wounded duardin was dead, before returning and remounting its horse. It turned the white steed east and, leaning low in the saddle, set off after Gotrek, Maleneth and Aziz.

CHAPTER TEN

They caught sight of the Eight Pillars as darkness crept over the dunes once again. Maleneth, moving ahead of the other two, crested a rise of craggy desert rocks and found it sprawling abruptly below them – the towering, sand-blasted pillars that gave the place its name, and the great pyramid structure that lay at the end of the ancient colonnade, the final resting place of some human desert lord and, according to the seer coven in Barkash, the site of an inscription bearing the location of the Axe of Grimnir. The crumbling structures lay at the end of a long gorge, flanked by sheer walls of arid yellow stone.

When they had first set out from Barkash on the back of Aziz's cart, the pack driver had told them that long ago a town had clustered around the pyramid, forever in the shadow of their entombed master. The slow, insidious work of the desert had wiped away any trace of the old settlement, but the recent affluence of the Triumvirate Cities had aroused interest in the Bone Desert and its potential secrets. Adventurers, artefact-hunters and looters had begun flocking to the Eight Pillars, lured by tall tales relating to the wealth the pyramid's founder had supposedly been buried with.

Their arrival had resulted in a new town springing up. Like Khaled-Tush, it was largely ramshackle, a conglomeration of wagons that had been converted into dwellings. Tents and lean-tos and rough huts of dirt and stone clustered like growths around the bases of each of the eight great pillars, the spaces between teeming with people. The sound of voices and the crack of picks and shovels rose up on the humid wind.

'It looks like trouble,' Maleneth said darkly, surveying the dilapidated camp-turned-settlement.

'No more than usual,' Gotrek said.

They descended to the bottom of the gorge and moved along the craggy path to the outskirts of the Pillars. Hysh was setting, and the cliffs on either side provided relief from its burning gaze. Maleneth was too weary to offer any sort of thanks for the reprieve. She was bone-tired and ravenous. A part of her wished she'd perished in the skyship crash. Surely whatever fate awaited her beyond death was preferable to the heat that had scorched and burned her arms, neck and face, the ache that had worked its way into her limbs, the thirst that had turned her throat raw or the hunger that gnawed at her insides.

Aziz seemed little better, limping along in her wake, but Gotrek appeared indefatigable. She was certain it was more than just the legendary endurance of the duardin race at work. Perhaps it was more, even, than the power of the Master Rune. Once Gotrek had decided upon something, nothing seemed capable of stopping him, least of all trifling things like physical exhaustion or hunger.

Gotrek had decided he would go to the Eight Pillars, and so to the Eight Pillars he would go.

As they neared the furthest-flung wagons, the sound of an explosion reverberated down the gorge. As it echoed away, smoke and dust rose in the distance to their right, near the base of the pyramid. No one in the encampment sprawling before Maleneth seemed surprised by the detonation, and she realised some wealthy treasure-seeker was probably using a form of explosive to crack open one of the tombs.

She wondered what the Priests of the Lightning thought of such desecration. They had tended the temple nestled into the mountains a few miles from the gorge for as long as any in the Bone Desert could remember. The priesthood had served the ruler whose tomb now lay before Maleneth, guiding him towards the will of Sigmar. The presence of the Order of the Azyr among the priesthood had been a more recent development, but it was an easy accommodation to make – they both served the Lightning God, and the temple gave the Order an outpost in Aqysh, in a region whose cities were growing in importance.

Maleneth had resolved to report there, whether Gotrek would go with her or not. Perhaps the Order would permit her to cease accompanying the irascible duardin.

'These manlings,' Gotrek growled as they moved in among the edges of the settlement, 'are they seeking the axe too? I'd sooner spend the rest of my days eating *grobi* dung than allow the woeful umgi of these realms to find it first.'

The words had been directed at Aziz. The cart driver raised weary eyes from his feet and shook his head.

'No, sellah,' he said. 'At least, I do not believe they seek anything so specific here. There are many legends about the riches of the Eight Pillars, not only of the axe.'

That much was clearly true. As they continued up the main track towards the pyramid Maleneth was afforded a proper view of the work being done by the prospectors. Not content with trying to break into the tomb itself, they were seeking to crack open the pillars as well. Rickety wooden scaffolding surrounded the nearest ones, and Maleneth could see dozens of men and youths, many stripped to their waists, hacking at the old structures with all manner of tools. The air rang with the sounds of hard labour, punctuated by the report of another excavation blast sounding down from further up the gorge.

'You still think you'll find the axe before everyone else?' she asked Gotrek as they trudged deeper into the camp. 'If there is an inscription within that tomb pointing to its location, dozens of hotheads and fools will be seeking it the moment it's translated.'

'The axe, *my* axe, won't be found unless it's meant to be found,' the duardin replied stoically.

'You know the Order of the Azyr would likely help you to find it,' Maleneth pressed. 'Our agents cover the Mortal Realms. Nothing passes unseen. We can help you track down its most likely resting place.'

'Or you will imprison me,' Gotrek replied, without looking at the aelf. 'You think I'm too dangerous, and that makes you afraid, aelf. So you will lock me away in your temple. Or you will try.'

Maleneth stifled her response, knowing he would only shoot back with something denigrating about her race.

'We need lodgings,' she said instead, directing the statement to Aziz. 'Have you visited the Eight Pillars before?'

'Twice,' he responded, his usual eagerness visibly crushed by the trials of the past two days. 'Both times carrying feed for the Master of Azalam. His contractors gave me space to sleep in one of their storage sheds.'

'Anywhere will do,' Maleneth said. 'We need to eat as well.'

'I will cook,' Aziz said, his spirits apparently lifted at least a little by the prospect. 'I still have the coin sellah gave me in Khaled-Tush. I will be able to buy much with it!'

Maleneth let the teamster take the lead, carrying them into the burrow-like network of rough buildings, scaffolding, shacks and wagons that nestled around one of the towering pillars. He spent long minutes haggling in his native desert tongue with a suspicious-looking man with an immaculately oiled black goatee, clad in the red robes of a Merport cattle guilder. Eventually the man conceded whatever was being debated with an exasperated wave of his hand, and motioned towards the cattle barns that sat in the shadow of the great stone column, leaning precariously between two rows of sheds being used to sift the pillar's broken stone.

'They say that at their core the pillars are solid gold,' Aziz explained as he led them into the dank shadows of the barn. The stench of animal dung and the scrape and scuffle of hooves in the dirt assailed Maleneth, and her keen eyes picked out a dozen tuskers herded together behind stalls at the far end of the barn. She grimaced. For a moment she contemplated once again demanding Gotrek accompany her to the Temple of the Lightning, but the duardin's stubbornness coupled with her own exhaustion overcame the words. She picked a heap of grubby straw fodder just inside the doorway and collapsed onto it.

'I will bring us food,' Aziz said.

'Anything you can find,' Maleneth agreed.

'I'm going to look at the pyramid,' Gotrek said. 'Don't follow me. Your blundering attracts too much attention.'

CHAPTER ELEVEN

Darkness was sliding along the gorge when Aziz returned and kindled a fire outside the barn door. He had been right about Gotrek's Fyreslayer gold going far. The pot he had purchased was soon full of an alluring mixture of beans, herbs and spices. Despite herself, Maleneth had slipped into a half-sleep as she waited, her usual care in such an unfamiliar place overcome by fatigue. It was not an easy rest – memories of Jakari and their forced separation haunted her for the first time in years. It was a relief when the aroma of Aziz's cooking woke her.

'The warabi beans add the flavour, and the spice unlocks it,' he said as she sat back on her haunches next to him, staring into the bubbling pot. He drew out a spoonful and held it out for her, nodding earnestly.

She was far too hungry to resist. It tasted good, but it only made her stomach ache all the more.

Gotrek arrived back soon after. He'd found or purchased fresh linen from somewhere and had bound his injured arm tightly. Going by the amount of blood staining the cloth, it would still need to be treated.

'How does the pyramid look?' Maleneth asked as he joined them at the fire. Aziz had begun doling out his broth into a trio of clay bowls he'd bought along with the food supplies.

'The entrance is sealed,' the Slayer said. 'The umgi are trying to blast their way inside, but they don't know the first thing about a mining charge or where to plant it.'

'And you're not going to enlighten them?'

Gotrek made a barking noise that Maleneth thought might be a laugh.

'Better to watch the manlings blow each other up. See how high the different pieces fly. I'll just get inside another way.'

'Another way?' Aziz asked, as he passed the bowls around.

'There is always another way,' Gotrek said, taking the bowl and sniffing it. 'What is this?'

'A recipe of my tribe,' Aziz said. 'We call it *kalem*. You will enjoy it, master duardin, I promise you.'

Gotrek took a sip, and grunted noncommittally. Maleneth had no such reservations – she was too hungry to show the Slayer's reserve. She gulped down the broth, enduring the strength of the spices Aziz had seasoned it with.

'I went up the gorge side,' Gotrek said, eyeing the flames of the fire burning low beneath Aziz's cooking pot. 'There are paths. Old paths. The rock has been marked with tunnel-work.'

'There are stories about hidden ways into the great pyramid,' Aziz said between a mouthful of warabi beans. 'Many have sought them, but none have succeeded.'

'I doubt many were dwarfs,' Gotrek said.

'If there are hidden passages, the priests of the Temple of the Lightning would likely know more about them,' Maleneth said, setting her bowl down momentarily. Her stomach was aching, and she chided herself for eating too quickly and too greedily. It had been years since she had last been pushed to such extremes of fatigue and hunger.

'For the last time, I won't go to see your accursed priests,' Gotrek spat. 'If you want this damned rune then why not draw those pretty little steak knives of yours, come over here and see if you can carve it out of my chest?'

The suggestion didn't appeal. A part of Maleneth knew she should stop pursuing the need to submit the Slayer to the Order of the Azyr, but this close to one of their outposts the opportunity was infuriating her. If she could turn him over to them, she could finally be rid of the duardin and his insufferable stubbornness.

'You won't find the axe you seek alone,' she pressed. 'The Eight Realms are vast – even the gods themselves cannot wander them at will and hope to perceive all things. Or perhaps you do not really seek the axe...' She paused. 'Felix. Was that his name?'

'Do not speak of the manling, aelf,' Gotrek growled. 'He is gone.'

Another blast rang through the gorge, reverberating from its sheer sides as though in harmony with the duardin's anger. Maleneth ignored it.

'The Order can help you,' she reiterated. 'If he lives, they can find him.'

'A rust plague on your damned Order! I told you, he is gone! I care not for him any more!'

Maleneth cackled gleefully. 'Again, another lie, duardin.'

Gotrek's response was not the one she expected. He didn't speak. Instead, his eye refocused past the cooking fire, and after a few seconds he uttered a curse in his strange dialect. Maleneth had just registered the word before a crashing noise made her leap to her feet, her half-empty bowl spilled into the dirt. She followed the duardin's gaze.

The explosion that had rung out just before wasn't another attempt to crack open the pyramid, or even one of the pillars. Whether deliberately or not, someone had set off explosive charges at the base of the western gorge face. Now a crashing sound was heralding an avalanche of shattered stone and dirt, as a portion of the gorge came tumbling down towards the nearest pillar and the makeshift camp surrounding it – the one the three of them had chosen for the night.

'The damned rats,' Gotrek muttered.

'Move!' Maleneth shouted, snatching her pack from the entrance to the animal shed. Hysh's light was suddenly bathing the pillar at their backs once more, the collapse of the top of the gorge revealing the lowering orb. It silhouetted a wall of dirt and dust that was plummeting with ponderous inevitability towards them.

Aziz was scrambling over the fire and away from the avalanche, his meal forgotten. Gotrek hadn't moved, and a part of Maleneth wondered if he wanted to stay where he was and greet the landslide head on, stone meeting stone. In her mind's eye she could imagine the Master Rune igniting, the rock tumbling to either side, broken apart by nothing but the duardin's unyielding resolve.

Then she realised Gotrek was running.

She followed.

The whole world was beginning to shake, the earth underfoot and the air about them shuddering with the weight of the approaching debris. The camp around them was descending into chaos as disbelieving prospectors finally realised what was happening and tried to flee. Screams and the lowing of panicked animals filled the air. Tents were torn and trampled and lean-tos collapsed. A cart was overturned in the stampede, its occupants trapped beneath its weight, their cries for help unheeded in the tumult. Maleneth found herself pressed in from both sides by a mass of stinking, white-eyed people as they poured from their shacks and caravans.

The crowd dragged them, and for all her speed and Gotrek's strength, it carried them along regardless of which direction they wanted to go. She could no longer see Aziz, and the thunder of the avalanche was now filling her ears, the ground tremoring so violently that whole groups of the fleeing mob were being thrown to the dirt, trampled by those rushing heedlessly on from behind them.

She tried to shout Gotrek's name, struggling to keep her feet in the press. A sudden pain in her arm made her gasp. She stumbled, face contorted, and brought her forearm up. Blood was streaming from a long slash in her pale flesh, cut from just above her wrist to just below her elbow. She clutched the wound with her other hand, hissing with pain, trying to see who or what had struck her, but amidst the swell of bodies it was impossible to tell. All the while the avalanche filled the world with thunder, a fury so great it seemed in that heart-racing, desperate moment that it was the death knell of creation itself.

Follow the duardin, child!

'Aelf!'

The barked word, now all too familiar, drew her attention back to Gotrek. The Slayer had ignited his greataxe, and the sight of its runic fires had served to give him the slightest amount of space. He snatched at Maleneth, managing to grasp her belt and draw her to his side.

'Dwarfs should never run,' he growled, turning back to the onrushing wall of dirt and rocks with his axe raised.

'Are you insane?' Maleneth shouted, her voice barely audible.

'No more than you,' Gotrek grunted, and began to charge back the way they had come.

Maleneth started to follow him instinctively before reason made her pause. Perhaps Gotrek was a demigod. Perhaps he could survive a collision with a falling cliff face. She had no such guarantees.

Foolish girl, snapped the hag. *I said follow him!*

'You wish me to stand before Khaine so soon,' Maleneth said bitterly. She was still clutching her wounded arm, her fingers soaked with blood.

I wish you to reach that spite-cursed pillar.

And finally Maleneth understood. He wasn't running at the avalanche. He was trying to reach the base of one of the Eight Pillars before the oncoming tide.

She followed him. The crowd was less dense now. Ahead she could see the ponderous morass of earth and rock shattering and eating up the encampment. One of the pillars stood just ahead of it, a tower of defiance, scarred and chipped by the tools of greedy mortals. Maleneth raced for its base, quickly catching up with Gotrek. Heart thundering and tired limbs flushed, she reached the pillar's shadow, then its Hysh-baked stone, slamming into its flank. Gotrek hit a moment later.

There was no time for words. The torrent of dirt engulfed them, slamming like the fist of a god into the other side of the pillar, thundering either side. The weight and momentum carried it round, but not all the way, leaving the aelf and the duardin standing in the clear wake created by the pillar's bulk. Maleneth shielded her face behind her uninjured arm as grit and stones battered them, and for what felt like an age it appeared the shifting tide of soil would wrap the pillar entirely, dragging them into its crushing embrace to be churned and ground up with the remains of the encampment and all those souls too slow to get out.

But it didn't. The avalanche had already expended a great deal of its force. It reached past the pillar on either side but didn't travel much further before it finally began to settle. The stonework of the pillar itself had shifted slightly, but held.

'Told you they don't know how to use mining charges,' Gotrek said.

Maleneth didn't reply. A pain had gripped her, a burning sensation running through her torso. She hissed, and the next thing she knew she was on her knees, hand clutching her wound and both arms clenched to her sides. Gotrek was saying something, but she couldn't make out what it was. Her hiss became a cry, and the pain surged to agony. It was as though a fire had been kindled inside her, the flames eating up her insides. She felt Gotrek's hand on her shoulder.

'The wound,' she managed to snarl from between clenched teeth. 'Someone... in the crowd... The wound is poisoned.'

CHAPTER TWELVE

High Priest Shal'ek was roused from his matins prayers by one of the notaries. The main prayer room of the temple was quiet, only a cluster of candles around the hammer altar giving light to the yellowing walls and rough-hewn stone pews.

'It is Zelja, your holiness,' the youth said. Shal'ek opened one eye, and scowled. He could never remember which notary was which.

'What is wrong with Zelja, boy?' the gaunt-faced priest demanded.

'There are travellers at the gate, your holiness. She sent me to inform you.'

Zelja, captain of the Temple Guard, knew well enough to turn away random pilgrims, especially when dawn was still only a glimmer over the distant dunes. Shal'ek assumed something more required his clarification, but that didn't stop him from snapping at the anonymous messenger.

'Captain Zelja does not need me to instruct her to follow her usual orders and tell them to begone. What does she want from me?'

Kneeling as he was towards the hammer altar, Shal'ek could not see the notary, but he didn't need to in order to sense the boy squirming.

'The captain... She reports that they may warrant your attention, your holiness. There are three of them, a human, a duardin and an aelf.'

Shal'ek's other eye opened, and his expression changed to one of consternation.

'The aelf and the duardin both seem to be injured,' the notary continued. 'The aelf is unconscious.'

'And what of the third one?' Shal'ek asked.

'Zelja says he is a desert trader.'

Shal'ek grunted, and stood. He offered a brief genuflection towards the hammer altar, traced the lightning sigil with two fingers and turned to the boy, who stiffly averted his eyes.

'Show me,' Shal'ek said.

'I'm going to count to ten,' bellowed a voice from beyond the temple's timber gateway. '*Ong!*'

Shal'ek approached the entrance, glaring, the notary scurrying at his heels. '*Tuk! Dwe!*'

'A duardin?' the high priest demanded of Captain Zelja. The veiled commander of the temple guard was standing next to the gate, her scimitar

65

drawn. A dozen of her men occupied the open stone parapet above, lit by
the braziers lining the wall top.

'*Fut!*'

'There is a human with him, and he seems to be supporting an aelf in the
garb of the Murder Temples,' Zelja added. 'They say she is dying.'

'*Sak! Siz! Set!*'

'Is it her?' Shal'ek demanded. 'One of the Order's wretches?'

The question went unanswered.

'*Odro! Nuk!*'

'Does Weiss know?' Shal'ek asked, stepping towards the viewing slit set
into the heavy doors.

'I have not sent anyone to wake him,' Zelja said.

'*Don!*'

Shal'ek set his eye to the slit opening. All he caught was a blur of movement, followed by an almighty bellow and a crash that made him stumble
backwards. He blinked. The edge of an axe, wickedly sharp, was gleaming an
inch from his nose. Had the sound of it cleaving clean through the temple's
front doors not sent him staggering back, it would have carved his skull in half.

There was a grunt from beyond the gate, and the axe head disappeared.

'H-he's hacking through the gate,' Shal'ek stammered.

'Archers,' Zelja commanded. There was a clatter above as the guards
nocked arrows to their bows.

'I wouldn't do that, manlings,' bellowed the voice from beyond the gate.
There was another shuddering impact, and the axe head reappeared amidst
a hail of splinters. 'I'd far rather be cutting heads instead of timber right
now. Give me an excuse.'

Zelja's guards looked to her, and she looked to Shal'ek. The high priest
tried to find an answer to the duardin's threat, but his eyes were fixated
on the axe as it reappeared for a third time, hacking through just above
the gate's locking bar. Another below – delivered with a strength and force
that seemed wholly unnatural – would surely break the gates wide open.

'The aelf with you,' declared a voice beside Shal'ek, startling him. Weiss
had appeared, clad only in a night shift, his podgy face pale from lack of
sleep. 'What is her name?'

The axe blows paused. There was a hint of a growled discussion from
beyond the gate. The voice called back.

'Some damned stupid aelf name. Witchblade.'

'And you,' called Weiss. 'You must be Gotrek Gurnisson.'

'Have I found the only manling in this cursed world with an ounce of
sense?' the voice demanded.

'It seems like it,' Weiss said, and then, speaking to Zelja, he ordered, 'Open
the gate, and be quick about it.'

'Are you mad?' Shal'ek hissed. 'That duardin is clearly insane. He will
slaughter all of us.'

'The aelf is a valued member of the Order of the Azyr,' Weiss said curtly.
'And the duardin, Gotrek... He is something else altogether. Something
beyond anything we can comprehend.'

Shal'ek's protestations were stilled by the opening of the scarred gate. A duardin strode in without hesitating. Weiss was right – he was unlike one Shal'ek had ever seen before. His scarred, tattooed skin bore only a single rune, crafted in the baleful image of the duardin god, and his huge rune-etched axe was wreathed in fire. The glare from his one remaining eye burned white-hot.

Shal'ek had spent his life in observance towards the gods. He had never anticipated standing before one. He whimpered.

'Well don't just stand there,' the duardin bellowed, making even Zelja cringe visibly. 'I've known better welcomes in the corpse-castles of Sylvania! The damned aelf wouldn't stop talking about you – the least you can do is help her!'

The duardin gestured behind him, at the two figures limping through the gate in his wake. One was a raggedy human, a desert pack driver by the cap he wore. The other, supported awkwardly by the boy, was a pallid aelf in purple silks and dark leather. She was unconscious, but as they crossed into the temple she convulsed against the boy's grip and was sick. There was blood in the vomit.

'You men,' Weiss barked at a gaggle of Shal'ek's priests, who had come from their sleeping dorms to stare. 'Take the aelf to the infirmary. And someone go and awaken Draz.'

Arch-Chirurgeon Abul Draz was woken by the temple's chief leecher. He came to with a gasp, grasping the man's smock.

'My apologies, sellah,' the leecher, Blemes, murmured, gently extracting himself from Draz's clutches. 'It is the high priest. He requires our presence.'

'What hour is it?' Draz asked groggily, sitting up in his cot. Blemes had come bearing a candle, its flickering light picking out the bare stone of Draz's sleeping cell. There was only the faintest hint of light from beyond the window shutters.

'Just after matins,' Blemes said. 'We have visitors, and they come bearing injuries.'

Draz pulled off his nightcap and swung his legs out over the side of the cot. The cold stone floor was a shock to his feet. The chill of the night still permeated the temple's ancient, cracked sandstone.

'They are in the infirmary,' Blemes went on, turning his back to allow Draz to dress. He did so, wondering as he pulled on his robes and rubbed sleep from his eyes just who could have arrived in the night and been permitted to enter. Since explorers had started digging around the Eight Pillars there had been more and more instances of people travelling up the high gorge to the temple, seeking aid and supplies. Shal'ek, High Priest of the Lightning, had ordered them all turned away. Only Weiss, the pale-faced representative of the Order of the Azyr attached to the temple's priesthood, had the power to overrule Shal'ek's judgements within the temple itself, and he rarely roused himself from his reports or the celestial auguries that cluttered his office.

'Lead on,' Draz told Blemes, tugging his robes straight and pulling on his work smock. He followed the leecher down the narrow, dusty corridor that connected his sleeping cell to the temple's infirmary.

The room was as small and spartan as the rest of the house of worship. It bore a washing stand, five sick cots, a cabinet of Draz's chirurgeon supplies – tinctures and vials, crushed herbs and poultice pots – and several jars of Blemes' leeches. It occasionally played host to a travelling pilgrim, or one of the temple's priests or notaries if they fell prey to the ague. It had certainly never serviced as unlikely looking a trio as those waiting for Draz.

He saw the duardin first. But for a single lion-headed pauldron, he was naked from the waist up, and covered in the marks of Hysh – blistered, peeling red skin, evidence of days spent in the Bone Desert. Draz recognised the red crest of the Fyreslayers, though he seemed to bear only a single fragment of ur-gold, a bright rune buried into his chest. The thickly muscled warrior turned, and Draz gasped as he saw his face. Half of it was wizened and deformed, as though it had aged centuries ahead of the rest of the duardin's body. The Slayer's single eye was stony, but flickered with forge-fire as it fell upon Draz.

'Chirurgeon,' said Weiss. The corpulent agent of the Order of the Azyr had been standing just inside the door when Draz entered, alongside High Priest Shal'ek. He was a small, pugnacious man, forever sweating and red-faced in the desert's heat, his embroidered, puffed sleeves, white stockings and starched ruff a garish contrast to the rustic sackcloth worn by the priesthood. He looked as though he'd dressed in a hurry.

'These pilgrims require your skills,' Weiss said, making a half-hearted gesture towards the duardin, who remained silent. For a moment, Draz thought he meant the Slayer's arm – it was crudely bound in strips of linen, stained and crusted with blood. Then he realised that the bed directly behind the duardin was occupied. A pale woman – an aelf – was laid out on it. A man was sitting on a stool on the opposite side, young and wide-eyed, wearing the dirt-encrusted brown half-cape and cap of a merchant's teamster.

'This aelf is a servant of the Order,' Weiss elaborated, sensing Draz's fear and confusion. 'She has been poisoned. The high priest and I desire that you and Blemes do all in your power to save her.'

Shal'ek, standing tall and lugubrious next to Weiss, nodded once. His sallow expression spoke volumes about his distrust towards the new arrivals, but clearly Weiss was in no mood to brook any argument – it was rare indeed to see him roused from his office.

'You're a healer?'

It was the duardin who had spoken, his parched voice like cracked desert rocks grinding together. Draz managed to nod. He had never heard of any form of close kinship between aelves and duardin before, yet the Slayer was standing over the stricken aelf like a guard dog. Draz eyed the wicked-looking edges of the heavy war axe slung over his back, glinting in the candlelight.

The duardin glared at him for what felt like an age, then finally stepped out of the way. Draz and Blemes approached, Draz kneeling beside the stricken aelf.

She was pale, even for one of her kind, her lips an unhealthy shade of blue. She was clad in tight-fighting leathers, though most of her arms were bared. Another strip of linen had been wrapped roughly around one, and was crusted with blood and yellow fluids.

Draz reached into his smock and pulled out a thin blade. He sensed the duardin tense at the sight of the naked steel, and he froze, but when the Slayer didn't say anything he reached down and gently slid the tool through the stiff cloth, cutting it free.

The wound beneath was crusted with more blood. Draz moved to the washing stand and wetted a strip of gauze. Blemes was at the cabinet, fishing through his jars for his leeches with a long prong. Draz returned to the aelf's side and began cleaning the wound. The woman stirred slightly.

'What is her name?' he asked, without looking up from his work.

'Maleneth,' the duardin said after a pause, giving the aelf name a rough Duardin inflection.

'And yours?'

'I am Gotrek Gurnisson.'

'You are a Fyreslayer?'

The words came easier to Draz as he focused on removing the dirt from the aelf's wound. They always did when he started his work. He had been a healer at the Temple of the Lightning all his life. No matter the patient, he was always willing to help those admitted by the priesthood. It was his calling in life, and he offered thanks to the Lightning every night that he had been bestowed with such a clear and simple purpose.

The duardin, Gotrek, hesitated before responding to his last question.

'I do not know if I am a Fyreslayer.'

'That is a curious answer.'

'This is a curious place, manling.'

Draz washed the blood from the gauze and knelt once more to expose the bared wound. It was long but shallow, running up the aelf's forearm. The cut was precise, the work of a thin blade expertly delivered. It was not in itself fatal, but it was clear enough that something else was seeking to push Maleneth through Shyish's door.

'Can she be saved?' Weiss asked from over his shoulder. 'She is an... agent that the Order would very much like to keep alive.'

'I will do all I can,' Draz responded. He placed his blade upon the bed-frame then withdrew two vials from his smock. Unstoppering the first, he pinched the aelf's nose, poured the contents into her mouth and massaged her throat until she swallowed the dark contents. 'I have given her an anti-dote known to combat most poisons, but I must still take a sample of her blood in case the poison should be rare and beyond its reach.'

He unstoppered the second vial, then once more picked up his blade and made a shallow incision in the aelf's arm, a finger's width from the main wound. He collected a few drops of blood from the small cut, then stop-pered the vial and dabbed the incision clean.

He rose, grunting slightly at the stiffness that had worked itself into his joints on the cold floor, then turned to Blemes.

'Will you apply clean dressings? I must see to this sample as swiftly as possible.'

'The leeches too?' Blemes asked. He already had one of the fat, black creatures curled around his prong.

'Yes, I don't see how that could do any harm. Apply them around the wound. They may be able to keep the worst of the poison at bay should the antidote falter.'

'How long?' Gotrek interrupted.

'Excuse me?'

'How long until you know whether the antidote has worked?'

'It is impossible to say just now. I may have to return for further samples.'

'I want you to move her,' Gotrek said.

'Move her?'

'You must have better beds than these,' the duardin growled, tapping one of the cot's legs with his boot.

'This is a simple monastery–' Draz began to say, but Weiss interrupted him.

'She can have my bed chamber.'

Draz frowned and nodded, wondering again just who the travellers were. He'd never heard of Weiss offering any sort of charitable concession in all the months he'd been assigned to the temple. And who was the third figure, the young desert trader? The youth had said nothing since Draz had entered, had hardly taken his eyes off the aelf. The intensity of his gaze was almost as unsettling as the barely restrained violence exuded by the scarred duardin.

Shal'ek summoned two of the older notaries to bear the aelf to Weiss' chamber. Gotrek and the human accompanied them, as did Blemes, with his leech jars and bandages. Draz took another corridor, down a set of worn stone steps, vial in one hand and a candle in the other. He passed under an archway at the bottom and set the candle's flame to a brazier on the wall. The rapidly strengthening firelight illuminated a vaulted room, buried into dry bedrock. Another archway beyond led into the temple's crypts, where generations of priests were interred in tiered niches. The looming darkness of that entrance always made Draz shudder, and he never passed over into the crypts proper – his business was with the living, and those who could still be saved.

That same business took him to the long table that dominated the otherwise bare chamber lying between the steps and the bones of the temple's priesthood. The objects on it were covered by a series of old cloths, but he carefully removed and rolled them up, each in turn, revealing an apparatus of beakers, candles, mortars and vials. He lit the candles, checked the metal framework holding various cups and glass tinctures together was properly set, and then seated himself at the bench running the length of the table.

He was tired, and he would have preferred to check his ingredients before assessing the sample. Time, however, was not on his side. He didn't need his years of experience to know that the aelf did not have long to live.

He unstoppered the vial of blood and allowed a drop of its contents to trickle into a beaker at the start of the connecting apparatus, murmuring a well-worn prayer to the Hammer and the Lightning as he did so. He watched the blood closely as it trickled through into another vial that had been stuffed with a grey, powdery substance. Rather than stain red, the powder turned a deep purple. Draz grunted and administered another drop, this time to a different section of the apparatus, a metal spoon held over one of the thick candle stubs. As the single droplet hissed and sizzled, Draz plucked a pinch of crushed herbs from a pot beside the candle and sprinkled them onto the spoon. He wrinkled his nose at the stink the cloying herbs gave off as they burned, but didn't take his eyes off the little wisps of black smoke that rose from the charred remains.

Still nothing.

He had one drop left, and then he would be forced to return to the aelf to take another sample. He didn't think either of her companions would approve of that.

He rubbed his eyes with his free hand, then shifted along the bench to the far end of the table. There a tincture of clear liquid was clasped in a claw-shaped holder over another candle, the stub almost lost in the sea of melted wax spread across the table's edge. He laid the side of his hand against the tincture to make sure it was at the correct temperature, then tipped the final drop of blood into the liquid within.

It turned pink. He wrinkled his nose, and was about to mutter something under his breath when the scrape of iron-shod boots on the stairway made him jump.

The whole table and its rickety construction shuddered at the suddenness of his movements. He froze. A figure was silhouetted against the light being thrown by the brazier, occupying the only route back up into the temple. The crest of hair and the brutal outline of the war axe made him unmistakable.

'You should not be here,' Draz stammered. 'I am trying to work.'

'Are you?' Gotrek asked, stepping into the light. The fire made his golden-red crest and beard look as though they were aflame, flickering with a heat of their own.

'Working at what?' he demanded, stamping down past the bench. Draz edged away.

'I am seeking to diagnose your companion's current state.'

'Her current state is that she's dying,' the duardin said bluntly, coming to a stop within arm's reach of Draz. He'd made no aggressive motions since appearing in the crypt, but the look in his solitary, stony eye made the chirurgeon shiver.

'She is,' he agreed hesitantly. 'But right now I do not know why.'

'Poison,' Gotrek barked. 'Any *wanaz* can see that.'

'Yes. She has been poisoned. But not from the wound she has sustained on her arm.'

The duardin's expression grew fiercer still, and Draz hurried to explain.

'None of the blood I took has shown any sign of poison. Whatever blade cut her arm, it does not seem to be responsible for her current state. It is certainly not in itself a fatal wound.'

The duardin stepped around Draz, looking into the darkness of the tombs beyond the entry chamber. For a moment he wondered whether he'd not heard him.

'I'm wanted dead, that is nothing new,' Gotrek said slowly, seemingly to himself. 'Nothing can bring me the doom I seek. That is also nothing new. Those are about the only things in these damned realms that I recognise. But the rats, they've been trying even harder than usual. By the grudges of the Eight Peaks, none of you understand. The horned one won't stop. And neither will I.'

The rambling comments made little sense to Draz. He shrugged, not wanting to rouse the addled duardin's anger by questioning him.

'Many wish harm upon the servants of the Order of the Azyr,' he said instead.

'The Order,' Gotrek echoed, still not looking at Draz. 'She spoke about them a lot. Wanted to come here even. I told her I wouldn't be lured in by her damned aelven trickery. I assumed if I took her here someone would look after her. Take her off my hands. After the last one...'

He trailed into silence. Draz shifted uncomfortably, wondering if he could reach the steps back up to the temple before the duardin. Perhaps he was drunk? He'd never been this close to one before, but everyone had heard tales of their fondness for ale. He certainly couldn't fathom any other means of enduring such horrific sunburn.

'The boy too,' Gotrek went on. 'The longer they're with me, the greater the danger. They don't understand anything about what it means to seek your doom. To be cast aside by the gods and to get back up and spit in their faces. It's just a game to them. Especially to the boy. He's watching over her right now. I should go tonight, before they realise I've left. Then perhaps I can find something worthy of my axe in these maddening realms. Is there not one beast or daemon out there capable of granting me a final doom?'

'W-who is the boy?' Draz asked, wanting to shift the conversation onto something more mundane than the Slayer's dark ramblings.

'A cart driver,' Gotrek said dismissively. 'He was our guide. Typical manling though – he was more trouble than anything else. You people in this new realm of yours, you're even less trustworthy than the ones I left behind. Treacherous, cowardly, or just too foolish.'

'He was guiding you to the Eight Pillars?'

Gotrek said nothing for a while, then rounded abruptly on Draz, making him cringe back.

'You said the wound didn't poison her?'

'No, she hasn't been poisoned by the cut to her arm,' Draz reiterated. 'I will need to take further samples, but I suspect it's the work of ingestion. I... I believe she has consumed the poison, probably in her last meal.'

'Her last meal,' Gotrek echoed, his gaze igniting. He cursed. 'It was never the rats.'

Draz said nothing, staring in fear at the duardin. For a moment, silence reigned in the crypt. Then, with a sudden burst of motion that made the chirurgeon yelp, Gotrek ran for the stairs.

CHAPTER THIRTEEN

Maleneth's insides felt as though they were being gnawed and chewed at by a thousand hungry vermin. It was the pain that dragged her back to consciousness, making her groan and grip the bed sheets.

Bed sheets. She was in bed, in a spartan room of yellow sandstone. A clay pitcher sat on a stone table beside the bed. It seemed to still be night – the room's shutters were closed and an oil lamp bracketed to the wall beside the door offered the only illumination.

She wasn't alone. Aziz was in the room too, standing over her. He seemed to go still when Maleneth looked up at him.

'The Runetamer told me to keep watch,' the teamster said, reaching for the pitcher. 'You must drink, sellah. The poison will dehydrate you.'

'You came back,' Maleneth croaked. Her throat was parched, and she flinched as fresh pain surged through her guts. She clutched her stomach with both hands and groaned.

'When I saw the rock coming down I ran,' Aziz admitted. 'I found the duardin carrying you when it settled. After everything, I decided I could not leave you both.'

'This is the Temple of the Lightning,' she managed to say.

'This is the temple,' Aziz agreed, holding out the water pitcher. 'The priesthood opened their doors to us when Gotrek showed them the token you carry. The token of the Order of the Azyr.'

Maleneth paused.

'I have never shown Gotrek the token,' Maleneth said slowly. Aziz didn't reply. Instead, he smashed the pitcher he had been proffering over her head. The clay shattered and water drenched the aelf as she was smacked down into the pillow. Her vision swam, and she gasped at the fresh, sudden pain that burst across her nose and the right side of her face.

A part of her mind, an aelven instinct further honed by decades of service to the Temple of Khaine, told her to move. She couldn't though. Everything else was pain and blinding starbursts of light. She managed to half raise one arm, slurring a curse, the subconscious part of her that was still capable of thought shrieking at her.

It had been Aziz. It had all been Aziz.

She passed out.

Consciousness was pain.

She lived.

Be still, child.

She obeyed her former mistress' command, even as she flinched away from the dagger she expected to feel digging into her breast. With agonised slowness, her vision returned. She blinked, reached up to wipe blood from her eyes. She couldn't. Her wrists had been bound to the bedposts.

She could taste blood. Aziz was standing at the foot of the bed, his boyish grin wicked in the candlelight. The sheets covering her were drenched crimson. She realised that almost none of it was hers.

A body was slumped against the side of the bed, the stone floor beneath it soaked. Maleneth recognised the simple habit of one of the temple's notaries. Judging by the blood covering Aziz's arms, he'd been the one who had murdered the boy and then carved his chest open. A heart, glistening and raw, lay in the bed beside her.

The sight of it made her shudder uncontrollably. Realisation rushed over her, turning her thoughts cold. It wasn't the skaven behind the assassination attempts. And they weren't directed at Gotrek either. They'd been coming for her.

There were many who wanted her dead, but none with the resources or the sadistic flare she'd witnessed since setting out for the Eight Pillars.

'Jakari,' she said, her voice thick with the blood clogging her broken nose.

'Correct,' Aziz said, offering a short bow.

'You were working for her from the beginning.'

'I was,' Aziz admitted. 'She hired me in Kalzuf. All of us, in fact, though the others proved to be... less than capable. The dragging sands, the poison combined with the avalanche, that was all my work. And here, the finale.'

'I should have realised she was behind it all at Khaled-Tush,' Maleneth murmured. 'Damn the duardin and his obsession with the rats.'

'The Seventeen Blades,' Aziz said. 'The dance that means so much to both of you. She felt it was a little too obvious but equally irresistible. Personally speaking, the Alharabi always charge too much. Their methods are so dramatic as well. It is far easier to just lose someone in the dragging sands.'

'You realigned the posts marking out the path,' Maleneth said, rage causing her to strain at her bonds. 'You intended to run all along. You had a horse tied at that trough, waiting for you.'

'It's true, I didn't expect to see you both together again at Khaled-Tush,' Aziz admitted with a shrug. 'I thought you'd abandon the duardin. You should've done. You hate him.'

'He is too dangerous to leave to his own devices,' Maleneth said, giving up on pulling at the ropes binding her wrists. 'But it wouldn't have made any difference even if I had, would it? It was never about Gotrek.'

Aziz shrugged again. 'He has enough bounties on his head already. You know Jakari has no interest in runes or fables of demigods.'

'She's here as well, isn't she? That is who I saw on the dunes, and then again from the skyship.'

'She cares for you a great deal,' Aziz said, his tone mocking. 'So much so that she was willing to double my price for the delivery of this final message, before I kill you and take your heart to her.'

'She is too much of a coward to face me on her own,' Maleneth snarled, spitting blood.

'Too wise to try to infiltrate an Azyr outpost when she could use an unassuming pack driver like me instead.'

'You brought down the skyship as well, didn't you?'

'I couldn't have those oafs compromising my client's wishes,' Aziz admitted. 'Duardin are so predictable. Their greed blinds them.'

'And this?' Maleneth snapped, nodding towards her arm, injured by the knife cut at the Eight Pillars.

'Oh, that was her. I don't think she could resist a little slice of her own.'

'All those people at Khaled-Tush, dead because of her obsession,' Maleneth hissed, her voice cracking with hatred. 'This time she's gone too far. Tell me where she is, right now, and I will kill you quickly. Refuse and I will give you to the mad duardin. You and she will both die, if only to stop others being caught up in the web of her bitterness.'

'I find that hard to believe,' Aziz smirked. 'Unless you intend to slay us from the afterlife. And you can stop trying to loosen your bonds, murderwitch. I know how to tie a knot.'

Maleneth froze, watching Aziz as he moved to her side and drew a long, thin dagger from where it had been concealed against his hip.

'I know when someone is just stalling for time as well,' he hissed. 'I expected more from a child of the temples, Witchblade.'

The sound of running feet reached Maleneth just before the blade fell. There was a crash, and she twisted her body desperately in the blood-drenched sheets as the door to the room blasted in. The knife thumped home, but not where Aziz had intended – her movement had caused it to punch into her side instead, making her grunt with pain.

The assassin didn't have time for a second blow. Rune blazing and axe ignited, Gotrek Gurnisson came thundering through the splintered doorway.

'*Thaggaz!*' the Slayer roared, leaping the bed as he went straight for Aziz. The young killer didn't consider meeting the duardin head-on. He turned and ran for the window, scrabbling wildly with the locked shutters.

'I shouldn't sully this axe with the blood of such a coward,' Gotrek snarled. 'You have as much courage as the ratmen, traitor. Now you'll die like one.'

He swung.

Aziz yelped like a snared rabbit, the horrible noise cut short by a gristly crunch. The fyrestorm greataxe cleaved him from shoulder to groin, his blood gouting across the shutters. The two halves fell like sheared meat, the gore almost dousing the greataxe's fiery core. Gotrek looked down at the grim remains for a few seconds, panting, anger still flushing his body. Then, without turning to Maleneth, he spoke.

'Never trust anyone who can't grow a beard.'

He turned to the bound aelf.

'That goes for you too, murderling.'

'If you count the Kharadrons, I think most of the things trying to kill us over the past few days have had beards,' Maleneth responded, eyes narrowed.

The Slayer glared around the room, his one eye ablaze, as though seeking out new enemies invisible to Maleneth.

'You worked it out then,' she said, looking with distaste at Aziz's remains, then flinching as her guts twisted, only this time it wasn't down to the poison. 'It wasn't the vermin after all.'

'For once,' Gotrek muttered.

'He was sent by a shadow of my past,' Maleneth went on, the feeling of being broiled alive beginning to lose its intensity. 'They all were. She won't stop until I'm dead.'

'I know the feeling, aelf.'

The Slayer appeared to accept that there was no one else in the room. The fires that seemed to pulse from the Master Rune and gleam in his bristling red-gold hair had dimmed. He stepped over to the bedside, grasped the cords binding Maleneth's wrists and snapped them.

'You brought me to the temple in the end,' she said, rubbing her wrists.

'Well I thought it was the only way to make you stop talking about this place and your damned Order. It was that or strangle you in your sleep, and there were enough *skaz* trying to do that already.'

'You relinquished the inscription about the Axe of Grimnir,' Maleneth said, brushing aside the duardin's gruff attempt at humour. 'You could have joined the party exploring the pillars. You chose to carry me here instead.'

'If I'd known you would keep babbling like this I'd have left you in the desert.'

'Thank you, Gotrek.'

The duardin grumbled something in his rough language, then sat heavily on the end of the bed, his doused axe laid across his lap.

'I need someone to explain this mad world to me,' he said quietly, almost to himself. He turned to look out of the window as the new day bled colour back into the dunes. 'If I'd known he had sent me here, I'd have spat in Grimnir's face.'

For a moment, the age that had once disfigured the side of the duardin's face seemed to return, and Maleneth found herself looking at an old grey-beard, his scarred flesh wizened, hunched over and alone as he stared out upon a strange reality that had been thrust upon him against his will. The illusion was gone in an instant, but the revelation it brought stayed with Maleneth. When Gotrek's greataxe ignited and he threw himself into the fight with the Master Rune blazing, it was easy to lend credence to stories of the Slayer's immortality. Seeing him now though, so isolated, so worn by all he had seen and all he had done, Maleneth found herself more convinced that he was no ordinary duardin than when she saw him roused to wrath. In all her time travelling the Mortal Realms, she had never known anyone or anything like him.

'You don't have to stay with me,' she said. He turned back to look at her, the aged side of his face lost in shadow. 'He was the last,' Maleneth elaborated, indicating Aziz. 'The last one sent to kill me. It's over, for now.'

'It's never over,' Gotrek said darkly.

They were silent, before Maleneth spoke again.

'The Axe of Grimnir then. You said there was another way to reach the inscription in the temple.'

'You are in no fit state to travel, even though your incessant prattling seems to imply that the antidote is working,' Gotrek said.

'Grant me until the morning, Slayer. You will need me if you're to convince the Order to let you leave.'

Gotrek scoffed. 'I wish they would try and stop me.'

'I'm sure the likes of Weiss would try. Besides, I'm not staying either. Jakari is still out there. Waiting.'

'You *elgi*,' Gotrek said, standing. 'If this is how you are with those you love, I cannot imagine how you treat your enemies.'

'You cannot even begin to imagine, Gotrek Gurnisson,' Maleneth said. The duardin let out something approximating a laugh. The crushing weight that Maleneth had seen, the one that she so rarely caught glimpses of when the Slayer's darkest memories beset him, had gone. Gotrek slung his axe over his shoulder, blood still running from its blade.

'I'll go tell the manling priests they've got some bodies to clear up. If you're not ready to move by the time the sun's up, aelf, I'm going without you.'

'If you so much as dare, I swear my fyresteel will spell your doom, duardin,' Maleneth said. A smile ghosted across her lips as the Slayer stomped out. Then she slumped back in the bloody bed, and finally let her eyes fall shut.

THE NEVERSPIKE

DARIUS HINKS

I glare at the ember-shot tide, listening to the hiss of the waves and the tick of my cooling armour. Escaping death is always so much harder than finding it. Returning from the underworlds has been like another Reforging, another flaying of my soul. My mind is as fractured and distorted as my armour, but slowly my memory pieces itself back together. Every one of my retinue has fallen. My anger flares. They faltered. They failed. They paid the price.

'We fight. We Kill.' My voice cracks with rage. 'We win.'

I am standing on a shoulder of the Slain Peak, three hundred feet above the Ardent Sea, drenched in blood and caked in soot. I look like one of the ruins that litter the foothills below. The Realmgate spat me into the shallows and my warhammers are still smouldering where the god-wrought metal punched through the heat of the Ardent.

I whisper the names of the fallen, in accusation rather than benediction, then turn inland, spilling ash from my blue-green armour. From this height I can see the length of the valley. At the far end is a stormkeep, silhouetted before the hammered-gold sky. Ipsala. Pride of the Zullan coast. Home to five glorious retinues of Celestial Vindicators, all of them veterans of the Realmgate Wars; the guardians of the Southern Wards. Two days' march. Then I will stand before warriors worthy of the name Stormcast Eternal. My own, vengeful kin. They will understand why I have returned. They would never fail me as the Hammers of Sigmar have done.

As I clamber down the slope, tongues of steam rush up through the blackened rocks, hissing and sighing.

'The Hammers of Sigmar did not fail you, Trachos. It was the other way around. You failed them.'

The accusation halts me in my tracks and my mind falls back to Shyish. My pulse drums as I recall pale, emaciated bodies, still smouldering in the ruins. Thin, broken limbs, grasping at smoke-filled air.

'I failed no one. The Hammers lacked steel.'

'You murdered those people.'

'I was relentless. As I must be. Those wretched souls *all* worshipped the Betrayer God. They bore the sigils of Nagash. None of them deserved mercy. The Hammers of Sigmar were blinded by pity. The fault was theirs.'

'What of their souls, Trachos? This is why you were made. You cannot simply abandon them.'

I limp down the slope, shaking my head, trying to rid myself of the wretched voice. I'd hoped to leave it in Nagash's underworlds. There's something unnatural about it. It's not simply my mind questioning itself – it's a distinct voice, ringing through my skull, accusing me.

'If you hadn't spent so long torching those huts, the Hammers of Sigmar would still be alive. You lost yourself in violence. You forgot what you were doing. The kill-fever took you.'

I clang my gauntleted fist against my helmet.

'What do you think they'll say when you reach the stormkeep? When you tell them how many men you've lost? What will you say when they ask you how it happened? How will you explain so many deaths? They will know, Trachos. They will know what's happening to you. Why would they send you back to Azyr? Your work is unfinished. They will send you back into the darkness.'

I can't go back. Not yet. Not until I can be sure of myself. I struggle to keep my voice level.

'The Hammers of Sigmar are to blame for what happened. They should have burned the place down before I ever reached it. The gheists were already leaving their roosts. We had to go before–'

'You're afraid to go back. You're a coward.'

'Who are you?' I cry. 'Get out of my–'

A howl rips through the air, silencing me, echoing across steam-shrouded peaks.

I crouch, a hammer in each hand. It was the cry of a beast, a large one by the sound of it.

Something moves on the next outcrop, a monstrous shape, coiling through the clouds.

Someone bellows a war cry, deep and savage, almost as bestial as the howl that preceded it. There's a flash of light and clang of metal hitting stone.

I look at Zyganium Keep. As soon as I reach it I can make my report and be gone. The voice in my head lies, but its presence troubles me. The gaps in my memory trouble me. I need to get home. I need to see the spires of Azyr and bathe in their holy light. I need to consult with the Lord-Celestant.

'You're afraid.'

'Never,' I mutter, but I know something is wrong. The voice is too clear. Too alien. Who is speaking to me?

There's another deafening howl and an answering battle cry, followed by the sound of smashing rocks. I peer into the steam clouds. There's something big fighting in there. The peaks are juddering like they're in the grip of an avalanche. I look up at the jagged slopes. Perhaps there *will* be an avalanche.

'Run home, Trachos. Hide. Before you lose what's left of your mind.'

I curse and turn away from the valley and the stormkeep, striding across the rocks towards the opposite crag, my boots pounding through the heat haze as I drop down into a crevasse and haul myself up the opposite side, climbing towards the sound of the fighting. Perhaps some of the Hammers of Sigmar made it back and are trying to reach Zyganium Keep? If there was a survivor, what might he say? My memories of Shyish are a shroud of screams and blood. What exactly *did* I do down there? *Could* some of the Hammers of Sigmar have survived? I did not see them all die. Sigmar's light fell from the clouds, slashing the gloom of Shyish, hauling some of their souls back to Azyr, but I could not count the blasts.

I look around. Slain Peak is a famously treacherous place. Skin-roasting geysers erupt constantly from brazier-pits, and landslides are common, but the wildlife is the real threat. If one of my men is here, I'm duty-bound to help him, whatever he might have seen in Shyish.

The sound of fighting grows more frantic as I crest the ridge and rush through the clouds, hammers glinting.

I break through the clouds and stagger to a halt in shock.

I've reached a broad, bowl-shaped hollow, a few hundred feet in circumference and ringed with tusks of rock. There are three figures at its centre and none of them are Stormcast Eternals. The first is inhumanly slender and pale, an aelf, dressed in black, clutching daggers and weaving back and forth, nimble and quick, looking for a chance to lunge. At her side is something peculiar. For a moment, I struggle to name him. He's shorter than a man, but clad in so much scarred, chiselled muscle that he looks like a piece of the mountain. He's a duardin, I decide, with the fiery mohawk and beard of a fyreslayer, but he's big – much bigger than any fyreslayer I've seen before. He's as broad as an ox and his biceps are like tree trunks. I would have placed him as a great king or lord if he didn't look so deranged. He's wearing a patch over one eye and there's a single metal rune embedded in his chest, burning with the ferocity of a fallen star. The rune is the source of the light I saw through the clouds. Even without using one of my implements, I can tell that it's unlike the runes worn by other fyreslayers. There's so much aetheric power radiating from it that the devices hung from my belt are crackling and humming in response.

The duardin is naked apart from a loincloth and, as his slab-like fists tighten, rune-light floods his frame, shimmering across his muscles and igniting a brazier at the head of his battleaxe. His gaze is wild and unfocused and there's sweat pouring down his filthy, tattooed limbs. There's such a thick animal stink coming from him that I can smell it a dozen feet away. He lets out another war cry and pounds across the rocks towards his foe.

When I see what he's about to attack, I can't help but laugh. It's a drake. One of the stone-clad behemoths that thrive in the brutal heat of the Slain Peak. It's as tall as a watchtower and its spreading wings block out the sky, throwing us all into shadow.

The duardin must be insane. Even I would baulk at tackling such a colossus.

The drake opens its long, sabre-crowded jaws and spews a landslide, hurling rock and scree across the hollow.

I shake my head and turn to leave. The duardin is doomed. There's nothing I could do to help even if I wished it.

The duardin keeps roaring as the rocks smash into him.

I hesitate, looking back.

Dust and flying debris fill the hollow and, for a moment, I'm blinded. When the clouds fade, I laugh again.

The duardin is still standing. There are mounds of rock and gravel heaped around him and he's shrouded in dust but the drake has failed to injure him.

I shake my head. That blast could have levelled a fortress.

The aelf is hunched next to him and she seems unharmed too, protected by his bulk.

The drake hesitates, confused, as the duardin shrugs off the rubble and rushes forwards, rune-light sparking in his beard and pulsing through his veins.

The drake recovers from its surprise and screams. Then it rears on its haunches and spews more rock.

Again, the hollow fills with noise and dust. Again, when it clears, the duardin is unharmed, chin raised defiantly, infernal light burning in his eye.

The drake leaps forwards, landing with such force that the rocks beneath my feet slide away and I stumble down into the hollow.

It swings a tail the size of an oak, bringing it down towards the duardin's head.

There's a seismic boom as the duardin smashes the tail away, parrying it as easily as a sword-strike.

The drake stumbles, claws scrambling on the rocks, vast wings kicking up dust clouds.

As the drake struggles to right itself, the duardin runs across the hollow, bounds off a rock and leaps through the air, axe gripped in both fists and raised over his head.

The drake spews more rock, but the duardin is too fast, slamming his axe into its chest like he's attacking a cliff face.

The drake is about to launch itself into the air when the aelf sprints through the dust clouds and plunges her daggers into its leg. The blades are clearly no ordinary weapons. They cut through the drake's stone hide and the aelf has to dive away as black, steaming blood hisses from the wound.

As the aelf rolls clear, the duardin climbs higher, slamming his axe into the drake's jaw, knocking its head back.

I race for cover as the creature staggers towards me, ripping rock from the walls and thrashing its wings.

The aelf flips onto her feet and plants her blades in the drake's other leg and, as the monster falls, the duardin slams his axe into its skull.

There's another resounding boom as the drake hits the rubble-strewn ground.

When the dust clears, I find myself face to face with the duardin.

He's standing on the stone carcass, glaring at me with his single, infernal eye, axe raised and beard sparking, his whole body trembling with violence.

'Maybe we should gut this one too?' His voice is a low snarl. He glances from me back to the aelf.

I raise my warhammers and face him side-on.

'Wait!' cries the aelf, rushing forwards and grabbing the duardin's arm. 'He's one of us.'

The duardin grips his axe tighter. 'One of *you*, maybe.'

'He serves Sigmar.' She steps in front of him.

The duardin looks unimpressed, but allows her to speak.

'I'm Maleneth,' she says, still gripping her daggers as she approaches me. 'I belong to the Order of Sigmar.'

She's a Khainite. I've dealt with the Murder Cults before. Her blades are most likely edged with poison. I keep my hammers raised.

I nod to the duardin. 'And this?'

She gives me a strange look. I can't tell if it's a warning or a plea. Despite fighting beside him, she does not look comfortable in his presence. 'Gotrek.'

This close, he cuts an even stranger figure. The light is fading from the rune in his chest, but it's still fierce enough to give his face a hellish aspect. I notice that one side of his head is oddly weathered, as though scorched by acid. His only concession to armour is a metal pauldron on his left shoulder, but that's clearly borrowed, its design too crude to be of duardin manufacture.

'Show your face, manling,' he growls, narrowing his eye. His beard bristles as he barges past the aelf and squares up to me. He slams into my armour and I stagger. His head barely reaches my chest but I feel like a cart has thudded into me.

I remove my helmet and glare back at him.

He holds my stare, then, just as I think he's about to attack, he shrugs and turns away. 'Another prancing knight.' He mutters something in his own language as he heads back over to the fallen drake.

I look at the aelf. 'Does *he* serve Sigmar?'

'I serve no one!' yells the dwarf, without looking back at me. 'Least of all gods.'

I give the aelf a questioning look, but she holds up a hand, indicating that I should wait until he is out of earshot.

'What is that rune in his chest?' I ask when the duardin has reached the fallen monster.

She speaks in an urgent whisper. 'I need to explain,' she begins, but then I cut her off.

'What's he doing?'

The duardin has clambered up onto the fallen drake and begun hacking at the carcass, filling the air with sparks and noise. Incredibly, his axe cuts through the stone scales, severing chunks of hide and spilling torrents of black gore. Blood hisses as it splashes across the ground.

'We're going to perform a rite,' she says, sounding weary. 'He's going to fish out the innards and then I'll inspect them. Hopefully it will work this time.'

'This time?'

'Someone told him that only drake entrails can point us in the right direction, but we've tried five times so far and I've found nothing but half-digested herdsmen.'

I can't hide my shock. 'This is the *sixth* drake you've killed?'

She nods. 'If you only count the winged ones.'

I stare at the duardin. 'What is he?'

'Gotrek, son of Gurni. Apparently he was born in somewhere called the

Everpeak and, if you believe what he says, he belongs to an earlier age than this – and another world, for that matter.'

I raise an eyebrow.

She still has that warning look in her eye. 'He's unlike any duardin I've ever met. He calls himself a Slayer, but he hates fyreslayers as much as anything else we've encountered. They said he's one of their gods, sent to help them, but that made him even angrier.' She looks over at him. 'He's not keen on gods.'

She scowls at me. 'Look, I want nothing more than to be rid of him, but that's the Master Rune of Blackhammer he's got jammed in his ribs. It's more powerful than you realise. I'm sworn to return it to Azyr.'

'To Azyr?' My pulse quickens. An idea starts to form.

She nods. 'But Gotrek has other ideas.'

'Then kill him. If the rune is needed in Azyr, why have you left it in the possession of a lunatic?'

'Did you see what he did to that drake?'

'I know your kind, assassin. Brute strength is no protection against you. You could scratch him in his sleep and he'd never wake.'

'He never sleeps,' she snaps, but she looks away, suddenly unwilling to meet my gaze. There's more to their relationship than she will admit.

'You like him.'

Her face darkens and she tightens her grip on her knives. 'He's a fool.'

'But?'

She glares at me, her eyes full of vitriol. I can't tell if she's angry with me or herself. 'It's not just the rune. There's something strange about him.'

I keep looking at her.

She spits, her rage palpable. 'I can't explain it. He says there's a doom hanging over him and, after spending all this time with him, I'm starting to understand what he means. He's unstoppable. Something wants him to succeed. Or some*one*.'

I nod. I've seen such things before. Primitive savages, sure of their destiny, oblivious to the facts, tumbling headlong through life, gathering doe-eyed disciples until they finally crash, taking everyone else with them. The aelf is beguiled by him. She mistakes his wild momentum for destiny. She's in thrall to his fearlessness, not seeing that it's only born of stupidity.

Gotrek laughs as he snaps the drake's shoulder bones apart, filling the air with a black fountain.

'You said you're killing these beasts because you're trying to find somewhere.'

She nods. 'The Neverspike.'

The name gives me pause. I've heard it before, but can't place it for a moment. 'Why?'

'Because of some drunk in Axantis. He told Gotrek that there's an immortal there – someone who has been bound to the rocks by Nagash. The drunk called him the Amethyst Prince. And now Gotrek's got in his head that, if this prince is an immortal, he must be from the same world he's from.'

My blood cools. 'I've heard of the Neverspike. Your drunk friend was right about the prince but the Neverspike is dangerous. It's a fragment of the underworld.'

She raises an eyebrow. 'Gotrek doesn't go anywhere unless it's dangerous.'

There's a thunderous slap as Gotrek rips the drake's stomach open and spills innards across the rocks.

'Aelf!' he cries, backing away from the wound, his arms drenched in blood and triumph flashing in his eye. 'What do you see?'

She hesitates. Still looking at me. Weighing me up. She wants me to leave. She's worried about what I might do to the Slayer. She's protective of him for some reason. It's the rune, I realise. She's worried I'll snatch the rune from under her nose. Then she'd have endured this boorish duardin for nothing. I smile as I follow her over to the mound of innards, my idea crystallising in my head. If the aelf can't take the rune to Azyr, I'll do it for her. No one could question my logic. What more important reason could I have for returning home? And then, in Azyr, I will rid myself of all these troubling memories and doubts. I will be renewed.

'You're doing it wrong,' I say after a few minutes of watching her poke at the sloppy mess, drawing bloody sigils and whispering pointless curses.

'What?' She looks up, her eyes flashing.

I take an aetherlabe from my belt and tighten the brass coil at its centre. Slender hoops whiz and click, orbiting its crystal dome until the gemstone inside starts to glow. I hold the device over the steaming intestines. Flies are already starting to gather but the mechanism is unaffected, picking up the aethionic currents with ease, whirring and clicking as its cogs fall into place.

The aelf's eyes widen. 'You're an ordinator.'

I ignore her, adjusting the device, closing in on the current.

Even the Slayer is intrigued. Some of the savagery fades from his face and I see a cunning I had not previously noticed.

'You're an engineer?' he says.

I say nothing.

He looks at me closely, then studies the various measuring instruments attached to my armour. There is a look of recognition in his eye and he mouths a few crude engineering terms.

I use my boot to move some of the intestines as the aetherlabe's teeth click into place.

I nod to a narrow ravine that leads from the hollow. 'The Neverspike is that way. You're only two days away.'

Gotrek laughs and slaps me on the shoulder, causing me to stagger. 'Finally! Someone with at least half a brain. What did I tell you, witch? We're almost there.'

He storms down the gulley, humming cheerfully to himself. His mood has changed in a moment from dour and fractious to eager and happy.

Maleneth is still kneeling in the drake's stomach, covered in blood. She looks at me in disbelief, then shakes her head and hurries after Gotrek, wiping the gore from her face.

* * *

'And this one?' says Gotrek, prodding another of my instruments with a stubby, spade-like finger.

We're hunkered in the lee of a scorched tree skeleton. Gotrek was keen to march through the night, but the aelf insisted we stop. The Slain Peak is even more dangerous in the dark than in daylight and the Slayer grudgingly agreed, still buoyed by the news we were close to the Neverspike.

'It looks like a connecting rod on a turbine,' he says.

He seems oddly knowledgeable about engineering. All his guesses are wrong, because he understands nothing about aetheric transference, but they are still *educated* guesses, based on a sound understanding of mechanics. I have never seen a savage so well-versed in science.

'It's an adylusscope,' I explain. 'A kind of orrery. It tracks the cycles of the realms and all the other heavenly bodies.' I would not usually be so open with a stranger, but the duardin will be dead in a few hours, so I allow myself a little pride, describing the power of my cosmolabes and other surveying equipment.

'And this?' His eye narrows as he looks at the inverussphere.

'It reverses aetheric polarity,' I explain, knowing he won't have any idea what I'm talking about. I baffle him with descriptions of all my instruments, going through them one by one, amused by the disdain on his face. He tuts and shakes his head, muttering something about shoddy work, even though he could never conceive of the machines' complexity.

The Slayer has a sack filled with skins of ale and we've been drinking for over an hour.

'Not bad for a manling,' he grunts as I empty another skin.

'You've no idea who or what I am,' I say. 'I could drink this for days and still be ready to fight. My flesh was forged in the Anvil of the Apotheosis, not prised from the womb of...' I hesitate, struggling to imagine what he was prised from.

The rune in his chest glimmers slightly, flashing in his eye, turning it crimson. Then he laughs and throws another skin at me.

'Let's see,' he says, grabbing another skin for himself and poking at part of my armour. 'What does this do?'

The aelf is somewhere back down the gulley, taking her turn to watch for drakes, so I allow myself to relax. Since I started drinking, the voice in my mind has fallen quiet and I'm feeling a little more at ease. Once the duardin is dead, I can dig the rune from his remains and be on my way. My return to Azyr will be far more glorious than I had expected if the aelf is even half right about the power of the rune – and by the way my instruments are behaving, she is. The witch is a fool to have let the Slayer live so long. He openly derides Sigmar, along with every other god he knows the name of. He's an enemy of the God-King. And he's an animal. Just like the drake he left steaming in the hollow. All he cares about is which of us can hold the most ale.

After another hour of drinking, I begin to feel odd. Gotrek's face shifts in the half-light, swelling and leering like a gargoyle. 'What *is* this?' I say, frowning at the skin I was drinking from.

'The first decent ale I've found in this sweaty armpit you call a realm.' He wipes froth from his beard with a forearm that looks like a thigh. Beer glistens on his scarred skin.

I have the disconcerting feeling that I'm drunk.

Gotrek lets out a deep, rattling belch.

'I need to rest,' I mutter, falling back against the tree stump, feeling as though the mountain is swaying beneath me.

Gotrek grins, revealing a jumble of broken teeth, then slumps back against a rock, reaching for another skin, ignorant of everything beyond the satisfaction of out-drinking me.

'So now you're murdering duardin?'

I wince as I walk. My head is already pounding from the ale I drank last night and the voice in my mind feels like fingernails scraping across the inside of my skull.

I'm not murdering anyone. He wants to reach the Neverspike and I'm taking him there.

'You know what will happen to him if he approaches the Amethyst Prince. Nagash put him there as punishment for defying him. He's there as an example. As soon as Gotrek touches him he'll be ripped apart by death magic.'

If he dies, it's because he's a fool. A dangerous fool. And a blasphemer to boot. He talks of killing the gods. Who would blame me for letting someone so stupid destroy themselves?

'The witch.'

I look around. She's clambering up the slope behind us, her eyes locked on me. She has spent all this time in service to an impious lunatic and she has done nothing to take the rune. When the duardin is dead, I'll deal with her. My fingers brush against one of my hammers. I already have a good idea how.

'Manling!' bellows Gotrek from further up the slope. 'You've earned your beer!'

I pick up my pace, clambering quickly over the rocks to reach the Slayer's side. We're perched on a ledge looking out over another drop and the sight that greets me is horribly familiar. Another world has been smashed into this one: Shyish. The Neverspike is an icy, iridescent spear of rock that juts from the mountain, completely alien from the sun-bleached crags that surround it. The rock is shimmering and rimy, edged with patches of ice. It has no place in the Realm of Fire and the air knows it, billowing around the shard in flickering, static-charged spirals. If we had approached from any other direction, the Neverspike would have remained hidden from view. It is clearly the work of a divine intelligence. Even in Shyish, the shard would not have been a natural formation – it is a single curved talon of rock, and at its summit there is a tall alcove that looks like a shrine. There is a fire burning in the alcove, purple and blue, death magic, engulfing the figure within. It's impossible to see the prince clearly from here, so I take out one of my looking glasses and turn the shaft until the prince comes into focus.

I grimace. He's rigid with pain, but still alive, after all these long centuries.

The flames are burning him, causing his skin to blister and peel, but he cannot die. His eyes are gone, melted into blackened sockets and his flesh looks like living ash, crumbling and flickering in the blaze, but his agony is eternal – a warning to all who would challenge the so-called God of Death.

I hand the looking glass to Gotrek and he mutters something in the duardin tongue, shaking his head as he sees the prince.

The Slayer is minutes away from death. Nagash's magic will not preserve Gotrek as it has done the prince; it will simply immolate him. It fascinates me that he can walk so blindly to his death.

'Why do you seek him?' I ask. 'What do you want?'

'Vengeance,' he snarls, taking the looking glass from his eye and handing it back to me. 'The gods lied to me, manling. They promised me a worthy doom, then stole it from me. They brought me to your wretched realms with no explanation. So I'm going to make them bloody pay.'

I am about to explain to Gotrek that the Amethyst Prince is not divine, and never was, when I realise the absurdity of arguing with someone who thinks he can kill gods. The Slayer is insane. I knew it the first moment I laid eyes on him. I look at the rune in his chest. The ur-gold is forged to resemble the face of a deranged, psychotic Slayer. It looks almost identical to Gotrek.

I nod and gesture to a narrow bridge. It leads across a sheer drop to the Neverspike. It's a single, slender arch of stone, soaring across the chasm like a hurled rope, suspended by some unseen artifice.

The aelf joins us as we make the final approach, grimacing as the air seems to attack us, lashing and hissing around our faces as we cross the bridge.

We are only halfway across when shapes assemble on the far side.

'Aye,' laughs the Slayer. 'Show us what you've got.'

As we get nearer, I see that the figures are corpses – the remains of men and women, lurching from the rocks that surround the spike. They are charred beyond recognition but they move with silent purpose, gripping swords and axes as they shuffle onto the bridge. I mutter a curse as I see that the whole spike is spawning similar figures. There are hundreds of them struggling to their feet.

Gotrek roars in delight and thunders across the bridge, his axe flashing as he raises it over his head.

Maleneth hisses a curse and barges past me, drawing her knives as she sprints after him.

I take my time, slowly drawing my hammers as Gotrek crashes into the blackened husks.

He burns brighter than the prince, hacking and roaring through the crush. Blackened bodies fly in every direction, tumbling into the crevasse. Gotrek barely breaks his stride, carving a path through the undead husks with Maleneth keeping pace, lunging and stabbing.

By the time I reach the end of the bridge, dozens of the revenants have been hacked to pieces, but there are plenty left to attack me. I stride out onto the Neverspike, hammering corpses aside, smashing the sorcery from their lifeless flesh.

We fight towards the burning prince, and the battle is bathed in the violet light of his pyre. Gotrek grows even more excited, hacking through the throng with even more ferocity.

'Hurry, manling!' he cries, waving me on.

I oblige, picking up my pace. When Gotrek dies, I need to be close. The aelf is not a worthy guardian of the rune. I must be on hand to pluck it from his ashes.

As we approach the alcove holding the Amethyst Prince, it becomes hard to see. The death magic is dazzling, bleeding from the tormented prince and flashing through rows of shuffling corpses, scattering light like strands of purple lightning.

I have to shield my eyes as I battle the final few feet.

I'm so dazzled that it takes me a moment to realise Gotrek has turned to face me. He's silhouetted by the unholy blaze, but I sense that his mood has changed.

'What–?' I manage to say before he pounds the haft of his axe into my stomach.

I'm so surprised I do not prepare myself for the blow. Breath explodes from my lungs. I double over in pain. It's like being hit by a felled tree.

Before I can straighten up he hits me again, pummelling the side of my helmet and sending me sprawling across the rocks. My hammers slip from my grip and clang down the slope towards the bridge.

When I manage to sit up, my vision is blurry from the blow, but I see that Gotrek is holding my inverussphere. Fury jolts through me. It's an incredibly sacred device, capable of reversing the polarity of aether currents.

'Thought you'd kill me?' There's a grim smile on his face. He hacks down another revenant but keeps his eye locked on me.

I throw an accusing look at the aelf, then remember I didn't share my plans with her.

The Slayer laughs. 'Drunks always talk in their sleep. Especially pompous manling drunks who can't hold their ale.'

'What?' I gasp.

He turns and fights his way up to the blazing prince, ignoring the fury of the flames as he cuts through the rows of undead.

'I'm not interested in princes,' he cries, adjusting the inverussphere with surprising skill.

I curse as I stagger to my feet, fending off revenants with my fists. Gotrek wasn't drunk when I told him how my devices work; he was listening carefully to every word.

He looks at the sky. 'My quarrel is with the *gods*!'

He turns a cog on the inverussphere and punches it into the prince's twitching body.

The light flares, blinding me, then vanishes, plunging the Neverspike into darkness.

Magic rips through the undead, tearing them from their feet and hurling them towards the alcove, lashing across the rocks with such ferocity that I fall again, tumbling across the stones towards the prince, caught like a leaf in a tempest.

Cords of aetheric lightning smash against the Neverspike, ripping the air with a deafening howl, rushing towards the alcove from the surrounding peaks.

Gotrek manages to stay on his feet, staggering but upright as the alcove becomes a vortex of shadows, smoke and body parts.

The Amethyst Prince howls in delight, finally freed from his torment, then disintegrates, obliterated like the rest of the undead, his ashes snatched by the whirlwind.

'Nagash!' howls Gotrek. 'The Slayer comes for *you!*'

He steps into the vortex, following the dead prince, bellowing a war cry as he vanishes from sight.

I try to crawl away, but the storm is too violent. I'm dragged, inexorably, towards the peak of the Neverspike.

There's a series of explosions as the Neverspike shatters, spraying amethyst lances into the darkness.

With a final, desperate lunge, I grab hold of the bridge, hanging on to a slender arch as rocks whistle past my head.

Then my fingers slip and I'm thrown forwards, my armour clashing against the rocks.

I hurl towards the vortex, surrounded by a storm of blackened corpses. Then the darkness takes me.

I howl as I feel the morbid chill of Shyish, soaking through my armour and eating into my arms. My memories clear, revealing in horrible clarity all the things I was trying to escape. But there *is* no escape from death.

As I fall I hear Gotrek, laughing and singing as he dives into the abyss.

GHOULSLAYER

DARIUS HINKS

PROLOGUE

One by one, the lights began to fade. They burned brighter for a moment, like votives kindled by a breath, then blinked into oblivion. All across the Eventide they slipped from view, and a shroud spread over the sea, mobile and impenetrable, consuming everything.

'What is it?' whispered Veliger. He was at the uppermost rib of the Twelfth Prominent, resting his elbow on the head of his scythe, leaning out from the battlements. He had manned the walls for decades, but he had never seen anything like this. 'There's Lord Samorin,' he whispered as, several leagues away, the Sixth Prominent pulsed brighter, its shell-like whirl illuminating the waves before the fortress sank from view, adding another pool of darkness to the growing void. Before the light faded something shimmered over the Eventide. It looked like gossamer caught in the breeze. 'Rain?' said Veliger, but there was something odd about how it flashed and banked.

Veliger wore the uniform of the Gravesward – a thick cloak of glossy white feathers clasped at the neck with an iron skull brooch and draped over lacquered black armour. He pulled the cloak closer as a breeze whipped through the shadows, even colder than usual, tightening around his chest and snatching his breath.

'And there goes Lord Ophion,' replied the figure next to him as another temple grew suddenly brighter. Meraspis wore the same uniform as Veliger. He was also carrying a scythe and a tall white shield designed to resemble a wing. Like Veliger, his head was gaunt, pale and hairless, but he was older, his forehead networked by lines and locked in a permanent frown.

They watched in silence as the fortress blazed then sank into the sea.

Veliger turned to look at the walls behind them, half expecting the light of their own temple to be fading. The Twelfth Prominent was unchanged. It was a mountainous edifice – a crumbling, spiral curve of bone, perched at the crest of an ancient, dusty wave. Souls burned at its heart like purple fire, bleeding through its walls, spilling amethyst over the peaks and troughs of the Eventide, and the fortress' outline was clouded by white moths, circling in their millions like sea spray crashing over a hull. Light shimmered across the moths, radiated through the walls and flashed in Veliger's eyes as he looked at Meraspis.

'What's happening?'

Meraspis did not seem to hear. He kept his gaze on the horizon. 'What if they *all* vanish?'

Veliger looked up at the heavens, imagining a world without light. The stars would not help – they were ghosts, echoes of the living realms, with no interest in illuminating the underworlds of Shyish. Without the light of the prominents, the Eventide would be in darkness.

As he stared into the growing darkness, Veliger heard an unfamiliar sound. It was like pebbles clattering across a table. At first it was distant and gentle, but as the minutes passed it grew louder, becoming a roar.

The two men looked at each other in confusion as millions of white shards rattled across the Eventide. The sea that had never moved suddenly looked storm-tossed, and as the downpour moved closer it crashed violently against the fortress walls, filling the night with a deafening roar.

Meraspis stepped forwards and reached out from the embrasure. 'Is that hail?'

Then he cursed and whirled away from Veliger, hissing in pain and clutching his hand.

'What?' cried Veliger, rushing over to him.

Meraspis shook his head, hunched over and gripping his hand. 'By the Shroud,' he muttered.

Veliger helped him stand, then gasped. Meraspis' flesh had been torn apart. The rain had punched through his skin and bone, tearing the ligaments so badly that his hand looked like a scrap of bloody meat.

Meraspis cradled his butchered hand in his good one, groaning, cursing and staring at the rain.

Most of the shards had punched straight through his palm, but one of them was still wedged between his knuckles, gleaming white against the dark, exposed flesh.

Veliger gently plucked it from the wound and peered at it. 'Bone?'

They both looked out at the storm, baffled.

Veliger dropped the shard and quickly bandaged Meraspis' hand. The cuts were deep. He doubted the hand could be saved. But he could at least stem the bleeding.

Meraspis grimaced as Veliger worked, but did not cry out, despite the terrible pain he must be in.

'We should go to Lord Aurun,' he said hoarsely.

Veliger looked south to their nearest neighbour, the Barren Points. It was still smouldering with a steady, unruffled light.

'Yes,' he agreed. 'Lord Aurun will know what to do. He'll know what this is.'

Meraspis straightened up and clutched his broken hand to his chest. 'Look,' he said, nodding out across the battlements. 'It's stopping.'

The storm was already fading, the bone shards hitting the walls with less violence as the clouds rushed off to the south.

They watched the storm move away across the Eventide, still shocked by what had happened, then Veliger fastened his helmet and checked that the rest of his armour was fully attached, turning on his heel and heading for the stairs. 'Aurun will know what this means. It will only take a couple of hours to get there.'

Meraspis shook his head. 'We can't leave the Unburied unattended. You go. I would slow you down anyway. I will wait here and tend to my wounds.'

Veliger hesitated, looking at Meraspis' hand, then nodded. 'Very well. I'll find a Cerement priest. I'll bring him back with me.'

Meraspis waved to the stairs. 'Just go. And go quickly.' He looked up at the clouds. 'Even your armour might not protect you for long if that storm comes back.'

Each fortress was linked to its neighbour by a bridge, miles-long walkways slung from the gates like iron tendrils. The bridges were called wynds, and they stretched over the Eventide in graceful arcs. Some were only wide enough for five men to pass down them side by side, others were vast highways, and all of them were illuminated by the light of the temples at each end. As Veliger sprinted down the south wynd, his boots clanged against the ancient metal, scattering dust and moths. It was a long time since anyone had passed this way. Each fortress was almost self-sufficient, able to feed its garrison for months before requiring new supplies from the capital. The guards at the Barren Points would be shocked to see him rushing towards them. No, he realised, correcting himself, they would not. They must have seen the lights fading too. They would know exactly why he was coming.

As he ran, Veliger could not stop thinking about Meraspis' ruined hand. How could weather do such a thing? Where had that storm come from?

Veliger had not gone far down the wynd when he heard the sound he had been dreading – the same ominous hiss he had heard earlier. Bones were falling across the Eventide again, filling the darkness with noise. He staggered to a halt, shaking his head and cursing. There was no way he could reach the Barren Points without the storm overtaking him. And what if his armour did not hold?

As he looked back at the fortress, he let out a horrified cry. A shadow had engulfed his home. The vast, curved surface of the Twelfth Prominent looked stained – as though someone had poured ink over its battlements.

Veliger stared harder and saw that the darkness was a heaving mass of smaller shapes – men, robed in shadow, flooding over the Eventide and climbing up the walls of the fortress like vermin. It was an attack. The idea was even more shocking than the bone rain. The prominents had not been attacked within living memory. The invaders were crossing the surface of the Eventide as though it were harmless. How could that be? The dead waves were lethal. No one could touch them and keep their sanity intact. Who were these people?

Veliger stumbled back the way he had come, dazed and muttering as the bone storm rushed towards him through the darkness.

He broke into a run, but it seemed agonisingly slow. With every step, the rain rushed towards him, crashing over the Eventide and rattling across the wynd.

He reached the end of the bridge and raced up the steps and through the fortress gates, dashing under the first roof he came to.

As he stood there, trying to catch his breath, the light blazed brighter, dazzling him. His eyes adjusted to the glare after a few seconds, and he saw a familiar figure sprinting towards him across the square.

'Meraspis!' he cried out, lowering his scythe.

The man crashed into him, sending them both toppling back down the steps.

Veliger rolled clear and leapt back onto his feet, moving with an agility borne of years of training.

'What are you doing, Meraspis, have you–?' His words died in his mouth as the man turned to face him. It was not Meraspis. It was a hunched, slavering wretch, a stooped horror with wild, staring eyes, whipcord limbs and flesh sagging from its bones. It looked like an animated cadaver. It was trembling and palsied, and its flesh was a dark, mottled grey, but it lunged at Veliger with shocking speed.

Veliger stepped back, moving without thought, led by the precepts of his training. His scythe flashed twice, slicing through the creature's torso, and it slapped to the floor in two halves.

Veliger staggered away, shaking his head, staring at the butchered corpse. 'What was that?'

With a shuddering groan, the corpse's upper half jerked into motion and began crawling towards Veliger, dragging itself with its hands, trailing innards, its eyes still rolling.

'Shroud!' cried Veliger, hacking furiously at the thing until it collapsed and finally lay still.

Veliger's relief was quickly replaced by a rush of horror. When he had looked back from the wynd, he had seen dozens of figures. What if they were all like this?

He gripped his scythe tighter and ran on, muttering in confusion.

Before he was halfway up the steps, the shadows began to shift and roll, rising up and gathering to block his way. Dozens of figures lurched towards him, their heads twitching and their breath coming in ragged gasps. They all resembled age-blackened corpses, shivering and frantic as they locked their blank, yellow gazes on him. Some clutched splinters of bone or fragments of broken weapons.

'Mordants,' whispered Veliger, feeling as though he were in a dream. He had heard tales of corpse-eaters but had never seen them first-hand. One or two occasionally sniffed their way into the prominents, but he had never heard of them attacking in these kinds of numbers. As Veliger looked at the tide of darkness gathering around him, he guessed that there must be hundreds of them clambering over the walls.

The mordants rushed towards him without a sound, twitching and juddering. They were like dumb animals that had taken human form.

Veliger staggered backwards, unbalanced by the ferocity of the assault, trying to stay calm, scything through the throng, filling the air with dark, treacly blood.

He charged up the steps, hacking and lunging and trying to break through the crush, but it was useless. The flesh-eaters forced him back until he lost his footing, nearly beheading himself in the process.

He leapt to his feet, hacked down more of the mordants and backed away, crying out in shock and anger.

The walls of the fortress burned brighter, scattering shadows across the square.

Several mordants broke from the main group and loped towards the wynd, their mindless gaze locked on the distant lights of Lord Aurun's fortress.

'No!' shouted Veliger, backing towards the bridge. 'You will not taint the Barren Points!'

The crowd rushed towards him. The prominent was now shining so brightly he could barely see.

He turned on his heel and raced back towards the bridge, barring the entrance to the wynd. He would not let the mordants go any further into the princedom.

Then the light of the fortress failed, plunging him into darkness.

Veliger could see nothing but an after-image of the walls, burned across his vision.

He heard breathing all around him in the dark –ragged, hoarse gasps, approaching from every direction.

There was a drum of rushing feet as the mordants attacked.

Veliger hefted his scythe back and forth, cutting down shapes he could not see, thudding the blade into thrashing limbs.

Hands clawed at his back and face, tearing at his armour, pulling him down.

Pain erupted across his body, and he heard the storm wash across the square, punching bones through his armour and skin.

Blood rushed into his eyes and he fell, crushed by the weight of bodies, howling in agony.

Your Celestial Highnesses,

I doubt very much that these missives will get further than the next ditch, but I feel duty-bound to make the attempt. Besides, it gives me solace to fantasise that, somewhere out there, beyond these grey doldrums, an educated soul is following my adventures and sympathising with the absurdity of my situation.

Despite the horrific nature of our departure from Slain Peak, I am still in the company of the doom-seeking Slayer. I am as surprised as anyone by this turn of events. Enduring his company is an achievement far surpassing any of the trials I endured in the Murder Temples. Forgive my self-pitying tone, your highnesses, but you cannot imagine a poorer travelling companion. He persists with his pompous claims of belonging to another, older, superior realm of existence, and the longer I spend in his company, the more I wonder if he might actually be right. It does not take a great leap of imagination to picture him crawling from some long-forgotten netherworld. He's a boor and an ignoramus, and he's prone to the most bewildering vacillations of temper.

During our passage across the Dwindlesea (see my previous report) he became infuriatingly enthused – deranged, in fact – howling at the oarsmen every time they faltered, obsessed with the idea of finding Nagash, genuinely seeming to believe he would find the God of Death waiting patiently for him on the next stretch of coast. Then, after we moored at Hopetide and found no such deity, he sank into an ale-steeped sulk, the like of which you can't imagine. So I now find myself languishing in a squalid hole called Klemp while the Slayer tries to drink himself to death. There's no sign of him dying, more's the pity, but that hasn't deterred him from making several valiant attempts. Rest assured, your highnesses, I will endure whatever indignities he throws my way and stay close to him at all times. The Rune of Blackhammer is still safe, secured on his corpulent person, and one way or another, I will bring it to you. The trust you placed in me was not misguided.

As an aside, I can report that this entire stretch of coastline is in a state of momentous uproar. The dominion of the Ruinous Powers is no longer secure, which is both good and bad news for the local populace. The underworlds are in a state of revolt. Spirits and revenants have reclaimed huge tracts of land in Nagash's name, while bands of brigands have started raiding from the north. The Realm of Death is in as much turmoil as anywhere else. Anyone who comes here expecting a peaceful afterlife will be sorely disappointed. Our journey from the coast took us past several Chaos dreadholds, and they were all ruined. And there was no sign of a counter-attack. This does not appear to be the work of Stormhosts, so I can only assume Nagash is responsible. The Klemp locals are preparing to flee, and the whole region is gripped by a kind of shared madness. Every crone and conjurer claims to have received visions concerning a terrible plague of undeath. They claim that Nagash has performed a great rite or conjuration that has given him absolute dominion over Shyish. There is much talk of levitating black pyramids and fleshless legions and the like, and it's hard to know how much – if any – of it is true, but there is definitely something afoot. It would seem the arch-necromancer has found a way to regain many of the territories he lost to Chaos.

As a second aside, I should mention that during the fight at the Neverspike, the Slayer and I gained an eccentric new travelling companion by the name of Trachos. He claims to belong to our order, and perhaps he once did, but the man is clearly insane. If he attempts any form of communication, disregard it. He does not know his own mind and he is not to be trusted. I shall make sure the rune does not fall into his hands and will leave him behind at the first opportunity.

   Your most loyal and faithful votary,
   Maleneth Witchblade

CHAPTER ONE

THE MUFFLED DRUM

Gotrek was snoring, attacking the night with brutal barks. Even asleep he was savage, hammering Maleneth's skull with every snort. The sound rattled through the Slayer's chest and shook the chain linking his ear to his nose. The brazier in his rune-axe was still smouldering, but the light had faded from his filthy muscles. He shifted, as though about to speak, let out a ripe belch and then lay still again. He had drunk for hours, downing ale like water, before finally collapsing next to an outhouse, surrounded by the corpses of brigands who had had the ill-conceived idea of trying to rob him. There was no dawn in this particular corner of Shyish, but even the endless gloom could not hide the rune buried in Gotrek's chest. A great slab of burnished power. The tie that bound her to him. The face of a god, glaring from his ribs, demanding that she hold her nerve.

She stepped gracefully through the dead, as though gliding through a ballroom, scattering flies and gore, a dagger held lightly in each hand. The Stormcast Eternal had gone, scouring Klemp for news of his own kind, and she was alone with the Slayer.

The heart-shaped silver amulet at her throat flickered, revealing the vial of blood at its core. *Now. This is your chance.*

Maleneth ignored the voice, creeping closer to the Slayer, wincing at his stench. He was grotesque. A graceless lump of scarred muscle, bristling with porcine hair and covered in knotted tattoos. Even by the low standards of the duardin race he was primitive – like a hog that had learned to stand and carry an axe. He was shorter than the brigands he had carved his bed from, but twice their width and built like a barn. The stale, sweet smell of beer shrouded the bodies, mixing with Gotrek's belches and stinging Maleneth's eyes. She could see the dregs glistening in his matted beard as she leant closer, keeping her eyes fixed on the rune. The rune stared back.

Despite her loathing she hesitated, knives trembling, inches from his body.

The amulet around her neck flickered again. *Coward.*

That was enough to spur her on. Her dead mistress was right. Klemp would soon be rubble, just like all the other towns they had passed through. The whole region was in uproar. And when the fighting started, who knew where the Slayer would end up? Once he was in one of his rages there was no way of predicting what he would do next. It was a miracle she had stayed with him this far. This might be her last chance. The Slayer's skin was like iron, though. She would need to punch the blade home with all her strength to get the poison into his bloodstream. She tightened her grip and leant back to strike.

'Maleneth.' The voice echoed down the alley, heavy with warning.

She whirled around, blades lowered.

Trachos' armour glimmered as he limped through the darkness, sparks flickering from his ruined leg plate. He was wearing his expressionless helmet, but she could tell by the way he moved, careful and slow, that he understood what she was planning. His head kicked to one side and light crackled from his mouth grille. He gripped the metal, holding it still, but the damage went deeper than the mask. All that god-wrought armour had done nothing to protect his mind.

He stopped near the corpses, staring at her, lights flickering behind his faceplate.

He remained silent, but the way he raised his warhammers spoke clearly enough. *That rune is mine.*

They stood like that for a long moment, glaring at each other across Gotrek's snorting bulk.

Trachos came closer, his metal boots crunching through broken weapons and shattered armour. The sky had grown paler, outlining him, and she saw how confidently he gripped the warhammers. Damaged or not, he was still a Stormcast Eternal. A scion of the thunder god. He was several feet taller than a normal man and, even broken, his plate armour made a fearsome sight.

Maleneth stepped through the pile of bodies, readying herself. She had always known this moment would come. They could not *both* claim the rune. There was a rent in Trachos' leg armour from his left knee to his left boot. It had been there when he first approached Maleneth months ago, wandering out of the hills like a deranged prophet. He was in desperate need of medicine, or repairs, or whatever help Stormcast Eternals received when they returned to the Celestial Realm. Every step he took was difficult, and his Azyrite armour sparked whenever he moved. She smiled. Usually, such a warrior would be a test for even her skills, but in this state he should be easy prey. There would be blood for Khaine this night.

Maleneth dragged one of her blades across a vial at her belt. The crystal broke in silence, but she could smell the venom as it spilled across the metal.

Trachos dropped into a crouch, hammers raised.

The two warriors tensed, preparing to strike.

'Grungni's arse beard!' cried Gotrek, lurching to his feet and grabbing his rune-axe. 'Don't you people know when you're beaten?'

He swayed, obviously confused, still drunk, piercing the night with his one, scowling eye, trying to focus, trying to spot an opponent. Seeing none, he turned to Maleneth.

'Aelf! Point me to the simpletons.'

Maleneth lowered her weapons and Trachos did the same. The chance was gone. She shook her head. 'All dead.' She backed away from Trachos with a warning glare.

Gotrek's face was locked in a thunderous scowl and his skin was as grey as the corpses. He kicked one of them. 'Lightweights. They could barely swing a sword. Even splitting skulls is no fun in your stinking realm.'

Trachos' hands trembled as he slid his hammers back into his belt. 'This is no realm of mine.'

'Nor mine,' said Maleneth, looking around at the peculiar hell Gotrek had led them to. The sky was the colour of old pewter, dull, bleak and riveted with stars. The stars did not shine but radiated a pitiless black. Points of absolute darkness surrounded by purple coronas, wounds in the sky, dripping fingers of pitch. And the town was equally grim. Crooked, ramshackle huts made of warped, colourless driftwood. There were panicked shouts in the distance and the sound of vehicles being hastily loaded. Columns of smoke stretched across the sky, signalling the approach of another army. They looked like claw marks on dead skin.

Gotrek muttered a duardin curse and picked his way through the corpses. 'Where's the ale?'

'You drank it,' replied Trachos.

The Slayer frowned and scratched his shaven head, causing his enormous, grease-slicked mohawk to tremble. Then he glared at the ground, his massive shoulders drooping and the haft of his greataxe hanging loosely in his grip. He whispered to himself, shaking his head, and Maleneth wondered what he was thinking. Was he remembering his home? The world he claimed was so superior to the Mortal Realms? She suspected most of his thoughts concerned his past. What else did he have? There was something tragic about him, she decided. He was like a fossil, revived by cruel necromancy and abandoned in a world where no one knew his face.

'You're right,' said Gotrek, looking up with a sudden smile. 'We need more ale.'

Maleneth shook her head in disbelief. She and Trachos were glaring at him. Anyone else would feel their hatred like a physical blow, but the Slayer was oblivious. He waved them back down the alley, away from the outbuilding, humming cheerfully to himself as he headed out onto the main street.

They stumbled into a chaotic scene. There were wicker cages rattling against every lintel and doorframe – hundreds of them, the size of a human head and crammed with teeth, skin and bones. Alongside the offerings to Nagash there were wooden eight-pointed stars, hastily hammered together and painted in gaudy colours. Braziers spewed clouds of blue embers across wooden icons that had been painted with the faces of daemons and saints. And all of this jostled happily against yellow hammer-shaped idols that had been scored with an approximation of Azyrite runes. Every corner revealed some desperate attempt to appease a god. And through this carnival of colours and shapes, people were rushing in every direction, hurling belongings from windows and clambering into carts. There was a cold wind whipping through the streets that seemed heavy with portent. Men and women howled at each other, arguing while their children fought in the dust, like a premonition of the violence about to be visited

on the town. For weeks, seers across the region had been wracked by agonising prophecies. Some sprouted mouths in their armpits and spewed
torrents of bile, others were visited by horrific, sanity-flaying visions, and
some had found their voices replaced by a bestial, guttural language they
could no more understand than silence. Whatever the nature of their vis-
itation, all of them agreed on one thing – death was coming to the region.
Most people had taken that as a cue to flee, but Gotrek, still furious at not
finding Nagash, had decided to stay, relishing the coming fight as a distraction if nothing else.

As Gotrek swaggered onto the wind-lashed street, he almost collided with
an enormous beast that was being led through the crowds – an armour-clad
mammoth, draped in furs and sacks and scraping tracks through the dirt
with its tusks. Dozens of fur-clad nomads were crowded into its howdah,
and more were swarming round it, driving it on with sticks and insults,
trying to goad more speed out of the plodding creature.

Gotrek halted, glaring at the nomads, and Maleneth guessed immediately what had annoyed him. She hated to admit it, but she was starting to
understand him. He was brutal and heartless in many respects, but there
were a few things that seemed to offend his primitive sensibilities. The sight
of a wild creature bound into servitude was one of them. For a moment,
she thought he might accost the nomads, but then he shook his head and
marched on, barging through the traders and making for the largest building
on the street, muttering into his beard.

Maleneth struggled to keep up as the Slayer booted the door open and
plunged into the gloomy interior of the Muffled Drum. Despite the scenes
of panic outside, Klemp's only inn was crowded with languorous, dazed
patrons – people so far gone they lacked the sense to try to save their own
skin, calling the prophecies scaremongering nonsense. There were more
nomads, wearing the same filthy furs as the travellers outside, but there
was also a bewildering array of other creeds and races – humans from every
corner of the Amethyst Princedoms and beyond. Maleneth saw hulking
savages from the east, as heavily tattooed as Gotrek and looking just as
uncouth. There were waif-like pilgrims, dressed in sackcloth and wearing
charcoal eye makeup that had been smeared by the beer they were lying in.
In one corner there was a party of duardin, dispossessed travellers, hunched
over their drinks and eyeing Gotrek from under battered crested helmets.

Gotrek made a point of ignoring the duardin and stormed straight across
the room to the bar, where a tall, fierce-looking woman was looming over
one of her customers, shaking him back and forth until coins fell from his
grip and rattled across the bar.

'Next time,' she snarled, 'it's your *guts* I'll spill.'

The man fell away from her, collapsing in a shocked heap on the floor before
scrabbling away on all fours as Gotrek strode past him and approached the
woman.

'Still no good,' said the Slayer, looking up at her.

She shook her head in disbelief, then leant across the bar and stared down
at him, peering at his impressive gut. 'You drank all of it?'

Gotrek pounded a fist against his stomach and belched. 'For all the good it did me.'

The woman looked at Maleneth as she reached the bar. 'He drank it all?'

Maleneth nodded, grudgingly, annoyed to notice that the landlady looked impressed.

Gotrek studied the bottles behind the woman. 'Got anything stronger?'

She stared at him. 'Are you with them?' she asked, nodding at the party of duardin.

Gotrek kept studying the drinks, ignoring the question. The only sign of a response was a slight tightening of his jaw.

She shrugged, taking a bottle from the shelf and placing it before him. It was the shape of an elongated teardrop and it was clearly ancient – a plump dollop of green, murky glass covered in dust and ash. There were fragments of something suspended in the liquid.

Gotrek grabbed the bottle and held it towards a fire that was crackling by the bar, squinting at the whirling sediment.

The woman grabbed one of his tree-trunk biceps. 'It's not cheap.'

Gotrek threw some coins at her, then continued eyeing the drink.

He jammed the cork into the bottle with his fat, dirty thumb, and a heady stink filled the room.

Maleneth coughed and put a hand to her face.

Gotrek sniffed the bottle and grimaced. 'It's not Bugman's.'

'Don't drink it then,' said Maleneth, remembering what had happened the last time the Slayer got drunk. There was no way they would leave Klemp intact if Gotrek picked a fight just as an army came over the horizon.

He gave her a warning glare.

'What about Nagash?' she said, the first thing that came to mind.

His scowl grew even more fierce, but he did not put the bottle to his lips.

'You dragged us all this way to find him.' Maleneth looked over at Trachos. He was standing a few feet away, watching the exchange, but as usual he seemed oblivious, locked in his own personal hell. Realising the Stormcast would be no help, she turned back to Gotrek. 'And now, just as his armies are about to reach us, you're going to drink yourself into a stupor. You could miss the very chance you've been looking for. The chance to face him. Or whatever it is you were hoping to achieve.'

Gotrek glowered. 'He's not here. Gods don't have the balls to lead from the front. Nagash will be hiding somewhere, like the rest of them.' He drank deeply from the bottle, holding Maleneth's gaze.

Then he paused for breath, threw more coins on the bar and took the bottle to one of the benches that lined the room. The wood groaned as he sat.

There was an elderly man sitting at the bench, and he watched with interest as Gotrek drank more of the foul-smelling stuff. He was tall and slender, sitting stiff-backed and proud, and as he sipped his drink he moved with the precise, delicate movements of an ascetic. Unlike everyone else in the Muffled Drum, he was immaculately dressed. His tunic, cloak and trousers were embroidered with golden thread, and his receding, slicked-back hair was so adorned with beads and semi-precious stones that it resembled a skullcap.

When Gotrek lowered the half-empty bottle onto the table, the man leant over and whispered, 'You have business with the necromancer?'

The drink had clearly not affected Gotrek yet. His hand shot out with surprising speed and locked around the man's scrawny neck.

'Who wants to know?'

A strange noise came from the man's chest. It might have been laughter.

Gotrek cursed. Rather than grabbing skin and bone, his hand had passed through the man's neck and was left holding a fistful of ash. The powder tumbled through his fingers as he snatched back his hand. He glared at the man.

For a fraction of a second, the old man had no neck, just a landslide of fine dust tumbling from his lower jaw onto his shoulders. It looked like sand in an hourglass. Then the dust solidified, and the man's neck reappeared. He stroked his greasy hair and looked at Gotrek, his eyes glittering and unfocused, as though he were looking into smoke.

Gotrek's cheeks flushed with rage and he gripped the haft of his greataxe. 'What are you? A spirit? In my day we burned the restless dead.'

'I'm quite well rested, thank you,' said the man, with a vague smile.

Maleneth and Trachos approached the table.

'What are you?' demanded Maleneth.

The man ignored her question, studying the rune in Gotrek's chest and the barbs on Maleneth's tight-fitting leathers. Then he looked at the shattered gilded sigmarite of Trachos' war gear. 'You don't look like servants of the Great Necromancer.'

'But you do,' said Gotrek, taking another swig from the green bottle. 'Why don't you...' He hesitated, looking at the bottle with a surprised expression, rolling his head loosely on his shoulders. 'Actually, this isn't bad.'

He looked over at the landlady and gave her a nod of approval.

To Maleneth's disbelief, the ridiculous woman blushed.

'Like you, Fyreslayer, I kneel to no god,' said the man, looking at Gotrek with an expression that was hard to read.

'I'm not a Fyreslayer, and you're nothing like me.' Gotrek stood up and started away from the table. He stumbled and had to grip the bench to steady himself. 'This *is* good.' He sat back down, and the bench gave another groan.

'Why do you wish to reach Nagash if you don't serve him?' asked the stranger.

'What *are* you?' repeated Maleneth, gripping her knife handles. 'Are you human?'

'I'm Kurin,' he replied, holding out a hand.

Maleneth eyed it suspiciously.

Gotrek had closed his eyes, leaning back against the wall, and when he opened them again, he had to blink repeatedly to focus.

'You're drunk,' muttered Maleneth.

Gotrek grinned. 'And you're ugly. But tomorrow I'll be ugly and you'll still be...' His words trailed off and he shook his head, frowning. 'No, wait... I mean, tomorrow I'll be ugly and you'll still be drunk.' He shook his head, muttering to himself, trying to remember the joke he had cracked every day for the last week.

'I belong to an order of magisters called the hush,' said the man, ignoring Gotrek's rambling. 'Shrivers, as some used to call us.'

'I've never heard of you,' replied Maleneth, eyeing the man with suspicion. There were a lot of people who would like to get their hands on the rune in Gotrek's chest. Perhaps it was no accident that Kurin was in the Muffled Drum at this particular moment.

'Not many have,' said Kurin. 'Our skills are no longer in much demand.'

'Skills?'

He held out his hand again, draping it before Maleneth in such a languid, aloof manner that she wondered if he was expecting her to kiss it. Then he flipped his hand around so it was palm up.

Maleneth, Gotrek and Trachos all leant closer, watching in surprise as the lines of his palm rose from his hand, spiralling up into the air like fine trails of smoke.

'Touch them,' he said.

Maleneth shook her head, and the other two leant back.

He shrugged. 'We're an ancient order. We ruled these kingdoms once, long before any of these ill-mannered barbarians who are currently trying to claim lordship. We are one with the dust. We share none of the failings of mankind – no doubts, no regrets, no grief, no shame. The sod is our flesh and the ground is our bed. It makes life simple. Mortal concerns do not bother us, so we have time to concentrate on more elevated matters.'

Gotrek managed to focus. 'You don't care about anything?' He picked a shred of meat from his beard, stared at it, then ate it. 'Doesn't sound particularly "elevated". Even I've managed that.'

Kurin smiled, his hand still outstretched, his skin still spinning a tiny storm. 'I sense that you care about more than you would like to admit. But I can shrive you of your crimes. We are able to see into souls, Slayer – we see their value and we see what haunts them. Take my hand, tell me what drives you to drink so eagerly, and I will take the memory from you.'

Gotrek sneered, but then hesitated and stared at the man's hand. 'Take it from me?'

The Slayer had never told Maleneth much about his former life, but she knew he wished to atone for a past deed. He sought glorious death in battle as a kind of penance. Her pulse quickened. If Gotrek was able to forget the thing he wanted to atone for, he would stop charging headlong towards his own destruction. She could simply lead him, like an offering, back home to Azyr, with Blackhammer's rune intact.

Kurin was still smiling. 'Or, if you do not wish to be rid of your painful past, I can give you a chance at reconciliation. I can rouse your ghosts, Slayer. I can drag your shadows into the light. Is there someone you would wish to accuse? Or apologise to? My reach is long.'

'A charlatan,' sneered Maleneth. 'I suppose you tell fortunes too. And how much does this all cost?'

'No money. Just honesty. Nagash has persecuted my order for countless generations.' Kurin waved vaguely, indicating the streets outside. 'And left me surrounded by people so stupid they worship all the gods when they should worship none.' He looked at the three of them in turn, with that half-smile still on his lips. 'And now I hear you three are *seeking* him. While every other wretch in Klemp is snivelling to Nagash, you want to take him on. It's a long time since I heard anything other than fear.' He looked at the rune in Gotrek's chest. 'There is something different about you.'

Maleneth nodded. 'So if we tell you why we're seeking the necromancer, you'll relieve Gotrek of his guilt?'

'If that's what he desires.'

The Slayer was still staring at Kurin's hand, but Maleneth sensed that his mind had slipped back into the past again. His usually fierce expression was gone, and robbed of its normal ferocity, his face looked brutalised rather than brutal –a shocking mess of scars and buckled bone.

'Do you?' prompted Kurin, an odd gleam in his eye.

Gotrek was staring so hard Maleneth wondered if the drink had finally made him catatonic. Then he laughed and leant back, relaxing as he took another swig. 'These realms are so damned subtle. I see what you're doing, sorcerer – you would rob me of my past and leave me beaming like an idiot. You would have me forget my oath.'

Kurin frowned, confused, shaking his head, but before he could disagree, Gotrek continued.

'There's no solace for me, wizard. No absolution. No bloody *shriving*. Not until I find my doom.' As the Slayer's anger grew, his words became more slurred. 'And, one way or another, the gods will give it to me.'

'Gotrek,' said Trachos. 'We have no idea why he wants to know your business.'

Maleneth looked up in surprise. The Stormcast Eternal hardly ever spoke, and when he did, it rarely made sense.

Gotrek laughed and leant close to Kurin, waving dismissively at Trachos. 'My friend here isn't digging with a full shovel. He thinks I need to *worry* about you. If he knew half the things I've slain, he'd know I don't need to worry about someone with brains for dust.' He shook his head. 'I mean dust for brains. You're muddling my thinking, damn you. Keep out of my head. The past is the one place I'm still happy to go. I'll thank you not to ruin it.'

Kurin nodded politely. 'Of course. I hope I have not offended you.'

Gotrek stared at the table and shook his head. 'Mind you, you've actually spoken the first sense I've heard since arriving in these realms. Gods *are* idiots. Worshipping gods is the pastime of idiots. You're right.' He waved clumsily at Maleneth and Trachos. 'This pair think they can earn a place at the head of some glorious, divine host if they make a prize of me.' He laughed. 'Look at them, dreaming of being holy footstools.'

Kurin smiled sadly. 'The curse of the devout. Praying so cheerfully to the cause of their pain.'

'Aye to that.' Gotrek's tone was grim as he clanked his bottle against the old man's drink. 'The gods are good for nothing,' he muttered. 'Apart from catching my axe.'

Maleneth shook her head, not keen on how the old man was hanging on Gotrek's every drunken word. 'Trachos is right,' she said. 'We should keep our business to ourselves.'

'*Our* business?' cried Gotrek. He scrambled up onto the table and bellowed at the room. 'It's my bloody business, and I'll share it with who I like!'

The buzz of conversation died away as everyone saw the crazed, over-sized Slayer swaying on the table.

Maleneth put her head in her hands.

'I've come here for Nagash!' shouted Gotrek, brandishing his axe. 'You cowardly whelps can run and hide all you like, but I'm going to find him and bury this useless blade in his useless skull.' He slammed the axe down and it split the table in half, hurling drinks and leaving Gotrek sprawled on the floor.

There was an explosion of yells and curses as people leapt to their feet, grabbing weapons and hurling abuse at Gotrek, outraged by his accusation of cowardice.

A glowering mob formed around the Slayer as he climbed to his feet and retrieved his weapon.

Maleneth drew her knives and leapt to his side, still cursing under her breath. Trachos grabbed his hammers from his belt and stood at Gotrek's other side. The trio made an unusual, impressive sight, and the drunks hesitated.

The duardin that had been watching Gotrek since he arrived rushed to stand with him, and Gotrek glared at them furiously.

'Don't come near me, you pathetic excuse for a dwarf,' he snarled, rounding on the nearest of them.

There was a chorus of gasps as the mob staggered away from Gotrek, clutching their throats and choking. The veins beneath their skin suddenly knotted together and began writhing like serpents. Some of the men dropped to their knees, murmuring and whimpering as they tried to breathe, while others stumbled towards the door.

'Wait!' cried Kurin, wiping pieces of table from his robes as he stood and crossed the room. He was holding up one of his hands with a beneficent smile. The creases of his palm had risen up in a miniature tornado again, whirling and twisting between his fingers. 'Lower your weapons, my friends. There is no need for discord. I'll pay for any spillages.'

He closed his fist, and breath exploded from dozens of lungs as people managed to breathe again.

There were more disgruntled cries, but no one attacked. They looked at Kurin even more warily than they did Gotrek. As they crawled back to their seats, muttering and wheezing, it occurred to Maleneth that until Gotrek had sat beside him, Kurin had been completely alone at the bench. No one had dared sit near him.

'You robbed me of a fight, wizard.' Gotrek hefted his axe a little higher and gave Kurin a warning look. 'And there's precious little else to do in–'

'I can reach Nagash,' Kurin said, smiling.

Gotrek froze.

Kurin's presence unnerved even the most hardened warriors in the room. As he walked slowly towards Gotrek, they backed away into the darkest corners of the inn. Maleneth had seen the same thing countless times. Few mortals were happy to risk the ire of a sorcerer.

Kurin nodded towards the street outside. 'We can talk in my rooms.' He carefully placed some coins on the bar and went to the door, waving for Gotrek to follow him.

The Slayer eyed him suspiciously, then shrugged and headed out into the gloom, Maleneth and Trachos rushing after him.

CHAPTER TWO

THE BONE RAIN

The sorcerer paused halfway across the street, staring at something. The mammoth was gone, but there were still crowds of people dashing back and forth and loading carts. Several had done the same as Kurin, halting to look back down the road in the direction of the town gates.

'God of Murder,' said Maleneth. 'What now?'

'Another gift from the gods,' said Kurin, calm despite the abomination that was spreading across the sky.

Beyond the gates the clouds were changing – swelling and trembling and forming mountainous black thunderheads. They were clearly not normal storm clouds. They were boiling out of an empty grey sky, like smoke pluming from a wound.

As more people noticed what was happening, the crowds became even more panicked. People screamed and abandoned the luggage they were trying to lug into carts. The wind grew in ferocity and bone cages broke free from the doorways, clattering down the street, scattering fingers and feathers as they whirled through the dust.

Maleneth coughed and gagged as dust filled her nostrils. There was an awful smell on the air –the heavy, thick stink of death. It was coming from the cloud forming on the horizon.

Drinkers spilled out of the Muffled Drum, pallid and swearing as they looked up at the approaching storm.

'This way,' called Kurin, waving in the opposite direction to the clouds, at a building back down the street.

Gotrek ignored him, planting his feet firmly apart and staring at the storm.

'Gotrek!' cried Maleneth. 'Whatever that is–' Her words were cut off as the inn's sign tore free and flew through the air, almost hitting her. She leapt aside and shielded her eyes as it smashed on the road, hurling shards of wood.

Gotrek was still leaning into the wind, grinning and testing the weight of his axe.

'Don't die here,' called Kurin, 'in this tiresome little town. Don't waste your energy on a place that's already been forgotten. I can show you how to reach Nagash.'

Gotrek looked back at him as the pieces of a broken shrine bounced off him – shards of bone and wire knotted with hair. He frowned. 'Tell me again why you would want to help me?'

'I see something in you, duardin. I have a feeling that–' Kurin tried to say more, but the storm was making it hard to breathe. Whatever the sorcerer was made of, his body was not bound by the same physics as anyone else's. He began to fragment and dissipate, buffeted violently by the reeking storm. For a moment, he seemed to collapse completely, snatched away by the wind, but then he reformed, his regal features tumbling back into place. 'We don't have long!' His voice reverberated down the street, laden with unnatural power.

Maleneth's legs carried her after him, moving of their own volition. She cursed as she realised the man had bewitched her.

Trachos was at Gotrek's side, hammers raised, weighted down by his hulking sigmarite armour as everyone else was being blown back down the street. The storm was now so violent that several carts were lying overturned in the whirling dust and doors were being ripped from their hinges and hurled through the air.

Gotrek was still looking at Kurin, who was flickering in and out of view, merging with the dust clouds. Then he shrugged and began walking towards the sorcerer, with Trachos staggering after him.

A porch near Maleneth broke free, and one of the beams thudded painfully into her calves. She fell and tumbled down the street, gasping and choking as she bounced over the hard ground. She slammed against the side of a wood store and managed to grab hold.

Fool, said her mistress. *You missed your chance. I said you would.*

Maleneth snarled, wanting to disagree, but she could barely see Gotrek now. He was just a vague, stocky silhouette in the dust, with Trachos looming over him, massive and unshakeable.

'Gotrek!' she cried, but at that moment, the cloud burst, splitting down the middle with a deafening boom and spewing rain on the road to Klemp.

No, it wasn't rain; it looked more like hail –hard, white shards that gleamed as they fell and kicked up dust as they hit the ground.

The hail rushed towards the town, and the few people still on the street dived for cover, leaping through doorways and slamming shutters.

Maleneth could see no sign of Gotrek or Trachos.

'No!' She hauled herself from the wood store and dived through a broken window into the house next to it. 'I won't lose that blessed rune! Not after all this!'

There was a man cowering in the room, hunkered down behind an overturned table. She glared at him as she crawled towards an opening where the wall had collapsed. As the wind sliced into her again, she saw that the hail had now reached the town and was tearing up the street like knives, drumming loudly across the packed earth and rushing towards her in a flashing wave.

The man gasped, staring at the hail as though it were a host of daemons.

His fear was infectious. Maleneth backed away from the opening and dropped down next to him.

'What is it?' she cried, struggling to be heard over the din.

He shook his head, not looking at her, still staring at the hail.

She pressed a blade to his throat. 'What *is* it?' she repeated with more vehemence.

He still kept looking at the storm, but this time he did at least answer. 'Bone rain!' He sounded demented. 'The death storm! Nagash's storm!'

'What do you mean?' she shouted, pressing the blade harder until blood formed at his throat.

'It means the mordants are coming!' He was about to say more when his face turned a worrying shade of purple and he fell back against the wall.

Maleneth was confused for a moment, then cursed as she remembered lacing her knife with venom when she had been about to fight Trachos.

'Idiot!' she whispered, glaring at the discoloured corpse.

She let him drop to the ground then ran through a doorway into the next room, still looking for the Slayer.

There was no sign of him, just more locals, cowering fearfully under a table as the storm lashed against the walls, sounding like waves breaking against a promontory.

Maleneth cursed when she saw there was nowhere left to go. She walked over to the barred door, but the family crouched under the table immediately began screaming.

'It's just hail,' she said, glaring at them, but she did not feel as confident as she sounded.

'It's bone rain!' gasped one of them, shaking his head furiously. 'It'll tear you apart!'

Maleneth frowned. 'What are you talking about?'

The man would say no more, wrapping his arms around his head and leaning against his family.

Maleneth hissed a curse and looked back at the door. 'This is ridiculous,' she whispered, but she did not go any further.

She began pacing around the room, flipping her knives from hand to hand, glowering at the people under the table and wondering where Trachos and Gotrek would be by now.

They will have gone with the sorcerer. Gotrek will be glad to see the back of you.

Not true, she thought. *The Slayer enjoys tormenting me. And he definitely has no love for Trachos.*

After ten minutes or so, the sound of the storm started to lessen.

'It's passing us by,' she whispered, itching to open the door.

The man under the table looked up at her, hope in his eyes. 'Wait,' he said, holding up a warning hand. 'Be sure.'

Maleneth wanted to hurl a knife into his pathetic face, but she held off from opening the door until the noise had completely died away. Then she carefully opened it a crack and peered out into the gloom.

The rain had gone, but the storm had left the street cluttered with all sorts of debris. Whole sections of houses had collapsed, leaving rooms exposed and scattering furniture through the dust.

There were people sprawled in the rubble, bleeding and crying out in pain, lacerated so badly they looked like they had survived a knife fight.

There were pieces of hail everywhere, creating a brittle carpet that crunched under Maleneth's boots as she walked out into the street. She stopped to look closer and saw that rather than being cold and glistening, they were dry, dusty shards.

Kurin, Gotrek and Trachos had emerged from the house opposite, and the sorcerer waved at the people lying bleeding in the dust. 'This is just the prelude.'

She shook her head, but then saw what Kurin meant. There were figures emerging from the storm, staggering through the dust clouds.

Maleneth laughed in disbelief as the first of them stumbled into view. It was as though the man were acting out a ridiculous performance. He was standing in an awkward, hunched posture, and his face was twisted in a deranged leer. Only his eyes robbed the scene of humour –they were staring and blank.

He hobbled towards Kurin, breathing heavily and flexing his bony hands. He was dressed in tattered scraps of armour and he moved like his body had been broken and only crudely repaired. He lurched and stumbled as though struggling to stand, but as he crossed the street he gained momentum, rushing through fence posts and charging.

Kurin watched the man's approach with no sign of concern, then, at the last moment, disintegrated into a cloud of dust, his would-be attacker lunging at the space he had just occupied before falling to the floor.

The man thrashed, panting and gasping, then stood and leapt at the nearest person. Unfortunately for him, that was Gotrek.

The Slayer swung his enormous greataxe with no sign of effort, sinking the blade deep into his attacker's skull.

The man staggered under the impact but did not fall. He looked confused as he reached up to touch the blade that was embedded in his head.

'You're dead,' prompted Gotrek.

The man snarled and tried to jump at him again.

The Slayer muttered a curse, wrenched the axe free and hacked it through his neck, sending his head bouncing through the dust.

For a few seconds the man carried on, staggering towards Gotrek with blood rushing down his chest.

Then he crashed to the ground and finally lay still.

'Gotrek,' said Trachos, waving one of his hammers down the street.

Dozens more people were lurching into the town, men and women dressed in bloody rags and twitching like marionettes. Their backs were so hunched that their spines jutted through their flesh, and their long, emaciated arms hung down to the ground so that they punched the dirt as they ran simian-like into the light.

'What devilry is this?' grunted Gotrek, looking at Maleneth.

She shook her head, drawing her knives as the blank-eyed mob rushed towards them.

'They're mordants,' said Kurin. He had reappeared a few feet away. Dust was still eddying around his robes, and his face took a moment to solidify. 'Their lord sends the bone rain in first. It gives them an easy victory.'

The mob limped and hopped down the street, their hands extended and twisted, like broken claws.

'What they lack in intellect,' said the sorcerer with a smile, 'they make up for in hunger.'

'Ghouls?' Gotrek sneered. 'I've met their like before.' He reeled drunkenly down the street, collided with an overturned cart then righted himself, raised his axe and hurled himself at the mob.

He landed with a flurry of blows, scattering limbs and heads.

Trachos limped to his side and began hammering the few creatures Gotrek had missed.

Maleneth gave Kurin a despairing look, but he just shrugged, seeming amused by the carnage.

'*Can* you get him to Nagash?' she cried, yelling over the sound of the fighting.

He nodded, still watching the fight.

As Gotrek and Trachos lunged and hacked, dozens more of the mordants were emerging from the storm, all moving with the same disjointed gait. They formed a ragged circle around the pair, closing in on them.

Gotrek and Trachos were hugely outnumbered, but Maleneth made no move to help. She had seen the Slayer face much worse odds without breaking into a sweat. As the crowds tried uselessly to swamp him, she turned to Kurin.

'Why would you help him?' she shouted, struggling to raise her voice over the howling wind.

'There is a change coming, aelf. I feel it in this wind. And I can see it in your friend. Getting him to Nagash could be a piece of the puzzle.'

Maleneth shook her head. 'Servants of the God-King do not–'

'I don't serve the God-King!' cried Gotrek, striding back towards them, leaving a heap of broken bodies in his wake.

'Not directly,' said Maleneth, 'but–'

'Not in any way!'

Kurin nodded in approval, then turned to Maleneth. 'And you? How many gods do you prostrate yourself before? Is Sigmar your only keeper?'

She glared at him. 'I'm an acolyte of the Hidden Temple, the Bloody-Handed, the Widowmaker. The Lord of Murder is my soul and my heart. But I'm–'

'But you're no fool,' interrupted Kurin. 'Whatever you swore to Khaine, Sigmar's Stormhosts are your only chance of survival. So your unshakeable faith is now shared with the storm god.'

Fury boiled through Maleneth. 'My queen communed with Khaine. She is the High Oracle, and she has prophesied the destruction of Chaos. Soon everyone will see the power of the Murder God.' She laughed. 'Turn your back on the gods if you like, wizard, but it won't help you escape their wrath.'

Kurin rolled his eyes.

Gotrek glanced back at the dead ghouls and then beyond the town walls, to the storm clouds that were still whipping through the darkness. 'How would you get me to Nagash?'

'I can do nothing unless we leave Klemp.'

Maleneth was about to ask another question when Kurin held up a hand for silence, nodding down the street.

Klemp was swarming with mordants. There were now hundreds of them, tearing down doors and clambering through windows. Screams knifed through the storm as the creatures dragged people from their homes, snarling and clawing, filling the air with blood.

'Into my rooms,' said Kurin, waving casually towards one of the buildings. 'Quickly.'

CHAPTER THREE

THE LAST OF THE HUSH

Trachos had to stoop to duck under the doorframe, and Gotrek had to turn sideways to fit through the narrow opening. The Slayer had finished the bottle he had bought in the Muffled Drum, and he was now so unsteady on his feet that he ripped half the doorframe away as he entered, trailing splintered wood and alcohol fumes. Kurin quickly barred the broken door, then lit a candle and held it up. The weak light revealed a hovel cluttered with mismatched furniture and the remains of uneaten meals. It was an eight-foot-by-eight-foot square, and there was something absurd about seeing Gotrek and Trachos squeezed into such a small, prosaic space.

'A smokescreen for the curious,' said Kurin, waving vaguely at the room.

The noise of fighting grew louder outside, and Kurin shook his head. 'We will have to be quick.' He took out a key and unlocked a door in the far wall, leading them into a second room, then locked the door behind them again. He carried the candle with him, and as they entered, the light flickered over dozens of silent, impassive faces.

Maleneth grabbed her knives, unsure what she was seeing. As her eyes adjusted to the faint light, she saw that the room was square, like the first one, but devoid of furniture. There were nine frail old men standing around the walls, but they were so motionless that Maleneth wondered if they were statues. They were dressed similarly to Kurin and looked almost identical to him, with the same long, aristocratic features and gangly limbs.

'What now?' demanded Maleneth. 'You've just trapped us in here. Those creatures won't take long to kick down your door!'

Kurin ignored her.

'Who are they?' demanded Gotrek, still swaying, looking at the nine motionless figures.

'My fellow shrivers,' replied Kurin, placing his hand on one of the old men's arms. 'This is all of us that remain. The last of the hush.' Muttering under his breath, he took the men's hands and linked them, creating a circle.

'Are they asleep?' asked Maleneth, finding the whole scene vaguely distasteful.

Kurin shrugged. 'We live in fragments and snatches, prolonging our span.'

Maleneth's distaste grew. The dank, dark room felt like a grave, and the silent men looked like corpses. It appalled her to think what people had been driven to in their determination to evade Nagash. 'What kind of existence is this? What kind of life is it?'

For the first time since they had met, Kurin's veneer cracked. 'This is victory. This is how we win.' His tone was brittle. 'Not through mindless devotion to callous gods.'

The noise of battle outside swelled louder. People were screaming and howling.

'Can you hear that?' demanded Maleneth. 'What are we doing in here? We need to get out of Klemp.'

Kurin regained his composure and waved a dismissive hand. 'We have time. No one passes through that door unless I permit it.' He looked at Gotrek. 'There *is* a way to Nagash. You must travel to Morbium.'

Gotrek shook his head. 'Morbium?'

'One of the Amethyst Princedoms. Not *all* of them fell. Some have remained hidden.' Kurin reached beneath his robes and drew out a chain of nine polished padlocks, each one engraved with a different rune. They clattered as he held them up and traced his bony fingers over the markings. Then he hung them around the necks of each of the silent men. 'Morbium,' he said as he worked, 'is one of the oldest of the underworlds, ruled by royal scholars known as Morn-Princes. Their knowledge of death magic is as vast as the Great Necromancer's. When Nagash tried to conquer their realm, the reigning Morn-Prince defied him. Nagash punished him for his temerity, but even as he took his revenge, he fell into the prince's trap. The Morn-Prince sacrificed himself so that Morbium could survive. A part of Nagash's power was channelled into a rite the Morn-Prince had spent years preparing. Morbium vanished, and however Nagash tormented the prince, he could never discover the location of the princedom. The Morn-Prince had engineered the rite in such a way that he did not know where he had sent his own people, only that they would escape the predations of the gods.'

Kurin explained all this with an approving tone in his voice. 'Nagash's arrogance blinds him to the subtlety of those he tries to subjugate.'

'Good for Morbium,' slurred Gotrek. 'How does that help me?'

'Things have changed. Nagash's power has grown. He has utilised a new, more powerful form of death magic. No one knows how, but he is suddenly able to drive back even the most powerful of the Chaos hosts. But it's not just the Bloodbound and the Rotbringers that have been affected. A plague of undeath has washed through Shyish. Defences that endured for a thousand years have toppled. And Morbium is no different. The wards so cleverly woven by the prince all those years ago are toppling, and the hidden jewel of the princedoms has been exposed. Morbium is one of the first underworlds, one of the oldest, and now it seems set to fall the same way as all the others. At the moment, there is no more than a crack in its wall, but it will widen.'

'Why does that make it a route to Nagash?' asked Maleneth.

'Because the wards that hid Morbium were created with Nagash's own power. Nagash is blind to it, but Morbium is bound to him. Still part of him. In a tower, in a city, in the heart of Morbium, there are stones that still remember Nagash. I have no idea who the current prince is, but he is linked to Nagash. He has a direct route to the Great Nadir.'

Gotrek grinned, revealing a mess of broken teeth. 'So if you take me to this Morn-Prince, he can *send* me to Nagash?'

Kurin looked at the ur-gold rune in Gotrek's chest. It was flashing in the candlelight, and the same heat was burning in the Slayer's eye. 'I think you are *fated* to reach him.'

The Slayer replied with the complete certainty of the completely drunk. 'Yes. I am. You're right.'

Trachos shook his head. 'We have never met this man before.'

Gotrek laughed. 'What would you have me do instead, manling? Run back to one of your stormkeeps so you can open my chest and see how this rune works?' He tapped the head of his axe on Trachos' breastplate, his eye burning malevolently. '*I* am not one of Sigmar's playthings.'

Gotrek shrugged. 'Besides, you saw what's happening outside. Wherever I go can't be any worse than this. And if there's even a chance of getting to grips with one of the gods, I'll take it.' He looked back at Kurin. 'I agree with you, wizard. I was meant to go to this Morbium.' His habitual scowl was replaced by a confused expression, and he began debating with himself. 'I've no truck with prophecies and soothsayers, but *something* brought me to this place. I'm here for a reason. I must be.'

Maleneth gave Trachos a despairing look. Every time the Slayer got this drunk, it led to disaster.

Kurin was still staring at Gotrek, obviously intrigued by him. He waved to the silent, motionless figures. 'If you really want to know why you're here, my brothers may be able to help.'

Gotrek scowled. 'I told you. My mind is my own. I'll not have you rooting around in there.'

'That's not all we do, Slayer. Is there anyone from your past who could help you? You say you're unsure why you were brought back. Back from where? Is there someone from your home who could help? A wandering spirit, perhaps –someone who might have the answer?'

'Pah!' Gotrek laughed. 'Mystic gibberish.'

Kurin smiled, saying nothing.

Gotrek peered into his face. 'You mean you can summon ghosts from one of these absurd realms?'

Kurin shrugged. 'Or another. I can summon whichever ghost you like – from whatever realm you choose.'

Gotrek scratched at his stubbly scalp and stomped around the dingy room. 'Anyone?'

Kurin nodded.

'Gotrek,' said Maleneth, shaking her head in disbelief. 'Listen to what's going on out there. We need to *leave*. You're drunk, and he's a fraud. Why would he want to help you? There must be something he's not telling us. Look at him. He's no more than a–'

Gotrek silenced her with a warning finger. 'He's spoken more sense in the last ten minutes than you've done in three months.'

Gotrek looked back at Kurin. 'There *is* a soul. A ghost I would wish to speak to.' He carried on circling the room, not meeting anyone's eye, drumming his blocky fingers on his axe. 'A poet. Felix Jaeger. I owe him an apology. I did not end things as I should have.'

Kurin's eyes glinted in the darkness. 'Felix Jaeger.' He placed his hand on Gotrek's forearm.

The Slayer moved as if to shrug him off, but something happening to one of the figures in the shadows stopped him. It shuddered, as though waking from a deep sleep.

Gotrek staggered over to it, seeming to forget that Kurin had hold of his arm.

The temperature dropped.

Maleneth glanced around, sensing the presence of something unearthly. She stepped to Gotrek's side and grimaced as she saw what was happening to the figure. The frail old man still had his eyes closed and still looked to be dead, with a ghastly complexion and no movement in his narrow chest, but something was happening to his skin. Just like on Kurin's palm in the Muffled Drum, the creases had risen up and begun moving, coiling and twisting in a silent dance.

As the miniature storm whipped across the lifeless figure, it began to blur his features and then transform them. They all watched in surprise as a new face began to appear, scarred and handsome.

'Is that you?' whispered Gotrek, staring at the face that was moving beneath the skin, as though trying to break the surface of water. 'Felix?'

'Are you really so gullible?' cried Maleneth. 'He's a charlatan! Can't you see? He's just showing you what you want to see. This is just a cheap trick designed to–'

'Can he speak?' demanded Gotrek, ignoring her.

'Give him a moment,' said Kurin. 'He's travelled a great distance to be here.'

The younger face finally broke through the surface of the older one. The man stared around the room in confusion, until his eyes came to rest on the Slayer.

'Gotrek!' His voice sounded muffled, like it was coming through a thick wall. 'Is that really you?' As it spoke, the figure lurched into life, reaching out and stumbling forwards, like the ghouls they had fought outside.

Gotrek grabbed the man's arms. 'Can you hear me?'

He nodded. 'You survived?' he said, sounding dazed.

For a moment Gotrek was too overcome to speak. When he finally answered, his voice was husky. 'I should have stayed with you, manling. They tricked me. Grimnir tricked me. The gods lied, Felix. Everything has been lost.'

The face behind the face smiled. 'If you're alive, not *everything* has been lost.' Then he frowned and looked back into the darkness, as though someone had called him. 'I can't stay,' he said, turning back to the Slayer.

'Forgive me,' growled Gotrek, still gripping his arms.

Maleneth shook her head, still unable to believe that the Slayer could fall for such obvious deception.

Felix smiled again. 'You are unforgivable, Gotrek. You always were.' Then his expression became serious. 'Make them pay. Make them pay for their lies.'

'Aye!' Gotrek was breathing heavily. 'I'm close. Nagash is within my reach. I'm going to bring his whole bloody palace down on his–' He frowned as the face under the skin vanished, leaving the sleeping face of the old man. 'Where's he gone?' Gotrek demanded, looking at Kurin.

Kurin frowned. 'You have him so clearly pinned in your memory. There should have been no problem talking to him. Something held him back. Something is keeping him from you – guarding his soul.'

Gotrek spat into the dust. 'Nagash. Who else?' He began pacing again, swinging his axe in a way that was far from ideal in such a small space. 'No matter. The manling was clear enough. Make them pay. And I will do. Starting with Nagash.' He paused and looked back at the now motionless figure, clearly still shaken by the whole exchange. Then he turned to Kurin. 'How do we get to Morbium?'

Kurin was still frowning, staring at the sleeping figure that had just been talking to Gotrek. Then he smiled, waving them back, outside the circle. He checked the chains around the old men'sst necks, adjusted the padlocks, then began muttering his incantation again. As he spoke, the hard-packed earth of the floor began to spiral and twist. A miniature storm raged between the silent figures, whirling and turning and causing Gotrek and the others to shield their faces.

When the dust cleared, Kurin was still smiling. There was a circular opening at his feet, with narrow steps leading down into the darkness.

'Follow me,' he said, descending. 'The entrance to Morbium is not far.'

CHAPTER FOUR

OATHBREAKERS AND FRAUDS

They emerged from an opening in a hillside, half a mile from the town.

Kurin did not pause for breath as he left the tunnel, and they had to move fast to keep up as their guide rushed into the half-light.

'Can we trust him?' asked Maleneth, eyeing the sorcerer as he slipped and scrambled down the rocky hillside.

'*Never* trust wizards,' laughed Gotrek in disbelief. 'Or aelves, for that matter.' He scowled at Trachos. 'Which only leaves you, unfortunately.' Then he shook his head. 'It's not Kurin I trust – it's Felix.' Gotrek's words were becoming less slurred. 'Besides, he got us out of Klemp, didn't he?'

They climbed down into a narrow valley, leaving Klemp behind and entering the strange landscape they had spent weeks travelling through since arriving at the coast. It was impossible to see more than a dozen feet or so due to the mist towers – sheer-sided, curved masses that soared up into the darkness for miles. This part of Shyish was relentlessly bleak. No breeze, no birdsong, no animal calls, no trace of mortality. Only one sound punctuated the darkness – the clang of a broken bell, far in the distance. It rang out every few seconds with heartbeat regularity. Maleneth remembered hearing it on the journey to Klemp, but she was surprised to hear it again now, nearly two days later. Time seemed frozen in Shyish. The realm seemed like a single, perpetual moment, hanging ominously over some terrible, imminent catastrophe.

Kurin hurried on, pausing every now and then to make sure they were still following him. Trachos' wounds caused him to grunt and mutter as he hauled his broken armour over increasingly rocky terrain, but he was far too proud to slow down or ask for help.

They travelled this way for several hours, and Gotrek began to grumble into his beard and complain that Maleneth had not thought to bring food from the Muffled Drum. Not for the first time, Maleneth wondered what Trachos would do if she rushed past him and sank a poisoned blade into the Slayer's back. It was little more than an idle daydream. Her mistress was right – Gotrek was more than a duardin. She had no idea if any of her toxins would work. And Trachos would almost certainly try to stop her. Whatever went on in that battle-ravaged head, he maintained a rigid code of honour. He would not condone a random murder, however entertaining it might be.

The sorcerer came to a halt next to a bleached, skeletal tree and crouched low, looking at something on the ground. There was a confusing mass of footprints.

'Mordants,' he said. 'But not from Klemp. These came from the south.'

Gotrek shrugged, then nodded at some tracks leading north. 'The morons were heading somewhere with a purpose. And little morons always follow big morons.'

They marched on, following the tracks, and after a while they spotted corpses, sprawled in the dust.

As they approached the bodies, Maleneth's lip curled in distaste. There were around thirty of them, twisted and feral, all wearing contorted snarls and scraps of bloody cloth. Mixed in with them were a few dead duardin, possibly the ones they had seen in the Muffled Drum. She raised an eyebrow and looked at the Slayer. 'I see your relatives made a good account of themselves.'

Gotrek glared at her for a moment, golden sparks flickering across his eye. Then he booted one of the dead ghouls and looked at the sorcerer. 'I didn't come here to fight these pitiful things. I came for a god.'

Maleneth shook her head. 'What in Sigmar's name would you do if you actually found Nagash?'

'I'd do nothing in *Sigmar's* name, aelf. A hammer-hurler's no better than a corpse-botherer. Once I've dealt with Nagash, the God-King is next.'

Trachos tensed and gripped his warhammers. His armour clicked as his head started twitching.

Gotrek laughed and slammed his chest into Trachos' armour, knocking him backwards. 'So there *is* someone in that bloody suit! That's the spirit, manling. Did Gotrek make you think a bad thought?'

Maleneth stepped back, trying to suppress a smile.

'You know nothing of Sigmar.' Trachos sounded furious, but he lowered his hammers and backed away, his head still twitching.

'I know more than you, manling. I know what happened last time he faced the Ruinous Powers. They *trounced* him. That's why he's hiding. That's why he's up there in... Where did you say he's snivelled off to?'

Trachos was clearly struggling to stay calm. 'The God-King will reunite the Mortal Realms. That which has been riven shall be reforged. Sigmar has sent his Stormhosts to–'

'Why?' The Slayer waved his rune-axe at the grey walls and up at the black stars. 'Why does he care for any of these stinking pits? I think he's had too many knocks to the head. Maybe he sits up there hitting himself with his own hammer? Maybe he's senile? Grungni's beard! There must be *something* wrong with him. He's as much a stranger here as I am. These are not his wars – these are not his people – any more than they're mine.'

'Then why drag us down here looking for the God of Death?' asked Maleneth. In truth, she did not really care, but it was amusing to see Gotrek upsetting Trachos. 'If you care nothing for these realms or these wars, why pit yourself against Nagash?'

'Because the gods *lied,* aelf. They're oathbreakers and frauds, the lot of them. They know the doom they promised me. They know what they swore.

But did they hold up their half of the bargain? No! And here they are, play-ing games and building empires, like they always do. I turned my back on my friends and my kin because of their lies.' His expression darkened. 'And a Slayer does not forget. Not *this* Slayer, anyhow. I hold true. I remember my bloody oaths. Even when others do not. They'll give me the doom I was promised.' He scowled. 'Or I'll give them a doom of their own.'

The sorcerer watched the exchange patiently. Then, when the trio fell quiet again, he nodded and continued, following the tracks on through the dust.

Maleneth winked at Trachos, then sauntered after Gotrek.

Kurin led them to one of the soaring mist walls, hesitated briefly, then plunged through it, disappearing from sight.

It was only when they got within a few feet of the mist that its true nature was revealed. It was a tangled vine of spirits – naked, emaciated wretches bound into vast circular prisons. Each of the chimney-like structures was miles tall. There must have been millions of spirits trapped in each one. As Gotrek approached, they screamed, thrashing and struggling, trying to reach him, but they were too tightly knotted to move. Some spoke words Maleneth understood, begging her to free them, sobbing for help.

Gotrek marched straight through the ghosts, following the sorcerer, head low and axe high, like he was shouldering his way through a snowdrift.

Trachos and Maleneth hesitated before the dead, chilled by the cries. Mal-eneth did not fear death any more than she feared violence, but the enormity of the torment was still overwhelming. So many lost voices. So many twisted faces. And she was going to endure it for that deluded hog, Gotrek.

Trachos stepped forwards, then halted. His head was twitching again. Every now and then, he seemed to notice who he was travelling with, as though it had never occurred to him before. This was one of those times. He stared at her.

'The Slayer is insane,' he said.

'Nothing gets past you.'

He continued staring at her.

She smiled at the irony. 'And we need to keep him alive until one of us can get that rune.'

She could see Trachos' eyes through the holes in his faceplate. They were as wild as the eyes of the ghouls. He was a taut string. She just needed to keep pushing. And when he snapped, the rune would be hers.

'Aelf!' roared Gotrek from somewhere up ahead.

She closed her eyes, then stepped into the mist with a sigh.

CHAPTER FIVE

THE IRON SHROUD

The wall of spirits was thick. As Maleneth staggered on, the cries became deafening. Deeper within, the ghosts summoned the strength to attack, their cold, waxy fingers clawing at her face.

After a few steps she was fighting, punching and kicking her way through the tangled limbs. The dead were desperate, trying to tear her skin, hungry for her warmth, craving her pulse. For a while she fought in silence, but as the attacks became more frantic she felt like she was drowning. She howled in defiance. Then, as the crush was about to overwhelm her, she burst through the other side of the wall and tumbled to the ground, gasping for breath.

The air was so thick and greasy that she gagged. It was like breathing cremation fumes. She lurched to her feet, coughing, and looked around.

They had entered another expanse of grey, encircled by another tower of mist. But there was a difference. In some places, the tower had collapsed, spilling ghosts across the ground. The spirits were trying to crawl away from the walls, but outside the mist their substance gave way, dissipating as they grasped at the air, thrashing across the ground like stranded fish. Gotrek was standing in the middle of the tower, and waves of spectral debris were crawling towards him, pleading and weeping. He seemed unaware of them. He was looking around in confusion.

'Where'd the wizard go?' he cried, glancing back at Maleneth.

Then he laughed as Trachos tumbled through the wall and landed with a clatter. 'Still with us, manling?'

Trachos did not reply.

'Get over here, *Lord Ordinator*,' said Gotrek, sneering Trachos' title.

Maleneth and Trachos hurried into the centre of the mist tower and stood next to the Slayer.

'Which way did he go?' asked Gotrek.

The spirits were whipping across the ground, kicking up dust. It was hard to see anything clearly.

Gotrek studied the astrological equipment fixed to Trachos' belt. 'Can one of your devices track him?'

Trachos staggered as ghosts whipped through the darkness, battering against his armour. 'What?' he gasped as he fended off the spectral shapes.

'Take that bloody hat off and you might hear me.' Gotrek tapped one of his slab-like fingers on Trachos' helmet. 'Where. Is. The. Wizard?'

'I am a Lord Ordinator,' replied Trachos, 'not a scout. These are instruments of Sigmar's divine will. They measure aetheonic currents. They plot the celestial spheres. They do not track conjurors.'

'The bell,' said Maleneth.

'What?' snarled Gotrek.

'I heard it earlier, and now it's louder. Do you hear?'

Gotrek looked at the ground, concentrating.

'We're getting closer to it,' Maleneth said. 'This...' She waved vaguely at the diaphanous structure that was collapsing all around them. 'This place is closer to wherever the bell is ringing. The creatures Kurin called mordants were heading towards it, so he might be too.'

Gotrek grinned and clapped her on the back so hard she staggered. He looked through the crowds of struggling spectres to the opposite side of the circular wall. It was the section that was most crumbled, and it was heaving with anguished souls. 'Of course. A bell means a building. And buildings mean civilisation.' He shrugged, grimacing at the bleak wasteland. 'Civilisation might be stretching it.'

'There's something else, too,' said Maleneth.

They all listened. Along with the bell there was a clamour – incoherent, bestial cries and a low, smashing sound, like a war engine pummelling a wall.

'Sounds like a fight!' Gotrek stomped off through the dust, waving for Maleneth to follow.

'That's a warning bell,' said Trachos, staring at the tumbling walls of mist. Maleneth nodded.

She turned to follow Gotrek, but Trachos grabbed her arm. 'No one gets the rune if he destroys himself.'

She looked at him, her expression neutral.

'And we can't keep him alive if we don't trust each other,' he continued.

Maleneth's smile was as cold as the dust. 'Of course you can trust me.' She jogged lightly away, weaving around the tumbling ghosts as she followed Gotrek.

Each tower of mist was more ruined than the previous one, and the spirits grew more desperate the further they went, but Gotrek strode on with purpose, heading unerringly towards the clanging bell. The closer they came to the sound, the more it mingled with the din of battle and the deep, seismic thudding they had heard earlier.

Finally, after breaking through a fifth wall, they saw the source of the din. Even by the standards of Shyish it was a macabre sight. Ghouls were clambering over a shrine, dozens of them, thrashing and snarling as they fought. The shrine was a splayed, claw-like structure perched on a rocky outcrop. It was made of stone, but its limbs were as sharp and twisted as a briar, hung low to the ground and knitted together in a jumble of knuckles and thorns. There were cylindrical cages hung at the end of each bristling limb, and in each cage there was a corpse. Some were no more than dusty skeletons while others were rot-bloated husks, bruise-dark and waxy, gleaming under a low-hanging moon. The corpses were moving, lunging and hacking at the ghouls, defending the shrine with silent determination.

At the sight of the frantic battle, Gotrek halted and let out an eager growl. He gripped his axe tightly and its brazier blazed with inner fire. 'We've found the puppet master!' he roared, pointing his weapon at the centre of the shrine.

At the heart of the stone briar there was a circular block, like a crooked pulpit, and inside it there was a slender man dressed in a white gown, his face hidden in a deep hood. He was waving a scythe back and forth, and with every sweep, the briar's limbs lashed out, tearing the ghouls apart and allowing the caged corpses to attack with rusting swords. It was grotesque and surreal. The monsters fought like animals, spitting and twitching, but the briar corpses were silent, even when their cages hit the ghouls with so much force they exploded, scattering shards of bone and flesh.

'A necromancer!' cried Gotrek, charging through the dust towards the shrine. There was a worrying gleam in his eye that Maleneth had seen before. His muscles were trembling and the rune in his chest shimmered with aetheric power.

Maleneth was about to follow when she noticed another shrine a few hundred yards away. It was similar to the one Gotrek was approaching, but it had collapsed. Ghouls were swarming over it from every direction, and as they reached its summit something strange was happening – they were vanishing from view, tumbling into it as though they were falling into a well. As the shrine crumbled, the spirit mist lashed down from the towers, spiralling around the crumbling stones.

'This is a wall,' she said.

Trachos stared at her.

She pointed one of her knives at the shapes in the distance. 'There are dozens of these things. They're a barrier.'

All of the shrines were under attack. Hundreds, perhaps thousands of ghouls were spilling from the mist and tearing down the stone briars. As the shrines crumbled, the spirit winds lashed around them like sails torn from their masts.

A bellowed war cry drew Maleneth's attention back to Gotrek. He drew back his axe and hurled it into the shrine wall, creating an explosion of shattered stone. Then he strode forwards, wrenched the axe free and began laying about himself, smashing mordants from the barbed limbs and bellowing. He made such a terrifying sight that even the ghouls hesitated, seemingly taken aback by the arrival of someone more deranged than they were.

The shrine heaved and lurched like an enormous crustacean, lashing out with its cages in an attempt to batter Gotrek away.

In his berserk state the Slayer was surprisingly agile. His short, muscular legs powered him through the tumult as he hacked chunks of stone from his path, howling the whole time.

The necromancer remained motionless, head down, his face still hidden in his hood, but it was clear he had noticed Gotrek's approach. The stone briar became a storm of lashing limbs and whirling blades.

A stone branch thudded into the Slayer as if to hurl him clear, but Gotrek gripped it tightly with one hand and headbutted it. The stone broke with an explosion of sparks, and for a moment Maleneth lost sight of the Slayer.

When the flash faded, she saw him halfway up the shrine, punching a ghoul and roaring with laughter, hauling himself through the contorted shapes.

She raced towards the shrine, dodging the mordants' grasping talons and leaping up onto the twisted mass, cutting down more of the creatures as she began to climb. When the Slayer was in the grip of a kill-fever, anything could happen. She had to get close enough to protect the rune.

Trachos lurched after her with a clatter of ruined armour. Then, absurdly, he launched into song. 'Oh, faint, deluded hearts!' he sang, his voice metallic and inhuman. 'The God-King hath descended!' Ever since Gotrek had dragged them down to the Realm of Death, the Stormcast had taken to singing hymns as he fought. Either his wounds had damaged his hearing or he had never had a musical ear. He turned every melody into a bludgeoning, tuneless dirge.

Maleneth weaved and ducked, planting kicks and dancing around lunges, but it was impossible to keep pace with Gotrek. Her blades flashed through necks and wrists, slicing the ghouls apart with calm efficiency. They tried to swarm over her, but she was too light on her feet, dancing away from them as blood-frenzy washed over her. At moments like this she could not deny her true faith. She fought in tribute to the Bloody-Handed God, making every cut as cruel and painful as she could, laughing mercilessly as the creatures tumbled away, gasping and choking, Khaine's symbol scored into their flesh.

There was an explosion of light, and the whole scene became a frozen tableau of silhouettes. Then the light vanished and Maleneth stumbled, blinded, as ghouls rushed at her.

Hot pain erupted across her back as claws raked over her skin.

She whirled around, lashing out blindly, cutting through muscle and cartilage as she jumped clear.

Once she had gained a safer vantage point she saw the source of the light. Trachos had taken some objects from his belt and clasped them together, forming a slender sceptre with an ornate mechanical cube at its head. The cube was trailing strands of smoke, and there was a charred heap where several ghouls had been standing.

'Steadfast and majestic!' boomed the Stormcast, still singing. 'Fiery hammer swinging!'

Maleneth grimaced and bounded up the shrine after Gotrek.

They reached the necromancer at the same moment, the howling Slayer barrelling through ghouls from one direction while Maleneth leapt gracefully from the other.

The necromancer whirled his scythe, and stone limbs stabbed towards the Slayer.

Gotrek was covered in blood and his grin was daemonic as he slammed his axe into the cages, shattering every corpse that tried to land a blow on him. He leapt through a storm of bone, blood and rock, grabbing the necromancer by the throat.

Maleneth arrived just in time to see the look of confusion on Gotrek's face as the hood fell back.

Rather than a wizened old man, there was a young woman staring back at the Slayer.

Gotrek froze, shocked into momentary silence.

The girl took her chance. As the Slayer hesitated, she sank her scythe into his chest.

There was another explosion, and this one was so powerful that it kicked Maleneth back from the pulpit, sending her crashing into the ghouls.

'Sound the starlit trumpets!' sang Trachos from somewhere nearby. 'Rouse the ardent host!'

'Trachos!' Maleneth howled, attacked on all sides and unable to rush after Gotrek.

The singing paused, and there were more flashes of light. Maleneth fought blind, weaving through the ghouls until she was back on the ground.

As her eyes adjusted to the glare, she saw Trachos swing his sceptre and hurl silver-blue flames. 'Never-ending glory!' he cried as the blast left a land-slide of charred body parts at her feet. 'Foes vanquished and unbound!'

Maleneth ducked and rounded on another mordant, opening its throat with a backhanded slash before leaping clear.

When she turned to look back at the fight, it was over. Gotrek had hacked down half the ghouls, and she and Trachos had dealt with the rest. The shrine was empty, its stone branches lying in the dust.

'Where is he?' she gasped, glancing at Trachos.

He did not seem to hear. His head was thrown back and he was still grip-ping the sceptre in both hands, aetheric energy sizzling around his gauntlets. He was still singing, but only to himself now, the words muffled and faint inside his helmet. Then he shook his head and lowered the sceptre, turning to face Maleneth. The light faded from his eyes and he suddenly looked dazed from his exertions. He leant on the sceptre as a crutch.

'He fell when the necromancer stabbed him.'

They both looked around.

'We need to get out of here,' said Maleneth, looking past the Stormcast Eternal to the mist towers. There were hundreds more ghouls approaching from every direction. Even with the Slayer they could never face down so many. 'That sorcerer you put so much faith in has abandoned us.'

She leapt over the dead bodies, looking for Gotrek and the sorcerer, lea-ving Trachos to stagger after her.

They found the girl first. She had rolled down through the nest of spiny stones and landed in a heap at the bottom of the shrine. Her hood was thrown back, so they could see her flushed, furious face. Her teeth were bared, and she glowered at Maleneth like she wanted to tear her throat out.

She tried to rise, but Maleneth held a knife against her throat, smiling. 'Just give me a reason.'

The woman was shivering with rage. 'The Unburied will endure.' Her eyes were so bloodshot they looked wholly red. 'Morbium eternal!'

'Unburied?' Maleneth glanced at Trachos for an explanation, but the Stormcast shrugged.

The woman sneered, her words thick with hate. 'Kill me. Be done with it. I don't know how you uncovered the Iron Shroud, but this will not be the end of us. The ancestors will endure. As was will always be. The past remains in the now. The Unburied will still be here when the traitor-god is overturned and the–'

'Your walls are falling,' interrupted Maleneth, annoyed by the woman's pompous tone. 'Take a look.' She hauled her to her feet and showed her the line of shrines. All of them were collapsing under the weight of the ghouls' attacks, surrounded by storms of mist.

'Morbium will endure,' snapped the woman, her fingers trembling, her weapon lost.

'Your spiky shrub is the only one still standing, and that's only thanks to Gotrek,' said Maleneth. At the mention of his name, she remembered that the girl had wounded the Slayer. 'Where is he?' she muttered, looking across the still-twitching bodies.

Trachos barged past her, striding through veils of mist, his sceptre shimmering.

'Wait!' demanded Maleneth, still crouched over the woman with her blade at her throat. 'What are you?' she said, wondering if there was any reason for letting her live. '*Are* you a necromancer?'

The woman looked appalled. 'I'm the High Priestess of the Cerement.'

'Good for you,' said Maleneth, pressing on the blade.

Gotrek staggered through the mist, dazed but apparently unharmed.

He shoved Maleneth aside and dragged the white-robed woman to her feet. He held up the scythe she'd used on him and tapped it against the rune in his chest. 'Aim higher, lass, if you get another chance.'

'Prince Volant will have your head,' hissed the woman. 'When he hears you attacked the Iron Shroud, there'll be no sorcery in all of Shyish that can protect you.'

'The Iron Shroud?' asked Gotrek.

Maleneth leant close, speaking with mock discretion. 'I think she means this impregnable edifice.' She pointed at the ruined shrines that trailed away from them in both directions.

'Attacked?' Gotrek shook his head. 'What are you talking about?' He looked at the tides of ghouls racing towards them. 'You think these things are *mine*?' He waved at the bodies that surrounded them and laughed. 'Perhaps you didn't notice me trimming their necks.'

The woman shook her head. 'Then who are you?'

'Gotrek, son of Gurni, born in the Everpeak and–'

'Gotrek,' said Maleneth, drawing the Slayer's attention to the host thundering towards them.

He grunted, annoyed at the interruption, and looked back at the woman. 'How do I get to your master?'

'Prince Volant?'

'Prince who?' Gotrek shook his head. 'Is that the Morn-Prince? Prince Volant? Is he the one who can get me to Nagash?'

The woman stared at him. 'Nagash? You're insane.'

Maleneth laughed. 'She's a sound judge of character, at least.'

'They're almost on us,' said Trachos.

Maleneth glanced at Gotrek. 'Any suggestions?' There were so many ghouls charging through the mist that the ground was trembling.

The woman looked past Gotrek to the approaching horde and then back at the shrine.

Gotrek caught the glance. 'Is there something you can do? What have you got in that shrine?'

'Why do you seek Nagash?' asked the woman. 'To pledge allegiance?'

'Allegiance?' Gotrek laughed. 'I didn't come here to bend the bloody knee.'

'Trachos,' said Maleneth. The ghouls were only moments away. She could see their rolling, feverish eyes and the blood on their teeth. 'Your staff?'

He nodded, whispered a prayer and adjusted the cogs around the sceptre's head. Energy shimmered down the metal, splashing light over his faceplate. The air crackled as he strode away, launching into another tuneless hymn. 'Stooping from celestial spires, he rides the storm to conquer!'

Maleneth looked back at Gotrek. Even now he seemed oblivious to the host rushing towards them. He was holding the woman's gaze.

The woman stared at the dead ghouls Gotrek had scattered around the shrine. Her expression was tormented.

'If you can do something, it needs to be now,' said Maleneth, infuriated by the woman's indecision.

They all staggered as Trachos hammered his sceptre down onto the ground. An aether-wave splashed through the mist, hitting the front ranks of the ghouls, and Trachos' song rose in volume and fervour.

The ghouls ignited like kindling, howling as they fell, shrouded in embers.

The woman's eyes widened. She looked at the wreckage of the other shrines and then at Gotrek's axe and the rune in his chest, both of which were still glowing.

'The Iron Shroud is both wall and door,' she said. 'If it is the will of the Unburied, I may be able to return to Morbium and take you with me.' Her eyes were still burning with hate and outrage, but she kept glancing back to the shrine and she made no attempt to attack.

'Morbium?' Gotrek shook his head. 'That's it. That's the one. Get us there quick, lass, and I might forgive you for trying to gut me.'

They staggered again as Trachos unleashed another wave of light, toppling more ghouls as his song reached a triumphant crescendo.

The young woman gripped her head, drumming her fingers on her skull. 'Prince Volant was right to send me out here. The Shroud *has* been breached.' She shook her head, glancing at the shrine. 'I have to reach him.'

'If he knows the way to Nagash, I'll get you to him,' said Gotrek. 'Consider that an oath.'

She glared at Gotrek but seemed to be considering his offer. 'If the mordants have breached the Shroud, I may need protection.'

Gotrek tapped his bloody axe. 'If protection is what you need–'

'Slayer!' cried Trachos, rushing back and smashing his sceptre into the face of a ghoul. Its skull detonated, scattering flames and grey matter.

Maleneth dodged the gore then stopped the next one with a flurry of knife blows, and Gotrek dropped a third, crumpling its skull with his axe.

'Follow me to the pulpit!' cried the woman. She clambered quickly up the gnarled, twisted mass of stone, waving for them to follow.

They climbed backwards up the stones, still facing the ghouls, parrying their attacks.

Gotrek grinned as he fought, scattering heads and limbs as he hurried after the woman. Trachos used his sceptre like a hammer, swinging it with almost as much ferocity as Gotrek, and every blow triggered a flash of Azyrite sorcery that flashed over his armour, catching on the lightning bolts and stars that decorated the polished plate. His song had become a meaningless jumble of unconnected words. 'Swift! Blessed! Heart! Strife!'

When they reached the centre of the shrine, the woman waved them into the pulpit and indicated that they should sit beside her on the knotted shapes.

'Press your palms to the stone!' she cried.

Maleneth rushed to Gotrek's side. 'Is there anyone you *won't* put your trust in?'

The Slayer laughed and nodded to the chaotic scenes around them. The ghouls were in such a frenzy that they were turning on each other, tearing at their crooked limbs in their desperation to reach the last standing shrine. 'Stay here if you like.'

Gotrek slapped his meaty hand down next to the woman's, gripping a spur of stone that jutted up from the centre of the pulpit.

Trachos pointed his sceptre and lightning ripped from the metal, tearing a ghoul's chest open before lashing through another one's head. 'There's no option,' he said, using the sceptre to club a ghoul that leapt at him from another direction. He put his hand down next to Gotrek's, the metal of his gauntlet clanging against the stone.

Maleneth looked at the red-faced woman. She had gripped the stone in both hands and closed her eyes, whispering furiously. Indigo flames flickered between her fingers, and a breeze washed through the pulpit, causing Maleneth to shiver and curse. This was necromancy, whatever the woman claimed. She could smell death magic on the air.

The shrine began to judder, crumbling under the weight of the ghouls.

Maleneth muttered another curse and put her hand on the stone.

Cold rushed through her, and she gasped in pain. She tried to pull her hand free, but it was frozen in place.

'What is this?' she hissed at the woman, but the priestess was oblivious to anything other than her incantation. Her eyes were closed, her head was tilted back, and she was mouthing arcane, sibilant phrases.

'If you have betrayed–' began Maleneth, but her words were drowned out by a deafening grinding sound as the stone briar tightened its grip, clenching like an enormous fist, enveloping them all in a cage of bristles.

Maleneth cried out as thorns punched into her. She tried again to wrench her hand free, but it was no use.

Dozens of crumbling tusks sliced into her, and as the world grew dark, the talisman at her neck spoke up, its voice full of derision.

You can't even die elegantly.

CHAPTER SIX

MORBIUM

'Ditch maid!' roared Gotrek.

Maleneth was in darkness, but the Slayer's bludgeoning tones could only mean one thing – she was still alive. She had mixed emotions about this.

'It's Witchblade,' she muttered, struggling to sit up. She was tightly bound and her arms were numb from blood loss. She cursed herself for not killing the priestess.

'Aye,' replied Gotrek, sounding infuriatingly cheerful. 'Ditch maid. Get off your arse. Look at this.'

Someone moved towards her, and there was a grind of shifting stones. As her face was uncovered, she saw the heavens whirling overhead. The strange black stars had vanished, replaced by the usual glittering constellations, but they were hazy and faint, as though seen through a gauze.

Maleneth's neck was stiff with cold, but she managed to turn and see who had uncovered her. It was Trachos, starlight shimmering over his battered mask.

'The priestess was telling the truth,' he said.

'This is Morbium,' said the priestess. Maleneth could not see her, but she recognised her taut, furious voice, coming from somewhere up ahead in the darkness. 'Soul prominent. Last bastion of the Gravesward and the royal demesne of Prince Volant, nineteenth heir to the Sable Throne and Morn-Prince of the Lingering Keep.'

Trachos moved more stone off Maleneth, and she managed to stand, slapping her legs and arms, summoning blood back into her limbs. The stone was the remnants of the shrine. Its thorny limbs were in pieces and the corpse cages shattered, leaving the bodies to spill onto the ground, where they now lay motionless.

She looked around. They were on a ruined quay, but it was a quay that hung out over the strangest sea Maleneth had ever seen. Its towering waves were all motionless, as though they had been hammered from iron. She stared at the bizarre view for a moment, wondering if the water was frozen, but while the air was chilly, she was sure it was not cold enough to freeze an entire ocean. The waves just seemed to be paused in a moment, like a sea that had been made for a stage set.

Piers jutted out across the lifeless tides, constructed from the same fractured bones as everything else. The scale of the place was shocking.

Maleneth had seen nothing so grand since leaving Hammerhal. Behind her, the quay joined an iron road, or a bridge of some kind, that led out across the sea, trailing off into the shadows.

'I haven't seen craftsmanship like this since the Hearth Halls of Karaz-a-Karak,' muttered Gotrek, staring out at the grand, crumbling piers. He almost sounded impressed. 'Who built this?' he asked, his breath coiling around him in the cold air.

The priestess was still picking her way from the ruined shrine and dusting her robes down, too dazed to realise she was being addressed. Maleneth noticed that she was mouthing words as she moved – numbers, by the look of it, as though she were counting something.

Gotrek repeated his question in even more bombastic tones, and the priestess looked up. 'The Morn-Prince,' she said. 'The *first* Morn-Prince, at the dawn of the Amethyst Princedoms.'

Gotrek stooped and picked up a piece of mangled metalwork. Even broken it was beautiful – intricately scored bone inlaid with strips of silver that depicted skulls and insect wings. 'Not bad for a bunch of ghost-botherers.'

'We do not "bother" our dead.' The priestess looked at her scythe, still tucked into Gotrek's belt, her eyes smouldering. Her face was flushed with anger, and Maleneth could see that she was struggling not to attack Gotrek. 'We watch over them just as they watch over us. We revere our ancestors.'

Maleneth nodded at the corpses slumped in the shrine's broken cages. 'Did you revere them?'

The woman sneered. 'They were mordants. I wiped their minds and turned them on their own kind. There are not worthy of anything more.'

'You're a witch?' Gotrek looked as though he had tasted something unpleasant.

'I am Lhosia, High Priestess of the Cerement. Spiritual adviser to the Morn-Prince.' She nodded towards the scythe at her belt. 'What power I have is tied to the ancestors.'

'Sounds like ghost-bothering to me,' grunted Gotrek, picking rubble from his mohawk.

Maleneth had climbed from the ruined shrine, and she stepped out towards Gotrek and Lhosia. 'This Morn-Prince you serve. We were told he could lead Gotrek to Nagash.'

The priestess frowned. 'Why would you *seek* the necromancer? Most people would do anything to avoid him.'

At the mention of Nagash, Gotrek's expression had soured. 'The gods owe me a doom. I don't care if it's the bone-head or the thunder-dunce – someone's going to give me what I was promised.' He waved his axe, causing its brazier to flicker. 'Either way, this thing will end up embedded in a god.'

Lhosia laughed in disbelief. 'You're at war with the gods?'

'We all are, lass. I'm just taking the fight to them.'

'The necromancer promised you something?' Lhosia glanced at Maleneth with a baffled expression.

Maleneth shrugged.

Gotrek's beard bristled. He stomped across the ruined metal, muttering in an archaic duardin tongue. 'I don't know who promised me what anymore,' he snapped, 'but I know I was robbed of my doom. Nagash knows what I'm owed. He'll remember me.'

There was a note of desperation in the Slayer's voice. Maleneth had the impression that Gotrek was propelled by fury more than facts. How much could he really remember? Was he seeking Nagash for revenge or because he didn't know what else to do? Did he just want to find someone who might know who he was? Since the moment she had met him, Maleneth had sensed that Gotrek was unsure why he was still alive. He was like a hound that had been kicked, bloodied and readied for the hunt, then thrown into a cage.

As Gotrek stormed around the ruins, swinging his axe and cursing, the rune in his chest started to glow.

'Can you get us to this prince of yours?' he demanded.

'I can,' said Lhosia. 'I *have* to reach him. He sent me to check that the borders of the princedom were sound, and they're in tatters. And if the mordants have breached the Iron Shroud, they could be anywhere.'

'What is this place?' asked Trachos. As usual, he seemed two steps removed from the conversation, consumed by whatever strange thoughts rattled around his helmet. He unclasped one of his devices from his armour and pointed its notched ellipses at the architecture. 'Why did you bring us here in particular?' He looked around at the empty streets and toppled buildings.

'It's my home,' Lhosia said. 'It was the easiest place for me to conjure from memory. Besides, before I do anything else I have to warn my family. The Iron Shroud is breached. Morbium has been revealed. I have to make sure our Unburied are safe.'

'It's a port,' said Gotrek.

She nodded. 'Some of your duardin kin used to pilot aether-ships here, before the fall of the princedoms. They called themselves Kharadron. They used to ship ore here. My ancestors fused it with bone to construct our temples.'

'There were dwarfs here?' Gotrek frowned, looking around the ruins with a suspicious expression.

Maleneth laughed. 'He's quite the celebrity amongst his own kind.' She lowered her voice to a mock whisper. 'They think *he's* a god. Oh, the irony...'

Lhosia stared at Gotrek's scarred, filthy muscles, looking even more baffled. 'A god? Why would they think that?'

Maleneth rolled her eyes. 'Because he crawled out of a hole and claimed it was the Realm of Chaos.'

'Slayers do not lie,' said Gotrek. 'The gods promised me a doom in the Realm of Chaos. Then the faithless bastards forgot about me. Now I'm here.' He peered into the ruins. 'Do dwarfs... I mean, do *duardin* still come here?'

Lhosia shook her head. 'No one comes here. When the other princedoms fell we built the Iron Shroud. Through the wisdom of the Unburied we hid ourselves from the necromancer and even from the Dark Gods. But without the Kharadron we lost contact with the other realms. We are alone.' She glanced at the corpses next to the shrine. 'Or, we were.'

'How can we reach your prince?' asked Maleneth.

Lhosia nodded to a building that looked more intact than the others. It resembled the bleached bowl of a skull, gleaming and chipped. 'My family is stationed here, guarding the ruins. They will have already seen that I'm here. It is only a small temple, but we have many Unburied loaning us their sight.' She waved for the others to follow as she began picking her way through the rubble towards the building.

'Unburied?' asked Maleneth. It was a strange word, and every time Lhosia spoke it there was reverence in her voice.

'The ancestors,' said Lhosia, glaring at her. 'The reason we are here. We exist to ensure their future. Our world is an antechamber to theirs – the world that is to come, where we shall join our forebears.'

Gotrek glanced up at that, seeming intrigued. He was about to speak when Lhosia faltered and came to a halt, squinting through the gloom at the building at the end of the pier.

Maleneth gripped her knives. 'What?'

'No light.' Lhosia's voice sounded odd. She nodded to the curved bone-white walls of the temple. The building was swathed in shadow and looked abandoned. She staggered on, looking dazed and troubled.

CHAPTER SEVEN

HARBINGERS

They rushed on, reaching the building together. It was a coiled teardrop of bone, edged with a silver tracery of symbols that Maleneth did not recognise. The bone looked ridged and grooved, as though made of irregular tiles. The silver glimmered in the starlight, but otherwise there was only darkness.

'Anyone there?' bellowed Gotrek, tapping the head of his axe against the walls.

There was an explosion of noise and movement.

Maleneth flipped gracefully back from the building, whipping her knives out of her leathers and landing in a crouch, only to find that Gotrek had disturbed nothing more dangerous than insects. What she had taken for tiles on the surface of the building were actually thousands of pale, diaphanous moths. They were now whirling around Gotrek and the others, fluttering against their faces and filling the air with a frenetic buzz.

Gotrek cursed and waved his axe around, nearly beheading Lhosia in the process. 'Damn things,' he grunted, trying to bat the insects away.

Maleneth laughed at the absurd sight of a Slayer doing battle with moths. 'You don't like them,' she snorted.

Gotrek glowered back at her. 'I like them a damn sight more than witch aelves.' He waded off through the fluttering cloud, muttering as he batted them away.

Maleneth was still laughing as she struggled after him, amazed by the ridiculousness of the Slayer. She had seen him kill beasts that could best armies and trade insults with a sylvaneth goddess. And here he was, cursing because a few insects were trapped in his beard.

'Stop!' cried Lhosia, grabbing Gotrek's axe and glaring at him in outrage. 'The harbingers! You'll offend them!'

Gotrek stared at her. 'The what?'

'She means the moths.' Maleneth laughed even harder. 'You're scared of them, and she's worried about offending them!'

'Where's the door?' cried Gotrek, scowling at Maleneth and then rounding on Lhosia. 'How do we get in?'

After a wary glance at Gotrek's axe, the priestess nodded and hurried past him, pointing her scythe at a bone archway that looked like the rib of a long-dead leviathan. Her eyes were wide with fear.

They all rushed after her, entering a circular courtyard with a hole at its centre and metal steps spiralling down into the darkness.

Lhosia hesitated at the top step, looking around the courtyard and shaking her head. She peered down into the darkness. 'Hello?' she called, taking a few steps down into the gloom. 'Mother? Father? It's Lhosia.'

A clattering echoed up the steps, followed by what sounded like a door slamming shut.

Lhosia glanced back at the others. Her pale, hard features twisted into a scowl.

Gotrek took the scythe from his belt and handed it to her.

She looked at the blade for a moment, then turned and dashed down the steps, vanishing from view.

Maleneth laughed again. 'By the Bloody-Handed, she's as eager to die as you are, Gotrek.'

'We need her alive if we're going to find this wretched prince,' he replied, and charged after Lhosia.

Maleneth turned to Trachos with a despairing look. The Stormcast took an instrument from his belt and fixed it to the head of his sceptre with a click. Cool blue light washed over Maleneth's shoulders, and she climbed down the steps after Gotrek and Lhosia, Trachos following closely behind.

She could make out the Slayer's squat, bulky form a few steps ahead as he halted in front of a doorway next to the priestess. The door was hanging from its hinges. As Trachos' light washed over an opening of curved, metal-edged bone, it revealed a glimpse of a large underground chamber beyond.

Lhosia swore under her breath and shook her head.

Gotrek grunted in annoyance and booted the door down, stomping into the room with his axe raised.

They rushed in after the Slayer, and Trachos' sceptre revealed a gruesome scene. Body parts were scattered across the floor, glistening in pools of blood and shrouded in fluttering moths.

Gotrek grimaced, but Lhosia fell to her knees as though she had been gut-punched, gasping, reaching out to the remains but not daring to touch them. Moths rose from the blood as her hands hovered over it.

Maleneth scoured the room for signs of the killer, but it was empty apart from the corpses, torn apart with such savagery that the whole chamber was splattered with gore. 'Impressive,' she muttered, nodding at the carnage.

Gotrek glanced at her and nodded to Lhosia.

Maleneth shrugged and gave him an apologetic smile.

The room was unfurnished apart from a few chairs arranged either side of a tall, curved door that led further into the temple. The door was ajar and there were trails of blood leading to it. A snuffling, grunting noise came from the next room, and then the sound of something heavy moving around.

'The Unburied,' whispered Lhosia, her words barely audible. She climbed slowly to her feet and staggered to the door.

Gotrek grabbed her arm and shook his head. 'Let me go first, lass,' he said, his voice softer than usual.

She wrenched her arm free and carried on, the others close behind.

Maleneth staggered to a halt on the other side, unable to understand what she was seeing. The room looked like a man-made orchard. The circular walls were punctuated by six trunk-like columns of bone that arched upwards and met in the centre of a domed ceiling. Each of the columns had a protruding limb about twelve feet in the air, and dangling from them was what looked like pale, rotten fruit, each one about the size of a man's head. No, realised Maleneth, they were more like cocoons – dusty, bone-white bundles, like elongated eggs made of paper strips. And they were not rotten – they had been attacked. The six cocoons had been slashed by claws or a knife, and dark, viscous liquid dripped from the shredded remains.

Lhosia howled at the sight of them, her expression more horrified than when she had seen the corpses in the previous room.

'What is this?' said Gotrek, reaching up to one of the torn cocoons.

'No!' cried Lhosia, her words rough with fury. 'They should not have been here! The prince swore that they would be moved!'

'What are they?' asked Maleneth, peering into one of the dangling sacks. She could see what looked like pieces of dried meat inside.

'The Unburied,' said Lhosia, her voice trembling.

'Your ancestors?' asked Maleneth.

'My grandmother!' gasped Lhosia. 'My great-grandfather! *His* great-grandmother! All of them. They were all–'

Gotrek silenced her by raising his hand and nodding to the next doorway. The light of Trachos' sceptre shone through into the next chamber, and there was something coming towards them.

Lhosia slumped against the wall, clutching her head. 'Prince Volant swore an oath.' She sounded furious. 'They should have been taken to the capital.'

One of the mechanisms fixed to Trachos' belt began to whirr and click. He looked like he was about to say something when the doorway exploded towards them.

Fragments of metal and bone filled the air as a huge shape smashed through, tearing half the wall down as it came.

'Grungni's Beard!' snarled Gotrek. 'That's more like it.'

The creature lumbered into the room, shrugging pieces of masonry from its shoulders. It was twice the height of Trachos. It was clearly a cousin of the ghouls they had fought on the borders of the princedom, with the same deranged eyes and slavering jaws, but it was massive, clad in thick, scarred muscle and bristling with mutant growth – every inch of its greasy flesh sported tusks of bone that jutted through its muscles like spines on a burr. Its face was smeared with the same dark liquid that dripped from the cocoons, and as it locked eyes on Gotrek, it let out a feral roar, dragging down more wall as it launched itself at the Slayer.

Gotrek answered with a roar of his own and leapt at the giant, swinging his axe as he flew through the air.

The blade flashed, thudding into the ghoul's chest with such force that the monster staggered back, carrying Gotrek with it. They smashed through the ruined doorway and landed in the room beyond.

Gotrek howled in annoyance as he stood atop the prone giant and tried to haul his axe free.

The blade refused to move. Rather than bleeding, the ghoul's chest had swallowed the axe head, puckering around it and holding it fast.

The ghoul rose to its feet and punched Gotrek with an enormous fist, sending him flying across the room. The Slayer smashed into a stone column and slammed to the floor.

'Gods,' he muttered as rubble pattered down on his scalp. 'You're a big lad.'

While Gotrek grabbed the broken column and tried to climb to his feet, Maleneth sprinted past him, knives drawn, and leapt at the monster's chest.

The ghoul lashed out with talons like swords, but Maleneth whirled out of reach, arching her back as she dodged the blow.

Before the monster knew what was happening, she dragged her blades across its throat and leapt away.

Maleneth landed with a curse. Her blades had remained embedded in the ghoul's neck. Just like Gotrek's axe, her weapons were being absorbed by the creature's flesh. Now that she saw it more clearly in Trachos' light, she realised that not only was the monster covered in spurs of bone, but also fragments of weapons – hilts and hafts jutted from between its ribs and shoulder blades, mementos from previous battles.

The ghoul locked its fist around Trachos' throat, lifted him into the air and slammed him into Gotrek like a club. They crashed to the floor just as Maleneth reached the monster, and the three of them ended up in a mangled heap.

They helped each other up and backed away, panting and limping.

Gotrek wiped blood and dust from his face. 'I didn't escape the Dark Gods to be pummelled by this oaf. Distract the bugger and I'll...' The Slayer's words trailed off as two more of the creatures stumbled into the room, just as massive and deformed as the first, their combined bulk almost filling the chamber. One was unarmed, but the second had wrenched a bone column free and was gripping it like a makeshift spear, its splintered point glistening with dark liquid.

'Three of them,' muttered Gotrek. 'And they swallow weapons...'

Maleneth was gripping her head, trying to quell the agony reverberating round her skull, and Trachos was leaning against the wall, sparks coiling around his neck brace as he took deep, ragged breaths.

Lhosia strode past Gotrek, gripping her scythe and glaring up at the three giants with no trace of fear. 'They murdered the Unburied.'

She sliced her scythe cleanly through one of the ghouls' legs, causing it to stagger, then whirled away into the shadows, swallowed by the darkness before the creatures could fight back.

Maleneth nodded, impressed by the girl's speed and bravery. She grabbed Trachos' sceptre from a shattered plinth and hurled it to him.

The Stormcast raised the light, dazzling the giants, as Gotrek bounded across the room and leapt for his axe again. 'Blazed pennants!' cried Trachos, launching into song as his sceptre shone brighter. 'And wondrous, gleaming pinions!'

The first ghoul staggered back into the other two, unbalanced by the impact of the Slayer slamming into it. As it fell, Gotrek roared in triumph, drowning out Trachos' song. Rune-light rippled across his knotted muscles, blazing in his beard.

With a final, ear-splitting roar, the Slayer ripped his axe from the monster's chest.

Gotrek cartwheeled backwards in an arc of blood, then rolled across the floor and charged back at the ghoul. This time, rather than sinking his axe into the monster's chest, he followed Lhosia's lead, swiping low and cutting through its ankle.

The monster fell heavily, smashing more columns and scattering cocoons.

As the ghoul landed, Maleneth dashed across the room, snatched a vial from her belt and hurled it into the monster's gaping mouth, dodging aside as it reached out to grab her.

Gotrek had already strode on to meet the other two giants. The first tried to land a punch, but the berserk Slayer was too fast and the blow only succeeded in smashing more bone from the walls.

Lhosia leapt from the shadows and hacked through the ankle of the next ghoul, sending it smashing to the floor before she vanished into the darkness again.

Maleneth was ready. The giant had hardly hit the ground before she hurled a vial down its throat and backed away.

Trachos marched past the downed ghouls and levelled his blazing sceptre at the one still standing, causing it to reel away from him, arms raised in front of its grotesque face.

Gotrek barrelled across the room and swung his axe with such force that it hacked straight through both of the ghoul's legs, dropping it in a shower of splintered bone. The creature slumped against the wall, and Maleneth hesitated, swaying from side to side as she tried to spot a route to its head. Then she had a better idea. She ran to the monster's butchered leg and punched her fist into the severed muscles, leaving a vial embedded deep beneath its pallid skin.

As Gotrek, Maleneth and Trachos backed away, Maleneth's poison took effect and the three giants began to smoulder. Smoke plumed from their mouths as they thrashed across the floor, clawing at their throats and eyes before erupting into flame.

The blaze was so ferocious that everyone was forced to back away to the doorway they had originally entered through.

Gotrek gave Maleneth and Trachos a grudging nod of respect. 'Not bad,' he yelled over the sound of the dying ghouls.

'The Unburied!' cried Lhosia, pointing her scythe at the door on the other side of the fire. The flames were spreading across the floor into the chamber the ghouls had emerged from. 'The others may still be alive! They'll be burned.'

Gotrek looked at the flames and laughed. 'Rather your paper eggs than us.'

Lhosia glared at him, still gripping the scythe. For a moment, Maleneth thought the priestess might try and attack the Slayer. Then she shook her head. 'Only the Unburied can guide me to Prince Volant. If you let them burn, you will never see the prince and you will never find Nagash. The prince could be anywhere in Morbium. And the princedom is vast – we could search for years and not find him. But the Unburied see all. They could tell me right now where Prince Volant is, and the best way to reach him without encountering more of the mordants.'

Gotrek stared at the fire. One side of his face was glossy with old scar tissue. He ran his finger over the burns. 'I've been through bigger fires.'

He turned to Trachos and Maleneth. 'Either of you know another way to find this prince?'

They shook their heads.

Gotrek gave his beard a thoughtful tug, looking at the priestess. Then he raced into the flames.

Maleneth cursed and headed after him, but the heat drove her back. 'Trachos!' she called. 'Your faith will protect you. Follow him!'

Trachos nodded and limped towards the fire.

'No, wait,' muttered Maleneth, putting her hand on his chest. 'I know what you'll do if he *has* immolated himself. You'll take the damned rune.' She glanced at Lhosia. 'Is there another way out of there?'

Lhosia nodded.

Trachos shoved Maleneth aside, heading for the flames again, raising his voice in skull-tightening song.

But before he reached the fire, Gotrek came charging back into the room, head down and cradling something, trailing sparks and smoke as he ran past Trachos and Maleneth and dropped to his knees, still laughing.

'Got it,' he said, standing up and grinning at Lhosia.

The priestess ran to him, ignoring the smoke and the heat as she prised his arms apart.

'Intact,' she whispered, gently lifting a cocoon from his grip. She closed her eyes and let her head fall gently against it.

'Now the others!' she said, staring back through the flames. 'There should be another cocoon, like this one.'

'It was empty.' Gotrek nodded at the mess scattered across the floor. 'Ruined like these.'

'You're lying!' Lhosia put the cocoon under one arm and drew her scythe, her lips quivering.

Gotrek raised an eyebrow, calmly ignoring the blade that was inches from his face.

Lhosia's eyes widened, and she drew the scythe back to strike.

Maleneth grabbed her arm. 'He doesn't lie. He really is that boring.'

The rage dimmed in Lhosia's eyes. 'All gone?' she muttered.

'Apart from that,' said Gotrek, nodding at the cocoon she carried.

Maleneth tried to get a better look at it, intrigued by the awe Lhosia obviously held it in. 'What is it?' she asked, struggling to see it clearly in the firelight. 'How is that your family?'

Lhosia sheathed her scythe and cradled the object like an infant. Then she nodded to the antechamber they had entered through. She walked towards it, indicating that they should follow. 'Let me show you.'

CHAPTER EIGHT

THE UNBURIED

Once they were gathered in the room, Gotrek shoved the door closed behind them, blocking out the heat and smoke.

Lhosia was still hugging the object and she gave them a wary look. 'You are not one of the Erebid. You do not understand the Unburied.'

Gotrek's expression darkened. 'I've just singed half my beard for this.'

'What is an Erebid?' asked Maleneth, amused by the woman's odd, nervous behaviour.

'I am.' Lhosia still sounded hollow and dazed, but she tried to explain. 'I mean, we are – the people of Morbium. It's what we call ourselves.' She waved them away. 'You must not stand so close. When I am communing with my ancestors I will be in a fragile state.'

Maleneth raised an eyebrow. 'Emotionally?'

'Physically. My form will change. You must not touch me until the rite is complete. If you touch me it won't only be me who is in danger. You will become part of the ritual. The Unburied will inhale your soul and your flesh will be transformed, made brittle. You will be drawn into your past lives and the past lives of the Unburied.'

'I have no idea what you're talking about,' grunted Gotrek. He gave Maleneth a warning glance. 'But I'll make sure no one interferes with your spell.'

Maleneth gasped in mock offence. 'Always, you doubt me, Slayer.'

'Stay away from me until I am done,' Lhosia said. 'Or you risk more than just your flesh.'

She headed over to one of the columns that arched up the walls of the chamber and sat down against it. She muttered quietly under her breath. It seemed to be some kind of song.

'Oh...' Maleneth rolled her eyes. 'She's a *wise* woman. I imagine she reads palms.' She gripped the knives at her belt and smirked. She could show Lhosia how to perform a rite that actually achieved something. And it would not require any lullabies.

As Maleneth strolled around the chamber, waiting for the rite to finish, she considered her next move. She'd had no option but to follow the Slayer this far, but what if there really was some way he could reach the God of Death? Nagash was known for many things, but sharing was not one of them. If Gotrek reached Nagash, the Slayer would be destroyed, his soul would be enslaved and the rune would be taken. She had to find a way to get her hands on it before this ridiculous quest got out of hand.

Maybe if you paid attention to your surroundings, you might learn something to your advantage, said her mistress, causing the amulet to pulse warmth across her chest.

Unlikely, she thought. A berserk hog, a babbling necrophile and a Stormcast Eternal who's so confused he can barely speak. They're not likely to offer much in the way of insight.

Something caught in Maleneth's hair. She batted it away, realising it was one of the pallid moths. Another one fluttered across her face and then another, until the air was busy with the things.

She cursed and tried to wave them away. They were fluttering past her in a great cloud, heading towards Lhosia. They landed on the priestess like a pale robe, covering her and the cocoon in humming wings.

Lhosia's hands were sinking into the surface of the cocoon, vanishing from sight. Then a pale light started to shimmer inside it, like a candle in a paper lantern. The surface of the cocoon gradually became transparent and, as the light burned brighter, the cocoon's contents became unmistakable. At first there was a flurry of tiny shapes, circling like gnats, then one began to grow and take shape. Maleneth could not help but laugh. There was such a contrast between the reverence in Lhosia's gaze and the pathetic, grotesque thing hanging in front of her. It looked like a wizened foetus, no bigger than a human head, but with the grey, weathered features of a decrepit old man. It had long, thin, grey hair and patchy stubble on its jaw. Its limbs were atrophied and wasted and its eyes were milk white.

Gotrek grimaced. 'I risked my life for a pickled corpse? How could that thing have got any more dead?'

'The Unburied endure,' replied Lhosia, speaking in hushed tones, her eyes still closed.

She moved her palms beneath the surface of the cocoon as its contents began to move.

Trachos muttered and Maleneth smirked as the shrivelled thing kicked its legs, disturbing whatever fluid suspended it inside the cocoon. Slowly, it raised a withered hand and pressed it against Lhosia's palm.

Lhosia whispered a prayer of thanks and, when she opened her eyes, the pupils and irises had vanished, leaving featureless white orbs. Then she began to undergo a more profound transformation. As the moths fidgeted across her robes, the dusty, white texture of the cocoon washed over her, turning her whole body into luminous bone. The light of the Unburied pulsed through her and caught on the wings of the moths as they spiralled around her.

Then the shape in the cocoon began to speak. No sound emerged but its mouth was opening and closing and Lhosia nodded in reply.

'How did you create such a revolting thing?' asked Maleneth.

'*We* did not do this,' Lhosia's voice sounded odd –like an echo. 'No mortal can preserve souls. Not by natural means, at least.' Lhosia nodded to the moths spinning around her. 'This is the power of the noctuid.'

'Noctuid?' Maleneth frowned. 'The moths?'

Lhosia nodded, her voice hushed. 'Harbingers. Our link to the next life. They weave the shrouds and preserve the spirit. Every one of our ancestors has been preserved this way for countless generations. We built our faith on the wisdom of our bloodline. Nothing lost. Nothing forgotten.'

Maleneth looked back towards the room containing the ruined cocoons. 'Until now, you mean.'

Lhosia's expression hardened. 'They should not have been left here. Each one of those cocoons held hundreds of souls.' She placed her other palm on the cocoon and whispered more prayers. The light was burning so brightly it looked like she had caught an amethyst star. The glare flashed over her hard, opalescent face, making her look like a work of devotional art.

'How will this thing lead us to your prince?' said Gotrek.

Anger flickered in Lhosia's eyes at the word 'thing' but she nodded. 'We are in a Separation Chamber. I have separated my soul from my flesh so I can speak with my ancestor.' She gave them all a stern look. 'You must be silent. If my concentration is broken, my form may be altered.'

'Your what?' laughed Maleneth.

'I have sundered my soul from my flesh. I am holding an image of my physical self in my mind so I may return to find it unchanged.'

Maleneth frowned at Gotrek and shook her head.

There was a long silence as Lhosia held the cocoon with her eyes closed, her hands still pressed beneath its surface. The only noise was a vague rattling sound coming from somewhere above. After several minutes, the shrivelled corpse mouthed more words and Lhosia nodded. There was another pause, then the priestess opened her eyes. The moths scattered from her skin and her flesh lost its shell-like texture, becoming normal again.

She took a deep breath, then looked up at them. 'The prince is headed to see Lord Aurun at the Barren Points. Not far from here. Three day's walk if we make good speed.'

'Good,' said Gotrek, striding away from the light and heading for the door. 'Then we should leave now.'

Maleneth and Trachos followed but Lhosia remained where she was, whispering to the tiny corpse.

'What's that sound?' said Gotrek, pausing by the door and looking up, noticing the rattling noise for the first time.

They all listened. It sounded as though someone were hurling stones at the roof.

Maleneth looked at Lhosia.

The priestess dragged her gaze from the cocoon and listened. Then she frowned, disconnecting her hands from the cocoon, extinguishing its inner light and rushing past Maleneth to the bottom of the stairs.

Maleneth and the others followed her as she climbed back up to the quay. The noise grew as they climbed the steps, becoming a fierce, rattling din, like coins poured onto metal.

As they reached the entrance hall they were greeted by a spectacular sight. The sky was a veil of glittering shards.

'I've never seen this,' said Lhosia. She stepped towards the opening at the end of the hall, her hand outstretched.

Gotrek grabbed her and shook his head. 'Watch out, lass.'

Lhosia glared at him and pulled her arm free.

'He's right,' said Maleneth. 'We've seen this before. In Klemp they call it bone rain.'

Lhosia shook her head. 'Bone rain?'

Gotrek grunted and stepped back, avoiding the shards that bounced towards him. 'Weather from Nagash. It'll cut through you like knives.'

They stood in silence for a while, stunned by the spectacle of the scene. It looked like they were trapped behind a waterfall spilled from the stars, and the sound was deafening, like waves crashing against rocks.

Eventually, Lhosia looked at Gotrek. 'When will it stop?'

He shook his head. 'Could be days for all I know.' He scowled. Then he looked past her, back into the temple, a hopeful gleam in his eye. 'Do you people have anything to drink?'

CHAPTER NINE

THE HOUNDS OF DINANN

The war had been brutal but brief. King Galan had not expected the level of resistance, but he had expected the glorious devotion of his men. The Hounds of Dinann. What army, in all the realms, could hope to stand against such warriors? Never had he felt so alive. He was almost grateful for the uprising. To rise from his fur-strewn throne and take up his spear one last time. One final war. The Great Wolf had smiled on him.

The traitors had taken hold of an outlying keep, burning effigies and flying their colours from the walls in defiance of his rule, but King Galan could taste victory. He was days away from ending the rebellion and returning order to the entire kingdom. Loyal vassals from every corner of his empire had flocked to his banner when word of the rebellion spread. There were reports coming in from all the major engagements, describing victory after victory. By the time he reached the capital, there would barely be a rebel left to face him. He looked around as he rode towards the keep. Ranks of spearmen were arrayed around him, their golden torcs gleaming in the darkness, their breastplates flashing as they followed him to the gates. Behind them came serried legions of foot soldiers, their pennants flying and their voices raised in song as the sigil of the hound fluttered in the wind.

'Surrender your arms!' cried Galan as he stopped his horse near the shattered gates. 'I am no tyrant. Handle yourselves with dignity and you can live. The battle is over. The Hounds of Dinann are not savages. There need be no slaughter.'

There was no reply. He could see figures rushing through the darkness up on the walls of the keep, readying their weapons and war machines for a final, desperate defence. He had expected no more, but he had fought the whole campaign with dignity and pride. He was no fool. He was old. He had not expected this last chance for glory, but now that it had been given to him he would show his men how a king should lead.

'Very well,' he called. 'We have given them a chance to kneel and they have refused. They have turned their back on the Great Wolf.'

He raised his spear and pointed it at the keep. 'Hounds of Dinann! Advance!'

There was an oceanic roar. His army surged past him, howling war cries and rattling spears on shields as they rushed forwards.

His men moved with such speed that they seemed to swarm up the walls with barely any need for ladders or hooks, washing over the battlements and pouring into the reeling defenders.

Howls and screams filled the night as King Galan rode towards the gates of the keep. He did not have to wait long before the doors flew open, revealing the victorious faces of his men as they drove the traitors back, washing the courtyard with blood and setting fire to the buildings inside the walls.

He strode over to one of the fallen defenders. The man was still alive, and as Galan offered him a helping hand he started to scream desperately, trying to drag his broken body away.

'What are you?' howled the man.

Galan frowned. It was a strange thing to say, even for a dying man. And it was not the first time he had been asked this question. 'What am I?' He laughed. 'I am your king.'

The man would not stop screaming, and eventually, the sound started to infuriate Galan. This had happened several times during the campaign. Every time he offered his hand, giving the wounded a last chance to surrender, they panicked and shrieked at him. He stooped down and pressed his hand over the man's mouth, trying to stifle his cries.

'There's no need for this,' he said. 'Lay down your weapons. Rejoin the Hounds.'

The man thrashed beneath him, blood flying everywhere.

Too much blood, realised Galan. He had a broken leg, but there were no cuts on him. Why was he bleeding?

The more Galan tried to calm him, the more the air filled with blood.

'What are you?' cried the man again, but Galan found it hard to concentrate and the voice grew distant.

The air turned crimson and Galan backed away, shaking his head, confused. As he stumbled away from the man, he realised how hungry he was. In fact, his craving seemed to have confused him. He'd imagined he was still on the battlefield, but hunger and exhaustion were playing tricks on him, throwing him back into the past. He laughed, realising he was already at the victory feast. He leant back in his chair and grabbed some meat from a platter on the table. It was so rare it was almost raw. Blood rushed down his chin as he ate, delighting in his well-earned appetite.

CHAPTER TEN

REMEMBRANCE

Gotrek grimaced as he drank the wine Lhosia had found, but Maleneth noticed that he had managed to empty another skin. A few hours had passed since the storm had begun, and there was now quite a pile of them lying around him on the platform, all empty. It looked like he had been fighting overgrown bats and was now sprawled on their carcasses. He nodded to a row of shields that covered the walls. 'What do they say?'

They were sitting in a circle, just inside the archway, silhouetted by the flashing rain. The torrent of bones bathed the group in ripples of light, making it look like they were under water. The temperature had dropped so they had lit a fire, with Lhosia seated to one side of the Slayer and Maleneth to the other. Trachos was opposite Gotrek, his head bowed as he muttered to the flames, his face still hidden behind his helmet.

'The shield poems?' Lhosia's words were slurred. Despite her earlier protestations, she had eventually agreed to drink some of the wine. She claimed never to have drunk before, but grief had clearly given her a thirst. 'They record the deeds of the Unburied. When an ancestor dies, we carve the story of their life into their shield and place it near the Separating Chamber. Then all who come seeking their wisdom will know how they lived and how they died.'

Gotrek bared his teeth in a grim smile. 'Death poems. We had such things where I come from.' He grabbed another wineskin, tore it open and drank, staring morosely at the fire.

'Where *do* you come from?' asked Lhosia. Maleneth had noticed that she kept steering the conversation away from herself and her loss, as though unwilling to share her grief with strangers.

Gotrek ignored her, hypnotised by the flames.

Lhosia looked at Maleneth.

'His world is gone,' she said. 'He says it was destroyed. Somewhere beyond the Mortal Realms. Although he won't say much else on the subject.' She sneered. 'He talks about his ancestors almost as much as you do.'

'You could never understand,' grunted Gotrek. 'You faithless aelves have no concept of history or tradition.' He waved at the shield poems. 'You have no regard for your elders, never mind your ancestors. All you care about is yourself.'

Maleneth shrugged. 'Someone has to.'

'My people respected the past and remembered their ancestors,' said Gotrek, giving Lhosia a sympathetic look. 'Much as you do. We recorded deeds on oath stones and…' His words trailed off and he shook his head, looking suddenly annoyed. 'What does it matter? They're all gone. All butchered. And, thanks to the treachery of the gods, I did nothing to help them.'

Lhosia was still holding the cocoon. There was no sign of the light or the figure inside. It looked like a rock, swaddled in dust and pale, fine-woven cloth. Maleneth noticed that she was counting again, mouthing the numbers in silence. Then she frowned and looked up at Gotrek. 'Why didn't you help your people?'

'Grimnir told me I was his heir. He tricked me into the Realm of Chaos, promising me that I would finally meet my doom. The mightiest doom ever achieved by a Slayer, he said. Lies, all of it.'

Gotrek lurched to his feet, staggering dangerously close to the archway. The bone shards were cutting into the ground just inches from where he stood, talking to the darkness. 'And while I languished in those wretched hells, forgotten, everything and everyone I knew was blown apart.' His voice grew hoarse. 'If I had remained to fight, I would have found a way to save them. But the gods tricked me. Everyone was killed and I was left alive. Sworn to die, and I outlived everyone! What could be crueller?'

It was the most Maleneth had heard Gotrek say about his journey to the Mortal Realms. The most she had heard him say on any subject, for that matter. Usually he just cursed, muttered or laughed. The wine had affected him differently to the ale he usually drank. He was still morose and bitter, but more willing to talk.

'What did you see in there?' she asked, trying to sound only half-interested, not wanting to spoil the moment by prying too eagerly.

Even Trachos ceased his muttering and looked up at Gotrek.

The Slayer stomped back over to the fire and sat down with a grunt, taking another swig of wine. 'Things with no names. Things beyond words. Citadels of sound. Songs of blood. Oceans of hate. You wouldn't understand even if I could show you. I couldn't understand them even as I saw them. For a long time I believed the lies. I believed that I *had* been given a great doom. To slaughter daemonic hosts for all eternity. Until I died or they did. But *nothing* dies in there. Not truly. I killed and was killed with no victory or defeat. The gods laughed at me.' His voice cracked with bitterness. 'Then forgot me.' He grabbed a burning stick from the fire and crushed it, the flames blinking in his eye, embers spiralling around his scarred face. 'They won't forget me again.'

He drank some more and fell quiet. His earlier high spirits had faded. Maleneth was about to ask Lhosia more about her own people when Trachos did something she had never seen him do before. He unclasped his neck brace and removed his helmet. The seals were dented and caked in filth, and they made a strange hissing sound as he prised them apart.

Even Gotrek looked up in surprise as the Stormcast Eternal's face was revealed. His hair was long, white and knotted into thick plaits. Released from his helmet, it tumbled down over the metal of his cuirass like ropes, giving him the appearance of an aged shaman. His skin was the colour of polished teak, and his face must once have been handsome in a fierce, leonine kind of way. It was not handsome now. Every inch was covered in scars. They were not the rippling burn marks that covered half of Gotrek's face, but deep, jagged cuts. One of them went right from his jaw to his forehead, wrenching his brow into a constant scowl. He looked warily at them, as though removing his helmet had made him feel exposed. 'How did you escape?' he said. Without his helmet on, Trachos' voice lost its thin, metallic quality and became a deep, rumbling tenor.

The combination of wine and surprise seemed to trick Gotrek out of his usual reticence. He stared at Trachos, then stared through him, as if picturing somewhere else.

'I began to see things,' he muttered. 'Things that had not happened yet, or maybe things that had happened long ago.' He shook his head. 'Losing my mind, I suppose. Fighting for so long. Furious at my betrayal. Struggling to remember my own name.'

He looked at Lhosia. 'I had a rememberer once too, like your shield poets. A manling. But not like most of that cowardly, cack-handed race. He was a skilled fighter. And brave with it. A good storysmith, too. He stood by me through everything. He would have come with me if I'd let him. Then, when the madness came over me, I thought I could see him, still alive, in some other world, preserved somehow through the long ages of my purgatory.' He laughed bitterly. 'I sometimes wonder if he's *here* somehow, in these damned worlds you call realms. But then I wonder if it was someone else I saw, leading me through the Realm of Chaos, bringing me through the flames.'

He seemed to notice everyone watching him and his face hardened. 'Whatever happened, my search spat me out into that ugly furnace you call Aqshy, surrounded by babbling idiots claiming to be Slayers. Descendants of Grimnir, they said. If they knew him like I do, they wouldn't be so keen to claim his kinship. Not one of them understands what a treacherous crook their god is.' He pounded the rune in his chest. 'They're as useless as him, though. So maybe they are his spawn. They made this bauble and then lacked the strength to use it.'

'What is it?' asked Lhosia, reaching out to touch it. She snatched her hand back as the rune singed her skin.

'Property of the Order of Azyr,' snapped Maleneth, giving her a warning glance.

Gotrek laughed, his mood lifting a little. 'Just you try and take it, aelf. He moved his beard aside, trying to look at the rune. He grimaced as he revealed its design – the face of a duardin ancestor god. 'Look at him, sitting in my bloody chest. Taunting me every time I see his stupid face.'

'*That's* Grimnir?' asked Lhosia.

'Aye. His likeness, at least.'

'You wear a symbol of a god you despise?'

'Not by choice, lass. It didn't bloody look like this when I planted it in my chest. Besides, it has its uses. What do they call this stuff, again?' he asked, looking at Maleneth.

'Ur-gold.' She rolled her eyes. 'The Fyreslayers say it's pieces of Grimnir, scattered across the realms.' She stared at the rune. 'Ridiculous, obviously, like all duardin legends, but ur-gold certainly has power. The Fyreslayers hammer it into their bodies to fuel their battle rage, but none of them are equal to the one in Gotrek.' She let her gaze caress the metal. 'This is the *Master* Rune, forged by Krag Blackhammer himself. And when Gotrek destroys himself, I will take it to Sigmaron.'

Maleneth's pulse raced as she considered what that would mean for her. *She* would be the one who had secured a weapon powerful enough to win the war for the realms. Her slate would be wiped clean. No one would care what she had done in the past. None of her enemies in Azyrheim would be able to lay a finger on her. Sigmar would probably make her a saint.

'So,' said Lhosia, frowning at Gotrek, 'when you talk of your doom, you mean you wish to destroy yourself?' She shook her head. 'You say your culture reveres ancestral wisdom, but you're prepared to throw away everything you know? What greater crime could there be than suicide? It's a betrayal of your ancestors *and* your descendants. You should preserve your wisdom. You should fight to pass on what you know.'

'I'm a Slayer, lass,' said Gotrek. 'I have to atone for...' His words trailed off and he shrugged. 'I have things to atone for, though no one here can remember them.' He drained the last dregs of his wine and grimaced. 'Gods, this is drakk's piss.'

They sat in silence again, listening to the rain and the flames. Then Lhosia looked at Trachos. 'And are you the Slayer's servant?'

Maleneth laughed.

'I serve the God-King,' replied Trachos. His brutal features were exaggerated by the firelight, making his face almost as savage as Gotrek's. His eyes looked like stars, smouldering under his furious brow. 'And the Order of Azyr.' He glanced at Maleneth. 'We both do.'

Lhosia looked from Trachos to Maleneth. The enmity between them was so obvious she asked her next question with a doubtful tone. 'You're working together?'

It was Gotrek's turn to laugh. 'The aelf wants the rune, and she doesn't care if that requires my death. Pretty boy here feels the same, but he's tying himself in knots trying to work out what the hammer-hurler would think is the right thing to do. He's desperate for the rune, but he doesn't want to behave badly. That's right, isn't it, smiler? You don't want to be a savage like me.'

Trachos' eyes flickered with emotion and his head kicked to one side, but he said nothing.

'You've been here before,' said Lhosia, leaning over to study Trachos' armour. 'You've been to the Amethyst Princedoms before.'

'What?' demanded Maleneth.

Lhosia pointed to the jumble of equipment that covered Trachos' belt. Tucked in amongst the measuring devices and weapons was a metal-framed hourglass filled with dust that shimmered as it moved. The piece was topped with an ornate, leering skull. —

'Or did you buy that from someone else who has been to the Amethyst Princedoms?'

Trachos grunted and covered the hourglass up. He looked angrier than ever, and his head twitched again.

Gotrek snorted in amusement. 'Something to hide?'

Trachos grabbed one of the wineskins and drank. He ignored Gotrek and Maleneth's intrigued expressions and turned to Lhosia. 'I fought with a retinue of Stormcast Eternals along the southern reaches of the Amethyst Princedoms. They were Hammers of Sigmar. My own retinues had been...' He hesitated, then tapped his turquoise armour. 'I belong to a Stormhost known as the Celestial Vindicators, but I was the last of my retinue. I was headed back to Azyr when I was attached to the Hammers of Sigmar. We were strangers to each other, but we fought well. We took back the Amalthea Keep then scoured the whole coast. No servant of Chaos now draws breath for nearly three hundred miles of those walls.'

Lhosia nodded. 'The Amalthea Keep. I know the name. The Radican Princes. In the ancient times they were our allies. There are still sacred texts written by Radican Princes held in the libraries of the Lingering Keep.' She shook her head. 'You have claimed back the keep? It is centuries, countless centuries since those lands were free of Chaos.'

Something flickered in Trachos' eyes, then vanished as quickly as it had come. 'We claimed the keep and the land around it. I was attached to the Hammers of Sigmar to perform a specific duty.' He tapped the devices clasped to his belt. 'My job was to send a signal to Azyr so that the rest of their Stormhost could find a route through the aether-void. While my comrades rounded up the locals and armed them, I helped the retinue responsible for repairing the keep.' He paused and took another deep swig of wine. 'Weeks passed. No word from Azyr.' He shook his head, frowning. 'Well, nothing I could recognise. Only howls and screams. Someone was trying to warn me. But it was like cries heard through a wall. "Necroquake" was the only word I could decipher, but I had no idea what that meant.

'We continued our work, scouring the plains for remnants of the Chaos dogs.' His gauntlet screeched as he crushed the wineskin tighter, as though imagining squeezing the life from someone. 'We had them on the run. We attacked. With ferocity. Such brutality. I showed the Hammers of Sigmar how Celestial Vindicators fight. Even the Bloodbound were not prepared. They had grown lax. They never expected anyone to try to reclaim the princedoms after so long. They thought these lands were theirs.'

His voice grew louder, as though he were addressing a crowd rather than three people sitting right next to him. 'But reclaim them we did! With barely a single loss. We tore down their idols and citadels. We ripped open their prisons. We freed wretched souls who hadn't seen light for decades. It was glorious. The hammer fell. The Bloodbound died.'

Maleneth took the wineskin gently from his hand, interrupting his memories. She took a sip and spoke quietly. 'And yet, when you approached me and the Slayer in Aqshy, you were alone. There were no Hammers of Sigmar with you when you found us on the Slain Peak.'

Trachos' head was shaking as he stared at her, rage bleeding from his eyes.

She slipped a hand discreetly to one of her knives, wondering if she had pushed him too far.

Trachos' anger subsided and he slumped back. 'We crushed Chaos. We did as we were forged to do. Those beasts could not break through the armour of our faith, but...' He hesitated. 'But Chaos is not the only threat in Shyish. The voices from Azyrheim grew fainter and more desperate, so we focused all our attention on fortifying the keep and arming the slaves we had freed. We knew it would not be long before word of our success reached the warlords in control of the rest of the princedom. We had taken the keep through speed and surprise, not through superior numbers. Without reinforcements we would be hard pressed. The slaves were terrified of us at first, but as the weeks wore on they saw a chance. A chance for revenge, if nothing else. Some still knew legends of the time before Chaos. Times when man lived free of tyranny. Under our care they grew stronger. Braver. We started moving out into the surrounding villages, fortifying them, spreading across the princedom. When the attacks came we were ready. And so were the mortals.

'But then we began to hear of other things.' His expression darkened. 'Cannibalism amongst the wretches we had armed and fed. We had shared Sigmar's word with them. We had told them that the Age of Chaos was over and that a new era had begun, but as soon as we left them to their own devices they fell back into savagery.' His voice trembled with rage. 'If people knew what we sacrificed to fight for these realms. If they knew what it meant. We are immortal but we–' He shook his head. 'After so long under the lash of Chaos, they had fallen back into the debased worship of the Blood God. Or, at least, that's what I thought. I rode out from the keep to see for myself what had happened.'

His voice fell quiet. 'It was not Chaos. They were not worshipping Khorne. I saw it as soon as I reached the nearest village. Worship of any kind was now beyond them. They were no longer human. They had crawled into the mass graves left by their oppressors and dug up the remains.' He grimaced. 'They were eating corpses, feeding on them like animals. After all we'd done for them, I could not understand it.' He pounded his fist against the ground, scattering embers. 'We freed them and they turned into animals. Couldn't they see that they were risking everything? They were leaving us open to attack. We saved them and they betrayed us! They did not even–' Trachos cut himself off again and shook his head.

'What did you do?' asked Maleneth, sensing that he was reluctant to finish the story.

Clearly the wine had had the same tongue-loosening effect on Trachos as it had on Gotrek. He looked torn, but he could not stop talking. Maleneth had seen humans like this before. Too ashamed to speak of their deeds but too tormented to stay silent.

'I was furious,' he muttered. 'Some of the Hammers of Sigmar were there and they tried to calm me, but I would not listen. I tore through the village. Those people were going to ruin everything, and I was determined not to...

I butchered them. All of them. I showed them how the God-King deals with those who betray their saviours.'

Maleneth shrugged. 'Seems reasonable. You saved them and they turned into ghouls. It's ill-mannered, if nothing else. I don't blame you for taking a hammer to them.'

Gotrek frowned. 'You said the other hammer-hurlers tried to hold you back. Why? You were doing the work of Sigmar. They were ghouls. Like the things we've fought here, in Morbium. Why shouldn't you slaughter them?'

Trachos would not meet their eyes, and his voice became flat. 'I was furious. It was a kind of madness. I could hear my comrades calling me, but their voices were like the screams of the aether-void. They made no sense. Like a pack of animals howling at me. My hammers rose and fell, smashed and crushed, filling my eyes with blood. Only exhaustion finally forced me to pause. And then I saw the bodies I had left.'

Maleneth nodded, finally guessing the truth. Finally understanding why Trachos' mind was as broken as his body. 'They weren't *all* ghouls, were they?'

Trachos did not answer.

'You were killing humans,' she continued. 'That's why the other Storm-cast Eternals were trying to stop you.'

Trachos spoke quietly. 'I walked back the way I had come, but I could not make sense of it all – of the corpses. Some were *definitely* the things I saw gnawing at the graves. But others were...' He shook his head.

Gotrek grimaced, drinking more wine.

Lhosia looked at Trachos with new eyes, appalled.

'What did the Hammers of Sigmar do?' asked Maleneth.

Trachos' voice was a dull monotone. 'Tried to control me. Tried to... I fought them off.'

Maleneth laughed incredulously. 'You *fought* them? Your own kind?'

'No! Not that. I fought them off. I don't mean I attacked them. Not that, at least. Even now, changed as I am, I would not harm one of Sigmar's own. But I resisted them. I abandoned them. I left them to their fate. I could not rid myself of the faces I saw. I still can't.'

Gotrek was looking thoughtfully at him and spoke with softer tones than usual. 'The gods make fools of us. All of us. You were there because they ordered you to be there.'

'The God-King did not order me to kill unarmed families.'

Gotrek glowered at the rain. 'When the gods talk of Order or Chaos, they just mean glory – *their* glory. They have no interest in what happens to the people who win them that glory.'

'Changed as you are?' said Maleneth.

Trachos shook his head, confused.

'That's what you said,' she continued. 'You said, "Changed as I am, I would not harm one of Sigmar's own."'

Trachos stared at Maleneth, and for the first time since they had met, she felt something other than amusement when she looked at him. She did not feel that she was looking into the eyes of a man. It was not a human gaze.

What were they, these Stormcast Eternals? She had never really considered it before, but now she felt a chill as she realised just how peculiar he was. In some ways, he seemed less human than the ghouls.

'I've lost myself,' he muttered, finally freeing her from his inhuman stare and looking back at the fire. 'I died for the first time at the battle of Visurgis. It was glorious. Agony, yes, but glorious. When I felt my soul, still intact, blazing in Sigmar's halls, hammered on the Anvil of Apotheosis, I knew I had been reborn. Reforged so that I could fight again. Then I died again, fighting greenskins at the Orrotha Pass. The pain was greater that time, but still, the glory was unimaginable. A chance to live again, to fight for the God-King, to fight against all that is wrong in the Mortal Realms.'

He looked up at the stars. 'The third time I died, the pain seemed like it would never end. Perhaps something was wrong? Perhaps I was too broken to be saved? I could not be sure. But the torture seemed endless. And that was not the worst of it. Once it was over, and I rejoined the host, I could not quite remember what it meant. Why were we fighting? Everything that had previously seemed so important felt like stage directions in a play, or the words of a song. Nothing seemed real.'

He turned to Gotrek, shaking his head. 'I could not remember my family. Not even the name of my father. Or the place of my birth.'

'And then you were sent to Shyish,' said Maleneth, guessing what came next.

He nodded, without meeting her eye. 'All I could remember was the songs. The hymns we learned in Azyr. Those glorious tunes. I sang them as I fought, praying that the words would hold me in check – that they would guide me when my mind could not. But the truth is that I do not know what I am. I have killed so many in Sigmar's name, thinking I was doing his work. But was I? Always?' He frowned and fell quiet again.

No one spoke for a while. Even Gotrek looked troubled by Trachos' speech.

Something occurred to Maleneth. 'What will happen to you when you return to Azyr? Word of your flight from Shyish might have reached them. Unless the Hammers of Sigmar all died. What will your commanders say when you return empty-handed and without your men?'

'I will not return empty-handed. I will submit to whatever judgement is deemed appropriate, but I will not return with only failure to report.' He gazed at the rune in Gotrek's chest. 'I will return with a prize.'

Gotrek's laughter boomed around the hall. 'Of course! You want me dead too, just like Ditch Maid. So you can cut this thing out of me and–'

'No.' Trachos tightened his fists. 'I am *not* a murderer. Whatever I did in the past. I will keep you alive. I will let no harm come to you until I can convince you to come with me to the Celestial City.'

Gotrek staggered to his feet, unsteady with drink, and grabbed his axe. 'Murder?' The calm, sympathetic tone had vanished from his voice, replaced by a savage roar. His face was contorted by rage and amusement. 'There need be no murder, manling. Face me in honest combat. *Earn* the bloody rune!'

Trachos remained seated. 'I will not. You are not a creature of Chaos or an agent of the Ruinous Powers. Nor are you a revenant summoned by the Great Necromancer.' He shook his head. 'In truth, none of us know what you are. I doubt you know yourself. I will not fight you.' He opened his hands and stared at the scarred, riveted palms of his gauntlets.

Gotrek stood for a moment longer, then dropped heavily back down beside the fire, grabbing another wineskin. His belligerence had lacked its usual fervour, almost as though he were going through the motions because it was expected of him. 'Pity,' he muttered.

Maleneth considered what she had just learned. A Stormcast Eternal whose faith had been shaken was far less of a threat than the hard-line zealot she had thought she was travelling with. There was no hope of convincing Gotrek to stroll up to Azyr and hand himself over to the Order to offer himself in service to the God-King. And if Trachos was too battle-weary to kill the Slayer and take the rune, that meant she was the only one with a chance of getting it back to Azyrheim. She leant back, sipping more wine, and grabbed some of the food Lhosia had fished out of the temple storerooms, feeling happier than she had for a while.

'And what about you?' asked Lhosia, turning to face her. 'Are you here to protect the Slayer too?'

Maleneth stifled a grin and Gotrek snorted.

'She'll protect me unless my death offers a better chance to get the rune,' he said.

Maleneth splayed her hand against her chest in mock offence.

'And what about the soul you carry?' asked Lhosia.

Maleneth laughed. 'You don't want to know what's in my soul, priestess.'

'No,' replied Lhosia. 'I don't mean *your* soul. I mean the one you carry around your neck.'

Trachos and Gotrek both glanced up, surprised.

Maleneth clasped her hand around the amulet.

She knows what you did! Her mistress laughed wildly, delighted by the turn of events. *How will you explain this one?*

'What do you mean?' Maleneth said, pitching her voice a little too loud. 'It's just a memento of a kill.'

Lhosia frowned, looking suspicious. 'Surely you know it's more than that? If not, I can help explain. I'm the High Priestess of the Cerement. Even the most shrouded spirit is visible to me. I see every soul in Morbium.'

Maleneth cursed inwardly. She needed to silence the idiot woman before she ruined everything.

'It's stopped,' said Trachos.

'What?' snapped Maleneth.

'The rain.'

'Finally!' cried Gotrek, leaping to his feet.

They watched as the last few shards rattled across the platform and ceased, then looked at Lhosia, but she was still staring at Maleneth's amulet.

Gotrek stomped out onto the platform, holding his palm up to the stars. 'Looks like marching weather!'

CHAPTER ELEVEN

SOMETHING MORE THAN BLOOD

While Trachos headed back into the temple to fetch supplies for the journey, Gotrek and the other two wandered around the platform, examining the damage, running their fingers over the scars that now covered every inch of the bone-work. There were still storm clouds overhead, glinting oddly as they rolled and swelled, but they were heading south, away from the quay.

When Trachos returned, he nodded to the far end of the platform, where wide, sweeping steps led up to the beginning of another huge structure. 'That way?'

'Yes,' said Lhosia. 'And we had better move fast. The whole princedom might be infested with those flesh-eaters. They could come back at any time.'

They climbed the steps and, despite Lhosia's request for urgency, had to pause at the top to admire the strangeness of the view. They stood at the entrance to a great road built of the same combination of bone and iron as the temple below. It swept out over the sea, curving as it vanished into the gloom. Far away, sections of it were illuminated by what looked like pale, low-hanging moons.

'The prominents,' explained Lhosia, nodding to the lights. 'Home to the living and the Unburied.' She looked pained. 'There should be far more of them. The whole sky should be lit up.' She turned and looked south, where there were almost no lights at all. One half of the sky was only punctuated by the faint spectral stars.

'They've been destroyed?' asked Maleneth.

'Perhaps. But even if they are still intact, they must have been defiled. They were built to preserve the souls of the Unburied. And the light of the Unburied should be visible from here. I had hoped that Prince Volant would have done as he planned and evacuated the occupants – keeping the Unburied and their guardians in the capital where we can keep them safe. But something must have gone wrong. My own temple had not been emptied. My family were still there when...' Lhosia shook her head.

Gotrek studied her for a moment, then peered down the road. 'Is *that* a fortress? Is that one of your "prominents"?'

Lhosia and the others came to stand next to him. There was a light flickering lower than the others, on the surface of the road. It was hard to gauge distances in such a strange landscape, but Maleneth guessed it was only four or five miles away. Rather than the blue lights of the others, this was a golden glow, the colour of flames.

'That would be the gatehouse,' said Lhosia. 'Each branch of the wynd is guarded at various points along its length by gatehouses.'

Gotrek waved his axe at the surface of the road. There were bloody footprints leading away into the distance. 'It looks like the gatehouse received the same visitors as this temple.'

Lhosia nodded. 'We should move. The sooner we reach the prince, the better.'

As the group rushed down the road, Maleneth heard a familiar voice in her head. *Did you hear what that girl said?*

She slowed down until the others were a few paces ahead of her. 'What?' she whispered, glancing down at the amulet hung from her neck.

Before she joined herself to the little dead thing – didn't you hear her? When she was talking about Separating Chambers. She said something interesting. Surprising, I know, from someone so ugly and boring, but she did.

Maleneth frowned. 'She said the Unburied could lead us to the prince and that the prince can help Gotrek find Nagash.'

Not that, simpleton. What did she say when she shooed you away?

'She said she had to concentrate. She said that if she lost her thread, there was a risk she might not return intact.' Maleneth stumbled to a halt, realising that her old mistress had a point. 'What did she mean by that?'

You always were such a poor student. So dim.

Maleneth smiled as she started walking again. 'And how does that reflect on you, mistress? Even someone this dim-witted was able to out-think you.'

You never out-thought me, you–

'I killed you.' Maleneth smiled. 'Surely that is the very definition of out-witting you?'

And what now, you ridiculous creature? What will become of you when you finally return home to Azyr?

'I will return with the rune. Nothing else will matter.'

That Slayer won't die. Can't you see that? He's not like the others. Even if you could get some poison through his thick hide he wouldn't notice. Something has changed him. Look at him! He talks about god-killing, but he's half god himself.

Maleneth nodded. 'The rune changed him. He's not like any other duardin I've met. He has so much power.'

It's not just the rune. Think what he was like when you first met him in the Fyreslayers' cells. That was before he took their Master Rune, but he was already unstoppable. Something more than blood burns in his veins.

'What do you want to tell me about the Separating Chamber?' snapped Maleneth, irritated by her mistress' games.

The amulet fell silent, and Maleneth whispered a curse.

She picked up her pace and caught up with the others as the road curved and gave them their first clear view of the gatehouse. It looked like a larger version of the cocoon Lhosia was carrying, like a pale, curved tear, built around a pair of large, leaf-shaped gates. It must have once been an impressive structure, but there were now flames washing across it, filling the darkness with embers and smoke. The walls had cracked in several places, dropping huge slabs of bone onto the road.

'No sign of mordants,' said Lhosia, hurrying on.

'Not that way,' laughed Gotrek, nodding back the way they had come. There were dark shapes pouring from the temple they had just left. Even from here, it was clear that there were hundreds of them.

Lhosia spat a curse and drew her scythe.

'We'll never outrun them,' said Maleneth. 'Look how fast they're closing the gap.'

'Move!' yelled Gotrek, waving them on to the gatehouse.

As they neared the building, they began to see bodies scattered across the road. At first it was only ghouls – identical to the wiry, semi-naked wretches they had fought on their way into the princedom. But then, a while later, they saw the corpse of a man who looked far less savage. It was a tall, powerfully built knight, dressed in black armour and a white, feathered cloak. His throat had been ripped out and he was clearly dead, but there were dozens of butchered ghouls lying all around him. Even in death, he was still gripping a bloody, two-handed scythe.

Lhosia shook her head. 'Gravesward. There's not much hope if even they can't hold these things back.'

'Hope's overrated,' said Gotrek. 'Sheer bloody-mindedness, that's the thing.'

As they reached the gatehouse they had to shield their eyes from the glare. The fire was ferocious.

'Not much good as a gate anymore,' laughed Gotrek. The front curve of the building had completely collapsed, consumed by the flames. It was possible to see the road on the far side, littered with more corpses. Again, they were mostly ghouls, but Maleneth spotted a few more of the black-armoured knights.

Gotrek crouched down on the road, looking at the metalwork at the base of the building. 'Is that an axle?' He glanced back at Lhosia. 'How do these gatehouses work? Do they just bar the way? Are they *just* gates? Or something more complicated?'

Lhosia shook her head and then nodded, her eyes narrowed. 'Yes, I see what you mean – they *are* more than just gates. It's possible to raise a section of the road, like a drawbridge. I'd have no idea how to operate it though.'

'Here's your chance, manling!' Gotrek grinned, pointing Trachos to the mechanism beneath the walls. 'You're an engineer, aren't you?' He stepped back and gazed up at the burning building. 'Looks like the whole structure works as a counterweight. We saw a bridge that worked this way when we were back in Nuln. Do you remember? The one that crossed the Reik.'

Trachos shook his head. 'Nuln?'

Gotrek rolled his eyes. 'No matter. The point is that we should be able to lift a section of the road up.' He examined the mass of arcane equipment at Trachos' belt. 'Does a fancy title like Lord Ordinator mean you know how to use a spanner?'

Trachos stared at Gotrek, clearly surprised. He shook his head. 'I have never seen this kind of design before.'

Gotrek jabbed him in the chest with a blocky finger. 'What are you scared of? Trying and failing? If you do nothing we die anyway.'

Trachos hesitated, then turned to the building, examining the layout. 'Perhaps.' He paced back and forth for a moment, then edged around the flames and dropped out of sight, climbing down into the mechanisms underneath the gatehouse. A few seconds later, clanging sounds rose up from the shadows.

Maleneth looked back down the road at the fast-approaching crowd of ghouls. 'I guess ten minutes. Maybe less.'

'We can do better than that,' said Gotrek, hefting his axe in both hands. 'Help the manling. He's more capable than he thinks. Call me when he's done.' He started pounding back down the road towards the ghouls. 'But don't be too quick. This looks like fun.' He howled a war cry, dropped his head and charged.

'They'll tear him apart,' muttered Lhosia.

Maleneth watched Gotrek go with exasperation. 'You really would think so, wouldn't you?'

She turned back to the fire and tried to spot Trachos. At first she could see no sign of the Stormcast, but then the sound of tuneless singing led her to him. He was wailing strident verses to himself as he worked. She held up her arm to shield her face as she approached the walls, feeling her hair shrivel in the heat.

Trachos was crouched on a framework of curved metal, grappling with a series of ash-covered cogs. He was holding what looked like a pair of riveted, golden callipers, and he was trying to fix them to the struts beneath the road.

There was a furious bellowing from behind as Gotrek reached the first ranks of ghouls. They were close enough that Maleneth could see their faces as the Slayer axed them down, scattering bones and blood.

She wondered whether to go and help Gotrek or stay with Trachos. 'Can you work it?' she called down to him.

Trachos' callipers were now clamped around one of the struts, and the tool was alive with aether-light. Trachos leant his weight against it, singing too loudly to hear Maleneth's question.

'Will it work?' she yelled.

He twisted around, shaking his head. 'No. The gates are warded by sorcery. I can see a lock, but we don't have the key.'

'The gatekeeper would have it!' cried Lhosia, peering through the ruined gate at the bodies on the other side. 'If you could get me into the building, I would be able to spot his corpse from the others. He might still be wearing the key.'

Maleneth stared at the wall of flames. 'We'd cook. We'll have to wait for it to die down.'

'No time,' said Trachos as he hauled himself back up onto the road, fastening the callipers back to his armour. He took his helmet from his belt and fixed it back in place, then took out both his hammers and marched towards the gates. He showed no sign of feeling the heat as he reached the inferno. He paused for a moment in front of the tall, bone-wrought doors. He leant forwards to peer at the hinges and nodded. As Gotrek careered through the crowds of ghouls, Trachos began to attack the gate, smashing the hinges repeatedly with his hammers, surrounding himself in clouds of sparks and smoke. The doors, already weakened by the flames, began to judder, and Trachos hit them with even more fury, swinging the hammers with such force that they began to spark and crackle. Finally, with a monstrous groan, the gates started to lean backwards.

Trachos retreated, lowering his hammers as they slammed down onto the road.

A wall of flames and smoke rolled towards Maleneth, forcing her back. Then the fire ebbed away to reveal the doors lying flat on the ground, still sparking and smoking but with nowhere near the same ferocity.

Trachos glanced at her. 'How fast can you run, Witchblade?'

She nodded and darted past him, sprinting over the toppled doors and dodging the flames until she reached the road on the far side.

Through the fire she saw Trachos march over to Lhosia. They exchanged words – Lhosia seemed hesitant. Then she nodded, and Trachos picked her up, throwing her over his shoulder like she was a bundle of clothes.

The rest of the gatehouse was still engulfed in flames, but as Trachos jogged through the fallen gates with Lhosia in his arms, he was able to protect her from the few still licking around the opening.

Even from this side of the building, Maleneth could see the absurd odds Gotrek faced. The Slayer looked like he was trying to hold back a tidal wave.

'The rune,' she muttered. She turned to Trachos. 'If they kill him...'

Trachos nodded. 'The key,' he said, looking at Lhosia. 'Which one of these bodies is the gatekeeper?'

Lhosia rushed back and forth. Apart from the dead knights, all the bodies were ghouls. She shook her head. 'None of them. He's not here!'

Maleneth moved further on down the road. 'Then he must have fled.'

'No.' Lhosia stared at the ruined building. 'The Gravesward would never have let him abandon his post. It would be treason.' She rushed from body to body, turning them over and shaking her head.

Gotrek cried out in frustration, and they all turned towards him.

The ghouls were driving him back. They could not manage to land a blow on him, so they were using sheer weight of numbers to overwhelm him, hurling themselves on the bodies of the fallen and creating a landslide of fists and claws.

'We need that key,' said Trachos, surveying the gruesome mess that surrounded them. 'Are you sure none of these are him?'

'Sure,' muttered Lhosia, 'but that makes no sense.'

There was another roar of defiance as the crowds pushed Gotrek back towards them.

So you die, said the voice from the blood vial, whispering smugly in Maleneth's head. *Slaughtered like cattle, miles from anywhere, in an abandoned gatehouse. A worthy end for someone like you.*

Maleneth hissed a curse. She cast her gaze over the ruined walls and the empty buildings on either side of the fallen gates. There were several doors, some smashed, some intact, all of them splattered with blood. 'I wonder,' she muttered.

'What?' said Trachos.

'Can you give me a few more minutes?' She nodded towards Gotrek. 'Can you help the hog hold them back for a little longer?'

He looked at her in silence for a moment, clearly suspicious. Then he shrugged and stumbled back through the flames, launching into another hymn. Maleneth guessed his logic – better to be near the rune than stuck with the murderous aelf. It didn't matter. As long as he could buy her a few more minutes.

As the road lit up with flashes of Azyrite sorcery, Maleneth rushed to the nearest ghoul corpse and dropped to her knees, whipping out her knives.

'It's already dead,' said Lhosia, staring at her in confusion.

Maleneth ignored her, slamming the blades down into the corpse's chest. There was a dull cracking sound as she wrenched them apart, ripping open the ribcage and revealing the glistening mess beneath.

Lhosia cursed in disgust and backed away.

You can't do this, said the voice of her dead mistress. *What are you thinking? You really are a fool. Do you think that just because you watched me at work, you can perform a blood sacrament?*

Maleneth thrust her hand into the wound and grabbed the still-warm heart, then stood up, ripping it from its cage in a spray of crimson. *I did more than watch you, mistress*, she thought. *You thought me a blunt-minded tool, but I was always preparing, always planning for the day I would take your place.*

With the blood still pumping, she began cutting the heart, gouging intricate sigils into the muscle, all of them centred on the symbol of her beloved, blood-thirsty lord, Khaine. When she had covered every inch of the heart, she cried out an invocation and the organ began to smoulder, spilling smoke between her fingers.

For a moment, nothing else happened. Maleneth cursed. Perhaps she *was* a fool, trying to pray to Khaine in such a rushed, slipshod way.

You absurd creature. If you'd really been learning from me you would know that–

Maleneth cried out and leant back, arching her back as Khaine's fervour jolted through her. She laughed in ecstasy. The blood rite had worked. The might of the Murder God shook her with such violence that she cried out to Lhosia. 'Help me! Hold the heart!'

Visions flooded her mind and, for a moment, they were utterly confusing. She was riding with proud warriors, clutching spears and pennants, charging into battle on glorious steeds. Their colours were unfamiliar, and the language was an ancient tongue that bore no relation to anything she had heard anywhere else in Shyish.

The riders were nothing like the black-armoured knights Lhosia had referred to as the Gravesward, but the landscape *was* familiar. The riders were charging down the same road she had just travelled – a highway of bone hung across the Eventide. The horsemen cried out as they saw the gatehouse up ahead. The building was still intact and there was no sign of a fire. Figures were racing back to the gates, but they were too late, caught unawares by the attack as the riders hurled spears and drew longswords, killing them before they could reach the mechanisms that raised the road.

The horsemen tore on into the gatehouse itself and began battling the defenders waiting inside – a ragtag mob of savage, sallow-faced barbarians clutching clubs and knives. Maleneth felt a wash of fury at the sight of these craven savages. Who were they to steal land from the Hounds of Dinann?

The savages fought desperately, but they were massively outnumbered and it was the work of moments to knock them from the walls and slice them apart.

There was another man in the gatehouse, though, unarmed but clearly a kinsman of the rest of the barbarians. He dashed away as the fighting began, bolting to a door at the bottom of a tower and slamming it shut behind him. Maleneth rushed towards him, outraged, but before she could reach the door, blood filled her vision and she fell heavily to the ground.

'What happened?' cried Lhosia, staring at Maleneth. The priestess was helping her grip the bleeding heart, her face a disgusted grimace as the gore flowed down her arms. 'What are you doing?'

Maleneth squeezed her eyes shut, confused, the words 'Hounds of Dinann' still echoing round her head. What did that mean? The gatehouse was in ruins again, flames rippling across the walls. There was no sign of the proud riders on their horses or the savages they had been fighting. She had no idea who any of the warriors might have been, but Khaine's vision had still told her what she needed to know. The door she saw slamming in the vision was still there, unchanged, with the same bloodstains across its handle and the same corpses piled in front of it.

'He's in there!' she gasped, dropping the heart and hurrying over to the door. The blood rite had left her exhausted and dazed, but also exhilarated. She had joined her soul to Khaine's! She could still feel his power hammering in her pulse. It was dizzying and wonderful. She grinned, waving for Lhosia to follow. 'Your gatekeeper is a coward. He's hiding.'

There was an explosion of shouts and splintering bone as Gotrek and Trachos staggered back through the broken gateway, hacking and lunging wildly at an enormous mound of grey bodies. The ghouls were as frenzied as Gotrek, oblivious to even the most horrific wounds as they tried to claw over the dead.

'Here!' cried Maleneth. 'Open this door!'

Gotrek barely broke his stride. He hacked the head from a ghoul, side-stepped a raking claw, slammed his face into the door, ripping it from its hinges, then lunged back into the scrum, blood sizzling on his chest rune.

The second the door fell, a figure tried to run at Maleneth, but she moved with fast, easy grace, dodging around him and then grabbing him by the collar, jolting him to a halt.

It was the man she had seen in her vision. He howled as he struggled to escape, staring at the legions of ghouls attacking Gotrek and Trachos.

Maleneth could not entirely blame the man for his fear. The creatures did make a horrific sight. She did not feel inclined to be sympathetic, though.

'Keys – quick!' she hissed in his ear, pulling him close and pressing one of her blades to his throat.

He scrambled at his belt and unclasped a bundle of keys, holding them up for her to see, his hand shaking violently.

Maleneth snatched them and let him go. As he sprinted past Lhosia and raced off down the road, Maleneth considered putting a knife in his back. She decided it would be a waste of a good weapon and turned away.

'Trachos!' she cried, hurling the keys.

He paused, mid-strike, and caught them.

Maleneth shook her head in disbelief as she rushed to join the fight. It looked like a mass burial falling on top of her.

Trachos sprinted away, leaving her alone with the Slayer. Gotrek was now using his head as a club, his face entirely crimson and covered in bits of skull and teeth. When he looked her way, there was no sign of recognition. He was like an animal in a feeding frenzy, tearing and clawing through the throng.

Maleneth had only been fighting for a few seconds when she realised that it was hopeless. There were too many. Cuts opened across her legs and face as the ghouls lashed out blindly, smothered by their own numbers.

'Pull back!' she gasped, though she knew the Slayer was too far gone to hear.

She was about to stagger free when the ground shook and she lurched backwards, struggling to keep her footing as the road heaved into motion.

'Trachos!' she cried. 'He did it!'

She backed away, knives raised, as the road began to rise, throwing ghouls dead and living towards her. She had to duck and weave as the bodies flew, crashing off the walls and bouncing down the slope. The brainless horrors could not seem to register what was happening, still trying to drag Gotrek down to the floor as it fell away from them. While dozens of ghouls hurtled towards Maleneth, many more fell back the way they had come, sliding from sight.

'Gotrek!' roared Trachos, reappearing on the road and battling his way towards the Slayer.

Gotrek was too busy smashing brains to hear.

'Gotrek!' repeated Trachos, slamming a hand down on the Slayer's shoulder.

Gotrek whirled round, snarling like a maddened dog and drawing back his axe to hack Trachos down. At the last moment he hesitated, finally noticing that the ground was rising beneath him.

'Manling!' he gasped, grinning through the blood.

More ghouls smashed into them both, and they staggered towards Maleneth, smashing the creatures away and reaching for handholds as they found themselves suddenly standing on a steep slope.

'Back here!' cried Maleneth, running down the slope to where the road was level again.

Lhosia was already there, staring up at the incredible scene in amazement.

As the gatehouse rocked back and gears whirred, the road lurched up into the air.

Gotrek and Trachos fell rather than ran the last few feet, and landed gasping and coughing beside Maleneth.

As she helped them up, ghouls began thudding down all around them, crashing onto the road with weird, wheezing groans.

Maleneth dealt with the first two, her knives slashing back and forth, then Gotrek and Trachos handled the others.

As the road juddered higher, it began to change. Iron and bone struts slid apart, splaying like the fingers of a hand, forming into a fan. After a few seconds, Maleneth laughed, realising what shape it was forming. The section of road that had risen up in the air, nearly fifty feet high, had created a piece of intricate sculpture – a pair of ancient, riveted wings, complete with the same spiralled markings that Maleneth had noticed in the temple.

'A moth?' she said, looking around for Lhosia.

Lhosia was gazing in wonder. For the first time since she had found her family's remains, it seemed as though her grief had been eclipsed by something. She nodded. 'A harbinger. Waiting here since the elder days. Ready to serve.'

Maleneth broke away to cut down some more of the ghouls that had fallen on their side of the wings. 'Very pretty. But I don't think we should spend too long admiring it.'

Gotrek nodded. He was panting heavily and drenched in ghoul blood. Usually, after such a brutal fight, he would seem pleased with himself, but he was staring at the rune in his chest with a furious expression on his face.

'Gotrek?' Maleneth said, trying to rouse him from his reverie.

It took a moment for his eye to focus on her, and when it did he was clearly thinking about something else. 'He's trying to...' He shook his head, looking increasingly annoyed.

'Who's trying to what?' she asked. The Slayer was moody at the best of times, but now he seemed confused.

'Bloody Grimnir,' muttered Gotrek, staring at the rune again and slapping one of his meaty hands over it, hiding the face of the Slayer god. 'When I was fighting, lost in the glory of it, the rune lent me its strength.'

She nodded. 'It's ur-gold. Fyreslayers don't hammer that stuff into themselves just for fun. You know that. That rune has been making you stronger ever since you took it from the Unbak Lodge.' She raised an eyebrow at the heaps of bodies. 'You've never minded before.'

'But Grimnir's still trying to get into my head!' Gotrek gripped the rune tighter, as though he wanted to tear it from his ribs. He was talking to himself as much as Maleneth. 'He's still trying to change me.'

Gotrek removed his hand from his chest and scowled furiously at the rune. 'He's trying to change me into *him*. Every time I use this bloody rune it gets worse.' Gotrek punched his own chest. 'Think again, Grimnir! I'm Gotrek! Son of Gurni! And I mean to stay that way.' He ran his fingers over the golden streaks threaded through his beard. 'None of these were here before I had the rune, were they?'

She shook her head.

'No more!' he growled. 'I've slain daemons and dragons without any help from you, Grimnir.' Gotrek stomped off down the road, still hurling abuse at the rune as he headed away from the gatehouse, trailing bits of hair and bloody flesh.

Lhosia followed him, cradling the tiny cocooned corpse of her ancestor and whispering to it.

Trachos limped after her, his head twitching and lightning flickering from the joints in his armour. He mumbled a hymn as he walked, celebrating their victory in a grating monotone.

Maleneth watched the strange trio go, shaking her head in disbelief. 'Am I the only one who's sane?' she asked the vial of blood at her neck.

CHAPTER TWELVE

THE MORN-PRINCE

Lord Aurun watched as a sleeping girl was lifted up into a cart. The driver took her carefully and placed her with the other sleeping children. She was around six or seven, younger than any of the others nestling in the sacks and blankets, and she looked tiny. As the cart rattled away from him, the girl looked like an infant, frail and defenceless. He tapped his scythe against the ground, feeling his pulse quicken. *I will not fail them*, he thought. *I have the strength to do this, and I* will not *fail*.

'No one would judge you if you left,' said a voice behind him.

'*Everyone* would judge me.' Aurun's voice was stern. 'Above all, the Unburied. And they would be right.'

He turned to face the man standing with him at the East Gate, a frail septuagenarian with sharp, brittle-looking features – a priest dressed in white robes. Corsos was hunched by age, and he was leaning on a femur as tall as he was. The enormous bone had been bleached and carved with sigils, and an iron padlock hung from one end. Corsos was the most senior priest in the Barren Points, and the intricately engraved lock was a symbol of his authority. Aurun had also seen him use it to club sense into some of the younger acolytes.

'We have lived through blessed times,' Aurun continued, gazing at the buildings behind Corsos. The prominent was almost empty. Most of the windows were dark. The only light came from the souls embedded in its heart. 'All these generations, hidden from everyone. Nothing required of us other than to watch and wait. Who in all the Mortal Realms has lived as we have? Who else has known this peace? And now, at the crucial moment, we have a chance to show our worth.'

Corsos nodded. 'The Morn-Prince will soon come. I have seen it. The Unburied have seen it. We need only hold the walls for another day or so. Prince Volant left the capital with a host unlike anything he has ever mustered before. It does not matter how all these mordants found their way into Morbium. None of them will leave.'

Aurun smiled. 'Bold words from a man armed with a bone. If you could have dragged yourself away from those holy texts, you would have made a good general.'

Corsos laughed and raised his arms, revealing his scrawny frame. 'I *do* have the physique of a hero.'

They both looked back at the train of disparate vehicles rolling away from the fortress, dwarfed by the vast, rigid breakers of the Eventide. 'Well,' said Aurun. 'Whether the prince arrives soon or not, the Barren Points will stand.'

They walked back through the gates towards the centre of the fortress. Soldiers in the black of the Gravesward were dashing from building to building, readying defences and fetching weapons before moving out to the city walls.

Aurun saluted them as he passed, filled with pride. These men had sworn their oaths as children. None of them knew what the words really meant. To serve in life and death. To preserve the Unburied, whatever the price. What does a child know of such things? But when he gave the orders for evacuation and allowed them the chance to leave with the civilians, not one of them had even considered going. The sky around them was almost entirely dark. The prominents had all died, dragged beneath the dead tides, their lights extinguished. But his men were like beacons, their lacquered armour flashing in the light of the Unburied. It was a glorious sight. Aurun had waited his whole life for this chance to prove himself, living in the shadow of the ancestors, with their tales of heroism and glory. And now he would have his chance to earn a place in their ranks, not as a subordinate but as an equal.

'Have you met the prince before?' asked Aurun.

Corsos shook his head. 'I have read all the histories of the Morn-Princes, though. I know they are more than men.'

Aurun nodded. 'Volant is larger than a normal man. And stronger. But I would not say he is more than us, Corsos. Merely different.'

'Do you like him?'

Aurun shook his head, surprised by the question. 'Like? "Like" would be a strange word to use in relation to Prince Volant. I respect him and I trust him, much as I think he trusts me.' He shrugged. 'He is hard to explain. But you should soon be able to judge him for yourself.'

Aurun spent another hour inspecting the defences and talking to his men. He had expected to find them anxious and afraid, but if anything, they seemed excited. He could understand it. They had spent their whole lives being told that they were born for one purpose, to protect their ancestors, and now they were going to have a chance to finally show that they were worthy of all that trust. The more time he spent talking to the men on the walls, the more proud he felt. Their excitement was infectious. They would easily hold the walls until Prince Volant arrived, and then he would explain to him why they need not leave. And then the people of the Barren Points would be free to return home.

As they climbed the walls and headed towards Aurun's chambers, excited voices rang out.

'The prince!' cried the men on the ramparts. 'All hail the Morn-Prince!'

All along the walls, the sound of horns rang out, bright and bold, seeming to drive back the shadows.

Aurun grabbed Corsos by the shoulder, and the two old friends grinned at each other.

* * *

Two worlds were visible to Prince Volant – the first was illusory, full of pain and doubt, and the second was true, full of life yet to be lived, where understanding would be attained. He alone in the princedom could see so clearly and so far, and his royal attire was designed to symbolise the duality of his vision. Like his subordinates in the Gravesward, he wore lacquered black armour and a white, feathered cloak, but his helmet was of a unique, ceremonial design. It was intricately worked so that one side resembled a snarling face, obsidian black and shockingly ferocious, and the other side was palest ivory, its expression serene. The Morn-Prince had a habit, perhaps a subconscious one, of turning his head as he talked, depending on which side of his mask best represented his mood. As he looked down from his saddle at Lord Aurun, only the black side of his mask was visible.

His steed was a skeleton drake, its gleaming bones clad in the same black as its rider. As the prince leant out from its back, the drake settled its enormous wings with a sound like rattling spears. Behind Volant were knights of the royal Gravesward, scythes gleaming and pennants trailing. Their steeds were smaller kin of the beast the prince was riding. It was an impressive sight. Aurun had never received such a visit before. In fact, he had never heard of *anyone* receiving such a visit.

Behind the pennants was a less cheerful reminder of the prince's power. Dozens of cylindrical cages were raised up on poles, swaying above the knights' heads, and each held a pitiful, emaciated wretch, stripped of their clothes and painted with runes. These were the Barred. They were men the prince had deemed unworthy –men who had failed to protect the Unburied. Some were already dead, dangling from their cages, but others would last for days, their cries growing weaker until they finally died from their wounds or lack of water.

'Did you receive my order?' said the prince. He spoke softly, but the words chimed through his helmet like a temple bell.

'Your highness, I did,' replied Aurun, determined not to be cowed before his men. 'But the messenger was wounded and confused. He did not make sense. And I'm afraid he did not survive more than a few days. Even if he had lived, I could not have complied with the order.'

The prince stared down at Aurun for a moment. They were outside the fortress, near where the wynd rose to meet its gaping North Gate. The Barren Points was one of the largest fortresses in the princedom, second only to the prince's own palace, the Lingering Keep. The light of the Unburied was pouring through the walls and flashing across the knights' scythes, making it hard for Aurun to see the prince. He had to hold up a hand to shield his eyes. The desperate cries of the Barred rang out from their cages, pitiful and deranged as they called for mercy. Aurun knew they were wasting their breath. Prince Volant was known for many things. Mercy was not one of them.

'We have ridden a long way to reach you, Lord Aurun,' prompted one of the prince's captains.

Aurun started, shocked to be addressed so casually by a subordinate.

He bit back an angry reply, conscious that the prince was still staring at him, and stepped back, waving the royal knights through the temple gates. He called for grooms and servants as the deathless steeds clanked past.

'Give me a few minutes,' said the prince as his attendants helped him from the drake. Aurun was not lacking in height, but the prince towered over him, eight or nine feet tall and bristling with lacquered ebon plate. His voice sounded like an echo in a crypt. 'Then join me in my chambers. We have only a few hours to prepare.'

Aurun hesitated, confused. He had been waiting for this moment for years, but now that it had come, it was not playing out how he had expected. He bowed, and was about to reply when he realised the prince had already strode off across the courtyard, preceded by a scurry of servants and courtiers.

Corsos looked as shocked as Aurun. 'A few hours to prepare for what?'

Aurun shook his head. The column of knights was still riding into the square, and as they passed, Aurun noticed that many of them were wounded, their armour gouged and battered, as though they had been grappling with animals. Their faces were speckled with blood, the crimson stark and shocking against their bone-white skin, and several looked little better than the prisoners suspended above their heads. More shocking than that were the numbers.

'Is that all of them?' whispered Corsos, his eyes wide as he leant on his bone staff, peering out through the gates.

They both stared in shock as they realised that there were no more knights coming down the wynd.

'That's barely two dozen men,' said Aurun, shaking his head. 'I thought this was meant to be the greatest host ever to ride out of the Lingering Keep. Did the Unburied give you no word of this? Did they make no mention of the prince's situation?'

Corsos looked uncomfortable. 'Nothing. But you know what I have already told you. They're troubled and strange. They do not speak with voices I am accustomed to. The last time I prayed to them, they–'

Lord Aurun silenced him with a wave of his hand, already aware of his friend's concerns. 'It matters not. We are prepared.' In fact, thought Aurun, if the prince's numbers were reduced, it would give him all the better chance to show what the men of the Barren Points were capable of. 'Do not let this interrupt the usual observances. Make sure everyone gathers for pallsong as usual. Fetch the shield poems from the reliquary and choose something appropriate. I will speak with the prince. When he learns how we have prepared for this day, he will want to come and sing with us.'

Corsos bowed. He turned to leave, but hesitated. 'My lord,' he said, nodding at the wounded knights. 'This must be to do with whatever made the other temples vanish. The prince must have come here because we are–'

'What happened at the other temples will not happen here.' Aurun raised his chin. 'We are different.' The haughty tones of Prince Volant had given him a new surge of determination. 'These are the Barren Points. We will not be sent into disarray by the negligence of others. We will not abandon our wards because others cannot tend to theirs.'

Corsos nodded, but seemed unable to drag his gaze from the darkness.

'Corsos!' called Aurun, heading back into the temple. 'Ready the shields. Gather the choir.'

'They're *gone?'* Aurun found a chair and sat, staring at the floor, his breath quickening.

The servants had put the prince in a room on the south face of the fortress with a balcony that overlooked the wynd. From up here, the huge iron bridge looked like a gossamer thread, glittering with hoarfrost, floating over a gelid storm. Volant's advisers were waiting outside in the hall, and the two knights were alone.

'Gone,' repeated the prince. 'Nearly half of our keeps. Thirty-two prominents.' His voice was rigid. He had removed his ceremonial helmet and his face was striking –pale and harsh, with brutal, angular features. 'There are many souls we will never recover.'

Aurun shook his head, dazed by the scale of the defeat. His chest felt tight. 'There must be a way. You are the Morn-Prince. Surely you are able to–'

'They are gone. You know why these temples were built, Lord Aurun. If our ancestors are not anchored to prominents, they go the way of every other soul.' The prince was squeezed awkwardly into the chair opposite Aurun, his voice dangerously soft. 'They go to the Nadir, Aurun. To the necromancer. They go to Nagash.'

Aurun gripped the arms of the chair. It was rare for anyone to use the name of the soul-thief so openly. 'But how? The Iron Shroud kept us hidden all this time. Even when the other princedoms fell. Why are we in danger now?'

'The Great Necromancer's power has grown. The Unburied tried to warn me, but Nagash's power has muffled their voices and muddied my vision. I knew there was a problem, but I thought I still had time. I thought I would still be able to complete my work. The necromancer has performed an act of great sorcery, Aurun. The Unburied showed me a black pyramid turned on its head, ripping souls from the sky. After all these centuries, the necromancer has played his final hand.' There was a fire snapping in the hearth beside them, and Volant stared into the flames. 'This is a new death magic. Whatever he has done is too powerful even for the Iron Shroud. Nothing is safe anymore, not even Morbium.'

Aurun thought of the little girl in the cart, out on the wynds, with only half a dozen Gravesward to watch over her.

Prince Volant leant closer. 'My messenger should have explained all of this. Why are you still here?' The two men had met before, as children, in the Lingering Keep, but Volant gave no sign of recognising Aurun. 'Why haven't you acted?' he demanded.

'Your messenger did talk of mordants destroying temples, but that is not a thing we need be concerned with here. We have heard the same vague warnings as you, my prince, and we have been preparing for months.' He tapped his armour. It was a new design, cunningly crafted by Aurun's artisans, beautifully engraved and studded with white gemstones. 'We have refined and strengthened our defences, your highness. Every aspect of the Barren Points has been tempered and readied. You have not seen us in action before, but now I will show you what this prominent is capable of. No mordants could hope to breach these walls, whatever Nagash has done.'

The prince studied him in silence, but Aurun noticed that he was gripping the arms of his chair so tightly that the wood was starting to creak.

'Where have they come from?' asked Aurun. 'I have heard of an occasional outbreak of flesh-eaters, but never whole armies entering the princedom.'

The prince stared at him for a moment longer, then replied in the same soft voice. 'The Iron Shroud has been damaged. Morbium has been revealed to the other princedoms – lands desecrated by the necromancer before you or I were born. The mordants can now see us. They can cross our borders as though we are just another territory. They have travelled down the wynds, murdering the gatekeepers. They're a plague, sweeping through the princedom, devouring everything. Our ancestors mean nothing to them. They are insane.'

Aurun felt the darkness pressing in, suffocating him. Then he recalled the legions of men he had trained and armed. 'We can stop them, your highness. This invasion will halt at the Barren Points. And the victory will be all the sweeter with you at our side. You have skill to match the necromancer. You are the Morn-Prince. The wisdom of the Unburied is in your blood. Their power is in your hands.'

'I am not a god. And I am no match for a god. What power I have is bound to the Lingering Keep. Outside my palace I can do little.' Volant's voice was still neutral, and Aurun could not gain any idea of what the prince was feeling. Was he furious or relieved?

'I intended to gather every soul in the princedom and return them to the capital.' Some of the rigidity had slipped from his voice, and for a moment, he just sounded like an exhausted man. 'I have lost hundreds of my own royal Gravesward.'

'Is he here, then? Is Nagash in Morbium?'

'No. The mordants are animals. They are revolting, inhuman things. But they bleed and they die. They are not born of necromancy. Perhaps they pay some kind of allegiance to Nagash, but they are too feral to be his true allies. They serve nothing but their own vile hunger. If the Great Necromancer's gaze had fallen on us, we would be facing spirit hosts rather than these mindless flesh-eaters. His sorcery has toppled our gates, but it was not specifically directed at us. He has summoned a great power and cast it over *all* the underworlds. All of Shyish. I do not think he has even noticed our existence yet. The mordants are savages. They have no idea what they've found.' Volant shrugged and poured himself a cup of wine. 'But they will destroy us just the same.'

'Destroy us? How could you say such a thing?'

The prince hesitated, then shook his head, the cold, flat tone returning to his voice. 'I can do little out here on the wynds, but it's a different matter in the capital. With the help of High Priestess Lhosia, I have been working on a new defence, a new Iron Shroud. We may not be able to safeguard the whole of Morbium anymore, but I have found a way to hide the Unburied in the capital, even against this new power the necromancer is wielding. I provided her with a powerful relic called the Cerement Stone. She is currently inspecting our defences, but I have been assembling the Unburied in the Lingering Keep so that when she returns, I can harness their souls through the stone and Lhosia's rites and preserve them.' He finished his wine and poured another cup. 'I have sent word to all the temples. Everyone who still can is heading to the capital. All the prominents have been destroyed or abandoned.' He paused. 'Apart from yours.'

'So that's why the lights have died?' Aurun looked out into the darkness. 'The Gravesward have taken the Unburied back to the capital?'

'You are not listening. Half the fortresses have been *destroyed*. They have sunk into the Eventide. The souls are gone. Caught in the nets of the necromancer. And without the souls of ancestors to keep them afloat, the prominents have fallen beneath the dead waters.' The prince shook his head. 'And I cannot guarantee that everyone who fled will make it to the Lingering Keep. The mordants are too numerous. They have taken many of the wynds. Even the Gravesward will have a hard fight crossing those bridges, especially when burdened with their ancestors' caskets.'

Aurun shook his head. Only the thought of the caged corpses outside stopped him laughing in disbelief. 'This *cannot* be, your highness. You would have me believe that in a matter of weeks Morbium has gone from impregnable to defeated. This princedom has defied the necromancer for centuries. How can it have so easily collapsed?'

Prince Volant sipped his wine, studying Aurun over the rim of his cup. 'The mordants are headed here next,' he said, ignoring the question. 'We heard word of them everywhere we went. Yours is the last light in the sky. They are coming for you.'

'Which is what you meant when you said we only had a few hours to prepare our defence. Why are we sitting here? I will muster the Gravesward and prepare the ballistae. The archers are already assembled. I will ready the defences.'

'You are not listening to me. There *is* no defence. Not out here on the wynds. You will return to the Lingering Keep. All of you, living and Unburied. You have a few hours to prepare for the journey and perform the necessary rites.' The prince looked around the room. 'The Barren Points is one of the largest citadels in the princedom. You have hundreds of Unburied here, contained within those twelve cocoons. Thousands, maybe. I will not risk losing them.'

Aurun sat up in his chair, trying to shrug off the grim atmosphere Volant had created. 'It's impossible,' he said, raising his voice. 'We cannot move the Unburied.'

Volant's eyes flickered and the arms of his chair creaked. 'In a matter of hours you will be besieged. Mordants will butcher you, and then they will destroy the Separating Chambers. Every soul in this fortress will be lost.'

Aurun was horrified by the prince's bleak manner. How could someone so unambitious, so lacking in faith, rule Morbium? He wondered if this despair and defeatism were the cause of the entire problem. 'You do not understand, your highness. It's not *possible* to move the Unburied. And even if it were, there would be no need.'

Prince Volant stood, his expression rigid as he loomed over Aurun, his massive frame all the more impressive in the tiny confines of the room. 'Every noble in Morbium has done as I ordered. Everyone has headed for the Lingering Keep. Only you have failed to obey. Only you have remained out here on the wynds, far from my reach, endangering the souls I have entrusted to you. Why is that, Aurun? And why have we had no word from you during all this time? Is there something you wish to hide?'

Aurun stood to face him. 'Are you accusing me of treason, your majesty?'

'Why are you still here?'

Aurun shook his head, biting back his rage. Then he waved to the door. 'Let me show you.'

The innermost coils of the fortress were like the chambers of a shell, spiralling and shimmering as they plunged deeper beneath the surface of the Eventide. The prominents had not been built by tools and hands but by the sorcery of an earlier age, when the gods still fought together against the Ruinous Powers and their supplicants could harness even the most violent aether currents. They were bone constructs, pale, translucent vessels woven from the air and suspended in a lifeless sea.

As the prince's attendants rushed through the streets, their torches quickly became superfluous. The ivory light radiating from the walls grew stronger as they approached the heart of the Barren Points. The chill grew the further they descended, and the damp air tasted of salt. Aurun led the way with Prince Volant at his side. Ahead of them went the elderly priest, Corsos, with a phalanx of Gravesward, their armour shimmering in the bone-light.

At each intersection they were met by a pair of priests clad in the white robes of their order, but Corsos waved them away with his bone staff, muttering prayers as the guards admitted them into the fortress' innermost districts. Finally, they reached a building even grander than the previous ones, constructed of the same intricately carved bone but blazing so brightly that Corsos squinted as he pushed the doors open.

They entered a vast circular hall with curving, spine-like columns that stretched up the walls and disappeared into a blazing inferno of amethyst light. The glare was so great that it was only just possible to make out the shapes of twelve cocoons hanging overhead. They were enmeshed in a labyrinth of pipes, chains and cables, all of which were shimmering.

Prince Volant strode into the middle of the hall, his iron-shod boots clanging across the bone floor as he looked up into the light.

'The Barren Points are unlike any other prominent,' said Lord Aurun, waving up at the machines. 'The Unburied are bound into the walls. The twelve caskets are part of the foundations. These engines were designed by the Kharadron at the dawn of the princedom.'

Volant shook his head. 'Do you think I don't know my own princedom,

Aurun? Did you think I knew nothing of how the Barren Points were designed? Remove the Unburied from these machines.'

'But, Prince–' began Aurun.

Volant spoke over him. 'There is no other way. Get everyone you can out of the city, then remove the Unburied from their cradles. There will be time to flee the fortress before it sinks.'

Aurun was too furious to respond, so Corsos spoke up on his behalf.

'Prince Volant, forgive me, but there *is* no way to remove the Unburied from the machines. The devices are alien and ancient. Their workings are a mystery even to the Unburied themselves. Only the duardin who built this hall could remove them. If we abandon the Barren Points, we will be abandoning the Unburied.'

Volant stared at him, then turned towards one of his own priests.

The man looked panicked. 'Dontidae Corsos is learned in matters concerning the Unburied. If he says it is so, then it must be so.'

Prince Volant was silent for several moments, gazing up at the machines and the cocoons embedded in them. 'How many are there?' he said eventually, his voice much quieter than before.

'Unburied?' said Lord Aurun. 'In all twelve cocoons? There must be over a thousand.'

Volant closed his eyes.

Aurun tried to hide his triumph. 'Your highness. We are prepared for this. We have sent everyone away who is not needed. This fortress is ready for war. We are ready for whatever the mordants can throw at us.'

Volant's voice sounded hollow. 'Show me.'

They marched from the Separating Chambers, and ten minutes later they were clambering up onto the ribs of the fortress, causing a noisy commotion as white-robed priests and black-armoured Gravesward dropped to their knees, whispering prayers as the prince passed by.

Once they had reached the battlements, Prince Volant inspected the defences, striding up and down the lines of men. He towered over them like a demigod, reordering the troops and repositioning the war engines.

'It is a fine sight,' said Corsos, speaking quietly in Aurun's ear as they surveyed the ranks of knights. Reinforcements from other prominents had been arriving all day, and it was the largest muster either of them had ever seen. As well as the knights, there were lines of archers dressed in a lightweight version of the black Gravesward armour, with white plumes on their caps in place of the feathered robes worn by the knights.

Aurun nodded, but his eye kept coming back to Prince Volant's knights. Volant had positioned them directly above the main gates into the fortress, and as they formed into ranks, Aurun was near enough to see how savagely they had been attacked. Gravesward armour was made of thick, lacquered leather, treated so cunningly that it formed into plates as hard as steel. But it had not been strong enough to protect the prince's men. Their wing-shaped shields were dented and their armour was torn, exposing deep, bloody wounds.

'How can mordants do that?' he asked as the prince returned to stand at his side.

'What?'

Aurun nodded to the wounded knights. 'What weapons do they use that can tear through our armour?'

Volant shook his head. 'No weapons. Only naked fury. They are deranged. It gives them unnatural strength.'

Volant looked around, frowning. 'Where are the rest of your men?'

Aurun nodded, trying to hide his pride. 'This is barely a third of our reserves, Morn-Prince. I have deployed the bulk of our army out on the wynd.' He nodded to the gatehouse barring the road, about half a mile out from the city gates. 'The approach to the fortress is only a hundred or so feet wide. There will be a bottleneck. My men will be able to hold the mordants back for as long as we need in such tight confines.' He smiled. 'Meanwhile, my archers will butcher them. They will never even reach the fortress.'

Prince Volant stared at Aurun. 'You have to call them back.'

A bell clanged, up on one of the towers.

'Too late,' muttered Volant, sounding dazed.

'What do you mean?' asked Aurun. 'Too late? Too late for what?'

The prince ignored him, stomping over to the walls and leaning out into the night.

A hush fell over the lines of knights as they all peered out into the darkness, straining to see what had triggered the alarm.

The bell clanged again, followed by another further down the wall, then dozens more followed suit, until the whole fortress rang to the sound of the alarm.

'The sea is moving,' muttered Corsos, confused. The black waves had started to ripple and surge for miles in every direction. 'How? The Eventide is solid. How can it move like a normal sea?'

'It's not the sea,' replied Volant.

'What do you...?' Aurun's words trailed off as he understood. The entire ocean, every mile of the Eventide, was swarming with crowds. Thousands of mordants were surging through the darkness.

'They're not using the wynds,' breathed Corsos, gripping his bone staff as though he were about to collapse. 'They're crossing the sea.'

'How?' cried Aurun as the dark legions poured past the gatehouses like an oil slick. 'It is impossible to walk on the Eventide!'

'Why?' said Prince Volant, sounding calm again despite the horror of the scene below.

'Because it means madness. No one can touch the Eventide without losing their mind.'

'How do you break a mind that has already been shattered?'

Aurun stared, trying to make sense of the numbers, but the prince climbed up a few steps, making himself look even more like a giant, and raised his scythe high into the air. 'The ancestors are with us!' he cried, his voice magnified somehow, so that every soldier and knight on the walls turned to face him. 'They're in our hearts! In our blades! Every generation of Erebid is on these walls. Those godless creatures have no idea what they're about to face. I came here because this is where the war will be won!'

The prince's voice boomed with such conviction that Aurun almost found himself believing him, even though he knew the prince had only come to order a retreat.

'Here is where we make our stand!' roared the prince. 'Today we end this sacrilege. Today we drive the mordants out!'

The soldiers on the walls raised their scythes and howled, full of right-eous fury, their fear forgotten.

Aurun remained silent. As the knights revelled in the glory of fighting with their prince, Aurun watched the gatehouse half a mile away vanish-ing under a tsunami of grey, feral bodies.

'Look at them,' he whispered, staring at the tides of ghouls rushing towards them.

'Look at *him*,' said Corsos, nodding at the prince.

Volant had returned to his skeleton steed and climbed up into the saddle. He looked like a figure from legend, head thrown back and scythe raised as his mount reared beneath him.

'Gravesward, to war!' he roared as the skeleton pounded its fleshless wings and launched him into the sky.

All along the wall, Volant's honour guard drove their steeds from the for-tress, gliding out into the darkness, pennants snapping.

The skeleton mounts looped in formation, like a single, mountainous ser-pent, then dived, plunging towards the wynd and the battle at the gatehouse.

Aurun shook his head, awed by the sight. Then he stood up straight, dusted down his armour and began marching through the lines of knights. His initial shock was fading. Nothing had changed. They were prepared for this. 'Ready the ballistae!' he cried, waving his scythe at the towers that punctuated the walls. War machines rumbled into view –huge iron bolt-throwers decorated with wings of bone, designed to resemble the moths that circled constantly overhead.

'Load the barrels!' he called, and huge, smoking vats of oil were ratch-eted up into place on the walls.

'Archers take aim!' Hundreds of bowmen rushed past the knights and readied their weapons, targeting the crowds surging towards the walls.

Aurun was ashamed of how he had hesitated at the sight of the mordants. The Morn-Prince had taken to the air with bravery and determination, despite the fact that he had never intended to make his stand here. None of this was as Volant had intended, but he had rallied the men with as much confidence as if this had been planned months ago. Aurun resolved to do the same. As he strode back and forth, howling his orders, his determination grew. The Unburied could not be moved, but neither would they be abandoned.

Corsos stumbled after him, gripping his bone staff. He had just opened his mouth to say something when he halted and peered out into the darkness.

The battle at the gatehouse was raging, a clamour echoing across the Eventide, but Corsos frowned and put a hand to his ear. 'What is that?' he cried.

Aurun paused to listen. 'What?' All he could hear was the din of battle and the sound of the bells ringing behind him.

Corsos held up a finger to silence him, still listening intently.

Then Aurun heard it –a thin, ululating shriek.

'What is that?' he muttered.

A captain rushed over to him, asking for clarity on his orders. Aurun answered his question, and by the time the captain had gone, the shriek was much clearer. It was quickly getting louder, and something about it caused Aurun's blood to cool. It was like dozens of tormented voices screaming in concert.

He shrugged and tried to ignore the sound as he saw that the mordants not attacking the gatehouse had now reached the foot of the fortress walls and were starting to climb up its twisting, claw-like buttresses.

'On my order!' he cried to the archers.

The mordants moved with unbelievable speed, scrambling up the walls like spiders bursting from an egg, swarming towards them with no need of ropes or hooks. The sight of them filled Aurun with revulsion. They were beings without souls. Men without minds. Vessels for a grotesque hunger and nothing else. He held his hatred in check, keeping his hand raised until he was sure they would be easy targets. Then he swept his hand down and launched hell.

A storm of arrows sliced into the mordants, tearing through their sagging flesh and ripping them away from the walls. Dozens tumbled back through the air, trailing arcs of blood and crashing into the mob below.

As the archers loosed wave after wave of arrows, the screaming sound grew so loud that some of them started to miss their marks, wincing and cursing as they shot.

'There!' said Corsos, pointing into the distance.

A shape was rushing through the clouds towards the fortress, a grotesque parody of the prince's skeleton steed. Rather than an elegant serpent of gleaming bones, it was an ugly, snub-faced thing, with ragged, fleshy wings and scraps of intestine trailing from its butchered chest. It looked like the carcass of an enormous bat, and its mouth was open, revealing long, cruel incisors and filling the air with that hideous shriek.

As the sound grew in volume, Aurun's head started to pound and he became gripped by an overwhelming sense of dread. His heart hammered in his chest, and his hands began to shake.

'A terrorgheist,' gasped Corsos.

Aurun shook his head, trying to escape the sound. 'A what?'

'It will send us mad!' cried Corsos, covering his ears. 'The sound will send us mad!'

Aurun looked across the wall and saw that some of the archers had staggered away from the battlements, shaking their heads and dropping their longbows. Even the lines of Gravesward standing behind them were lowering their scythes, gripping their heads and cursing.

'Block your ears!' shouted Aurun. He grabbed some dust from the ground, spat in it and jammed it in his ears, waving for his men to do the same. 'Block out the noise!'

All along the wall, knights and soldiers dropped to their knees, seizing fistfuls of dirt and trying to cram it into their ears.

The dust lessened the sound for a moment, but as the terrorgheist hurtled towards the walls, the noise became unbearable.

'Fire the ballistae!' cried Aurun, and the men in the towers struggled to comply, triggering their war machines as best they could while reeling from the sound.

The bolts went wide, whistling off into the clouds as the terrorgheist crashed into the battlements, hurling bone and masonry in every direction as it waded onto the top of the wall, screaming furiously at the soldiers scrambling for cover.

The monster was huge –thirty or forty feet long, with enormous leathery wings that thrashed violently as it tried to find a steady perch on the wall.

With the archers scattering, the Gravesward rushed towards the creature, raising their scythes to attack.

The monster hit them with a scream like a body blow, causing them to stumble and stagger. Most of them failed to land a blow, and those that did only hacked through flaps of dead, ragged skin.

The terrorgheist's head lunged forwards and ripped through the knights.

Aurun stumbled through the carnage, dodging around staggering knights in his attempt to reach the monster.

This close, the scream was horrific. It felt like his head was being split open, and he struggled to see clearly, his eyes were so full of tears. There was also a nauseating smell pouring from the monster's heaving carcass. Several of the knights near Aurun were doubled over, gagging on the foetid stink.

He reached the creature and landed a blow, slamming his scythe into its chest. The blade cut easily through the exposed ribs, but the wound had no effect. The terrorgheist did not even seem to notice him as it dropped a fresh corpse from its mouth and waded into the crush of archers and knights, locking its jaws around another man and ripping him in two.

Aurun tried to attack again, but before he could, the monster reared back and let out its loudest screech yet.

Aurun fell to his knees, deafened and in so much pain that he could not see.

Other knights collapsed all around him, helpless to defend themselves as the monster lurched forwards, ripping and tearing, filling the air with blood and howls.

The scream grew until Aurun curled into a foetal position, his muscles locked with cramp and his breath caught in his chest. His lungs burned and his oxygen-starved brain began to withdraw into itself. The cries of his men and the scream of the terrorgheist faded, becoming distant and vague, as though he were remembering his death rather than experiencing it.

Light burned into Aurun's mind, and he mouthed a prayer, preparing to meet his ancestors. Then he realised that as the light grew, the terrorgheist's scream was faltering. His vision was also returning. He saw that the light was not in his mind, but burning through the walls of the fortress. It was the amethyst fire of the Unburied.

His muscles loosened enough for him to breathe, and he managed to sit up and look around. All across the wall, men were struggling to rise as the scream dropped away, but rather than attacking, they were staring up in shock.

The Morn-Prince was circling overhead.

He still had his scythe raised, and he had been transformed by the Unburied. Their fire had leapt from the walls of the fortress and ignited his armour. He was burning with the power of the ancestors.

Prince Volant lashed out with his scythe, and purple light ripped through the air, slamming into the terrorgheist's face.

The monster fell backwards, pounding its wings, trying to right itself as amethyst fire drummed into its flesh, engulfing it in sparks and smoke.

The terrorgheist launched itself from the wall and locked its jaws on the neck of Volant's steed. The winged goliaths looped and dived, screaming and roaring as they tore at each other.

'The walls!' cried Aurun as dozens of figures poured over the battlements. He cursed when he realised that whatever happened to the terrorgheist now, it had done its job. While it kept his men occupied, the mordants had scaled the walls and were now pouring into the fortress.

He rallied the knights nearest to him and led a charge, howling as he cut down the first mordant to reach him.

It was frenzied and desperate. The mordants clawed at the knights like animals, and there were so many of them, flooding onto the walls with a roar of snarls and grunts.

Aurun staggered backwards, swiping, hacking and slipping on blood. The knights around him fought with the same furious, silent determination and managed to hold their ground until a massive shape crashed down beside them, sending a violent tremor through the walls and causing everyone to stagger.

Aurun dragged himself clear of the scrum, up onto the battlements, and saw that the two winged monsters had crashed to the ground.

Volant slammed onto the wall and rolled away as his steed collapsed and fell in the other direction.

The terrorgheist leant back and opened its bloody jaws, preparing to scream again, but Volant's armour was still ablaze with the power of his ancestors, and he hurled it from his scythe.

The terrorgheist's head jolted back, and as it tried to shake away the flames, Prince Volant dived across the wall and sank the full length of his curved blade into the monster's skull.

The creature jolted upwards, trying to fling the prince away, but he gripped the haft of his scythe and yanked it down, splitting its head in two.

Archers and Gravesward cheered as the terrorgheist crashed to the ground, juddered, then lay still.

The Morn-Prince turned to face his men, light still shining from his black armour. He held his scythe aloft, trailing strands of blood from the blade, and his men howled even louder.

'The Unburied are with us!' cried Prince Volant. 'Now and forever. And when this battle is-'

His words became a pained cough and he stumbled forwards.

Then he dropped to his knees, revealing the figure standing behind him. It was a mordant, and it was gripping a bloodstained shard of iron as long as its arm. It stood over the prince, panting hungrily, about to pounce on him, but dozens of arrows kicked it backwards through the air, sending it hurtling from the battlements.

'To the prince!' howled Aurun, running through the battle and climbing up the terrorgheist's corpse.

Gravesward formed a circle around Volant, holding back waves of mordants.

As the flesh-eaters continued tumbling onto the wall in great crowds, swamping the fortress' defenders, Lord Aurun dropped to Prince Volant's side and grabbed his bloody armour.

At first he thought the prince was dead, but then Volant coughed, spraying blood through the mouth grille of his helmet.

He managed to sit up and grab Aurun's arm. 'We've lost the gatehouse. Can you hold the wall?'

Aurun nodded, then glanced around. 'No,' he admitted. He was determined to show the same fortitude as the prince, but he could not deny what he was seeing. Thanks to the terrorgheist, the mordants were flowing freely over the battlements. As well as the ones climbing over the embrasures, there were some with wings, like smaller versions of the terrorgheist's mighty pinions. There was no way to use the oil or war machines. 'The walls are lost.'

He thought the prince would be outraged, but he simply nodded, pulling Aurun closer. 'Get your men to the Unburied. I need time to think.' He coughed and stiffened in pain, then grabbed Aurun again, his voice growing more steady. 'Fight every inch of the way.'

CHAPTER THIRTEEN

THE VICTORY FEAST

'What happened to us?' asked Queen Nia. She was seated at King Galan's side, at the head of the feast. Lords Miach and Melvas looked up at her words, but Galan knew she was talking to him. The war had ignited something in her soul. Her tiredness was gone, her bitterness forgotten. She looked wonderful – twenty years younger and flushed with pride. The firelight flashed in her glistening eyes, and he realised he could not remember the last time she had looked at him with such passion and focus.

He reached out and took her hand. 'What do you mean?'

She nodded at the Great Hall. They were surrounded by victorious warriors, vassals and kinsmen, their faces ruddy from wine and the heat of the fire, their eyes burning with pride as they leant back in their chairs or danced through the smoke. 'How did we forget this?' she said. 'How did we forget how to live?'

Galan laughed and drank more of his wine. 'It is not our place to choose the why and the when. The Great Wolf chose this moment to rouse his pack. We must just be grateful that he remembered us. He is behind everything. This rebellion would not have come as a surprise to him. I believe he sent us these traitors as a test –a final chance to prove our strength and loyalty.'

She smiled, squeezing his hand so hard it hurt. 'I love you.'

Galan raised her hand to his lips and kissed her fingers. 'I saw you at the gates, my love. So brave. So beautiful. You looked like a goddess – like Netona reborn.'

She blushed and looked away, then raised her chin and looked proudly down the table, the very image of a noble regent. For years she had hidden in her chambers, nursing a hurt he could not ease, the agony of not giving him an heir, but now she looked as though she had rid herself of a terrible weight, no longer hunched, no longer bowed. The lines on her face no longer looked like the cruel wounds of time, but badges of honour.

Galan turned to the warrior seated at his other side, Lord Melvas. 'What news from Lord Curac?'

Melvas was drowsy with exhaustion and drink, and his gaze was fixed on the dancers and musicians at the far end of the table. He sat up and rubbed his face, struggling to focus on his king.

Galan laughed. 'No one celebrates as well as you, my old friend.'

Melvas gave him a rueful grin. 'I have waited until tonight, King Galan.

We will be on the road for two days or more after this. I will have plenty of time to recover before we reach the capital.'

'Then Curac has won?'

Melvas grinned. 'Very nearly. It took less than a day to reach the northernmost castle. He's attacking it as we speak. If the traitors refuse to surrender, Curac will take their heads just as easily as those of all the others.'

'Then he has no need of our aid?'

'No, your majesty.' Melvas emptied his goblet and poured himself another glass of wine. 'We are free to enjoy the fruits of our labours. And then, in the morning, we can set off for the capital.'

King Galan closed his eyes, picturing the scene. Once the Hounds of Dinann had captured the capital, the whole kingdom would be his once more. The sign of the Wolf would fly from every castle in the land, and the bards would sing of the day King Galan and Queen Nia crushed the rebels who had turned their backs on a thousand years of tradition and fealty.

He sensed Melvas watching him.

'I can't eat with you staring at my ear,' laughed the king. 'Speak your mind. What are you worried about now?'

'Curac could join us within a few days, your majesty.'

Galan shook his head. 'Not this again.' On another night, his general's doubt might have annoyed him, but he was in such good spirits that he smiled. 'Speed is everything, Melvas. I have told you this from the day we left Ruad. The rebels are a disorganised rabble, but if we give them time to join together against us, this war could become a tedious slog. I will not end my days locked in some drawn-out tussle over a backwater I had forgotten the name of until a few weeks ago. We move fast. We take their heads before they have time to get them together and form an alliance. We don't *need* the extra numbers from Curac.' He nodded at the meat heaped on Melvas' plate. 'You're just getting too comfortable here. You want to spend a few more days stuffing your gut.'

Melvas was about to protest, but Galan held up a hand to silence him. 'I'm joking! You're a good man, Melvas. Would I let you lead the Hounds if you weren't?' He shook his head. 'But I won't wait here for Curac. I needed him to take the north so that we wouldn't have an enemy at our backs, but you tell me he's dealing with that, so we will set off for the capital tomorrow. If Curac is as good as you claim, he will join us quickly enough to see me plant the false king's head on the battlements.'

Melvas seemed about to argue again when Queen Nia laughed at him. 'Know when you're beaten, Melvas. We'll leave in the morning.'

The warrior held up his hands and smiled. 'I'm not fool enough to argue with both of you.' He rose slowly to his feet, holding the back of his chair to steady himself. 'So I will dance.' He bowed, almost falling in the process, then stumbled down the length of the table towards the dance at the far end. As he went, warriors reached out, grabbing his hand and patting him on the back, roaring his name.

Galan was still smiling as he turned to Nia. 'Are we going to let that rogue have all the fun?'

She looked shocked. 'You haven't asked me to dance since...' She frowned. 'Have you *ever* asked me to dance?'

He shook his head in mock outrage, then stood and bowed to her. 'Queen Nia, heroine of Sarum Keep, will you consent to dance with me?'

She raised an eyebrow. 'Will your back hold out?'

He laughed as he took her hand and crossed the hall. People backed away, forming an impromptu processional, bowing, smiling and raising their drinks.

As their regents approached, the musicians struck up a new tune, playing faster and louder, and Nia laughed as Galan whirled her into the dance.

Faces blurred as the king turned at pace, lifting his queen off her feet and crushing her to his chest.

Colour and sound blazed in his mind, ignited by the wine and his quickening heart. Some of the dancers were swinging red ribbons, and as he spun, King Galan found himself surrounded by a spiral of crimson strands.

CHAPTER FOURTEEN

THE BARREN POINTS

The road headed south for a mile before it started to bend west and climb towards the stars. Gotrek walked just a few paces from the edge, staring out into the void and shaking his head. 'What do you call these roads again?' he asked, looking back at Lhosia.

'These are the wynds,' she replied. 'This is the Great South Wynd, one of the largest highways in the princedom. From here we will pass the Sceptred Wynd and the Wynd of Foreknowing. Beyond that we will reach the Barren Points, home of Lord Aurun, Warden of the Northern Climbs. There we shall find Prince Volant.'

Gotrek nodded and looked back out from the road. 'How are these things suspended? Sorcery?'

'The wynds are the veins of the princedom. They are hung from the prominents.'

'The prominents are your fortresses?' asked Maleneth, studying the few lights that still shone on the horizon.

Lhosia nodded. 'And our temples and homes. The greatest of them are vast. There are thousands of people in a fortress like the Barren Points or the Lingering Keep. There are many kinds of–' She cut off mid-sentence and stared up at the empty tracts of ocean.

'The Lingering Keep?' asked Maleneth.

'Morbium's capital,' said Lhosia, her voice flat. 'Home of Prince Volant, and home to the Amethyst Princes since the dawn of time.'

Gotrek was still gazing out at the lonely lights of the temples. 'So the roads are hung from your cities, but what keeps the cities afloat?'

'The Unburied,' said Lhosia, touching the cocoon she carried. 'We preserve our ancestors, and they, in turn, loan us their immortal power, feeding life into the prominents. Or at least, that's how it has always been until now.'

They trudged on in silence for a while, the only sound coming from Trachos' twisted boot as he dragged it along behind him. After walking for a few hours, his limp had become even more pronounced. Maleneth imagined he would like to rest but was too proud to ask. The thought of his stoical, grimacing silence made the journey slightly more entertaining.

Every dozen yards or so, they passed another corpse – either a dismembered ghoul, one of the knights in a flamboyant, feathered cloak or one of Morbium's civilians – pale, emaciated wretches like Lhosia, dressed in white or dark purple robes. Every one of the corpses was surrounded by a mobile shroud of tiny moths that scattered when Maleneth and the others approached, filling the darkness with movement and noise. It took a few minutes for Maleneth to realise that one of the bodies up ahead was still moving, trying to fend off the moths.

'Gotrek,' she said, nodding towards the struggling shape.

He nodded and veered back into the centre of the road, slinging his axe from his back as he reached the man.

When the Slayer hauled the terrified wretch to his feet, Maleneth recognised his face. 'The gatekeeper,' she laughed. 'You didn't get far.'

'Traitor!' cried Lhosia, barging past Maleneth to confront him. 'How dare you abandon your post? If you had done your duty, the mordants could have been halted. How could you hide yourself away while the Gravesward fought for their lives?'

The man tried to pull away from her, shaking his head, but he was trapped firmly in Gotrek's iron grip. 'High priestess... forgive me.' His voice was shrill. 'What could I do?'

'What you were trained to do!' Lhosia exclaimed. 'What you were sworn to do!' Her voice was taut with rage. Maleneth sensed that she was venting all the grief and rage that had been tormenting her since she had left the port. She drew her scythe and brandished it at the quaking man. 'Your cowardice will have risked countless souls! I should execute you for your–'

'They came so fast,' said the gatekeeper, shaking his head. 'There was no time to lock the gates or raise the wynd. Even the Gravesward could not hold them back.' His eyes flicked towards Lhosia. 'I've never seen so many mordants. Where are they coming from? Why are the prominents growing dark?'

'The Iron Shroud has been breached,' said Lhosia, not looking at the man. 'Something has broken through the power of the Unburied. We have been revealed to the rest of the princedoms.'

The gatekeeper looked like he might be sick. He shook his head and muttered something to himself. 'You're headed somewhere,' he said. 'Where?'

'Prince Volant is at the Barren Points. And I have promised to take this duardin to him.'

The man stepped away from Gotrek, staring at him in confusion, taking in the chest rune and the streaks of gold in his beard and mohawk. Then he turned towards Maleneth.

Her leathers were drenched in gore and her hair was clotted with blood, sticking up from her head at a deranged angle. She gave him a friendly wink.

'Take me with you, priestess,' he gasped, looking back at Lhosia. 'Don't leave me with these...'

Maleneth wondered whether he was more afraid of her or the ghouls.

Lhosia did not meet his eye, but nodded.

'Only if you can keep up,' said Gotrek, and marched off down the road.

As the road climbed higher, they saw other highways passing beneath them, criss-crossing the sea, made of the same amalgamation of bone and iron. After a few hours, lights began to wash over the metal, coming from up ahead.

'Is this it?' asked Maleneth, peering at the distant shape. 'Is this the fortress where we will find your prince?'

Lhosia nodded.

Maleneth looked again at the shape in the distance, frowning as they walked towards it. 'Did you say the lights come from the...' She hesitated, gesturing at the cocoon Lhosia carried. 'From those things?'

Again Lhosia nodded. 'The Unburied.'

'And did you say that your prince took all the Unburied back to your capital, so that they would be safe from the flesh-eaters?'

Lhosia hesitated, staring at the lights.

'It would appear he's overlooked some,' said Maleneth.

The priestess strode on, gripping her scythe and picking up her pace.

'Finally!' grunted Gotrek, jogging after her. 'Someone with a sense of urgency.'

The Barren Points were nothing like the fortress they had seen at the port. Rather than a shell-like spiral curve, it resembled an overgrown version of the shrine where they had first met Lhosia – a gnarled, briar-like tangle of bone towers, each knotted around the others to make an impenetrable tangle. The whole tormented mass reached up like flames, as large as a city and as strange as everything else they had seen in the princedom. Somewhere deep inside the knotted walls was the source of the purple light, which spilled through the gaps between the towers, landing on the sea in a jumble of rippling shafts.

'Looks as buggered as the last place,' said Gotrek.

The far side of the fortress had collapsed, and hundreds of fires littered the ruined walls. There were figures battling through the fumes, silhouetted by the flames. Even from half a mile away, it was clear that most of the figures were ghouls. They were breaching the walls in a way that no sane warrior would attempt, swarming over the defences like rats, scrabbling over each other in a frenzy to reach the defenders that had gathered to face them. War engines hurled comet-like missiles, huge spheres of purple flame that exploded on impact, drenching the ghouls in liquid heat and adding to the fires that were spreading quickly through their ranks, but the shots were wild and sporadic.

Lhosia stared at the carnage. 'If the Barren Points fall, there is nothing to stop them taking the Northern Wards.'

'Are they more of your sacred moths?' asked Maleneth, peering at the clouds of tiny shapes that tumbled around the fighting.

Lhosia frowned in puzzlement, shaking her head.

'We would not see moths from this distance,' said Trachos. He took a carved ivory box from his belt and flicked a clasp on its side. A dozen linked boxes rattled out of it, each one smaller than the previous one, creating a long, square-sided tube. He snapped the clasp back, locking the boxes in place, then held the tube up to his helmet, looking through a lens at the narrow end. He muttered something and handed the spyglass to Maleneth.

She grimaced as the scene over the walls swam into focus. The flying shapes were ghouls with vast leathery wings, and as the knights reeled away from them, the creatures swooped down and tore them apart. 'No one is leading the defence,' she said. 'Look. It's mayhem. Where is this prince you've been telling us so much about? Is he the kind of prince that directs his troops from the local hostelry?'

They each took a turn with Trachos' spyglass, but when it came to Gotrek, he held it for a long time, muttering under his breath. 'There are thousands of ghouls at the front gates. They're everywhere. I presume the gates on this side will be locked, and I don't fancy our chances of climbing the walls. Any ideas how we get in?'

Lhosia was still staring at the battle on the walls. 'Where is the prince? Or Lord Aurun?'

'Priestess,' said Maleneth, causing her to turn round in surprise. 'Can you get us in? I can't imagine it will be long before the ghouls take a look at this side of the fortress.'

'Of course. I have my own routes into all of the prominents.' She waved at the approach to the gates, where several smaller paths snaked away from the main one, then started to hurry on along the road. 'Quickly.'

As they neared the fortress walls, they heard the sound of winged ghouls whirling overhead in the darkness. Some of them were making a thin, scraping, gasping sound. It was like a knife being dragged across porcelain. Maleneth would have found the noise easier to cope with if Trachos hadn't tried to drown it out with another grating hymn. He tried to look proud and triumphant as he marched on, but his wounds made him more tragic than fearsome.

Think how easy it would be to lace one of your knives and jam it through those splits in his armour, whispered her mistress.

'I serve the God-King,' she muttered. 'I serve something bigger than myself. You wouldn't understand what that's like.'

You were meant to serve me! You serve yourself before any god. And you need Gotrek dead if you're going to claim the rune for yourself. How else can you guarantee that he won't end up marching back into Azyr with it?

'Look at him. He's half dead already. I just need to bide my time and he'll do the job for me. That way I'll get the rune without breaking the oaths I swore in Azyrheim. The Order of Azyr won't last long if we murder each other every time there's a chance of glory.'

You're getting soft in your old age. You care about him.

Maleneth laughed. 'I haven't changed *that* much.'

'This way,' said Lhosia, leading them down a side road that followed the curve of the fortress walls, heading down as it went.

Maleneth glanced up. This close, the fortress looked even stranger, like a forest of heat-warped bones.

'Look out!' cried the gatekeeper as a ghoul dived at them from its perch on the wall.

Maleneth cursed. The thing was huge, like the ghouls they had faced at the port.

Gotrek ran at the wall of the fortress with such speed that he managed to take a few steps up its sheer side and hurl himself into the air.

The ghoul screamed in confusion as the full weight of the Slayer hit its back. It struggled furiously, forcing everyone to back away, blinded by clouds of dust, but Gotrek was still laughing as he struggled to keep his footing on the monster. He reached down, grabbed its chin and snapped its neck.

Maleneth ducked as another ghoul attacked, but she was too slow and a fist slammed into the side of her head. She stumbled like a drunk, swerving across the road. Then her breath exploded from her lungs as she tripped over rubble and thudded to the ground.

She was vaguely aware of a figure standing over her, fending off the ghouls, but she did not realise who it was until she heard Trachos' voice, booming out, 'Mallus-born and fiery-eyed! Godly lightning in my hand! Turning back the darksome tide! From Sigmar's golden starlit land!'

As the dust cleared, she saw him battling for her life, chin high and voice raised in triumph. He whirled his hammers back and forth, ignoring his wounds and his pain, smashing down every ghoul that scrambled towards her, punching sigmarite into their deranged faces. There was something horribly desperate in his words. It did not stem from fear of the ghouls, she realised, but fear of his own state of mind.

With a few of the ghouls down, the screams were more bearable and Maleneth managed to stand, staring at Trachos as he staggered away from her, dragging his ruined leg and looking for another target.

'You're such a dunce,' she said. 'Why were you protecting me? Without me around you'd have a chance of getting that rune.'

'I will protect you with whatever strength Sigmar spares me, Maleneth Witchblade, servant of the God-King.'

She rolled her eyes. 'So brave.'

'This way!' cried Lhosia, dashing under an archway and continuing on down the road.

Maleneth ran after her and Trachos followed as quickly as he could, but Gotrek stayed in the centre of the road, roaring at the horrors above. Some were clambering over the walls and others were pounding torn, rotten wings as they circled overhead. Deranged as they were, the ghouls appeared reluctant to go anywhere near a raging Slayer. 'Get down here!' he cried. 'Or on my oath, I'll sprout wings and come up there after you!'

'Gotrek!' shouted Maleneth, waving her knives at the archway. 'The prince! He's in the fortress, remember?'

Gotrek grunted, gave the ghouls one last glare, then stamped through the carnage towards the arch, shrugging gore from his massive shoulders.

The road followed the curve of the wall, and after a few minutes, the clamour of battle began to fade.

They passed through a low arch. Lhosia unlocked a small hidden door, and they entered the fortress, emerging onto a wide paved area surrounded by windows and doors, all of which had been shuttered and barred. They could hear battle all around them, but there was no sign of soldiers or ghouls. The place seemed to have been overlooked as the fighting raged all around it.

The glow they had seen outside the fortress was brighter here, and the buildings looked like shards of alabaster held before a fire, pale and shimmering with amethyst light. Lhosia looked furious as she studied the lights. 'The Unburied should be safely in the capital by now. I explained to the prince. We didn't need to lose a single soul, as long as he took them to the Lingering Keep.' She waved her scythe at the lights. 'And here they are, still at risk, surrounded by mordants.'

'Where is he, lass?' said Gotrek, wiping blood from his face as he trudged into the square.

She shook her head and gestured them on, across the square. She led them to a narrow lane that looped up behind one of the buildings, lined with dozens of market stalls.

As they neared the top of the steep road, the sounds of fighting grew louder.

They readied their weapons as they crested the hill and saw another square spread out below them.

A brutal clash was in full swing. Gravesward, black-armoured archers and white-robed priests were all backing slowly into the square as mordants tumbled from every wall and roof. The ghouls were in such a frenzy that they were killing themselves to reach the defenders, leaping from rooftops and smashing themselves across the flagstones or else being crushed by the weight of bodies.

The scene was dominated by an enormous fossilised serpent that towered over the soldiers, its bleached-bone wings rattling as it lashed at the ghouls, flinging them through the air.

The Erebid numbered no more than a couple of hundred, but every building was carpeted with frenzied ghouls and more were looping overhead, pounding their wings as they looked for a place to attack. Maleneth guessed that in the streets around the square alone, there must have been thousands of the creatures, all thrashing wildly as they tried to reach the scythe-wielding knights. The Erebid had formed a tight circle around one of their fallen comrades. Maleneth struggled to see the wounded warrior they were so desperate to protect, but he looked to be unconscious, slumped in the arms of another knight. It was a desperate scene. The Erebid were massively outnumbered, and most of them were bleeding from multiple wounds. As they backed into the square, mordants rushed towards them from every direction, spilling out of streets and windows in a flood of grey, mottled flesh.

'This is not a fight we can win,' said Maleneth, searching around for a place to take cover. 'We need to think carefully about how we–'

'Who's the prince?' bellowed Gotrek, swinging his axe cheerfully as he strode out into the square.

CHAPTER FIFTEEN

THE HIDDEN CITY

Most of the Gravesward were too busy fighting to register Gotrek's question, but some looked round in surprise at the sight of a Slayer storming towards them.

Maleneth cursed and ran after Gotrek, with Trachos and Lhosia following close behind. The gatekeeper took his chance to flee, sprinting off up a side street.

Ghouls dashed at Gotrek as he broke from the shadows, but he hacked them down without breaking his stride.

'Halt!' cried one of the knights, breaking from the fight to level a scythe at Gotrek. 'Who are you?'

The skeletal drake reared up behind him, a furious edifice of bone, locking its empty eye sockets on the Slayer.

'I could ask the same of you,' replied Gotrek, glaring at the knight, clearly unimpressed by the massive beast looming over him.

Maleneth muttered another curse.

'You're clearly not the defenders of this fort,' continued the Slayer, 'or you'd be up on the walls instead of hiding down here.'

Maleneth had to step aside as a ghoul broke from the scrum and leapt at her, its face rigid with bloodlust. She opened its throat and booted it into another of the creatures, then bounded over the first one and hammered a knife into both their faces. She flipped clear and landed at Gotrek's side. Her pulse was hammering, willing her to abandon herself to the slaughter, but she held her bloodlust at bay.

A knight pushed through the crush, trying to reach Gotrek. It was the warrior carrying the fallen knight.

'Who are you?' he called, struggling under the weight of his burden.

'Where's your prince?' shouted Gotrek, punching a ghoul to the ground and slamming his axe through its neck. 'Well? Anyone got a tongue in their head?'

'Take their weapons,' said the knight. His armour was more ornate than the others', engraved and filigreed and studded with white gemstones.

The Slayer rumbled with laughter, gripping his axe in boulder-sized fists and dropping into a battle stance. 'Just you bloody try.'

The knights hesitated, thrown by Gotrek's psychotic grin.

The Slayer shrugged, swapping the axe from hand to hand. 'Not much of a weapon, to be fair.' He tapped it against his chest rune with a clang. 'I got it from the same mewling runts who made this. But it'll do for the likes of you.'

The knights staggered backwards as ghouls continued to pour from the surrounding streets. Trachos limped past them, pummelling ghouls and singing.

'Wait!' cried the knight in the ornate armour. 'Lhosia?' He pushed towards her, still dragging the fallen warrior, but then hesitated when he got within arm's reach of Gotrek.

'Lord Aurun,' said Lhosia, rushing past Gotrek and embracing the knight. He smiled, clearly shocked.

'Prince Volant!' said Aurun, looking down at the man in his arms. 'It's the high priestess!'

'*You're* the Morn-Prince?' cried Gotrek, striding towards the prone knight.

There was a loud clatter as the Gravesward locked ranks, raising shields and readying scythes.

'Wait!' Lhosia raised a hand. 'The duardin is not an enemy. I would not have reached you without his help. He killed countless mordants to get me here.'

The prince managed to raise himself up and look at Gotrek.

It was only then that Maleneth realised how big he was –almost twice as tall as her, larger than Trachos, even. His armour was filthy and damaged, but he was unmistakably the leader. His face was hidden inside a tall black-and-white helmet that displayed a snarling face on one side and a serene smile on the other.

'Your majesty,' said Lhosia, backing away.

'Who are you, duardin?' gasped the huge knight, ignoring Lhosia. His voice was rough with pain, and there was blood pooling beneath him. 'Why do you fight for Morbium?'

The ghouls surged forwards again, and there was a flurry of blows as the knights struggled to hold them back.

'I'm Gotrek Gurnisson,' bellowed the Slayer over the din, 'and I fight exclusively for Gotrek Gurnisson.' He hacked down a pair of ghouls with one savage swipe. 'I'm here because I've been told you can get me to Nagash.'

'Nagash?' Prince Volant turned to Lhosia, shaking his head. He had to pause as more ghouls broke through the lines of knights. There was a furious flurry of scythes, and then, when there was another gap in the fighting, Volant stared at Gotrek. 'No *sane* person wants to reach the Great Necromancer.'

Gotrek laughed. 'Sane?' He waved his bloody axe at Lhosia, still holding the cocooned corpse she had taken from the docks. 'You live in bones and worship moths.'

Prince Volant looked past Gotrek towards Maleneth. But before he could say anything, the ground juddered and the sounds of distant battle swelled in volume. A low, booming explosion echoed down the streets.

'Grungni,' muttered Gotrek as a shadow loomed over the city. It looked like a column of smoke pluming from a volcano.

'What *is* that?' said Maleneth as the shape moved into the light.

'A mordant,' said Prince Volant, his tone bleak.

The ghoul looked similar to the others apart from its size – it was a colossus, hundreds of feet tall and teeming with legions of smaller ghouls. It smashed an enormous fist down into the battlements, destroying the rows of explosive charges lined up for the ballistae. Flames blossomed through the walls, lighting up the giant's grotesque face. It was just as hunched and sinewy as its smaller kin, but there was a gleam of cruel intelligence in its eyes, quite different from all the others. It dragged its fist sideways through the battlements, hurling men and war machines through the air and creating another drum roll of explosions.

'To the Separating Chambers,' snapped Volant, turning towards Lord Aurun. 'Protect the Unburied.'

Aurun nodded and ordered his men back across the square. They were completely surrounded and it was slow going, but the knights fought with impressive discipline, carving a path through the frantic crowds.

The fury of the fighting made more conversation impossible, so Gotrek, Maleneth and Trachos fought alongside the knights in silence as they made for a building on the far side of the square.

It was a huge, undulating structure built in an architectural style unlike anything Maleneth had seen before. It looked like a marquee of white silk, frozen at the moment its peaks were caught in a breeze, all ripples and bulges, but it was made of the same hard, bone-like material as the rest of the fortress.

'Into the Hidden City,' shouted Aurun, waving for everyone to follow him as he dragged the prince up the steps with the help of some of his men.

As most of the knights formed a semicircle at the bottom of the steps, raising their shields, Aurun unlocked the door, flinging it open and spilling purple light over the battle.

They hurried inside, hurling ghouls back down the steps as they backed into the hall. There was a fierce scrum at the threshold before the knights managed to shut the doors with a resounding slam.

'Bar them!' cried Lord Aurun, leaving the prince on the floor and rushing back to the doors. They were vast, imposing things wrought of iron-threaded bone, with thick crossbars mounted on either side. As Aurun waved his men back and forth they slammed the bars down. When each bar landed, it triggered a mechanism that whirred like an enormous timepiece, turning and interlocking and creating a lattice of bolts.

The sound of the mechanisms seemed to draw Trachos out of his habitual daydream, and he wandered over to them, fingering the locks with interest.

'What is this place?' asked Maleneth, looking up at the distant vaulted ceiling. There were twelve cocoons, identical to the one Lhosia was carrying.

'Who are you?' demanded Prince Volant, still sprawled on the floor and clutching his wounds. His skeleton steed was circling him protectively, its hollow gaze locked on Gotrek and Maleneth.

'I serve the Order of Azyr.' Maleneth nodded at Trachos, who was still studying the locks. 'We're escorting the Slayer through the princedoms.'

'You serve Sigmar?' The prince waved at Gotrek, who was stomping around the hall, staring up at the ceiling. '*He* doesn't. Why are you helping him?'

Maleneth spoke up quickly before Trachos could tell the entire crowd about the rune. 'He's unusually powerful. And he's an enemy of the Chaos Gods.'

'*Any* gods,' clarified Gotrek. He walked over to the prince. 'Get me to Nagash and I'll demonstrate.'

The prince removed his helmet and studied Gotrek. Like the rest of the Erebid, Volant's head was pale and hairless, but unlike the others, his face was inked with a complex spiral of tattoos – slender black lines that coiled down from his eyes, mimicking the markings of a moth's wings. His long, angular face was unmistakably regal, but it was twisted by pain. He gasped as he climbed to his feet, towering over everyone present. He stooped and tapped Gotrek's rune with a long, tapered finger. 'And this?'

Maleneth struggled to hold back a curse, wondering if there was anyone in the Mortal Realms who *wouldn't* immediately pick up on the rune's importance.

Gotrek laughed bitterly. 'The reason for my sudden popularity.'

Prince Volant waited patiently for him to elaborate.

The Slayer shrugged. 'Just a rune. And a bloody ugly one at that. Can you get me to Nagash?'

'Why would I help you?'

Gotrek made a low growling sound, but before he could respond, Lhosia strode across the room and addressed the prince, her face rigid with anger.

'We've come from the Anceps Docks. The Unburied were left to the mordants.' Her voice trembled as she waved at the cocoons hanging overhead. 'As they have been here. You swore that you would get the ancestors back to the capital, Prince Volant.'

'You swore the Iron Shroud would hold long enough for me to do so.' The prince's nonchalant mask slipped and his eyes flashed. 'Do you think you're the only one who cares for the safety of the ancestors?' He pointed at Aurun. 'I sent an order for the Unburied to be moved months ago, and when I arrived, only hours ahead of destruction, I find Lord Aurun doing nothing.'

'Nothing?' Lord Aurun looked outraged. 'We can't move the Unburied, high priestess,' he said, addressing Lhosia. 'I have explained all this to the Morn-Prince. We stayed here to defend them because it's either that or abandon them. They're bound into the workings of the fortress. They're part of the old duardin engines. It would take months to separate them from the architecture. Years, maybe.'

Lhosia shook her head, looking up at the cogs and wheels fixed into the ceiling. 'The Unburied are *trapped*?'

Aurun nodded. 'The forefathers completed their work here.' He tapped the haft of his scythe on the cobbles. 'This was the final prominent to be completed. They sealed it with the souls of the Unburied and then sailed back to the Lingering Keep. The Unburied are bound by mechanisms too complex to understand. And even if we could understand them, we don't know how the Kharadron powered these machines. And there's no way I could have broken the ancestors out before the mordants arrived.'

Maleneth shook her head. 'Did you say sailed? How could anyone sail in this place? Your sea isn't liquid. It looks like it's made of lead.'

'It's impossible to cross the Eventide now,' said Aurun. 'Even touching it means madness and death. But our forefathers crossed it regularly. They had to –there were no wynds until they built them. They borrowed engineering skills from the Kharadron. They brought the Unburied here in great engines that were able to cross the Eventide.'

Gotrek's eye glazed over. Maleneth had seen this happen before. It tended to precede either sleep, an idea or an explosion of extreme violence. It was worryingly hard to predict which.

'Right,' said the Slayer, looking up at the Morn-Prince. 'I have business with a god.' He waved his axe at the moth-shrouded shapes hanging overhead. 'How about this – I get your corpse eggs back to your capital, and you tell me how to reach Nagash?'

Lord Aurun laughed incredulously, and the prince simply stared.

'Well?' demanded Gotrek as something heavy boomed against the doors. 'My guess is that you have five minutes before the morons break in and start chewing your skulls. Do you want my help or not?'

'You're insane,' replied the prince.

'Agreed. If I get these twelve cocoons to safety, will you get me to Nagash?'

There was another blow at the door, and it gave a low groan as the frame started to give.

'Brace it!' cried Lord Aurun, waving more of his men towards it. 'Jam your scythes against the metal!'

Gotrek was still standing in front of the prince, waiting for an answer.

Volant winced and staggered. Knights rushed to help him, but he shrugged them off. He frowned at Gotrek, as though struggling to make him out in the dazzling light. 'You are peculiar. Quite unlike anyone I have ever met.'

Gotrek shrugged.

The door shook again, and the soldiers cried out as they tried to hold back the weight.

'How could you get the Unburied to the capital?' asked the prince. 'Lord Aurun says it would take weeks to break those machines.'

Gotrek turned to Lord Aurun. 'Are these doors the only way out?'

'There's another exit, but it only leads to the Eventide. The chambers at the rear of the hall join with the city walls, and then there's nothing there but dead sea and the *Spindrift*.'

'The *Spindrift*?'

'An aether-ship. The transportation used by the forefathers when they built the prominents –before they made the wynds.'

'An airship?' Gotrek shook his head. 'Why in the blazes aren't you using it?'

'It's a useless relic,' replied Aurun. 'Powered the same way as those.' He waved his scythe at the machines overhead.

Gotrek looked over at Trachos. The Stormcast Eternal was helping Aurun's men as they struggled to hold the door.

'Right,' he said, turning back to the prince. 'If I rescue your corpse sacks, you'll help me reach Nagash, agreed?'

Prince Volant sneered and seemed about to dismiss Gotrek again, but the Slayer's tone was so confident that he hesitated.

'He has a habit of surprising people,' said Maleneth. 'And he's *tediously* honest. If he says he can do it, he probably can.'

'How?' asked the prince, his expression a mixture of outrage and intrigue.

'Tell them, manling,' Gotrek called over to the Stormcast Eternal.

Trachos was not following the conversation. He was staring at the mechanical doors, muttering to himself.

'Trachos!' shouted Maleneth.

He looked over. As usual, his face was hidden behind his helmet's gleaming deathmask, and it was hard to know what he was thinking.

Gotrek waved him over. 'The moth people want their corpses back. They need them out of those machines.' He gestured with his axe at the ceiling. 'Duardin engineering. Shouldn't be hard to untangle.'

Trachos stared at the Slayer in silence, as though he had forgotten who Gotrek was.

Maleneth felt like jamming knives into his helmet.

The prince waved a dismissive hand. 'These people are ridiculous.' He turned away. 'Aurun! Get some of your archers up on those balconies. Fast!'

A low rumbling started in Gotrek's chest, and he stood up to his full – if not very impressive – height. He gripped his greataxe, and Maleneth saw quite clearly what was coming next. The prince was about to find out what happened to pompous nobles who refused to take Gotrek seriously.

'They're like the engines in Azyr,' said Trachos, talking to the ceiling. 'In the Sigmarabulum. In the alchemical forges. Those machines were designed almost entirely by duardin engineering guilds. These look similar.'

Maleneth looked from Trachos to Gotrek and back again, realisation dawning. 'You've studied duardin engineering?'

Trachos was still talking to the ceiling. 'Of course. Most of Azyr is built on the principles of duardin engineering. I have studied several methods of containing aetheric matter – Baraz Cylinders, Gromthi Coils. They're no different to any other...' He shook his head and began mumbling to himself.

Gotrek nodded. 'Between the two of us, we could untether these cocoons.'

Trachos lowered his gaze from the ceiling and stared at Gotrek. 'What?'

Gotrek's grin froze on his face, and he gripped his axe tighter. 'I said we could *release* them, you tin-headed lump.'

'Oh. Yes, perhaps. It would require an influx of aetheric energy.' Trachos tapped some of the arcane devices jangling at his belt. 'I should be able to trigger the correct currents.'

Gotrek had just opened his mouth to say more when the doors gave way.

CHAPTER SIXTEEN

THE MASTER RUNE OF KRAG BLACKHAMMER

Maleneth ducked as bone and iron whistled through the air.

Tree-sized fingers clawed at the doors, ripping away the frame, causing the walls to crumble.

Then, as the giant ghoul backed away, hundreds of its smaller kin poured into the hall, howling and snorting, their eyes rolling with kill-frenzy.

'Shield wall!' cried Lord Aurun, and the Gravesward locked together, forming a row of tightly packed shields just before the ghouls crashed into them.

The knights staggered under the impact but held their position. As one, they swiped their scythes beneath their shields, cutting the legs from the creatures. Ghouls slapped to the floor, thrashing in their own blood.

'Trachos!' bellowed Gotrek, waving at the stairs that lined the walls. 'Get those bodies down!' He was running as he shouted, rushing to join the battle. He vaulted a toppled column and leapt over the shield wall with a joyous howl, crashing into the heart of the ghouls.

Prince Volant waved Lord Aurun and Maleneth over. 'Help me up!' he called, pointing at his steed.

The skeleton drake had already lowered its head in readiness, but Aurun shook his head. 'Morn-Prince! Your wounds!'

'It's an order, Lord Aurun.'

Maleneth scoured the hall for the other exit, cursing as she realised she might have to abandon her plans, after all she had endured. They were cornered like rats. It was going to be a massacre.

The other doors lead to the sea. There's no point trying them. Her mistress' voice was not as sneering as usual. It sounded alarmed. *You heard them. Walk on those dead waters and you'll lose your mind. There's nowhere to go.*

Maleneth hissed in annoyance. Her mistress was right. Her only chance was that Gotrek's lunatic plan might somehow work. Trachos was still only halfway up the wall, struggling to climb because of his wounds. 'Your prince will last longer on that thing than on the floor,' she muttered, glancing at Aurun. 'Get him on there.'

Aurun looked appalled that she was addressing him in such a commanding tone, but he gave a grudging nod and, between them, they hauled Volant up onto his mount.

The prince seemed reinvigorated to be looming over the fighting, and he raised his scythe. 'Morbium eternal!' His steed reared beneath him and the Gravesward roared in reply, their shield wall unbroken as they cut down row after row of ghouls.

Volant's drake jerked its head forwards, jaws gaping, spewing a column of dust across the hall. It hit the ghouls with such force that it carved a path through the centre of the scrum, toppling dozens of the creatures. But as Maleneth climbed some rubble for a better view, she saw that the blast was doing more than simply knocking them over. As they tried to rise, their movements grew stiff and awkward and their flesh hardened. Within a few seconds, every ghoul that had been hit was lying cracked and life-less on the ground.

Maleneth nodded, impressed, then remembered Gotrek. 'The Slayer is out there!' she cried.

'Aye!' shouted Gotrek, climbing onto the toppled door, the head of a ghoul in one hand and his axe in the other. He raised the weapon and grinned.

'Watch out for Gotrek!' she called to Prince Volant, pointing at the Slayer.

He nodded and cried out the same command, and his steed vomited more dust in the opposite direction.

Trachos was still struggling to reach the ceiling, so Maleneth bounded up the steps. As she approached him, she shook her head in disbelief. The idiot was singing to himself, as though he were enjoying a moment of quiet reflection.

She grabbed his arm and hauled him up the last few steps. They reached a balcony suspended just below the ceiling, and were now within arm's reach of the machines. Trachos' song faltered.

'Incredible workmanship,' he said, removing his helmet and fastening it to his belt so that he could study the devices in more detail.

'We're about to *die*,' said Maleneth.

Trachos fixed her with a flat, blank stare. 'I will not die.'

'Oh, well that's all fine then.'

He continued staring at her.

'The machines, Trachos,' she prompted. 'Can you make them work?'

He looked back at the engines and the rows of pale ovoid shapes they cradled.

From up here Maleneth could see the twelve cocoons clearly. They were just like the one Lhosia carried – like oversized eggs wrapped in dusty gauze. Now that she knew what they contained, she found the sight of them revolting.

'Think of all those withered little corpses,' she muttered.

Trachos shrugged. 'Gotrek won't leave without the prince, and the prince won't leave without the corpses.'

There was an explosion of howls from below as the ghouls broke through the shield wall. Knights scrambled to block the gap, but it was like trying to stem a ruptured dam. Ghouls rushed in every direction, leaping and claw-ing and tearing soldiers to the ground.

'Quickly!' cried Maleneth. 'Get those things out!'

Trachos turned back to the machines. He singled out a particular piece of the workings and rotated cogs with his fingers, clicking them into a new position, aligning the duardin runes engraved into the ancient metal.

Maleneth laughed with relief as light shimmered through the metalwork, edging its wheels and levers.

The fighting became a desperate rout. Gravesward staggered in every direction, trying to fend off claws and teeth as their shields were ripped from their grip.

Gotrek whirled through the carnage, hacking, laughing and lunging.

'His rune,' whispered Maleneth.

Trachos was too engrossed in his work to hear. He had taken a spherical golden cage from his belt and fixed it to the cogs. The instrument was pulsing with the same light as the rest of the ceiling and making a bright ticking sound.

Maleneth stared at Gotrek. He was lost in the moment, fighting so ferociously that Grimnir's face was blazing in his chest. His blocky, savage features looked like they were rising from a brazier, underlit by a hellish glow. 'It will change him,' she muttered.

Trachos paused. 'What?'

'The rune.' She pointed one of her knives at Gotrek. 'It's consuming him.'

Trachos stared blankly at Gotrek's frenzied attacks, then went back to turning the cogs.

The lights flashed brighter over the ceiling and he nodded, taking another instrument from his belt and attaching it to the first.

'To me!' cried Prince Volant, still clinging weakly to the back of his steed as he waved his scythe. 'Form a circle!'

His soldiers tried to cross the room towards him, but so many ghouls had crushed into the hall that many of the knights were surrounded. Lord Aurun led a group of soldiers to the prince, and they formed an island of black armour in the heaving mass of grey.

'If we don't go now it's over,' said Maleneth, leaning over Trachos, trying to understand what he was doing.

Every part of the machinery was flickering, and there was a low humming emanating from the cradles holding the Unburied, but Trachos shook his head and backed away, leaving his implements hanging from the cogs.

'Not enough power.'

'What?' Trachos was nearly twice as tall as Maleneth and clad in hulking sigmarite, but she reached up, grabbed his arm and hauled him round to face her. 'You're giving up?' She shook her head in disbelief, waving at the battle that was ending below them. The Gravesward around Prince Volant were falling fast, vanishing beneath mounds of frantic ghouls. 'If we don't get these things out, we're all going to be butchered.' She pulled him close. 'You might not die, Trachos, but what will your next Reforging be like? And what will be left when you come out the other side?'

He loomed over her, his voice taut. 'I *know* what this means for me, Witch-blade, but I still don't have the power to trigger those engines. They've been inert too long. It would take massive amounts of aether-fire to reignite them.'

Down below, the prince's steed let out an unearthly scream as ghouls tore into it, snapping bones in its legs even as it lashed out with foot-long claws. The prince howled a command and the drake spat more lethal dust, but it was like punching a mountain. Ghouls continued tumbling towards the prince.

'Try again!' Maleneth shouted, infuriated by Trachos' fatalistic tone. 'Even if I have to drag you–'

He barged past her, whipping his hammers from his belt.

Her fighter's instinct told her to duck, and she heard a crack of breaking bone.

She whirled around, knives drawn, to see ghouls lurching and scrambling up the steps.

'Get to the knights!' she gasped.

Trachos nodded, and they began fighting their way back down the steps.

Maleneth tried to kill as she had been trained, to honour the Murder God with every cut, but she was too mired in grasping limbs. The best she could do was use her momentum to bound over the heads and shoulders of the ghouls.

Trachos resorted to similar tactics, using his weighty, armour-clad bulk to smash through the crush.

By the time they reached the bottom steps, Maleneth could barely see, her face was so drenched in blood, but she managed to stagger into the circle of knights around Prince Volant.

Trachos punched his way after her and began hammering anyone who broke through the lines. He was unusually quiet, fighting in grim silence and glancing up at the machines still glowing overhead.

Gotrek was a few feet away, fighting outside the circle, his face locked in a scowl.

'What happened?' he cried, snatching a glance at Trachos.

'It can't be done!' yelled Trachos.

Gotrek attacked the ghouls with renewed fury, his axe a golden blur. 'Can't be done?' His words were contorted by rage.

The Slayer battled towards the base of a toppled column and climbed up onto it, wiping his face and staring out at the deranged figures crashing around him. He looked like the captain of a listing ship, standing at the prow as waves swelled around him.

'So *this* is my doom?' The rune in his chest was blazing constantly now, fuelled by kill-fever. 'These wretched things? In this wretched place?' He was talking to himself more than Trachos. 'I'm glad you never lived to see it, manling. It would not have been worthy of a poem.' He pounded the dazzling rune. 'Redeem yourself, Grimnir! Give me something better!'

At the far end of the hall, the door shook, hurling masonry through the air as the giant tried to shoulder its way into the chamber. Its grotesque face was so vast that only half of it was visible through the tumbling walls.

Gotrek laughed. 'Aye, I suppose *he'll* do.'

The Slayer glanced back at the group battling around the prince. 'Get out!' he shouted. 'I can't save your dead, but I can save you. I'll hold the morons back. Go. While you can.'

Lord Aurun called out to his men, waving them forwards. 'To the Slayer!'

'Don't be a fool!' yelled Gotrek. 'Go!'

As the Gravesward charged, Aurun cried out. Despite the carnage, he sounded clear and determined. 'What are we without the wisdom of our forebears? What use living if we lose the past?'

Gotrek's eyes flashed, and for once it was with something other than rage. 'Well said!' He bared his teeth in a grin, looking back at Lord Aurun. 'Well bloody said, manling!'

He raised his axe, letting the fury of the rune blast from his chest and up into the blade. He looked like a fallen comet, burning as the world collapsed around it. 'Then we meet our dooms together!' He locked his single, burning eye on the colossus at the far side of the hall. 'And that one's mine!'

Maleneth struggled to keep her footing as the knights shoved their way deeper into the ghouls. 'No!' she spat. 'I refuse to die *here.*'

Knight after knight fell, shields torn from their grip and necks ripped open. It was grotesque. And brutal. Whatever Gotrek thought, Maleneth saw nothing noble in the sacrifice. These men were dying for no reason, which might be fine for them, but not for a Bride of Khaine.

She fought furiously, buying time to think, but it was all going to be over in minutes.

There was no way to reach the exit at the back of the hall on her own – there were too many ghouls in the way. She looked to where Gotrek was charging head down through the creatures, making for the giant. He was consumed by his determination to reach the grotesque monster, burning so brightly now that it was hard to look at him.

'God of Murder,' gasped Maleneth. 'Why didn't I think of it? Trachos!' she howled, opening a ghoul's belly and standing on its back as it doubled over, raising herself over the crush.

Trachos was only a few feet away. His turquoise armour had been painted crimson by blood, but he was still swinging his hammers, towering over the battle. He looked her way.

'Power!' she cried, dodging a blow and trying to point at Gotrek.

Trachos shook his head, confused.

'The rune!' she shouted, enraged by his stupidity. 'The Rune of Blackhammer! Power!'

Trachos hesitated, only for a moment, but it was enough for a wave of ghouls to attack him. He fell, vanishing beneath the crowd of bodies.

'*Damn* you!' howled Maleneth, shaking her head violently as she fended off another blow.

Don't be a fool, said her mistress. **What do you know of engineering?**

'He hesitated!' she snapped, too far gone to care if anyone heard her addressing a ghost. 'Trachos hesitated. Because I'm right!'

She shrugged off the despair that had been threatening to overwhelm her and leapt from the back of the ghoul, landing on the shoulders of another one. Determination and hope thrilled through her veins, giving her a furious surge of energy. She bounded from one wretch to the next, moving so fast that they barely registered her footfall before she had leapt clear.

In a few seconds Maleneth left the Gravesward behind and crossed the hall, arriving next to Gotrek with a final, acrobatic leap.

The Slayer turned on his heel, axe raised, ready to behead her, his face contorted.

'Gotrek!' she said, holding out her knife in warning, squinting into the inferno that had engulfed him. 'It's me!'

Recognition flickered across his eye. He axed down a pair of ghouls without looking away from Maleneth.

'Aelf?' His voice was hoarse from shouting. He looked barely recognisable. Golden light was slicing through the pores of his skin and rippling across his mohawk. He looked like a weapon plucked from a forge.

They were a few feet from the wall, and Maleneth pointed at the pipes stretching to the ceiling. They were still shimmering with the power Trachos had triggered.

'The machines...' she said, but her words faltered as Gotrek stepped closer. The sweating, porcine oaf had vanished, and she found herself facing something quite different. He looked like an avatar of war, gilded with bloodlust and burning with power.

Gotrek dealt out a storm of brutal blows, cutting a path around Maleneth. Then he shook his head. 'It's my time, aelf.' Even his voice sounded different – deep and calm rather than harsh and boorish.

He turned to go.

'No!' cried Maleneth, leaping in front of him.

Fury burned in Gotrek's eye. 'Step aside!'

Maleneth saw one last chance. One hope of survival. She shook her head, crouching before him. It was suicide, but she gripped her knives and dropped into a battle stance.

Gotrek glowered, outraged, and swung his axe at her head.

She ducked, rolling clear, and Gotrek was thrown forwards by the force of his blow.

His greataxe smashed into the shimmering pipes.

Power rushed through him, pouring from the rune down the haft of his axe and into the machines.

Maleneth was hurled backwards, engulfed in white heat.

CHAPTER SEVENTEEN

THE LAIR OF THE GREAT WOLF

'For Dinann!' howled King Galan, standing in his stirrups and lifting his spear.

'For Dinann!' His soldiers filled the night with noise, their horses rearing and screaming, pounding their armoured hooves on the dusty road.

Nia was at his side, triumphant on her white destrier, grinning as she raised her spear. She was bold and beautiful, her auburn hair plaited down her back and her voice as ferocious as any of the men's.

The Hounds of Dinann kicked their horses into a canter, and the highway rang to the sound of metal-shod hooves.

The capital was still half a mile away, but Galan could already see soldiers rushing to man the battlements.

'These are our lands,' said Nia, her voice hoarse with anger. 'The birthright of the Dinann. The lair of the Great Wolf. How could they fail us so badly? What could have driven them to betray us?'

Galan waved his spear at their glorious host. 'Who cares? It will soon be over. This battle might be larger than the others, but it will be just as decisive. And when we are done, the kingdom will be restored and we can end our days in peace. We can be proud of our reign, Nia.'

She held his gaze, and an unspoken thought passed between them.

He leant closer. 'We might not have produced heirs, but we have rebuilt the kingdom and given our people hope. That is worth far more. We *can* be proud, Nia.'

'Your majesty,' said Lord Melvas, steering his horse towards Galan.

Nia smiled at Galan and rode away, chin raised and eyes flashing.

Melvas looked troubled, and Galan slowed his horse to speak with him. The warrior seemed unable to talk, grimacing and struggling to meet Galan's eye.

'What is it, man?' Usually, Galan would have found his general's awkwardness amusing, but not on the cusp of battle. 'Speak up.'

Melvas shook his head. 'I'm not sure...' He still looked pained. 'Now that I come to say it, it sounds absurd.'

'Pull yourself together, Melvas. I can't have you pulling faces and cowering when we're about to attack. What *is* it?'

Melvas frowned. 'This morning, when I was inspecting the rearguard, I saw the strangest thing. For a moment, I thought I saw the men eating something...'

'What are you talking about, Melvas?' snapped the king. 'Eating what?'

He grimaced. 'It looked like they were eating the men they had just killed.'

'Eating the bodies? What are you talking about? You're saying they were cannibals?'

Melvas stared at him a little longer, then laughed and shook his head. 'I know. It's absurd. Forgive me, your highness. I think I really *did* drink too much at the feast.'

Galan leant closer. 'We've been fighting too long and sleeping too little, all of us.' He slapped Melvas on the back. 'Soon you'll be back at home with your feet up, boasting about how you did all the real work.' He laughed. 'Cannibals!'

Melvas tried to smile, but his eyes remained fixed and dull.

'Galan?' called Nia from the other side of the road. 'Is there a problem?'

'Only Melvas' inability to hold his drink! I warned him this would happen!' She laughed and rode on.

Galan pulled Melvas so close their faces were almost touching. 'We are about to end this uprising. The men will be looking to you for guidance. Understand?'

Melvas nodded and sat up in his saddle. 'Of course.'

Galan loosed his arm, and the general's horse carried him back into the flow of riders. Melvas barked orders as he went, but his commands lacked their usual vigour.

Galan shook his head and rode on, frowning until he saw Nia, just ahead of him, laughing with one of the men, radiant and glorious.

'For Dinann!' he howled, grinning.

The host echoed his call.

CHAPTER EIGHTEEN

THE SPINDRIFT

Maleneth's breath exploded from her lungs as she landed, hard, on the floor. As she lay there, dazed and breathless, blinded by dazzling light, a great roaring came from somewhere and the ground started to shudder.

'Gotrek!' she gasped, her throat full of ash.

You've killed him! Finally!

Maleneth's skull was pounding where it had hit the floor, and nausea rushed through her as she stood, swaying, surrounded by coruscating light.

'Nice work, aelf,' boomed Gotrek, staggering through the glare. 'If in doubt, blow it up. Always a good plan.'

She tried to speak, to explain herself, but her breath was still trapped painfully in her lungs.

Gotrek's bludgeoning tone told her that he was himself once more. Whatever transformation had been threatening to overcome him had ceased. He was the hog again. He laughed. 'Did you *attack* me?'

'The cocoons,' she said, taking a deep, juddering breath. 'The power of the Master Rune. You sent it into the machines.'

He shook his head, looking at her as though she were insane. Then he laughed. 'By Grungni. Only an aelf could be so devious. If that's worked, I'll buy you a barrel of Bugman's.'

He hauled her across the hall, carving a path through the dazed ghouls until the light dimmed and they saw the effects of the blast.

The explosion had given the Gravesward a chance to regroup around their prince. There were more of them left than Maleneth had guessed, and they had locked their shields back together, forming a circular wall that bristled with scythes. Trachos was there too. His armour was even more damaged than the last time she had seen him, but he was still standing, staring up at the ceiling.

Maleneth followed his gaze and laughed. 'It worked!'

The pulleys and chains that held the Unburied were jolting and unfolding like spider legs, snapping and clicking as they lowered the cocoons.

'Gravesward, advance!' cried Lord Aurun, leading the knights forwards. 'Keep the mordants from the Unburied.'

As Maleneth's eyes adjusted to the light, she saw that the blast had torn through the ghouls. Her own body was unharmed, as were the Gravesward, but the aether-fire had devastated the mordants, burning flesh from their limbs and leaving most of them lying broken and smouldering.

'The aether-fire,' she muttered. 'It burned through them.'

The Gravesward crashed into the wounded revenants, avenging the brothers they had lost on the walls. The slaughter that followed was quiet but brutal. The hall rang to the sound of scythes cutting through meat and bone.

The far side of the building had almost entirely collapsed, its facade scattered across the square outside, and the giant ghoul was towering over the rubble, shielding its eyes from the blaze.

'Get the corpse eggs,' shouted Gotrek, running across the hall. 'I'll deal with Tiny.'

Maleneth whirled around and sprinted back towards Trachos. His neck armour was damaged and something was happening to the burnished sigmarite –it was pulsing with inner light, as though there were flames moving beneath its surface.

Lhosia was beside him, staring up at the unfurling machines with a rapt expression on her face. 'It's a miracle,' she whispered, looking from the ceiling to Trachos.

'It's engineering.' There was no pain in his voice. If anything, Maleneth thought, his tone seemed lighter than usual. He sounded almost pleased.

Prince Volant rode over to them, his enormous steed moving in a swaying, drunken gait similar to the wretches that had wounded it. The prince stared over the heads of his men, to the doors at the far side of the hall, where Gotrek was running towards the giant.

'What is he?' It was hard to tell if Volant was impressed or disgusted.

'Demented,' snapped Maleneth. 'Anyway, *I* was the one who had the idea to–'

'Look!' cried Lhosia.

The columns had reached the floor of the chamber, and at the base of each was a cocoon, lying safely on the debris-strewn floor.

'Quickly!' Prince Volant waved his honour guard towards them. 'Gather up the Unburied. That was only a fraction of the mordants. More could arrive at any moment.'

Rune-light was still shimmering through the columns, and the knights became silhouettes as they lifted the cocoons from their cradles.

Another shudder rocked through the hall, causing them all to stagger.

Maleneth wondered if the whole place was coming down, then realised that the noise had come from outside. The giant ghoul had fallen backwards across the square and toppled into the buildings opposite, smashing walls and sending up clouds of dust. The Slayer was just visible, like a dazzling ember on its chest, roaring as he hacked repeatedly with his axe.

Prince Volant shook his head as his men brought the cocoons towards him. 'Leave the hall. Make for the East Gate. We'll see if that wynd is still clear.'

'No!' said Lhosia. 'They'll be on us before we get half a mile.' She waved at the cocoons. 'Think how slow we'll be carrying those.'

'What do you suggest?' snapped Volant. 'Waiting in here for the next attack? We will be–'

He had to pause as, outside in the square, the giant fell through another building, rune-light flashing across its skull as Gotrek attacked its face.

'Use that,' said Trachos, nodding to the back of the hall, towards a looming, shell-like curve that reached almost as high as the ceiling.

Maleneth shook her head. 'What?'

'The aether-ship,' replied Trachos.

'The *Spindrift*?' said Lhosia. 'Do you think you could revive it the same way as the other machines?'

Trachos shrugged. 'Why not? Duardin engineering is built to last. It's probably just inert.'

Prince Volant shook his head. 'The forefathers used obscure techniques – the rune-science of the Kharadron.'

Trachos nodded. 'They used aether-gold.' He peered at the vessel. 'Is it likely to have been plundered?'

Lhosia looked appalled by the suggestion, and Volant shook his head. 'We revere the past. Our relics are sacred to us.'

Trachos nodded and limped off to the back of the hall.

Maleneth rushed after him. He had taken out his sceptre and clicked a new device to its head. It looked like a square goblet, formed of wire mesh and studded with gems.

The aether-ship was in the one part of the hall not illuminated by the light of the Unburied –a gloomy, barrel-vaulted recess like the undercroft of a cathedral. The half-visible leviathan loomed from the shadows like a promontory on a stretch of coast.

The mesh at the end of Trachos' sceptre blazed into life, spilling fingers of cool blue light.

'Khaine,' whispered Maleneth as the light washed over the prow. The figurehead was in the shape of a fierce, howling face, with a long, stylised beard and a thunderous brow. The face was as large as a house, and as Trachos' light glinted across the tarnished metal, it seemed to glower and snarl.

'It looks like him,' said Maleneth.

Trachos glanced back at her. 'Who?'

'The hog. Gotrek.'

Trachos nodded. 'Whatever he is now, he was a duardin once. The shipwrights who made this were too.'

He strode over to the hull and climbed onto an iron ladder that led up between the gun ports. A thunderclap of moths exploded from the darkness, thousands of them, alighting from every corner of the ship.

Maleneth shielded her face, and Trachos had to pause until the tumult ceased, then continued climbing. Maleneth wondered at the size of the vessel. She guessed it was fifty feet tall from rudder to gunwale, and she could just make out an armour-plated dome rising from the deck. It looked more like an impregnable fortress than a ship.

The moths had disturbed centuries of dust, and as she stepped onto the deck, Maleneth felt as though she had walked into a sandstorm. She coughed and cursed as she looked around. The vessel was unlike any ship she had ever seen. The deck was built in the shape of an enormous cross. It was actually four decks, arranged like the spokes of a wheel and linked by a circular walkway. The whole thing was like an enormous cog.

With the dust still whirling around her, she stumbled after the hazy silhouette of the Stormcast Eternal. He reached the dome at the intersection of the four decks, the hub of the 'wheel', and dropped to one knee, taking another device from his belt. There was a whirr and a click, and just as Maleneth reached him, a circular hatch opened in the deck. It slid aside with a mechanised rattle, and pulses of light shimmered under Trachos, flickering over the ruined plates of his armour.

Without a word, he turned around and climbed down into the darkness. Maleneth hurried after him.

Trachos' light flashed over a tangled forest of pipes and cogs. The belly of the ship was crammed with machinery, and as it flickered into view, Maleneth was surprised to see how well preserved it was.

'No rust,' she said, touching a row of pistons, tracing her finger over the carefully worked metal. Every inch was engraved with runes.

Trachos' faceplate looked almost as fierce as the ship's figurehead. The usual impassive gaze of his Stormcast Eternal helmet was rent beyond recognition, and with the light of his sceptre washing over the buckled metal he seemed to leer at her. He turned back to the machines and began working at them.

The light grew brighter, shimmering across cables and turbines, just as it had on the machines outside, then flickered and died.

Trachos took out the pair of callipers he had used at the gatehouse, measuring and twisting the mechanisms. He worked calmly at first, but after a few minutes he grew agitated, muttering curses under his breath.

He clanged the callipers against the pipes and strode across the engine room, examining cables and wiring and tapping gauges.

'It should be working!' He wrenched a circular hatch open and prodded the workings inside the case. 'The aether-gold *is* still here. There's no reason for the engines not to fire.'

He halted, spotting something in the forest of pipes and levers. 'Of course!' He grabbed it. 'The conduits have split. There's no pressure.'

Maleneth stepped closer and saw the two lengths of cable he was holding. Unlike everything else, they had perished and crumbled.

'Aether-gold is corrosive.' Trachos dropped the pipes and wiped his gauntlets on his armour. 'The Kharadron probably replace these conduits regularly to keep them working.'

'So we can't fire up the engines?'

'We'd need some way to channel the aether-gold.' Trachos stared up at the hatch. 'It's not so different from the machines that were holding the Unburied.'

'So we could use Gotrek's rune again?'

'Perhaps. If he's happy to come down here and let the aether-power blast through him. If he doesn't mind being used as an engine part.'

Maleneth raised an eyebrow. 'Ah...'

They stood in silence for a moment, then heard footfalls up on the deck and clambered back up the ladder, weapons readied.

It was Gotrek. He was trembling with battle fury and staring wildly.

Rune-light rippled over his skin and his beard, spilling through the gloom. The knights of the Gravesward were behind him, carrying the cocoons onto the deck under the watchful eye of Prince Volant. Lhosia was there too, standing with the prince, and the pair were locked in a whispered debate.

'Did you kill it?' asked Maleneth as she rushed towards Gotrek.

'What?'

'The giant ghoul.'

He shrugged. 'He won't be breaking any more doors, let's put it that way. Unless someone puts his ugly head on a battering ram.'

'What do you intend to do?' asked Prince Volant, looming over Gotrek. 'You swore to preserve the Unburied, and we are running out of time.'

Gotrek looked at Trachos.

'The engines are intact,' said Trachos. 'And there's plenty of aether-gold on board. We just need a conduit – a way to channel the power. A powerful piece of ur-gold would do it.'

Gotrek nodded, then realisation dawned in his eye. 'Me? You want to use me as an engine part?'

'Your rune is powerful enough to channel the aether-gold.' Trachos' voice remained dull and flat. 'Nothing else could handle it.'

Gotrek tapped the rune. 'And what would be left of me when the journey was over? How much would be Gotrek and how much would be Grimnir?'

His beard bristled, and he looked so furious that Maleneth backed away, readying herself to dodge his axe.

'Grungni's teeth,' he snarled, scowling at the rune. It was still rippling with energy. The aether-light was spreading from the rune into Gotrek's veins, pulsing across his chest and revealing the arteries beneath his scarred skin. It looked like rivulets of molten gold passing under his ribs.

'I refuse to keep doing this,' said Gotrek, not looking at Maleneth. 'I did not come all this way to give my soul to the one god who betrayed me more than any other.'

Trachos grabbed one of his massive biceps. 'There *is* another way.'

Gotrek glanced up at the Stormcast Eternal in shock. Then he glowered. 'What way is that? Trot meekly into one of Sigmar's sparkly towers and prostrate myself before his greatness? Oh, Hammer Lord, let me comb your mighty beard! That sort of thing?'

'There's no need to worship him. Your soul is your own. Your faith is your own. The Order of Azyr only needs the power you wield.'

'And how exactly would you get it out of me? Last time I checked, my ribs weren't hinged.'

Trachos seemed oblivious to Gotrek's rage. 'The power isn't just in you. It's *part* of you. If you harnessed it in Sigmar's name we could–'

'In Sigmar's name?' Gotrek's face flushed with anger and the rune pulsed brighter. He slammed against Trachos, about to yell something else, when they were interrupted by the sound of fighting back in the hall.

'Mordants!' cried several Gravesward as they ran towards the ship, struggling under the weight of the last few cocoons. 'Hundreds of them.'

Volant cursed. He knelt down so that he was facing the Slayer. His tone was an awkward mix of outrage and desperation. 'I *could* send you to Nagash, Gotrek, son of Gurni, but only if you get my ancestors to the Lingering Keep. And only if we leave *right* now.'

A growl rumbled up from Gotrek's chest and he gripped his mohawk, wrenching his hair back and forth as though trying to rip it out. He stared at the shapes rushing through the shadows towards the ship, muttering angrily under his breath. Then he nodded, spat on the deck and climbed down the hatch, waving for Trachos to follow him.

Maleneth shook her head. 'I never dreamed he'd do it.' She looked at the cocoons. 'I suggest you tie those things down.'

CHAPTER NINETEEN

THE EVENTIDE

I refuse to be sick, thought Maleneth as the world turned around her. Even over the roar of the engines, she could hear people groaning and vomiting across the deck. She had lashed herself to the railings, but the ship was shaking so violently that she was covered in bruises.

'God of Murder,' she groaned. 'How long will this take?'

'Hours at most!' cried Lord Aurun from a few feet away. He looked exhilarated. 'Look how fast the *Spindrift* is!'

She shook her head and looked out at the sea. The waves were shimmering, illuminated by the ship's blue-green light. It gave them the illusion of movement, and seen in such snatched glimpses, it could almost have been a natural sea. Rather than crashing through the breakers, though, the aether-ship was lurching drunkenly over them, gliding a few feet above the pitted surface, hurled by the arcane science of its Kharadron-wrought engines. Light knifed through the seams in its iron hull, splitting Morbium's endless dark.

Every now and then she heard Gotrek cry out, his voice rising up from beneath her like the howl of a wounded leviathan. Trachos was down in the engine room with him, battling to harness the aether-gold Gotrek was channelling, but Maleneth was glad to be nowhere near them. There were alternating bouts of anger, confusion and excitement in the Slayer's voice. He sounded even more unstable than usual. Even though he was hidden from her, his presence was unmissable –beams of golden light were shining up through the deck plating. It looked like the ship had a piece of the sun stowed in its bilges.

At the end of another deck she could see Prince Volant, standing unaided at the wheel, legs apart as he struggled to keep his footing. Lhosia was at his side, tied to the gunwale and cradling one of the Unburied. She was crying out instructions to the prince, and he responded by wrenching the levers and handles that surrounded the huge brass wheel.

'What did I do to deserve this?' muttered Maleneth.

Murder the one person who ever cared for you?

Despite her nausea, Maleneth laughed. '*Cared* for me? Cared for my blood, you mean. And only in the way a cat cares for a mouse.'

You never understood me, Witchblade.

'I understood you as well as I needed.'

And look where it got you.

'It's got me within reach of that rune. And once I have it, no one in Azyrheim will say a word against me. I'll be the hero of the Order. The hero of the age! Sigmar himself will want to meet me.'

You're no closer to getting your hands on that thing. I've told you the key, but you're too ignorant to listen.

'The key? What key? And why would I listen to you? What possible reason could you have to help me?'

Anger crept into her mistress' voice. *Khaine. You're as dim-witted as the Slayer. What do you think will happen to me if you die down here?*

Maleneth rarely heard anything other than derision from the blood amulet. There was something intriguing about this new, furious tone. She started to pay attention. 'You're already dead. What does it matter to you if I live or die?'

Whatever this is, it is not death, Witchblade. Do you think this is just your subconscious speaking to you? Do you think I'm merely a fragment of your mind?

Maleneth shrugged. 'The thought had occurred.'

Her mistress' anger grew as she was forced to speak so plainly. *Idiot girl. You have captured a facet of my soul. While you live I retain a portion of life. A wretched morsel, admittedly, and attached to your disastrous existence, but it is all I have.*

Maleneth cradled the amulet in her hand, studying the dark liquid at its heart, smiling. 'Yes, the most suitable torment I could think of. Letting a piece of you live on, powerless, watching me ascend to the heights you dreamed of.'

Play your facile games, Witchblade, but if you do not steal that rune from the Slayer, neither of us will leave Shyish.

'Then cease your prattling and stop talking in riddles. If you really want to help me, if you really do have an idea, share it.' She took the blood vial from the amulet and dangled it over the rolling deck. 'If my games are so facile, perhaps I will abandon them? Perhaps I will rob you of your chance to watch my ascension?'

Put that back! I will tell you what I saw.

'You will.' Maleneth smiled, rolling the vial between her fingers, revelling in the power she held over her former betrayer. 'And you will do it quickly.'

Khaine curse you. I will make you pay. I will–

'You will dribble across this deck and be forgotten. Unless you speak up quickly.'

Very well! I will speak so plainly even you might understand. Do you remember watching the priestess commune with her ancestor?

Maleneth nodded.

What did she say?

Maleneth laughed. 'She warned us to keep away because she would be so "fragile".'

Exactly – her body grew brittle and she warned you not to touch her. And the padlock she wears around her neck. Can you remember what happened to that?

'Nothing. *Nothing* happened to it.'

Precisely. Her flesh was transformed. She grew brittle and weak, but her necklace was unchanged. What if the Slayer were transformed in such a way? He would be so brittle and weak he could be smashed like porcelain.

Maleneth slumped back against the gunwale, her pulse racing. 'Of course. And the rune would be left intact.'

It's ur-gold. Tempered by that duardin rune master back in Aqshy. And Gotrek's not truly a Fyreslayer. He has no interest in their god. That rune does not belong in his body. If you destroyed his flesh, the Rune of Black-hammer would be left in the broken shards.

'And how would we move this ship if Gotrek was dead?'

Think! You only need the rune to channel the ship's power. You don't need the oaf.

Maleneth shook her head, still dubious. '*Why* are you helping me?'

You're all I have, you fool. If I don't help you, you will die down here and I will be... I will be nothing.

There was genuine emotion in the voice. Maleneth could not believe her mistress was telling the absolute truth, but perhaps it was part of the truth. And the idea was a good one. She laughed. 'And how do you suggest I convince Gotrek Gurnisson to worship moths and hug corpses?'

Even in a mind as barren as yours, some of my training must have taken root. Think. I have given you the key. Find a way to use it.

Maleneth shook her head. 'He would never–'

She gasped. 'Khaine.' All across the deck, Gotrek's rune-light blazed brighter, dazzling her again.

'Valaya's teeth!' howled the Slayer. It sounded like he was in pain.

Maleneth was blinded for several unpleasant minutes. She tried crawling into a foetal position to ease the nausea, but that made her feel like she was one of the cadavers in the cocoons. She tried standing to see if that was any better, just as Gotrek let out another howl.

A few seconds later, Maleneth breathed a sigh of relief. The aether-ship was slowing down. The spinning motion of the decks grew slower and slower until, with a final, metallic screech of gears, the whole thing ground to a halt.

After all the noise and movement that had preceded it, the quiet was eerie. Everyone on the deck glanced around in confusion.

Maleneth stood on trembling legs and looked out across the waves. There was nothing but the peaks and troughs of the Eventide. 'Lord Aurun?' she called out. 'What is this? Why have we stopped?'

The knight shook his head, frowning as he looked up towards Lhosia and Prince Volant.

The prince strode across the deck and stamped on the hatch to the engine room. 'Slayer! What happened?'

There was no answer.

Maleneth muttered a curse and untied herself, then staggered across to the hatch. 'Let me speak to him,' she said, opening it and climbing down the ladder.

The engines were still sparking with rune-light, and she spied Trachos way down in the bilges, at the bottom of a second ladder. She continued down and rushed over to him. The air was hazy with bitter-smelling smoke, and it took her a moment to spot Gotrek, sprawled against the engines. His muscle-bloated frame was shimmering with energy. He looked like a star chart, covered in lines and intersections, all centred on the rune.

'Grimnir's taking me,' he grunted. 'And I'll not stand for it!' Dozens of cables dangled from his chest where Trachos had attached him to the ship's engines. 'I'm not a bloody fuel pipe!'

Trachos shook his head. 'The Master Rune is the only way to channel the aether-gold. And without aether-gold we have no way to move this ship.'

Prince Volant had climbed down after Maleneth. He leant through the acrid fumes. 'You swore an oath. Are you breaking your word?'

Gotrek struggled to his feet and glared up at Volant. 'I'm no oathbreaker. I'll get your moth eggs home.' He looked down at the rune. 'But there has to be a better way.'

He jostled the cables and scowled at Trachos. 'This rune is a vampire, manling. Think of something else.' Rune-fire flashed across his beard as he talked. 'Another hour of this and there'll be nothing left of me.'

Trachos rattled the broken cables. 'These are ruined. We need your rune.'

Now. Now's your chance!

The voice spoke with such vehemence that Maleneth half expected the others to hear it.

She looked from the raging Slayer to Trachos and then to Lhosia, who was halfway down the ladder, watching the exchange. She thought hard about what her mistress had said. If she could convince the Slayer to commune with the corpses, he would be vulnerable, and the rune would be within her grasp.

'Is there a way...?' she began, her voice faltering, unsure what she was going to say.

Everyone turned to stare at her.

She looked up at Lhosia. 'Did you say the Unburied power your fortresses?'

Lhosia nodded.

'I wonder...' She shrugged, ready to be ridiculed. 'Could they help us use Gotrek's rune in some *other* way? If your ancestors could see it – if they could understand its nature – could they release its power without causing Gotrek to be changed like this? If they could channel the power from the rune, it could still work as a conduit for the aether-gold.'

Volant shook his head, but Lhosia peered at Gotrek with interest.

'I do not understand the nature of that rune, but the Unburied understand most things. Some were alive when the Kharadron sold us the *Spindrift*. One way or another, I'm sure they could help.' She looked back up towards the deck. 'If Gotrek were willing to join me in communion with the Unburied...'

Gotrek backed away, his eye flashing. 'Join you? You want to join me to those *things*? Not a chance.' He started to climb up the ladder, and the others followed.

'You would only need to sit with me to join the communion,' said Lhosia as she emerged onto the deck.

'No.' Gotrek was stomping around, glaring at the cocoons.

'We need to do *something*,' said Lord Aurun, staring out across the sea. 'Look.'

They all peered into the darkness.

'What is that?' asked Maleneth. With the rune-light gone, it was hard to see far across the waves. 'Is the sea moving?'

Prince Volant muttered a curse and shook his head. 'Archers!' he cried. 'Ready your bows!' He turned to the scythe-wielding knights gathered around them. 'Prepare to be boarded.'

Maleneth crossed the deck and leant out over the rail until her eyes made sense of the movement. Thousands of ghouls were rushing over the Eventide, scrambling up the dusty waves and sprinting towards the ship.

There was a rattle of armour as the knights drew scythes and raised shields while the archers rushed into position.

Try him again. Force him.

Maleneth rushed over to Gotrek, who was glowering at the approaching horde.

'Look how many there are,' she whispered, leaning close.

'I can take them.' He rolled his shoulders with a cracking sound and raised his axe.

At what cost? prompted the voice in her head.

'At what cost?' she echoed, waving a knife at the massing shadows. 'What will be left of you when the fighting is done? You'll have to call on every ounce of the rune's power.'

He glared at her, then down at the rune with even more anger.

'Think about it,' she said. 'If these Unburied know half as much as the priestess thinks they do, they may be able to find a way for you to use the rune's power without giving yourself to Grimnir. Wouldn't that answer all of your problems?'

Lhosia was standing a few feet away, watching the exchange. 'I believe they could help,' she said.

'Get this ship moving!' roared Prince Volant, striding across the deck to where his steed was waiting. 'I will hold them as long as I can.'

'You're going out there alone?' Gotrek looked impressed.

Volant nodded as he mounted the skeleton drake. 'I won't lose these souls to those animals.'

The creature spread its skinless wings and pounded them, hanging over the ship as the prince stared down at Gotrek. Volant kicked his steed into motion and rocketed off into the darkness, hurtling towards the approaching horde.

Gotrek watched him go in silence. The rage slipped from his gnarled features, and Maleneth was surprised to see how the prince's words had moved him.

He respects him, she realised. She looked at the knights waiting around the ship in stoic silence, prepared to die for their ancestors. *He likes them.*

Light flashed in the darkness as Prince Volant reached the first wave of ghouls. He scythed trails of amethyst through the night, lashing out at the teeming figures beneath him.

'Archers!' cried Lord Aurun from a few feet further up the deck. 'On my order!'

There was a clatter of arrows being nocked.

Gotrek gave Maleneth one last glare, then turned to Lhosia and nodded. 'Do it quickly. Before I change my mind.'

Stand ready. Watch for him changing. The Stormcast Eternal will try to protect him if he realises what you're doing.

Trachos was nearby, watching Gotrek and Lhosia in silence.

Maleneth was about to suggest he head below decks to examine the engines, but then she forgot all about him, entranced by the bizarre transformation taking place.

Lhosia had sunk one hand into the cocoon and begun singing. The rag-like covering started to glow, revealing twitching shapes beneath as Lhosia placed her other hand on Gotrek's rune.

As Lhosia murmured her song, Gotrek's weathered muscles started to lose their chestnut colour, turning the same ash-white as the cocoon.

'Grungni's oath,' he whispered, his skin becoming a white carapace.

'Keep still,' murmured Lhosia. 'And close your eyes.'

Maleneth had been so amazed by the transformation that she had momentarily forgotten why she had engineered the whole fiasco. She stepped closer, gripping her knives, pleased to see that Trachos was too busy staring at Gotrek to notice what she was doing.

She flinched as a dreadful shriek rang through the night.

Trachos whirled around and the Erebid soldiers staggered, lowering their weapons. Only Lhosia seemed unaffected, so far gone in her ritual that she was oblivious to the noise. Gotrek cursed, but remained still.

Now!

Maleneth ignored her mistress, looking out across the sea for the source of the horrific screech.

There was a flash of purple light, and Volant's steed hurtled beneath a looming shadow.

The shadow let out another scream, even louder than the first.

Pain seared through Maleneth's skull. It was like knives jamming into her head.

Aurun ordered to his men to loose their arrows, but the archers were reeling in pain and their shots hit nothing but air.

Gotrek growled, tormented by the sound but unable to cover his ears. As he snarled, the rune in his chest pulsed back into life, scattering glimmers of light between Lhosia's fingers and sparking in his eye.

'What's happening?' gasped Maleneth as rune-light flashed through Lhosia's robes, down her arm and into the cocoon.

The figure within flashed like kindling and Lhosia gasped.

The anger faded from Gotrek's eye as he stared down the deck. 'I see them,' he muttered, sounding dazed.

Now!

Maleneth ignored the voice in her head. She had followed Gotrek's gaze and seen something incredible. Across the ship, every one of the cocoons was lighting up, mirroring the one in Lhosia's arms and burning with rune-light. The light rippled across the metal deck and shimmered down the pipes that ran under the gunwales.

Something juddered beneath Maleneth's feet, then settled into a steady rumble.

'The aether-gold,' said Trachos, hurrying back to the hatch and vanishing below decks.

Maleneth gasped in agony as the screech sliced into her head again.

Prince Volant was directly overhead, thirty feet or so above the ship's dome, locked in battle with a grotesque mockery of his own steed – an undead horror, its wings trailing shreds of dead skin and its jaws ripped back in a fixed snarl. This was the source of the dreadful shrieking. The creatures clawed and snapped as Volant lashed out with his scythe.

Out on the Eventide, the ghouls were slipping and tumbling across the waves, and some had reached the *Spindrift*. The ship was drifting so low that the creatures were able to bound up its hull and clamber over the railings.

The Gravesward raised their shields as slavering wretches slammed into them.

Aurun leapt into the fray, howling orders. Scythes flashed, scattering limbs and sending ghouls toppling from the ship.

'It's moving!' cried Maleneth, dodging a headless mordant as it slapped onto the deck. She looked around in wonder as the Unburied burned brighter and the ship screeched into motion, turning around its central dome.

Prince Volant crowed in triumph, bathed in arcane light as he beheaded the screaming monster. It thrashed its vast, bat-like wings, then flipped backwards, crashing into the crowds of ghouls.

The prince swooped across the deck. 'Lash yourselves to the ship! Tie yourselves down!'

As the *Spindrift* picked up speed, lots of the monsters fell back onto the waves below, but some were still loose on the deck.

While the soldiers obeyed the prince and began tying themselves to masts and gunwales, Lord Aurun strode across the decks, hacking furiously at the ghouls and hurling them over the railings.

Maleneth dashed to his side, opening the throat of a mordant that was about to pounce on him from behind. Aurun turned in time to see her rip the blade out and kick the gasping creature over the railings. He nodded in thanks before striding past her to return the favour, slicing his scythe through a ghoul that was about to leap on Maleneth.

They weaved across the deck, protecting the Erebid as the ship gained speed, juddering and rolling so violently that Maleneth felt as though she were drunk, reeling and staggering as she fought.

'Bravely done, aelf,' gasped Lord Aurun as he stumbled past her, making for the dome. 'Now tie yourself to something!'

She fell backwards, the motion of the aether-ship wrong-footing her, sending her plummeting through the air towards the Eventide.

A hand locked around her wrist, jolting her arm painfully in its socket as someone hauled her back onto the deck, lashing her quickly to the ship before it lurched again.

'You're making a habit of this,' she gasped when she realised who her saviour was.

Trachos nodded as he checked the ropes he had used to secure her. 'I'll take that as a thank you.'

His turn of phrase was so natural she laughed in surprise. 'Was that a *joke?*'

He made a sound that might have been a laugh.

'What happened to you?' She tried to peer through the eyeholes in his helmet. Hearing Trachos speak so normally seemed even more miraculous than the power ripping through Gotrek and Lhosia.

When he had finished checking his knots, Trachos sat back against the railings, shaking his head. 'Your plan is working. The Unburied are somehow directing the rune-fire down into the engines. Aether-gold is flowing freely through the engine.'

Maleneth shook her head in disbelief. The last thing she had expected was that her absurd plan would work. She gripped the railings as the decks turned faster around the dome.

Trachos looked over to where the bone-white Slayer was still sitting with the priestess, surrounded by a nimbus of aetheric currents. Unlike everyone else on board, they were calm, not tied down in any way, fixed to the spot by the energy burning through them, linking their brittle shells to the cocoons lying around the ship.

'He...' said Trachos, shaking his head as if unable to complete his thought.

'Gotrek?' Maleneth frowned. '*He* what?'

Trachos sounded confused. 'I was forged in the light of Sigendil, by the will of the God-King. Sorcery has no power over me. And yet I feel the Slayer has changed me in some way.'

'*Something* has changed. You sound almost intelligible.'

'The Slayer had faith in me,' he muttered. 'When I did not.'

Maleneth laughed in disbelief. 'I have never understood humans, Stormcast Eternals even less so. You sound like those dispossessed duardin who wanted to pray to him.'

'I raised the gatehouse,' Trachos replied gruffly. 'I freed those cocoons, when the Erebid thought it was impossible. I made this vessel move.' He looked up at the spinning stars. 'I felt Sigmar's power working through me again, as surely as I did when I was first forged in Azyr.'

Maleneth leant closer to him, lowering her voice. 'So?'

He laughed. The sound did not seem at home, coming from his battle-scored faceplate. 'I think, perhaps, I am starting to make peace with my god. And it would not have happened without the Slayer.' He looked back at Gotrek. 'What *is* he, Witchblade?'

Maleneth was about to mock his reverent tone, but as she glanced at

Gotrek, hurling the *Spindrift* through the dark, haloed by the souls of the Unburied, the words snagged in her throat.

CHAPTER TWENTY

THE LINGERING KEEP

Maleneth was shocked to realise that she had fallen asleep. The motion of the *Spindrift* had settled into a steady, loping rhythm, and she had gone untold days without rest, but she still cursed as she woke, grabbing her knives and glancing around for attackers.

Trachos was at her side, his massive, battered armour shielding her from the wind. Beyond the ship the darkness was absolute, but Gotrek and Lhosia were still engulfed in a dazzling corona, scattering splashes of purple and gold over the Eventide.

The grinding of the engines was unchanged, but there was a new sound rising, an oceanic roar that Maleneth guessed was the reason she had awoken.

'What is that?' she asked, but as the decks completed another rotation, her question was answered. Up ahead, just a few miles away from the prow of the *Spindrift*, was a colossal fortress. It was the largest structure she had seen since arriving in Shyish, and it was built in the same style as the Barren Points – a tangled briar of iron and bone, curving and bur-like with looping, knotted towers. It burned purple on the horizon, like a sinking violet sun.

'The capital,' replied Trachos. His voice had regained some of the automaton-like coldness. 'They call it the Lingering Keep.'

'That noise.' She frowned. 'Is that cheering?'

He nodded and pointed past the prow.

A few hundred feet ahead of the ship, Prince Volant was flying through the flashing lights, leading his honour guard of mounted knights. His scythe was held victoriously over his head, and the crowds on the city walls had raised their voices in tribute.

'You'd think he'd won a war,' she sneered. 'Rather than organising a hasty retreat.'

'He has returned to them. Perhaps they did not expect him to.' Trachos pointed at the cocoons on the deck. 'And he has returned with these.'

They both fell quiet as they watched the city rushing towards them, taking a moment to study the strangeness of the place. As its sharp, thorny details grew clearer, Maleneth realised just how vast it was. It was almost on the scale of the free cities built by her own order. There was a curved, tusk-like tower right at its centre, many hundreds of feet tall, soaring over the rest of the barb-like structures, glittering with narrow arrow-slit windows. 'Prince Volant's palace, I presume,' she said, pointing it out.

'No. I heard Lord Aurun talking while you were asleep. That tower is called the Halls of Separation. That's where the Erebid need to take their ancestors.' Again, he surprised Maleneth with how normal he sounded. 'How unique those buildings are. I have never seen such strange architecture. I wonder if in all of Shyish there are two underworlds that look the same. We all have such a different idea of what lies beyond the grave.'

'There will be no grave for you.' She raised her knife in the air with a dramatic flourish. 'You live on! Stormcast Eternal! Unfettered by mortality! A light in the darkness! Burning for all eternity!'

He studied her from behind his battered faceplate. 'You're mocking me.'

Maleneth lowered her blade and shook her head. 'I *was*, but you're too damned earnest for it to be any fun.'

He maintained his stare. 'I had a normal life. I was a mortal man before Sigmar chose me to join his Stormhosts. I was destined to live, hate, love and die just like everyone else.' He looked at the approaching city. 'Who knows, perhaps this would have been *my* afterlife? I do not even recall what nation I belonged to before I became...' He tapped his armour. 'Before I was remade in Sigmar's image. But whatever fate was allotted to me has been taken. I serve the God-King. And nothing else matters.'

Maleneth shrugged. 'What more could you want? You serve your god through strength and courage. You spill blood in his name. You rid the realms of his enemies. Isn't that enough?'

'As long as I can remember whose blood to spill.' He shook his head. 'My god is not like yours, aelf. Khaine requires you to give him blood and power. He has no interest beyond that. The God-King does not seek power merely for its own sake.'

She sneered. 'You really have been reborn, haven't you? Have you forgotten what happened to you last time you were in Shyish? Are you so sure Sigmar's creations are as perfect and divine as all that? Are you really so different from me?' She leant closer. 'Why did Sigmar send hammer-wielding killers into the realms? Was it to broker peace? Was it to negotiate a truce? No. He sent you to wreak murder and ruin. Your god is no different from mine. Every time you crush another skull, Sigmar smiles, Lord Ordinator. Every drop of blood is a tribute.'

'You're wrong. Sigmar sent his Stormhosts to free mankind from the yoke of its oppressors. To save it from tyranny.'

'And what about when you were killing those unarmed families, Trachos? Were you freeing them from tyranny?' Maleneth's voice was full of scorn, but she realised, to her surprise, that she was genuinely interested to hear his answer.

Trachos nodded. 'I *have* strayed close to the precipice. But now I see that there is hope, even with this tiny ember of humanity I have left, I can–'

The cheers suddenly grew in fervour, drowning Trachos out, and she saw that they had nearly reached the city walls.

'What?' she said, wanting to hear what Trachos had to say, but it seemed he could not hear her over the din.

They both stood up and watched over the railings as the rotations of the *Spindrift* began to slow.

The light around Gotrek and the priestess faded, giving the pair a less divine appearance.

Your chance is almost gone, said Maleneth's former mistress. *In a few more minutes he will be flesh and blood again. You'll have to move now if you want to get that rune.*

He's surrounded by soldiers, Maleneth thought. *And he's in the process of saving all of our lives. Do you really expect me to plant a knife in him now?*

She untied herself and climbed stiffly to her feet, slapping her cramped limbs and stretching her back until the *Spindrift* was steady enough for her to cross the deck and approach the Slayer.

Trachos clanked after her.

You'll have no chance with the Stormcast Eternal watching. Get him away. Trick him into going below decks.

Maleneth ignored the voice, staring at Gotrek. His eyes were closed and, like Lhosia, he was sitting completely still. His skin was still pale and shell-like, and he looked more like a statue than a living being. Robbed of his erratic, surly manner and bombastic voice, he seemed an entirely different proposition. Traces of light still played around him, and she could almost imagine that the people of Morbium were cheering for him rather than their prince. They certainly would be if they knew what he had done.

Something is happening here, she thought. *Something is happening with this Slayer. He is not like anything I have encountered before.*

Fool. Stop being pathetic! Look! His skin is almost normal again. Do it now.

It's more than just the rune, she decided. *He is destined for something. Whatever he thinks of gods, I think one of them has sent him here. He must have some kind of divine patron. How else could he have faced everything he has faced, with so little planning or logic, and still be alive? He's brutish and thoughtless and has no ounce of finesse, but nothing touches him. How can that be? Something is* propelling *him through these trials, directing him and loading him with power. And if I killed him here, now, I would never know what it was – or what Gotrek is. What he's here for.*

Blood of Khaine! What are you talking about? He's not propelled by a god – he's propelled by stupidity. There's no divinity in that sweating lump. Look at him! You said it yourself – he's a talking hog, too ignorant to recognise the danger he keeps throwing himself in. The only thing he's here for is to destroy himself in the most vainglorious way possible. There is nothing to be gained by letting him live. Kill him now, while you have the chance. Give him the doom he wants, or you will die here. With these vile people. And so will I.

Maleneth shook her head.

Gotrek opened his eyes, blinking and confused, looking as if he had spent a night drinking. He caught sight of Maleneth and Trachos, watching him in dazed wonder.

'Grungni's balls. Why are you looking at me like that?'

Lhosia opened her eyes at the sound of his voice and gazed at the lights, fading quickly around the deck as the *Spindrift* slowed. 'It worked,' she said, glancing over the prow at the city as she lifted her hand from Gotrek's rune.

Gotrek stood, rolled his shoulders and sniffed, making a long, liquid rattling sound. 'What next, lass?' He stomped over to the railing and looked out at the prince and the walls of the Lingering Keep. 'Where do we need to take these things before your prince will consider them saved?'

Lhosia gently removed her hand from the cocoon, and across the ship, the lights began to fade. 'Incredible,' she whispered. 'I've never seen anything like it. They were *all* present. Every one of the Unburied. There were a thousand souls on this ship.'

'Priestess!' bellowed Gotrek, waving her over to the railings and nodding to the city. 'What now?'

Lord Aurun staggered towards them, flanked by Gravesward. He was covered in cuts and bruises, but his eyes were bright.

'Now the prince will perform his rite.' He gestured at the cocoons. 'With the Unburied assembled in the Lingering Keep, he will be able to save them.' He smiled at Lhosia. 'The prince told me you and he will harness the light of a magic stone. He said you will rebuild the Iron Shroud and put an end to this invasion.'

The wonder faded from Lhosia's eyes. 'Would that it were that simple, old friend. The prince has a powerful relic called the Cerement Stone. He believes that with the Unburied in the Lingering Keep, he and I will be able to channel their power into the stone and create a new ward, strong enough to protect them. We will be able to keep them safe from the mordants. It will be a *kind* of Iron Shroud, but not one that will protect the whole princedom.' She looked back the way they had come, at the vast darkness that had once been lit by the prominents. 'Nothing can be done for the rest of Morbium.'

'But if we are locked away in the capital, what will become of us?' said Aurun. 'Wouldn't we starve?'

'The prince has not shared all the details with me.' She shook her head, looking grim. 'He said nothing of our survival, only of the Unburied.'

Aurun frowned as the ship's momentum carried them over the final approach to the city and the ship rumbled to a halt. It bumped to a stop alongside a broad wynd that led to a set of enormous gates forged to resemble folded wings, mirroring the shield designs of the Gravesward. The highway teemed with refugees, hundreds of exhausted-looking people hauling carts and sacks towards the city. Many of them were wounded, and they all looked emaciated, but they were cheering Prince Volant with even more gusto than the soldiers on the battlements.

The soldiers on the boat leapt to action, hurling ropes to the wynd, where gaunt-faced refugees grabbed them and tied the aether-ship to the metal road.

Lord Aurun led the way down a gangplank, proud and victorious, waving to people like a monarch as the rest of the ship's passengers trailed after him.

Gotrek was right beside Aurun, looking eagerly up at the city gates as Maleneth and Trachos hurried after him.

The Gravesward formed an avenue of shields for them to march down, and as Prince Volant soared overhead, over the city walls, Aurun and the others marched through the gates, entering a square crowded with hundreds more refugees and soldiers.

The noise was incredible. The people saw the cocoons and cheered even louder, crying, 'Morbium Eternal!'

Prince Volant landed in the centre of the square, his bone steed clattering against the flagstones. He dropped from his saddle, attempting to look triumphant but unable to completely hide the fact that he was injured. He moved in awkward, sudden lurches, but waved his men away when they rushed to help.

'I have kept the oath of the Morn-Princes!' he cried, looming over the crowd. 'I will never abandon our past!' He waved his scythe at the cocoons, which were being carried into the square. 'We *will* endure!'

The crowd hurled his words back at him.

'Incredible,' whispered Maleneth to Gotrek. 'They've lost their entire kingdom and now they're cheering a half-dead prince.'

Gotrek glared at her. 'They kept their oath. That means nothing to an aelf, but it means a lot to them. I thought these realms were peopled solely by treacherous thagi and cack-handed morons. But these people are prepared to risk everything for the honour of their ancestors.' He took a deep breath, threw back his shoulders and punched his chest. 'It does me good, aelf. It does me good to see this. Perhaps not *all* of the old ways have been forgotten.'

They joined the crowd around Prince Volant as he continued his speech, describing the battles he had fought to save the Unburied as more and more people crushed into the square.

'They look worse than their pet corpses,' muttered Maleneth. 'And what do they think will happen when the ghouls get here?'

Gotrek was about to answer when a loud clattering sound announced the approach of more soldiers. A column of Gravesward entered the square, riding beneath an arch and heading straight for the prince. They were mounted on wingless versions of the prince's skeleton steed, and their armour showed no signs of battle, shimmering with a dull lustre in the light that spilled through the streets. There was a carriage at the head of the column that looked like a mobile ossuary – an elaborate construction of sharpened bones led by four bleached, fleshless horses. As the carriage reached Volant, a knight climbed down. He wore a wreath of iron rose petals and held himself with the casual, languid bearing of an aristocrat.

'Your majesty!' the noble called out across the noise of the crowd. 'The Unburied prophesied your return, but it is wonderful to see you so soon.'

Prince Volant laughed. 'Soon?' He gazed out across the crowd, studying the crowded streets. 'We must talk, Captain Ridens.'

The captain nodded and gestured to a nearby building. 'The chapter house, your majesty. We will have privacy in there.'

The knights made another colonnade of shields, and they passed through the crowds and approached a tall, narrow building that looked quite different from those around it. Most of the architecture that lined the square was built of the same bone-like contortions as the rest of the city, but this building was a slab of ink-black stone and its design was simple and unadorned. The only decoration was a pair of folded white moth wings on the door.

The captain led the way inside, closely followed by Prince Volant, who had to stoop under the doorframe, High Priestess Lhosia, Gotrek, Maleneth, Trachos and finally Lord Aurun and a detachment of Gravesward. Aurun ordered some of his men to stand watch outside, then slammed the door.

The entrance was long, narrow and lined with crackling torches. It led into a wide circular chamber with a domed roof and twelve alcoves spread equally around its circumference. In each alcove was a white shield, forged in the shape of a wing and carved with small lines of text.

There was a circular stone table at the centre of the room, and Prince Volant strode across to lean over it, fists pressed to the stone and head bowed. He was breathing heavily.

'Your majesty,' said Lord Aurun, hurrying towards him. 'We must tend to your wounds. Let me send for an apothecary.'

Volant removed his black-and-white helmet and dropped it onto the table with a clang, then waved Aurun away. 'Later.' He glanced at one of the soldiers. 'Food. And water.'

The knight nodded and hurried away as Volant turned towards the captain. 'Tell me everything.'

He nodded, speaking quickly. 'The garrisons from the prominents have been deployed across the city walls, as you instructed.'

'How many?'

'Nearly four thousand, your highness.'

'How many archers?'

The captain hesitated. 'There are four thousand men in total, your majesty. Roughly two thousand Gravesward. The rest are archers, assorted foot soldiers and militia.'

Volant stared at him for a moment. He sighed and nodded. 'And the Unburied?'

'Other than those you have just brought from the Barren Points, every surviving cocoon has been taken to the Halls of Separation, as you instructed.'

Volant nodded again. 'The host that follows in our footsteps is larger than anything we anticipated. Four thousand soldiers will not suffice.'

The captain paled, but before he could reply, the prince continued.

'But neither would fifty thousand. Our only hope is to hold the walls until I and the high priestess have completed the rite. With the power of the Unburied gathered together in a single location, we can use the Cerement Stone to guarantee their future.'

The captain nodded. 'We have positioned the men exactly as you ordered, your majesty.'

'I will see for myself before I leave the walls.' Volant grimaced and pressed a hand to his side, closing his eyes. Then he noticed that the captain was looking awkwardly at him. 'Anything else?'

The captain nodded. 'Something peculiar happened at the Sariphi Docks. The relics...' He frowned, struggling to explain himself. 'The relics began moving. And making noises.'

'Relics? Which relics?'

'The aether-ships, Morn-Prince – the ironclads and frigates. They were shaking and rattling, shedding light from their hulls. Some of them moved with such force that they damaged the nearby buildings.'

Volant glanced at Gotrek and Lhosia.

Gotrek shrugged and looked at Trachos. 'Blame the manling.'

The captain had not looked at Gotrek or Trachos properly until that moment. He now stared at them in surprise.

'Your companions, your majesty. Are they the cause of the problems at the docks?'

Trachos shrugged. 'The old Kharadron devices form a network across your whole princedom. In triggering the duardin mechanisms at the Barren Points, it's possible I have also triggered engines here.'

'Triggered them?' said the captain. 'What do you mean?'

'If that's everything, I will inspect the walls,' said Volant, ignoring the captain's question and waving to the door.

'One minute.' Gotrek held up his hand, and Prince Volant halted. 'We had a deal. I saved your corpse eggs. Now it's time to keep your side of the bargain.'

'Nothing is saved yet,' replied the prince. 'The mordants will be here within hours. We need to hold these walls until the high priestess and I have performed our rite, or the Unburied will be destroyed along with everything else.'

Gotrek narrowed his eye. 'Get them to the capital. That was the deal. You owe me a god.'

'You swore to *save* them,' said Volant, speaking softly despite Gotrek's bullish tone.

Maleneth noticed that the prince spoke to the Slayer very differently to the way he addressed the captain. The impatience was gone. He was talking to Gotrek as an equal.

'You have shown bravery and skill beyond anything I would expect to see in a non-Erebid. And there is power in you that goes beyond my understanding. I thought you were insane when you spoke of challenging Nagash, but now...' Volant shrugged. 'Now I think you might just be destined for something greater than the rest of us, Gotrek Gurnisson.'

'That's as maybe,' he muttered, 'but I did not come here to fight your wars.'

Volant shook his head. 'I am not asking you to fight our wars. I would ask only this – lend me your axe and your courage one last time. Today will either rob us of thousands of years of tradition or see us victorious, preserving the dignity of our elders as the rest of Shyish falls to ruin. If you will help my knights hold the city walls, I can go with Lhosia to the Halls of Separation and make my forefathers proud, either by my triumph or by my glorious death.'

Gotrek looked at the shields mounted in the alcoves and the poems carved into them. There was a long, tense moment as he seemed to forget about his surroundings. 'I lost everything,' he said finally, his voice low. 'And now I'm stuck in this shoddy, mannish age.' He scowled at Maleneth. 'Surrounded by people who care nothing for tradition and respect.' He met the prince's eye and nodded. 'It would do me good to fight for something again. To fight alongside someone who wishes to preserve rather than change.' Gotrek nodded. 'I'll hold the wall for you, Morn-Prince.'

He stepped closer and tapped his axe on the prince's armour. 'But know this. I will also hold you to your oath. When those cocoons are safe, you send me to Nagash.' He spat on the floor. 'Or you will have something worse than ghouls to worry about.'

Prince Volant nodded. 'We have an understanding.'

CHAPTER TWENTY-ONE

THE GHOUL KING

The Morn-Prince ordered Lord Aurun to accompany Lhosia and the Unburied to the Halls of Separation, promising to join them shortly, then led Gotrek to the battlements above the city gates. As Maleneth and Trachos followed, they received shocked glances from the soldiers who lined the steps. Maleneth smiled at them, conscious of how white and hungry her grin would look in her bloodstained face. She was probably the first aelf they had ever seen. She was keen to make the right impression.

'We spied the mordants even before we saw you approaching,' said Captain Ridens as they climbed the stairs inside one of the thorn-like towers that lined the walls. 'Every survivor who reached us brought news of them, explaining that the prominents had been taken.' He grimaced, shaking his head. 'They described terrible things, all of them. But it was not until two days ago that we started to see what they were talking about.'

They reached the top of the tower and stepped out onto the curtain wall. A chill wind lashed against Maleneth, and ranks of soldiers backed away, bowing, as they made space for the prince to approach the wall.

He stared out into the darkness. 'What do you mean? I can't see any mordants out there.'

The captain nodded to some soldiers further down the wall, standing beside a catapult the size of a house. They leapt into action, lighting tapers and fastening bundles of dried wood to the weapon. There was a rattle of whirring cogs as the catapult sent an arc of fire towards the stars. It landed with an explosion of sparks, half a mile from the city, splashing light over the Eventide.

Maleneth hissed in disgust. Lit up briefly by the explosion were lines of ghouls. She had seen plenty of the creatures by this point, so it was not their crooked, hunched bodies that shocked her, nor the gore dripping from their wasted arms. It was their lack of movement. Every ghoul she had seen was frenzied, but the light had revealed lines of motionless flesh-eaters. They had gathered in ranks, like a normal, reasonable army. Seeing them like that, standing with such a vile pretence of sanity, was worse than watching them leap and claw.

'How long have they been like that?' she said as the light faded, leaving her with a disturbing after-image.

Captain Ridens looked at Prince Volant, who nodded.

'For five days.'

'They've been standing there for five days?' Maleneth laughed in disbelief. 'Doing nothing?'

The captain nodded. 'Survivors from the other prominents say this is unusual – that the mordants are not usually so well ordered.'

'Damn right,' she muttered. 'What *is* this?' she asked Gotrek. 'What are they doing?'

The Slayer shrugged. 'Looks like they're waiting for a command.'

'A command from whom? And how would they follow an order even if it came? They have no minds.'

Prince Volant replied without taking his gaze from the darkness. 'The histories talk of such behaviour. It is not unheard of. Mordants have been known to act with reason in the presence of a...' He hesitated, looking for the right word. 'A leader of some kind.'

'A leader?' Maleneth was incredulous. 'You saw them. They're like wolves fighting over a carcass. They can't recognise leadership skills. They couldn't distinguish a leader from a thigh bone.'

The prince looked past her to Trachos. The Stormcast Eternal had taken out his square-framed spyglass and was adjusting its nest of lenses, flipping clasps and turning rows of polished brass cogs. He held the device up to one of the eyeholes in his helmet.

'Can you see in the dark with that machine?' asked Volant, but Trachos did not answer. He stood in silence for several seconds, looking in different directions, until he spotted something and gave a grunt of recognition.

He handed the device to Gotrek and pointed out past the wynd that led to the gates.

Gotrek looked where Trachos was indicating and laughed. 'Well, would you look at that. *He's* impressively ugly.'

Maleneth snatched the spyglass from him and stared through the lens. By some cunning artifice of its Azyrite makers, the device was able to penetrate the pitch dark. It was not true vision but a ghostly approximation of sight. Lines of ghouls simmered into view, as if they were painted in smoke, faint, ephemeral and grotesque.

'What do you mean?' she asked. 'Who's ugly?' She flinched, forgetting that she was looking into the distance as a revolting shape filled the eyepiece. It was a monstrous, snub-faced creature, like the one Prince Volant had battled over the *Spindrift*, but this one was saddled and ridden by one of the large species of ghouls. The rider was as corpse-grey and withered as all the other mordants, but where they hunched and lurched, this one affected an attitude of regal disdain, reins held loosely in one listless hand and its chin raised in haughty indifference. Of all the flesh-eaters she had seen since reaching Shyish, this was the first one that Maleneth had found truly shocking. Its flesh had the same rotten, rag-like texture as the others, and its eyes were the same blank, oversized orbs, but unlike all the rest, this creature was dressed in scraps of armour and carried a rusty longsword on its back. As it shifted in its saddle, Maleneth realised that the ghoul was even wearing a dented circle of metal on its gleaming pate.

'It thinks it's still a man,' she said, with a mixture of amusement and unease. There was something unnerving about seeing such a debased creature assuming the air of a noble warrior.

'There are more of them,' she laughed as she spotted other riders circling the one with the crown. There were half a dozen or so, all with the same bat-like steeds and the same absurd facade of regal bearing. Some of them carried shields and pennants, as though they were proud knights, and one of them was riding side-saddle, as though it were a noblewoman heading out on a hunt with her courtiers and servants.

Prince Volant held out his hand and she handed the device up to him. 'I have not seen them behave like this before,' he said after studying the strange figures. 'What does it mean?' He looked at Captain Ridens. 'Have you seen this? Mordants behaving like nobles?'

Captain Ridens seemed unnerved every time Volant so much as glanced his way. At this question he looked distinctly panicked. 'Your majesty,' he mumbled. 'I do not understand the question.'

Volant handed Ridens the spyglass and directed him to the riders circling above the army.

Ridens paled. 'Those things were not there last time we fired the flares, Morn-Prince. They must have been following close behind you. I have heard...' He lowered the spyglass and looked up at the prince. 'The survivors all have something terrible to tell. Some spoke of a ruler of the mordants, leading them into battle as if they were rational, human soldiers.'

Maleneth frowned up at the prince. 'Did you say ghouls have been known to act with reason in the presence of a "leader"?'

Volant nodded. 'According to the histories.'

Gotrek grinned. 'Then this might be even more interesting than the last scrap. At the Barren Points they were like drunks trying to find their own feet, but if they fight like actual soldiers, in those kinds of numbers...'

'It might not matter,' said Trachos, still staring out into the darkness.

'What do you mean?' asked Maleneth.

'Lift the spyglass a little higher. Look past the ghouls.'

Volant did as Trachos suggested. 'Nothing,' he said after a moment. 'Storm clouds. Nothing else.'

Maleneth stared at Trachos with a feeling of grim realisation. 'Storm clouds?'

He nodded. 'Bone rain. Coming fast.'

CHAPTER TWENTY-TWO

SHELTER FROM THE STORM

The streets of the Lingering Keep were already chaotic before Prince Volant sounded the alert. When he ordered everyone to take cover, there was a stampede. Screams rang out through the city. People clawed at doors and dived through windows. There was a desperate battle to find shelter as thunderheads rushed through the night. There were some in the city who had seen the results of the bone rain, and fear spread like a plague, leaving people as frantic and deranged as the monsters gathering beyond the walls.

Even those who had not seen it before could tell this was no natural storm. Mountainous clouds boiled into view, flickering with amethyst and enveloping the wynds, hurtling towards the gates that had only been slammed minutes earlier as the last few arrivals scrambled into the Lingering Keep.

Maleneth sprinted through the madness, dodging mobs of panicked refugees. She had almost crossed the square when she realised Gotrek was way behind her, walking casually from the walls, his axe slung nonchalantly over his shoulder.

'Slayer!' she yelled.

Trachos was at her side, and they both stopped to wait for him.

Volant and his captain were at the centre of a crossroads, yelling orders to the soldiers and trying to marshal the crowds into some kind of order. There was such a panic that the Gravesward had to form ranks and raise shields, driving people back to avoid a crush.

'There are empty houses and temples in the eastern quarter!' shouted Volant, climbing onto his steed and launching it over the crowd. Its wings dragged clouds of dust as Volant tried to redirect the people. He waved his scythe. 'Head that way!'

The mob was too deranged to respond, so Volant spoke to the skeleton drake and it opened its jaws in a roar so loud it cut over the noise of the approaching storm.

Finally some of the people paid attention, allowing the Gravesward to shepherd them away, relieving the bottleneck at the crossroads, but new crowds surged into the square from other directions and the situation was soon even worse.

'The storm will hit in minutes,' said Trachos. He and Maleneth had stepped out of the flow of bodies, climbing up a flight of colonnaded steps that led to a set of doors. The Stormcast Eternal was looking through his spyglass at the clouds. 'These people are not going to make it.'

Gotrek shoved his way through the mob and stomped up the steps. He looked sullen. 'Nagash is scared. That's what this is all about. He's doing everything he can to stop me reaching him. He's swamping this city in skull-chewers so the Morn-Prince can't send me to him.' He glared at the carnage in the square. 'And it's not going to work.'

'I can never decide whether to be impressed or amused by you,' said Maleneth. She waved one of her knives at the scene below – thousands of desperate, fear-maddened people, clambering over each other as a cataclysmic storm gathered overhead. It looked like an apocalypse. 'Does nothing here give you pause? Is there nothing about this situation that makes you think you might *not* be destined to reach Nagash?'

Gotrek laughed. 'Bloody aelves. So quick to accept defeat. That was always your problem. Comes of being knock-kneed poetry readers.'

He looked up at Trachos. 'We need to reach these Halls of Separation everyone keeps blathering on about. That's where the prince sent the ghost eggs. We'll go there and stand watch over the doors. I'll take on every ghoul in the realms if I have to, until the priestess has finished her spell, but I'd rather guard a door than a city.'

Maleneth pointed at the tusk-shaped spire looming over the city. 'The Halls of Separation are miles away, and Trachos just told you the storm will hit in minutes. You have the legs of a pot-bellied pig. How exactly do you intend to outrun those clouds?'

Gotrek shrugged. 'The manling will work something out.'

Trachos stared at him. Then he nodded and stood a little taller.

Maleneth rolled her eyes. 'How does this lump-headed brute have such an effect on people? How has *he* made you believe in yourself again, Trachos? How can your faith have been renewed by a god-hating savage?'

Trachos ignored her, peering around at the architecture. 'This is an advanced civilisation, by the look of the buildings.' He waved at an ornate arch reaching over their heads. 'They have preserved things most realms lost in the Age of Chaos. These techniques must date back to the time before Chaos, when Sigmar still walked the realms. I see his hand in every–'

'Sigmar?' guffawed Gotrek. 'You can't lay everything at the feet of the hammer-dunce! These people have learned some half-decent engineering skills, and that can only have come from dwarfs. Or at least those pale shadows of dwarfs you call duardin.'

Screams broke out not far from where they were talking as the Graves-ward began using their scythes on the crowd, cutting people down in an attempt to save others who were being crushed by the mob. As the crowd heaved in a new direction, bone carriages splintered and toppled and flesh-less horses panicked, trampling through the mayhem, their black plumes bobbing as they tried to find a way out.

'*Minutes* away, you said,' reminded Maleneth, waving at the looming clouds. 'Perhaps now isn't the time to discuss engineering?'

Trachos was still facing Gotrek. 'If the Erebid built their city on duardin principles, how would they have dealt with sanitation?'

Gotrek shrugged. 'Latrines. Sewers.'

'Have you lost your final shreds of sanity?' muttered Maleneth.

But Gotrek was grinning. 'Sewers – of course.'

Trachos studied the facade of the building they had climbed up to. 'That ironwork looks like waste pipes.' He leant out from the steps and looked down to the corner of the building. 'We could follow that outlet and see where it leads.'

'You want to crawl through the sewers?' asked Maleneth. 'For miles?'

'Nowhere is safer than underground,' replied Gotrek. 'Besides, which would you prefer, muck or bone rain?'

Trachos led them back down the steps, muttering and glancing back at the walls of the building as he tried to follow the route of the pipes.

At the bottom of the stairs they hit the crowd. Maleneth grimaced as people crashed into her, but the bulk of a Slayer and a Stormcast Eternal was enough to smash through the crush. Trachos waved them on, heading round to the corner of the building.

As they left the main flow of people, clouds began sailing over the walls.

Some of the soldiers managed to force their way down from the battlements, but others took cover in towers and archways, looking as though they were preparing to battle the weather.

'Here,' said Trachos, hurrying down an alleyway at the side of the building. He reached a metal hatch and stamped on it with his boot, creating a loud, reverberating clang.

Gotrek grinned. 'Good work, manling!' He climbed up onto an overturned cart and looked over the heaving crowds.

'Morn-Prince!' he howled, but there was no sign of Volant.

The noise of the crowds and the growing storm drowned out even the Slayer's booming tones.

'Gotrek!' cried Trachos as he levered the hatch open and revealed a flight of stone steps leading down into the darkness. 'We have to go now.'

'Where *is* that blessed prince?' snarled Gotrek, his cheeks flushing with anger. 'He needs to order these people into the sewers or they'll all be massacred. Morn-Prince!' he bellowed, his eye sparking, but there was no reply.

Maleneth ducked past Trachos and climbed down the steps, descending into the darkness. Glimmers of white shimmered over the walls. 'It's now or never,' she said, looking back at Trachos.

'Morn-Prince!' cried Gotrek a third time. The gold sparks in his eye were mirrored by a flash from the rune in his chest, and his words tore through the city, charged with the power of the rune, ringing out with such fury that people staggered.

The sneer fell from Maleneth's face. Gotrek's cry sounded like the voice of a god.

The mayhem ceased. Everyone in the square turned to face him.

'The sewers, you imbeciles!' Gotrek's face was purple. 'Get under-ground!'

People stared at the Slayer, clearly shocked, then did as he ordered, sprinting for drain hatches and sewers.

A few seconds later a bright rattling sound filled the city as the downpour arrived, crashing over the walls like waves of broken teeth.

Gotrek leapt down from the cart and raced towards Maleneth and Trachos with hundreds of terrified people following him, all trying to escape the deluge.

'Go!' cried Gotrek, pounding down the steps and disappearing into the darkness. There was a loud splash as he disappeared from sight.

Maleneth grimaced at the thick stench that rushed up in his wake. 'Smells as bad as him,' she muttered, hurrying down the steps.

CHAPTER TWENTY-THREE

THE ASCENSION OF KING GALAN

'The Wolf is with us!' cried King Galan as he felt his steed changing beneath him, its bones snapping and elongating and its muscles swelling. He could feel the undeniable power of his lord as the horse became a sinewy armoured drake, with vast taloned wings and powerful reptilian jaws. The creature pounded its wings and lifted him from the road, up over sun-drenched wheat fields. On his back he could feel the weight of his ancient longsword, Rancour. He had sworn not to draw it until he had the leader of the rebels kneeling before him. The sword had been blessed by Shadow Priests on the eve of the war, impregnated with the might of the Wolf, but he would not fritter its sorcery on any old warrior – he would unleash it with great ceremony on the head of his would-be usurper, with the Hounds of Dinann witnessing his righteous fury.

Nia and Lord Melvas were with him, their steeds elevated by the same miracle as his own. Other lords of the Dinann followed quickly after, laughing in wonder as their horses' hooves became claws and their flanks sprouted wings. They left the road and began racing through the air, trailing tails through the early dawn as their riders raised spears and howled.

The same miracle had occurred at each of the previous battles, but Galan still felt his pulse racing as he looked down at his army, charging into battle below him.

'One last time!' cried Nia, grinning at him from a few feet away.

'One last time!' he laughed, gripping his spear as he rushed towards the battlements.

The traitors were so awed by the miracle of the Wolf that Galan landed on the walls to find them already abandoned. The rogues who had seized the castle were scrambling for cover, tumbling down the steps and fleeing across the courtyard.

Some of them had managed to injure themselves in their desperation to escape, and as King Galan rode down the walls, he reached a group of bloodied, terrified wretches who tried to crawl away at his approach.

'I offered you mercy at every turn,' he said, pointing his spear at one of the gibbering wrecks, who was slipping and stumbling towards him, shaking his head.

The soldier muttered and cursed, unable to meet his eye, and Galan finally understood what was happening. He could not believe he had not suspected it before. The glorious victories, miracles like the drakes, the terror in the eyes of his victims –they all pointed to one thing: he was *ascending*. The oldest of all the prophecies had come to pass – the prophecy of the Wolf Lord. This was why the Shadow Priests had imbued Rancour with such power. This must be why his later years had been so quiet and lacking in glory. The Great Wolf had been waiting for this moment to raise him up and show him the glory that had always been his due.

Nia's drake landed beside him on the wall, and she leant out from her saddle, slamming her spear into the man's chest. He staggered away, dazed, then fell as she wrenched her weapon free. 'Not much of a fight,' she said with a smile, glancing around at the few wounded soldiers left on the walls. They were all flinching and cowering, as though attacked by invisible foes.

'I'm changing, Nia,' Galan said, his voice trembling with the glory of his revelation.

She looked at him in shock. Then she clearly saw the pride and power in his face, and her smile broadened. 'As are we all, my love.'

She drove her horse on down the wall, drawing her longsword and cutting down everyone in her path as the other lords landed, looking around in wonder at the abandoned battlements.

'There is still work to do!' cried Galan, pointing his spear down into the courtyard and the streets beyond. There were hundreds of wounded and fleeing soldiers. Lots were running into buildings to hide, but many were crawling into sewers, fleeing underground like rats. 'The traitors refused every entreaty to peace. Show no mercy!'

He clicked his heels and his drake leapt from the wall, hurtling down towards the crowds. Figures scattered as he landed, not even trying to defend themselves.

'What is this?' called Nia, landing near him. 'They battled so hard to hold the outlying keeps, and now, now that we reach the capital, they have no fight in them.'

Galan sat back in his saddle, watching the slaughter. 'They know they've lost.' He looked around the castle. 'It's even bigger than I expected.'

She raised an eyebrow. 'Maybe this is a more suitable place to rule from?'

'No,' replied Galan. 'I will make an example of this city. I will leave no brick standing. I will raze it to the ground. And if anyone considers challenging my rule again, they will only need to look here to see what their fate will be.'

He pointed to a bright, gleaming needle of white stone. 'Make for the central keep. The ringleaders will be there.'

Galan turned to the lords who were landing in the courtyard behind him. 'Open the gates, assemble the men. Gather the war machines. Bring this city down.'

CHAPTER TWENTY-FOUR

SACRAMENT OF BLOOD

Trachos' light flashed over barrel-vaulted ceilings, revealing the incredible age of the sewers. The stones had been rounded and smoothed by the centuries, slumping and swelling in places, as though bloated by tumours. It looked like they were crawling through diseased innards.

The foetid river running down the tunnel was knee-deep on Maleneth, but that meant Gotrek was wading up to his thighs. The water had no chance of slowing the Slayer though. While Trachos called out directions, a brass compass in one hand and his blazing sceptre in the other, Gotrek raced through the filth, vaulting pipes and leaping over the remains of old cave-ins.

'This is more like it!' he shouted, his greataxe slung across his back as he rushed through the darkness. He slapped the wall. 'Good, solid work. I could be back in the Eight Peaks.'

Trachos looked to Maleneth for an explanation.

She shrugged. 'He shares your enthusiasm for drains. How nice.'

'The north pipe,' said Trachos, casting light down another tunnel.

Gotrek nodded, humming cheerfully to himself as he splashed off in that direction.

'How long will this take?' Maleneth asked, catching up with Trachos.

'It looks like the main sewer runs from the central tower out to the city walls. We should be able to take a more direct route than if we were above ground. We might be there in less than an hour.'

She was about to reply when the tunnels juddered. Dust and brick fell from overhead, throwing up splashes of muck and clouds of flies, and Maleneth would have fallen if Trachos hadn't grabbed her arm.

'Prince of Murder,' she said. 'What was that?'

He shook his head. 'Maybe Nagash's storms are powerful enough to shake city walls?'

'I don't think so. It didn't seem like that in Klemp. I think that's the flesh-eaters entering the city.'

He strode on through the sewer, hurrying after the disappearing shape of Gotrek. 'Ghouls? How could they shake walls?'

'Siege engines?'

Trachos shook his head. 'You've seen them. How would they have the skill to use war machines?'

'Remember that giant?' she said, racing after him. 'The thing that Gotrek fought in the Barren Points? Perhaps they have creatures like that up there?'

He glanced at her, then nodded. 'We need to move faster.'

They ran as fast as they could through the effluence, but after a few minutes there was another tremor, then another, and Maleneth found herself struggling to keep up with Gotrek.

'What if he succeeds?' she gasped, swatting flies away.

'What?'

'What if we make it to the tower and Gotrek holds back the ghouls until the prince performs his spell?'

He shrugged. 'We have to hope that Lhosia and Prince Volant are right – that her rite will protect this city.'

'They said it would protect the *Unburied*. That's not quite the same thing.'

'What option do we have?'

'None, but that's not really what I meant, anyway. If this works how Gotrek hopes it will – if the Erebid really *do* send him to Nagash – what will you do then?'

Trachos glanced at her. 'I will…' He hurried on, shaking his head. 'I will go with him.'

'Really?' She nodded to Gotrek. His broad, hulking shape was clearly picked out in Trachos' light, and they could hear him humming cheerfully to himself and laughing at jokes he was muttering under his breath. 'You'd follow *that* to the Lord of Undeath?'

'Whenever you speak of him, your voice is full of such bile.'

She laughed. 'Of course. Look at him. Who wouldn't find him ridi–'

'But…' Trachos looked at her again. 'Since the Barren Points, I hear something else in your voice too.'

'What?'

'You have seen the same thing I have seen. The Slayer is not just some wandering brigand. He's important. He *means* something. He's here for a reason. The priestess saw it too. And so does the Morn-Prince. Gotrek has more than his own doom riding on those tattooed shoulders.'

She sneered, but could not find it in herself to disagree.

'What will *you* do if he succeeds?' asked Trachos. 'If they send him to Nagash, will you just stay here?'

'I don't know!' she snapped. 'None of my options seem particularly enticing at the moment.'

She was about to change the subject when an explosion rocked through the sewer, bathing her in amethyst light.

They fell into the muck, unbalanced by a tremor even more violent than the preceding ones.

Maleneth thrashed under the water for a moment, then lurched from the filth, cursing and spitting.

Gotrek was up ahead, shrugging off rubble and looking up at an opening that had appeared in the ceiling. A column of purple light was shining down through the hole and it framed the Slayer, picking him out of the darkness.

'Trachos,' hissed Maleneth, realising that his torchlight had faded.

She whirled around, scattering flies and water. The light from overhead was enough to reveal him, trapped beneath the surface of the water, pinned in place by a huge section of pipe that had been dislodged by the blast.

'Can you breathe underwater?' she muttered, rushing back towards him, realising how little she knew about Sigmar's storm-born warriors.

She could see him straining in the murk, trying to heave the shattered masonry off his chest.

Let the dullard die, said the voice in her head. *Good riddance.*

To Maleneth's surprise, she found that she was not willing to leave Trachos behind. Something about their conversations had intrigued her. And she felt that they were unfinished. Besides, she had a feeling that Trachos might still prove to be the key to getting the rune back to Azyr.

She grabbed the fallen pipe, trying to heave it away. It was impossible – she could not shift it an inch, even with Trachos shoving from the other side. Bubbles rushed from his armour and he thrashed furiously.

'Gotrek!' she cried. The Slayer had backed away to the far side of the hole in the ceiling and there were now shapes in the column of light that separated her from him – pale, glittering shards clattering down through the hole.

'Bone rain,' she muttered.

It was hard to see Gotrek clearly through the downpour, but she could tell he was shaking his head, powerless to reach her.

She looked the other way, back down the tunnel, and saw pale purple light coming from that direction too. 'Another hole,' she muttered. 'The whole place is coming down.'

Trachos twisted violently under the water, straining and bucking against the pipe.

She grabbed it again and pulled with all her strength, but it was hopeless.

'Khaine,' she wheezed, backing away and shaking her head. As she watched Trachos drowning, an unexpected fury washed through her. If she had engineered his death, she might have seen matters differently, but the idea of him being taken against her will was infuriating. 'We *need* you,' she muttered, trying again to shift the stone.

Light flickered over the walls and flashed in her eyes. She thought for a moment that another hole had opened in the ceiling, but it was Trachos' torch, shining beneath the surface of the water and throwing rippling lights across the arched ceiling.

'Gotrek!' she shouted again, but she knew it was useless. If the Slayer passed through that curtain of rain, he would be cut apart like anyone else.

Splashes echoed down the tunnel and she turned to see a hunched, loping shape lurching into view. Even in silhouette, she could recognise the wiry, twisted frame of a ghoul.

She cursed and backed away from Trachos, whipping her knives from her belt as more ghouls rushed from the shadows, their pus-yellow eyes flashing in the light of Trachos' torch.

She could see the Stormcast Eternal watching her from underwater as his struggles grew weaker.

'What can I do?' she said, taking another step away from him as the crowd of ghouls thundered through the sewer, twitching and grunting as they splashed through the effluence. There were dozens of them, just minutes away, and even more dropping into view behind.

'Well?' she demanded. 'Any advice?'

You should have killed the Slayer. Then you wouldn't be stuck down here with your back to the bone rain and flesh-eaters about to rip your lungs open.

'Thanks,' she said. 'Very helpful.'

She looked up the tunnel again. Gotrek had gone, carrying on without them. It made sense. The Slayer had never made any pretence of friendship. If he had ever had friends they had died a long time ago. But, absurdly, she still felt an odd sense of betrayal. In the months that she had travelled with the Slayer, she had begun to feel as though their fates were somehow entwined.

'I'm a fool,' she muttered. The first of the ghouls was only a minute or two away. She could see its black, jagged teeth drooling saliva as it tried to fix its febrile gaze on her.

Give us a death to be proud of. There was none of the usual venom in her mistress' voice. She sounded unusually calm. *Show Khaine we deserve a place at his side. These things bleed. Cut prayers into them.*

A cruel smile stretched across Maleneth's face. There were far too many ghouls for her to win this fight. There was no need to play it safe. Her mistress was right – she may as well abandon herself to the glory of the kill. She could revel in the bloodshed and devote herself, body and soul, to the Lord of Murder.

'In mine hand is the power and the might,' she whispered, dropping into a battle stance. 'None may withstand me. By the Will of Khaine I will bathe in the blood of mine enemies.'

Not far from where she was standing, Trachos finally became still, but Maleneth had already forgotten him. There was nothing left in her mind but the moves of a lethal dance.

She lashed out as the first ghoul reached her, spinning on her heel in an elegant pirouette to open its throat and send it crashing into the water.

A bright umbrella of blood engulfed her, and she sighed with pleasure before sidestepping the next ghoul, hammering her knives into its back and ripping it apart with an ecstatic howl.

The kills merged into a fluid ballet of hacks and lunges. Maleneth flipped and rolled, singing to Khaine as she opened throats in his name. Her mistress howled along with every cut.

CHAPTER TWENTY-FIVE

A TEST OF FAITH

King Galan rode hard through blood-filled streets, howling orders as the city toppled around him. Ancient towers and sprawling manses were pulled to the ground, and as the traitors fled in panic, his men cut them down. It was brutal and merciless, a massacre the like of which he had never witnessed before. For a moment, he wondered if he had gone too far. Had he become the kind of tyrant he had always sworn to oppose?

Nia saw the hesitation in his eye. 'This is the only way,' she gasped, plunging her spear into another back and wrenching her drake round to face him. 'When people hear of this victory they must quake. They must be horrified and appalled by the fate of these people.'

Galan nodded. They had discussed this many times on the road to the capital. He was old. And without an heir. If people believed they could turn on the crown without fear of death, the kingdom would not survive another year. This was his last chance to show what became of anyone who tried to claim independence. And yet... As his soldiers tore down statues and performed far worse atrocities in his name, his battle lust left him. 'To the tower,' he said, pointing his spear at the building that dominated the whole city. 'Once I find the ringleader and introduce him to Rancour, in front of the whole city, our message will be clear. And then we can finally rest.'

He ducked as, in the next street, a huge temple collapsed, pulverised by one of his war engines, sending a writhing tower of dust up into the hazy summer heat. A powerful sense of purpose rushed through him. The wounded rebels were all fleeing to the tower at the centre of the city. Once he reached that building, he would ascend. He was sure of it. He would breach that central keep and butcher everyone inside, and then the Great Wolf would crown him not just king, but immortal Wolf Lord.

He glanced at Nia, grinning despite the carnage boiling all around him. And Nia would be his eternal queen. This was why they had come – not just to quell a foolish rebellion, but to reach this point and be elevated to a new life.

He grabbed Nia's arm. 'I can feel him riding with us.' He pointed his spear at the tower, and his voice trembled. 'He's in there, I know it. Today, we will walk at his side!'

She stared at him, her eyes glistening.

And they rode on, killing with more fury than ever before.

CHAPTER TWENTY-SIX

A PATH THROUGH THE DARKNESS

Maleneth lost herself to the ritual of sacred murder. She abandoned every thought of Sigmar and the Order and thought only of Khaine, moving with more speed, cruelty and elegance than she ever had before. Bodies piled up around her, scored with holy sigils and drained of blood, until finally, inevitably, the sheer volume of them began to overwhelm her. As the piles of dead collapsed towards her, she stumbled, banged against the sewer wall and fell cursing to her knees in the water.

A ghoul locked its bony hand around her neck, but she sliced through the wrist, cutting the hand free and staggering clear as the mordant lunged after her, oblivious to the blood rushing from its arm.

As Maleneth backed away, cutting down more ghouls, she trod on something hard and cold under the water.

It was Trachos' sceptre, shining through the murk.

Still fighting, she crouched and grabbed the golden rod.

The ghouls stumbled, dazzled by Azyrite sorcery. The thing was covered in runes and dials, like all of Trachos' equipment, but Maleneth did not attempt to decipher its workings – she simply used it as a club, smashing it into the face of the next ghoul to reach her and scattering beams of frigid light through its shattered skull.

The sceptre proved a useful weapon, but the memory of Trachos dulled some of her fervour. She glanced over at the fallen pipe. His turquoise armour was still visible, but he was no longer moving.

Khaine's hunger still pounded through her veins, but another thought was now vying for her attention. An idea had occurred to her. She vaulted a ghoul and splashed down near Trachos.

She jammed the sceptre into the water, forcing it under the fallen pipe. Then she stood on it, using her weight to try to lever the masonry off Trachos.

The sceptre was made of the same unyielding alloy as Trachos' armour, and it took her weight, lifting the pipe up from the water.

Maleneth balanced on it like an acrobat, ducking and swaying as she fought, then fell back as Trachos rose like a river god, swinging his hammers furiously and driving the ghouls back.

'Don't expect my help every time you fall over,' she gasped, dodging to Trachos' side and fighting with her back to his.

He laughed, but it turned into a series of hacking, liquid coughs. He managed to keep fighting, but he looked like he could barely stand.

'Gotrek?' he managed to gasp.

She shook her head.

He snarled in frustration, lashing out at the ghouls with growing strength. 'He needs you!'

'What?' In the confusion of the fighting, she wondered if she had misheard him.

'Gotrek needs you,' said Trachos. 'You're his sanity.'

She laughed. 'You dunce. I've been looking for a way to get rid of that oaf since the first day I met him.'

'Then why are you still with him?'

Maleneth thought of how she had failed to kill the Slayer on the *Spindrift*, when it would have been so easy.

Trachos pointed at the sceptre Maleneth had left sticking out from beneath the fallen pipe. 'I have an idea,' he coughed, blood spraying from his helmet. 'On the count of three.'

'On the count of three what?'

'Jump.'

They were now so completely surrounded by ghouls that she could no longer see the walls of the tunnel. 'Where?'

He started counting.

'Wait!' Maleneth cast around for a place to leap, but he ignored her, and as he reached three she jumped, landing feet first on a ghoul's shoulders and knocking it back into the others.

Trachos moved at the same moment, but rather than jumping clear, he dropped down onto the sceptre wedged beneath the pipe.

The metal held even under his weight, and it levered the remains of the pipe from the wall. Bricks and mortar smashed into the tunnel, along with a deafening torrent of water.

Maleneth fell back, knocked from her feet. She scrambled to right herself, but jumping clear had kept her from being washed away by the sudden influx of water.

Bodies and stones thudded into her, and as the water rose, she thought she might suffer the same fate she had just spared Trachos.

She tumbled backwards, coughing and cursing, then managed to leap from the stinking water and get back on her feet.

'What in the name of Khaine are you doing?' she cried as she saw Trachos a few feet away, the sceptre in one hand, a hammer in his other.

He punched his hammer into a knot of ghouls and nodded to the opening he had made.

'It will rejoin the main tunnel further up.'

Maleneth glanced at the quickly rising water. 'So will our corpses.'

She leapt past him, diving into the tunnel. She had only moved a few feet when she realised that Trachos was not with her. She twisted to look back over her shoulder.

Trachos had staggered away from her, hammering his way into the centre of the ghouls.

'Go!' he cried, glancing towards her as the ghouls boiled over him, tearing at his armour. Cracks of light appeared in his neck brace –tiny fingers of lightning that danced across his armour, scorching the air and flinging shadows across the walls.

'Now!' he yelled, a furious warning in his voice, as he hurled his sceptre towards her.

She caught the sceptre, but instead of fleeing, she scrambled back down the pipe towards him. The water was already up to her waist and the walls were juddering, filling the sewers with a worrying groaning sound.

'What are you doing?' demanded Trachos, smashing more ghouls back into the water.

She glared at him. 'It's your fault I'm down here. You're going to lead me out.'

'It's not safe to be near me,' he grunted, grabbing the neck brace of his battleplate, causing more sparks to slash through the gloom. 'I'm damaged.'

'Who isn't?' She threw his sceptre back to him. 'Lead me out.' The water was now up to her chest. '*You're* no Slayer. Doom-seeking doesn't suit you. Stop looking for a glorious death. I'll never get out of this wretched place without you to lead me. It's a damned labyrinth. Without you and your machines, I'll wander down here forever.'

He hissed a curse and used the sceptre to punch through the ghouls, pushing back towards the hole he had torn in the wall.

'Follow me!' he said as he clambered up into the pipe.

The mordants tried to rush after them, but after Maleneth had killed the first few, the way became clogged with twitching bodies. Dozens more tried to cram into the pipe, but they were so frenzied they only compounded the problem, jamming it with thrashing limbs.

'This way!' called Trachos, wading on through the water, his torchlight flickering over wet, mossy bricks.

As she hurried after him, she noticed something. 'The water's rising in here too!'

He nodded without pausing to look back. 'The whole system is flooding. Something is destroying the city.'

Water was spraying from overhead, and every now and then came a resounding boom that caused the structure to shudder as though it had been punched.

'Is this thing going to come down?'

Trachos nodded, pausing at a crossroads and pointing his sceptre down each route, shining blue light into the darkness as he tried to decide which way to go. 'Something is smashing through it.'

He took out a small, golden box and flipped back the lid to reveal whirling needles in a polished wooden frame. He stared at them until they stopped spinning and all pointed in the same direction, then snapped the box shut and waded on through the water.

They had not gone more than a few steps when there was another boom, much closer this time, and a shuddering crash as the ceiling behind them gave way, filling the tunnel with bricks and clouds of dust. When the dust cleared, Maleneth saw that the way back was completely blocked by fallen rubble.

The water was now almost as high as it had been out in the main sewer. Maleneth was waist-deep in filth.

'Don't worry,' said Trachos, carrying on. 'My aetherlabe was clear – there is an exit up here that will lead back to a larger pipe.'

He rushed on towards a rusty, circular door with an iron wheel for a handle, similar to the doors on the *Spindrift*. He grabbed the wheel and tried to turn it, but the mechanism started to crumble in his grip, shedding lumps of rusty metal.

The water was up to Maleneth's chest. She moved to Trachos' side and grabbed the wheel, lending the Stormcast Eternal all her strength.

More rusty metal came away, but there was no sign of the thing turning.

The tunnel was shaken by another booming blow, and the sound was now so loud that there was no mistaking the truth – something big was headed their way.

Trachos handed her his sceptre and took something else from his belt. It looked like a sapphire encased in silver, and as he raised it over his head, light shimmered in the heart of the stone. With his other hand, he unclasped his helmet and removed it, letting his white plaits tumble down his breastplate.

Maleneth gasped at the sight of his face. It was even more brutal than the last time she had seen it –the mass of old scars had been joined by a new kind of injury. In several places, the rough mahogany of his skin had changed, covered now by a tracery of silver capillaries that glittered and flashed as he moved. There were pulses of light blinking across his cheeks and jaw where the silver threads were most numerous.

'What's happening to you?' she said, but Trachos did not seem to hear. His eyes were closed, and he pressed the blue gemstone to his forehead.

The walls shook again. 'Whatever that is, it's close,' she muttered.

Trachos was mouthing words. He took the stone away from his face and shook his head, looking at Maleneth. 'This is the only way.' He returned the stone to his belt and turned back to the rusted door. 'There is no other route back to the main sewer.'

The water was up to Maleneth's chin by this point, and she cursed. The wheel that opened the door was now completely submerged. She ducked under the surface and tried to grab it, but her hands could not even grip it in the filthy water.

'What now?' she gasped as she stood back up.

Trachos shook his head, looking at the wall of rubble behind them. 'We could try digging.'

She laughed, stepping on some broken bricks and hauling herself a little further away from the quickly rising water.

The walls shook with so much fury that she fell. From underwater she saw Trachos stagger backwards, away from the rusty door, bathed in light and trying to shield his un-armoured face.

She leapt back up out of the water and came face to face with a demented, blood-splattered snarl.

'What are you two playing at?' yelled Gotrek, framed by the door he had just destroyed. 'I have a god to slay.'

CHAPTER TWENTY-SEVEN

THE FLESH-EATER COURT

'I'm touched that you came back for us,' said Maleneth as the Slayer dragged her through the remains of the door.

Gotrek ignored her, grimacing at the sparking silver veins shimmering across Trachos' face. 'Grungni's teeth. No wonder you wear a hat.'

Trachos looked puzzled, reaching up to touch his cheek.

Maleneth staggered on up the pipe, struggling to keep her head above water. 'Can we compare wounds later?'

For a while they were swimming more than walking, but eventually they reached another intersection and tumbled back down into the main sewer, sliding and bouncing over the rubble until they landed with a crash at the bottom of the main concourse.

The water was only about a foot deep, and they sat there for a while panting and coughing. Even the Slayer seemed tired, leaning back against a broken support strut and massaging his massive forearms.

'If you two stop dawdling we might reach that tower before the whole city comes down.' He waved his axe at the various openings that led off the main pipe. 'I hope for your sake that you know which way to go, manling.'

Trachos was studying his reflection in the surface of his helmet and muttering to himself.

'It won't get any less ugly,' said Gotrek. 'Can you get us to the tower or not?'

Trachos fixed his helmet back in place and nodded. 'You only needed to keep going straight on. I told you, the main sewer leads from the tower.'

Gotrek shrugged and climbed to his feet. 'Let's get moving then.'

'But you already knew that,' said Maleneth. 'Trachos told us the route when we first came down here.' She gave the Slayer a wry smile. 'You were still in the main tunnel. You weren't lost. You didn't *need* to come back for us. I think you missed us.'

Gotrek glared at her, then stomped off up the tunnel. 'I just wanted to make sure I didn't wander around down here till doomsday.'

Maleneth winced as she stood and stumbled after him. Every inch of her was bruised and cut, and she could not remember the last time she had eaten.

'Aelves,' snorted Gotrek. 'No stamina.'

She shook her head in disbelief. 'Every time I start to think you might be *slightly* interesting, you open your mouth. Then I remember that you're an irascible infant trapped in the body of an ale-infused boar.'

Gotrek snorted and spat. 'What's an irascible?'

'Don't play the fool,' she muttered. 'You're absurd enough.'

'It's stopped again!' called Trachos.

They looked back down the pipe and saw that he had halted near one of the holes spilling light down from the streets above.

'The bone rain has stopped,' he said, shining his torch across the opening.

'What of it?' said Gotrek, walking back to him. 'You said the sewers were the most direct way.'

'But they're flooding.' Trachos waved his light over the water rising all around them. 'It's not as high yet as it was in the smaller tunnels, but it will be soon. And this whole structure is unstable. Whatever has been shaking the city has dislodged the foundations.'

He waded to the far side of the tunnel and shoved a fallen column.

Gotrek and Maleneth backed away as the masonry toppled towards them, smashing against the edge of the opening above and creating a crumbling ramp back up to the street.

Gotrek barged past her and clambered up the column. 'Keep up, aelf. You don't want pretty boy fishing this rune out of my corpse while you're still swimming with turds.'

She gripped her knives tighter as she climbed up after him, amazed to think that she had actually been pleased to see his face a few minutes ago.

They emerged to a scene of such desolation that it halted them in their tracks.

The storm had been brief but apocalyptic. Roofs had collapsed and windows had shattered, and scattered across the streets in every direction, people were crawling through the wreckage, clutching wounds or sobbing over the corpses of their kin.

Even Gotrek looked shocked. The tower at the city's heart was burning brighter than ever, bathing everything in the amethyst pall of death magic, and the desolation was terrible to look at.

Gotrek grimaced at the wounded and the dying. 'The prince could have got them underground quicker. This could have been avoided.' He nodded at the tower. 'Looks like something big is happening in there.' He rushed across the street, clambering over wrecked carts and carriages and ignoring the pitiful figures heaped around him.

As Maleneth and Trachos staggered after him, he dropped down into an empty street and hurried past the facade of what looked to be a temple, wrought of the same pale, bone-like curves as the other buildings they had seen. There were broad, sweeping steps leading up to it, and dozens of wounded people were sprawled across them, obviously struck down before they had managed to reach the temple doors.

Maleneth and Trachos tried to keep pace with Gotrek, but they were both carrying dozens of injuries, and by the time they dropped down into the street, he was far in the distance, running down a broad, empty boulevard that led to the foot of the tower.

People were sprawled all around them, groaning in pain and fear, both soldiers and civilians, cut apart and defenceless – and ghouls were rushing towards them from every direction.

'This is a deliberate tactic,' Maleneth said, shaking her head, surprised she had not realised sooner. 'Their leader must be some kind of sorcerer. He hurls this bone rain at his enemies, and then, by the time the mordants arrive, there's nothing left to fight.'

One of the ghouls was just a few feet away, and as she passed, it leapt at her. She dodged easily, lashing out with her knives as the spitting wretch stumbled on, spilling its blood across the dusty road.

As the ghoul thudded to the ground, dozens more lurched towards her, grunting and grabbing pieces of wreckage.

Trachos hammered two into oblivion, humming as he fought, and Maleneth cut down more, but there were already hundreds spilling from the streets, tearing at each other in their frenzy to feed.

Maleneth and Trachos ran on along the one remaining path through the mob and reached the approach to the tower.

Gotrek was almost at the doors, silhouetted by the light leaking through the walls, when something odd happened.

The ghouls backed away, moving in unison, as though responding to a silent command.

Maleneth staggered to a halt, confused. 'What are they doing?' The ghouls were acting as if they had regained control of their senses, shuffling together and even trying to form regimented lines, like an army of drunks attempting to look sober for a parade. 'Are they ghouls or not?'

Trachos waved her on. 'It doesn't matter – we need to reach that tower. Volant will be waiting in the Halls of Separation.'

Maleneth shook her head as she studied the crowds. 'It's like they're still human.' She gave Trachos a warning look. 'Surely you, of all people, want to know what you're killing?'

He slowed to a halt and looked around. 'They're flesh-eaters.'

The ghouls were still hunched, aberrant horrors, convulsing and snatching, but they were trying to form orderly lines and none of them were making any attempt to attack. They had made a living colonnade down the length of the boulevard, and dozens more were joining their ranks every second. Maleneth guessed that there must already be a few hundred.

Gotrek halted and looked back at the grotesque parade while Maleneth and Trachos jogged towards him.

'What are they playing at?' he demanded as they reached him. 'Why are they doing this?'

They both shook their heads and stared back down the boulevard. There was now a vast crowd of the flesh-eaters, huddled together in a strange semblance of order. Many of them still wore shreds of clothing, and some might have almost passed for normal if not for their blank eyes and awkward, jerking limbs.

'Maybe that's why,' said Trachos, pointing his sceptre towards the city walls.

Maleneth stared into the distant gloom and saw what looked like a flock of birds soaring over the rooftops, heading straight for them. She quickly realised the truth. They were the huge, bat-like things they had seen through Trachos' spyglass on the city walls. She heard their dreadful, screeching cry echoing through the streets.

'Khaine's blood,' she hissed. 'Not these things again.'

'No,' said Gotrek, jabbing his axe at the winged monsters. 'They are not the same.' He laughed as they flew closer and were lit up by the light of the tower. 'These are noble steeds.'

The riders were straight-backed and proud, their chins raised, and banners trailed from their saddles. Some wore pieces of broken barrel on their heads, like crowns, and some carried pieces of wreckage on their arms, as though they were shields. But their flesh was as ravaged as the figures lined up to greet them, and their bodies were just as gnarled and misshapen.

'It's the Ghoul King!' roared Gotrek, grinning. 'How regal he looks on his giant, dead bat.'

Maleneth waved a knife at the expectant crowds of ghouls lined up in front of them. 'What would happen to these legions of flesh-eaters if you killed their noble leader?'

Gotrek raised an eyebrow. 'Interesting idea.'

'We need to enter the tower,' said Trachos. 'Gotrek has sworn to guard the Unburied until the prince and Lhosia have performed their spell.'

Maleneth shook her head. 'A spell that will save the Unburied, but not necessarily us. They were notably vague on that point.' She pointed at the surrounding streets. Ghouls were shuffling closer from every direction, lining up with the others. 'Can you see how many of these things there are? And look over there.' She pointed further out into the city, back the way they had come. Columns of figures were marching beneath the Ghoul King, countless hundreds of mordants arriving from the Eventide.

Gotrek sucked at his beard, frowning, considering her words.

Then the light in the tower pulsed with renewed energy, scattering beams across the underside of the clouds, and a bell rang out, dull and tuneless, like the one they had heard when they first reached the borders of Morbium.

They all turned to look at the building. It was like a coiled white tusk, peppered with circular windows. The smooth, honeycombed walls were made of polished bone, and as the light grew, the tower looked like a shimmering flame.

'Something's happening up there!' cried Gotrek, scowling. 'They've bloody started without me.' He waved his axe at the army gathering behind them. 'There will be plenty of time to deal with these morons.' With that he turned and raced through the doors of the tower.

Maleneth and Trachos followed him into an atrium, slamming the doors shut behind them. The smooth, undulating walls of the tower contained no floors, only a single spiral staircase at its centre, surrounded by a wide, open, circular space. The staircase climbed to a central platform hundreds of feet above, and the walls were hung with thousands of white, wing-shaped shields, all covered in lines of poetry. There was something eerie about such an enormous space, devoid of rooms or furniture and bathed in purple light, and Maleneth paused for a moment, shaking her head. She felt as though she was in a dream.

The light was coming from about halfway up the walls, where the shields were replaced by hundreds of cocoons that nestled in the curves, burning with inner light. After the noise and violence of the last few days, Maleneth was shocked to find that the tower was quiet. Other than the echoes of the bell, there was a strange, peaceful hush. The screeching of the terrorgheists had been silenced as soon as they shut the doors. It was as though they had stepped into another realm.

She looked out through the nearest window and saw that the ruined city was still there, along with the crowds of ghouls, but their din had been silenced.

'Witchblade,' said Trachos, rushing past her and heading up the stairs.

She snapped out of her reverie and saw that the Slayer was climbing up into the light, moving fast.

Maleneth ran over to the staircase. The spiral was broad and shallow, but circling at such a pace still made her dizzy after a few minutes of running, and the building was so huge that she felt as though she was making no progress, turning without climbing in a soundless void.

The bell rang out again. Inside the tower it was deafening, and Maleneth cursed, clamping her hands over her ears as the sound reverberated through her skull.

Just as the ringing seemed to be fading, the wall of the tower caved in, slabs of bone and metal tumbling across the steps.

Maleneth dropped into a crouch as a terrorgheist screamed into view, thrashing its wings and hurling broken masonry across the staircase.

There was a ghoul on the monster's back, wearing a crown and a preposterous air of nobility. The rider carried a rusted, crooked spear, and it pointed the ridiculous weapon at Gotrek, who was still racing up the steps, not far from the circular platform at the top of the tower.

A second terrorgheist smashed through the walls, causing more of the building to topple and revealing the rows of rooftops outside.

The creatures were enormous and revolting, skin trailing from their bones in ragged shreds and rotten intestines snaking behind them as they turned. They both had the same pug-nosed, bat-like faces, and at a signal from the Ghoul King they screamed in unison.

Maleneth howled, but her voice was lost beneath the screeching of the terrorgheists.

Trachos had halted a few steps further up. He was shaking in pain, and the sparks around his helmet had grown worse, dancing across his pauldrons and down his chest armour.

She managed to climb up towards him, still crying out as the terrorgheists whirled around them, screeching and pounding their wings.

Trachos was struggling to stand, but she grabbed his arm and hauled him to his feet. He leant on her shoulder, almost crushing her with his armoured bulk, before righting himself and starting to limp up the stairs.

Something hurtled out from the upper steps and slammed into one of the terrorgheists. The creature pounded its wings, trying to maintain its position as its rider stood in the saddle, straining to see what had hit its steed.

'Gotrek,' mouthed Maleneth, guessing the nature of the projectile even before she saw the Slayer clamber up the terrorgheist's neck, grin furiously and slam his axe into its skull.

CHAPTER TWENTY-EIGHT

RANCOUR

'Nia!' cried King Galan as the traitor beheaded her steed.

Her drake slumped beneath her and plunged towards distant flagstones.

Galan kicked his mount forwards, steering it after her. He hurtled past the steps at the centre of the tower, struggling to hold his reins.

Nia's steed trailed crimson as it looped and fell, but he could still see his queen, hanging onto its ridged back. The traitor was there too – squat and heavy and gripping an axe almost as tall as he was. His head was shaven apart from a central strip greased with so much animal fat that the hair stood up in a flame-like crest. He was climbing over the dead animal even as it fell, still trying to reach Nia, drawing back his axe to strike again.

'No!' howled Galan, driving his drake towards the ground as he tried to ready his spear and take aim.

His steed swooped low and slammed into Nia's drake seconds before it landed, sending all of them tumbling across the floor. Galan was hurled from his mount and thudded into the wall, losing his spear as he hit the stones.

He sat there for a moment, too dazed to move, staring up at the hollow tower, trying to remember who he was. There was a circular window nearby that looked out onto the wide boulevard. His men were gathering outside, preparing to attack, and the sight of them filled Galan with pride. They had fought their way through the city with ease, and their chins were raised in triumph as they rode towards him, colours flying in the breeze. Behind them, his war machines were laying waste to the city, pulverising everything.

'Galan!' cried Nia.

She was lying a dozen feet away, at the foot of the stairs, pinned beneath her dead drake and struggling to breathe.

He groaned at the sight of her, unable to hide his shock. She had been crushed. There was blood rushing from her armour and her hips were twisted at a revoltingly unnatural angle.

'Galan?' she called again.

The traitor with the mohawk was on the other side of the stairs, looking equally dazed, massaging his face as he used his axe to lever himself back onto his feet.

Galan rushed over to Nia and tried to shift the dead drake. It was impossible. The beast was the size of a full-grown oak.

Nia reached up to him, no fear in her voice, only frustration. 'Damn it.' She strained to move. 'Can you move it?'

He wanted to scream and pull away. To see his love like this was more painful than anything he could have ever imagined. But he knelt next to her, forcing himself to meet her feverish gaze.

'Why do you look at me like that?' she croaked, struggling to breathe. The colour was draining quickly from her face as the pool of blood spread around her. She nodded, slowly, and settled back against the floor.

Galan could think of nothing to say. A numbness seized him at the thought of life without her.

She gripped his arm, smiling through her pain. 'We have almost done it, Galan. We are almost there. *You* are almost there.'

There was a thud of boots as the Hounds of Dinann entered the tower and dismounted. Their triumphant expressions faded when they saw Galan holding their dying queen. They stumbled to a halt, lowering their spears.

'Melvas and the others are here,' he said, struggling to speak. 'Rest for a while, and I will come back for you when the traitors are dead. Then we will fetch the healers to–'

She silenced him with a horrific smile. 'No lies. I see the truth in your eyes. No healer can help me now. But I'm not afraid of death, Galan. This is all I ever wanted. To die in battle, with you by my side. I would rather this than any number of–' Her words were interrupted by a violent coughing fit.

'I could never have been a king without you,' he said.

She tried to nod, but the coughing grew worse until she was choking. Her grip on his arm tightened and she pressed her already blue lips against his skin, giving him a last, long kiss. Then she lay back, still smiling as her final breath rattled from her chest.

Galan stared at her, his own breath stalling in his lungs. He gently touched her silver wedding ring, tracing the runes, remembering the day he had put it on her hand.

Then he saw someone striding towards him across the atrium.

Fury jolted through him, forcing him to take the breath he had been holding back. It was the barbarian with the crest of golden hair – the muscle-bound savage who had murdered his queen.

Galan forgot his grief and lurched to his feet. He did not care who the strange-looking warrior was. Nia's murder would not go unavenged. He reached over his shoulder and found, to his relief, that Rancour was still there. He drew the longsword and gripped it in both hands, feeling its sorcery pulsing through its handle. Then he rushed at the barbarian.

'King of the ghouls!' cried the savage, laughing as he saw Galan coming towards him. 'Finally we meet!'

It was only now that he was so close that Galan saw how short the warrior was. He had an absurdly muscular frame, but his head only came level with Galan's chest. Galan had never encountered a duardin before, but he was educated enough to know that this must be one.

'On your knees, murderer,' he cried, drawing Rancour back to strike.

The duardin laughed again, clearly unimpressed. 'Are you trying to talk? With half your neck missing?'

Galan faltered, unsure what the barbarian was talking about. He touched his neck, but found no wounds.

'Tricks won't save you,' he hissed.

He hefted the ensorcelled blade with all the strength he could muster, aiming for the duardin's mocking grin.

The savage parried, but as the sword struck the axe, sorcery erupted from Rancour's blade, hurling him backwards in a storm of darkness, as though he were buried under gauzy black sheets.

The duardin cried out in annoyance as he tried to fight his way through the darkness. He swung his axe furiously, causing a flame to shimmer in the metal, but the harder he fought, the more dense the darkness grew, tightening around him like a net.

'Curse you!' he roared, staggering from side to side, unable to free himself.

Galan circled him, relishing the moment.

Then he came to a halt, noticing something strange. There was a golden face embedded in the duardin's chest, and as the warrior struggled to escape Rancour's sorcery, the metal mask pulsed with inner fire, glowing like an enormous ember.

As the duardin reeled back and forth, howling in outrage, Galan stepped quietly towards him, drawing back Rancour, feeling its seething power. The blade was charged with the might of the Great Wolf. It was blessed with sorcery so powerful it would cut through anything – even the golden rune.

But as the rune-light flooded into Galan's eyes, he felt a strange sensation. It was as though the breeze were blowing through his neck rather than against it. He remembered the duardin's strange insult and reached up to touch his throat. His fingers brushed wet, torn meat.

Cold dread gripped him, as though he were waking from a dream, but he still could not tear his gaze from the rune in the duardin's chest. The light burned through his mind, twisting his thoughts, giving him the most peculiar sensation that he was not who he thought he was.

Pain exploded in Galan's chest as a blade jutted out from between his ribs.

'No need to look so grave,' whispered a sardonic voice in his ear.

He staggered forwards, and his attacker wrenched the blade sideways as he fell, tearing his flesh apart.

Galan hit the floor in a fountain of blood and looked back to see a sneering aelf standing over him, whipcord thin and clad in barbed, blood-splattered leathers.

He tried to rise, but she put her boot on his chest, holding him down and waving a disapproving finger. He collapsed back onto the floor, dizzy with blood loss.

The aelf strolled away with the sprightly, elegant steps of a dancer, heading over to the duardin.

From where Galan was lying, he could see Nia's dead drake and the soldiers who had entered the tower. Only, they weren't soldiers at all. They were something else – grey, twisted horrors, with torn flesh and leering, lipless mouths. Rather than watching over their fallen queen, they were hunched over her steed, tearing hungrily at its flank, ripping its muscles, filling their mouths with blood.

He could just see Nia's outstretched hand, mottled and grey, like rotten meat. Then he saw the wedding ring, glinting on her bloodless finger.

With his last breath, he whispered her name.

CHAPTER TWENTY-NINE

FEEDING FRENZY

'Bloody wizards,' muttered Gotrek as the darkness dropped away from him. He stamped on the shadows that tumbled across the floor and writhed away from him. Within seconds, they had all faded and he was left glowering at the flagstones. He caught sight of Maleneth, still holding her knife with the dead ghoul at her feet.

'Saved by an *aelf*,' he groaned.

She laughed at his ingratitude. 'Ah, but you're a charmer, Gotrek Gurnisson –humble and eloquent in equal measure. You always know just the right thing to say. Truly, you are a credit to your species.'

He glared at her, embers dancing in his furnace-like eye.

Maleneth tensed and gripped her knives.

Then a broad grin spread across Gotrek's face. 'You're almost funny,' he laughed. 'For a backstabbing aelf.'

She bowed with an exaggerated flourish. 'I can but try.'

One of the ghouls reared up from the dead horse, its throat jammed with meat and blood rushing down its skin. It reached out towards them, groaning hungrily, but before it could take a step, another mordant dragged it to the floor and began eating it, snarling and gasping as it ripped flesh with its teeth.

Maleneth and Gotrek watched, bemused, as the ghouls all turned on each other in a snorting, growling kill-frenzy. They seemed oblivious to anything but the body nearest to them, and they quickly devolved into a heap of thrashing limbs and clawing fingers.

Through the windows, Maleneth could see the ghouls gathered outside in the boulevard, and they were all behaving the same way. They abandoned all pretence of being an army and turned on each other, lunging at whoever was nearest. Even the terrorgheists had joined the carnage, diving from the rooftops and devouring creatures they had previously fought alongside. 'What in the name of Khaine are they doing?'

Gotrek watched the carnage, shaking his head. 'Even ghouls usually manage to attack someone other than themselves.'

'You killed their leader,' called Trachos from the stairs above. 'These things have no minds of their own. They were only acting with a purpose because of that.' He waved his sceptre at the Ghoul King's corpse. 'You have achieved what the prince asked of you.'

'What do you mean?' said Gotrek. He nodded at the cocoons up in the rafters of the tower. 'They're not saved yet.'

'You have saved them from the ghouls. The flesh-eaters will be so busy devouring each other, the Erebid will have no problem slaughtering them when Prince Volant summons them back out of the sewers.'

Gotrek glanced at Maleneth, and she gave him another exaggerated curtsy, delighting in the fact that she had done his job for him.

'All that remains now is for Volant and Lhosia to perform the rite they spoke of,' she said. 'To fire up their magic stone and protect the Erebid from future invasions.'

Gotrek looked up towards the top of the tower. The hexagonal platform in its eaves was shining so brightly he had to shield his eyes. 'Let's get up there before they get so excited they forget what they promised me.'

CHAPTER THIRTY

DEATHWISE

As they reached the building's upper levels, they found themselves surrounded by Unburied. Maleneth remembered what Lhosia had said about each cocoon carrying hundreds, even thousands of souls, and she marvelled when she saw that the walls were covered in countless hundreds of them. They were all cradled in niches of smooth bone, like seeds in an enormous white pod, and the nearer they were to the platform, the brighter they shone. As she ran, Maleneth felt as though she were racing into the heart of a star with giant embers tumbling all around her, burning as they fell. The platform was made of the same pale, translucent material as everything else, and shadowy figures were walking across the surface, passing back and forth above her head.

They were still several minutes away from the platform when Maleneth cried out in alarm and stumbled to a halt.

'Keep moving, aelf!' snapped Gotrek, glancing back at her. As soon as he saw what had happened to her, he stopped too.

'What are you doing?' he demanded.

'Doing? I did nothing!' she said, staring at her arms. Her skin was naturally pale, but it had been transformed, turned into the same bone-like substance as the walls. Even her clothes had changed to the same material. 'This is what happened to you!' she cried, pointing at the rows of cocoons. 'When you joined yourself to those things. It's happening to you now! Look!'

Gotrek exclaimed in annoyance. His leathery, tattooed muscles now resembled dusty alabaster, as did the plate of armour on his shoulder. He stared at his palm, grimacing at the change in his flesh.

'Don't move!' called Trachos.

'Don't move? What do you mean, don't move? We need to get up there.' Gotrek turned to continue up the stairs.

'Remember what the priestess told you,' said Trachos. 'You're fragile in that state. Tread carefully.'

Gotrek halted and looked back. 'And what about you?'

Trachos' armour was now the same chalky white as everything else. He shook his head, staring at his arms.

'Ha!' crowed Maleneth. 'Not so eternal after all. Tread carefully yourself!'

The figures overhead suddenly rushed to one side of the platform, and the cocoons on the walls pulsed even brighter.

'Sod this,' grunted Gotrek, and carried on up the stairs, but he was moving noticeably slower.

The final stretch of steps opened into a fan shape as they led onto the platform. Gotrek, Trachos and Maleneth walked out into the light together, shielding their eyes as they stepped onto the smooth, powdery floor, gripping their weapons. It occurred to Maleneth that they were moving like old comrades in arms, standing side by side, trusting each other implicitly. As soon as she noticed this, she sidestepped away from the other two, muttering in annoyance.

As Maleneth grew accustomed to the light, she saw that her skin had regained its normal appearance. The others were the same. The transformation that had overtaken them on the stairs had ceased as soon as they stepped up onto the dais.

There were a dozen people assembled on the platform. To her left was Lord Aurun, flanked by six knights of the Gravesward. He looked like he was about to be crowned – chin raised, shoulders back and eyes gleaming with pride.

In the centre of the platform were High Priestess Lhosia, three other priests and the towering shape of Prince Volant. The priests were standing in a circle around the prince, arms raised and hands clasped, and Volant was kneeling. It looked like he was holding an exploding star. Thousands of white moths fluttered around his hands, forming a ball of teeming, flashing wings.

Gotrek opened his mouth, but before he could speak, Prince Volant's voice rang out through the lights. His words were cracked with pain but still sure and proud.

'Deathwise we fly, rescued from life and cradled by sod. From the tombs of fell-handed forefathers, red-scarred and charred, death-tongued and hale, we bring faith, we bring hope, we bring eternity.'

Maleneth wanted to announce their arrival, but the air was so heavy with sorcery that she dared not speak for fear of triggering some kind of transformation.

Lhosia echoed Volant's invocation, and then the prince spoke again. His voice was lower this time, and more resonant, echoing through the shadows. 'Deathwise we fly, rescued from life and cradled by sod. From the tombs of fell-handed forefathers, red-scarred and charred, death-tongued and hale, we bring treasurelings. We bring gifts. We bring offerings to the deep, deepest dark.'

This time the words had a dramatic effect. The cocoons in the walls pulsed, then grew dark. There was a pair of small braziers positioned at the top of the steps, and if it weren't for their flames, the whole platform would have been plunged into darkness.

'Those are not the words,' said Lhosia, backing away, breaking the circle and staring up at the prince. 'What are you doing?'

When Lhosia had loosed her grip, some of the moths had flown away, scattering over the platform and fluttering up, into the spire of the tower.

Volant looked up through the clouds of whirling insects, his face grim.

CHAPTER THIRTY-ONE

THE CEREMENT STONE

The prince was not wearing his helmet, and as he turned to face Gotrek, his eyes creased into a slight smile.

'You made it.' He ignored the confused-looking priests and walked over to the Slayer. 'I hoped you would, but the odds were long. You are a unique individual, Gotrek Gurnisson. A rare find.'

Lhosia was staring at the dark cocoons on the walls, looking increasingly more outraged. 'What are you doing, Morn-Prince? Why did you alter the rite?'

'You hoped I would make it?' said Gotrek. 'What are you talking about?'

Volant watched Gotrek with glazed, lifeless eyes. He looked like he was intoxicated. 'You hold the gods in the contempt they deserve.' He waved a dismissive hand at everyone else on the platform. 'When you said you had come to bring your fury down on Nagash, it made my heart sing, Gotrek. We are of a similar mind, you and I. And you have done great work, bringing these souls here.' He pointed at the small patch of darkness hanging in the centre of the moths. 'I could never have managed this without you.'

Lhosia and the other Erebid stared at the prince, mystified, as he continued.

'This offering guarantees the future of the Erebid.'

Gotrek shook his head. 'Offering?'

Volant looked sadly at Lhosia. 'We've kept our ancestors hidden for all these centuries. But now we are undone. The Lord of Undeath has harnessed a power beyond anything he has wielded before. We can no longer just cling to our prayers and hope to outrun the tide.'

'What have you done?' asked Lhosia quietly.

'I have gathered hundreds of divine souls,' said Volant, glancing at the dark shape in the centre of the moths. 'Souls that have eluded Nagash for centuries.'

Lord Aurun glared at the Morn-Prince, gripping his scythe with such fury that his arms were shaking.

Maleneth looked at where Volant had been kneeling and saw a shimmer of purple in the ball of moths. It was a gemstone, faceted and dark.

'Do you mean that the Cerement Stone will *preserve* the Unburied?' said Lhosia.

Prince Volant shook his head, suddenly seeming tired. He massaged his scalp as he paced across the dais, distorting the intricate tattoos on his face.

'Nothing preserves life except power. I see that now. For a long time I thought there might be another way, but now I see that the only way to gain freedom from the gods is to *buy* it. Prayers, devotions, ancestor worship... It's all meaningless. But offerings win the favour of any god. And thanks to this duardin, the Cerement Stone has captured more souls than I could ever have hoped. And now it will send them to Nagash.'

'Nagash?' gasped Lhosia, glancing over at Lord Aurun, her face drained of colour.

'Seize him!' howled Lord Aurun, pointing his scythe at the sorcerer. 'He's a *traitor!*'

Aurun and the Gravesward rushed forwards, weapons raised, but Prince Volant shook his head despairingly at them. Just as they were about to reach him, he lashed out with his scythe, slicing through armour and hurling his attackers across the dais.

The knights stumbled and fell, clutching their throats and chests. There was a loud clattering as scythes and shields bounced across the floor.

Aurun leapt to his feet and attacked again, but Volant clubbed him down, towering over the knight and pummelling him with the haft of his scythe.

The prince looked around at the gasping knights, then nodded and addressed Gotrek again.

'This tower is linked to Nagash's own citadel, and I have now linked it to the Cerement Stone as well. I have all the souls I need to complete the ritual – I can now do as I promised and send you with them. You can finally confront your past.'

'What?' Gotrek shook his head. 'Why? Why would you send your ancestors to Nagash? After everything you people said about your forebears.'

The prince's expression darkened. 'Morbium is gone!' He waved dismissively at Lord Aurun. 'No one else here has the sense to see it, but I realised the truth weeks ago. *Months* ago. And I have been living with it ever since, knowing that everything we have worked for all these centuries has come to nothing. Knowing that every one of the prominents will sink beneath the Eventide. It shamed me, Gotrek Gurnisson!' His voice cracked. 'I was going to be the one Morn-Prince who failed to preserve his bloodline. The one ruler of Morbium who let memories be lost! The Great Necromancer was going to take everything! Every trace of our past.

'At first I thought there might be a way to find an offering *outside* Morbium. I employed shrivers to scour the princedoms, looking for a gift that would be fit for a god – some way to buy our safety. But it was hopeless. What single individual would satisfy Nagash? I needed more. Only the Unburied would appease the Great Necromancer. These souls that have eluded him for so long.'

'Kurin?' laughed Maleneth. 'He was working for you?' She looked triumphantly at Gotrek. 'I told you that conjuror in Klemp was a fraud. He was fishing for victims to send to Nagash. I bet he was delighted when he heard you say you *wanted* to go to him!'

Gotrek glared at her, but Volant did not hear Maleneth's words, too intent on justifying his actions to the Slayer.

'Once the rite is complete,' he continued, 'Nagash will take ownership of the Unburied. The Cerement Stone will send every one of them to him. The Lingering Keep will sink beneath the waves like all the other prominents, and every soul will go to the necromancer. Then I will be–'

'Nagash's servant,' said Gotrek, his lip curling in disgust.

'I serve *no one!*' snapped Volant, finally losing his veneer of calm. All around the dais, the Gravesward were clambering to their feet, clutching wounds, but the prince ignored them.

'For now,' he said, his voice still taut, 'Nagash has the upper hand. But let a few centuries pass, and Sigmar will hold sway, or maybe some other god that has yet to emerge from the aether-void. Who knows? What matters is that as the gods rise and fall, the bloodline of the Morn-Princes will endure. With the souls of the Unburied I have bought myself safe passage. I have bought a chance for at least one of the Erebid to escape the Nadir. I will survive, and begin again.'

Lhosia hissed a curse and moved to attack, but her acolytes held her back as Volant raised his scythe, saving her from being cut down.

Gotrek looked thoughtfully at the struggling figures on the dais, considering the prince's words. 'If you're sending these souls to Nagash to buy yourself peace, why would you send me? I'm not after peace. I'm not some willing victim. I came for vengeance.'

Volant shrugged. 'And I believe you might find it.' He peered down at Gotrek. 'Your soul has been altered. You are more than mortal but better than a god.' He shook his head. 'I have no idea what you are, but perhaps you *will* destroy Nagash. Perhaps that is why you were brought to these realms – to end all these schisms and power plays. I'm sending these souls to buy freedom from tyranny, but if you destroy Nagash, there will *be* no tyranny.'

'And if I fail to destroy him?'

'Then I have presented the arch-necromancer with an even greater present than I promised. Your soul would be the jewel in his crown. What matters is that I will be far away, taking my bloodline beyond the reach of arrogant, self-absorbed gods.'

Trachos unclasped his hammers from his belt and tensed, ready to attack, but then paused and looked at Gotrek, as if waiting to see how the Slayer would respond.

Is Gotrek our leader now? wondered Maleneth. *Is that what we have come to?* The idea appalled her. *Do we just follow him whatever he decides to do?* She was struggling to understand why, but both she and Trachos seemed to be in Gotrek's thrall.

Strike him down then! Stick a knife in that fat neck. Try another poison.

Maleneth shook her head. There was such a powerful, momentous feeling in the air that she could not bear the idea of ending this scene before it had been played out. She had to know what would become of the Slayer. And of the Erebid.

'People have been promising they'll get me to Nagash since I arrived in this wretched hole,' snarled Gotrek. 'So far it's come to nothing.'

Volant waved Gotrek over to the cloud of moths and pointed to the gem at its centre. 'Place your hand on the Cerement Stone. I am about to finish the ritual – the stone will send you to Nagashizzar. You will see Nagash *today*. Have your vengeance, Gotrek, or answers, or whatever it is you seek.'

Gotrek stepped closer, reaching out to touch the stone.

'Gotrek!' cried Trachos, finally breaking his silence. 'This man is a–'

Volant whispered and amethyst light leapt from the stone, blazing around his scythe. 'This stone is part of me!' he shouted. 'I'm bound to it, and it to me.' He swung the blade, hurling purple flame. 'Together, we are invincible!'

Trachos staggered, clutching his gorget, bathed in light. He dropped to his knees with a clang, sparks tumbling down his chest. As he struggled, the purple lights grew brighter, eating into his armour, causing him to convulse and kick.

Maleneth shook her head. For a long time she would have gladly watched the Stormcast Eternal die, but not at the hands of this pompous prince. There was nothing she hated more than someone who lied better than she did.

'Gotrek,' she said, but before she could get any more words out, Volant lashed out again, hurling more light. Pain knifed into her throat, and she dropped to the floor beside Trachos, unable to breathe.

Gotrek glanced back at her, his expression blank. As she clawed at her throat, feeling the strength drain from her limbs, the Slayer studied Prince Volant. For what seemed like an age, Gotrek looked from Volant to the stone and the people dying on the dais.

'I have been in these realms for months,' he said finally. 'And I had given up hope of finding anyone who thinks like me.'

Maleneth felt a rush of hopelessness as Gotrek placed his hand on Volant's shoulder. 'And now, in this lightless pit, I see that I was wrong to despair. Not everyone in these realms is as stupid as I thought.'

Maleneth's vision grew dark as her oxygen-starved brain lost hold on reality. She pictured scenes from her past, from the Khainite Murder Temples where she had learned to pray through violence, and the halls of the Azyrite scholars, where she had first understood the power of Sigmar's Stormhosts. The scenes merged and coalesced as her consciousness slipped away.

Gotrek smiled at Prince Volant.

Then he smashed the Cerement Stone with his axe, hurling crimson shards through the air.

Volant roared and reeled across the platform, clutching his face.

Moths whirled around Gotrek's axe, flashing against the fyresteel.

The walls lit up as the cocoons pulsed back into life.

Maleneth managed to gasp a choking breath as the flames dropped away from her.

With fragments of the Cerement Stone still tinkling across the floor, Gotrek strolled after the howling prince.

'I thought these realms were blind to the things that really matter,' he said, 'but the people of Morbium have proved me wrong. They value tradition. They respect their ancestors. They record every detail of their past. They *believe* in something. They believe hard enough to fight and to die for it.'

Lhosia, Trachos and the others were still gasping for breath and trying to sit as Gotrek reached Volant and pointed his axe at him. 'And they deserve better than to be betrayed by their own lord.' He glanced at Maleneth. 'I was wrong. Whatever I've lost, there *are* still things worth fighting for. Even here.'

Volant had fallen to his knees, and cracks had spread over his face. He looked like he was about to be sick. 'I placed all of my power in that stone.' His voice was a strangled hiss. He glared at Gotrek. 'You will rue the day you–'

His words were cut off, along with his head, as Lhosia's scythe slammed through his throat.

CHAPTER THIRTY-TWO

A THING OF VALUE

Gotrek stood brooding over Volant's shattered remains, passion burning in his one good eye. The prince looked like a broken vase, hundreds of pale shards, each showing a jumbled glimpse of his face.

All around the dais, people were climbing to their feet, gasping and coughing and struggling for breath.

Maleneth gave Trachos her hand, and Lhosia's acolytes rushed to steady the priestess as she staggered away from the prince's corpse, staring at her bloody scythe.

Lord Aurun and the Gravesward grabbed their weapons and dusted down their armour.

'You could have gone with him to Nagash.' Maleneth was, once again, baffled by the Slayer's behaviour. 'You could have fulfilled your destiny. You could have met your doom.'

Gotrek nodded, staring at Volant's splintered corpse, his expression grim. 'Aye.'

Trachos walked across the platform and stood next to the Slayer. His breath was wheezing inside his helmet and he was clutching the rent in his neck armour, but he managed to stand straight and there was no sign of the tremors that had troubled him before.

'I thought you and the prince were of one mind,' sneered Maleneth. 'I thought you would see yourself in him.'

In the harsh light of the Unburied, Gotrek's face looked more weathered and beaten than ever. 'I did. I did see myself in him. And I did not like what I saw.'

'What do you mean?' asked Trachos.

Gotrek shrugged. 'He cared for nothing but his own future. He was deluding himself that he was fighting for his race, but he was just a coward. I might not have been so sure.' He turned towards Lord Aurun and Lhosia. 'If I had not seen your bravery.' He placed his hand over the rune in his scarred chest. 'The gods haven't tainted everything. Not yet. So perhaps I was sent here to...' He shook his head. 'Perhaps I came here to do *more* than die?'

They all fell quiet again as Gotrek wrestled with his thoughts. Even Maleneth felt reluctant to interrupt.

'What about your old friend?' she said after a while. 'Felix, was it? He wanted you to come here, didn't he? And face Nagash.'

Gotrek scowled. 'Maybe the wizard in Klemp was tricking me? He did have the look of a charlatan. Or perhaps Felix wanted me to come here to stop Prince Volant.' He lowered his voice. 'Besides, the manling is dead. Long dead. Which makes me a gullible fool.'

Lhosia spoke up, looking at Gotrek with newfound respect. 'You saved the Unburied. You saved all of us. But what will we do now?' She was addressing him like a subordinate requesting orders. 'The city is still conquered. If everything Volant told us is a lie, then there is *no* rite that will save them. There is no new Iron Shroud.' She looked at the shards of Cerement Stone. 'The mordants are everywhere, and we have no way to escape them.'

'Then we make our stand here,' said Lord Aurun in strident tones. 'We will not abandon a single soul. We will hold this tower until our dying breaths. The Lingering Keep is not lost while we live.'

The Gravesward clanged their scythes against their breastplates, but Lhosia looked doubtful.

'Think,' said Aurun. 'Most of our men should have reached the sewers before the rain hit. I can muster them. However many mordants there are out there, they will have a hard fight making it up these stairs with a thousand archers firing down on them and a shield wall waiting at the top.'

One of the knights saluted. 'I will sound the horns, my lord.'

'Wait,' said Gotrek, halting the knight before he reached the stairs. He looked at Aurun. 'The halls of my ancestors were filled with the corpses of warriors who died defending their homes. It is an honourable way to die.'

Aurun tilted his head in a slight bow. 'You have given us another chance, Slayer. Whatever the odds, we will fight on.'

Gotrek nodded. 'You are brave, and honourable, but...' He shook his head, frowning. 'Perhaps, like me, you can do more than just die with honour? I never expected to find anything of worth in these realms. *People* of worth. And now that I have found a thing of value, I wonder if there is a way to preserve it.'

Aurun shook his head. 'We will not abandon our ancestors.'

'Nor should you. But perhaps you could abandon something else.'

Gotrek was staring into the middle distance, his expression rigid. 'I come from a proud race. As proud as your own. And in our pride, we refused to change. We refused to move on.' He glanced at the rune in his chest. 'And we died. All that pride, all that wisdom, sacrificed for bricks and mortar.' He waved at the building around them. 'For towers like this. To honour the past is good, and right, Lord Aurun, but to be enslaved by it is another matter.'

'What are you suggesting?' asked Lhosia.

Gotrek pointed with his axe at the rows of cocoons that lined the tower walls. 'Your duty is to the Unburied, not this city. And the Unburied can be moved. You could die here, fighting until the end – and by Grungni I would honour your memory for doing it – or you could take them away and find a new place to live, find a new *way* to live.'

'How?' demanded Aurun. 'Where could we go?'

Gotrek shrugged and waved at the ruins outside, smoking and crowded with feasting ghouls. 'What could be worse than this? And now Nagash has thrown your borders open to the other princedoms, there will be plenty more ghouls coming your way. Along with any other army that happens to be passing.'

Maleneth shook her head. 'Even if we could fight our way to the gates, the wynds would be crawling with mordants. How could we go anywhere?'

Gotrek looked at Trachos and raised an eyebrow.

'Yes.' Trachos' voice was hoarse but confident. 'I can do it.'

'Do *what?*' demanded Maleneth, irritated that they seemed to be sharing secrets.

Gotrek turned back to Aurun. 'When we first reached the city, we spoke to someone in the chapter house – a captain. He spoke of strange happenings at the docks.'

'Captain Ridens, yes. He said something had triggered the old Kharadron engines. The aether-ships. He said they lit up.' Aurun looked at Trachos. 'You said you might be responsible.'

Trachos nodded. 'At the Barren Points I ignited power lines that run beneath the whole of the Eventide. They date back to whenever the princedom was first colonised.'

'So the aether-ships are working again?' said Lhosia. 'Could you pilot them?'

'They might be working. Some of them, at least.'

Lhosia gripped Gotrek's arm. 'Then we could cross the Eventide. With the Iron Shroud gone, we would be free to cross the underworlds. With you to help us, we could find a new home, another corner of Shyish, far from the mordants.'

Gotrek gave a grim laugh. 'I've seen this realm. You won't like it. But there are other places.' He nodded towards Maleneth and Trachos. 'Places where people like this hold sway rather than Nagash.'

Lhosia shook her head. 'But could we reach the docks?' She looked out through a window. Seen from so high, the city was like an ant's nest, teeming with life as mordants flooded from every direction.

'Have you noticed that none of them are attacking us?' said Maleneth. 'Since *I* killed their king, I mean.'

Trachos nodded. 'They are leaderless. They are no longer an army.'

'They'll still try to chew your face off,' grunted Gotrek, 'but they're quite busy killing each other. We should be able to cut a path through them once you muster your men.'

'Lhosia, is there any reason the Unburied can't be moved?' Lord Aurun said.

She seemed dazed by the direction of the conversation, but she shook her head, waving to her acolytes. 'We could perform the necessary rituals. It would take a few hours, but it can be done.'

'Then perhaps we could save them,' muttered Aurun.

Gotrek stretched, rolling his massive shoulders and arching his back, causing the face in his chest to glint in the torchlight. 'I gave you my word I'd save them.' He clanged the haft of his axe on the floor and unleashed one of his terrifying grins. 'And I keep my bloody oaths.'

* * *

For someone who professed no interest in religion, Maleneth was constantly surprised by Gotrek's unshakeable faith. He believed resolutely in his own indestructibility. He wore self-belief like a suit of inch-thick plate.

He marched back out into the city like he was taking an evening stroll with nothing more pressing on his mind than finding a tavern. There were hundreds of ghouls crowded into the boulevard, thousands more in the surrounding streets, and he was blind to all of them, leaving the Gravesward to cut them down as he chatted calmly to Lord Aurun, asking for directions to the docks and discussing options for a destination. As they walked and talked, Maleneth noticed how animated Aurun was becoming – despite everything that had happened, despite the destruction all around him, he seemed excited. Gotrek had no trace of diplomacy, no tact, no desire to be political, but he had turned the Erebid noble into an eager convert and given him hope in the face of ruin.

Behind them, Erebid priests hauled their ancestors into the streets, abandoning centuries of religion on the word of a one-eyed duardin with an ale-matted beard and a face that looked dredged from a wreck.

'How does he do it?' muttered Maleneth.

Trachos was a few paces behind her, readying his hammers as the ghouls started to gather, sniffing the air and slavering. 'He's headed somewhere,' he said. 'It's written in his face.'

'To his grave,' she said, but she could not make her cynicism ring true. She knew what Trachos meant. Everyone else was limping through life, but Gotrek was charging.

She drew her knives and grinned, wading into the fight.

CHAPTER THIRTY-THREE

GHOST SHIPS

Gotrek staggered down to the quayside, wiping sweat from his face and laughing. He glanced back at Trachos, who was a few paces behind him, cleaning blood from his hammers. 'On my oath, manling, what a sight. That's the most glorious thing I've seen since falling into these wretched hells.'

Trachos looked up from his hammers and nodded in agreement.

Arrayed before them, glimmering in the darkness, were six vast edifices – colossal duardin faces, wrought of metal and wearing coats of faded, peeling paint. The figureheads towered over Gotrek, grander even than the one on the *Spindrift* and just as ferocious –savage, battle-hungry goliaths, roaring in silence, lit up by the fires of the burning city. They were of a different design to the *Spindrift*. They looked more like traditional ships, but were forged of iron and brass and topped by enormous metal spheres. Runes were painted across the hulls and mechanical weapons bristled from every gunwale.

Gotrek placed his hand on the first prow he reached, patting the ancient riveted metal with a low, resonant clang. 'I don't have much time for the Kharadron, but this *is* impressive. Proper, sturdy engineering. Almost reminds me of honest, well-crafted dwarf work. It will do me good to travel this way.'

Lhosia followed him to the ship, and over the next ten minutes, hundreds more people poured down onto the quayside – civilians and priests, flanked by lines of Gravesward, fleeing from the carnage behind them. The Lingering Keep was aflame. As buildings had collapsed, destroyed by the confused, rampaging ghouls, fires broke out, whipping through the corpse-filled streets and engulfing the city's temples and townhouses. The tower where Prince Volant had died had collapsed not long after the Gravesward removed the Unburied. The whole structure had been weakened by the terrorgheists, and there was now a column of whirling dust and embers where it had once stood.

Lord Aurun had seemed reinvigorated since Gotrek suggested leaving the city. He had taken command of Prince Volant's armies without a moment's thought, ordering them to form a defensive perimeter around the docks until the city's surviving civilians had made it down to the quayside. The bone rain had massacred many of the refugees, and the ghouls had killed even more, but there were still thousands of people left to swarm around the ancient ships, filling the air with a panicked clamour, laden with belongings and, in the case of the priests, cradling the cocoons that held the Unburied.

'Not much of a fight, eh?' said Gotrek as Lord Aurun made his way through the crowds.

Aurun nodded. 'They seem more interested in destroying each other than attacking us.'

'They are only the beginning,' said Trachos, his tone bleak. 'I have seen this happen in other underworlds. First come the creatures you call mordants, and then, once the kingdom is in tatters, the spirit hosts arrive, led by Nagash's own generals.'

Aurun looked back at the flames. 'I understand. The princedom is gone. I knew that the moment I heard Prince Volant's lies. It is time to begin again.'

Lhosia gazed up at the vast, furious face that loomed over them. 'But can we really leave? What will you do? How do we make them sail again?'

Trachos headed over to a ladder that reached up the side of the hull. 'If these ships still have aether-gold on board, as the *Spindrift* did, we should only have one problem.'

He started to climb, his sigmarite boots hammering on the ladder's metal rungs.

Gotrek nodded, looking pleased with himself. Then he frowned, staring up at Trachos. '*What* problem?'

Maleneth might have been imagining it, but she thought she heard a trace of humour in Trachos' reply.

'The conduits. They will most likely have corroded, as they did on the *Spindrift*. We'll need some way to channel the fuel.' He hesitated. 'A powerful piece of ur-gold would do it.'

Gotrek looked at his chest rune with a furious expression, preparing to howl an insult at Trachos.

Maleneth started to laugh.

Your Celestial Highnesses,

Forgive the break in communication, but after leaving Klemp, the Slayer's quest to find Nagash took a strange turn that led me beyond the reach of even the most dedicated Azyrite agents. I will spare you the details, at least until I return to Azyr, but suffice to say, I am still in Gotrek's company, as is the Stormcast Eternal, Lord Ordinator Trachos. We have finished our delightful sojourn in the Amethyst Princedoms and are now on the road to a storm-keep recommended by Trachos. It is a large fortress known as Hammerskáld, where I hope to find a messenger who can carry this missive to you. I find it hard to explain exactly how this has come to pass, but we will reach Hammerskáld travelling in a fleet of ancient Kharadron aether-ships, with a dispossessed nation trailing in our wake. The entire population of a forgotten under-world has adopted Gotrek as their holy saviour. Since leaving their homeland, many of their priests have painted stripes on their heads in mimicry of his greasy mohawk, and soldiers have hammered their weapons into new shapes in an attempt to make them resemble the Slayer's axe. It is singularly the most absurd thing I have ever seen – pale-faced waifs, in their hundreds, attempting to emulate the heavy tread of an inebriated duardin.

By all the gods of all the realms, I swear that I have no idea how such a thing is possible. But along with the absurdity of it, I sense something else. It is hard to explain, but I sense a signifi-cance to all of this that I cannot quite explain in words. I imagine you now think me as deluded as the refugees, but if you could see him, hauling an entire diaspora through these ruined hells, you might understand. He has an inexplicable magnetism. He attracts people as easily as he attracts flies. They are drawn to him, caught in his trajectory, convinced he can help even though he is so clearly unable to help himself.

He takes no pleasure in it, mind. Where others would delight in such adoration, Gotrek considers it an inconvenience, hurling abuse at his followers, demanding they leave him in peace and stop asking him so many questions. If it weren't for the alcohol they keep offering him, I think he would have jumped overboard days ago. He has clearly come to regret his newfound altruism. I imagine we will leave Hammerskáld without this fervid host in tow.

But I digress. The Master Rune is still safe, but I feel no closer to convincing the Slayer that he should return with me to Azyr. I had hoped he might do so as soon as we reach Hammerskáld, but I am troubled to report that he is now in the grips of a new obses-sion. Despite the dreadful ordeals we endured in the princedoms, he seems to have quite abandoned his mission to face Nagash. He now assures me that he can 'fix' the Mortal Realms if he can lay his hands on an axe he once owned. Apparently, the enormous

Fyreslayer greataxe he currently wields is not impressive enough. He says it hinders his ability to teach the realms any 'bloody sense,' so he has set himself the challenge of retrieving a weapon that probably never existed beyond the addled confines of his own ale-steeped brain.

I am painfully aware that my return to Azyr is terribly over-due, your highnesses. And I imagine that you have despaired of me ever bringing you the rune. Perhaps you have even sent other agents of the Order to replace me and complete the job. But I will give you this warning – the Slayer will not be fooled, bought or strong-armed. For all his hatred of gods, he is the closest thing I have ever met to one. I have still to decide if he is a tragic simple-ton or the greatest hero of the age, but whatever he is, I am closer to understanding him than anyone else alive. And I am therefore your best chance of harnessing the rune for Sigmar's crusade. For Khaine and the God-King, I swear I will find a way to claim this elusive prize. And, while doing so, I shall also endeavour to solve the infuriating enigma of Gotrek Gurnisson.

Your most loyal and faithful votary,
Maleneth Witchblade

GITSLAYER

DARIUS HINKS

PROLOGUE

'Cretins,' muttered Gotrek, watching the river belch and hiss in the wake of the *Sigmaron Star*. They had only set sail an hour ago but the spires of Anvilgard were already fading into the dusk, swallowed by clouds of yellow steam.

'You sound surprised.' Maleneth leant on the gunwale and looked out at the charred trees stooping over the river. 'I thought you'd designated *everyone* in the realms a cretin.'

His brow bristled. 'There are degrees.'

Maleneth studied him. His hulking frame was half hidden in the steam. With his knotted tattoos and crest of greasy hair he looked like the sculptures on the riverbank. Brutal and portentous. Like the weather-beaten shoulder of a mountain. There was an ugly magnificence to him that Maleneth pretended not to notice. 'It was your idea to visit the wretched city,' she said. 'If you desire the company of Sigmar's devoted then why won't you let me take you to Azyr?'

'Desire their company? Why would I want to spend time with starry-eyed Sigmar followers?'

Maleneth shook her head. 'You'd stroll into a burning keep if you thought you could knock heads with someone, but when I talk about the celestial majesty of Azyr, a place where people walk free from the shadow of Chaos, you look like you're going to explode. It makes no sense. What could be so bad about spending time with people who don't want to kill us?' She grimaced and waved back down the river. 'And look where we end up instead. Wading through the fish markets of Anvilgard. Khaine's teeth. I'll never be rid of that stink.' She sniffed her sleeve. 'In fact, it seems to be getting worse.' She looked out at the trees. They seemed to be reaching out to her through the seething mist. 'The whole jungle's rank. It's like a cauldron. Why did you drag me out here? Are you still tormenting yourself with memories of dead friends? Are you still thinking that you can somehow bring them back?'

Gotrek drew himself up to his full height, which still left him looking up at her. 'The only torment is listening to you.'

'Without me you'd probably still be in that Fyreslayer lodge.' She tapped the cold rune in his chest. 'Without me you wouldn't have this.'

Gotrek gripped her hand. 'That's nothing to boast about.'

She removed her hand from his. 'You've had plenty of chances to be rid of me. You *want* me around.'

'Don't flatter yourself.' Gotrek was about to say more when the ship juddered, as though run aground.

Captain Verloza was standing a few feet away and she approached them with a nonchalant swagger that made Maleneth's jaw clench. The woman thought that being master of one boat made her a person of significance and power. If Gotrek had not expressly forbidden it, Maleneth would have taught her a lesson in real power. She was around thirty or forty years old, as far as Maleneth could guess. Humans aged so quickly it barely seemed worth pinning down their age. She was small, wiry and narrow-hipped with skin like scuffed leather. She had a scarred, stubbly scalp and the air of a retired pit fighter. She was oblivious to most forms of danger, was rarely sober, always spoke her mind and had absolutely no respect for authority. Maleneth knew from the moment they met that Gotrek would like her.

'Apologies,' said the captain. 'We don't usually bounce off every rock. The river must be in one of its playful moods.'

Maleneth looked down at the amber-coloured waves. Steam boiled up from them constantly and there were lights flickering beneath the surface. 'Is it water?'

Verloza smiled. 'Were you thinking of going for a paddle?'

Gotrek snorted.

'No,' said Verloza, 'it's not water. Some say it's lava but that's nonsense. The *Star* has a metal hull, but if this was lava we'd have sunk within half a mile of Anvilgard. My guess is that it's acid. Either way, it would eat through you in minutes.' She smirked. 'I'm sure in the "celestial majesty of Azyr" one can bathe in much prettier rivers.'

Gotrek laughed. 'You don't want to know what she bathes in.' Prior to docking at Anvilgard, they had spent several weeks with the captain, exploring the Charwind Coast, and Gotrek seemed to have decided that Captain Verloza was the one worthwhile person in Aqshy. Maleneth had no doubt that the captain would soon find an excuse to fetch more of the grog she and Gotrek were so partial to.

A deckhand rushed over and whispered in Verloza's ear.

'Silt rats,' said the captain as the boat juddered again.

'Grungni's teeth.' Gotrek stumbled and had to grab the railing. 'Rats?'

Verloza grinned. 'We grow 'em big out here. Come and see.'

As they neared the bow of the ship, Maleneth heard the familiar sound of off-key singing. Trachos, their Stormcast Eternal travelling companion, was stomping through the steam, armour glinting as he towered over deckhands, raising his voice to the heavens. Trachos claimed to have some connection to Maleneth's order, but she was never sure whether to believe him. He had fought several campaigns in the underworlds of Shyish and the experience had left his mind as ragged as his armour. He had seemed unhinged since the day they met him but he had become even more confused over the last few months. Maleneth would not have been surprised to find that he was the cause of the ship's lurches, but as they came closer, she saw that there was a genuine threat – Verloza's crew had gathered at the railing, glaives and harpoons pointed at something rising from the acid.

Verloza leapt up onto the gunwale and dangled out into the spray, hanging from the rigging and peering down at the river.

The boat shook again, causing most of the crew to stagger, but Verloza remained where she was, swaying over the hissing currents. She grinned and pointed her harpoon at something near the hull. 'Here it comes! Ready yourselves.'

Steam billowed up over the railing, causing everyone to gasp and back away. There was a thud as something slammed onto the deck.

As the fumes dissipated Maleneth saw what looked like a statue made of old fish scales and riverweed. This was the source of the smell, she realised, covering her nose. Everyone backed away as the thing moved, raising a brutal-looking club. It rose to its full height, towering over the sailors, and smashed a man to the deck, crushing his skull with a single blow.

Verloza howled, but before she could move, Gotrek strode forwards and punched the thing in the groin. It doubled over, gasping, and Gotrek sliced his axe down, sending the monster's head thudding across the deck. Acid hissed from the severed neck, causing the deck to steam and smoulder.

Gotrek peered at the corpse. 'A river troll?'

Verloza frowned, then nodded. 'I suppose. We call them troggoths. River's full of 'em.'

She glanced at Trachos, who was still singing, although only to himself now, mumbling the words inside his brutal, impassive helmet.

Trachos caught her gaze and stared at her. 'The Antiana Gate will hold. Chaos spawn will *never* enter Azyr.'

Verloza gave Gotrek a confused look. 'Azyr?'

Gotrek was too busy peering at the dead troggoth to register her question.

Maleneth leant over to Verloza. 'Trachos fights his own wars. Special ones that happen in his head.'

Before she could say anything else, the boat rocked again and there was an explosion of screams. She whirled around, knives raised, as something heavy thudded down behind her.

Stooped, steam-shrouded shapes clambered into view, seven or eight feet tall and armoured in dripping scales. Their faces were vaguely humanoid but they were so ugly they resembled the grotesques on a fortress wall. They had spikes running down their backs and ears like glistening fins.

Verloza looked shocked. Then she waved her crew forwards. 'Get in a line! Get those rats off my ship!' She dropped from the rigging, bounded across the deck and hurled her harpoon into the face of the first monster.

The brute barely registered the wound. It pounded across the deck towards her, trailed by flies, the harpoon jutting from its face. As it ran, it yanked the weapon from its forehead, spilling acid and adding to the stink of fish guts.

It slammed its shoulder into the fore mast, ripped up a large section of the deck and sent the captain tumbling head over heels.

Verloza landed heavily but managed to raise her sword as the troggoth loomed over her.

She had no need to use the blade. The troggoth crashed to the deck as its head rolled away.

Gotrek nodded at Verloza, his axe blade fizzing with acid. 'I would have paid more for the passage if you'd told me there was entertainment.'

Verloza shook her head. 'I've never seen them attack in these numbers before. Something's got them all worked up.'

'This is an idiot magnet,' said Gotrek, tapping the rune in his chest. 'And there are a lot of idiots.'

Verloza shrugged. 'Not to worry. They're big but there's nothing between their ears. I can't see us–'

Before she could finish, more troggoths stomped into view and both crew and passengers found themselves occupied.

As Verloza, Gotrek and the others rushed to attack, Maleneth found herself with her back to the gunwale as a troggoth charged in her direction. She easily sidestepped the mouldering plank it aimed at her head. The troggoth grunted in confusion as it saw her standing at its side with a smile on her face.

The thing looked even more confused as its head lolled against its chest, giving it an upside-down view of the battle, its neck neatly severed by Maleneth's knives. She backed away as the monster slammed onto the deck.

'Sigmar's balls!' cried Verloza, leaping across the rigging. 'This must be the whole family.' She was grinning, but it looked forced. The ship was quickly filling up with troggoths. Maleneth counted at least twenty. Several of Verloza's crewmen had already been killed. There were bodies on the deck and a few more dissolving in the river. Upstream she saw dozens more troggoths rising from the riverweed, spitting acid and raising weapons.

Maleneth spied the Slayer at the stern of the ship, laughing as he lunged and hacked, charging through the monsters and scattering limbs. She could see by his expression what was happening – he was losing himself to kill-fever. He would soon be oblivious to everything but the pulse hammering in his ears. 'Gotrek!' she cried. 'We should turn back! Look up ahead. There are too many.'

Gotrek swung his axe with even more savagery. 'There are exactly the *right* number. This is the first fun I've had since reaching this stinking city.' He looked around, his face a crimson mask, his eye glassy. 'What say you, captain?'

Verloza was not far from him, surrounded by her crew, fighting furiously but being driven back towards the railings. She tried to match his grin but she was clearly struggling. There were now a dozen dead crewmembers lying on the deck. 'I've never seen so many,' she managed to gasp. 'Perhaps we should turn back.'

'Bugger that.' Gotrek headbutted a troggoth so hard he toppled a whole pile of them. Then he climbed the heap, beheaded the monsters and charged towards Verloza.

Before he could reach her, another mob of troggoths tumbled over the gunwale and blocked his way, raining blows on the Slayer with makeshift clubs and salvaged weapons. Gotrek parried, cursed, then pointed at a shape in the river. 'We'll make a stand on that island. Gotrek Gurnisson does not flee from river trolls.'

Verloza nodded, but she was drenched in blood and acid and more of her crew were falling every second.

Trachos strode through the carnage swinging his hammers with calm precision, his chin raised proudly as a hymn boomed from his helmet. Despite the tears in his buckled armour he smashed through the giant creatures with as much ease as Gotrek, cracking skulls to the rhythm of his song.

Maleneth leapt onto the rigging and hurled a fistful of barbs. The blades were poison-laced and they hissed as they sliced into the monsters' hides, releasing lethal toxins. As more thundered towards her, she raced across the rigging towards the prow of the ship to look at the island Gotrek had mentioned. The *Sigmaron Star* was rushing towards it, caught in the current. Gotrek was right that they would soon be grounded. And troggoths were rising from the shallows all around it. Fifty, maybe more, all preparing to storm the ship.

'This is madness!' She looked back towards the Slayer. 'We have to turn this ship around!'

'Captain?' Gotrek looked over at Verloza. 'Are you with me?'

Verloza's face was grey and her blows were growing weaker. Half her crew were injured or dead. She shook her head.

'Bah! Leave it to the Slayer!' Gotrek smashed his way to the ship's wheel, steering the vessel straight for the island. 'I was killing trolls when your ancestors were living in caves.'

The ship juddered as it hit the island and the fighting paused as people fell or struggled to right themselves.

Gotrek barrelled through the reeling shapes and leapt over the prow, plunging through the steam and landing on the shore. He had started climbing to the summit when the island shook, hurling him onto his back and sending him sliding down towards the acid.

The tremor was so violent that the *Sigmaron Star* slid back into the river, pulling away from the island.

'Earthquake?' muttered Maleneth, hurling her barbs and dropping lightly to the deck. Combatants were staggering in every direction, struggling to land blows as the ship lurched.

The troggoths that had been gathering around the island began clambering onto the ship, rushing at Verloza's crew.

'Get back over here!' howled Maleneth. 'They've tricked you! They just wanted you out of the way!'

'Rubbish!' Gotrek stood and charged back towards the ship, but it was too late for him to make the leap. 'They don't have the brains to play tricks.' The Slayer paced around on the island as it continued shifting beneath him.

Then the river exploded, hurling geysers of acid and steam into the air and hiding the island from sight.

Maleneth struggled to stay on her feet as the ship rocked and troggoths attacked her from every direction. She looked for the captain but the scene was too chaotic to make anything out clearly. Figures were lurching through the spray, howling as monsters piled onto the deck. 'Verloza?' she cried.

The columns of acid fell away to reveal something even more disturbing.

The island Gotrek was standing on was rising from the river and, as tonnes of weed and mud fell away, Maleneth saw that rather than being a lump of rock, it was the head of a serpent – a snake five times the size of the *Sigmaron Star*. It towered over the trees as it uncoiled, shrugging off rocks and acid.

Gotrek howled with a mixture of rage and amusement, clinging on to its head.

The serpent hissed in response, fixing Gotrek with an eye that was as big as the Slayer. The hiss was so loud that Maleneth thought the sound might split her skull. The distraction was enough for her to miss her footing and one of the troggoths managed to punch the side of her head. She pinwheeled through the air and slammed into the side of Verloza's cabin. Blood filled her eyes. Pain lanced through her cheek.

We're not dying here, said a voice in Maleneth's mind, emanating from the amulet at her neck. *Not at the hands of some walking sewage. Get up. Do something.* The voice belonged to Maleneth's former mistress, a Khainite aelf she'd murdered years earlier. Maleneth wore her soul as a battle trophy, preserved in a vial of blood at the heart of the amulet. She carried her mistress with her for the sheer joy of tormenting her, but on occasion, her barbed comments were actually useful, spurring her into action.

Maleneth staggered to her feet in time to sidestep another punch. The cabin wall collapsed under the blow and her attacker fell through the wreckage.

Maleneth leapt onto the troggoth's back and climbed back onto the rigging. Troggoths tried to follow but only succeeded in wrecking more of the ship. The *Sigmaron Star* was rocking with increasing violence and, in her peripheral vision, she could see the serpent still rising from the river, shedding torrents of water, but she had more urgent matters to deal with. She took a lash from her belt and spat blood onto it. As the blood splashed across the leather she whispered a prayer, invoking Khaine's presence. To her delight, she felt a stab of agony through her hand.

He's here.

Maleneth nodded, baring her teeth in a bloody grin. 'For the Bloody-Handed One.' The whip coiled and writhed in her grip, struggling to free itself as an unnatural darkness washed over the battle, casting twisted shadows across the deck.

Maleneth whispered another prayer, then hurled the whip into the scrum beneath her feet. It thrashed as it fell then rippled away through the fight, lashing out as it tumbled through the troggoths. They tried to defend themselves but the whip snaked through them at incredible speed, slicing through necks and eyes.

Maleneth allowed herself a few seconds to enjoy the spectacle, then climbed higher and looked back at the island. 'Khaine's teeth,' she muttered. 'He's using the rune.'

He said he'd never use it again.

'What choice does he have? That thing's half snake, half mountain.' Gotrek looked like an ember smouldering in a heap of ash. Maleneth's spell had plunged the valley into darkness but the serpent was lit up by the infernal glow radiating from Gotrek's chest. The enormous creature was tightening around Gotrek, attempting to crush him. It looked like it had caught a flame. Gotrek was barely visible in the blaze, but Maleneth could hear him roaring as he struggled to break free.

'He's giving in to the rune,' she muttered. 'He's going to let it–'

There was another explosion.

The serpent hissed and fell backwards, sending waves crashing against the *Sigmaron Star*. Maleneth gripped the rigging as the whole valley shuddered. Rocks and trees tumbled down the riverbank, kicking up spray and noise.

Gotrek leapt at the serpent's head, his axe and chest burning.

The snake opened its mouth revoltingly wide but Gotrek swiped his axe to the right and cut its lower jaw away, sending it crashing down into the river. The fire in Gotrek's chest burned brighter and flooded into the runic tattoos that covered his skin. He hacked and hacked again, cleaving chunks of snake flesh and surrounding himself in gouts of acid. The snake swayed then fell, plunging straight towards the *Sigmaron Star*.

There was an explosion of acid and sparks as the snake crashed into the deck.

Maleneth was hurled backwards by the impact and hit her head as she landed, feeling a sharp pain run down her spine. The strength went from her legs, and as the ship began listing onto its side, she slid across the bloody deck, crashing into the mast.

Gotrek pounded through the carnage, dealing out blows with his axe and howling a war cry. The snake was dead, sprawled across the deck of the lurching ship, but Gotrek showed no sign of relenting. He was hacking at the ship itself, rending metal and oak as he ripped through the cabins. People were screaming and running, diving for cover, but Maleneth could not move, mesmerised by the intensity of Gotrek's rage. There was no thought in his eye, just dazzling, untrammelled fury.

'He's going to kill us all,' she whispered as the ship crumpled before his wrath.

There was another blast, so violent that Maleneth lost her grip. Her head bounced painfully on the deck and she lost consciousness.

Wake up.

Maleneth lay there for a moment, enjoying the pleasant sensation of warmth playing over her skin. 'Not yet,' she muttered. The act of speaking sent a splash of pain across her skull. 'Gotrek,' she gasped, sitting up. She was on the riverbank, half sunk in the mud. A dozen feet away, a piece of the *Sigmaron Star*'s deck was slowly dissolving in the acid. Flames licked across the wreckage, lighting up the mounds of bodies that were lying all around her – troggoths mostly, but also some humans, heaped in piles and shifting in the current. Their flesh had melted away, leaving little more than gore-stained skeletons, and each time the river lapped over them, a little more of the remains disintegrated.

Where's the rune?

Maleneth stood, unleashing several more explosions of pain, and looked down the valley. There was no sign of the serpent, or Gotrek. Then she realised that the serpent *was* there – it was sprawled in the river, half sunk, looking like a chain of islands. 'He did it.' She looked around at all the dead troggoths. 'We did it.'

But where is the rune?

'Gotrek will be around.' She wiped some of the filth from her face, looking through the smoke. 'He'll be celebrating. With ale.' As Maleneth tried to reassure her mistress, she could not help noticing that there were no sounds of celebration. She began picking her way through the bodies, keeping an eye out for signs of movement. A few crewmembers were still alive but their flesh was melting fast where the river had touched it. In a few more minutes they would be dead. Some of them called out to her for help as she passed, but she rolled her eyes and strode on, looking for the Slayer. After a victory like this he would have a thirst on him. If she didn't intercede quickly she would be stuck here for days as he drank his way through the ship's cargo. The thought of the ship made her realise that the *Sigmaron Star* was no more. Gotrek's rampage had sent the whole vessel to the riverbed.

She headed away from the melting piece of deck, marching through whirling steam as she headed upriver in the direction of the dead serpent. Perhaps he would still be nearby, gloating over his kill.

'Maleneth.' Trachos' voice echoed through the smoke and it took her a moment to locate him. He was back near the piece of deck she had just walked away from.

'Did you get me to the shore?' she asked.

'Yes.'

She nodded. 'I thought so. Gotrek would have left me to melt, wouldn't he?'

As was often the case, the aftermath of a battle seemed to give Trachos a moment of clarity. He replied clearly, with no trace of the madness that usually plagued him. 'He would not have known you, Witchblade. He was too far gone. He did not know me either.'

'Have you seen him?'

He pointed the Slayer out, and her heart sank as she saw him. He was sitting on another piece of wreckage, his massive shoulders rounded and slumped. *Damn*, she thought, *he's already drunk.*

Trachos knelt down by a dying sailor, speaking to him in gentle tones. Maleneth shook her head in disbelief. Whatever Sigmar had meant to forge Trachos into, it was not this. At some point in his past he had fallen below the standards he set himself, so now he was tediously pious, seeking ways to assuage his guilt by helping people who should be helping themselves. Usually to the sound of an atonal hymn. She ignored him and headed on towards the Slayer.

There were bodies melting all around him, humans mostly, and the piece of burning wreckage threw him into silhouette as she approached from behind.

'All praise the Slayer,' she said. 'Victorious again. Did you–?'

Her words stalled as she saw his face.

Gotrek's expression was black. He was staring at the mud with such ferocity that Maleneth half expected it to catch alight. She had seen him sink into these moods before. They could last for weeks.

'You won!' She waved at the dead serpent and the troggoth corpses. 'What in the name of the gods can you be angry about now?'

Gotrek said nothing, but Maleneth noticed that he was staring at one corpse in particular. There was little left to distinguish it, but Maleneth saw from a scrap of clothing that it was Captain Verloza. She laughed. 'Don't tell me you're *grieving*. Not over a buck-toothed fishwife? You're a Slayer. Slaying things is your job.'

Gotrek turned his withering gaze on her. She resisted the urge to back away, but any further comments stalled on her lips.

The Slayer's muscles were as taut as his stare. Maleneth realised she was one word away from triggering violence. She sat down near him, wracking her brains for something soothing to say. 'They were ugly and stupid, Gotrek. Does it matter if they're dead?'

His jaw clenched. Maleneth sensed she had not struck the right tone.

She licked her lips and thought carefully. 'You were trying to protect them, weren't you? Is that right? In which case is it your fault they didn't survive?'

'I killed them. I sank their ship.'

Maleneth found Gotrek's attitude peculiar even by his standards. 'These people ply this river all the time. They know the risks. They could have–'

'Verloza wanted to turn back.' Gotrek glanced at his axe, blood-drenched and lying in the mud. 'I was only thinking of myself.'

'When do you think of anyone else? Apart from that dead poet you always carp on about. This is a victory, Gotrek. Celebrate it.'

He spat. 'Tripe. These realms are so damned skewed they've dragged me to your level. I'm not some murdering aelf.' He kicked the nearest corpse, splashing acid into the flames. 'This isn't victory. This is slaughter. I've behaved more like a dim-witted greenskin than a proud son of the Everpeak.' Gotrek frowned and his face was so ridged with scars that it seemed to collapse, like boulders grinding against each other.

Maleneth felt a cold chill of premonition, guessing where the Slayer's mind was headed. She spoke quickly, trying to steer his thoughts in a new direction. 'We need to get back to the city. There could be more troggoths out here. If you've lost your love of–'

'It's the rune.'

Maleneth shook her head, but before she could speak, Gotrek continued. 'It *is* changing me.'

'It's not the damned rune. How many times have you told me that Slayers seek ever-bigger foes to pit themselves against? A *lot* of times. I've learned a lot more information about Slayers than I will ever need and I know that this is not unusual. You said you've hunted every kind of daemon, drake and greenskin.' She waved at the dead serpent that was slowly sinking from view. 'This is nothing new.'

He stared at Verloza's remains. 'I sank their ship. I killed them. And these were good people. They were going about their lives in the best way they could. There's no honour in this.'

Maleneth felt like striking him. 'What does it matter? They were nobodies. They were nothing.'

'What would you know about it? What would you know of honour? Of pride? Of decency? Of anything? You say you serve Sigmar but you're as mealy-mouthed as any other aelf. I'm a *dawi*. Do you understand? A dawi. My honour is my life and without it I'm nothing. I didn't swear my Slayer oath to bring shame on my ancestors, to bring shame on the memory of Karaz-a-Karak.' He glared at his slab-like fists. 'I'm the last. The last of my kind. If I can't uphold my ancestors' honour then who can?' He punched the rune. 'This thing's poisoning me. Making me a savage.' He stood, grabbed his axe from the mud and pointed it at the sky. 'Well you picked the wrong dwarf! I'm Gotrek Gurnisson! Not some plaything of the gods! I'm no bloody savage!' He stomped through the wreckage, hacking chunks from it and surrounding himself in a storm of sparks.

'Who could call *you* savage?' said Maleneth with a raised eyebrow, but she kept her voice low.

Gotrek spent the next few minutes attacking the riverbank, then turned to face Maleneth. He was silhouetted by flames, his face in shadow, but he was shaking and she could hear the fury in his voice. 'This thing is coming out, aelf. I won't have it in my chest any more. I won't be ruled by it. Someone in these realms must have an ounce of brains. I'll find them. I'll set them to work on it. I'll not rest until it's gone.'

Your Celestial Highnesses,

I encountered your agent in Anvilgard and I understand the frustrations expressed in your letter. However, if you will forgive the impertinence, I would like to request that you do not send me messages via agents who skulk from the shadows of inns. I would never knowingly inflict harm on a servant of the Order of Azyr, but when someone lunges at me from behind a stack of barrels I cut first and ask questions later. As a result of my (honest) mistake, much of your message was obscured by blood. I am assuming the lines ending 'return to Azyrheim' refer to my oft-stated mission to return home with the Slayer's rune so that we may harness it for the good of our military campaigns. At present, it is still embedded securely in Gotrek's chest, but I am edging closer to winning his confidence and convincing him to bring it to you. I have yet to find out exactly why he is so averse to coming to Azyr, but I sense that by repeatedly goading him I will eventually needle the truth out of him. It is not, as I at first thought, that he fears being in the clutches of our divine order. He does not fear anything. And we have visited several stormkeeps and Sigmarite outposts during our travels. It is the Celestial Realm itself that he is hostile to. The suggestion of going there sends him into the most apoplectic rages. I shall not be deterred, however. Perhaps when I finally understand his reasoning, I can allay his fears.

As you know, we have recently visited the port of Anvilgard. (What a glum, sweaty place.) Prior to that we spent an interminable few months trawling the steaming bogs of the surrounding Charwind Coast. The Slayer dragged us there on one of his obscure whims. He has abandoned, for now at least, his fanciful belief that he can recover an axe he might have once owned in a world that might never have existed. He also seems to have accepted that his former friend Felix (inhabitant of aforesaid world) is dead and not likely to recover from that condition any time soon. If I am honest, I have no idea what he intended to find in the lava-cooked puddles of the Charwind Coast, but thankfully he still sees me as a useful guide. He has no grasp of social mores or, for that matter, basic geography, and he has an impressive skill for making enemies, so he has become increasingly reliant on me (much to his annoyance).

After deciding Anvilgard is populated by 'sour-faced simpletons,' the Slayer led us back out into the acid swamps that cover this whole region. I believe he was looking for nothing more than something to sink his axe into and, just a few miles from the city, we found it. We were attacked by river monsters. Gotrek, of course, made short work of them, but rather than lifting his mood, as it should have done, the experience sent him into another of his maddening sulks. A few local deckhands were killed in the encounter and Gotrek has become obsessed by the idea that he has behaved dishonourably.

After the trail of corpses he has left across the realms, this newfound morality is frankly absurd, but as you may imagine, trying to reason with him is not an option. Once he latches on to an idea there is no force beneath the stars that can rid him of it until he moves onto another fixation. He has decided that the rune is responsible for his 'dishonourable behaviour' and he has sworn to have the thing removed from his chest. That may sound like progress – if he were to extract the rune, my commission would become a lot easier. I would no longer have to try to guess his reasons for avoiding Azyr if I had the rune. However, Gotrek's plan concerns those self-serving opportunists, the Kharadron Overlords. The Slayer has heard of a city, one of their cloud-borne sky-ports called Barak-Urbaz, in which duardin engineers have developed aethermatic engines capable of extracting metals by alchemical means. He is now set on the idea that the Kharadron will be able to suck Blackhammer's Master Rune out of his body without killing him and allow him to become, well, whatever he was before the rune was in his chest.

Gotrek's latest obsession presents me with a new difficulty – if the Kharadron really are able to remove the rune I doubt very much that they will hand it over to me. They are conniving profiteers and they will seek to harness the rune's power to further their own endeavours.

I have been unable to sway Gotrek from his course but I have devised a plan to ensure that our stay in Barak-Urbaz will be brief. I shall simply ensure that the initial attempts to remove the rune fail. I shall only have to do this a few times and he will decide the entire city is worthless. I should have no trouble contacting you from Barak-Urbaz, so I shall keep you abreast of developments.

As an aside, I think your letter made mention of rumours concerning my departure from Azyrheim. It is hard to read through the bloodstains, but I think you make mention of murders and deceit. Let me assure you that I only ever act in the interests of our order and any slanderous tales being spread about my methods will be a result of jealousy. We shall see what my detractors have to say when I return to you with Blackhammer's Master Rune – a weapon so powerful it would enable Sigmar's Stormhosts to strike further into the realms than ever before. Having seen the rune in action, I can assure you that our initial estimations of its power fall way short of its true strength. I truly believe that this thing will turn the tide of the war for the realms and grant Sigmar's armies victory after victory.

As a second aside, let me mention that the Stormcast Eternal Trachos is still travelling with me. I accept your assurance that he is linked to our order and, in truth, I have to admit that he has proved useful on several occasions. While Gotrek had a clear *purpose, Trachos seemed to shake off his delusions and behave in a less erratic way. However, since Gotrek sank into this latest bout of despondency, Trachos has also lost his way. He has developed a peculiar devotion to Gotrek, and with the Slayer lost in morose introspection, Trachos has become more confused than ever. He is as physically powerful as any Stormcast Eternal, so his fractured state of mind makes him something of a powder keg.*

I shall send more news once we reach Barak-Urbaz. In the meantime, I would request that you base your judgements of me on my actions rather than the tales circling Azyrheim. I have been unwavering in my determination to bring the rune to you, and I remain,

Your most loyal and faithful votary,
Maleneth Witchblade

CHAPTER ONE

Maleneth paused at the end of an iron gangplank and cursed, lost in the clouds, surrounded by a forest of clanking leviathans. In Barak-Urbaz nothing was entirely visible, obscured by banks of smoke and drowned by the din of industry. And yet, even here she could not escape Gotrek. Alarmed cries echoed towards her, distorted by the smog. Wherever the Slayer went, howls of protest soon followed. And booming over the clamour was Gotrek's own voice, raging and savage.

Maleneth felt a flicker of amusement from the amulet at her chest. The vial of blood spoke directly into her thoughts. *He sounds particularly annoyed.* Her dead mistress was right. She could hear people running and things breaking. Maleneth toyed with her knife, muttered to herself, then hurried on.

Their lodgings were in the Stromez Quarter, or the Obscurfjard, as the older signs referred to it, but Maleneth had yet to distinguish any difference between the sky-port's various districts. She had spent the last few hours in the Skoggyn Quarter and, aside from being even more ash-clogged, it consisted of exactly the same oil-spurting forges as everywhere else. To be in Barak-Urbaz was to be lost in the workings of a great machine, assailed by gears and pistons, deafened by the roar of smokestacks. To Maleneth's heightened senses it was a brimstone hell. Everywhere she looked there were mechanisms the size of mountains – fifty-foot tilt-hammers that landed with an arterial thud, jolting the city like an iron pulse. Nitrous mills belched alchemical smoke, filling her every breath with the taste of metal. Antimony pumps groaned like subterranean monsters. Maleneth had seen Kharadron architecture before, but Barak-Urbaz was more frenzied and pungent than anything she had ever experienced. It was like being surrounded by worker drones in a mechanised hive, with everyone building, extracting and refining in an orgy of growth and consumption. As she raced along a suspended walkway she had to dodge clanking vehicles – smaller, track-bound cousins of the Kharadron airships that rushed by just a few feet above her head. Further up there was an endless train of gyrohaulers, airborne freight carriers that hissed and spat as they rushed overhead. And on every steaming hulk she could see the famed Kharadron endrineers, hanging from railings and prows with no thought for safety, wrenching cogs and hammering plates even as the vehicles screamed through the air. For all her revulsion, Maleneth had to concede that they were unlike any people she had ever encountered before. While other nations fought for survival or grovelled for mercy, the Kharadron were in a state of endless evolution, constructing and inventing at such a pace that one could almost believe they would outstrip the hungry grasp of Chaos.

Maleneth tried to ignore the general din and focus on the commotion around Gotrek. She dropped lightly from the walkway and landed on another iron road, stepped back as a phaeton thundered past, then headed on towards her lodgings.

Squat figures turned to face her as she neared the tumult. The Kharadron were all as short as Gotrek, barely coming up to her chest, and most of those she had encountered so far made themselves even more ungainly by wearing bulky flight suits – creaking outfits of metal and rubber topped with riveted, ugly helmets. The Kharadron Overlords claimed the overalls protected them from the toxic clouds, but Maleneth doubted there would be any toxins if it weren't for the Kharadron forges. Even her superior, aelven physique had been affected. Within a day of reaching the city in the clouds, her lungs had begun to rattle and her eyes streamed constantly. She would not lower herself to wearing one of the cumbersome Kharadron flight suits, even if they made one to fit her slender figure, but had to wear a piece of cloth over her mouth every time she ventured outside or she would find herself coughing blood. It had taken months to get from Anvilgard to the Realmgate that brought them here, and Maleneth found it particularly galling that, after such a long journey, they had managed to find a place where the air was just as toxic as the Charwind Coast.

A group of Kharadron grumbled as she passed. She glared at them until they backed away into the fumes, huddling protectively around a rattling brazier and glowering through the eyeholes in their helmets. Despite being hung above the clouds, this quarter of the sky-port was sunk in a stygian gloom, blanketed in purple and black clouds, so the streets and walkways were lit by aether-filled brass spheres that clinked against the hull-like walls. The unnatural light lent everything it touched an otherworldly air, and as Maleneth scowled at the endrineers it felt like she was staring at ghosts.

Despite the filth and noise, Barak-Urbaz was one of the safest places in the entire realm – in any of the realms outside of Azyr, for that matter. As a result, the Stromez Quarter was mostly given over to teetering stacks of buildings called *khordryn* – a form of accommodation reserved for the travellers who poured into the city. The Kharadron were canny and always eager to do business with outsiders, but they also liked their foreigners where they could see them. Urbaz was famed as a cosmopolitan melting pot, but Maleneth had noticed how closely the Kharadron guarded their grand-looking guildhalls. There were clearly things they did not wish to share.

A duardin called Brior raced towards her through the fumes. Even through the hammered metal of his mask she could see his panic. 'You have to talk to him!' He reached out to grab her arm.

She sidestepped and drew her knife in such a fluid motion that it took Brior a moment to realise his throat was about to be opened.

He backed away, hands raised.

'What has he done?' she asked, keeping the knife raised.

'I...' Brior shook his head. 'It's hard to explain. He's *so* angry.'

'About what?'

'Everything. He said he's going to knock Barak-Urbaz out of the clouds.'

Maleneth nodded.

'And he's arguing with someone in there. *Roaring* at him. And I can't hear any replies.' Brior looked even more anguished. 'By the Code! What if he's killed someone? You promised me when I let you the rooms you would keep him–'

'Arguing? Who would be stupid enough to argue with Gotrek Gurnisson? Was it Trachos?'

'Who?'

'The Stormcast Eternal. The Sigmarite who travels with us.'

Brior looked almost as concerned by the thought of Trachos as he did Gotrek. 'I haven't seen him all day. He left shortly after you.' Brior leant closer to her and lowered his voice, glancing around. 'He told me to muster the host and meet him at Heavenhall. What does that mean? What host? Where is Heavenhall?'

Maleneth cursed under her breath. Trachos' delusions had become more severe since Gotrek had latched on to his latest obsession. How could she have offended Khaine so badly she ended up with such ridiculous companions?

By letting oafs like this live.

Maleneth could not argue with that logic, but she resisted the urge to gut Brior and continued on her way.

There was a crowd gathered outside the khordryn and she recognised some of them. It was their fellow guests – mostly humans but also some duardin exiles and even a few aelves. At the sight of Maleneth they grew more enraged, rushing towards her and demanding recompense. Some of their belongings were scattered across the gantries along with pieces of the khordryn's facade.

As the guests caught sight of Maleneth's expression and the knife in her hand they halted. They continued yelling, however, calling for her to get Gotrek away from them.

Brior nodded eagerly. 'Perhaps it would be for the best. If the Fyreslayer is so unhappy with the rooms you could–'

Maleneth rounded on him. 'Is that what triggered this? Did you call him a *Fyreslayer*?'

'No!' Brior hesitated, wiped his eye lenses and shook his head. 'I don't think. No, I'm sure I didn't. I remember you said he preferred to be called a dwarf, so I called him a dwarf. To be honest, though, I've tried not to talk to him at all.'

'Very wise.' She looked up at the broken windows. Gotrek's cries were booming out through the smoke. He sounded furious at whoever had entered his rooms. 'Conversation is not his strong point.'

She rushed across a gangplank, heading into the khordryn.

Brior followed. 'It would be best though, don't you think?'

'What?'

'If you and the Fyre... if you and the dwarf found other lodgings. Somewhere more to his liking.'

Maleneth laughed. '*Liking?* I'd have to travel a long way before I found something to his liking. Besides, you said there are no rooms available anywhere else. Something to do with the moon?'

He grimaced. 'Kazak-drung. The grot moon. It's almost full. And what little of Ayadah was still free is now falling to the greenskins.' For a moment he looked troubled, then he brightened. 'So everyone is looking for a place in Barak-Urbaz. We've never had so many visitors. Most of the khordryn are full.'

'*All* of them are full, you said.' They were inside now, and Maleneth paused at the foot of a spiral staircase. 'That was why I was willing to pay such an absurd amount for these tin boxes you call rooms.'

Brior tried to back away, but Maleneth's hand lashed out and grabbed the pauldron of his flight suit while the other pressed her knife to his throat. 'Were you lying?'

'Grungni be blessed, madam, no. Of course not. But if your friend is so unhappy here, I could see if a room has come available since you arrived.' He hesitated. 'They might not be quite so reasonably priced as my own premises, but I would be willing to act as an agent on your behalf, for a small fee, and I have many friends over in–'

'Gotrek's right.' Maleneth leant close. 'You're all money-leeching worms.'

They were interrupted by a loud cracking sound. It sounded like a door being torn in half.

Brior gasped and shook his head. 'He *can't* stay.'

'Do you want to tell him?'

Brior said nothing.

Maleneth nodded. Then she let him go and headed up the stairs, picking her way between buckled furniture and torn drapes. The only illumination came from an aether lamp, crackling in the gloom, but it was an easy enough matter to locate their rooms. Gotrek's rage was echoing through the hammered bulkheads, punctuated by the sound of metal hitting metal.

She reached the door to their rooms and paused. Maleneth was no coward. She had survived years in Khainite Murder Temples, fought in Sigmar's wars of reclamation and seen dead rise to claim the living, but Gotrek was unlike anything she had ever seen before. She took a moment to whisper a prayer to Khaine, sliced her knife across her palm and kissed the spilled blood. Vigour flooded her limbs. Then she gently pushed the door open.

The room was a mess. The lights had been ripped from their sconces and even Maleneth's aelven eyes struggled to make sense of what she was seeing. There was broken furniture everywhere. Gotrek was a hulking shadow at the centre of the destruction, silhouetted by the brazier in his axe. His back was to Maleneth, but she could see that he was taking deep, juddering breaths.

Unable to see who had driven him into such a frenzy, Maleneth edged closer, knives raised, trying to see round Gotrek's barrel-like frame.

'Blood of Grungni,' growled Gotrek, spraying saliva through the air and drawing back his axe to strike.

'Gotrek?' said Maleneth, dropping into a fighting stance.

'Liars!' roared Gotrek, spinning round with surprising agility and swinging his axe at her head.

The weapon trailed embers as it slammed into the doorframe, shearing off a slab of metal.

Maleneth dodged the blow, tumbling back onto her feet on the opposite side of the room.

Gotrek wrenched his axe free, hurling more sparks.

As he steadied himself for another blow, Maleneth looked around to see who had driven him into such a rage. Dented metal lay scattered in heaps and a broken heating pipe was spewing steam, but she was fairly sure that there was no one else in the room. She felt a rush of anger. 'You're getting worse.'

Gotrek's eye was glassy and unseeing as he swung at her face.

She ducked and the blade clanged into a bedpost, causing another flash of sparks.

Gotrek's momentum sent him tumbling into the wall and Maleneth realised he had been drinking. To her endless regret, the brewmasters of Barak-Urbaz produced an ale called hazkal that was so strong Gotrek considered it almost palatable. 'What are you talking about, aelf?' Gotrek staggered away from her, batting embers from his beard. His eye was burning as fiercely as his axe. Maleneth had seen him like this before. The violence he had wreaked so far was nothing to what he was capable of.

Maleneth tried to change her tone to something more placatory but the best she could manage was sardonic. 'You and Trachos are both losing your grip. You're fighting people that don't exist. Next thing you know you'll be joining him on his imaginary crusades.' She waved at the wreckage. 'There's *nobody* in here.'

Gotrek moved with the agility of a practised drunk, grabbing her by the shoulders and slamming her against the wall. His ale-reek breath made her eyes water but she held his gaze. 'You're fighting furniture, Gotrek.'

His voice was a dangerous whisper. 'I'm trying to use the toy *you* bought from that trader.'

Maleneth had supplied Gotrek with so much junk that it took her a moment to remember which deception she needed to repeat. 'Ah, the chain-grip.' She spotted the machine lying near a broken bed. An oval-shaped brass case crammed with slender chains. The seller had told Gotrek it had alchemical properties but she had ensured it was now only good for an ornament. It was the latest in a succession of devices she had secretly disabled, hoping to rid Gotrek of his belief that Kharadron machines could help him.

She planted one of her boots in Gotrek's groin and the Slayer loosed his grip, stumbling away and cursing as she dropped into a crouch.

Before he could lash out again, she leapt across the room and grabbed the device from the floor. To her amazement, the mechanism was ticking, cogs spinning and chains clicking through the housing. 'You fixed it? Blood of Khaine. How did you–?'

Gotrek's fist hit the wall near her head, hurling her across the room. She felt a strange sense of serenity, feeling as though she were floating through a fragment of time. Then she slammed into the opposite wall, the air exploded from her lungs and she lost her sense of tranquillity. Blood rushed down her face and she had the unpleasant sensation that her head was no longer attached to her neck.

The door opened a crack and Brior peered in, whispering nervously, 'There's a room in the Starkhad Quarter. Your master would prefer it there, I'm sure. Lots of colourful, foreign types. I could haggle on your behalf if you–'

Maleneth slammed the door, eliciting a surprised yelp from Brior. She rolled aside, instinct warning her that Gotrek's axe was likely to follow his fist, but there was no attack. She flipped back onto her feet and saw that he was engrossed in the device again. His fingers were like battered ingots but he managed to use them with surprising dexterity, making adjustments and flicking clasps.

'Cack-handed sky dwarfs.' He peered at the device. 'Another bloody drop valve. Why in the name of Valaya's teeth would anyone put that in there?' There was a bright click as Gotrek snapped something from the mechanism. His eye flashed as the chain started moving again, then the light died as the mechanism clicked to a halt. He stared at the strip of silver he had taken out. It dangled in his grip like a metal worm. 'Only a moron would put this in there. And it was exactly the same with all the other machines we've found.'

Maleneth felt a flash of panic. He had noticed the aetheric inhibiters she had been planting in his devices.

Gotrek was studying the thing so intently that Maleneth felt sure he was about to make a connection between it and her. Then he dropped it to the floor and punched the wall, splitting another heat pipe and adding to the clouds of steam.

Maleneth rolled across the rubble and grabbed the inhibiter while Gotrek was looking the other way, secreting it safely in her leathers. The thing had been expensive. And she had no way of buying another one.

'I could secure the rooms for a vastly reduced price,' hissed Brior, peering round the door again.

She booted it shut, pleased to hear him fall over on the other side. Then she padded over to Gotrek, wiping blood from her face and keeping a safe distance. Perhaps she was wrong to say he was going the way of Trachos, but he was clearly losing himself. Since the loss of the *Sigmaron Star* and her crew he had become even more irascible. She had always struggled to gauge his mood but now it was easy. He was either furious or drunk. Usually both.

She tried even harder to sound sympathetic and this time she almost managed it. 'Can't you see this is a fool's errand? All these endrineers and aether-khemists have nothing to offer you.' She looked at the rune flickering in his chest. 'They can't turn that thing off any more than you can. But if you come with me, back to Azyr, we can harness its power. I don't know why you're so set against it, but if you let me take you to Azyrheim we can turn that rune into a weapon against Chaos.'

'A weapon for that dolt, Sigmar, you mean.' Gotrek's eye blazed as he swung his axe.

Maleneth leapt aside but there was no need. She was not the target.

The chain-grip exploded as Gotrek's axe slammed into it, tossing springs and cogs across the room. 'I am no one's weapon.' Gotrek levelled his finger at Maleneth. 'Not yours, not Grimnir's and certainly not that of some flaxen-haired farm boy with delusions of godhood.' He kicked the broken machine across the floor. 'These Kharadron are shoddy endrinkuli, but even bad dwarfish engineering outstrips anything else in the Mortal Realms. That thing could have actually worked if it weren't for the drop valve. I almost had it going.'

Maleneth stared at him. He was a constant surprise. He played the part of belligerent oaf so well that it was easy to forget how sharp-witted he was. He had a savant-like affinity with anything mechanical. She had done everything she could to ensure the device could never work but Gotrek had come worryingly close to fixing it.

Gotrek punched the rune. Veins of light leaked from it, spilling across his beer-slick chest. 'We're not leaving this city until I get this out.' His eye flashed again and Maleneth backed away. 'Maybe it's Grimnir in there and maybe it's not, but either way it has no place in my chest.' His words grew strained. 'In my bloody *head.*'

The door flew open, spilling Brior into the room and revealing a towering, armoured figure.

Trachos strode through the doorway, oblivious to the supine landlord. He was a mess. Trachos' ghosts had returned in force. His blue-green battle-plate was dented and rent and it sparked constantly. He looked like one of the broken devices Gotrek had tried to fix. Part of his faceplate had cracked but there was no glimpse of a face beneath, just flickers of light and flashes of irradiated bone. Stormcast Eternals were figures of awe wherever they went, but Trachos was more than that now. People would cross the street not to be near him – several streets. He moved with the mechanical gait of an automaton and his head flicked constantly from side to side, as though trying to rid itself of troubling thoughts.

He walked over to Gotrek and nodded at him, scattering sparks through the gloom.

Gotrek, Maleneth and Brior stared at him.

Trachos showed no sign of noticing the awkward pause, looking down at the Slayer through the eyeholes of his mangled helmet.

Brior climbed to his feet and dusted himself down. He edged closer to Trachos with the air of someone approaching a wounded animal. 'I was just explaining to your friends that I have found you some superior rooms in the–'

'We're leaving the city,' said Maleneth, speaking over him with a warning glare. She looked up at Trachos. 'Nothing Gotrek has tried has had any effect on his rune. These duardin are all talk. Not one of them has any actual skill.'

Trachos nodded, and Maleneth was pleased to see that he had not entirely lost his grip on reality. 'There is only one place in all the realms where you could harness that rune – the Anvil of Apotheosis, in the halls of High Sigmaron itself, where the God-King waits. The astrologions of the Lunar Spheres know how–'

'Let Sigmar sit up there playing with his spheres.' Gotrek was clearly furious at the suggestion. 'This Slayer won't hide away in glittering heavens while the Ruinous Powers hold sway below. Besides, I don't want to *harness* the bloody rune, I want rid of it.' He slammed it with the haft of his axe, making it flash like a disturbed ember. 'Rid of all the gods and their trinkets. Then, when I have my mind back, I'll finally be able to think straight.'

Brior spoke quickly, before Maleneth could interrupt him again. 'Master dwarf, I could help.'

Maleneth was about to order him from the room but Gotrek spoke first. 'How?'

Brior looked closer at the rune in Gotrek's chest. 'It's ur-gold?'

'Aye.' Gotrek's lip curled. 'With a seam of mischief running through it. The damned thing is poison.'

Brior nodded. 'The Fyreslayers. They hunt ur-gold obsessively. They hoard it.' He shook his head. 'Grungni knows why. They hide it in their mountain holds and hammer it into their skin, but if they *spent* some of it they could stop living like savages, with their bare chests and mohawks and...' Brior's words trailed off as he remembered what Gotrek looked like. 'Not that there's anything wrong with a rustic style of dress,' he continued quickly. 'It's just that–'

Gotrek tapped the rune. 'You said you could help.'

'What is it you want?' Brior glanced at Maleneth and Trachos, who were both glaring at him. 'Your friends seem to think–'

'They're not my friends and they don't think. There's a leaden-headed ape in Azyr who thinks for them. I want this thing out of my chest, but I don't want to breathe my last on an alchemist's slab. A Slayer doesn't die on a table. I need to survive so I can die properly.'

Brior removed his helmet, letting his long, plaited beard tumble down his rubber flight suit. He peered closer at the rune. 'It's buried in your ribs. Removing it without killing you would be hard, even for a skilled chirurgeon.'

Gotrek's face flushed with colour, highlighting the terrible scars that covered one side of his face.

Brior spoke quickly. 'But I know Barak-Urbaz's finest aether-khemists – Captain Thialf Solmundsson, Guildmaster Horbrand, Admiral Skuldsson, all of them. I don't know if they could remove the rune, but they're masters of everything metallurgical. If the rune contains aetheric power they would be able to extract it using their engines and braziers. Even if they couldn't remove the rune they could...' He struggled to find the word. 'They could nullify it. I'm sure they could.'

Maleneth cursed herself for not slitting Brior's throat when she had the chance. 'Gotrek. Look at him. He's an idiot, just like all the others. None of these people have a clue what that rune means.'

'Ah, but you do, don't you, aelf?' Gotrek scowled. 'It's a leash.'

Trachos shook his head. 'Not a leash. A boon. With this rune you can be more than you were. You can be a great weapon against Chaos.'

Maleneth nodded eagerly. 'He's right, Gotrek. Think of all the things you've seen, in these realms and the ones you were born in. Think of the madness and ruin. And you have it in your power to make a difference.' Unexpectedly, she found that she was speaking with genuine passion. 'Most of us can only fight on the sidelines, but you can actually *do* something. If you use that rune you can-'

'Use it?' Gotrek's expression darkened. 'Have you forgotten what happens when I use it? Have you forgotten what I did to the *Sigmaron Star*?'

Maleneth was genuinely baffled. 'You killed some sailors. Why are you so fixated on that? What is the significance of a few deckhands when balanced against the fate of the realms?'

'*I* did not kill them, aelf. You saw what happened. I was not using the rune as a weapon – the rune was using me. Maybe it was *him* using me.'

Maleneth knew better than to be drawn into an argument with Gotrek, but he was so infuriating she could not help herself. 'Him? You mean Grimnir? A god who, if he ever existed at all, is widely held to be dead now. *He* made you kill people, did he? Because he lives in your chest now. A god. In your chest. Telling you to do things. Can you hear yourself? You accuse Trachos and me of being in thrall to a god but at least it's a god that exists.'

Trachos gripped Maleneth and Gotrek by their shoulders and leant close. 'The lord-celestant,' he whispered. 'Do you hear him?'

Maleneth frowned, then closed her eyes in despair.

'Thialf Solmundsson could help,' said Brior hesitantly, looking from Trachos to Maleneth. 'He's a lord of industry now, one of the wealthiest magnates in the city, but he made his fortune through metallurgy. There's no form of metal he can't tame. If there is something in that rune you want extracting, he could do it.'

Maleneth shoved Trachos aside, furious that his rambling had given Brior another chance to speak.

She jabbed the duardin in the chest. 'You have no idea what you're doing.'

'Take me to this Solmundsson,' said Gotrek.

Brior grinned. 'I'll have a contract drawn up immediately. My terms will be reasonable. I shall require payment up front for the-'

Gotrek tapped his axe against Brior's chest. 'No contracts. Help me get shot of this rune and you'll be rewarded.'

Brior's grin faltered.

Gotrek strode from the room, taking some door frame with him. 'My word is my bond.'

Brior moved to follow, but Maleneth halted him at the threshold. 'I don't know what game you're playing, but if anything happens to that rune, I will take you apart. Slowly. With my thumbs.'

Aero-endrins roared overhead as Gotrek and the others headed out onto the street. Some were so vast they looked like ironclad mountains and it seemed incredible to Maleneth that they could stay aloft. They carried huge lightning-charged spheres in place of masts and clusters of pipes that fed the energy down the length of the hulls. From the street level it looked like gun-laden leviathans were swimming through the smog, turning in shoals and causing the air to grind.

Gotrek and Maleneth glared at the crowd that was still gathered by the doors and Brior waved some of his servants over. 'Go to the dwarf's room and clear it up. Itemise all the damage. I want a full inventory. Draw up a list of every expense.' As his servants rushed back into the khordryn, Brior dusted himself down and stood as tall as he could. His panicked demeanour had been replaced with an absurd air of pride as he led Gotrek through the crowd.

'Stand aside!' he cried, waving an ornate cane he had grabbed from the hall. It was a thick bronze staff, topped with an intricately worked anvil. 'We have business with Thialf Solmundsson.'

A few of the Kharadron guests looked impressed by the name, but most people continued demanding recompense.

Brior shook his head sadly. 'Check clause five of your tenancy agreements, my friends. I cannot be held liable for the indiscretions of my guests. If you have a complaint you must raise it with Gotrek Gurnisson here.'

Gotrek looked around, treating the assembled guests to a fierce stare.

Nobody approached.

Gotrek nodded and waved his axe at the pipe-clogged streets. 'Which way?'

Brior beckoned and strode off, still waving his cane. 'Captain Solmundsson lives in the Starkhad Quarter, near the aerostatic dock. We'll need to fly.'

Gotrek nodded, and they marched off down the street with the crowd still gawping at them.

CHAPTER TWO

'Gizzit.'

Scragfang tapped the puffball with his knife. It was several inches taller than him and there was light pulsing in its flesh, but he told himself not to be afraid. He was here on the Loonking's business. A royal envoy. He wore long black robes, intricately stitched with images of the Bad Moon's face. He had a thick necklace of polished teeth hung around his neck. His bony fingers were crowded with jewelled rings and his nose rattled with silver hoops. He was *someone*. A regal prophet. No one could touch him. He pushed the blade deeper, splitting the spongey skin, smelling the goodness. 'Gizzit.'

Gibbermarsh was brighter than the rest of the Asylum. Circles of fungus carpeted the valley and all of them were lit up in the same way as the puffball, spilling a wan, listless glow over the tree-high toadstools that surrounded them, but Scragfang did not mind the glare. It was nothing like sunlight. If anything, the circles of light accentuated the pall, deepening the shadows, adding to the comforting claustrophobia. Plump, quivering grubs whirled through the drizzle, banking and catching the light on their wings as they devoured each other in a perpetual feeding frenzy. Rich, rotten aromas wafted through the mist, making such a heady concoction that Scragfang's nose began to twitch. Scragfang's appetites had long ago blurred the boundaries between real and unreal. He was never entirely sure which things were in the world and which were in his head. He was followed, constantly, by a swarm of winged feet. They all had his face grinning from their soles and laughed at everything he said. Even though they looked incredibly vivid, no one else saw them and he was fairly sure they were only in his head.

Scragfang pushed his blade futher into the puffball. The stink thickened and black pus spilled from the pallid skin. The puffball was one of the most powerful scryshrooms in the whole marsh. It had given Scragfang some of his most useful prophecies. But it was prone to mood swings and he had yet to fully tame it, so he stood as far back as he could, leaning away from its flesh. A shape swam into view, forcing its way through the membranous gloop, blinking and grimacing as it emerged into the warm rain. Its face was almost identical to Scragfang's – green-skinned, pinched and hateful with vivid red eyes huddled next to a hooked nose.

'Scragfang,' gurgled the face, sneezing snot and spores. 'Gizzit wot?'

'An 'eadache.' Scragfang waved his knife, trying to swat some of the grinning feet away. 'I ain't got nuffin. Gis an 'eadache or I'll cutcha.'

The face sneered. 'You ain't got the guts.'

Scragfang pressed his nose against the leering face. 'Gizz. It.'

The face continued smirking as it slithered back into the puffball's innards. Then a scrawny hand emerged, holding a lump of flesh.

Scragfang snatched it and swallowed it whole.

For a moment nothing happened and Scragfang was about to use his knife again. Then the puffball blazed brighter. Even then, the glare was not unpleasant. It was cool and gibbous, soothing rather than scorching. Scragfang giggled and shuffled closer, staring into the light, letting it fill his mind. He felt so proud. No one knew Gibbermarsh like he did. Even the Loonking himself had no idea how Scragfang gained his visions. No one knew about this grove or all the others he had sniffed out. The back of Scragfang's head was fused with a wart-covered death cap and, as the light grew, the fungus began to quiver and ooze.

Scragfang giggled as the puffball changed shape, assuming the glorious, pockmarked visage of the Bad Moon. Scragfang danced and whistled. It had worked again.

Mangleback edged into the light, giggling along with him. Mangleback had been moonstruck too. He had not gained the dizzying insights that had enabled Scragfang's meteoric rise, but he was transformed in so many other ways that his original form was barely recognisable. He almost resembled a fungal crustacean. In place of a carapace, he had a gilled, powdery mushroom cap and his legs were pale, ribbed stems that ended in puckered cups. His goblinoid face was still visible though, peering out from beneath his spongey carapace, and he grinned as Scragfang danced. He reached up to a sack on his domed back, took out some finger bells and a whistle and began to play, accompanying Scragfang's dance with clangs and peeps and joining him in his dance through the mud.

The sound of the whistle snaked through Scragfang's brain until he saw it was a serpent, coiling round the face of the Bad Moon, sliding past swarms of giggling feet and catching spores on its forked tongue. Scragfang leapt at the moon, trying to chase the serpent. The moon shattered like the surface of a pool and Scragfang found himself falling through the heavens. The snake was ahead of him and it turned to look back, revealing that it now had the hooked, grinning face of the Bad Moon. Or was it Mangleback?

'Why settle for second place?'

Scragfang was too busy laughing to catch the words at first.

'Wozzat? Second face?'

The face whirled around him in the darkness, still grinning. 'Why let da Loonking have all da fun?'

Scragfang stopped laughing as he realised it was Mangleback speaking. Was this a test?

''Cause 'e's da boss?'

'Does da Bad Moon only need one servant? D'ya fink he can laugh *too* much?'

Scragfang could not quite understand where the conversation was leading. Part of his mind knew that this serpent was actually just Mangleback's whistle, looping round the drizzly grove, but the other part of him felt a great sense of moment, as though he was on the cusp of revelation. This had happened several times since he was moonstruck and it was why the Loonking had placed him in such a high position. 'I int gonna upset Skragrott, ya moron. I int gonna steal 'is place.'

The darkness vanished and Scragfang howled as sunlight filled his eyes. He thrashed and hissed, trying to shield his face, then he realised that there was no pain. The sun was not real. Just another vision. He opened his eyes and saw a dreadful, sunlit city, filled with stunties and their shiny, wheezing machines. Mangleback's whistle was still playing and the notes carried Scragfang through the clouds, guiding him past the facades of buildings and rows of moored sky-ships. It was awful. Even in a vision, Scragfang found it agony to look at. Everything was so bright. So hard. Wherever he looked, light glared from polished hulls and gleaming pillars.

'Imagine if everywhere was like dis,' said the moon or Mangleback, speaking into Scragfang's mind. 'Fulla light. No scrap of dark. No scrap of shadow. No scrap of fog. Nuthin' wet. Nuthin' sticky.'

Scragfang's song turned into a wail of defiance. 'The Loonking will kill 'em first.'

The moon sounded amused. 'All of them? Look at da guns. An da bombs. An all of it up in the sky, away from the damp and the dark.'

'Wot then?' demanded Scragfang.

'We needs a weapon. Not just a measly army. Not just a piddly joke. A real belly-splitter.'

'Wot weapon?'

But the moon did not reply. It rippled and split, disintegrating before vanishing completely. Scragfang realised he was alone, falling through the clouds towards metal streets. He panicked, then remembered that none of it was real. He was still in the grove, talking to Mangleback beside the puffball. He tried to stay calm as he hurtled towards the largest building. Flames were spilling from the roof and sections of the walls were toppling, lashed by lightning.

Scragfang shielded his face as he plunged through the fire, and then he saw it. A golden rune shining in the chest of a stuntie who had a tall crest of hair. It was horrible and wonderful. As bright as old Frazzlegit himself. But he could smell its power. It filled his quivering nostrils with a sense of destiny. It burned even brighter as the stuntie rushed through falling rubble to save his companion, a skinny murder aelf. They were both disgusting.

Then the vision shifted. Scragfang saw a vast metal face on the front of the big building. It was dreadful and fierce, staring down at him. But then he saw the face exploding, erupting into flame. And then he understood. If he could steal the power of that magic rune, he would become more powerful than anyone before him. That was what the blazing face meant. That was what the Bad Moon was trying to tell him. That was why it had returned. It wanted him to get the rune and turn it on the sky-city, and then watch it collapse and burn. It was the one they called Barak-Urbaz. The one that had stopped the Loonking taking control of Ayadah. What a wonderful joke – using stuntie magic to destroy their greatest city. And once that city was gone, the Moonclans would be free to spread the Everdank. The final obstacle would be gone. All thanks to Scragfang. His heart pounded as he imagined himself on a great throne. Even more impressive than the Loonking's.

'Get that rune's power an you'll be safe.' It was definitely Mangleback talking. His moist croak was unmistakable. 'From everyone. Even da Loonking.'

The good feeling vanished. Scragfang felt a rush of the old fear. He reeled away from the puffball, returned his mind to the rainy grove and ordered Mangleback to cease playing. 'Wotcha mean, safe? I'm the Loonking's chief flippin' sniffer. He gave me da zoggin fang!' Scragfang waved his knife, a pale shard of loonstone. 'Why'd 'e gimme 'is best sticker if 'e wants me dead? I'm 'is best seeker.'

As the music ceased, Scragfang lay panting in the mud, watching the winged feet glide through the darkness. They were grinning at him. Of all the things he'd seen in the Gibbermarsh, nothing had hit him with such a sense of urgency and importance. That blazing stuntie face was so apocalyptic and magnificent. He was sure it meant the end of the sky-city. But Mangleback's words had ruined everything. Now all he could think about was the fear.

The feet fluttered away as Mangleback scuttled towards him, eyes flashing as he looked at the puffball.

Scragfang calmed his breathing and stood up. 'Wotcha gimme the fear for? Why'd ya say that?'

'Say wot?'

'About bein' safe. Who's safer 'n me? Chief sniffer to the Loonking. Best seeker in the Asylum.'

Mangleback shrugged, a gesture that raised his whole mushroom cap up from his fleshy limbs. 'Who's safe? Always a good question, Fang. We're all safe while the Loonking needs us. Not so safe when 'e don't. Precarious, I'd call it.'

The fear became a torrent. 'Why wouldn't Skragrott need me any more? I'm 'is best zoggin sniffer. I told him where all da floating boats are. I told him where all da sky castles are. All those stunties are dying thanks to my visions. 'E needs me.'

Mangleback shrugged again. 'Well, yes, 'e'll need ya until he's ready.'

'Ready for wot?'

'Ready ta start da Everdank, ready to snuff out old Frazzlegit and make da uplands dark as it is down 'ere. He does need ya to 'elp 'im find stuff until then. But once 'e's king of everywhere, once the light's gone and everywhere is cool and sticky, 'e's gonna look around and see what threats are left, ain't 'e?'

'Threat? Wotcha mean, threat? I ain't a zoggin threat.'

Mangleback leant close, filling Scragfang's nostrils with his meaty aroma. 'Da best sniffer. Da best finker. Da best seeker. Don't ya fink that might make someone nervous if they woz meant to be the king? Da big boss. Da ruler of all the clans. I reckon it might, Scrag. I reckon it might make 'im wonder if it's wise to let you keep snuffling around down 'ere in this marsh. I reckon he might wonder if he should take that sticker back off ya and put it somewhere you don't like.'

Scragfang was breathing so fast his head was getting light. 'You've been chewing too many corpse caps. I'm 'is most loyal servant.'

'Are you? Have you *really* never wondered if you needed to protect yerself? Have you really never wondered about takin' 'is place?'

Scragfang rubbed his nose again and said nothing.

'Not many of us gets close to da Loonking,' said Mangleback. 'Not like you, Fang. 'E's got your number. 'E knows everyfin aboutcha.'

Scragfang stomped around the grove, glancing back at the puffball. The smell of the vision was still on the air. He could still see the stuntie with the miniature Frazzlegit in his chest.

'This is summat special,' whispered Mangleback. 'Summat big. Ain't it, Scrag? Maybe the biggest joke of all.'

Scragfang grinned despite himself, thinking about the vast, burning stuntie face on the building. If he sucked all that power into his loonblade he could wreak such glorious havoc. The whole sky-city would die. The Bad Moon would laugh for an age. 'It was big,' he muttered.

'Then don't tell 'im! Don't let 'im 'ave it. If this is the big one, this could be your last chance.'

Scragfang nodded. Mangleback was always right. Always helping him. 'Yer right. Let's keep it quiet.' He smiled. 'Play yer pipe again.'

Mangleback blew into his whistle and Scragfang started to sing, his voice thin and shrill.

> *Splitskulls worming, dripping clagg,*
> *Withering sprouts and mucal gag,*
> *Lurking greylugs ooze and scrag,*
> *Scragfang, Scragfang, splitting clagg.*
> *Bringing ruin, bringing snag,*
> *Scragfang, Scragfang, dripping clagg.*

As he sang, Scragfang's head filled with visions again. He had never been so blessed with loonsight. He saw himself at the head of a mob, hurtling through clouds. They landed on a sky-ship and stole the aelf that the stuntie loved so much. The stuntie was furious at the kidnapping. So furious that he had to follow them back to the Asylum and down into Gibbermarsh, right into the centre of Slathermere, where Scragfang was at his most powerful. Then Scragfang saw fire and destruction on a glorious scale – buildings toppling and flagstones splitting as the stuntie face blazed. All the while, the Bad Moon laughed hysterically overhead, and at the heart of the madness he saw himself, the architect of it all, powerful and triumphant, dragging ruin across the realm.

Then the puffball grew dark again and the visions faded. There was no sign of the cut he had made. 'You're right,' he whispered, struggling to stay calm. 'I should keep it to misself. Just for now. Just until I can understand it.'

'Exactly!' Mangleback scampered round him, turning in circles. 'Just for now. Until you know wotcha dealing wiv. You can always tell da Loonking later, once you've thunked a bit more.'

Scragfang nodded, then glared at Mangleback. 'I ain't no traitor though. Understand? Not to 'im. I'm playin' it safe. Dat's all. Just checkin' da lie of da land.'

'Exactly.'

'Exactly.'

CHAPTER THREE

It was only from the air that Maleneth was able to fully appreciate the mind-bending scale of the sky-port. Ugly and gaudy as it was, she could not deny that it was an incredible feat of engineering. It stretched into the clouds for miles in every direction, a vast grid of bridges, aqueducts and highways, all wrought of ornately worked metal and held aloft by the arcane aether-tech of the Kharadron. Legions of shipwrights, millwrights, master builders and industrialists had created something impossible – a continental slab of districts linked by arterial pipes and spiralling walkways.

They were travelling on one of the smaller endrins, no bigger than a small frigate, and Maleneth was clinging to the handrail, peering down through the smoke. The fumes were dense but every now and then fierce winds would snatch them away, revealing a glimpse of gleaming beerhalls, growling refineries and squat, steam-pumping mills. After a few miles, Maleneth was greeted by an even more peculiar sight. As the clouds parted, she saw that the metal architecture had vanished and they were flying over a forest of ruptured meat. As they flew further, she realised that she was looking at the carcass of a colossal creature. There were tiny shapes eating into it – Kharadron vehicles, cutting into the meat like they were working at the seam of a mine. The monster must have been half a mile long and it clearly hadn't died recently. The stench of putrefaction was so thick that it even broke through the chemical stink of the smoke. The carcass had been cut in some places and butchered in others, but she could just about make out the thing's original shape – a winged serpent, but larger than a stormkeep.

Gotrek and Trachos came to look and Brior nodded proudly. 'Where others see a fearsome predator, we see a source of meat, bones and leather – materials to be refined and sold. The beast you see there is a solarian wyvern. Captain Arngrin harpooned it nearly a year ago and he's still not harvested half of its value. He's employed riggers, packers and eviscerators from across the whole of Barak-Urbaz and he'll make himself a guildmaster in the process.' Brior spoke with awe in his voice as he watched the machines at work. 'He'll be one of the wealthiest captains in any sky-port from here to Barak-Nar.'

Maleneth shrugged. 'But what is all this for?' She waved to a vast, pillared guildhall, flanked by statues of duardin gods. 'You mock the Fyreslayers for hording ur-gold, but what's the purpose of your wealth? Is it a tribute to the gods?'

Brior was wearing his helmet, but even through the eyeholes of his face-plate Maleneth saw his confusion. 'Well, yes, that is part of the reason. We pay our respects to Grungni, of course we do, but...' He shook his head. 'We seek wealth because it creates this.' The clouds had engulfed them again, but he waved in the direction of the city. 'It has enabled us to lift ourselves from the mire. The enemy might rule the lands but we rule the sky. Do you see? Every year more of the realm falls to the grots. But as they spread their mists and shadows we build, growing wealthier and more powerful. We use our wealth to arm ourselves. We don't need Grungni to save us. We'll be our own saviours. We have moved beyond the need for gods.'

Gotrek was watching Brior closely, and Maleneth thought he might be impressed by the speech. The idea of not needing gods must certainly strike a chord with him.

Then the clouds rolled away to reveal a new vista. The mountainous corpse had been replaced by a district far grander than any they had seen before. The buildings were gilded and bold, proud palaces studded with aether-lights. It was like flying over spilled treasure.

Gotrek shook his head, his tone dark. 'You're following a well-trodden path. And it ends badly. I heard this kind of talk in the holds of Karak Azul and even in the Everpeak. And it laid ruin to better dwarfs than you.' He waved at the overwrought architecture. 'Whatever you tell yourself, you're hunting wealth for its own sake. Filching and pilfering when you should be crushing your foes. You're flying above the clouds but you may as well be a miser under a mountain. Hunger has blinded you. It will consume you.'

Brior stiffened. 'When the downsiders are on their knees, butchered by the greenskins, it will be the Kharadron Overlords they call to for help.'

Gotrek laughed. 'Then they're doomed. You'll be too busy counting coins to hear them.'

Brior seemed on the verge of saying more, then he shook his head and strode off across the deck to speak with the captain.

Maleneth patted the Slayer on the back. 'Always making friends.' She leant close. 'Tell me. The world that you speak so fondly of, the one you can't get back to. Are you *sure* it was destroyed? Or did you just offend so many people they *pretended* to die? I bet they're still there, having a cel-ebration without you, congratulating themselves on their lack of Gotrek.'

Gotrek was about to reply when Brior hurried back over. His anger had vanished. 'We're there. And Thialf Solmundsson has already sent word that he is happy to grant you an audience.' He looked absurdly excited. 'He is one of the wealthiest guildmasters in Barak-Urbaz. He's already a captain despite being barely sixty.'

The ship was already dropping through the clouds, turning wide loops around one of the golden palaces. It was as ridiculous as all the others, with a gilded facade that had been worked into the stylised rendering of a dwarf's howling face, with the gaping mouth spewing a tongue of polished steps. The face looked similar to the rune in Gotrek's chest, and as the ship dropped towards a gleaming courtyard, the Slayer gripped his axe tighter and glared at Brior. The whole building seemed to have been built to support chimneys. They were all wrought of metal, but that was the only uniform thing about them – some were tall and slender while others were plump, bowl-like structures. The largest were bigger than some of the surrounding buildings and all of them were circled by flotillas of sky-ships, drifting over the palace like metal raptors, glinting in the thermals.

As the aether-ship passed through banks of smoke, Maleneth coughed and sneezed. By the time she could see clearly again, the ship had settled at the centre of a cog-shaped courtyard and there were dozens of Kharadron gathered to meet them. They were clad in the same suits as Brior, but where his was dirty and dented, theirs were as ornate and polished as the building they had spilled from. At the head of the group was an even more impressive duardin. His flight suit was almost entirely constructed of gleaming plate and he carried a filigreed hammer connected to an anvil-shaped backpack.

As the crew lowered the landing ramp, the decorative-looking duardin approached, his chin raised disdainfully.

Gotrek snorted. 'He looks like he's got one of those chimneys stuck up his arse.'

Maleneth felt warmth at her chest as her dead mistress spoke up. *These people might actually get that thing out of his chest.*

That's no concern of yours, thought Maleneth. *Why would it matter to you if they took the rune?*

Always the slow student. Much as I would like to see you flayed alive for killing me, you're my only link to the Mortal Realms. If you fail to protect that rune, you're as good as dead. And if you die, I die.

They're not going to do anything to the rune. You've seen what these people are like. They might be able to build cities in the sky, but none of them can touch that rune. They're charlatans. They can generate wealth, but that's where their genius ends.

Brior waved them down the ramp as the grand-looking official swaggered over to greet them.

'Greetings. I am Alrik Grimullsson, adept of the Worshipful Company of Endrinwrights and chief steward to Captain Solmundsson, guildmaster and prime warden of the Solmund Company.'

Brior performed the awkward duardin equivalent of a bow. 'I am Brior, son of Briorn. An honour.' Brior looked up at the chimneystacks, shaking his head. 'What your master has achieved here is an inspiration to us all.'

Alrik nodded. 'Welcome, Brior son of Briorn.' He looked at Gotrek. 'And your companion.'

Brior gestured for Alrik to lead them into the palace. 'My friend is eager to speak with Captain Solmundsson. May we proceed?'

Alrik said nothing, studying them with his chin still raised.

Maleneth sensed that he was enjoying the moment, and she had to resist the urge to make a sharp comment.

Alrik finally nodded, and with an elaborate flourish he gestured for his honour guard to lead the way.

'Wazzock,' muttered Gotrek.

The courtyard was so vast it took several minutes to reach the sweeping stairs that curved up to the gaping mouth. No part of the building was constructed of stone. Every inch was wrought of metal and studded with semi-precious jewels. The columns around the entrance had been worked into the shape of bared teeth, and as fumes banked around them, they seemed to move.

The party passed through the opening like ants entering the mouth of a leviathan. The growl of distant engines shook through the walls and up through the floor, adding to Maleneth's impression that she was walking into a monster. More guards were waiting for them inside a grand entrance hall, all clad in the same ostentatious livery. Maleneth noticed that Gotrek was surveying the grandeur with the same disdain she felt. She had spent so long in his company that she was beginning to spot subtle differences between his various scowls. He clearly disapproved of the brazen display of wealth, but there was something more than that in his gaze. He was muttering under his breath and she sensed that he was annoyed with himself. Was he jealous of all this wealth, despite himself?

'An impressive haul,' she said, smiling coyly at him.

He muttered and picked up his pace, stomping across the polished floor.

She laughed. If nothing else, she was becoming expert at needling him.

They were escorted across the entrance hall and on through a succession of increasingly impressive chambers until, finally, they reached a throne room. There was a broad oval dais at the far end, topped with three absurdly grand-looking chairs that each stood on a broad golden slab covered in runes. Gotrek and the others were led to the foot of the steps and left to stand before the central throne.

Brior removed his helmet with a hiss of escaping gas and stared at the finery.

Gotrek glowered at the empty seats. 'Is he an engineer or an emperor?'

'He's a grand warden of the Solmund Company,' replied Alrik sternly.

Brior tugged at his beard and smiled apologetically at Alrik before turning to Gotrek. 'Captain Solmundsson has mining operations and trade fleets established in three different realms. He's one of the most successful merchant lords in the city.' He pointed out rows of elaborately wrought runes that covered the wall drapes. 'The Solmund Company holds more trade contracts than any other business concern in history. We're extremely honoured to have been granted an audience with him. He's one of the most respect–'

Gotrek held up a hand. 'What are you, his mother?'

Brior was about to reply but Gotrek silenced him with a glare, waving his axe at the throne. 'Where is he?'

'Captain Solmundsson knows you're waiting,' replied Alrik.

Gotrek stomped up the steps towards the thrones, swinging his axe. 'Does he?'

'Wait!' Brior hurried after him, grabbing his arm, but Gotrek shrugged him off and strode towards the central throne. 'Like everything in the realms.'

He tapped his axe against the throne and peered at the designs worked into it. 'Looks reasonable until you get close. Whoever made this had too many thumbs.'

Alrik signalled to the guards and they approached the dais, guns raised.

'Guests must wait at the foot of the steps.' Alrik's voice was taut. 'Keep away from the throne.'

Gotrek raised an eyebrow. 'Or what?'

Maleneth's hand dropped to the hilts of her knives. It was incredible how quickly things could turn sour when Gotrek was involved.

Before the guards reached Gotrek, the sound of voices filtered into the hall, emerging from a doorway leading deeper into the palace.

Alrik clanged his hammer on the floor. 'Resume your places.'

To Maleneth's surprise, Gotrek did as requested and climbed down the steps to rejoin the group, glaring at the guards, who still had their guns trained on him.

The voices grew louder and one rang out above the others, speaking quickly and with great enthusiasm to the accompaniment of dozens of iron-shod boots clanging on a metal floor. Then, a few seconds later, a crowd of Kharadron deck officers entered the hall. They were all clad in a variation of Alrik's bulky uniform, equally grand-looking but draped with pieces of scientific equipment. At the centre of the group, gesticulating furiously, was a Kharadron who was even more grandly attired than the others. His helmet had been forged to resemble the face of a duardin ancestor god and the eyeholes were framed by black gemstones. He wore the same baggy suit as the others but it was trimmed with silver, and around his neck was a cog-shaped medallion hung on a thick chain. Maleneth was in no doubt that this absurdly gilded duardin was Solmundsson.

Solmundsson paused at the entrance to the hall and held up a hand to one of his officers. 'Three ships, you say?'

The officer had a long, forked black beard that hung outside his armour, and he was the largest Kharadron Maleneth had seen so far, almost as large as the Slayer. He towered over the other officers as he nodded at Solmundsson. 'All destroyed. The storms are so fierce now and the grots attacked from the clouds. They've captured an ironclad and refitted it somehow so they can fly it. The moon's almost full and there's nothing the grots won't attempt. Our ships went down before they could reach the seams, even the *Zul-Maraz*. Dozens of lives were lost.'

Solmundsson looked at the floor. 'Damned grots. They get bolder by the day.' Then he nodded and gripped the officer by the shoulder. 'We will face losses like these, Thorrik. It's inevitable. At least until Kazak-drung starts to wane. But we must not be cowed by the grot moon.' He waved at the architecture. 'Every inch of this is built of bravery and sacrifice. You know it, and they knew it. They knew the risks and they took them anyway.'

Thorrik nodded and replied sternly, 'May the ancestors welcome them.'

'May the ancestors welcome them,' echoed Solmundsson, still gripping Thorrik's shoulder. 'You're sure it was three ships?'

'Yes, captain. Three. We have already contacted our underwriters and informed the guilds.'

'But we sent four ships. There was a frigate.'

'Aye, captain. The *Brynduraz*. We think it reached the seam.'

Solmundsson stared at him. 'So the *Brynduraz* got *through*. Despite the greenskins. And where one can go, more may follow. There is great loss of life here but that is not the only story. We're talking about the richest seam in the whole aetherstratus. Do you realise the significance of this? If we can harness that we could deal the greenskins a sore blow.'

'We don't *know* the *Brynduraz* got through, though, captain. We just have no record of it being destroyed by the grots.'

'Then send more ships and find out. Ten. No, twenty. Repeat the process. Find the *Brynduraz*.'

Thorrik nodded, slowly.

'There's *always* a way, First Officer Thorrik,' said Solmundsson.

Thorrik was about to reply when Gotrek strode over.

'Is this going to take long?'

Solmundsson glanced at Gotrek, was about to ignore him, then looked back at him in shock, taking in his massive, tattooed frame and the metal in his chest. 'The Slayer. And the rune.' He waved his officers away and stepped closer. 'I am Captain Solmundsson. And you are?'

'Gotrek. Son of Gurni. From the Everpeak. Trachos over there is one of Sigmar's hammer maidens and this smarmy backstabber is an aelf.'

Solmundsson looked surprised by Gotrek's vitriol. Then he nodded his head in a slight bow and stepped closer, looking at the rune rather than Gotrek's face. 'Fascinating. I've never seen anything like it. And it...' He looked at Gotrek. 'Does it light up when you're excited?'

Gotrek raised an eyebrow. 'Excited?'

'When you're angry. Does it glow in the heat of battle?'

'It does all manner of irritating things. Can you get it out?'

Solmundsson looked at the rune again, as though hypnotised. 'Incredible. This is nothing like any of the Fyreslayer runes I've seen before.' He reached out, his fingers just inches from the metal. 'Yes, of course I can remove it. There is no ore, vapour or alloy that I cannot bend to my will.'

Gotrek looked at the gemstones on the captain's armour. 'And what do you charge for the bending of wills?'

'Things of value rarely come cheap, Slayer, but I can rid you of this rune and I doubt you will find anyone else who can.'

The voice of Maleneth's former mistress rushed through her. *He might actually do this.*

Maleneth stepped between Gotrek and Solmundsson, glaring down at the captain. 'If you remove the rune we can give you nothing in return.'

Solmundsson removed his fierce-looking helmet to reveal a surprisingly young face. His beard was blond and short by duardin standards. His features were as blunt and craggy as any duardin's, but his eyes shone with a playful enthusiasm. He smiled broadly and nodded at the rune. 'You wish to be rid of this rune. I am happy to take it off your hands. No other payment is required.'

'We do *not* wish to be rid of the rune!' Maleneth spat. 'It is the property of the Order of Azyr. It must be taken to Azyrheim. Not given away to someone who has no idea of its importance.'

Solmundsson laughed in a good-natured way. 'It would appear that the rune's owner has other ideas.'

'You're making a dangerous mistake.' Maleneth waved at Trachos, who was watching the exchange from a few feet away. 'Azyr is full of Storm-hosts ready to turn on those who hinder Sigmar's crusade. Do you want the God-King for an enemy?'

Solmundsson laughed again. 'We're the Kharadron. Strangers are just enemies we haven't met yet. Outside of our guilds no one has our interests at heart. But we're not talking about Sigmar's possessions, are we?' He looked at Gotrek. 'Are you one of Sigmar's soldiers? Do you serve in a Stormhost?'

Gotrek clenched his jaw.

'I sense he does not.' Solmundsson's tone was still friendly, but he was clearly used to getting his own way. 'Therefore, I see no reason why this Slayer and I may not do business as we see fit.'

'It belongs to Sigmar.' Maleneth's fingers itched to grab one of the vials that nestled inside her leathers. A quick draught of poison would wipe that infuriating smile from his face.

'And yet here it is, in the chest of your friend.' Solmundsson looked over at Alrik. 'Chief steward. Remind me, what does the statute of fiscal limitations in subclause eighty-seven-B of the Code have to say about the possession and sale of aetheric metal?'

Alrik replied without hesitation. 'Possession of said artefacts confers ownership after more than six months have elapsed, unless expressly refuted by the sky-lords of the Geldraad.'

Solmundsson nodded and looked at Gotrek. 'Would you say that rune has been in your chest for six months or longer?'

Gotrek's lip curled. 'A damn sight longer.'

Solmundsson spoke in soft, conciliatory tones, smiling at Maleneth. 'There's no need for an argument. There is no one in the realms better qualified to remove this rune. I shall stabilise it and then examine its composition. If it turns out that you're right, and it may be of use in Sigmar's campaigns, then I will barter with your superiors. Your enemies are my enemies. And everything is for sale at the right price. I'm not in the business of hoodwinking anyone, aelf. I always aim to be clear. If I remove this rune, it will be mine to do with as I please.'

Maleneth turned to Gotrek. 'Think about what you're doing. You know the power of that rune. Are you really going to hand it over to someone you've just met? Like a worthless trinket? Can you really just give it away?'

'Happily.'

Solmundsson looked intrigued. 'Why? Has it poisoned you? Is it making you ill?'

'It's poisoned my mind, beardling. It has made it so I can't think clearly, and when I try to fight, it becomes worse.'

'It adds to your strength?'

'And turns me into a fool. Makes it so I can't recognise friend from foe.'

Solmundsson nodded. 'Then you must let me help. I can rid you of your curse, Gotrek, son of Gurni. Science can always find a way.' He waved to a servant. 'Prepare rooms and see that my guests have all that they require.'

'Rooms?' Gotrek frowned. 'I didn't come here to be your bloody guest, endrinkuli. If you can get this thing out then do it. Or I'll look elsewhere.'

Solmundsson looked taken aback. Then he laughed. 'Very well. No time like the present.' He gave some quick, whispered orders to his officers then spoke to the officer who had been talking to him when he first entered. 'Have the ships prepared, First Officer Thorrik. This damned moon will not stop us. The grots have taken too much already. We cannot let any more seams go. But do not let the ships leave until I am done with our friends here. I intend to accompany you myself this time.'

'Captain.' Thorrik's voice was brittle. 'You can trust me.'

'I do not doubt it, First Officer Thorrik. But I want to be there when we finally break through.'

Thorrik hesitated, then saluted and strode from the throne room, heading off with all the other officers.

'And who are you?' asked Solmundsson, noticing Brior standing a few feet away, looking terrified.

Brior stammered and stumbled over his words until Alrik came to his rescue, announcing him in disdainful tones. 'The innkeeper Brior Briornsson. He alerted us to the rune's existence, your honour.' As Alrik spoke, he looked firmly into the middle distance, avoiding Solmundsson's gaze.

Solmundsson clapped Brior firmly on the back. 'Good work!' He waved a servant over. 'Have him flown home.'

Brior finally managed to speak. 'Captain. There is the small matter of my personal recompense. I was the one who–'

Solmundsson held up a hand. 'This is a company matter now.'

Brior gaped in shock as he was steered back towards the exit.

Solmundsson looked back at Gotrek, Maleneth and Trachos, clearly intrigued by all three of them. Then he clapped his hands together and nodded to a doorway on the opposite side of the hall. He waved Alrik and his guards on and strode across the throne room after them, calling out commands as he went, sending underlings scattering in various directions.

'Trachos,' hissed Maleneth, alerting him to the fact that they were leaving. 'We have to stop this.'

'Stop what?'

Maleneth resisted the urge to stab him. 'Stop these Kharadron leeches stealing the master rune.'

Trachos stared at her, then at Gotrek, who was already halfway across the throne room. 'No need.'

'What do you mean? If we lose that rune neither of us will ever be able to return to Azyrheim. Use whatever's left in your skull. We can't let the rune fall into the hands of this duardin. Who knows what harm he might do to the thing while removing it. The rune was not made by aether-science – it was forged by the deranged magic of Fyreslayer runesmiths. Solmundsson has no idea how powerful it is.'

'Exactly. He has no idea what it is, Maleneth.'

Maleneth hissed in exasperation and, seeing she would get no help from the Stormcast Eternal, hurried after Gotrek and the others.

They entered a long hallway lined with statue-filled alcoves. Each statue, rather than showing a figure, was sculpted to resemble a ship in the Solmund fleet – ironclads and frigates, mining vessels and cargo ships, all rendered in such detail that Maleneth could see crewmembers on the decks.

Solmundsson glanced back and noticed her looking. 'The Solmund Company has one of the largest sky-fleets in all of Chamon. And we have plans for expansion on a scale no one has witnessed before in this or any other realm.'

Maleneth shook her head. 'I was just wondering how such ugly tubs manage to stay aloft.'

Solmundsson waited for her to catch up. 'Forgive me, I think I missed your name.'

'Maleneth Witchblade. And I'm not impressed by any of this. I've met your kind before. You're deluded. You think you can make your way in life through industry and gumption, with no need of divine influence. You think energy and optimism will save you.'

Solmundsson shrugged. 'Optimism is a good start, wouldn't you say?'

Up ahead, Gotrek let out a derisive snort.

They reached a pair of double doors designed to resemble the rearing prow of a sky-ship. From the other side came the sound of hammering and banging. While Solmundsson's aides rattled keys as big as their forearms, Maleneth leant closer to him. 'Despair serves no purpose but you'll feel it all the same if Sigmar's Stormhosts fail. A cheery disposition won't preserve you from daemons.'

Solmundsson smiled and gestured for her to step through the opening doors as the din rushed out to meet them. 'This might.'

She entered what looked like a cross between an armoury and a laboratory. Everywhere she looked there were workshops, braziers, furnaces and anvils as duardin worked on weapons and engines, half hidden by plumes of smoke and embers.

Solmundsson looked around proudly. 'If the greenskins find a way to scale the clouds and reach Barak-Urbaz they will find us waiting, and armed with the latest aethermatic guns. All the wealth we generate is being invested here, building and developing weaponry that is more advanced than anything else in the realms.'

Gotrek and Maleneth shared a glance and, again, she had the worrying feeling that they were thinking alike. The Kharadron were impressive but complacent. As she and the Slayer crossed the realms they had seen first-hand how tenuous the bulwark against Chaos was. Solmundsson was deluded if he thought greenskins were the only threat.

They passed through the crowded workshops and descended into the lower levels of the building. Down here, the corridors resembled the companionways of a ship – riveted metal tubes punctuated every few dozen feet by thick, wheel-handled doors. As they went lower, the sound of engines grew so loud that Solmundsson had to yell to be heard. 'You may feel some discomfort as we enter the sublimation chambers.'

Maleneth was about to ask what he meant when she realised that an odd sensation was affecting her balance. The floor and walls seemed oddly fluid, as though they were melting. Gotrek pounded on, oblivious, but she noticed that Trachos was affected too, stumbling and reaching out to steady himself.

Solmundsson and the other Kharadron all donned their helmets and checked the seals on their flight suits, and as they passed through another circular door, Solmundsson's guards took rubber overalls from the walls and offered them to Maleneth, Gotrek and Trachos.

She raised an eyebrow, indicating how unlikely the thing was to fit her slender frame, designed as it was for someone who was only four and a half feet tall. Gotrek waved the thing away too, and Trachos seemed to have no comprehension of what it was.

Solmundsson hesitated, shrugged, then ordered his guards to open the next door.

Maleneth gripped the wall as she entered a room so peculiar it took her a moment to understand it. It was a large circular chamber filled with lenses. Everywhere she looked, curved discs refracted light pouring down from somewhere high overhead. The floor of the chamber was like a huge brass dial, clicking as it turned, and the lenses were suspended above it on a framework of gears and dials. As the lenses turned, they cast rainbow colours through the air.

Gotrek, Maleneth and Trachos hesitated, taking in the spectacle of the place. Maleneth caught Gotrek's eye and saw that he was as impressed as she was.

'They might not be complete morons,' muttered the Slayer.

Maleneth shrugged, but she could not quite bring herself to disagree.

The noise of the engines was deafening and Solmundsson had to shout even louder as he directed them across the chamber. 'These are not the machines we need for your rune. Let me show you the way.'

Kharadron endrineers were gathered in several parts of the room, adjusting mechanisms. Some of them saluted Solmundsson as he headed to the centre of the chamber. He led Maleneth and the others to what looked like an egg-shaped cage. It was twice as tall as Maleneth and the gaps between the bars were filled with panes of glass so polished that she could barely look at them. The cage was fixed to a metal base riveted to the centre of the chamber. There were endrineers and aether-khemists gathered inside and outside the device, and at the sight of Solmundsson they downed their tools and rushed over to greet him. He nodded as they relayed a torrent of information that, to Maleneth's ears, sounded like jargon. She still felt oddly drunk, and by this point it was starting to make her feel quite ill. She knew she might only have moments to save the rune, but she felt so nauseous and confused she was struggling to even stand up.

'Gotrek!' she managed to cry. 'That rune came to you for a reason. You were meant to have it.'

Gotrek's laughter boomed out over the sound of the machines. 'I thought I was just a barrier to your success, aelf. Am I your saviour now?'

Flattering the oaf only made Maleneth feel even sicker, but she had to try something. And invoking his pride seemed worth a try. 'You found your way to that rune from another world. It can't have been by accident. You were fated to have it. You can't simply discard it like an unwanted gift.'

'It is unwanted. And I won't be ruled by it.' Gotrek looked at Solmundsson. 'What do I do?' He approached the walls of the cage. 'Is this the machine?'

Solmundsson shook his head. 'The frame is merely a precaution. The real treasure is inside. A volatising lens! The only one in existence.' He tapped the glass, pointing to a crystal inside the cage. It was a pyramid of blue glass, no bigger than a fist, and it seemed underwhelming in comparison to the monstrous machines that surrounded it. 'Isn't she glorious? Based on a design of my own invention. I call it the "burning glass"! Applied correctly, it is able to separate one substrate from another!' He looked at Gotrek. 'With that lens, I can remove the rune. Is that what you want? There will be some... discomfort.'

Gotrek peered into the cage at the crystal. 'Do it.'

Solmundsson nodded to one of the flight-suited technicians, who then dashed across the hall, calling out commands and waving to his colleagues.

Do something, you imbecile.

The voice in Maleneth's head added to the nausea caused by the forest of lenses and she slumped against Trachos, who stopped her from falling by grabbing her arm.

'We have to act,' she said, staring up at him as she tried to stand.

He shook his head, impassive as ever. 'The duardin have no power over Sigmar or his servants.'

Maleneth cursed and shoved away from him, managing to stay upright as she staggered over to the egg-shaped cage. Alrik and his guards were locked in conversation with the technicians and Solmundsson was showing Gotrek some aspect of the machine. Maleneth circled the device, and while everyone was occupied, she took the silver worm from her pocket and looked at it. It wriggled in her grip, still active.

Quickly!

She shook her head. *This is different. Disabling those other devices just made them harmless. But if this one malfunctions it could kill him.*

And? Remember your faith, Witchblade. Remember who you are. If he dies, he dies. It does not matter. But you are the blood of Khaine.

And I serve the Order of Azyr. Or at least I will if I get this damned rune back to Azyrheim.

I don't care what oaths you've sworn to Sigmar, you're a bride of Khaine. A scion of the murder cults. And you certainly do not serve that sweaty oaf. What matters now is that Solmundsson does not get his hands on the rune.

Maleneth hated to admit it, but her mistress was right. Without the rune she was nothing. She leant closer and dropped the silver worm onto the frame.

As though in response, the hall shuddered and the drone of engines shifted up in pitch. Kharadron were rushing in every direction, pouring oil into braziers and hammering pieces of ore. Clouds of smoke rolled through the chamber, obscuring most of the rotating lenses and giving Maleneth a moment in which she could work unseen. Knowing that the inhibiter might not be enough, she took her knife to some of the cables and pipes attached to the frame, cutting through anything that looked important. Then she backed away.

For a moment she felt relief, then as the fumes cleared she felt a cold dread, staring at the pipework where she had planted her device. Incredibly, she realised that she did not want Gotrek to die. It was absurd, but when she imagined him dead, she felt a rush of alarm.

Maleneth walked back over to the egg-shaped cage, but at that moment, the engines surged again and lights began blinking through the smoke, flashing through the facets of the crystal.

Stay back, hissed her mistress.

'Stay back!' howled Alrik as he and his guards formed a circle around the machine.

'Wait!' yelled Maleneth, but her words were drowned out as light spilled from inside the cage. To her horror, she saw that Gotrek was already inside, strapped to an upright gurney with the crystal lens near his chest.

'Keep away!' cried Solmundsson, rushing towards her. 'Do not touch the volatising engine!'

When Maleneth refused to stop, Alrik's guards raised their guns and took aim.

'It would be dangerous for you,' explained Solmundsson as he reached her and steered her back towards where everyone else was waiting.

'What about *him*?' she demanded. 'He's inside the cage.'

'He will be given an elixir that will induce an artificial sleep.' Solmundsson indicated a flight-suited endrineer who was entering the cage, stepping with great care and carrying a copper cup. 'In such a state his mind and body will be unaffected by the process.'

Upon reaching Gotrek, the endrineer held the cup out to Gotrek's mouth. The Slayer was reluctant at first, glaring at the drink. Then he nodded and let the technician hold it to his lips.

Once Gotrek had emptied the cup, the endrineer stepped back to observe him.

After a few seconds, Gotrek shrugged and looked out through the cage's glass walls.

The endrineer hesitated, then left the machine and approached Solmundsson. 'He swallowed the whole draft, your honour, but he's still awake.'

Solmundsson shook his head. 'That was enough to stun a fire drake.' He thought for a moment, then spoke to another technician. 'Give him another,' he said finally, looking back at the endrineer.

'Is that safe, captain?'

'Look at him. It's safe.'

The endrineer nodded, fetched more of the liquid from another duardin and headed back into the cage.

Gotrek swallowed it without question this time and even gave a vague nod of approval, but still nothing happened.

Solmundsson laughed and looked at Maleneth. 'Grungni's beard. Where did you find him?'

'You have to stop this,' demanded Maleneth. 'You have no right to endanger that rune.'

Solmundsson thought for a moment, then nodded and waved at the endrineers near the machine. 'Back away. Close the doors.'

Maleneth spat a curse and drew her knife, only to find a circle of guns pointing at her.

Solmundsson smiled. 'It's understandable that you feel concern for your friend, but if he's strong enough to resist the elixir, he'll be strong enough to survive the volatising process.'

Maleneth counted the guards and gauged her chances. Kharadron aethermatic guns were superior to the flintlock variety she had seen humans use. She might take a few of the guards down, but the others would blow her apart before she got anywhere near Gotrek. She cursed her impulsiveness. *You made me do this*, she thought.

Happy to help.

Maleneth was about to threaten Solmundsson when a fan of energy burst from the crystal pyramid and drenched the room in light. As the beams refracted and flashed in Maleneth's eyes, the engines grew louder and the floor shook with more violence.

As the light radiated from the cage Gotrek became a silhouette, dark and hulking at the centre of the blaze.

'That lens is a marvel!' cried Solmundsson. 'It's my masterpiece. No bigger than my hand but powerful enough to defy physics. It can separate element from element and ore from ore.'

As Solmundsson spoke, his assistants were busying themselves around the cage, adjusting the angles of lenses and tightening parts of the iron framework.

As the light grew brighter, Maleneth realised it was burning most fiercely at Gotrek's chest. It looked like a star trapped in his lungs. The energy spread from Gotrek and shimmered across the hall.

'Are you ready?' cried Solmundsson, addressing a duardin who was operating a machine that looked like a metal coffin.

The endrineer nodded.

Solmundsson gave Maleneth a final, proud smile then brought his hand down in a chopping motion.

The cage exploded.

CHAPTER FOUR

Dunngol sprinted through the darkness, clutching Sigmar to his chest, racing across the silvery hills and making for the line of trees at the far side of the valley. As he ran, he kept his gaze fixed on the ground, refusing to think about the Hexmoon. He could feel it watching him, its sneering eyes burning into his neck as he stumbled and scrambled over the rocks.

'Not far,' he gasped, clutching Sigmar a little tighter. The doll smelled of dust and straw but he could *feel* the God-King's presence. He could feel it as clearly as he could his own pulse hammering in his temples.

Dunngol had not risked taking many belongings from the longhouse. He needed to move fast. But the elders had insisted he at least take his longsword and his grandfather's old shield. If the grots spotted him, he was ready to fight. He would not stop. He would not let the moon take the rest of the villagers. Too many of them had already died. A memory made his breath catch in his throat and he stumbled to a halt, his mind filling with the terrible scenes of the last few days. Since the grots came he had watched his entire family die. Death was never far away in Ayadah, but this was different. Some had been killed by the grots, but that was not the worst of it. The most horrific attack had come from the Hexmoon. He pictured its first victim, screaming as she died. They looked like boils at first, but then blossomed into plump, grinning faces – miniature likenesses of the Hexmoon that covered her body, growing larger until her screams were strangled and finally ceased, her face hidden by yellow mushroom caps, grinning as they spiralled from her broken body. She was the first of many. Only those who locked themselves in the longhouse survived, huddled around Sigmar and howling prayers, trying to drown out the screams. The Kharadron would come, they said. The Kharadron would come. The duardin needed the ore that the villagers mined and they would protect their investment. With their science and their machines they had always kept the village safe. This would be no different.

Then, as the days ground on, the curse even took hold in the longhouse, warping the congregation's flesh and leaving a heap of broken corpses around the altar. Some grew deranged, praying to other gods. Even praying to the Hexmoon itself. And then, finally, the elders saw the truth. Someone had to take word to the Kharadron Overlords. Someone had to leave the longhouse. Even though the surrounding hills were full of grots, someone had to leave the village. They had not needed to say Dunngol's name. Only he knew the forest and the lands that lay beyond the mines.

He shook his head, trying to rid himself of the memory, then continued running across the rocky valley floor. He reached the far side and began climbing, keeping his thoughts on the forest and the hope it contained.

Giggles echoed through the valley.

'No,' whispered Dunngol. The grots had seen him. Or smelled him. He glanced back down into the valley and saw small, hooded shapes scrambling over the rocks. They were no bigger than children but they moved with shocking speed, cackling and laughing. Blades flashed in the moonlight, and as the grots looked up at him he caught glimpses of their faces – gaunt, leering faces that resembled the moon gliding overhead.

Dunngol whispered urgent prayers to Sigmar as he carried the doll up the rocks, cutting his hands and scraping his knees in his frenzy to get away. He could feel the moon laughing at his pain and fear. At first he had thought the moon simply resembled a face, but he now knew the truth. It was not a moon at all. It was a daemon. Sent to test their faith. Sent to purge all those who had not armoured their souls.

He reached the summit and ran towards the trees, crossing a broad hollow, desperate to escape the dreadful light. Animals scattered as he entered the gloom, vaulting fallen trunks and scrambling over ditches. He ran blind for several minutes, not caring about a route. Only caring that he left the grots behind. The sound of giggling faded. He whispered to Sigmar, looking into the doll's face. 'They can't follow. No one knows these woods like me.'

He paused and leant against a mossy tree trunk, breathing hard as he tried to get his bearings. Before moving into the village he had lived in these woods. It was many years since he had risked returning, but after staring through the shadows, he spotted one of the paths he had played on as a child. He kissed the straw doll and hurried on, filled with an odd sense that he had slipped back in time. As he went deeper into the woods, he began to hear the grots again, their shrill voices echoing through the trees as they tried to follow him, but he could tell they were lost, heading in every direction but the one he had taken. On he went, running for hours down winding paths and clambering through bracken until the voices faded again.

Finally, after hours of fleeing through the forest, he broke from the trees and ran back out into the moonlight. Up ahead, the land ended at a sheer drop – a cliff that looked down over a vast, bottomless chasm. He whispered a prayer of thanks to the doll and hurried towards the building perched at the cliff edge.

The dome was as strange as he remembered. Rather than thatch and mud it was built from rune-scored metal. The walls were covered in tubes and pieces of machinery, and at the front of the dome there was a broad platform that hung out over the drop. In his youth, Dunngol had watched fearfully as the Kharadron docked their huge, gleaming sky-ships, unloading crates and barrels and taking ore mined by the villagers. The old duardin who guarded the dome was called Nothri, and sometimes he used to give

Dunngol scraps of food and pieces of clothing. Dunngol had not seen Nothri for years but he was sure he would remember him. There was no ship there now, but Nothri was at home. Dunngol could tell by the smoke billowing from a flue on the side of the dome.

He hurried onto the platform and found that the door was open. He dared not call out for fear of being heard by the grots, so he crept quietly into the building, hurrying through the rooms.

At the back of the dome he found Nothri, surrounded by crates and sleeping on a bunk. Immediately, he sensed that something was wrong. Nothri would never sleep with the dome left unlocked. Then he noticed something else. The smoke he had seen from outside was not coming from a hearth or a brand – it was coming from Nothri himself.

'He's burning,' whispered Dunngol, but even as he said it, he knew it was wrong. The room was deathly cold. There was no fire.

He edged slowly towards the bunk, his panic growing.

He reached out and gently turned Nothri over.

The duardin collapsed, crumbling into a cloud as his clothes slumped onto the bunk. It was not smoke.

'Spores,' gasped Dunngol.

Nothri's remains were a mass of lemon-coloured mushrooms, all with the moon's face, all grinning at him as they exhaled more spores. Dunngol coughed and spluttered as they filled his lungs.

He screamed and raced from the dome. Tears streamed down his face as he felt something start to move and grow, deep in his chest.

As he ran he realised he had left Sigmar lying in the hut. His howls echoed as he raced back into the forest, repeating and multiplying until they sounded like many voices, all laughing.

CHAPTER FIVE

Maleneth fell back, gasping, as shards of crystal cut her skin. Her breath exploded from her lungs as she landed heavily on the floor, blinded. Then, as the light faded, she began to see the mayhem her inhibiter had caused. The explosion had torn holes in the walls, and in some places the super-structure had split, causing the building to slump. Acrid fumes blew into the hall, whistling through the shattered walls. Everywhere she looked, people were sprawled on the floor, clutching wounds or struggling to stand. Some were dead, their rubber flight suits cut to ribbons, but it was not the Kharadron Maleneth was concerned about.

'Gotrek,' she croaked, lifting herself onto one elbow and looking towards the centre of the hall. Where the cage had been there was now a smoulder-ing crater. There was no sign of the machine or Gotrek, just a gaping hole looking down over the building's lower levels.

'I told you,' said Trachos, striding through the whirling dust and helping her to her feet. 'They can't touch the rune.'

'Idiot,' she muttered. 'This was my doing.'

Trachos stared at her.

She shook her head. 'One of us had to do something. We have to find–'

Before she could finish, the floor lurched and there was a screech of rending metal.

'To the exit!' cried Alrik, staggering towards them. His helmet was gone and his beard was soaked with blood. 'The walls are giving way!'

Everyone began struggling through the mess, trying to reach the doors, but in several places the floor was already impassable, either split apart or littered with broken machine parts.

Maleneth leant on Trachos, and together they walked in the opposite direction to everyone else, heading back towards the centre of the blast.

'Gotrek!' cried Maleneth. 'Khaine, where are you?' She felt a rising panic as they reached the hole in the floor. The lower levels were also collapsing.

Solmundsson staggered through the wreckage towards them and shoved them back the way they had come. He was gripping the glass pyramid in his hand, staring at it. 'I can't understand it. It makes no sense. It should have worked.'

'We need to find Gotrek,' said Trachos, walking off. He began picking through the wreckage. 'He will be here somewhere.'

Solmundsson shook his head, still staring at the crystal. 'We have to go. The Slayer will not have...' He raised the burning glass, peering through its facets. 'The volatising beam broke loose. I've never seen anything like it.' His voice shook. 'The Fyreslayer rune was too powerful. It resisted. How is that possible? It must have repelled the beam. Almost as though it were defending itself.'

Maleneth decided not to reveal the real reason for the lens' failure. 'If the process was unsuccessful where's the rune?'

They all staggered as another section of wall crashed down, kicking up clouds of dust and powdered glass.

Solmundsson pocketed the lens then nodded weakly at the rent in the floor.

'Captain!' called Alrik from the far side of hall. 'We have to leave!'

'We can search the lower levels,' gasped Solmundsson, waving for Maleneth to follow as he headed away from the crater. 'But we need to get out of here.'

They joined the general rush of figures racing for the exit, but when they reached the doors there was no sign of Trachos. Maleneth rolled her eyes as she saw that he had paused halfway across the chamber to help some wounded Kharadron.

'He's a noble soul,' said Solmundsson, pausing to look back at the Stormcast Eternal.

Maleneth smiled sweetly. 'He's an idiot.' Then she limped off down the hallway, determined to reach the rune before anyone else. The Kharadron had guns but she had subtler methods of killing. She might salvage something from this disaster yet. As she ran with the others, dodging falling pillars and toppling statues, she wondered if the entire complex was about to come down. The reverberations from the initial blast seemed to be growing rather than fading. As she dodged the falling debris, she realised that the knot in her stomach was not concern for her own safety. Infuriatingly, she was thinking about Gotrek. After all her thoughts of murdering him, she now felt a chill at the thought that she might have succeeded.

By the time she staggered out into the fume-filled courtyard, there were hundreds of Solmund Company workers pouring from the building. Maleneth ran down the steps and did not pause to look back until she was a hundred feet away. The snarling face on the front of the building had slumped to the left, ripping through several windows and causing one of the largest cooling towers to sag in the opposite direction.

Maleneth flinched as a shadow rushed towards her.

She whirled around to see Gotrek holding a support strut that would have crushed her if he had not caught it.

He let it clatter to the ground and nodded at the face on the front of the building. 'If that thing comes down they're all buggered.'

Maleneth stared at him, thinking about what she would now look like if he had not saved her by catching the strut. She could not quite bring herself to thank him though. 'You don't look any worse than last time I saw you,' she said.

Gotrek spat. 'That lens couldn't hurt the feelings of an aelf. I thought Solmundsson–' He had to pause as more metal clattered down. 'I thought Solmundsson might be less of an idiot than the others, but I was wrong. He's just as bad.'

'*None* of these people have anything to offer you. They can't influence the Blackhammer's Master Rune for good or ill, but they will continue to rob us blind. We should get out of Barak-Urbaz. Surely you can see that now?'

Gotrek looked at her in silence. It was one of those rare occasions when his mask slipped and she caught a glimpse of how weary he was. How wounded. Not a physical hurt but something deeper. His gaze hardened and the snarl returned to his mouth. 'One way or another, this rune is coming out. I won't be its slave.'

She nodded, feeling almost as weary as he looked, but before she could reply a new sound flooded the courtyard – the thunder of turbines and the roar of engines. They looked around to see a sky-ship landing at the centre of the courtyard, whipping up dust and causing the people fleeing the building to back away, shielding their faces.

'Different colours,' said Gotrek, and Maleneth saw that he was right – the ship was not painted in the livery of the Solmund Company. As it landed, the crew that poured down its gangplanks and mag-ladders wore a different uniform to Solmundsson's soldiers – crimson flight suits with bronze-coloured helmets and weapons.

'They don't look like a rescue party,' she muttered, noticing that most of the crew had raised their weapons as they rushed towards the mayhem. She jumped to her feet and took out her knives.

'You looked pleased,' said Gotrek, still seated on the rubble.

'What?' She looked back at him.

'When you saw me. You were pleased I was alive.' There was no mockery in Gotrek's tone, or pleasure for that matter. Only surprise.

'Don't be ridiculous.' She waved a knife at his chest. 'I was pleased you hadn't destroyed the rune.'

He studied her in silence, his expression unreadable. Yet again, she had the troubling sensation that his savagery was a mask. But a mask for what?

'Who are you, Gotrek?' she snapped. 'What's *actually* going on in that ugly head?'

He stared through her, speaking to the drifting fumes, as though on the cusp of a great revelation. 'I wonder what was in that drink. It wasn't too bad.'

'Join the others!' cried one of the crimson-clad Kharadron, rushing towards them.

Gotrek scowled and raised his axe. Without thinking, Maleneth dropped into place beside him, knives raised, guarding the spot that his dead friend used to protect. It was a role that already felt familiar and right. Sometimes she felt that she was the one being possessed by the past, not Gotrek.

'Who're you giving orders to?' snarled Gotrek, glaring at the approaching group with such force that they staggered to a halt and looked at each other for reassurance. There was a clattering sound as they raised their guns.

'Try me,' growled Gotrek. His beard bristled and he began testing the weight of his axe, slapping it against his palm. A low, snarling sound rumbled in his chest.

Maleneth's blood surged as she sensed Gotrek's rage growing. She could feel him edging towards an explosion and she revelled in the thought of impending violence. It would be good to finally show the Kharadron what she thought of them. Then she hesitated. There were thirty, perhaps forty of them. She turned to Gotrek. 'Is this a good idea?'

Gotrek spat on the ground. 'It's a bloody great idea.'

The duardin soldiers were advancing cautiously, guns trained on Gotrek, and Maleneth realised that Gotrek was moments away from one of his berserk states. The Kharadron sensed it too. They looked edgy and unsure. They would shoot first and think about the consequences later. She battled to dampen her own bloodlust so that she could avert disaster. 'These people are not your enemy, Gotrek.' She turned to face him, trying to sound as though she cared about what happened to the Kharadron. 'Remember what you said on the *Sigmaron Star*. Honour and ancestors, remember. Would killing these people be honourable?'

Gotrek ignored her, then cursed as he noticed that the rune in his chest was shimmering. He let the head of his axe clang to the floor and muttered.

'Join the others over there,' said the leader of the soldiers, waving his gun at a crowd gathering nearing the sky-ship.

Gotrek stared at him.

The soldier took a step backwards, his gun rattling in his grip.

Gotrek grunted in disgust. But then he did as requested, trudging through falling debris towards the crowd.

They were still thirty feet from the ship when Solmundsson spotted Gotrek. He rushed over, flanked by Alrik and dozens of Kharadron guards. He shook his head as he saw the rune still intact. 'Not a scratch.'

'Captain Solmundsson?' cried one of the guards.

'Yes?'

'I have orders from the council. We are to accompany you to Admiralty Hall. Along with the...' The soldier hesitated. 'Along with your guests.'

Solmundsson was not wearing his helmet and Maleneth noticed a flicker of pain pass across his face as he watched the explosions on the far side of the courtyard. Then he nodded stiffly, regaining his composure. 'Of course. I was already intending to bring news of my latest discovery. Is the council in session?'

'The admirals and guildmasters have been summoned to an emergency hearing by the Lord Admiral himself.' The soldier looked at Gotrek. 'To discuss recent developments.'

Gotrek barged past the soldier and marched up to Solmundsson. 'I'm not interested in your bloody council meetings. You told me you could get this thing out.'

Rather than being cowed by Gotrek's fierce tone, Solmundsson smiled at him. 'It's far more powerful than I imagined. The Fyreslayer runemasters have surpassed themselves.'

Gotrek was about to yell something but Solmundsson continued quickly, still smiling. 'I have an idea. But I will need the written approval of the admiralty and the guildmasters.' He waved at the sky-ship looming over them. 'So this emergency council is perfectly timed.' He clapped Gotrek on the shoulder. 'Perhaps the ancestor gods are watching over us after all? Perhaps Grungni has—'

Gotrek grabbed Solmundsson's neck armour. 'Grungni won't help you, beardling, if you let me down.'

There was a rattling sound as the Kharadron turned their guns on Gotrek.

Gotrek leant closer to Solmundsson. 'I'm not known for my tolerance.'

The captain maintained his cheerful smile. 'There's always a way, Gotrek. Trust me.'

Maleneth tensed. This was exactly the kind of comment that could result in a beheading. To her surprise, Gotrek seemed wrong-footed by the captain's confidence. The Slayer grunted dismissively but backed away and made no move to attack Solmundsson. Maleneth was starting to see how Solmundsson had managed to reach such a high rank at such a young age.

Solmundsson strode up a gangplank onto the sky-ship, carrying himself with such a confident swagger that it looked like he had summoned the ship himself. Meanwhile, behind him, another section of his palace collapsed, filling the air with glowing shards.

CHAPTER SIX

'We needs a meetin', said Scragfang, struggling to suppress the hysteria boiling through his innards. 'Da whole Gobbapalooza.' He licked his lips, shocked by the ideas worming through his mind. Could he go through with something so big? He remembered the certainty in the moon's voice and nodded. 'We need ta get da whole mob ta Slathermere.'

'Wozzit mean?' Mangleback scuttled through the mire, squelching through the marsh. 'That song, wozzit mean?' Mangleback's expression was devious, as though he were amused by a private joke. 'Drippin' clagg?'

'Drippin' clagg. It means I'm gonna bring the Everdank down on Barak-Urbaz. It means summat big's comin'. Big news for me. Dat's wot.' He frowned. 'It'll take a while ta get da others. They're all over Slathermere.'

Mangleback draped a reassuring stem over Scragfang's shoulder. 'No need ta worry. I 'ad a sense this'd be big. I sent word. They're all comin'.'

'They're already on their way?'

'You're not the only one touched by the Gloomspite. I see fings too. I saw you was on to summat big an' I let the others know. Told 'em you'd 'ave summat important to announce.'

Scragfang shoved the tentacle away. 'Idiot! They'll blab.' He stamped furiously in the mud. 'And if they've blabbed, da Loonking probably already knows. An 'e'll want to know why I'd keep a secret from him.' Scragfang's voice rose to a screech. 'Wot 'ave ya done? I'd never have even thought of this if it wasn't for you.'

Mangleback hugged him again. 'I ain't that stupid. I told them it'd be in *their* interests if no one knew nuffin. They pricked up their ears at that. Dey won't wanna risk sharing anything they could keep for themselves.'

Scragfang took a deep breath and nodded, slightly reassured. That was true – the rest of the Gobbapalooza would happily keep secrets if they thought it was to their advantage.

'Who'd ya invite?'

'Boglob. Stinkeye. Lord Zogdrakk.'

'Zogdrakk? Really?' Scragfang grimaced.

'Funds, Scrag, 'e's got da funds.'

''E gets on my wick.' Scragfang clambered up the side of the valley with Mangleback hurrying after him. 'All that "thou" and "one" and stuff.' The ground was springy and moist, and as Scragfang climbed, the Asylum stirred, sensing prey. Blusher tufts and mucus caps popped from the gloop, eyes blinking, trying to lasso him with tendrils. Scragfang barely registered the attacks. Since being moonstruck, there was little in the Gibbermarsh that could touch him. Which was why the Loonking sought him out – which was why he was so trusted. At the thought of the Loonking's cruel face Scragfang faltered, wondering, again, if he really dared to attempt this ruse.

A candle-scab rushed towards him through the rain, gills rippling as it stooped to engulf his head.

Scragfang howled a muffled curse, choking on mucus as he lashed out with his loonblade. The knife cut easily through the downy flesh. The candle-scab gurgled and tumbled away, clutching its wound, making a mournful burbling sound.

'Try it!' screamed Scragfang, turning on his heel and waving his loon-blade at the shapes shuffling towards him. The Asylum was always hungry. Every piece of fungus wanted to grow and consume. An outsider would not survive an hour in its brackish swamps, but Scragfang knew how to handle himself. His voice was shrill. 'I'll cutcha ta pieces!'

His blade spilled cool light, revealing the fungal host gathered around him. Think-cups were hovering over his head, gossamer wings whirring as they circled, and crested stinkhorns were stomping through the muck, their cyclopean eyes staring hungrily. And behind them were even larger pred-ators. There was a scryer's saddle, like a scabby, mobile hill with a mouth, and a whole herd of scud plates, spinning through the mist, scattering brain milk as they twirled through the air.

Scragfang nodded, his resolve hardening. They all sensed that he was destined for greatness. They wanted a taste of destiny. He took some death parasols from his bag and gulped the mushrooms down, relishing the earthy taste. Then, as his attackers swarmed closer, he spat a curse and sliced his knife through the air. Silver flames burst from the mud, enveloping the shapes that surrounded him. The think-cups popped like fireworks, hurling pulp. The others ignited in equally spectacular fashion, and for a few seconds Scragfang was surrounded by a storm of gills and stems. When the flames died down to a pale, flickering glow, Scragfang strode on with Mangleback scurrying close behind.

They headed out across the marsh, keeping their heads low and their pace quick. Nowhere in the Asylum was truly exposed. The Loonking used it to grow his scryshrooms and plot his wars, so he kept it well hidden. The roof was always overhead, jagged and moist, but still, of all the places Scragfang had to visit, the marsh was the biggest. It spread out for miles in every direction and the roof seemed unnaturally high. It made him feel like he was out under the stars, at the mercy of the wind and the open sky.

They climbed the hill on the far side and were met by the sight of his beloved Slathermere. The upper levels were carved from the still-living head of a gargant. And not just any gargant. All gargants were colossal, but this thing must have been like a mountain. Its grimacing head domi-nated the marsh. Its skin was covered in firemould and it radiated cool light, like a moon that had broken the surface of a pool. Half the grots in

Gibbermarsh called Slathermere their home. Beneath its shimmering bulk there were miles of twisting tunnels, caves, boltholes and underground pools, all teeming with exotic fungi. It was one of the most crowded locations in the whole Asylum. With so many clans living together, fights were a common occurrence, but no one was ever foolish enough to tangle with the Loonking's most trusted finker and Scragfang lived in relative peace. Slathermere was the first place he had ever known happiness.

Lights led towards the gargant's head from every direction – heads and bodies, encased in fungus but still alive, gibbering and screaming and filling the clammy air with their voices. Each of them was dusted with firemould spores and they formed a glimmering halo around the gargant's head, like fireflies circling a flame. The sound of their voices gave the Gibbermarsh its name and Scragfang paused to savour it, closing his eyes, enjoying the torrent of agony that drifted across the twilit water. There were humie heads, stuntie heads, aelf heads and the heads of countless other races, all gasping in the darkness. It never failed to amuse Scragfang that all of them would have wished to stop the Everdank but now they were here, aiding him with every babbled scream.

He trudged on through the muck, and after a while he spotted sentries milling around the holes in the gargant's neck. Even from half a mile away, he could see that many of them were accompanied by squigs. Squigs were one of the simpler life forms in the Asylum but also one of the deadliest. They were little more than spherical heads on legs – spheres of crimson muscle with jaws so wide their heads seemed to hinge each time they opened their mouths – but they were incredibly violent and their teeth were *very* sharp. The sentries had the squigs on chains, but they were struggling to hold the creatures back as they snapped and drooled, straining at their leashes. Scragfang knew that he should consider squigs his slaves, but he was secretly terrified of them. Not for the first time, he wondered how he would cope if he didn't have Mangleback to look out for him. He suppressed the thought, determined that Mangleback would not find out how much he relied upon him.

They kept on, feet squelching, but it was slow going as the mud grew deeper, so Scragfang put two fingers to his lips and whistled. The sound echoed out across the lake, and almost immediately shapes slithered from the mud. The first segmapede to reach them was too small to be ridden, but the second was so large that Scragfang and Mangleback could both climb on.

Scragfang held out a handful of tiny mushrooms called clag bonnets and the creature snatched them in its mandibles, devouring them eagerly. Lights flickered in its segmented body and it surged forwards, carrying them quickly over the final stretch of marsh, using its rippling skirt of legs to hurtle across the water as though it were weightless.

'I'll do da talking,' said Scragfang, straining to look back over his shoulder at Mangleback.

'Course.' Mangleback smiled. 'It's your plan.'

'Exactly,' snapped Scragfang, but as he said it, he had a niggling sensation that it might *not* be his plan. He never would have considered double-crossing the Loonking if Mangleback hadn't given him the fear.

He wanted to raise the point with Mangleback but then he would look like a weak fool, so he just nodded firmly.

The segmapede rushed them across the marsh so fast Scragfang barely had time to listen to the forest of severed heads swaying over the water, but he heard enough to feel even more sure that he had to act. Many of the heads were screaming about the Bad Moon. That was a sure sign that it would soon be full. 'I have to get it soon,' he muttered.

They leapt from the segmapede at the entrance to the caves, under the canopy of the gargant's chin. The guards bowed and yanked at the squigs' leashes as Scragfang and Mangleback hurried towards them. Stories of Scragfang's high standing were widespread. No one wanted to get in his way.

They passed the squigs and headed in through the largest cave mouth. As always, Scragfang had to pause to giggle at the scene. There were hundreds of grots rushing back and forth, most bearing the sigil of the Bad Moon on their shields and robes. Some were on foot but many were mounted on vast swamp creatures – spiders big enough to be saddled and mucus-coated glop snails that were even bigger, along with a whole host of moist, glistening steeds that slithered and scuttled through the shadows. There was always a carnival air to the entrance cave. Half the crowd was busy fighting, drinking and eating while the other half whirled in blissful confusion, pounding drums, hammering gongs and squealing through whistles. Mangleback gave Scragfang a gentle shove, dragging his attention from the hilarious sights. Scragfang nodded and they rushed through the crowd, heading out of the cave and jogging down a steep, glistening incline towards the lower levels. As soon as they entered the main cave network, Scragfang started to relax a little. It was only here, in the shadows beneath Slathermere, that he felt truly safe, with no big open spaces hanging over him and the comforting drip of the stalactites. There was firemould here too, glittering in the encrusted walls, but it was a wan, gentle glow and Scragfang felt his confidence increasing the deeper he went.

'I told 'em to wait at Murkseat,' said Mangleback, his suckers popping from the stone as he ran.

Scragfang nodded. He did not entirely trust any of the Gobbapalooza, but at least in such a small cave they would not be able to bring their guards and squigs along. And it was in those deepest holds, far beneath Slathermere, that he felt able to glare them all down.

The floor shook and they both had to pause and lean against the wall. They did not comment on the tremor. There was no need. They both knew what was happening. Every now and then, the gargant's head would stir and realise it no longer had a body. It would shift and groan for a few seconds, before the toxic mould on its skin sent it back into a fitful sleep.

Once the shaking had stopped, the two grots headed on down into the gloom. As they neared the cave called the Murkseat, Scragfang saw a crowd of grots waiting at the entrance. Everyone backed away as Scragfang approached, making room for him to pass. Even the guard squigs shuffled back, their huge crimson tongues lolling as they watched the shaman.

The Murkseat was a small oval cave with a low roof. It was unexceptional, apart from the bowl-shaped bracket of fungus at its centre. The fungus was a vivid saffron yellow and served as a large cushion. Most of the Gobbapalooza were sprawled across it as they watched Scragfang enter. The largest was Boglob. He claimed to be descended from some larger species of greenskin and was twice the size of anyone else in the Gobbapalooza – almost as tall as a human. He wore a suit of plate armour formed of gnarled bracket fungus that entirely encased his broad frame. He looked more like a rotten tree stump than a grot. Unlike tree stumps, however, Boglob was never still. As Scragfang entered the Murkseat Boglob was stomping back and forth, waving a scythe in his encrusted fist and glaring at everyone. At the sight of Scragfang and Mangleback, he spat and brandished the scythe at him.

Sitting nearest to Scragfang was Lord Zogdrakk, an absurd-looking figure draped in stolen finery. He was wearing a crown twice the size of his bony head that forced his ears to stick out at right angles from his skull. He was swathed in purple silk robes and his hand was resting on a golden sceptre topped with a fist-sized ruby. As he saw Scragfang, he raised his chin in a magisterial sneer, tilting his head so the light flickered across the golden hoops in his ear.

Behind Lord Zogdrakk was a grot so hunched, scarred and wizened that he looked like charred kindling. Stinkeye was the alchemist of the group. He was dressed in filthy, torn robes and his twisted body was testament to how far he had pushed his art in service of the Bad Moon. His head was dominated by a single blue-tinged eye that filled most of his face. His body was wracked by constant tremors, and with every rattling breath he exhaled green embers. The embers plumed around his eye and snaked from his hood, adding to the impression that he was half spirit creature. He was draped in so many alembics, flasks and medicine glasses that he clinked as he shook.

'Big news!' exclaimed Scragfang, attempting to sound confident. 'You best get prepared for a change.'

Stinkeye remained silent, squinting at Scragfang as his vials bubbled and steamed. Boglob growled like a whipped dog, baring his teeth. But Lord Zogdrakk strode towards Scragfang, his shoulders thrown back and his sceptre clacking on the floor.

'Change?' His voice was pinched and thin as he tried to emulate a human noble. 'Has thou finally got a grip of thou's headaches?'

'Think bigger,' said Mangleback, scuttling into the cave and sounding almost as pompous as Lord Zogdrakk. 'Scragfang's seen 'is biggest prophecy yet. Ain'tcha, Scragfang? 'Ee's seen our next target.'

Zogdrakk yawned theatrically. '*Another* fat sky stuntie, I suppose.'

Scragfang found his confidence wilting under Lord Zogdrakk's regal glare, but he tried to hide his fear. 'Way bigger.'

Lord Zogdrakk ran his fingers through the pelt that covered his chest and continued staring at Scragfang. 'One's listening.'

Stinkeye climbed from the fungus, moving in palsied lurches and filling Scragfang's nose with the smell of brimstone. His voice was a whisper, scraped from a ruined throat. 'Er, an' wot's da Loonking got to say about dis?'

''E don't need to know nuffin,' replied Mangleback, jumping into the awkward pause. 'Yet.'

Stinkeye gave Lord Zogdrakk a sideways glance. 'Really? Seems odd.'

Boglob had been staring at his scythe, not following the ex-change, but at this comment he stomped across the cave and jabbed one of his fingers into Stinkeye's chest. 'Ya callin' me odd?'

Stinkeye staggered backwards, creating a din of clinking bottles and snorting more embers. 'Dimwit.' He placed a trembling hand on one of his glass beakers. 'I'll melt yer stinkin' gizzard.'

Boglob snarled and shook his head violently, and continued pacing around the cave.

'Oi!' snapped Scragfang, aware of how easily things could descend into carnage. 'Listen. Dis *is* big. We's gonna try summat different.'

Lord Zogdrakk assumed another grand pose, draping his hand over the pommel of his sceptre, placing one leg forward with the knee bent and tilting his head back even further. 'Wot haft thou in mind?'

'Da Bad Moon's almost full,' replied Scragfang. 'An 'e's right over all them stuntie sky caves.'

Stinkeye shrugged, still gripping the glass beaker and glaring at Boglob. 'Er, so? 'E's risen before. An', er, we're already killin' da shiny stunties. Thanks to da Loonking, we're spreadin' shadow faster 'n a bad smell. Why'd ya wanna keep stuff from 'im?'

'Because,' snapped Mangleback, 'the Loonking's already gettin' tired of us. 'E don't want no competition. Scragfang's seen the big one. The big scrap. The Everdank's nearly 'ere. But d'ya think the Loonking will just pat us all on our little noses?' Mangleback dragged a finger across his throat. 'That's wot we'll get.'

Stinkeye gave Mangleback a doubtful look. ''E ain't never 'ad shamans like us.' He nodded at Scragfang. ''Specially 'im.' He shook one of his bottles, creating a brief, dazzling flash of light. 'We're sparky. Powerful.'

Mangleback looked around at all of them. '*Too* powerful. We's a threat. An' the Loonking knows it.'

Lord Zogdrakk wiped the back of his hand across his brow, affecting dismay. 'Dat's a filthy slander. I ain't never been nuffin but loyal. Dat's why da Loonking comes ta me for gear. 'E knows one's 'is most loyal servant. I ain't never thought about stabbin' 'im in da back.'

Stinkeye raised his eyebrow.

'I've seen how to start the Everdank,' said Scragfang. 'I've seen 'ow we can show the Bad Moon the best joke of all.'

Lord Zogdrakk narrowed his eyes. 'Wot joke?'

Everyone fell quiet. Even Boglob stopped stamping around the cave and Mangleback looked eagerly at Scragfang, nodding for him to speak.

'Da Bad Moon showed me a special stuntie. A Fyreslayer wiv magic metal in his chest.' He paused for dramatic effect. 'Metal so powerful it could blow up Barak-Urbaz.'

Stinkeye looked intrigued. 'Er, what's it look like?'

'Like gold, until da Fyreslayer gets mad. Then it's a comet in his chest, blastin' an smashin'.'

Stinkeye looked at Lord Zogdrakk then back at Scragfang, narrowing his eye. 'An', er, how'd ya fink we'd get it? Just pop up to Barak-Urbaz an' ask?'

Scragfang grinned. 'I seen a way ta bring him 'ere.' He waved his knife. 'So I can use da fang on 'im.'

'Yer gonna stick 'im?' leered Boglob, waving his scythe in Scragfang's face.

Scragfang carefully moved the blade away. 'I ain't gonna zoggin fight 'im. The rune magic is too strong.' Scragfang waved his knife. 'But the fang can suck it out.'

Zogdrakk frowned. 'And 'ow, forsooth, is thou gonna get da Fyreslayer down 'ere to Gibbermarsh?'

Scragfang felt a rush of pride and triumph. 'I've been *shown* da way. Da Fyreslayer's gonna leave Urbaz on a sky-ship.'

Stinkeye laughed, wheezing embers. 'Er, 'e ain't gonna come 'ere though, is 'e? No stuntie's gonna come down to the Asylum lookin' for 'elp.'

Scragfang drew back his shoulders and tried to employ the pompous tones Lord Zogdrakk always used. 'I studied 'im. 'E's got a *loyal* friend. Someone 'e loves and trusts. A murder aelf. We'll reach their sky-ship, catch the murder aelf and bring 'er to da Asylum. Once the Fyreslayer realises 'e'll be down 'ere like spores from a lungwart. 'E'll be *desperate* ta get 'er back.'

'An' then you'll cut 'im,' snarled Boglob, slicing the air with his scythe and spitting again.

Scragfang stared at him for a moment, slowly shaking his head, before continuing. He waved his knife at the cave. 'If I gets da Fyreslayer 'ere everyfin's gonna boot off. Barak-Urbaz will fall! I seen its face meltin'. I'll do what the Loonking couldn't.'

Lord Zogdrakk waved his sceptre at Scragfang. 'An' ow, exactly, is thou gonna get ta da sky-ship? The overground's a big place. An' da sky's even bigger. It goes right up to da sky roof.'

Stinkeye sniggered inside his hood. 'Da sky ain't got a roof.'

Zogdrakk rose to his full, unimpressive height and pointed his sceptre at Stinkeye. 'Thou arst a moron. Everyfin's gotta zoggin roof. Wotcha fink stops the mountains floatin' off?' Zogdrakk snorted and gave Mangleback a sideways glance. 'An Stinkeye claims ta be *clever*.'

Stinkeye's lip curled and he gripped one of the bottles strapped to his filthy robes.

Mangleback held up one of his tendrils. 'Use yer noggins for a minute. Scragfang's given us an amazin' chance.'

'Er, amazin' chance for who?' hissed Stinkeye, still sneering. He waved his bottle at Scragfang. 'Even if 'e does nick a murder aelf, 'ow's it gonna benefit me? You called us 'ere sayin' we'd learn summat to our advantage. I can see, er, *nuffin* to my advantage. Scragfang's mad or 'e's a prophet. Either way it don't mean nuffin for me.' He waved the bottle at Lord Zogdrakk and Boglob. 'Or any of us apart from maybe you. An dat's only cuz yer always so far up Scragfang's rear ya might manage to get a place on 'is throne as a cushion.'

Mangleback scuttled around the cave, his tentacles popping on the muddy floor. 'If Scragfang became the new Loonking, 'e's gonna need a new court. An' oo's 'e gonna choose? Weedy scrag-brains 'e ain't never met? Or 'is own Gobbapalooza wot 'e's worked with for years.'

Stinkeye looked unconvinced. Then he looked at Scragfang and his expression softened. 'Er, well, is dat true?'

'I ain't got no chance of making this work if you ain't in it with me,' he replied. 'An' if I do end up as the new Loonking, I ain't gonna 'ave a clue how ta rule without you lot ta help me.' Scragfang meant every word. His mind was a powerful weapon but he knew it was cracked. One of the smiling feet was hovering a few inches in front of his face, gurning cheerfully. Scragfang shook his head. 'I needs ya.'

Stinkeye let out a long breath and lowered his bottle. 'Maybe then. Maybe I could, er, 'elp.'

Scragfang grinned at him. 'Once I've nicked da Fyreslayer's magic, Barak-Urbaz is gonna come crashin' down. An then we're gonna spread Everdank. We'll be masters of everyfin.' His head began to pound with excitement. 'It'll be zoggin glorious. One big, bloody, hilarious slaughter.'

Boglob's eyes widened and he gripped his scythe tighter, looking at Mangleback. 'Is 'e right?'

Mangleback turned in a circle. 'Oh, Boglob. 'E's right all right.'

Boglob grinned and smacked the handle of his scythe against his helmet. He hit himself so hard that he staggered across the cave and slammed into the wall, unearthing a cloud of mould spores.

When the clouds had cleared, Stinkeye hopped from his seat and walked over to Scragfang. ''Ow are ya gonna reach da sky-ship?'

Lord Zogdrakk tapped his sceptre against his chest, causing his jewellery to rattle. 'One may'st be able to assist. Ast thou knowst one 'ast the finest herd of squigs this side of the Stagnant Peak. It would be a small matter ta make them fliers.' He gave Stinkeye a grudging nod. 'I've seen thou doest it plenty o' times before. Thou's got medicine to make 'em sprout wings.' He bowed to Scragfang. 'It'd be an honour to gift one's finest beasts in da great cause of thou's decension.'

'It's "ascension",' muttered Stinkeye.

Lord Zogdrakk raised his chin and adopted an even more magisterial expression, continuing to address Scragfang. 'I'm at your service.'

Scragfang thought for a moment. 'Squigs might be useful as a diversion.'

Zogdrakk frowned and mouthed the word.

Stinkeye shook his head in despair. 'Distract the stunties while we're nickin' the murder aelf.'

Scragfang nodded. 'Exactly.'

Stinkeye rubbed his mould-encrusted eye, looking doubtful. 'We'd still get spotted though. There's nowhere to hide on a shiny ship. Everyfin's a zoggin mirror.' He nodded at Scragfang. 'Ya said it yerself. We need ta be *cleverer*.' He waved everyone close and looked around the cave. ''As any of you heard of gassy rotters?'

'Never,' said Lord Zogdrakk.

Stinkeye grinned. 'It's a kind of death cap. A special kind. Ones dat float in da Weeping Brook.'

Scragfang nodded. '*Brain* rotters we used to call 'em. One mouthful an' ya don't know yer face from yer arse.'

Stinkeye leant even closer. So close Scragfang could see the slime oozing from his charred pores. 'Brain rotters is right.' He tapped a teardrop-shaped bottle at his belt. 'Ever tried 'em wiv powdered webcap?'

Scragfang shook his head. 'Rotters and webcap? Never tried it, Stinkeye. Wotsit do?'

Stinkeye bared his black tooth stumps in a grin. 'It unlocks yer brain.'

Scragfang looked at the feet fluttering over his head. 'My brain don't need no unlockin'.'

Stinkeye laughed. 'I mean it unlocks yer brain so it can fly.'

'I'm flyin' most of da time.'

Lord Zogdrakk held up a warty finger, causing his rings to glitter and flash. 'I believe one understands wot he's ramblin' about, Scragfang. He don't mean it maketh thou confused. He's imperlicating that it frees yer mind ta go somewhere else. Somewhere yer body can't.'

Stinkeye nodded. 'Old flash hat is right. It's a way to get out of yer 'ead.' His whisper grew even quieter. 'An get in someone *else's*.'

Mangleback did a circular, scampering dance. 'Ya could get inside the murder aelf's 'ead. You could make 'er walk off the sky-ship onta one of Lord Zogdrakk's squigs. Then fly 'er here and Zog's yer uncle, da Fyreslayer follows.'

Stinkeye shook his head and leant back from the huddle. As he moved, more embers erupted from his robes, causing the others to cough and splutter. 'Er, no, Mangleback. Dat ain't gonna work. Two reasons. One, we don't know where the sky-ship's gonna be. Two, ya don't wanna get in an aelf's mind. It's messed up in there. They don't fink right. You'd either crack or just get booted out. A stuntie's 'ead is bad enough, but you don't wanna try an aelf.'

'So wot's yer idea?' asked Scragfang, sensing from the gleam in his eye that he had one.

'You've seen Barak-Urbaz with yer moonsight, is dat right?'

'Yeah.'

Stinkeye licked his blackened canine. 'Then ya could go there. I mean, er, yer mind could go there. Take a dunk in the, er, Weeping Brook and you'll be flyin'. Yer body would flop but yer mind would whiz. An wiv yer visions ta guide ya, there'd be no problem gettin' to da Fyreslayer.'

'An wot then?' Scragfang felt a rush of the fear. 'Try an' get in 'is 'ead?'

'No.' Stinkeye started limping around the cave, trailing smells and spores. 'I don't reckon' ya wanna go in there. Borrow the body of someone in da Fyreslayer's mob. Someone who'll travel wiv 'im on da sky-ship. Then, all ya gotta do, er, is spy.' Stinkeye had been talking to the shadows as he hobbled round the cave, but now he looked back at Scragfang with such excitement that his convulsions paused. 'Then, when we turn up, use yer borrowed body to sling da aelf on one of our squigs.'

Everything had sounded fine to Scragfang until this point. The idea of tricking the aelf or subduing her, without the help of the others, sounded terrifying.

Boglob noticed his crestfallen expression. 'Let me do it!' He waved his scythe with such violence that everyone reeled away from their seats.

The thought of someone else getting near the rune without him made Scragfang even more nervous. He noticed that Mangleback was looking at him, nodding slightly. 'No,' said Scragfang, trying to sound impressive. 'It was my vision. It 'as ta be me.'

Stinkeye nodded eagerly and resumed his shivering spasms as he started limping around the cave. 'We just need to getcha to da brook.'

Lord Zogdrakk rested one hand on the head of his sceptre, raised his chin and spoke into the middle distance. 'One has onest minor concern about da plan, Stinkeye.'

He halted, wheezing and juddering as he sneered at him. 'Lemme guess. It's, er, that yer a great zoggin coward. An yer worried ya might get a dint in yer crown. Is that yer, er, minor concern?'

Boglob burst into laughter and began ambling around the cave on all fours like an ape, punching the ground and chanting, 'Minor concern! Minor concern!'

Lord Zogdrakk turned with regal slowness to Scragfang and Mangleback. 'If onest presence ain't no longer required, onest can leave. But 'ave a fink about how you'll reach dat sky-ship wivout squigs.'

'Oi!' snapped Scragfang.

Stinkeye and Boglob halted, taken aback by Scragfang's forceful tone.

Scragfang was equally shocked by the power in his voice. So much so that, for a moment, he forgot what he was going to say. Then Mangleback gave him an encouraging nod and he managed to continue. 'We's got an amazin' chance 'ere, boys. Da Bad Moon's given me a chance ta do summat really funny. But we ain't gonna get nowhere if we're spendin' all our time callin' each other names until someone gets a sticker in da throat.'

To Scragfang's amazement, they all sat back down on the seat. 'Good,' he said, giving Mangleback a quick sideways glance. 'Now, I reckon Stinkeye is right. I reckon it's worth tryin' his rotter idea.' He looked at Stinkeye. 'Can you get us to da right spot?'

Stinkeye tried to answer but broke into a coughing fit, spraying embers around the cave. Everyone backed away, trying to avoid the toxic spores, until he took a swig from a bottle and managed to control himself. 'Yes,' he wheezed. He glanced at Lord Zogdrakk. 'We'll need some of yer squigs though. It's a few miles to da Weeping Brook.'

Zogdrakk ignored him but bowed low to Scragfang. 'Woteva thou desirest, though canst 'ave.'

There was a pause and Scragfang was pleased to notice that everyone looked his way, waiting for his response. 'Right,' he said, still feeling like he was embarking on a ride he hadn't entirely signed up for. 'Get da squigs. Take me ta da brook. Let's get this zoggin started.'

CHAPTER SEVEN

Maleneth shook her head. 'Do you get the sense they're trying to compensate for something?' Each building they reached in Barak-Urbaz was more overwrought than the last. Admiralty Hall was a monstrous cluster of gromril-framed domes. She counted six, each large enough to dwarf the sky-trawlers drifting overhead. The domes merged into each other, giving the hall a strangely organic appearance, as if a geyser of molten metal had bubbled up through the city. But it was not the domes she found so absurd. Straddling the whole structure was a colossal statue, not of an ancestor god but of a nameless Kharadron captain, his boots planted firmly on the domes as he reached up into the sky, grasping the boiling limbs of a harkraken. She frowned as they were led across a broad square. 'No amount of science can defy the will of the gods.'

Captain Solmundsson was only a few paces ahead. 'We do not defy them. But we can't wait for divine intervention. The greenskins do not wait. They do not allow time for prayers to be answered.'

The soldiers led them up a broad flight of steps into an entrance hall. Maleneth paused at the threshold, taken aback by an enormous fossil that was suspended from the ceiling. It was hundreds of feet long and appeared to be some kind of winged whale. The hall was lined with alcoves containing the fossils of other beasts, but none were on such a vast scale.

The others had not paused and she hurried after them, joining a press of Kharadron who were heading for an archway beyond the fossil's tail. Pillars in the curved walls cradled aether-lights, but they had been angled to leave much of the chamber in shadow. This, combined with the angular shapes in the architecture, gave Maleneth the peculiar sensation that rather than being hung in the clouds, the hall was a vast cave sunk deep below the ground, lit by smouldering brands.

They passed through several colonnaded hallways and then finally emerged into a rectangular hall built on the same absurd scale as the entrance. It was long and lined with tiered benches that radiated up from a central rectangular pit. The pit was dominated by a long table and an aethermatic orrery – a nest of polished metal ellipses that were rotating slowly around each other, glinting in the aether light and casting shadows across the lower tiers of the hall. The design was more Azyrite than Kharadron and she guessed it must have been a gift, or perhaps a collaboration between the human and duardin races. The chamber looked large enough to seat several hundred Kharadron but there were fewer than a hundred in the room, all gathered in the lower terraces or seated around the table.

Maleneth and the others were led down several flights of stairs towards this group as Kharadron servants dashed past them, hurrying through archways carrying scrolls and casting wary glances at Gotrek. As she passed near the walls, Maleneth saw that they were lined with bookcases that were stuffed with thousands of logbooks, ship manifests, charter scrolls and sky charts. She reached out to touch one, but a guard waved her on with his gun.

When they reached the crowd at the base of the chamber, Maleneth was surprised to see that some of the Kharadron were not wearing the sturdy flight suits she was used to seeing. Many of them had their heads uncovered and were dressed in flamboyant finery, their beards and tunics dripping with jewels and precious metals. They radiated wealth and pride and they whispered to each other as they saw Gotrek approaching. In front of the chattering merchants was a row of Kharadron dressed more like Solmundsson – finely worked flight suits encased in plates of rune-inscribed armour and topped with imposing filigreed helmets. They carried an impressive array of ornamental weapons and badges of office, and so many of them were smoking pipes that the pit was thick with fumes.

There was a place reserved at the table and the soldiers ushered Solmundsson and his guards towards it, then led Gotrek, Maleneth and Trachos through the smoke to a bench on one of the terraces near the table.

Maleneth was shocked by Gotrek's behaviour. She would have expected him to rail at being ushered around like a servant, but he was oddly compliant, sitting where he was ordered and looking up at the ceiling in silence. Maleneth glanced at Trachos to see if he had noticed the Slayer's strange behaviour, but he was staring at the orrery down in the pit.

As the others sat down and waited patiently for whatever was about to happen, Maleneth paced up and down past the benches, muttering under her breath and waving away the smoke. Were the Kharadron going to imprison them? Execute them? She had her knives and her poisons but there were dozens of armed soldiers lining the hall, all carrying aethermatic weapons. If this turned into a fight Gotrek would probably be the only one who left the hall alive.

Trachos wandered over to the orrery and leant close, peering at the mechanism.

Maleneth hurried over to Trachos' side. 'Stay with the Slayer. I might need you.'

Trachos ignored her and addressed one of the gilt lions on the frame, speaking in an urgent whisper. 'Can you hear me? Lord-Celestant?'

Maleneth stared at him in disbelief.

Trachos circled the orrery, looking through the hoops and spheres. The whole device was only five feet in circumference, but he seemed to have decided that there was a Stormcast Eternal inside. 'I have atoned,' he gasped, gripping the frame.

Maleneth grabbed his arm and wrenched him away. 'It's empty, Trachos! Look! There's no one in there!'

'How do you know?' he muttered.

Before Maleneth could think of an answer, a low booming sound reverberated round the hall. It sounded like a hunting horn. There was a clattering as all the Kharadron rose from their seats and pulled their shoulders back. Maleneth dragged Trachos away from the orrery and back to the seats beside Gotrek.

The noise grew louder as a channel opened between the rows of benches – the metal plates folded away like toppling cards to form a path into the hall. Maleneth peered through the gloom and smoke, struggling to make out the strange object that was approaching. At first, she thought it was a boulder, rumbling slowly down the slope towards them, but then she saw the glint of moving pistons and heard the rattle of cogs and realised it was a machine. As it plunged through the smoke she saw it was similar to the galvanic phaetons that circled the city, but built to carry a single, claw-shaped throne. Slumped on the throne was the oldest, largest duardin she had ever seen. His white beard trailed over his enormous gut and snaked around his boots. His master-wrought armour was a vivid lapis blue and edged with golden trim, and he had the pelt of a sky serpent draped over his shoulders. He wore no helmet and his face looked like the aftermath of a landslide, so mangled by scars that his slab of a nose formed a crooked Z and his mouth was locked in a permanent grimace. One of his arms was missing and had been replaced with one forged of golden metal and studded with gems. He was smoking a pipe so large the bowl was nested between his feet. Both of his eyes were featureless white orbs.

'Lord Admiral Solmund,' intoned the assembled duardin, thumping their chests and bowing their heads.

The Lord Admiral gave a barely perceptible nod as his throne trundled to a halt. The machine was surrounded by gold-clad honour guards carrying ornamental skypikes, and as the throne settled onto the floor with a hiss of hydraulics they positioned themselves around it, clutching their mechanised spears in a manner that indicated they were far from ceremonial.

A captain rose from his seat at the table. 'Lord Admiral Solmund. In accordance with article twelve, subclause fifteen, we beg your permission to forgo the usual–'

The Lord Admiral interrupted with a dismissive wave of his hand, while continuing to draw heavily on his pipe.

The captain hesitated, then nodded. 'Lord Admiral. We have called this emergency council to discuss the incidents in the Starlokh shipyard, the Jarnskogg mills, a khordryn in the Stromez Quarter and the endrinhouses of Solmundsson Palace. Since our last gathering, Lord Admiral, it has come to light that all of these incidents, as well as the fires in the Brog Market and surrounding bakeries, were a result of the actions of one...' The captain frowned and turned to a guildmaster sitting on a bench behind him. The two whispered and the guildmaster shook his head furiously. The captain nodded and looked back at the Lord Admiral. 'These events were all caused by the actions of a foreigner by the name of Gotrek Gurnisson, who is sitting...' The captain squinted through the pipe fumes that were trailing round his face, then pointed in Gotrek's direction. 'Over there, beside the Khainite aelf who was his accomplice in several of these misdemeanours. All of the events have incurred extremely expensive damage to property and equipment, and the final incident...' He glanced at Captain Solmundsson. 'Was by far the worst, resulting in the destruction of large portions of Solmundsson Palace and a tremor so powerful that it damaged berths at the nearby Cogsmiths' Guildhouse.'

A murmur of discontent rippled through the merchants and guildmasters and several of them banged weapons on the floor, creating a din that echoed up into the domed ceiling.

The captain nodded eagerly and paused, clearly expecting a reply from the Lord Admiral.

The Lord Admiral said nothing, taking another drag on his pipe.

The captain looked flustered by the lack of response and his cheeks flushed with anger. 'Lord Admiral, someone has to recompense the guildmasters.'

Gotrek's patience finally ran out. 'I'm right here, you talking trinket.' He left his seat and marched out in front of the audience, gripping his axe and glaring up at the captain. 'Get off yer fat arse and come over here. I'll recompense you in the face.'

Guards rushed towards Gotrek, guns raised and armour rattling.

The captain flushed even darker and clanged the handle of his hammer on the floor. 'How *dare* you! Barak-Urbaz is not like the squalid, muck-strewn caves you Fyreslayers call home. This is–'

'I'm no bloody Fyreslayer!' Gotrek marched towards the guards and they took a step backwards, preparing to fire.

The captain bellowed in outrage and began shoving his way through the crowd towards Gotrek, causing a great commotion as the other Kharadron tried to step aside.

'Halt!' The Lord Admiral's voice boomed around the hall with such power that even Gotrek stopped in his tracks.

Almost all of the Kharadron rose to their feet, hurling insults at Gotrek and defending the captain.

'Silence,' growled the Lord Admiral, and Maleneth realised that his throne was amplifying his voice, either through mechanical or magical means. It sounded like the voice of the ancestor gods looking down from the ceiling.

'Out!'

The captains and guildmasters looked around in confusion, wondering who was being addressed.

'Get out!' repeated the Lord Admiral. 'The lot of you!'

Still they hesitated.

'Out!' bellowed Lord Admiral Solmund, gesturing to his honour guard, who promptly pointed their skypikes at the crowd.

'Apart from you,' growled the Lord Admiral as Captain Solmundsson started to leave. He nodded at Gotrek. 'And them.'

There were a few more moments of confusion as the captains, merchant lords and guildmasters all realised that they were being dismissed from the council they had summoned. Then, driven on by the Lord Admiral's sightless glare, they began shuffling down the terraces, muttering and harrumphing as they headed towards the exits, casting furious glances back at Gotrek.

It took several minutes for them all to leave, during which Gotrek paced back and forth, gripping his axe and glaring up at the Lord Admiral. Once the council members had all left, the Lord Admiral and his honour guard were left alone with Gotrek, Maleneth, Trachos and Captain Solmundsson.

The Lord Admiral took another long drag on his pipe and waved for them to approach. Gotrek was muttering as he headed over towards him, but Maleneth caught an intrigued look in his eye. From what little she knew of Gotrek's beliefs, age and long beards were two of the only things he showed any respect for – and the Lord Admiral was blessed on both counts.

As they reached the mechanised throne, the Lord Admiral broke into what Maleneth took to be a coughing fit. It took a few seconds for her to realise he was laughing.

'A talking trinket.' The Lord Admiral shook his head. 'Not a bad description considering you've only just met Captain Thorlagg.'

Gotrek glowered. 'Are you mocking me?'

'No, you great wazzock, I'm complimenting you.' He held his pipe out in Gotrek's direction. 'First honest words anyone's spoken in my earshot for years.'

Gotrek hesitated, still frowning, then grabbed the pipe and took a deep drag. 'Blood of Valaya.' He closed his eye and tilted his head back, savouring the flavour. 'Not bad.'

The Lord Admiral nodded. 'Not bad. High praise from a... from a what? You say you're not a Fyreslayer.'

Gotrek handed the pipe back. 'I'm a who, not a what. I'm Gotrek son of Gurni, and no, I'm not a gold-hugging simpleton. I'm a *true* Slayer. Forged in the Worlds Edge Mountains. I swore my Slayer oath in a world that no longer exists. A *better* world.'

The Lord Admiral took another drag on his pipe. 'Some of the Fyreslayers are making strange claims about you. I spoke to a half-soaked runeson from the Greyfyrd who wouldn't shut up about you. He was deep in his cups, to be fair, but he blathered on about you like you were some kind of saviour. Something more than duardin. He had the sense not to tell me all of his lodge's secrets, but I gleaned enough. Enough to know that they hold you in high regard. They'd bend the knee to you if you let them.'

Gotrek curled his lip. 'They've hammered too much metal into their legs to bend them.'

The Lord Admiral's eyes creased in amusement. Then his expression grew serious. 'They're still duardin. And I've no desire to put myself on a war footing with kinfolk, however distant.' He handed the pipe back to Gotrek. 'Which leaves me with a predicament.'

Gotrek took a drag and answered through a cloud of pipe smoke. 'What's that?'

'The Fyreslayers want to worship you and my guildmasters want to put your head on a pole.'

'Let them try.'

'Is it a fight you've come looking for, then? Have you come here to pit yourself against me, Gotrek, son of Gurni?'

Gotrek's expression remained neutral. 'I've no quarrel with you.'

'And yet my people tell me you have caused untold amounts of damage.'

'Because your people are liars. They swore to rid me of this damned rune and not one of them has the means to touch it.'

'And was my son trying to rid you of the rune when he blew up his palace?'

Gotrek glanced at Solmundsson. 'Your *son*. Of course. Yes, he's very skilled at boasting but not so skilled at doing.'

Solmundsson approached and took out the blue crystal, holding it up to his father. 'The rune resisted the burning glass. Repelled it. I've never seen anything like it.'

'You sound very pleased, Thialf,' rumbled the Lord Admiral, 'for someone who just destroyed half his palace.' He leant forwards in his throne. 'Our palace.'

Solmundsson grinned, missing his father's furious tone. 'It's incredible. It's like nothing else from the Fyreslayer magmaholds. Even the Vostarg runes couldn't endure the burning glass, but this thing can. It's unique, father. Uniquely powerful. It could be exactly what we need.'

The Lord Admiral nodded. Then turned his head in Gotrek's direction. 'And you wish to be rid of it?'

'I do.'

Lord Admiral Solmund waved one of his attendants over and muttered something. The servant rushed away.

'This requires thinking,' said the Lord Admiral as the servant reappeared with a keg and some tankards. 'Which requires a slaked thirst.'

Gotrek nodded seriously as the servant handed him a tankard. 'Wise words never left a dry throat.'

Lord Admiral Solmund laughed. 'My great-grandfather used to say that every day. Just before his breakfast.'

Gotrek growled as he drank and Maleneth realised he was laughing. She rolled her eyes. These two oafs had never met before. Gotrek had ruined half the city. Awnd now they were acting like old friends.

'Sit.' The Lord Admiral waved at the nearest seats. 'No need to stand on ceremony. We're not talking trinkets.'

Gotrek snorted again, spitting beer into his beard. He proceeded to suck it back up with a sound that made Maleneth want to kick him. 'Ai! This is more like it. Reminds me of Thengeln's Golden Preserve.'

She waved away the cup she was offered. 'What is there to discuss? Your son has just admitted that his devices can't touch the rune.'

'It is beyond his understanding,' said Trachos.

The Lord Admiral tilted his head, seeming to consider Trachos. 'He understands more than you think, soldier of Sigmar. It's not just those who hide in Azyr who have learned to read. My son may be impetuous but he's not dim-witted. Thialf's mechanisms are more subtle than you might guess. Lack of knowledge is not the problem here.'

'What then?' asked Gotrek, cheerfully holding out his cup to a servant.

'Lack of power.' The Lord Admiral ran his mechanical hand over his beard. 'We have refined the sublimation process beyond anything achieved in the other sky-keeps. We have uncovered the great mysteries of metal. Struck the richest seams. Harnessed the most wilful elements. No one has achieved as much.'

Solmundsson nodded eagerly. 'My aethermatic coils may have failed but there could be other power sources in Ayadah that would work. Other ways we could fuel the burning glass.'

Gotrek picked something out of his beer, peered at it, then ate it. 'Aya-who?'

The Lord Admiral was looking in the direction of his son, nodding. Then he looked back towards Gotrek, following the sound of his voice. He laughed. 'You really are from another world.' He waved vaguely at the distant doors. 'Ayadah is the name of this land. The place we're hanging above. The whole continent, from here to the Bitten Gulf.'

'Your realm?'

'A contested realm.' The Lord Admiral grimaced. 'In truth, if anyone can claim dominion it would be the damned greenskins. The grots snivel from every pit and puddle. And since Kazak-drung appeared in the sky they've tripled in number. The moon has driven them into a frenzy. We built our keeps in the clouds long ago, to escape the minions of the Dark Gods, but these days it's greenskins we have to watch out for.'

'*Grobi* scum.' Gotrek held out his tankard again. 'Nothing bloody changes.'

'They're a damned nuisance. Our profits have been halved. Since Kazak-drung returned the Moonclans have spread their infernal gloom even further than before. And wherever they go our fleets disappear, swallowed by skies that used to be clear. Dozens of our zonbeks have been lost and it's getting worse.'

'Zonbeks?'

'Glowbeacons. Skyborne keeps that guard our sky-paths. They're heavily fortified and they used to be able to resist even the most determined greenskin attacks. Until Kazak-drung began to wax.' The Lord Admiral frowned, then looked in Gotrek's direction. 'But if we had a weapon powerful enough to reclaim our keeps we could turn back the tide. A weapon like your rune.'

'I'd give it gladly.' Gotrek glanced at Solmundsson. 'What did you mean when you spoke of other power sources?'

Solmundsson hesitated and looked at his father.

The Lord Admiral shrugged. 'The legends are muttered by every drunk from here to the Yhorn Mountains. There's no need to be coy.' He yanked a lever and his throne rumbled into life, adding gouts of steam to the clouds of pipe smoke. 'Let's discuss it in the map room.'

As the mechanised throne clattered across the chamber, the Lord Admiral's guards steered it with their pikes, directing it back towards the entrance the Lord Admiral had arrived through.

Solmundsson waved for Gotrek and the others to follow. 'Everything always looks better on a map.' He grinned. 'Don't you think?'

CHAPTER EIGHT

Vaspero stared at the Slaughter Stone, trying to blank out the sounds of battle. The walls were crowded with refugees from the surrounding villages but no one paid him any heed. Everyone was either scurrying for cover or rushing to the walls. Men, women or children, it did not matter. They all clutched weapons with the same grim determination. Hain had once been a proud city. Trading partnerships with the Kharadron Overlords had brought them wealth and security. But then, a few months ago, the Kharadron ships had stopped coming, and Vaspero's people had been forced into a less palatable allegiance. The local cannibal tribes had demanded blood tributes in return for protection. As long as the people of Hain fed the Slaughter Stone, chanting prayers to a hungry god called Khorne, the marauders kept Hain free from the greenskin tribes. Until the Killing Moon came. Then even the cannibals stopped coming, slaughtered by the myriad goblinoid creatures that swarmed up from the swamps. Now the people of Hain had nothing to lean on but their own fear.

As Vaspero tried to listen to the Slaughter Stone he heard the clash of spears and shields overhead. The latest influx of refugees had doubled their numbers and it looked like Hain might actually be able to repel the attack. The greenskins were everywhere, crawling the walls like vermin, gripping blades in their teeth and vaulting the battlements with screeches of laughter. But they were wretched, stunted things, only waist high to a man of Hain. A few hours earlier, Vaspero had even allowed his men to open the gates and sally forth, taking the fight out to the greenskins and driving them back to the swamplands around the river. The grots had already returned in even greater numbers, but the people of Hain now saw hope. The city walls were not just vast, they were made of riveted, reinforced metal. They had been built centuries earlier, with the engineering skills of the Kharadron Overlords. They were rusted and dented, but they were also bolstered by powerful, unfathomable aether-science. Even the fiercest blow left no mark. The greenskins had wheeled great war machines from the swamps but it was pointless. The boulders bounced uselessly away, crushing grots rather than the people of Hain. The sun had not risen for weeks, and as the Killing Moon waxed it drove the grots into a kill frenzy, but they still could not breach the gleaming metal walls.

Vaspero should have felt pleased but his mind was not on the battle, or the power of the Kharadron engineering – it was fixed on the Slaughter Stone. He stepped closer, peering through the gloom at the bloodstained rock. It was carved to resemble the lower half of a skull, forming a huge bowl at the centre of the courtyard. The cannibals had left it when the Kharadron stopped coming, demanding heads be offered to it every week and the bodies cast into the pits beneath the jaw. As high priest, it had been Vaspero's duty to name the chosen ones. He had borne this role with stoicism.

There was a brief lull in the fighting and Vaspero heard the whisper again. It was half in his head and half in the dusty skull. 'Liar.' Vaspero gripped his hair, horrified by how clear the voice had become. He had almost convinced himself that it was a delusion brought on by exhaustion. He had not slept properly for days, standing with the warriors at the battlements, willing them to victory, and he felt so tired it was almost like being drunk. He had told himself that the voice must be his sleep-starved brain playing tricks on him. But now, as he placed his hand on the Slaughter Stone, there could be no doubt. The words were horribly clear. 'You lied to them.'

For the first time, Vaspero actually recognised the voice. It was his older brother. One of the first sacrifices made to the stone.

'Kirn?' he whispered. 'Is that you?'

'Of course it's me, you lying worm.'

Vaspero walked round the skull, letting his fingers scrape the pitted stone. 'How? How are you alive?'

'Because you lied. You told them Khorne wanted me. You told them it was my name in the bones. And you know it was yours.'

'The bones were wrong!' Vaspero's pulse quickened as the old rage rushed through him. He looked around, horrified at the thought someone else might hear the exchange. No one was paying any attention. The fighting on the walls had grown fiercer and the courtyard was emptying as the newcomers rushed to grab spears and shields. 'Only I can protect the city,' hissed Vaspero, placing his mouth near the skull. 'If you had ruled Hain it would have fallen to the cannibals, or the Moonclans, or someone else. Only I have the wit to keep us safe. The Blood God meant for you to die. It was a mistake. It had to be you.'

'You lied. I know you did.'

'How?'

'Because I didn't die. I was not the chosen one, you were. Khorne did not want me. So I've been waiting down here. All this time. Waiting until I had the strength to rise and tell them all the truth about what you did.'

'It can't be true. I saw your head. I saw you die. And I saw you buried under the skull, along with all the others.'

'I lived. Because my time had not come. And once the moon waxes full I will rise, my dear brother, and everyone will know what you are. They loved me more than you. You know they wanted me to rule in your stead. So you lied. But you cannot fool a god, Vaspero. You can lie to our people but not to Khorne.'

'It's you who is lying!' Vaspero reeled away from the Slaughter Stone, shaking his head. 'You died. I saw your head. You *cannot* be down there.'

Vaspero stumbled across the courtyard and headed back to his royal chambers. He hurled himself on his bed and lay in the dark, hands clamped over his ears as he waited in fear for the voice to come again. The voice did not return, and outside, the sounds of battle faded as the grots drew back, readying themselves for the next assault.

Vaspero tried desperately to sleep, sure that would be the answer to his madness. Because it had to be madness. What other explanation could there be? How could his brother have survived all this time beneath the Slaughter Stone? How could he be preparing to rise? It made no sense.

Finally, after an hour of torment, Vaspero gave up trying to sleep and looked out of his circular window. The fighting had now ceased completely. The defenders were slumped behind the rusty walls, either sleeping or tending to wounds as the Killing Moon blazed overhead, giving the scene the flat, artificial appearance of a stage set. Vaspero drank wine but it did nothing to calm his nerves. An idea had been building in him the whole time he was trying to sleep. It was a hateful, horrible idea, but he could not be rid of it. And now, he realised, while most people were sleeping, might be his only chance to try it. The lookouts would not be facing into the courtyard, but out towards the river where the greenskins were waiting to attack. No one would be watching the Slaughter Stone.

He took another swig of wine for courage then marched from his chambers, doing his best to look sane. When he headed out into the moonlight he saw that he was right – the courtyard was empty. After days of fighting, everyone who could was sleeping. He strode over to the stone and took a ring of keys from his robes. Then, after a final look around, he climbed up into the base of the skull. At the skull's base there was a thick stone hatch, scored with runes and barred with locks. Knowing he would not be visible from outside the skull, Vaspero knelt down, unlocked the hatch and opened it.

The stink of rotting meat rushed up to greet him. The last sacrifice had been less than a week ago, but already the bodies were starting to decay.

'It's too late,' said Kirn, his voice echoing through Vaspero's head. 'I will tell them.'

'You're the liar,' gasped Vaspero. 'You're not in here. It can't be true. You were worm food months ago. I won't listen to you any more.'

'I'm here. And when the Killing Moon is full I will rise. I will tell them what you did.'

Vaspero groaned with a mixture of rage, fear and disgust. Then he plunged his hands into the bodies. Flies and maggots engulfed him as he began heaving the dead aside, uncovering the steps that led down into the pits beneath the skull. Before they had been used for the sacrifices they had stored food, but now they were a charnel house. Vaspero gagged and cursed as he fought down through the blood. His brother was one of the first to die. He would have to dig deep to prove Kirn was not really down there. But, despite the gore and the smell, Vaspero refused to stop. He had to be sure. He had to reach the bottom.

He had only clawed down a few feet when Kirn started to laugh. 'Thanks for your help, brother.'

'No,' gasped Vaspero as he saw the corpses starting to jostle and shift. 'You *can't* be there.'

He backed away, blood dripping from his hands, as a figure rose from the slop.

Vaspero was so horrified that it took him a moment to realise it was not Kirn. It was not even a human. The face grinning up at him belonged to one of the greenskins.

Before Vaspero could react, the grot slid a knife into his belly.

Vaspero stumbled, then dropped backwards onto the steps, landing with a thud in the rotting meat.

The grot laughed as it scurried over him, and as his life rushed out of him, Vaspero watched dozens more of the creatures race up the steps, giggling and singing to the Killing Moon, howling with delight as they finally breached the city.

CHAPTER NINE

Scragfang tried to look regal as the squig jolted beneath him, rattling his bones and forcing him to clutch tightly on to the reins. They had crossed the Gibbermarsh basin and climbed to the higher ground a few miles from Slathermere. Even from this distance, the vast, slack-jawed gargant head dominated the view, shimmering with firemould and haloed by spores.

The rest of the Gobbapalooza were riding their squigs a respectful distance behind Scragfang, as though he were already the Loonking. This meant they could not hear him curse and mutter every time the squig leapt particularly high. However stern he made his commands, the wretched creature seemed to sense his fear, careering through the brackish pools in a wild, drunken manner that made it increasingly hard to remain in the saddle. Mangleback and the rest of the Gobbapalooza were flanked by Lord Zogdrakk's heavily armed grots, but Scragfang had insisted that they keep the group small. The last thing he needed was people in Slathermere asking questions about the expedition. It was unusual for him to drag the whole Gobbapalooza out with him and not everyone in Slathermere was an idiot. It would only take one clever guess to ruin everything, and if the Loonking found out what Scragfang was up to, he knew exactly what would happen – he would join the muttering legions that grew in the Gibbermarsh.

They rode up a series of rocky inclines, like the foothills of a mountain, crossed another boggy valley, climbed more slopes and finally, after hours of riding, they looked down across the Weeping Brook. It was a winding trickle of sluggish black liquid that snaked through a mire of puffballs, candle-scabs and stinkhorns. Everything in the valley was dusted with firemould and every gill, cap and tendril glowed, shimmering with pallid light. It looked like the Weeping Brook was winding through white, glimmering fur.

As soon as the party reached the slopes above the valley the fungi below began to stir, rippling up towards them with a chorus of squelches and pops. There were hundreds of carnivorous killers, and even Scragfang might have been hard pushed to cut through them all, but before he had the chance to worry about it, Stinkeye raced past, riding his squig with far more confidence than him, and dealt with the situation. He placed one of his bottles in a small hand-held catapult, uncorked it and fired it out over the mass of tubes and domes. There was a flash of light as the contents rained down and erupted into colourless flames. A whining sound filled the air as toadstools and puffballs scrambled to escape. The flames were too fast, rippling across rubbery flesh and causing a series of loud pops. Within a minute, there was a charred, smouldering path leading down to the brook and the rest of the nearby predators were busy trying to distance themselves from Stinkeye.

He turned, nodded at Scragfang and then waited, his squig panting and hopping beneath him. No one spoke, and it took Scragfang a moment to realise that they were all waiting for his lead again. He kicked his steed a few times with no effect, and then, when it finally did respond, it bolted down the slope at such a frenzied pace that he barely managed to cling on.

As he reached the banks of the brook he was glad to jump off the thing and hand the reins to one of Lord Zogdrakk's soldiers. Then he walked slowly to the edge of the river while the others dismounted behind him. He was not sure what was flowing through the brook, but it was not water. The ink-black liquid moved at a sluggish pace, and every time a bubble popped on its glossy surface it released pungent fumes. The feet that always followed Scragfang were splashing and rolling in it, chuckling and grinning. 'Is it tar?' he asked them, forgetting for a moment that he was not alone.

'Where ist da rotters?' said Lord Zogdrakk, coming to stand beside him. He prodded the liquid with his sceptre, causing another explosion of noxious gas.

Stinkeye lurched through the mud, blinking his membranous eye, staring into the blackness. 'Er, everywhere. Da whole river's full of 'em.' He looked at Scragfang. 'Ya need ta get right in though. Get yer 'ead under.'

Scragfang looked at the viscous liquid and shrugged. He had done far worse. He moved towards the river and searched for a part of the bank to climb down.

'Oi!' laughed Stinkeye. 'Dis first.' He grabbed another green vial and held it up, shaking the powder inside it. 'Webcap! Da rotters don't do nuffin wivout webcap.'

Scragfang nodded and headed back over to him while the others all gathered round. Lord Zogdrakk was sneering at the surrounding muck with a disdainful expression, pretending to be disgusted, Mangleback was watching Scragfang eagerly from beneath his pulpy shell and Boglob was swinging punches at the air, jogging on the spot, splashing mud over the others and hissing at imaginary foes.

'Tastes good.' Stinkeye grinned as he held the bottle out to Scragfang with a trembling hand. 'Ya only need a tiny...' His words trailed off as he saw that Scragfang had already downed the entire contents.

Scragfang noticed Stinkeye's shocked expression. 'Wot?' He looked at the empty vial. 'Too much?'

'Er.' Stinkeye scratched at his burnt forehead, dislodging flakes of blackened skin. 'I'm sure it's fine.'

Scragfang felt a buzzing sensation on his tongue. ''Ow much should I 'ave 'ad?'

'Er, well, no need ta worry,' Stinkeye said, giving him an unconvincing grin. 'I just ain't seen anyone glug a whole bottle before. I bet it's fine.'

Scragfang felt a rush of fear and looked around at the banks of fungus. 'Do

I need an antidote? Slug tufts usually...' He paused as he noticed something peculiar – he could *see* himself talking. He could see his own gaunt features, his own crimson eyes, his own enormous ears and nose. His features had gone slack and his eyes had a glassy look to them. He swayed forwards on his feet, and if the others hadn't grabbed him he would have fallen face-first into the mud.

'Quick!' cried Stinkeye. ''E's losin' it. 'E's crackin'. Get 'im in. Get 'is 'ead under!'

As Scragfang watched from his peculiar vantage point, he saw the others drag him to the edge of the river and sling him into the black liquid. His body hit the surface with a loud slap, but he only felt the pain as a distant sensation, as though it did not really belong to him.

'Swallow da rotters!' cried Stinkeye as Scragfang sank into the gloop. His bony limbs were visible for a moment, floating on the surface, then he vanished from sight with a gurgling sound.

As Scragfang watched himself disappear into the brook, he found that he was still able to control his physical self. He forced his mouth to open and drink some of the river, feeling the gritty spores that Stinkeye called gassy rotters. He chewed and swallowed then waited to see what happened next. For a while, nothing did. His vantage point continued to drift higher. He was looking down on Stinkeye and Mangleback and the others and soon he could see the lights of the whole valley spread out beneath him like a carpet of moonlit jewels. *It's so pretty*, he thought, watching the fields of stems and caps as they pressed cautiously back towards the brook, trailing clouds of spores. He was just about to try to speak to the others when a belch rocked through his body. The explosion of gas was so violent that the valley whirled around him. Then he opened his eyes and saw nothing but pitch dark. Warm, cloying liquid was pressing down on every inch of his body and he realised he had returned to his flesh. He tried to speak, but the tar-like substance flooded his mouth and silenced him. Panic gripped him as he realised he could not breathe. He was about to try to swim when another violent belch exploded up from his guts. He clamped his eyes closed as the gas thundered through him. When he opened them again, he was horrified to find he was overground, gliding above a forest of iron trees. The moon was shining down on the rusty boughs, which were so vivid they had to be real. Prismatic clouds were hurrying past him and he could hear the distant clang of rocks tumbling into ravines. This was Skrappa Spill – the region above the Asylum. The Loonking had covered most of it in a protective shroud of gloom and drizzle, so Scragfang guessed he must be looking down over the borderlands, where the Spill merged with lands still ruled by humies and stunties. Scragfang had spent his entire life consuming mind-splitting morels, dream-inducing death caps and prophetic puffballs, but he had never eaten anything that affected him this quickly and this powerfully. He found the experience horrific – to be adrift in the roofless sky was worse than anything he could have imagined. 'Stinkeye,' he whispered, 'wot do I do next? 'Ow do I get da zoggin–?'

Before Scragfang could finish his question he belched again. The burp was so ferocious that he was momentarily blinded. When he could see once more, the metal boughs had vanished and he was on the moonlit roof of a building. He was still in the overground and he was surrounded by humies and stunties. They were all rushing down a narrow street, clutching weapons and strapping on pieces of armour. He cowered back from the edge of the roof, then laughed at himself as he remembered his body was back in the Asylum, under the Weeping Brook. He had never had a chance to observe a humie lair at such close quarters, and after checking there was no visible part of him, he moved back towards the edge of the roof and looked down at the crowd. He felt a rush of panic as some of them turned his way. Then he realised they were looking past him, up into the sky. Whatever they were staring at was clearly horrific. The stunties were all wearing metal masks, but Scragfang could see the faces of the humies and their eyes were wide with terror. Scragfang turned slowly around then laughed in relief. It was the moon, grinning down at him.

He stepped from the roof and glided gently down amongst them, laughing at how awful they looked. The humies were all half-starved, with sunken cheeks and staring eyes and ragged clothes. And the stunties, who usually looked so shiny and annoying, were battered and limping, with blood leaking from their masks. Several of them were clutching at wounds and they were clearly exhausted, stumbling along as though pressed down by great weights. There was a humie at the head of the mob, clad in more impressive armour than the rest. He was carrying a tattered banner with a twin-tailed comet stitched across it and he was bellowing at the others to keep moving, pointing his banner to a crossroads at the end of the narrow street. But every few seconds he glanced up at the moon and whispered a prayer. Scragfang drifted near his scarred face and spat insults at him, giggling as the man staggered on, oblivious.

The crowd reached the crossroads and dozens of them immediately fell back, black-flighted arrows sticking from their chests and heads. The roar of battle washed over Scragfang as the soldiers dived behind overturned carts and hastily erected stockades. It was a chaotic scene and Scragfang forgot his purpose for a moment, laughing wildly at the destruction. Many of the buildings were collapsing, their tall, teetering facades smashed into asymmetry and robed in flames. The firelight silhouetted the soldiers, making them resemble flickering shadow puppets as they raced back and forth. The stunties were firing metal guns that barked and crackled and the humies were shooting arrows, but the fight was clearly not going their way. Scragfang drifted out across the battle and felt a rush of pride as he saw the invaders. They were grots, just like him – the Moonclans of Skrappa Spill, perhaps even from the Asylum. They were riding a howdah-backed spider so big it was smashing through the walls of buildings, scattering rubble and flames as it scuttled towards the defenders. The stunties fired a deafening barrage of shots. The spider stumbled as two of its legs crumpled beneath its mandibles, causing the grots in the howdah to scream and giggle, clinging to the rickety frame. The arachnid's face slammed into the road, throwing up a cloud of dust and sending several of the grot archers somersaulting through the air while the others laughed hysterically.

The humies and stunties gave a weak cheer, but their victory was short-lived. As the spider struggled to right itself, another three skittered into view, rushing past it and racing down the street. Some of the soldiers managed to fire again, but most were busy desperately trying to reload their guns and several had given up altogether, sitting on the ground with dazed expressions on their faces as they looked up at the moon.

The grots in the howdahs clanged gongs and screeched battle songs as they loosed another volley.

Dozens of the humies and stunties fell back, bristling with black arrows. Those that could limped away, diving through the smoke, trying to escape the column of spiders that was now rushing into view. Scragfang giggled. There were dozens of the towering creatures, all crowded with grot mobs. As they attacked, Scragfang drifted on through the streets, delighted to see that the grots were taking control of the whole city. It looked like a big one, too, surrounded by a fifty-foot stone wall, topped with towers and crenellations and statues of their hammer-wielding storm god. The Loonking had trashed most of the humie lairs, but this one must have been big enough to last longer than the others. Not any more though. There were grots boiling up from every cellar and drain, flooding the streets with screeches and braying laughter. While grots swarmed from below, more of the spiders were clambering over the fortifications, dragging their bloated abdomens through the corpses as they hurled webs at the surviving soldiers. In a large square he found a stuntie sky-ship, tipped onto its side and covered in flames. Stunties and humies were battling to stifle the flames but a series of explosions drove them back, just as a huge mob of grots rushed towards them. Scragfang nodded eagerly, in awe of the Loonking's cunning. If it wasn't for Barak-Urbaz he would have gained complete control of the whole region. The memory of Barak-Urbaz reminded Scragfang why he was here, drifting through the flames and smoke. *Da rune*, he thought, recalling the slab of metal sunk in the Fyreslayer's chest.

He looked around for Stinkeye, wondering what he was meant to do now, but there was no sign of the Gobbapalooza. He could not see the Weeping Brook or any of his friends. He was alone in the battle. He wracked his brains, trying to think how he could proceed. He was meant to be sending his brain to Urbaz, not stuck down here on the ground in this humie lair. But how would he move? Then he grinned as an idea occurred to him. He swallowed hard and let out a loud, rattling burp. The gassy rotters immediately did their trick. The battle swam around him like water rushing down a sinkhole, creating a blur of masonry, spiders and grots. Shapes and colours blurred into a single, busy darkness, then, with a dizzying rush, he tumbled into another scene.

Scragfang drifted across a wind-lashed sea towards a drifting metal sphere silhouetted by the light of the Bad Moon. The sphere was covered with pipes, vents and runes and there were plumes of smoke pouring from its chimneys. *Stunties*, thought Scragfang, recognising the style of the architecture, but this was not Barak-Urbaz. It was far too small. It was just a single floating building hanging a few hundred feet above the waves.

The sea was not water but molten metal and the air shimmered with heat and fumes. Hovering near the sphere was a vehicle that looked like it might once have been a stuntie sky-ship, or, rather, it looked like several sky-ships that had been mangled together to make something far more amusing. The prow had been hammered into a crescent-moon shape and painted with a cruel grin, and where the spherical engines should have been, there were now three huge puffballs, pulsing with inner light and hazed by clouds of spores. Someone had painted scowling, ugly faces on the puffballs and given them scribbly, messy beards. Scragfang laughed as he realised they were meant to be stunties.

As Scragfang glided closer he saw that, like the city he had just seen, the floating building was under attack. Plumes of rainbow-coloured smoke were pouring from its circular windows along with the sound of shouts and gunfire.

He passed through one of the windows and entered a hall that was slashed by beams of moonlight. The room followed the design of the tower's exterior – curved metal plates crowded with mechanical devices. There were glowing orbs hung in alcoves and dozens of figures were dashing through the flickering light. Masked stunties, like the ones he had just left. Many of them were sprawled on the floor, injured or dead, and the rest were firing guns and harpoons, launching deafening volleys at the figures attacking them. Scragfang felt another rush of pride as he saw that here, too, it was Bad Moon grots who were attacking. They were pouring through a hole they had ripped in the wall, emboldened by the moon and swarming over the stunties. The defenders fought with grim determination but they were hugely outnumbered. As Scragfang watched, hundreds of his kin scurried into the room, loosing arrows and waving knives. The grots were only chest high to the stunties but they rushed over them in a frenzy. The stunties drew swords and began hacking wildly, but for every grot they cut down, dozens more surged forwards.

One of the stunties climbed from the scrum and up onto a statue at the centre of the hall. The statue was like an exaggerated version of the stunties' masks – a fierce, bearded face forged of polished metal. The stuntie stood proudly on it, looking down at the crowds of grots, his chin raised and blood glistening on his uniform. Scragfang guessed he must be the boss. He surveyed the fighting with disdain, one boot resting on the edge of the statue. Dozens of grots clambered up the sculpture and lunged at him but he barely moved, blasting them away with calm, well-placed shots from his pistol and cutting them down with his cutlass.

The other grots hesitated, unnerved by the ease with which he was dispatching their kin. The stuntie boss watched the fighting for a moment then called out a command. Scragfang could not understand the gruff, barked words, but the meaning was clear. All the surviving stunties broke away from the fight and charged across the hall towards him, cracking grot heads with their fists and lashing out with their cutlasses. They clambered up the sides of the statue and made a circle, raising swords and guns as the grots gathered around them. There was a moment of quiet as the stunties glared down at the crowd, trying to catch their breath.

Then there was a scuffling sound at the back of the hall as grots parted to make a path for a newcomer. Intrigued, Scragfang floated over their heads to see who they were bowing and fawning to. It was another grot, but he was clearly a great shaman. He was wearing a tall metal hat hammered into the shape of a crescent moon and was leaning on a twisted staff topped with a knotted fist of toadstools. He grinned as he made his way towards the statue. The stunties waited in silence, loading their guns and helping stragglers up onto the top of the statue. The shaman came to a stop a few feet away and scratched thoughtfully at his behind, grinning toothlessly at the stunties. Then, moving with surprising speed, he hurled a glass vial onto the floor and raised his staff. As the vial shattered, it produced a cloud of lurid gas that whirled around the head of the shaman's weapon. The stunties began firing. The grots surged forwards.

Scragfang belched again and the scene melted into a vibrant splash of colours that whirled around him and hurled him in a new direction. When his vision cleared he found himself immersed in another moonlit battle, seeing more grots swarming over another foe. This happened again and again. With each belch he was cast across the realm into a new corner of Chamon, and after dozens of these leaps he began to panic. This was not what Stinkeye had planned. He was not meant to be travelling from battle to battle, he was meant to be in Barak-Urbaz, spying on the Fyreslayer and finding out where he was headed. His pulse quickened as he realised he was in danger of messing everything up. If he failed to get the rune he was ruined. He had no doubts about the rest of the Gobbapalooza. He could trust Mangleback, but the others would only stand by him if he was a success – they would drop him the moment he looked to be failing. And they would have no qualms about telling the Loonking what he had tried to do.

Scragfang tried to ignore the battles that unfurled before him so he could send his mind back to the Weeping Brook. It was useless. He could no more control his thoughts than he had been able to control Lord Zogdrakk's squig. Fear made him determined, though, and he tried again, picturing Stinkeye's burnt features, trying to get back to him. Finally, after several minutes of panic, he managed to achieve something. A faint voice swam through his consciousness. There was always a chorus of voices babbling in Scragfang's head, mostly telling him to break things, but he had learned to recognise them and this was a new sound, one that had nothing to do with his fractured sanity. It was Stinkeye. 'Da rune! Fink on it! Paint a picture in yer 'ead!'

Scragfang tried to do as he ordered, but it was hard to remember the exact shape. There was still a battle raging around him and every time he managed to picture the rune, a wall collapsed or a window exploded, breaking his concentration. He took himself away from the fighting and stared into a pool of blood, trying to conjure a scene from the gore. As the liquid rippled and slopped, shaken by a sky-ship rumbling overhead, he remembered a fragment of detail – the Fyreslayer only had one eye. He was not cyclopean, like Stinkeye – he had a scar running across one side of his face and wore an eye patch over the mess where an eye used to be. This single, insignificant detail was enough. It was like looking at tree bark from a new angle and suddenly seeing a face. More of the scene swam into view, exactly as he had seen it in the vision in the grove – the Fyreslayer with the crest of hair and the rune and the spiteful-looking aelf at his side. From these two figures a whole city sprouted – a hideous metal metropolis crowded with engines and sky-ships.

Scragfang's mind floated through the city towards a room where the Fyreslayer was talking with a stuntie who looked to be some kind of king, slumped in a huge wheeled throne. There was a big crowd of stunties chuffing on pipes. Some were guarding the king, while others were studying maps and scrolls and some were gawping at the Fyreslayer. Scragfang felt a rush of elation. *This is actually going to work*, he thought. *That's him. Just like the moon showed me.* He glided through the fumes, away from the Fyreslayer and the king, looking around at the other stunties. He singled out the dimmest, most low-browed specimen he could spot and leapt into his skull.

CHAPTER TEN

The Lord Admiral led Maleneth and the others along a pillar-lined passageway that headed downwards, taking them deeper underneath Admiralty Hall. Maleneth tried to maintain her sneering expression but she could not help noticing the grandeur of the place. As they passed openings she glimpsed halls like the insides of mountains, crowded with metal walkways and statues and thronging with duardin. She would never have believed that anywhere outside of Azyr could seem so untainted by the predations of Chaos. These people were not just surviving, they were thriving. Building wonders in the deeps of their sky-city. Gotrek strode beside the throne, chatting amiably with the Lord Admiral. The two ancient duardin were irritatingly similar in manner – gruff, plain-speaking and full of low wit. Maleneth stayed a few paces back so she would not have to endure their tedious banter.

'Is he your king?' she asked Solmundsson.

'We have no kings, Maleneth. Such things have been consigned to the past. My father is the city's most senior representative of the Geldraad, our ruling body. But his power is checked by several measures. The city's guildmasters hold as much power as he does. He cannot simply overrule them.' He shrugged. 'Mind you, it would be a foolish guildmaster who ignored the will of the Geldraad. Besides, we have the council and the Code. Most eventualities are covered by the statutes laid down by our forefathers.'

'How incredibly dull.' Maleneth thought of the glorious, bloody contests in the Murder Temples where she grew up and almost pitied the duardin with their tedious codes and guilds.

Solmundsson waved at the gleaming aether-endrins moored in the chamber they were passing. 'Power is not dull, Maleneth. Defeat is dull.'

Maleneth was about to reply when a pair of doors slammed open, filling the passageway with light as the Lord Admiral led them into another grand hall. This one was a circular, bowl-shaped amphitheatre built around a machine larger and more convoluted than any they had seen so far. It was a golden cylinder covered in thousands of duardin runes, and there were dozens of horizontal bars arrayed from its sides, glinting and flashing as the central column slowly turned, powered by some unseen engine. The thing was so tall Maleneth struggled to make out the details higher up, but as they approached its base she saw that there were hundreds of cables snaking away from its sides, trailing out of sight through holes in the floor. Interspersed between the cables were rows of pillared alcoves, each of which contained a statue of a muscular duardin, hands raised above their heads and biceps bulging, giving the impression that they were supporting the weight of the entire sky-port. The noise of the engines was like an earth tremor and the floor juddered beneath Maleneth's feet.

'Brunnakh's Capstan,' said the Lord Admiral, pausing his throne for a moment to admire the structure. Smoke was pouring down its sides and pooling at its base and there was a crimson glow slicing out through its riveted plates, giving the whole thing a vaguely daemonic appearance.

'The heart of Barak-Urbaz,' said Solmundsson, looking at Maleneth.

'A metal can?'

Solmundsson looked shocked and was about to say more, but the Lord Admiral waved them on across the hall. Sweaty, oil-splattered duardin crowded every inch of the chamber, working at machines and dragging equipment. They saluted the Lord Admiral as he passed, pounding their chests and nodding their heads, but he did not pause, driving his throne towards another magnificent doorway.

The din of the capstan died away as they passed through a series of smaller circular chambers. The first few were engine rooms and armouries, but after that, they took on a less utilitarian appearance, filled with polished, gilded furniture and crowded bookcases. Finally, they came to a map room. The walls were lined with beautiful navigation charts that described the movement of air currents and heavenly bodies.

The Lord Admiral waved them all to seats, then sent Solmundsson to a ceiling-high bookcase.

Solmundsson rushed over, clambered up a ladder and began sliding books from the shelf, unleashing clouds of dust. Then he placed all of them back bar one and brought it over to his father, flicking through the pages and pointing to a particular passage. 'The Great Maker trod these lands before any of us. Even our finest works are only a shadow of his skill. If anyone built a forge equal to this task, it will be him.'

The Lord Admiral nodded and smiled.

'Grungni?' laughed Gotrek. 'He was here? Floating about in these sky cities?'

The Lord Admiral shook his head. 'This was the elder ages, the Age of Myth, before the coming of Chaos.' He glanced at Trachos. 'And Sigmar's Stormhosts.'

Solmundsson stared eagerly at the book in his hands. 'The Forge Father built great wonders in these lands, Slayer. In the Age of Myth he was here, in Chamon, leading his people to victory.'

Gotrek looked unimpressed. 'He was here until the fighting started.'

Solmundsson was too busy leafing through the book to notice the jibe. Maleneth's seat was close enough for her to look over his shoulder to study the pages. She could not read the angular runes but it was obviously a book of maps. Unlike the ones on the walls, these showed locations on the ground and most seemed to be mountain keeps – fortresses hewn from rock, similar to those built by the Fyreslayers.

'Some of the old keeps still exist,' said Solmundsson. 'Most are ruined, of course, after so many centuries, but there are still treasures to be found in the deeps – great wonders of engineering that we can still learn from. It could well be that in one of these lost keeps I could find the power to complete the sublimation process.' He stabbed his fingers at an illustration of a mountain hold. 'Somewhere like the Iron Karak.'

The Lord Admiral nodded, still smiling.

'The Lost Forge City,' continued Solmundsson. 'The home of the Master Smith himself. The finest, greatest example of his skill in the realms.'

Gotrek massaged his jaw and stared into the middle distance. He tried to sound unimpressed, but Maleneth could see he was intrigued. 'Grungni built it?'

The Lord Admiral took another deep drag, his lungs rattling as he savoured the flavour. Then he waved the pipe. 'It was taken though. Centuries ago. You know that as well as anyone, boy. Those ruins are full of ratkin.'

'But there are so many tunnels leading into it. Many that have probably never been unearthed by the ratkin. Hidden ways known only to us.' Solmundsson tapped the map. 'Ways that are detailed in these very books.'

'This all sounds horribly familiar,' interrupted Maleneth. 'Gotrek has been boring me with stories of lost mountain holds since the day I met him, but I've yet to see one. Is this forge city real? Somewhere that's still intact and we could actually find?'

The Lord Admiral shrugged. 'Finding the Iron Karak would be hard. Even more so since the grot moon returned. Moonclans have covered the whole damned continent in their wretched fogs and swamps. And it's getting worse by the day. Even before you got near the ratkin' – he tilted his head in Gotrek's direction – 'you'd have to get through lands teeming with "grobi scum", as you called them.'

Maleneth looked from father to son and finally saw what was going on. She cursed herself for not realising sooner. 'They're tricking you, Gotrek. Can't you see it? They just want you to clear out this old ruin for them. They want you to drive out the ratmen so they can get their forge city back. I doubt there's anything in there that could help you get that rune out.'

The Lord Admiral gave her a good-natured smile that was identical to the one his son had annoyed her with earlier. 'Nothing gets past an aelf, eh?' He laughed. 'I'm not one to play games. Yes, I admit it, I swore an oath many years ago to reclaim that city in the name of my ancestors.' He tapped his pipe on some of the runes that covered the block under his seat. 'And I never forget an oath. It cuts me like a knife to think of vermin defiling our ancestors' home. And with the might of Grungni's forges we could build fleets and weapons that would make my son's current efforts look like toys. We could cleanse these lands of the greenskin scourge and the ratkin and every other vile species that has stained Grungni's holds with their presence.' He slammed his metal fist on the arm of his claw-throne, moving so suddenly that some of his attendants flinched. 'We could take back what is ours.'

Maleneth expected Gotrek to rage at being manipulated, but he shrugged. 'I thought you people cared only about the size of your coffers. At least you have the sense to think beyond that. Driving greenskins from your ancestral halls is a worthy goal. So it's not my rune you're after, then? It's this lost city?'

The Lord Admiral shrugged. 'I'll take both if I can get them.'

Solmundsson looked dumbfounded, staring at his father. 'You knew I'd suggest going to the Iron Karak?'

The Lord Admiral looked in Gotrek's direction. 'They grow a bit of chin fluff and think they can outwit their elders.'

Gotrek snorted.

Let him go, sneered Maleneth's mistress. *If the greenskins don't gut him the ratkin will. And you can be on hand to get the rune. If he somehow survives, and that fool Solmundsson gets the rune out, you can make short work of him and still get the rune. But nothing's going to happen if Gotrek stays here exchanging beard anecdotes.*

Maleneth had no desire to search out a mountain keep full of skaven, but for the moment she could think of no alternative. She had learned long ago that the best course was often to wait for an opportunity to arise. She said nothing.

Solmundsson was beaming. 'The smithies of Grungni. Anything would be possible. I'm sure I would be able to complete the transformation in the Halls of the Great Maker.'

'Halls full of skaven?' said Trachos, surprising Maleneth with his grasp of the conversation. 'Surely they will have ruined the anvils?'

'You don't understand,' replied the Lord Admiral.

Solmundsson nodded. 'The power of the Iron Karak does not lie in its contents. It's in its bones. If the legends are true, the whole superstructure is an aetheric fulcrum. The Saga of Ulfrikh Ironboots says the city's foundations are built from changestone – vast chamonite pillars that are built over runes of formation. If that's true, and I could align a burning glass to those sacred lines, I could transform anything.'

'Legends and sagas,' muttered Maleneth. 'Is that what you base your decisions on? You people are deranged.'

Gotrek sipped his beer thoughtfully, ignoring Maleneth and looking at the Lord Admiral. 'So you get my rune and you take back your city and you survive a little longer.'

The Lord Admiral's expression darkened. 'Is it wrong to want to survive? We're the Kharadron Overlords. We find opportunities where we can. I'll use whatever I damned well need to clear these lands of my enemies, whether it be aether-science or the runecraft of my forbears. The nature of the weapon is not the point. The point is wielding it with honour.'

'With honour?' Gotrek looked into the middle distance. 'There's the rub.'

The Lord Admiral studied him. 'Honour means different things to different folk, Slayer. What does it mean to you?'

Emotions flashed across Gotrek's face – anger, pain, determination. He seemed on the verge of shouting something, then slumped back in his chair looking dejected. 'Damned if I can bloody remember.' He took another swig of beer. 'But I know it means more than just surviving.'

The Lord Admiral thought for a moment, running his metal fingers down the length of his beard. 'I can see you think little of us, Slayer, but you are the one who arrived in our city uninvited and began wreaking havoc.'

Gotrek curled his lip but did not reply.

The Lord Admiral sighed and shook his head. 'I don't claim to be perfect, Slayer. I know there's more to honour than simply survival, but how will we debate the finer points if we're dead? Besides, if you want to talk about honour, look to your own deeds. We'll all be judged if Doomgron really does come. The worthy will be weighed against the unworthy.'

Gotrek frowned, sipping more beer. 'Who's Doom Ron?'

The Lord Admiral shook his head. 'It's not a who, it's a when. Doomgron. It's something the Fyreslayers blather on about, and to be honest, it might be as untrue as the rest of their superstitious claptrap. They've spent so long living in magma pits they've cooked their brains. But...' He frowned and took a drag on his pipe, the embers flashing in his blank eyes. 'But Doomgron has been mentioned so many times I do wonder if they might not be on to something.' He waved his pipe at the scrolls that lined the walls. 'Even our own logbooks and manifests make mention of it. And I've spoken to some of our dispossessed kin who mutter the word "Doomgron" into their cups. The tales chime with each other. They say that a day will come, a day of judgement, when the greatest heroes shall be called to war by Grungni himself. And in that final battle the slag shall be divided from the gold. Grungni will judge which of his children fight with honour and which do not.'

Gotrek sneered. 'Grungni? Show his face in a battle? He's more likely to show his arse as he legs it.'

Again, Maleneth could see through his bluster. His derisive tone did not convince her. He had recognised something in the Lord Admiral and was keen to hear what he said.

'I'm not in thrall to any god, Slayer, Grungni included. The Fyreslayers sing songs about Grimnir rising to save them. And many of our duardin kin make similar claims about Grungni. I treat most of it like the useless clinker it is, but you're not the only one who's thought about how to be worthy of his ancestors. And this talk of Doomgron... I sometimes wonder if there might not be something in it.' He leant forwards in his throne. 'The Kharadron are survivors, Gotrek. We've been forged, hammered and tempered. But survival is not our only purpose. Not mine, at least. I don't intend to shame my ancestors. I mean to honour them.' He shrugged. 'And what if Doomgron is just another daft Fyreslayer myth? The facts remain the same. We'll all be judged. It might be by the ghosts of the past or it might be by the scholars of the future, but our deeds will be weighed and measured.' He leant closer to Gotrek. 'Nothing we do goes unseen. I know that.' He tapped his pipe against the cogs turning on his chair. 'For every action there is a reaction. And the greater the force, the greater the effect.'

Gotrek's face fell into an expression Maleneth had not seen him wear before. He looked uncomfortable, as though the Lord Admiral's blind stare had breached some hidden corner of his soul. He placed his leathery palm across the rune and looked away.

There was a moment of awkward silence, then one of Solmundsson's guards spoke up, causing everyone to look at him in surprise. 'So, which way da we go?'

CHAPTER ELEVEN

Scragfang cursed as everyone looked round at him in surprise. He had not meant to ask his question out loud. Being inside the stuntie's head was not a pleasant experience. He had imagined it would just be like looking through a window, but his host's thoughts kept seeping into his. He kept seeing glimpses of the duardin's memories and they were all full of dazzling sunlight, clear, open skies and dizzying views of the world seen from the clouds. He could also feel his host reacting to his presence, straining to drive him out. There was a peculiar battle taking place. The power of the rotters was growing by the second, and Scragfang had no problem exerting his will, but the stuntie's mind kept finding cracks to seep up through. If Scragfang relaxed his guard, the duardin might be able to snatch control of his own vocal cords and shout for help. It was this constant need for vigilance, added to the revolting visions of sunny horizons, that caused Scragfang to blurt out his question.

Luckily the Fyreslayer did not look his way, staring gloomily at the elderly, blind king, but several of the other stunties did. Some looked amused but most glared at him, as though he had broken some rule of etiquette.

There was an awkward pause and Scragfang felt a rush of panic. Could they see him? Did they know he was spying on them?

'Which way *would* it be?'

Scragfang relaxed as the gravelly voice dragged the attention from him. It was the Fyreslayer. He clearly *had* heard Scragfang's question. He did not look over towards him, but turned to face the blind stuntie again. 'If we did do this, how would we reach Grungni's city?'

The blind king looked pleased. 'Then you do think the journey worthwhile, Gotrek?'

The Fyreslayer shrugged. 'I swore an oath. I swore that I would regain my honour by dying a worthy death. Centuries have passed. Worlds have died. And I'm still bloody here. So, if I'm going to be stuck here for a while I'd better find something that is worthwhile.' The Fyreslayer looked angry, but Scragfang guessed from the deep creases in his brow that he only ever looked angry. 'I still don't believe in any of this.' The Fyreslayer waved at the gilded columns that surrounded them, glittering in the artificial light. 'It's not enough. Hiding up here is almost as bad as Sigmar hiding in Azyr.' He shrugged. 'But you, Lord Admiral, do actually speak some sense. We'll all be ancestors one day. And we'll all be judged. More importantly' – he held up his tankard – 'you're the first person to give me something drinkable since I got here.' He tapped the drink. 'And most of my best decisions have come from a cup.'

The blind king looked troubled by Gotrek's words, but he raised his tankard and nodded. 'Aye to that.'

The Fyreslayer continued glowering for a moment, then his face cracked into a smile and he laughed. Soon all of the duardin were roaring with laughter and Scragfang looked around at them, confused, wondering if he had missed something. He had always thought that he and the rest of the Gobbapalooza were pretty cracked, but the stunties seemed even more deranged. After laughing and drinking for several minutes, the Fyreslayer stood up and launched into a song, and after a moment's confusion all the other duardin joined in, roaring out the words 'Ho! Ho!' until a great, raucous chorus filled the chamber.

> *Two barrels more and I'll hit the floor,*
> *Ho! Ho! Fill me up some more!*
> *Three barrels more and I'll split the door,*
> *Ho! Ho! Fill me up some more!*
> *Half a gallon, half a pint,*
> *Ho! Ho! Fill me up some more!*
> *Four barrels more and I'll hit the floor,*
> *Ho! Ho! Fill me up some more!*

Scragfang mumbled along, pretending to know the words, which in fairness were not hard to grasp. As he looked around, baffled, he saw that he was not the only one who found the whole thing peculiar. The murder aelf, standing just a few feet away from the Fyreslayer, was watching the display with a look of withering derision. She was gripping the knives at her belt and Scragfang could tell from her expression that she wanted to hurl them at the duardin. Perhaps she was jealous of the Fyreslayer's affection for the blind king? She must care greatly for Gotrek, he decided, to endure the company of the other duardin. He grinned as he thought about his plan. Stealing her was going to work perfectly.

As he watched the murder aelf, congratulating himself on his genius, Scragfang noticed something peculiar – something no one else seemed to be aware of. The aelf was talking to a piece of jewellery that was hung around her neck – an amulet. She was not talking out loud, but with her mind. Scragfang realised that the rotters had shown him something about her that she wanted hidden – he was hearing a secret conversation. There was someone *in* the amulet. Or, at least, there was the spirit of a person in there. And it was telling the aelf what to do.

To Scragfang's relief, Gotrek finished his song and the din subsided. Then, before Scragfang's ears had a chance to recover, the blind king swigged his drink, struggled into a standing position, raised his cup and launched into a new song.

The barmaid only has one eye, but she won't let my throat go dry!
Keep your gold and keep your queens, I'll love Brenna till I die!
The barmaid only has one leg, but she won't let my throat go dry!
Keep your gold and keep your queens, I'll love Brenna till I die!
The barmaid only has one tooth, but she won't let my throat go dry!
Keep your gold and keep your queens, I'll love Brenna till I die!

The sound of the duardin voices battered against Scragfang's mind. Their songs were as hard and resounding as their city. Scragfang wanted to clamp his hands over his ears but he knew that would draw more attention to himself. To his dismay, rather than winding down, the stunties seemed to be just getting going. At a signal from the blind king, the party left the map room and headed out into a large banquet hall filled with benches. The king called out to his servants and they hurried away and returned bearing trays laden with barrels of ale, alongside loaves of fresh bread, slabs of cheese and hunks of cold meat. Rather than deciding on a course of action, which would have enabled Scragfang to learn their route, they began a raucous, drink-fuelled feast. As they drank they launched into more songs, all with almost identical tunes and themes. Every one of them concerned the pleasures of drinking, the heartache of not being able to drink or the unlimited amounts they would like to drink. The songs drew more duardin to the hall, who brought with them more food and drink and a selection of drums and horns. Soon there was a large celebration taking place and everyone had completely forgotten the matter of journeying north.

Scragfang turned to the duardin next to him, and while trying to stamp his foot in time to the beat, he raised his voice over the racket. 'Wot route do ya fink we'd take?'

The stuntie frowned and cupped his hand to his ear.

Scragfang shouted louder and tried to sound like a duardin. 'Wot route dooo yoooo think we'd take?'

The duardin laughed. Then he grabbed a tankard from a passing tray and thrust it at Scragfang, spilling foam from the brim. 'This one!'

Scragfang smiled nervously and took the cup. Then he realised that the duardin was staring at him. *He's seen me*, he thought, panicking again. *He knows who I am.* Then he realised the duardin was just confused as to why Scragfang had not downed his ale.

He swallowed hard, then raised the tankard to his lips and began to drink. It did not taste quite as bad as he expected. There was something yeasty and earthy about it that reminded him of the brew Mangleback made from mottled milk caps. To his relief he was able to finish the drink. He proudly held up the empty cup to the stuntie to prove he had emptied it.

The stuntie misunderstood the gesture and handed Scragfang another full tankard.

Again, he stared at Scragfang, grinning at him through broken teeth and an ale-sodden beard. Scragfang felt more confident the second time and emptied the cup in a few quick gulps. This time he found it positively enjoyable, and as he swallowed the last few dregs he began to feel pleasantly light-headed.

'Reminds me of Scab Cap Brew,' he muttered.

The stuntie shook his head, unable to hear over the sound of singing. Then he handed Scragfang a third tankard. This time, he took it eagerly. The more he drank, the less afraid he felt and the more confident he became that he would go undiscovered. The ale was making him feel more like a real stuntie. He actually felt a peculiar sense of companionship with the duardin, who was grinning enthusiastically at him as he drank.

Ten minutes later, Scragfang had emptied six tankards and was staggering through the crowd with his arm slung over the stuntie's shoulder. His head was spinning wonderfully and, to his amazement, the words of the songs were starting to make sense. He even managed to sing along. The stuntie was called Knut and he led him to a long, bench-lined table crowded with singing drunks. They flopped onto a bench and drank so much ale that Scragfang forgot all about his reason for coming to the city. All he could think about was how hilarious the situation was. He, a Bad Moon shaman, was drinking happily with the stunties he was going to destroy.

'You're a good friend, Ornolf!' yelled Knut, clunking his tankard against Scragfang's.

'I'm Scragfang!' he replied.

Knut's smile froze on his face. 'Scragfang? Sounds like a damned grot name.'

Scragfang giggled hysterically. 'I *am* a grot.'

Knut stared. Then he burst into deep-bellied laughter and clapped Scragfang on the shoulder. 'A grot!' He slammed his forehead on the table. Then he looked back at Scragfang, shaking with mirth. 'Me too. I'm *king* of the grots.'

'The Loonking!' laughed Scragfang.

'Yes!' Knut snorted ale from his nose. 'Loony king! I'm the Loony king! King of the loonies! Here to wage war on my brain!' He grabbed an armful of tankards and pulled them towards him. As he did so, he elbowed the stuntie next to him, spilling his drink. It was one of the ornately armoured stunties who had been guarding the blind king. He rose from the bench and glared at Knut.

'That was my beer.'

'And I'm the Loony king!' cried Knut, still laughing.

The other stuntie planted his fist in Knut's face.

Knut slammed into Scragfang and they toppled onto the floor, scattering tankards and causing more stunties to howl. Someone punched the guard in golden armour and more drinks went flying.

Scragfang, like all of his kind, had been born with razor-sharp survival instincts. Even drunk, he had the sense to roll clear and stagger away as a huge fight erupted around the table. A storm of tankards and flying fists rushed through the hall as stuntie slammed into stuntie. The sound of singing was replaced by the howl of curses and the crunch of breaking noses. Scragfang lurched and weaved through the mayhem, making for an empty corner. As he ran, his ale-clumsy legs managed to tie themselves together and he fell forwards, smashing his face into the back of another stuntie's head and causing him to drop his drink.

The stuntie whirled around, bellowing furiously, and Scragfang's heart sank as he saw it was the Fyreslayer.

He was about to apologise when a rock-like fist slammed into his face and sent him gliding through the air. He passed over the heads of several stunties and crashed back down into the group fighting round the bench. He took another painful blow to the side of his head and tumbled to the floor.

He rolled to a halt and found himself face to face with Knut. Knut's face was smeared with blood and the skin around his left eye was already darkening into an impressive bruise, but he laughed at the sight of Scragfang, spitting out a tooth and handing him one of the tankards he had dragged under the table. Scragfang looked at him in disbelief, then, realising he had no better options, took the proffered drink and gulped it down.

As the fighting around the table grew more intense, Scragfang and Knut worked through their collection of drinks, leaning against each other in quiet camaraderie until, after several more cupfuls, Scragfang finally passed out.

CHAPTER TWELVE

Scragfang enjoyed the sense of darkness pressing over him, filling his thoughts with warm, comforting quiet. Then he realised his lungs were straining and he could not breathe. He pounded his limbs and broke the surface of the Weeping Brook.

'There!' cried Mangleback, scuttling down the riverbank towards him, casting one of his tentacles out like a fishing line.

Stinkeye and the others rushed from the gloom and gathered round Mangleback.

'Does thou know da route?' called Lord Zogdrakk.

'No,' gasped Scragfang. Even though he was back in his own body, he still felt horribly drunk, and he struggled to focus on the figures gathered at the riverbank. 'Not yet.' He reached out through the cloying liquid, trying to grasp the limb Mangleback had extended, but it was no use. The brook seemed to be gripping him in place. However hard he tried to kick his legs, they barely moved.

'Dive down again,' wheezed Stinkeye. 'We need da route if we're gonna get to steal the aelf.'

'I'm zoggin drownin'!' cried Scragfang, furious at Stinkeye's nonchalant tone. 'I ain't goin' back in! 'Ow long was I in there? An hour?'

They all shook their heads. 'U've only been under a few seconds,' said Mangleback.

'It's just the rotters messin' wiv yer 'ead,' said Stinkeye. 'U've only been under for a moment, but the brook gives ya hours of scrying time. Don' worry 'bout drownin'.'

Mangleback nodded eagerly. 'I promise, if yer under for more than a few seconds, I'll come an' fish ya out.'

They all looked at him in expectant silence as he kicked his legs and glared back at them. 'By the moon,' he muttered. 'This betta zoggin work.' Then he rolled over and dived back beneath the ink-black liquid.

The drinking hall was filled with a mixture of snores and groans. Scragfang lifted himself up on one elbow and looked out from under the table. Most of the stunties were slumped in a stupor, sprawled across benches, drenched in beer and blood. Lights were still flickering overhead, and after wiping his eyes, Scragfang saw that not everyone was comatose. Not far from where he was lying, at the end of a long table, the Fyreslayer was talking with the blind king. Despite the copious amounts of ale they had consumed, neither of them seemed at all drunk. They were hunched over a map with some of the other stunties. The murder aelf was there too, along with a much taller figure that Scragfang could not quite make out in the shifting light.

Scragfang tried to stand but there was a weight crushing him to the floor. It took him a moment to realise that the heap of armour and vomit was Knut. He heaved the snoring stuntie aside and crawled out from beneath the bench. There was no natural light in the drinking hall, so it was impossible to know how much time had passed, but he guessed, by the fact that most of the stunties were in such a deep sleep, that the fighting and drinking must have ended quite a while ago. He cursed under his breath as he staggered towards the group around the blind king. What if he had missed the details of their plan?

To his relief, Scragfang saw that they were all leaning over a map and one of the stunties had drawn lines across it in red ink. No one paid any attention as he joined them.

The stuntie who was talking wore amour almost as impressive as the blind king's and seemed to be an expert in navigation. 'We may have trouble in this pass,' he said, tapping the map, 'where Holmkel Leadfist slew the Cobalt Serpent. Greenskins hold all the surrounding peaks.'

The blind king shook his head. 'Nonsense, Thialf. We have a zonbek at the Valdrakh Pass. Captain Ragni still holds sway in those hills.'

'Sorry, father,' said the stuntie in grand armour. 'Ragni is dead. The Valdrakh zonbek fell just last month. Do you remember the messages we had from Sirikh? The greenskins used the same flying steeds they've been sending against our mining fleets. Captain Ragni was massively outnumbered. Had you forgotten?'

The blind king sat up in his throne and scowled in the direction of his son. 'Aye, of course I bloody remember. It's just the ale muddying my thoughts.' He looked at the Fyreslayer. 'Damned beardling. Likes to make out I'm senile so he can worm his way into this throne a little sooner.'

Thialf looked appalled. 'That is *not* what I meant.'

'No matter. If the Valdrakh Pass is unsafe, how do you intend to reach the lost city?'

The Fyreslayer shook his head. 'Surely you can just fly *over* the mountains. Your sky-ships can go higher than those peaks. You mine things from the clouds, don't you?'

'The height's not the problem,' replied Thialf. 'There are more gargants living in those peaks than the rest of the realm put together. Flying over them would mean we'd face an airborne avalanche. The gargants hurl rocks in impressive numbers. It's impossible to get through without taking damage to the hull. No, it has to be the Valdrakh Pass. I just wanted to be clear that it's the riskiest part of the journey. It's a narrow, steep-sided crevasse. If greenskins attacked us there it would be a tough fight.'

The Fyreslayer laughed. 'Can grobi fly now?'

'After a fashion,' replied the blind king. 'They ride monsters that are like winged mouths. Squigs, they call them. Big lumps of muscle that chew through armour and bone in seconds.'

The Fyreslayer's lip curled and he tapped his axe on the floor. 'If green-skins are your only problem then there isn't a problem. Leave 'em to me, along with their flying squigs.'

The blind king laughed. 'It sounds like our friend here can deal with the Moonclans. You just need to make sure you can get your ship to Valdrakh Pass.' He paused to draw on his pipe, then, after blowing smoke across the table, pointed the pipe at his son. 'But you have developed a worrying ability to lose ships. Can I be sure you're the right person to handle this commission?'

'Commission?' Thialf looked surprised. 'I imagined this would be a family matter.'

The blind king chuffed on his pipe again, the embers lighting up his featureless eyes. 'Damned if I'm taking all the risk.' He waved his pipe at the figures sprawled all around them, still snoring and groaning. 'If we tell the guildmasters they have a shot at reclaiming the lost forge city they'll trip over their beards to fund the expedition.'

'Have you so little trust in me, father?' Thialf waved at the gilded pipes that covered the walls, studded with jewels and rune-inscribed shields. 'Half of this wealth came from me. I can do this, father. I will get us to the forges, remove Gotrek's rune from his chest and reclaim the Iron Karak.'

'You're still drunk, Thialf. Do you think a single ship is going to take back the Iron Karak? Even a whole fleet? The grots have taken every inch of land around there, and once you get past them, the ruins themselves are infested with ratkin.' He shook his head and took another drag on his pipe. 'No, if we're going to do this, we do it properly. First, you take this Slayer and see if you can even find the place. None of our maps agree on its exact location and I don't trust any of the captains who claim to have seen it. If you can find it, pin down the location and bring me proof it's still standing. Then we will show your evidence to the guildmasters and fund a full-scale invasion.'

'They'd never agree to it,' said Thialf. 'Not when we're so hard pressed, on so many fronts. Grots are conquering the whole of Ayadah, father. None of the admirals would want to call back their fleets. It would risk every one of their cloud mines.'

'They would risk anything for the Iron Karak,' said the blind stuntie with a grim smile. 'As long as you get proof of its existence. Think about it, lad. The might of Grungni's Fingers. Chamonite pillars. Slabs of changestone taller than this hall. Think what we could do with that power. Barak-Urbaz would become the most powerful of all the sky-ports. We'd drive those damned Moonclans back into the ground and make the whole continent safe for honest traders.'

The Fyreslayer had been picking up empty tankards, peering hopefully into each one, but at this he looked up. 'How does this one-ship plan help me get the rune out of my chest?'

The blind stuntie nodded. 'As things stand, small numbers are your best chance of getting to the city and getting inside. I can't guarantee a full-scale invasion will ever happen, but despite his careless habits with my ships, I am pretty sure my son could get you to the Iron Karak. You tell me you're not afraid of a few ratkin, so–'

'Afraid?' The Fyreslayer slammed his fist on the table, rattling all the empty cups.

The old stuntie nodded and continued. 'So you should have no problem getting my son and his crew to one of Grungni's changestone pillars. At that point, Thialf can tap into more power than he's ever dreamt of. He can hook you up to his... What did you call it?'

'It's a volatising lens, father. I call it the burning glass.' He glanced at the Fyreslayer. 'It may be in need of some repair work.'

'Whatever,' grumbled the blind stuntie, looking back in the direction of the Fyreslayer. 'My son will patch up his crystal, bring it to the Iron Karak and then, once you get him to one of the changestone pillars, he will use it to blast that thing out of your ribs. All I ask is that you help my people get out of that place and bring me proof of its existence.' He took another drag on his pipe. 'What you do after that is your own business.' He waved his pipe at the murder aelf and the tall figure Scragfang had noticed earlier. 'I'm sure these Sigmarite fanatics can find a way for you to do something "honourable".'

Scragfang peered through the pipe smoke and finally saw who was standing next to the aelf. He let out an involuntary gasp. It was a Stormcast Eternal clad in thick, battered armour and gripping a pair of brutal-looking warhammers.

'Ornolf?' cried the blind king, turning in Scragfang's direction. 'What in the name of Grungni has got into you?'

'Sorry,' muttered Scragfang, doing his best to sound gruff.

The king continued glaring at him for a moment, before looking back towards the Fyreslayer. 'But I would hope, Gotrek, son of Gurni, that when you see the might of the Iron Karak, and the wonders of its hidden deeps, you might consider lending your strength to the people who share your ancestry. We have the same blood running in our veins, Gotrek. And I have spent many years asking the same questions you have. Maybe we could answer them together?'

The Fyreslayer said nothing.

The king looked back towards his son. 'I'll trust you, lad, once you've shown me that you can get a ship to those ruins and get it out again. Do you understand? Do this thing and there will be no question mark hanging over your rank.'

Thialf paled. Then he nodded and punched his chest.

The king nodded, seeming satisfied, then slumped back in his throne to continue smoking.

The conversation moved on to the details of the location they were trying to reach, but Scragfang was no longer interested. He had what he needed. Valdrakh Pass. The name was new to him but he had looked hard at the map and fixed the location in his mind. That was where he would make his move. As Lord Zogdrakk's mobs attacked, the crew would be too busy to notice anything strange going on. In the confusion of the fighting, it would be an easy matter to trick Maleneth into the arms of Mangleback and the others. He grinned as he backed away from the table, belching his way back into his own body.

CHAPTER THIRTEEN

Moonlight flashed across the deck of the *Angaz-Kár* as Maleneth strode towards the prow. It was the capital ship in the Solmund fleet and even she had to admit it was impressive. Despite being twice the size, it was essentially the same design as the ironclad vessels that she had seen before, but where some Kharadron ships were utilitarian in appearance, the *Angaz-Kár* was gilded and polished to such a degree that it blazed every time it banked through a cloud. It was so large that it had a smaller vessel called a gunhauler attached to the hull and more engines than she had ever seen on one ship. Deckhands and endrinriggers bustled all around her, manning the rigging and stoking the engines, but none of them were singing. Maleneth had observed Kharadron on their ships before and they usually sang constantly. This was what they lived for, to be slicing through the breeze with valleys and peaks far below, but this journey was different. The moonlight had stolen the words from their throats. They worked in grim silence, averting their gaze from the face hanging overhead. Maleneth did the same. She had made the mistake of looking at the moon when it first broke through the clouds and she had almost screamed in horror. She could feel it up there, glaring down at her, but she kept her gaze on the deck, hoping it would not take long for the clouds to close again.

The endrins thrummed and the whole vessel bristled with aether-guns of every conceivable design. It was an airborne armoury. It was hard to spot an inch of hull that did not sport a lethal instrument of war. The crew were all dressed in spotless flight suits covered in gold trim that gleamed as brightly as the ship's hull. Captain Solmundsson had removed his helmet and climbed up onto the railing, and was now hanging from the ship by one hand, perched over the empty sky, eyes closed as the wind whipped through his beard. He alone seemed immune to the pall that had fallen over the crew. 'Do you feel it, Gotrek?' he said. 'Freedom.'

They had only left the sky-port a few hours ago but they had already left Barak-Urbaz far behind in the clouds. Gotrek was standing at Maleneth's side with Trachos a few feet behind, and he looked distinctly unimpressed. 'I'd rather be in the belly of a mountain. In the Hearth Halls of Karaz-a-Karak, with my feet up by a fire and a pint of Bugman's in my hand.'

He gave Maleneth a sideways glance, as if she were likely to understand what he was talking about. Every now and then he slipped into the past and forgot that she was not his old companion who had died in the World-that-Was. He was such an addled dotard that it would have been funny if he wasn't also the most dangerous person she knew.

'I've told you before,' she said, 'I have no idea what a Bugman's is. Nor do I wish to think about your feet.'

He turned his grizzled face towards her, blinking, like he was trying to bring the real world back into focus. 'Aye, true enough. You have no idea. About anything.'

She leant so close their faces were almost touching, speaking in a gentle whisper. 'I hate you.'

Gotrek bared his teeth in a brutal grin.

Solmundsson savoured the wind for a moment longer, then clanged back down onto the deck and strode over to them. 'I've spent too long at home. It does me good to be back out among the elements again. This is the way to live. Standing on the deck of a proud ship with the wind lashing through the...' His smile faltered as he saw Gotrek's grim expression. 'Does this not stir your soul, Slayer?'

'It stirs my guts. Has your pilot ever heard of a straight line?'

Solmundsson laughed. 'You'll get used to it. Everyone finds it strange at first. But trust me. After a few days of this, you'll feel like you were born to it. Even I–'

Maleneth held up her hand to silence him. 'Did you say *days*?' She was feeling quite nauseous herself. 'How far is it to the Iron Karak?'

Solmundsson shrugged. 'Hard to say, as I've never succeeded in finding it before.'

He said this in such a jolly tone that it took all of Maleneth's will not to draw a knife. She looked at Gotrek. 'Why are you giving time to these idiots? I've always considered your intolerance to be one of your few virtues. Now you're letting this grinning oaf hurl us round the sky in a tin bath looking for a city that might never have existed.'

'Captain!' cried a voice from overhead. 'Wyrms, twelve degrees starboard.'

'Man the carbines!' replied the captain, still sounding cheerful. 'Come and see,' he said, heading over to the gunwale. 'See how we have become the masters of the sky.'

They followed him over to the railings as deckhands rushed to their weapons.

'Do you see?' Solmundsson pointed at the clouds swirling beneath them.

Gotrek squinted through the railings. 'See what?'

Maleneth shook her head, unable to spot anything unusual, beyond the fact that she was sailing in the sky.

Solmundsson handed Gotrek a copper spyglass covered in runes. 'To the east.'

Gotrek grunted. 'Is that what passes for a dragon in your...' He frowned. 'Very well, I see there are quite a few of them, but they're hardly bigger than me.' He handed the spyglass back to Solmundsson. 'Am I supposed to be impressed?'

Solmundsson handed the spyglass to Maleneth. 'Not dragons,' he said as Maleneth focused in on a swarm of undulating shapes rushing towards them. 'Phosgene wyrms. And they're hungry. They've caught the scent of our aether-gold.'

'They look like ghosts,' said Maleneth. 'Are they spirits? I can see through them.'

'No,' said Solmundsson. 'Not spirits. Their flesh is an amalgam of sinew and toxic gas.' He unclasped his helmet from his belt and fixed it over his head with a hiss of escaping air, hiding his bright, cheerful face behind a grim mask. 'Sniff the air and you'll probably smell them even from here.'

'Smells quite pleasant,' said Maleneth. 'Like fresh blood.'

Solmundsson cast her a sideways glance. 'Breathe enough of it and it will choke you.'

'I'm not wearing one of these damned things,' grunted Gotrek, tapping Solmundsson's helmet.

Solmundsson shrugged. 'No need. I don't intend letting them anywhere near the *Angaz-Kár.*'

'Choose your targets!' he cried, climbing up onto the railing and turning to face his crew. 'Ready the torpedoes! Hold your fire until I give the order!'

Maleneth tried to look as unimpressed as Gotrek, but as the wyrms spiralled up towards them, she was shocked to see how many there were. It looked like a large flock of birds was banking and weaving towards them. 'How many would you say there are?' she asked Trachos.

Trachos was staring up at the moon, muttering something.

'Trachos!' she snapped.

He turned to face her, moonlight glinting over his cracked faceplate. 'We will not hold the gate.' His voiced clanged like a broken bell. 'The revenants have taken the outer walls.'

'How many?' she demanded, losing patience. She reached up and grabbed the back of his helmet, intending to turn his face towards the approaching wyrms. 'Khaine!' she hissed, snatching her hand back and gripping it. 'What's happening to you?' Touching his armour had been like putting her hand in a fire.

The contact had clearly affected him too. Light pulsed behind his faceplate and he reeled away, raising one of his hammers in a warding gesture. The collection of esoteric devices at his belt sparked and shimmered, making worrying ticking sounds.

'I barely touched you,' she muttered. For a while, she had begun to think of Trachos as a useful ally. But in recent months he had become so strange she barely knew him. It seemed odd to her, but she almost felt like she had lost a friend.

'It's me!' she snapped. 'Maleneth. We're with Gotrek Gurnisson. Remember?'

He stared at her as the deckhands hurried past, obeying Solmundsson's orders. 'I remember you, Witchblade.' He looked around the ship. 'This is not Anvilgard.'

'Anvilgard? Khaine. No, you dolt. Of course it's not. We left Aqshy months ago. We're in Chamon. We came to Barak-Urbaz.' She waved at the crew. 'We're with the Kharadron Overlords.'

Trachos fell silent again.

'Stay with me, dammit,' said Maleneth. 'It's bad enough that Gotrek's only got half a foot in reality. You claim to have a connection to the Order of Azyr and you swore to help me with...' She hesitated and looked at Gotrek. 'With *that*.'

Trachos fiddled with the equipment slung from his armour, silencing the ticking sounds. 'I thought I was back in the underworlds. Newly forged. Facing the revenants again.' His tone was bleak. 'I thought my brothers were still with me.'

'Get a hold of yourself! Your men never left Shyish and you've told me several times that it was your fault. And you said you'd make amends by helping me get this oaf or his rune back to Azyrheim. Do you remember?'

He lowered his hammer and looked at Gotrek. 'I remember pieces.'

Captain Solmundsson was growing more excited as the flock of creatures approached his ship, and Gotrek had climbed up beside him on the railing to watch. Maleneth shook her head in despair. 'Stay with me, Trachos. The hog is about to go into one of his killing frenzies, I can sense it. We can't lose him over the side of this ship. Even he might not survive falling from the heavens.'

Trachos shook his head. 'What am I, Witchblade?'

'An idiot. Damn you. I'd knock some sense into you but your armour would fry my hand again. You're a Stormcast Eternal. You lost half your mind during a campaign in Shyish but that still leaves you with more brains than these tin-hatted fools.' As she spoke, she had a horrible suspicion that she was starting to sound like Gotrek, but she continued. 'The Order of Azyr. Remember? I work for it and you said you would aid me. We are sworn to root out Sigmar's enemies and do whatever we can to aid the God-King's cause.'

Trachos looked around the glinting, silver-splashed vessel and spoke in hushed tones. 'I can't find myself.'

The vial of blood at Maleneth's throat spoke up. *He's a dead man walking. Don't waste your time.*

Maleneth knew her mistress was right, but she felt inexplicably annoyed that Trachos was slipping away from her. He had fought for Sigmar for longer than anyone she knew and she could not accept that this was the fate of all who served the God-King. 'What was that song you were always singing? "He rides the storm to conquer," was it? Something about mighty pinions?'

Trachos began mumbling the words and nodded in recognition. 'Yes. The songs. I do remember the songs.'

Maleneth breathed a sigh of relief and was about to say more when the deckhands cried out.

'Open fire!' shouted Captain Solmundsson, and the deck lit up with muzzle flares and detonations.

Maleneth had to grip the railing to steady herself as the ship lurched and rolled. Clouds of aether smoke blossomed all around her and she struggled to see what was happening. Then she staggered back a few paces and saw that a second group of winged serpents had reached the ship from a different

direction and were circling overhead. As they attacked they made a scraping sound, like blades being sharpened on a whetstone.

Guns hammered and Maleneth continued backing away from the tumult
until her back collided with a bulkhead. She heard Gotrek's familiar bellow
and then saw him charge through the fumes, swinging his axe at the shapes
hurtling past. His blade connected with one of the serpents, but rather than
slicing through muscle and scales it triggered an explosion that hurled the
Slayer back across the deck, leaving him lying at Maleneth's feet. The wyrm
reformed from the smoke like ink pooling in water. Then it banked and
rushed towards Gotrek.

'Gazul's sword,' grunted Gotrek, staggering to his feet and readying his
axe for another swing. 'Smoke dragons? Can't these realms do anything
properly?'

As the wyrm shot across the deck it opened its billowing jaws to consume the Slayer.

Then the creature exploded again. But this time, rather than reforming, it
fell to the deck in a shower of black crystals, making a sound like hailstones.

Captain Solmundsson jogged through the smoke, gripping a pistol with
a glowing muzzle. 'Hold your breath! Don't breathe the fumes.'

Too late, thought Maleneth as her head swam sickeningly. She stumbled
and might have fallen, but Gotrek grabbed her roughly by the arm and
held her up.

'Too rich for your delicate constitution?' he grunted, but she could hear
that he was wheezing too.

'Head to the prow,' said Solmundsson, waving them up the deck.

Maleneth assumed Gotrek would refuse, but he nodded and helped her
walk as she continued to battle a rising nausea.

Solmundsson headed back into the melee, howling orders to his crew.

Maleneth and Gotrek had almost got clear of the fighting when another
sinuous shape rushed through the fumes. Gotrek cursed and dropped Maleneth on the deck, raising his axe and turning to face the approaching creature.

The wyrm was larger than the last one and aether-current flashed beneath
its transparent hide. As it reached Gotrek it opened its jaws and screamed.
Then it detonated in a ball of yellow smoke, sending shards tinkling across
the deck.

Maleneth expected to see Captain Solmundsson emerge from the fumes
again, but she was surprised to see Trachos limp into view. He was gripping
one of the aether-charged devices that adorned his armour – a fist-sized
metal cage that he folded away as he reached them, slotting it back into
place. He nodded in greeting then seemed at a loss what to do.

Gotrek looked even more annoyed at being saved by Trachos than he had
at being saved by Solmundsson. 'I was going to deal with it,' he growled,
still gripping his axe.

'Only if you used the rune,' said Maleneth, giving him a pointed look.

Gotrek's face darkened. 'It takes more than a smoking lizard to stop me.'

She smirked. 'That's why you've just been rescued twice in as many
minutes.'

'Bah!' Gotrek looked around for another target. 'I'll show you how much I need this damned rune.'

He paced back and forth, squinting through the smoke, but it quickly became clear that the fight was already over. The deck was littered with black crystals and the fumes were drifting away, snatched by the breeze as the ship rushed through the clouds.

Captain Solmundsson marched across the deck towards them. He had removed his helmet again and there was a grin on his face. 'See? Not everything in the realms can be bludgeoned into submission. But we have developed weapons that can dissolve matter into its most basic elements.' He took out the burning glass and tapped it. 'We rule through the careful application of aether-science.'

Gotrek glowered at the crystal, then looked at Solmundsson. 'You could have set a different course. You could have avoided them. That was all for show, wasn't it? You just wanted to demonstrate your fancy toys. But you hadn't seen that second flock coming, had you?'

Solmundsson was about to reply, but before he could speak, Gotrek jabbed a finger in his chest. 'No more games. Get me to your damned city and get this thing out of my chest. Or I'll see how well you fly without a ship.'

CHAPTER FOURTEEN

'It was one of Solmund Company's earliest zonbeks,' said Captain Solmundsson, leaning against the railings. 'The Valdrakh Pass has always been a key route for our trade fleets.'

It was several hours since the smoke dragons had attacked and Maleneth was standing at the prow of the ship with Solmundsson, Gotrek and Trachos. There was a wall of mountains up ahead. They looked ominous and impenetrable in the darkness, but she could see the slender pass Solmundsson was referring to – a blade of moonlight bisecting a great slab of shadow.

'And now you've lost control of it?' she said.

Solmundsson looked pained. 'We held it for centuries, and many others like it, but the grots have multiplied beyond anything we've ever seen before. As fast as we build, they tear down. And wherever they strike, the land changes. Kingdoms that were once bright and noble fall into shadow and mist. And things grow in the darkness. But we'll drive them out. The grot clans cannot stop progress. We will find a way.' He nodded to himself. 'There's always a way.'

The ship was thundering through the night at such a speed that Maleneth could see the mountains rushing closer. It was not long before she could see the ruined zonbek drifting into view, its domes and walkways listing sadly in the clouds. 'Wealth isn't enough,' she said. 'You're right, Gotrek. There's your proof.'

Captain Solmundsson was called away by one of his officers, so Maleneth, Gotrek and Trachos were left alone as they neared the zonbek. The closer they came, the more surreal it looked. The outpost had been stripped to a buckled skeleton, but some of its engines were still working and hung over the mountain pass, turning slowly in the thermals, trailing rusty pipes like innards hanging from a corpse. Most of the metalwork had vanished beneath a coat of rust. Then, as the ship's course took it within a hundred feet of the ruin, she saw that it was actually fungus – a skin of toadstools, brackets, parasols and lichens that were all the same gory colour. The red growths added to the impression of the fort being a chewed corpse, glistening and rippling in the breeze.

Gotrek grunted. 'They think they can buy safety but nothing is permanent. Not wealth, not power, not even faith.'

Trachos was at Gotrek's side, leaning heavily against the railing. 'What about honour? I heard you talking about that with the Lord Admiral. Is that as fleeting as wealth and weapons?'

'Maybe not.' Gotrek looked at Trachos. 'But you don't have to worry about that, do you? You have blind, block-headed faith. All you have to do is follow the pronouncements of that dimwit in Azyr.'

'So I thought. And now, here I am, with a trail of butchered innocents in my wake, a body on the verge of collapse and a mind beyond repair. You say nothing is permanent, but some things *are*. However many times I die, Sigmar will remake me and send me back to these realms. Send me back to kill and die. And each time it happens I lose the last shreds of who I was. And now I am such a stranger to myself that I can't see what makes me less of a monster than those serpents we just fought. At least they only attack to feed. I can't remember why I'm fighting.' He held up one of his battered warhammers and looked at the pitted metal. 'Block-headed faith doesn't seem so comforting any more.'

Gotrek stared at him, then shook his head. 'Aye. It's all a bloody mess, Trachos.'

Maleneth looked up in surprise. She could not remember the last time she had heard Gotrek use Trachos' name. Not without a derisive snarl.

Gotrek touched one of the tattoos that knotted around his muscles. 'I remember when I was a knee-high beardling, in the halls of my forefathers, I knew exactly what set me apart from the monsters. I knew the worth of oaths, grudges and finely made things. I was a dawi. We were different. Better. We carried the honour of our ancestors in our shields and our oath-stones. In our hearts and fists. We remembered the old ways. Old truths. Courage and pride. Hearth and hold. Oath and honour.'

'And now your hearths are gone,' said Trachos. 'So are your holds. What use is the rest without them?'

Gotrek's eye flashed. 'I wondered the same. But now I think I have the right of it. It came to me when I was talking with the Lord Admiral. Our honour wasn't there to protect the holds, it was the other way round. We built strongholds to protect our honour.' He tapped his brutal brow. 'Honour lies in here.' He looked at Trachos. 'Let everything else go, Trachos, but not that. And if you slip, find a way to set yourself right again. We have to remember why we're fighting.' He nodded at the ruined zonbek. 'Or end up like that.'

The two old warriors stared at each other in silence.

Maleneth started to speak then stopped herself.

Gotrek glared at her. 'You have no idea what we're talking about, aelf. You think honour is a dirty word.'

She licked her lips, troubled by where her mind was going. 'Actually...' She shook her head, still struggling to spit the words out.

'Actually what?' asked Trachos.

She grimaced, sneered and muttered. 'Nothing... well... perhaps... perhaps I see *some* things the way you do.'

Gotrek frowned, then laughed. 'If you weren't an aelf, I'd say you've learned to think about something other than yourself.'

Maleneth's feeling of kinship vanished as quickly as it came. 'You're the one who won't think of others. You talk of living with honour and remembering why we fight, but they're just empty words. When I suggest going to Azyr, so that rune can be harnessed for the war against Chaos, all you can think of is your own ego.' She began pacing up and down across the deck. 'You've never given me one good reason why you won't go. You'll go anywhere apart from the one place where you could actually do some good. Why is that?'

Gotrek's expression darkened. 'I will never set foot in Azyr. It doesn't matter how many tricks you pull or how many lies you whisper, I will never come within a thousand miles of Sigmar or his snivelling lap dogs.'

Maleneth waved at Trachos. 'Do you call this a snivelling lap dog? This "honourable" warrior that you feel such kinship with was forged in Azyr. Sigmar's Stormhosts are worth something and you know it. They've driven the Chaos legions back from regions that have been enslaved for centuries. The Stormcast Eternals are liberating the realms, Gotrek. Do you understand? Liberating them. Slowly, painfully, they're driving the Ruinous Powers back. They're clawing sanity from madness.'

'Is this your idea of sanity?' Gotrek clanged his axe against Trachos' dented armour. 'Sigmar's taken decent, brave men and broken them to his will. Just like every god that came before. Because he doesn't care. The gods are vain, conceited lunatics. And they won't rest until your worlds are as ruined as my world.' He reeled away from them, shaking his head, talking to himself rather than Maleneth. 'If I went there. Imagine it. If I went to Azyr... I would see it. The horror of what he's done.'

Maleneth looked at Trachos. 'What's he talking about?'

Trachos was watching Gotrek closely but said nothing.

'You're deranged!' she yelled, marching after Gotrek. 'No. Worse than that. You're a coward. I don't know what it is you're afraid of in Azyr, but–'

Gotrek rounded on her, grabbing her by the arm and shaking her. 'I am afraid of nothing! And if you think I am, I...'

His words trailed off. When he shook her, Gotrek had dislodged something from her leathers – a small strip of metal that had clattered onto the deck.

As he stooped to pick it up his eye widened. 'Grungni's teeth.' He held the piece of metal higher and squinted at it. 'A drop valve. Like the ones from Barak-Urbaz.'

Maleneth backed away. 'What?'

Gotrek followed, waving the piece of metal at her. His voice went dangerously low. 'It's *yours*? The valve is yours? You put them in all those devices? *You* stopped them working?'

Trachos looked at the valve, then at Maleneth. 'What is he talking about? What is this thing?'

Maleneth could have lied her way out of the situation, but anger washed away her fear. 'Oh, don't play the innocent, Trachos. You wanted to stop him as much as me. You were just too addled to know how. We couldn't let him use those Kharadron toys. We couldn't let him get the rune out. You know we couldn't. They would have taken it.'

Gotrek's voice was a taut whisper as he looked at the rune in his chest. 'They would have worked. All those machines would have worked. But *you* disabled them.'

'Of course I did!' She leant against him, hissing into his face. 'What if those things had actually worked? Do you think I'd let you give the rune away!' She waved at the crew rushing all around them. 'Let you give it to these idiots and let them melt it down to make statues of themselves or to fuel a machine even more clever and pointless than all their other machines? This rune is going to Azyr, by Khaine! How many times do I have to tell you before your thick duardin skull lets the information through? I'll die before I let you–'

Gotrek grabbed her throat and slammed her against a copper smoke-stack, drawing back his axe. 'You *will* bloody die.'

His lip curled as he saw Maleneth had a knife held to his throat.

Trachos placed a hand on Gotrek's wrist. 'She was doing what she thought right. Think about what you just said. Think about who you are. Think about honour.'

Gotrek howled and swung his axe.

There was an explosion of light. Maleneth was hurled backwards across the deck.

She landed hard and rolled clear, expecting another blow to land. None came, and as the light faded she saw that Trachos was locked in a struggle with Gotrek. He had raised both his hammers to block the Slayer's axe and he was now staggering backwards under the duardin's weight.

'Stand aside!' roared Gotrek, his voice contorted by fury.

'She is not your enemy!' cried Trachos, dropping to one knee as Gotrek's axe edged towards the faceplate of his helmet.

'I will not be lied to!' cried Gotrek, kicking Trachos and sending him clattering into the railings. He spotted Maleneth and charged towards her, drawing back his axe, its brazier flashing and sparking. Then he cursed and shook his head as a shower of small objects began bouncing off his shoulders and back. 'What is this?'

The momentary distraction gave Maleneth time to leap forwards and kick him hard in the throat.

Gotrek stumbled backwards, making a choking sound, and Maleneth paced after him, knives raised. All thoughts of the rune went from her head. She forgot about everything but her desire to kill. She flipped through the air and plunged the blades towards Gotrek's face.

He parried with shocking speed, bringing the haft of his axe up into her gut. Breath exploded from her lungs, pain washed through her and she landed awkwardly on the deck, struggling to breathe.

How can he move so quickly? demanded her mistress. *He looks like a burnt hog.*

Maleneth managed to stagger clear as Gotrek's axe hammered down into the deck, leaving a ragged dent in the metal.

'You're lying to yourself,' she spat, righting herself and lunging at him. This time she was faster than he was. Her knives left two bloody gashes across his chest and he bellowed in annoyance. The poison on her blades would have killed most enemies in an instant, but the Slayer just grimaced, slapping a hand over the wounds and muttering curses. 'You say you want to live with honour,' she continued, flipping away from him, 'but really you only care about your guilty conscience.' She turned to look back at him, levelling a knife at his face. 'You're too obsessed with your past to care about everyone else's future.'

Gotrek pounded towards her, his expression thunderous, but before either of them could land another blow, more of the shapes thudded into them and the sound of violence erupted all around.

Trachos batted the shapes away with calm precision, but Gotrek was slipping into one of his berserk rages, lashing out, howling and reeling like a drunk.

Nice work, Maleneth, sneered her mistress. *Now he'll tear the whole place apart.*

Maleneth paused and looked around, wondering what was happening to the ship. Was this one of the avalanches Captain Solmundsson had warned of?

'Squigs,' said Trachos, calmly crushing one with his hammer and splattering his armour with gunk.

Maleneth grimaced in disgust as she saw that Trachos was right. Dozens of crimson, spherical creatures were thudding down onto the *Angaz-Kár*, each no bigger than a man's head, with stumpy legs, tiny eyes and mouths that filled most of their faces. Some bounced like balls while others spread grubby wings and whirred through the air, attacking like carnivorous insects.

Gotrek was still trying to reach Maleneth but the squigs were blocking his way. Maleneth backed away from the bellowing Slayer, looked out over the railings and saw a nauseating sight. The sky was full of squigs. They were being hurled by catapults mounted on the backs of larger squigs borne on rickety, mechanical wings. The bigger squigs were teeming with greenskins – wizened little grots dressed in black robes and armed with spears and bows.

As the squigs thudded to the deck and bounced off the machinery, Maleneth felt teeth tearing through her flesh as some of the creatures latched on to her limbs, chewing furiously. She whirled away, slashing at the squigs with her knives and filling the air with splashes of black, treacly blood. What followed was too frenzied and confusing to properly be called a battle. The *Angaz-Kár* was laden with weapons but most of them were too large and powerful to be turned against the creatures rolling across the deck. The crew raised cutlasses and fired pistols, but there were so many squigs pouring down on them they struggled to get a clear shot.

Maleneth gasped and staggered backwards as one of the squigs gnawed furiously at her bicep. She cut the thing away and stamped furiously on its corpse. For a moment she lost sight of the Slayer, surrounded by gunfire and falling squigs, then saw Gotrek trapped near the prow. He had given up attacking the rain of squigs and was now assaulting the ship. He had pummelled one of the rotary masts, knocking it from its axel and creating a thick column of steam that rushed up from its broken base. The rune was burning in his chest, making his beard look like it was on fire, and his tattoos were like streams of lava running down his grimy muscles. Trachos was nearby, trying to reason with the Slayer and fend off squigs at the same time. Gotrek was clearly deaf to his pleas.

'It's the *Sigmaron Star* all over again,' hissed Maleneth. 'He's a damned moron.'

Some of the crew hesitated, lowering their guns and harpoons, shocked by the sight of the enraged Slayer. Maleneth had to concede that he made a terrifying sight. He was chopping through hunks of machinery, filling the air with sparks, and his eye was burning with inner fire. He was even more frenzied than the squigs, spitting and twitching as he ripped the ship apart.

The fighting was so intense and the situation was so infuriating that she found it hard to think clearly. She backed away from the Slayer, cut through a storm of squigs and climbed up onto a cooling vent to get a better vantage point. The whole deck was covered in squigs of various sizes and they were tearing the duardin apart. Some were as small as the ones she had first seen, but others were like fleshy boulders, bounding through the battle with limbs and innards trailing from their gaping maws. Hovering in the sky, all around the *Angaz-Kár* there were even larger squigs laden with howdahs, and the grots onboard them were squealing and wailing hysterically, clanging gongs and turning cartwheels. There was something strange about the attack though. None of the grots were trying to board the ship and half of the giant squigs were not even approaching the battle, beating their mechanical wings and hovering in wait, dozens of feet away from the *Angaz-Kár*.

Maleneth could see no sign of Captain Solmundsson, so she dropped back to the deck and sprinted through the fighting. The violence had grown even more frenzied. There was blood and aethershot flying everywhere and the miniature squigs were like a cloud of teeth, chewing and tearing. They were so ferocious that some of them had turned on the ship itself, using their powerful jaws to rip through machinery and rigging.

As Maleneth whirled and flipped through the battle she felt blood lust well up from her chest. She turned every lunge into an elegant dance, moving in such a fluid way that she barely seemed to be fighting at all. As she pirouetted through clouds of blood, warmth pulsed at her neck and her dead mistress spoke to her from the amulet. *You need to get away from the others.*

'What are you talking about?' gasped Maleneth, pausing mid-lunge to look down at the vial of blood.

You need to go to the back of the boat.

Maleneth looked back that way and saw that the fighting was less fierce near the stern of the ship. 'Why?' she gasped, cutting down another small squig and dodging the attack of a larger one.

Trust me, she said. *I have an idea. But we need to be alone.*

'Trust you?' Maleneth laughed. *I'm not that desperate yet*, she thought. *And you're talking rubbish. I need to find the captain and find out what he's planning. He said this pass would be dangerous. He must have some idea of what to do. Why would I cower at the back of the ship?*

You have to listen to me, insisted her mistress.

Maleneth hesitated. There was something unusual about the voice. Her mistress sounded oddly sincere. The scorn that usually filled her voice was absent. *You sound like you actually mean what you're saying,* she thought. Then she remembered the point that her mistress had made several times as they crossed the realms – if Maleneth died, her mistress died. They were bound by blood magic, and as much as Maleneth's mistress might despise her killer, she was terrified by the thought of her death.

Quickly, to the stern. It's your only chance of surviving this.

Maleneth wavered for a moment longer, then sighed and turned back the way she had come. 'This better be good,' she said, vaulting over a squig and bounding off another one.

Get to da back of da ship. I'm bringing her there now.

'Bringing her?' Maleneth hesitated. 'Who?'

She felt an unfamiliar sensation radiate from the amulet, as though her mistress were annoyed at herself, or even afraid.

'What's going on?' she demanded as she rammed both her knives down into a squig and hurled it over the railings. In the years since she had captured her mistress' soul, she had never known her to be so nervous and strange. There was something intriguing about the whole conversation, and she picked up her pace, eager to see what pathetic form of mischief her mistress was attempting.

You'll see when we get there. I have a way we can get out of this.

The fighting surged towards Maleneth, forcing her backwards. She lashed out with her knives, sending pieces of squig flying, but she was forced back towards the railing before she could reach the rear of the ship.

'Tell me what you're talking about!' snapped Maleneth as she was crushed against the metal by the weight of struggling bodies.

I have a way to get us out of here.

'Out of where?' Maleneth jumped lightly up onto the railing, hanging out over the clouds as she gripped the rigging. 'Out of this realm? What do you mean?'

To Maleneth's surprise, she saw Trachos, pummelling his way back down the deck towards her. There was a cluster of squigs trailing from his armour, gnashing at the charmed metal, but he was paying no attention to them. He seemed set on reaching Maleneth.

I mean that I can get us off this sky-ship before it goes down.

'Witchblade!' cried Trachos, heaving through the crush and pointing at something behind her.

Maleneth struggled to hold on as a weight slammed down onto the deck. It was a giant squig, larger than any of the ones she had seen so far, and its grotesque face grinned at her, blocking out the battle and the rest of the ship. All she could see was its row of pus-yellow eyes and stockade-like teeth. Its mouth gaped, revealing a ridged, fleshy interior and surrounding Maleneth in a foetid stink. Then it staggered to one side as an explosion lit up its flank.

Trachos strode through the smoke, still thumping the smaller squigs with one hammer as he took a device from his belt and hurled it at the giant squig, triggering a second, deafening blast.

The Stormcast limped towards Maleneth, his way still blocked by dozens of the smaller squigs. He looked even worse than he had a few minutes ago. His armour was sparking, and every time he landed a hammer blow his body juddered. He showed no sign of stopping though, making straight for her.

'I'm fine, you idiot,' she muttered, realising that Trachos seemed to think she needed rescuing.

She's here! cried her mistress. **At the railing!**

'Who?' Maleneth looked around but only saw squigs and Solmundsson's crew. 'What in the name of Khaine are you talking about?'

Before her mistress could reply the Slayer waded into view, covered in bloody wheals as he chopped through the crowd. His rage seemed to have dimmed and he was trying to reach Trachos.

At that moment, a figure leapt from the howdah on the back of the giant squig. It was one of the grots and it was dressed in an absurd costume. It looked like a child in a pageant, dressed as a king. It was wearing luxurious purple robes and a crown that was almost as tall as the grot itself. It scurried towards Gotrek and then halted, raising a jewel-topped staff with a regal gesture and crying out a command. A wave of smaller squigs rushed forwards and engulfed Gotrek, driving him back. The Slayer howled again, unable to shake off the blanket of snorting heads. He stamped repeatedly, popping several of them and covering himself in slime and spores, but there were so many squigs that he stumbled under the weight of them.

Some of the squigs rushed at Maleneth and she almost fell from the railing, barely hanging on with one hand as she lashed out with the other, batting squigs away and trying to knock them from her leathers.

The giant squig was still trying to right itself after Trachos' blasts and the Stormcast Eternal marched past it, approached the royal-looking grot and shattered its skull with a single hammer blow, leaving the creature crumpled on the deck.

Another grot dropped from the howdah – a hunched, wretched-looking thing with burnt skin and a single oversized eye that filled most of its face. It barely seemed able to walk, leaning on a carved bone staff, but as Trachos drew back one of his hammers to strike again, the grot snatched a glass sphere from its belt and hurled it at him.

The glass shattered on Trachos' armour, engulfing him in a cloud of yellow spores. The Stormcast fell to the deck and the fighting faltered as everyone coughed and spluttered, struggling to see. When the spores cleared, Trachos was lying on his back, buried under a heap of fungal growths. Yellow, gnarled brackets had latched on to his armour, making him look like a barnacled wreck. As they stretched and grew, acid oozed from their flesh, dragging smoke from his armour. Without a sound, Trachos staggered to his feet and managed to rip some of the smouldering brackets away.

'Get away from them, Maleneth!' bellowed Trachos, his voice cracking, as he limped towards her. 'They want *you*!'

Maleneth halted, watching in stunned silence as the Stormcast battled to reach her.

There was a flash of aether-fire. Trachos staggered as a bright rent opened in the chest plate of his armour.

To Maleneth's shock, she saw that one of Solmundsson's Kharadron had shot the Stormcast Eternal. His aethermatic pistol was still raised, the muzzle still glowing. He adjusted his aim and prepared to fire again, but at that moment a wave of squigs slammed into him.

'What in the name of Khaine is going on,' she muttered as the duardin vanished into the scrum.

As she tried to make sense of the fighting, Maleneth saw a creature that seemed to defy classification. It looked like a crustacean but was actually a colony of bracket fungus with rubbery tentacles for legs. It scuttled towards the stooped, burnt-looking grot and turned it to face Maleneth.

By this point, Trachos was almost entirely hidden by fungus, but still he refused to stop. He charged at the burnt grot, trying to raise one of his hammers.

The grot flinched and raised its staff in a defensive gesture, but at that moment, another greenskin leapt through the air and collided with Trachos' chest. This one was larger than the others and it was wearing fungal armour that looked almost identical to the growths on Trachos. Its momentum sent Trachos crashing back into a row of Kharadron, and the whole group fell to the deck.

Trachos rolled free and managed to stand, even though his armour was covered in growths. 'Gotrek!' he cried, whirling around and looking for the Slayer. 'They're after Maleneth!'

The Slayer rose from the throng, weighed down by dozens of squigs, his muscles straining.

'After me?' laughed Maleneth. 'What are you talking about?'

The crustacean-like creature scrambled backwards, letting out a thin shriek, but the burnt grot took the chance to leap back onto the large squig and haul the other creature up after it.

Trachos began limping across the deck again, and he had almost reached Maleneth when the large, armoured grot rose up behind him and slammed a scythe into his back.

There was a flash of sparks as Trachos fell to his knees, then the pair of them vanished from sight as a vertical shaft of lightning slammed down onto the deck. It stayed there for a moment, a vast column of light crackling down from the heavens, turning slowly and spitting electricity through the crowd. Then it vanished.

Everyone stumbled to a halt, staring in shock.

Maleneth staggered backwards, blinded by the afterglow, ears ringing from the noise of the blast. *He's dead.*

All the fighting had stopped. Even the squigs had paused, halted by some bestial instinct as the final strands of lightning dissipated. There was no sign of Trachos where the lightning had struck, but there was a molten, glowing hole in the deck, trailing wisps of smoke and embers.

Maleneth dropped back down onto the deck, shaking her head, staggering towards the light, knives raised.

She was halfway there when the giant squig pounded its wooden wings and launched itself back into the air. Some of the surviving grots were clambering up ropes and ladders back into the howdah.

Maleneth was so fixated on reaching the spot where Trachos had fallen that she did not pay any attention as the squig banked overhead and hovered directly above her.

At the last moment, Maleneth paused and looked up, and saw a bottle flying towards her. She cried out as spores billowed around her, filling her lungs and stealing her breath.

She staggered and coughed, struggling to breathe. Then, finally, she managed to howl a single word – 'Gotrek!'

As the spores choked her, Maleneth dropped to her knees. Dozens of moist strands wrapped around her body, stinging her skin as they tightened. She gasped and cursed. The spores had entirely blocked her throat and nostrils. She could not breathe. Dizziness washed over her and she fell to the deck.

The armoured grot was rushing in her direction when Gotrek broke from the crush and smashed his axe through the centre of its helmet. The Slayer struck with such force that his blade sliced the monster neatly in two. Then Gotrek seemed to forget about the fighting again, staring at the spot where Trachos had fallen.

Maleneth tried to call out to the Slayer again, but the words would not come. Her lungs were burning and her vision was growing dark.

Then she saw the duardin who had shot Trachos. He looked panicked as he rushed towards Gotrek. 'Have you seen?' he cried. 'They're takin' da aelf.'

Gotrek looked up, his face a mask of blood and fury.

The Kharadron stumbled, looking terrified, but he continued yelling. 'They're taking her to da Loonking's Asylum! Ta Slathermere!'

Maleneth felt consciousness slipping away from her. She seemed to be watching Gotrek down a long, dark tunnel.

Gotrek shrugged. 'Good riddance,' he spat, slamming his axe into a squig.

'But she's yer friend,' gasped the duardin.

Gotrek laughed bitterly and stomped away, dealing out another flurry of axe blows.

Maleneth felt her body rising from the deck as the darkness swallowed her.

CHAPTER FIFTEEN

'There's an imperfection in the glass.' Prince Elaz was peering into one of the six mirrors that lined his bedchamber, stroking the surface, a pained expression on his face.

Toldos thought of his master as a 'he', but in truth, Elaz belonged to both sexes. Or perhaps neither. He was unique in form and thought. Elegant and strong, delicate and brutal. Utterly perfect. Toldos loved his prince and would have died for him without hesitation. To see him dismayed was a torment, and Toldos rushed to the mirror. The prince was right. In the top corner of the mirror there was a small, crescent-shaped mark. Toldos pulled his silk sleeve over his palm and rubbed gently at it. Then he rubbed harder, his pulse quickening as he realised that the mark was beneath the glass. 'I will have it replaced immediately, highness.' Seeing that the prince was deeply disturbed, he led him gently to his bed and helped him under the sheets. 'Rest, your highness. By the time you wake, everything shall be as it was. I promise.'

Elaz nodded, but the unease remained in his eyes. Toldos waited until he settled and finally slept. Then he placed a hand on the prince's perfect shoulder, filled with a terrible sadness. This was all wrong. This should have been a time for celebration. For years, the sky-fleets of Barak-Urbaz had been a thorn in their side. It had been impossible to build a principality worthy of Slaanesh while the Kharadron hounded them at every turn, obliterating their elegant hosts from the skies and dropping explosives onto their ivory palaces. But in the past few months the sky-fleets had withdrawn, abandoning the region and rushing to fight on another front. Elaz had finally achieved his god-given potential, massacring the humans and aelves that stood in his way and reconquering huge swathes of Ayadah. He had claimed so many fortresses and outposts that his reign was assured. If the fleets of Barak-Urbaz ever returned, they would find themselves attacked from all sides. And in Elaz they would find a prince who was so gilded with unearthly power that he was more like a demigod than a man. It should have been the time of the prince's ultimate triumph, but tragedy had befallen him. A tragedy so strange and obscure that not even his most loyal servant could help him.

Just as he should have been leading his hosts to victory, the prince had become crippled by an inexplicable obsession. Rather than reclaiming territories that were no longer protected by Kharadron, he stayed in his mirrored bedchamber, spending days with his nose an inch from the glass, staring into his own eyes. His wars of expansion had been halted on the cusp of triumph, but Prince Elaz no longer cared. He no longer cared about anything beyond his own beautiful face.

Elaz would sleep for many hours, but Toldos still rushed through the palace, calling out commands to his subordinates. The flawed mirror could not be repaired. It would have to be replaced entirely with an exact replica. Most of the palace's bedchambers were mirrored but the replacement would need to fit in the existing frame and match the lustre of the other five mirrors. The prince would notice even a tiny inconsistency. The next few hours were fraught, and by the time he collapsed into his bed, Toldos was trembling. He had to drink several glasses of wine before he could finally sleep.

'You promised me,' said the prince as Toldos entered his chamber the next morning. The prince's face was ashen and he was staring at the replacement mirror.

Toldos hesitated in the doorway, shaking his head. The wine had been a mistake. He had woken with such a clouded, pounding head that he could not understand what the prince was talking about.

'The imperfection!' snapped Elaz. 'It's still there.'

Toldos hurried across the polished floor. 'Impossible, highness, the mirror has been...' His words trailed off as he reached the mirror and saw that the mark had returned. It was in exactly the same place as before.

'It's larger,' whispered Elaz, staring at Toldos. 'Do you see? It's getting worse.'

Toldos was about to deny it, but then he realised that the prince was right. The shape had almost doubled in size. The previous night it had been the size of a coin. Now it was as large as a fist. And it was less of a crescent now – more like a half-moon. As he looked closer, Toldos imagined he could see a face in the shape – a leering mouth and hard, tiny eyes. 'It can't be there,' he said, trying desperately to think how this could have happened. He had supervised the work himself and watched the old mirror being destroyed. How could the mark still be there? Again, he tried to calm the prince, and again, he waited at his side until he slept. Then he rushed from the chamber and called out for his attendants, demanding that the mirror be replaced again.

By the time evening came Toldos was twitching and muttering to himself. He spent a long time staring at the new mirror before he would let it be taken to the prince's bedchamber. He peered into every inch, looking for even the tiniest imperfection, terrified that he might have missed something. Elaz's mind was bright and wonderful but it was also brittle. One more shock like the last one and it might shatter. Toldos could not bear the idea of his master suffering. He ordered his underlings to examine the mirror too, and by the time he finally crawled into his bed his mind was filled with images of his own face, staring back at him from the darkness.

He was woken by howls of alarm. The palace was in uproar. Servants were rushing back and forth and hammering at his door. 'It's back!' howled someone as Toldos sprinted to the prince's rooms. He entered to find Elaz crumpled on the floor, sobbing and pointing at the mirror.

'What are you doing to me?' howled Elaz. 'I can't bear it. Get it out! Get it out! Make it go!'

Toldos felt as though he were still dreaming as he approached the mirror and saw the mark was there again. It was even bigger, nearly as large as a head, and it was almost a perfect sphere. But it was not the size of the thing that caused his stomach to lurch – it was the face. There was no mistaking it now – a sneering, lunatic face, grinning at him from inside the mirror.

'It's a moon,' sobbed Elaz.

Toldos' breath caught in his throat. The prince was right. The face was not human. Its skin was dusty and rugged, the texture of rock, and there was a silver light shining from its craters and peaks. But the eyes were livid red, like blood drops, and filled with such madness that Toldos had to look away. 'Smash it!' he howled, waving the servants over. 'Tear it down!' Then he staggered over to the prince and slumped onto the floor beside him, whispering a prayer for both of them.

As the servants began dismantling the frame, Toldos summoned the prince's chirurgeons, and then, once Elaz was in drug-induced sleep, he strode from the room, cursing his moment of weakness, determined not to fail the prince. He spent the day talking to merchants and artisans, and by evening he was in possession of a completely new mirror. The materials had all been sourced from outside the palace and the artisans swore on their lives that there was no way the prince would find an imperfection.

That night Toldos went to bed sober and at peace. He was sure that the new mirror would solve the problem. Perhaps the lustre would not exactly match the older glass, but that would be less of a torment to the prince than the leering moon.

Toldos woke early to the sounds of a calm, peaceful palace. Servants bustled around his room, opening the windows and preparing his breakfast. He dressed quickly and left his breakfast, hurrying through the palace to the prince's chambers. There were no sounds of distress as he approached the door and Toldos whispered a prayer of thanks as he entered.

He hurried to the mirror and, to his delight, there was no blemish on the glass – no sign of the hideous, grinning moon that had been there the day before. 'Finally,' he sighed, turning to the bed, 'we are rid of it.'

The bed was empty.

Toldos rushed over and whipped back the sheets, his heart racing. 'No matter,' he said, whispering to himself. 'The prince often used to rise early, before all this madness with the mirrors.' He asked the servants if they had seen Elaz, but none of them had. Then, just as Toldos was beginning to panic again, one of the cooks mentioned that they had seen someone heading into the cellars just before dawn. The cook had thought nothing of it at the time, but as he described the figure to Toldos he realised that it might have been the prince.

'The cellars?' Toldos was baffled, but he was so relieved by the sight of the unblemished mirror that nothing could quite dampen his mood. Not wishing to embarrass the prince, he dismissed the servants and headed off towards the cellars alone. The door was open at the top of the steps, and as Toldos hurried down them, he noticed someone slumped on the flagstones below. 'Prince,' he gasped, hurrying down. 'Did you fall? Are you hurt?'

As he placed his hands on the neck he knew he was touching a corpse. The skin was as cold as the stone floor. He flipped the body over, then backed away, gasping in disgust. It was not the prince but one of the servants. Toldos could only tell by the man's uniform though. His face was so mutilated there was no way of recognising him. There was a deep gash that had cut through both his eyes and drenched him in blood, and his throat had been slit.

Toldos gently lowered the corpse back to the floor and looked around the cellars. They had been carved from the rock beneath the palace and consisted of a network of rough-hewn tunnels crowded with barrels, sacks and crates. 'Prince?' he called, snatching a brand from the wall and lighting it. As light billowed over the piles of food he saw a second figure hunched over one of the crates, weeping softly. It was Elaz.

'Highness,' cried Toldos, rushing over to him. 'What ails you? The moon has gone. We are free of it. Do not worry about this servant. Whatever happened can be–'

His words stalled in his throat as the prince stood and turned to face him. Elaz's beautiful face was gone, replaced with the leering, crater-strewn monstrosity from the mirror. The prince's head had been transformed into a pockmarked moon with blood-drop eyes.

'Do not look at me!' screamed Elaz, raising a bloody knife and charging at Toldos.

CHAPTER SIXTEEN

Maleneth woke up coughing, her mouth full of dust. She opened her eyes and saw the clouds rushing by. For a moment she thought she was still on the deck of the *Angaz-Kár*, but then she saw the Kharadron sky-ship several miles away from where she was lying, still surrounded by smoke and squigs as it drifted over the Valdrakh Pass. The vessel was listing and she could make out signs of fighting on the deck and engines. She watched the battle sleepily, wondering how long it would take for Gotrek to relent and use the rune. The thought of Gotrek gave her a jolt of realisation. Why was she not with him?

'What's this?' she gasped, trying to sit up. She was tightly bound and only managed to lift her head. She was on the back of the giant squig and there was a group of grots huddled round her, amusement flickering in their crimson eyes. Most of them were like grots she had seen before – hunched, withered greenskins only a couple of feet tall with ridiculous, hooked noses, but two of them were even more grotesque than the others. One was the walking bracket of fungus she had seen on the *Angaz-Kár*, with its skirt of fleshy legs skittering beneath its domed back and a leering face squashed between cushions of fungal growth. The other was the burnt, wizened grot. It looked like charred remains and its face was dominated by a single blue eye that rolled constantly in a bubble of tacky liquid.

The sight of Maleneth waking up sent the grots into a frenzy. They all laughed and then proceeded to dance around her, clanging finger bells and tooting whistles.

Maleneth strained at her bonds again but they refused to give. She looked around for her weapons but the crab-like grot grinned and held up her knives, waving them and scuttling gleefully just out of her reach. Then it pointed out the moist net that covered her body.

'Blood of Khaine, you'll pay for this,' she hissed, glaring at the hideous creature. As her head cleared, she realised that the grot must have lassoed her on the deck of the *Angaz-Kár*. 'I'll flay you for a week. For a lifetime. I'll show you pain like nothing you have ever imagined.'

Maleneth howled the words with such vehemence that the grots ceased their dance and looked at the crab-like mutant.

The grot seemed troubled for a moment, then it looked at Maleneth's bonds and grinned again, waving the knives gleefully and performing another jig, scuttling in circles across the squig's back. Then it leant close, filling her vision with its rubbery, fruit-like bulk. Deep under its shell, the creature's face crumpled into a grimace and it made a peculiar gargling sound in its throat. Maleneth tried to move her head, guessing that the thing was about to vomit. Then, with a juddering retch, it managed to spit out a word. 'You,' it coughed, as though trying to eject food. The grot clearly found it immensely difficult to form an aelven word, but Maleneth was shocked that it had even attempted such a feat. She had never heard of grots speaking in anything other than their own garbled screeches. To her amazement, the creature managed to spew more strangled words. 'Are... da one who... will... be... flayed.'

The mutant leant back, gasping for breath as the other grots looked on in awe, clearly impressed by its language skills.

Bloodlust shuddered through Maleneth as she remembered how they had captured her. She felt the indignity of her position. She could think of nothing more shameful than being captured by these absurd, pathetic creatures. She stared at the crab-like grot, memorising every detail of its appearance. 'No,' she breathed. 'I won't kill you – I'll keep you alive. By Khaine, I swear it. I will find a way to prolong your life so I can torment you for the rest of my days.'

The thing leant close again, filling her nostrils with an earthy stink. 'Nah.' It grinned. 'Don't fink so. Other way round.'

Maleneth moaned with a fury so intense that it was almost like ecstasy, but she could not break free.

I did not think you could sink any lower, snarled her dead mistress. *But you have brought shame on both of us. How could you let these ridiculous things capture you?*

'It's your fault!' cried Maleneth, causing the grots to flinch. 'You sent me to the back of the ship. You sent me away from the Slayer. If I hadn't listened to you I wouldn't be in this mess.'

The grots looked at Maleneth in confusion, then turned to each other and started giggling again. She ignored them. 'You said you were bringing someone to me!'

You wretched simpleton. Why would I send you into danger? One of these grots spoke through me. It was telling the others that it was bringing you. It was you that was being discussed. They just spoke into your head.

'But it was your voice!'

They're sorcerers, you idiot. Look at that burnt one with its vials and bottles. They can harness the aether with their drugs and rituals just as we do in the Murder Temples.

As Maleneth saw how much of a fool she had been, her rage spiralled. She spat at the crab creature. 'You'll scream for a century!'

The grots laughed harder and danced around her again. The burnt one in the robes rattled as it leapt and twirled, its bottles clanking. Then, as the others watched with rapt expressions, it used its charred fingers to take a speck of something from its robes and press it into Maleneth's forearm.

'Khaine's teeth,' she hissed. 'What are you doing?'

The black speck disappeared beneath her skin like a pebble dropping through the surface of a pool.

'What was that?' she howled, wrenching her arm back and forth as though she could shake the thing out.

The grots loomed over her, still grinning as they stared at her arm. Maleneth felt an odd bubbling sensation under her skin, and then a dark patch appeared, like a bruise. The bubbling sensation grew and the dark patch began to ripple, like wind-lashed water.

They've poisoned you. Maleneth could hear panic in her mistress' voice. *They've poisoned us. We're going to die on this flying slug.*

Maleneth took a deep breath and tried to calm herself by reciting one of the old blood rites. 'No,' she said once she had steadied her breathing. 'That makes no sense. Why would they catch me if they just want to kill me?' She looked around at the grots' faces, taking in their repulsive, leering expressions. 'They could have killed me on the *Angaz-Kár*. Why would they go to the effort of talking through you and getting me away from the ship?'

The crab-like grot nodded, still baring his yellowed fangs in a grin. 'Bait.'

'Bait?' Maleneth shook her head. 'Bait to catch what?'

The creature raised an eyebrow and attempted to look smug. 'Da Slayer.'

Maleneth stared in disbelief. Then she laughed, genuinely amused. 'Gotrek? You've captured me because you're after Gotrek? Why in the name of the gods would you *want* him to follow you? He'll turn you into paste.'

The grot smirked. 'Da rune.'

This, at least, made some sense, but Maleneth still found the situation hilarious. 'And you think he'll come after me? He hates me. You morons. He'll be *glad* you've taken me.' She found herself laughing and groaning at the same time. 'By the Murder God, you're even stupider than he is.'

The grot frowned and managed to force a few more aelven words out. ''E 'ates you?'

'Yes. Of course. He despises me. He was about to behead me when you interrupted him.'

The grot seemed increasingly troubled. It backed away and spoke in an urgent whisper to the others. The music stopped and they all began to look equally worried. They turned and stared at her in silence for a moment, peering at her suspiciously. Then the crab-shaped one nodded slowly and a devious look came into its eyes. 'Yer trickin' us,' it said, the smirk returning to its distorted features.

Maleneth groaned. Then she shrugged. 'It doesn't matter what you think. I'll find a way to escape and then you will find out what happens to–'

Something popped out of Maleneth's arm, sending a trickle of blood across her skin. Nausea washed through her as she saw what it was. A plump, crimson-capped toadstool had grown from her muscle, ruining the elegant shape of her Khaine-wrought limb. 'Damn you!' she cried, wrenching her arm back and forth again, trying to dislodge the fungus. 'Get it out of me!'

As she railed and bucked against her restraints another toadstool speared up through her skin next to the first one. This time it was slender, pointed and pale yellow. As Maleneth watched in horror, a whole cluster of colourful toadstools sprouted from her arm. 'No!' she howled, horrified at such a gro-tesque perversion of her flesh. Everything she did in life was a tribute to the Murder God. Every kill was a prayer. But how would she be able to perform a worthy tribute if her flesh became as ungainly as the grots'? How would she fight with elegance and skill? She looked in terror at the grot that was like a scuttling bracket of fungus. She could not become like that.

'Stop this and I'll help you!' she gasped, breathless with desperation. 'I hate the Slayer as much as he hates me. If you loose these bonds, I swear I will help you catch him. I can tell you his plans and methods. I can teach you everything about him. I know what he means to do and where he means to go. With me as an ally you can get him wherever you need him to be.' She managed to lift her head a few inches from the squig's back and look out into the clouds. She could only see sky. 'Where is it you're taking me? Where is it you want Gotrek to go?'

The grots all smirked and continued staring at her.

'Damn you!' screamed Maleneth as she felt the dreadful bubbling sensa-tion moving under her skin, spreading further up her arm. 'Without my help you will never get the Slayer. Only I know how he thinks. You're making a mistake. He won't follow me. I betrayed him!' The word 'betrayed' caused Maleneth to halt. Why did it sit so awkwardly in her mouth? What could be wrong with betraying Gotrek? He was a boorish, arrogant hog and he cared nothing for her or the Sigmarite cause. So why did she feel a rush of panic at the thought that she had betrayed him?

Because you've ruined everything, you idiot. Your one chance was to keep him on your side. How will you get that rune to Azyr now? He's heading off with those sky miners while you lie here turning into... into whatever they're going to turn you into.

Maleneth knew her mistress was right. Her plan had failed spectacu-larly – but that was not the reason for her anguish. She had been in worse situations and always found a way through. Khaine was with her. She would find a way to escape and she would make the crab creature pay. No, there was something else going on. When she thought of Gotrek and Trachos and recalled all the times they had saved her, she felt a pang for something she had lost. She remembered Trachos' final moments on the *Angaz-Kár*. She knew what that lightning bolt meant. The fate he had so dreaded had come to pass. He had been destroyed again and now he would be remade in Azyr, losing whatever shreds of memory he had left. He had been so badly wounded that he must have seen what would happen, but he still refused to let her go. He would not give up on her. An unfamiliar emotion threatened to overwhelm her. She crushed it, knowing it for the weakness it was. What need did she have for companionship? All she needed was the strength of Khaine. If Trachos wanted to destroy himself for her benefit then he was a fool. She would not have done the same for him. Another shape sliced up through her skin. It looked like purple, frilly coral, shivering in the wind. Maleneth felt sick as she looked at it. Her whole arm was undulating and shivering. How would she honour Khaine now? She would be as clumsy as a human. Fury washed through her. She was ruined.

Perhaps you could cut the arm off?

Maleneth was about to curse when she realised that, for once, her mistress was not mocking her.

The Kharadron are deluded fools but they make incredible machines. If you removed your arm, they might be able to build you something elegant and balanced enough to replace it. Perhaps it could even enhance your performances?

It would not be the flesh Khaine gifted me, she thought, but the idea was not so absurd. The way the thing looked mattered far less than how lethal it was. And she certainly could not continue her life with her arm as it was now.

'Gotrek won't follow me!' she spat, jolting against the bonds again. 'Your only chance is to let me help you.'

The crab-like grot leant close again, a knowing smile on its face. 'Yer lyin.'

'I'm not lying, you idiot. You have to let me free.'

The grot laughed. 'When we reach da Asylum.' It tapped one of the toadstools wobbling on her arm. 'Then we'll plant ya.'

Maleneth's fury escaped from her throat in a thin whine, but she managed to stay calm enough to think. They had her knives but she was a daughter of Khaine. She was armed in ways the grots could never guess at. She just had to wait for the right moment. The time for revenge would come, but it could not be here, up in the clouds on the back of this monster. She could kill the grots easily enough, but she would not be able to control their winged steed. She would be thrown to her death. She took a deep breath and calmed herself by imagining all the ways she could hurt the crab creature. She just had to be patient. Once they landed, she could kill the others and drug the leader so she could deal with it at her leisure. She slumped back and closed her eyes, trying to ignore the revolting sensation in her arm as her muscles swelled and shifted under her skin.

After a while, seeing she was not going to do anything else entertaining, the grots lost interest in her and hunkered down at the front of their steed, peering out into the clouds. Hours passed and Maleneth's thoughts wandered, soothed by the beating of the monster's wings. She moved with a jolt and realised, to her surprise, that she had fallen asleep. It must have been the after effects of the grot poison. There was no way of knowing how long had passed, but the scene around her had changed. The moonlit clouds had vanished and the monster was now flying through a dark, clammy mist. It was hard to see anything clearly, but there were tall shapes rushing by on either side. The mist was so thick that they could have been either mountain peaks or treetops, but Maleneth guessed it was the latter. It was hard to say why, but she sensed they had dropped much lower to the ground. Autumn seemed to have arrived while she slept. The mist was heavy with the scent of mouldering leaves and the air was dank. She heard the creak of old boughs and realised her guess had been right – they were near the ground. The grots were paying no attention to her, leaning out over the walls of the howdah, looking into the mist. They were bathed in a dirty light and Maleneth moaned in horror as she saw her arm. It was bloated out of all recognition. It looked like a cankerous tree trunk.

The robed, burnt-looking grot heard her and turned around. It tapped the crab-like one, who scuttled back to leer at her. 'We're back. Da Asylum.'

Maleneth's heart was racing. If they were going to land soon, it would not be long before she could have her revenge on this creature. If she was no longer worthy of Khaine, Maleneth had only one reason to keep living – to make this creature pay. 'What is the Asylum?' she asked, straining to keep her voice calm.

'Home.' The grot sounded absurdly cheerful, as though chatting to an old friend. 'An' home of da Loonking.'

'But what is it?' The moronic creature seemed quite happy to answer any question she asked, so Maleneth continued. 'A fortress? A cave? A hole in the ground?'

The grot waved its tendrils in a vague gesture. 'A world.'

'What do you mean? You've taken me out of Chamon? Out of this realm?' The grot nodded eagerly. 'To da Asylum. Where we feed our dreams.'

The creature was clearly insane. They were all clearly insane. Maleneth guessed that what the grot called another world was most likely a mountain hold or a city complex.

One of the other grots called out and looked back, waving at something in the mist. The surrounding lights seemed larger or nearer and the sound of groaning bark had been joined by the screech and patter of small creatures. The grots' steed pounded its wings a few last times and flopped into a pool, kicking up a wave of mud and insects.

CHAPTER SEVENTEEN

Captain Solmundsson lowered his cutlass and leant against the railing, trying to catch his breath. The attack was over. The deck of the *Angaz-Kár* was littered with corpses but the swarm of monsters was dispersing. The greenskins were steering their mounts back into the clouds, clanging gongs and blasting horns in the darkness.

'They're retreating!' he bellowed, leaping up onto one of the endrins and raising his blade. He tried to sound triumphant, but he did not feel it. Over half of his crew had been butchered or strangled by hideous growths. And the greenskins were withdrawing at the moment of victory. Something felt wrong. Why were they leaving just as they were about to take the ship?

His crew replied with a ragged chorus of cheers, but they sounded as doubtful as Solmundsson felt. The ship was listing to one side and there was smoke billowing through a hole in her deck plating. He dropped from the endrin and strode over to his chief endrineer, Khorstun. 'Get those fires put out,' he said.

Khorstun saluted and limped away, calling to other endrineers as he went.

Solmundsson felt a rising wave of fury and grief as he looked around the ship. Every inch of the deck was heaped with the dead and dying. Doubt loomed at the back of his thoughts. What had he done? He had been so sure they would reach the lost city he had not considered the consequences of failure. He recalled his final conversations with his father before he left Barak-Urbaz. Lord Admiral Solmund had summoned him to a private talk the day before they set out. 'This has to work,' he had said, speaking with an urgency that shocked him. 'The Moonclans have us in a headlock. I have not said this openly to anyone but you, but Barak-Urbaz is no longer safe. The grots are closing in from every direction. This damned moon is spreading their darkness right across Ayadah. They're taking every one of our border forts. We have to find a new weapon. We need a way to halt the Loonking before the moon is full.' Solmundsson remembered how shocked he had been to hear his father talk that way. The idea that Barak-Urbaz itself might fall had never entered his thoughts.

He stooped to help one of his riggers into a sitting position, carefully removing the duardin's broken helmet and handing him a flask of water. The rigger nodded in thanks, looking at Solmundsson with absolute trust. That look helped Solmundsson shake off his doubts for a while. He began stomping across the deck, helping his crewmen and calling out orders. As always, he found that being active gave him his sense of purpose. 'There's always a way,' he said, repeating the phrase with increasing conviction as he marched back and forth through the smoke, righting pieces of toppled equipment and hacking at wounded squigs with his cutlass.

Then he spotted the Slayer, crouched near the centre of the deck. He hurried over to him and then halted a few feet away, shocked by what he saw. Trachos' death had torn a hole right through the ship, melting and warping the plates and blackening the metal. This must be one of the main causes of the ship's engine problems, realised Solmundsson. There were sparks of energy flickering through the dark, and scattered around the Slayer were fragments of the Stormcast Eternal's armour. Most of him seemed to have been obliterated by the blast, leaving little more than a charred silhouette, but there were a few scraps of metal left, blinking and flashing. Gotrek was holding one of the pieces, but as Solmundsson watched, the metal pulsed and vanished, leaving just a few traces of dust in the Slayer's hand. One by one, all the other pieces vanished in the same way, until all that remained was the rent in the deck.

Gotrek remained hunched over the spot for a moment, then noticed Solmundsson and stood, turning to face him. The Slayer's expression was rigid and hard to read. He let go of the ash he was holding and let the breeze whip it away across the deck.

Solmundsson frowned. 'How will he ever join his ancestors if he is endlessly reborn?'

Gotrek watched the ash fade into the night. 'Ancestors? He couldn't even remember his own parents.' The Slayer looked back at the hole in the deck and muttered into his beard, 'Why, Trachos? She was a damned liar. And she hated you.'

Solmundsson shook his head. 'Maleneth?'

'Aye. Trachos was trying to reach her. The grobi scum dragged her off the deck. Up onto that flying lump of gristle. But Trachos gave them a hard time first. Grungni knows why, but he was determined to stop them taking her.' He waved his axe at the mounds of squigs and grots lying around the hole. 'They didn't expect this. He fought well. And with honour.' He was still talking to himself more than to Solmundsson. 'But why? The only thing he could remember was that he had to avoid being killed. There was so little of him left and he knew what would happen if he was...' He waved his axe at the hole. 'If this happened.'

'But I thought Stormcast Eternals lived forever. I thought they were immortal.'

'In body, perhaps, but not in mind.' Gotrek sounded angry at Trachos rather than troubled at his passing. 'He's thrown away his past trying to help that traitorous aelf.'

'Traitor?' Solmundsson waved his cutlass at the dead bodies of his crew. 'Is this because of her? Did she help them? Is that why they took her? Is she in league with the Moonclans?'

'She's only in league with herself.' Gotrek ground his teeth and his eye flashed. 'She betrayed me long before we got out here. She's been tricking me since the moment we reached Barak-Urbaz. She made it so that I couldn't disable this rune.'

'How? What do you mean?'

Gotrek shrugged. 'She had some kind of gadget. A drop valve she planted in everything I tried to use on this damned rune.'

'I knew it!'

'Knew what?'

'The burning glass could have worked.' He tapped the pouch on his belt that contained the crystal. '*Should* have worked. But her drop valve must have shorted the aether-current. I thought it was strange. The burning glass has never failed before. Your aelf friend was responsible.'

'Friend?' Gotrek laughed bitterly and looked at the rune in his chest.

Solmundsson noticed that the rune was cold and inert. 'You did not use the ur-gold. You could have turned it on the greenskins.' His pulse quickened as he followed the thought to its conclusion. 'You could have saved my crew.'

Gotrek glared at him. 'Don't you have any ears under that hat?' He tapped the rune. 'It's not a weapon I can turn on and off at will. It's poison. If I'd let it rule me your whole crew would be dead, not just half.'

Solmundsson did not really understand, but Gotrek looked ready to behead him so he let the matter drop. He looked back at the shape Trachos had left. 'Did *he* know about the treachery? Did he know she was a traitor?'

Gotrek was about to yell something. Then the fire faded from his eye and he looked confused. 'Aye. He knew.' He shook his head. 'And he still died for her.' He stomped off across the deck.

'She's stable,' said Endrineer Khorstun, hobbling over towards Solmundsson, his face covered in oil and sweat. 'She'll need to be completely refitted when we return to Barak-Urbaz, but I can keep her moving until then.'

Solmundsson clapped him on the shoulder. 'Good work, Khorstun.' Then he looked across the deck. All the uninjured crewmen were tending to their fallen comrades, binding wounds or repairing flight suits. 'Help treat the wounded. We won't continue to the Iron Karak until we've helped everyone we can.'

The endrineer hesitated, looking pained.

'What is it?' asked Solmundsson.

'We should be able to make it back to Barak-Urbaz, captain,' said Khorstun. 'But there's no way we could reach the Iron Karak. Based on the routes we studied in Barak-Urbaz, there's no way we could get that far now. We're halfway there at best. There's too much damage to the endrins. And we've shed half our fuel. We can make it home, but any other route would be impossible.'

Solmundsson stared at him, battling anger. He bit back harsh words and nodded. 'See to the wounded.'

As Khorstun saluted and headed off to help, Solmundsson stood erect and proud, but once the endrineer was out of sight he clenched his fists. 'I can't return to Barak-Urbaz now. There has to be a way.' He felt the moon grinning down at him but refused to look up, knowing how confused he would feel if he met its gaze. 'There has to be something I can do.' He looked around for the Slayer, recalling what a glorious sight he had made when he was fighting the grots. He was like one of the ancestor gods forged into the ceiling of Admiralty Hall. He spotted Gotrek over at the railing, looking out into the clouds at the quickly disappearing squigs. The grots had flown their steeds with impressive speed and were already fading into the darkness, moonlight glinting on their weapons. Solmundsson joined Gotrek and gazed out at them. 'They nearly took the ship,' he said, speaking quietly so that only Gotrek would hear.

Gotrek snorted. 'They wouldn't have taken it with me onboard.'

'That's hard to argue with. But when they left they had the upper hand. A few more minutes of that and my crew would have been wiped out and the ship would have gone into a nosedive. Perhaps you could have survived that, but we wouldn't. I don't understand why the grots withdrew when they did.'

Gotrek shrugged. 'They seemed more interested in Maleneth than your ship.'

'Dat's right,' said a rigger who was standing nearby. 'Dey came for da aelf.'

Solmundsson had not noticed him until that moment, and it took him a moment to recall his name. 'What's that, Ornolf?'

Ornolf was shaking and hunched over, as though gripped by fever, and his flight suit was torn. He was so weary he was struggling to speak, his words seeming to choke him. 'Dey took da aelf to da Loonking's Asylum. I heard 'em say it. To a place called Slathermere.'

'They spoke words you could recognise?' Solmundsson shook his head. 'Are you sure?'

Ornolf looked distressed, flinching and avoiding Solmundsson's eye. 'Da... The aelf said it. She said dat's where they're goin'. To a place called Slathermere.'

Solmundsson looked at Gotrek. 'Could Maleneth speak to greenskins?'

Gotrek shrugged.

Ornolf tried to say more but his words were gibberish.

'You sound awful,' said Solmundsson, taking Ornolf's arm before he dropped to the ground. He waved a deck officer over. 'Get him to a bunk.'

Ornolf tried to protest, but his words remained jumbled and Solmundsson ordered the officer to take him away.

'What's the Loonking's Asylum?' asked Gotrek, narrowing his eye. 'And Slathermere?'

'I've never heard of Slathermere, but the Asylum is reputed to be the home of our enemy. The Loonking is a powerful greenskin warlord that holds sway over Skrappa Spill.' Solmundsson grimaced. 'And most of Ayadah, for that matter. The Asylum is his home. I don't know if it's a fortress or a tunnel network, but it's located somewhere under Skrappa Spill.'

Gotrek looked at the disappearing squigs again, then back at the hole caused by Trachos' death. He backed away from the railing and started pacing. 'So you know where the greenskins are coming from?' He glared at Solmundsson. 'And you leave them there, undisturbed, to do what they like? You don't do anything about it?'

'You don't understand. Skrappa Spill is hidden in an endless night. The grots have turned the place into a netherworld. No one can get near the place. And the Loonking's Asylum is buried somewhere *beneath* it. Only a lunatic would go there.'

'So you let these flying half-pints raid your fleets and trash your sky-forts?' Gotrek's ire was growing as he stomped back and forth. 'And leave their king to fortify his home in peace? Is this how the mighty Kharadron sky lords treat their enemies? You hide from them?'

'We don't *hide*, Gotrek, we plan. The guildmasters and admirals would not launch fleets into unmapped territory with no idea of what we'd face there.' Even as he argued with the Slayer, Solmundsson sensed that there was something else going on. The Slayer's rage was not really caused by Kharadron inaction. He was not really railing against the Loonking. He was angry about something else. The loss of the Stormcast Eternal, perhaps? Solmundsson looked back at the distant swarm of squigs. *Perhaps it's her*, he wondered. *Maleneth. Is he troubled by her loss?* Solmundsson had already spent enough time in the Slayer's company to know that asking Gotrek would be a mistake. He decided to change the subject. 'We've suffered serious losses, Gotrek, and my ship is damaged, but I'll find a way for us to continue the journey to the Iron Karak. Trachos need not have died in vain. We can still remove that rune and–'

'Remove the bloody rune?' Gotrek's beard bristled and his face turned the colour of raw meat. 'Do you think I'm going to waltz off looking for lost cities now?'

Solmundsson was speechless. He did not know whether to laugh or weep. The Slayer was clearly insane. 'You *don't* want to find the Iron Karak?'

'Of course I bloody don't!' Gotrek clanked his axe against the railing. 'What are you thinking? That's not where we should be going!'

'What am I thinking?' muttered Solmundsson, with a sinking sensation in his guts as he considered what he had sacrificed to drag a maniac halfway across Ayadah. With Gotrek still scowling furiously at him, Solmundsson decided to risk one more question. 'Where *should* we be going?'

'To this damned Asylum!' Gotrek began pacing back and forth across the deck, muttering to himself and swinging his axe. 'You can't run a kingdom like this. Leaving your worst enemy to fester like a wound. You need to root them out. What's the use in building castles in the clouds if greenskins rule everything else?' Emotion flashed in his eye, but Solmundsson sensed it was not just rage now. There was something else. Excitement, perhaps? Mischief, maybe? It was impossible to be sure. 'How far are we from Skrappa Spill?'

Solmundsson shrugged. 'We're skirting its eastern borders. But why...' A troubling realisation hit him. 'You're not thinking that we–?'

'Why did you bring me up here?' asked Gotrek.

'To find a way to harness your rune.'

'What for?'

'To halt the advance of the greenskins before the moon waxes full. To derail them somehow.'

Gotrek stopped pacing back and forth. 'You want to rid yourselves of these moon-loving grobi. You want to stop them dragging ships from the skies and robbing your legitimately stolen gold.'

'Stolen? I can assure you that the Kharadron Code is quite clear on–'

'You need a distraction. You need a way to drag those filthy grobi back to their home before they take yours.' Gotrek stopped next to Solmundsson and gripped his shoulder. 'Get me to the Asylum. I'll make such a mess you'll have every greenskin in the realm scrambling back there.'

Solmundsson shook his head in disbelief. Then he thought about the news his endrineer had just given him. The *Angaz-Kár* would never reach the Iron Karak, but it might reach Skrappa Spill. The thought of returning empty-handed appalled him, and there was something infectious about the Slayer's determination. 'I wonder...' he muttered, holding Gotrek's fierce gaze.

Gotrek smiled. It was an unnerving sight. 'Take the fight to them. I've slain far worse than grobi. On my oath, beardling. Get me to this bloody Asylum and I'll butcher half of them before they have time to grab their stupid little bows. And while they're busy chewing my axe the moon will wane and Barak-Urbaz will be safe.'

Solmundsson was struggling to keep up with the Slayer's sudden change of heart. He nodded at the rune. 'And what about that?'

'It can wait. Grungni's teeth, beardling, you need to stop mucking about with fart dragons and deal with the real threat. Maybe the ancestors will forgive you for living in cloud houses, but not if you let greenskins butcher everyone.' Gotrek was growing angrier by the second. 'I saw some of this land before we bought passage to Barak-Urbaz. The aelf dragged me round all sorts of hovels. I saw things that you should be ashamed of.' Gotrek gripped the railing so hard it started to buckle. 'It's a slaughterhouse down there. Everyone's either hiding from the moon or being diced by the greenskins. And you think you can let these grobi swan about in a secret cave? You think you can just abandon everyone to their deaths?'

Solmundsson took a step back, sensing the violence simmering up through Gotrek's words, but he refused to accept the charges being laid at the feet of his people. 'We have abandoned no one. If anything, *we* were abandoned. But we found a way to rise from the scum. We built weapons and fleets that can withstand anything our enemies throw at us.'

Gotrek turned his glare back on Solmundsson. 'And for what? What have you achieved? If greenskins can loot and murder at their leisure, what's the point of your clever toys?'

Solmundsson was not given to rage, but the Slayer's words left him breathless with anger. 'The realms are full of such degenerate species. Why would you single the Kharadron out for criticism?'

'Because you should bloody well know better.' Gotrek lowered his voice, but the rage was still burning in his eye. 'Because somewhere deep in your gold-plated past you were dawi once. And you should start acting like it. Besides, if Barak-Urbaz is all you care about, you still need to get me to the gobbos. If you don't let me make some noise down there you won't have a city to return to.'

While they had been talking, First Officer Thorrik had approached and begun following the exchange.

Solmundsson took a deep breath and turned to him. 'What would be our best course, if we *were* to approach Skrappa Spill?'

Thorrik had removed his helmet to treat a wound and his proud, craggy features were visible. His long, forked beard was drenched with blood and his face was drained of colour, but he looked as fierce as always. Solmundsson had sailed with Thorrik on countless expeditions and he rarely saw him look surprised. This was one of those times. 'Skrappa Spill, captain? In a single vessel? Without support from the admiralty or the guilds?'

Hearing the idea spoken out loud in such uncertain terms caused Solmundsson's pulse to quicken. He forgot his anger at Gotrek for a moment and saw that there was some merit in it. 'Perhaps,' he said, drumming his fingers on the railing and glancing at Gotrek. 'Who would expect it? It would be an act of madness.'

Thorrik raised an eyebrow. 'It would.'

'Which means no one could predict it,' continued Solmundsson. 'Think about it, Thorrik. Every one of our recent expeditions has floundered. Our fleets are attacked with unerring accuracy. Every move we make is anticipated by the grots. Every decision made in Admiralty Hall is met by a countermove. Every attack is pre-empted. The Moonclans predict our every move, through treachery or espionage or whatever dark rites they perform in their caves.' He stared out into the silvery clouds. 'But who could predict this? It was not planned and it makes no sense. A single ship, striking deep into their territory. And bringing an unstoppable weapon into the Asylum. They could not predict it because we did not predict it.' Solmundsson could hear his words running together as he spoke faster. He paused and took a deep breath. 'The grot armies are scattered across Ayadah. And not just Ayadah. They're striking against every sky-port in the realm, and they're doing it because the moon is almost full. They think they're unstoppable. But they don't know we've heard of the Asylum. They would never see this coming. Imagine their surprise if we get the Slayer in there and he causes the same havoc he was causing in Barak-Urbaz.'

Thorrik looked at Gotrek with obvious distrust and was clearly about to say something, but his expression hardened and he fixed his gaze somewhere over Solmundsson's shoulder. 'Aye, captain.'

Gotrek looked at Solmundsson with a peculiar mix of grief, rage and eagerness. 'Maybe there *is* some dwarf in the duardin.' He gripped his axe and clanged the haft on the deck. 'Get this tub on the ground and I'll teach the greenskins how real dawi fight. I'll show them how we deal with people who wreck our forts.'

Solmundsson and Thorrik had both glanced at each other when Gotrek used the word 'our'.

He caught their look and his face flushed, but he said nothing.

First Officer Thorrik frowned. 'Captain, even if we were to head into Skrappa Spill, how would we find the Asylum? None of our charts have placed it with any accuracy.' He gave Gotrek a hard look. 'Despite the Slayer's suggestion, Kharadron fleets have tried to find the place, but they either failed to locate it or never returned. Do you have newer charts than the ones I've seen? Ones that pin down the route?'

Solmundsson would not accept such a challenge from most of his crew, but Thorrik was a veteran of countless voyages and he had earned the right to speak without fear of censure. 'Not as such,' he replied, 'but I have you and the best crew ever assembled by the Solmund Company. And the *Angaz-Kár* is the finest ship in the fleet. If anyone could find the Asylum, it's us.'

Gotrek stared at them in disbelief. 'You're all soft in the head.' He pointed his axe at a shape fading into the distance. 'Follow the bloody squig.'

CHAPTER EIGHTEEN

Are you going to let them do that to you?

Maleneth could not remember hearing her mistress sound so unnerved. Even when she still had a body to protect she had been relentlessly fearless, but the things growing in the Asylum were so horrific that even Maleneth struggled to stay calm. When she had first awoken, she had assumed she was in a vast, moonlit swamp, but as the grots dragged her down a muddy, winding road, she started to see glimpses of distant rock walls arcing up overhead and realised she was in an enormous cave. Rather than moonlight, the swamp was illuminated by a strange forest that surrounded the road. She saw overgrown forms of fungus – translucent puffballs, shaggy parasols and rings of lemon-coloured toadstools, all glowing with a pale inner light. The glow throbbed like a pulse and revealed people staring out from the stems and frills. Some of the fungi bore no more than a fragment of a face or a pair of slender hands, but others were almost entirely humanoid, enveloped in gelatinous flesh but still recognisable as people. Some stared blankly as Maleneth staggered past, their mouths slack and silent, but others were screaming, begging to be released.

Maleneth was not afraid of pain and suffering, but even she found the sight revolting. There was no beauty to this, no art. The marsh was fly-crowded and noisy and its captives made an ugly sight, gasping and straining against their fleshy prisons. She stopped to look at one. It was a toadstool, taller than her and containing an aelf who was trapped but still intact. He was not one of Maleneth's Khainite kin, but the symbols on his robes marked him as a citizen of Azyr. A sorcerer. And a powerful one by the looks of him. Under normal circumstances she would have been glad to stand beside him on a battlefield, but as he reached out towards her, Maleneth recoiled in disgust. 'Get me out,' he whispered, his eyes wide. Part of his mouth was covered by the toadstool's flesh and his words were muffled. 'I beg you.' Then a grot yanked Maleneth's chains and hauled her forwards through the mud, leaving the sorcerer to clutch uselessly at the air.

'Scryshrooms,' said a voice behind her.

Maleneth was still tightly bound, but she managed to look back over her shoulder. The grot that looked like a walking bracket of fungus was scuttling along behind her through the swamp with an amused grin on its face. 'Dey show us fings.'

Maleneth strained against her bonds with such violence her guard stumbled. She managed to launch herself at the crab-like creature. Her fists were shackled but she pounded them into the grot's face. The creature buckled, squealing. She drew back her fists to strike again but dozens of wiry arms wrenched her away and hurled her into the muck. Her breath exploded from her lungs as she thudded against an enormous puffball, but she dropped into a crouch and prepared to launch another attack.

'Stupid witch,' hissed the crab-like grot, its legs thrashing furiously in the mud as it backed away from her. Grots surrounded her. They were tiny, feeble-looking things, no more than three feet tall, but there were dozens and all of them had raised bows with the arrows pointed at her face.

Not now, you idiot girl. They'll turn you into a pincushion. Wait. Be patient.

Maleneth slumped back against the fungus and relaxed her muscles. Her mistress was right. She might manage to throttle a few before they killed her, but she would never get near the one she wanted – the smug-faced mutant that had captured her. She had to bide her time. She had promised Khaine she would make the creature pay for the damage to her flesh and she must not go back on her word.

Her guard grabbed hold of the chain and tried to pull her back to her feet, but something caught on the back of Maleneth's head and she could not move. Pain exploded across the back of her skull as the grot yanked at the chain, spitting curses and failing to move her.

'Wait!' she hissed. 'I'm stuck, damn you.' Maleneth tried to pull her head away from the puffball but it would not budge. As she struggled the fungus shivered and glowing spores billowed around her, alighting on her face and chest and causing her to glow.

The guard called to the crab-like grot. Maleneth had no idea what the guard was saying, but the way it was pointing at the back of her head did not fill her with confidence. She struggled to move again but the pain was worse and she could now feel that something soft and warm was wrapping itself around the back of her skull.

It's swallowing you! Move your legs, you lazy wretch.

Maleneth pulled with all her strength, but her head would not move and the pain became so intense that she had to give up and slump back against the puffball's flesh.

The crab-like grot scrambled to its feet and scuttled in circles, looking panicked. Then it rushed away, heading back down the road, barging the other grots aside as it vanished into the gloom.

'Don't leave me like this!' cried Maleneth, but the creature was already out of sight. 'I'll have to do it now,' she hissed, using her tongue to feel for one of the capsules hidden in her molars.

No, you fool! They'll fill you full of arrows before you take two steps.

'I'm sinking into this thing!' gasped Maleneth, horror gripping her as she felt the rubbery surface roll over her ears. The swamp's chorus of screams was muffled as Maleneth's head sank slowly into the puffball. She could still hear the cries but they sounded distant and strange, as though heard from underwater.

Ignoring her mistress, she prepared to bite down on the capsule and blow poison into the faces of the grots. Then she hesitated. How would that help? She would blow the venom into their faces, killing the grots nearest to her, but she would still be trapped in the puffball. She tried again to move her head but the pain was horrific. The fungus had seeped through her skull, joining itself to her. It was eating her. No, she realised, not eating. It was turning her into one of the pitiful captives that lined the road. Maleneth had rarely felt true panic, but this was too much. The thought of spending the rest of her long life here, trapped in a revolting lump of fungus, was enough to make her howl.

The crab-like grot scuttled back into view, followed by the robed, burnt one. The burnt grot shook its head furiously as it saw Maleneth. Then it shoved past the grots with the bows and hurried over to her, taking something from its sodden robes.

As the grot leant close and its face filled her vision, Maleneth felt her sanity cracking. She could feel the puffball's flesh rolling over her cheeks towards her eyes. It was like sinking beneath mud. And the face hanging in front of her was a nightmarish sight. The grot's face was not just charred but slick with a clear, glue-like liquid that oozed from its eye. The fruit of the puffball burned brighter, as though a fire had been kindled in it.

As despair threatened to overcome her, Maleneth called out in fear and outrage. To her surprise, the name she cried was not Khaine.

'Gotrek!' she howled.

CHAPTER NINETEEN

'Grungni's oath.' Gotrek stumbled away from the railing, shaking his head.

Captain Solmundsson reached out to grab the Slayer's arm before he slammed into First Officer Thorrik. They were standing on the foredeck of the *Angaz-Kár*, surrounded by crewmembers. Everyone looked over in surprise at Gotrek's outburst.

'Are you well?' asked Solmundsson once he had steadied the Slayer.

Gotrek growled and shrugged him off, but the way he gripped the railing revealed how shaken he was. 'I saw her.'

Solmundsson shook his head. 'Who?'

'The aelf. In my head.' Gotrek slapped the head of his axe against his palm. 'She's bloody haunting me.'

It was two days since they had repaired the ship and set sail from Valdrakh Pass, and they were now deep into the uncharted regions over Skrappa Spill. Solmundsson had not mentioned it in front of his crew, but he was worried. They had barely crossed Skrappa Spill's eastern borders when the moon lurched towards them, moving so close it was like he could reach out and touch its leering face. And as the moon swelled to a grotesque size the sky billowed away from it, revolted by its presence. The normal rules of physics were crumbling. Clouds were whirling around its pitted bulk, and they were made of silver shards that rattled against the hull. The ship lurched wildly, battered by turbulence, but the shards of silver caused the most damage, splitting fuel tanks and slicing into the crew.

'Even dead she won't let me escape her prattling,' grunted Gotrek.

Solmundsson studied the Slayer, confused by him. Gotrek had only mentioned Maleneth in derisive tones, but Solmundsson was becoming more and more convinced that the Slayer's reason for coming to Skrappa Spill was to follow her. He clearly cared for her, but he refused to acknowledge it, perhaps even to himself, stating repeatedly that they were only here to 'rid the realm of grobi scum.'

'We don't know that she's dead,' said Solmundsson. 'Ornolf said she was captured and bound. Why would they do that just to kill her?'

'Do you think I care if she's alive or dead?' Gotrek snarled. 'They can feed her to their squigs for all I care. I just want her out of my head.'

'Captain,' said First Officer Thorrik, pointing to a shape up ahead in the storm. 'Look! The straggler. We're still with it.'

Solmundsson took out his spyglass and looked through the downpour. It took him a moment to focus on the spherical shape, but then he nodded. It was one of the winged, grot-carrying squigs. He grinned. They had not seen it for nearly an hour, and he had begun to lose hope. 'Good.'

'It's not the one that took the aelf,' said Thorrik, 'but it's part of the same group. I recognise the shape of the howdah.'

'So it will be heading to the same place,' said Solmundsson. 'To the Asylum.'

Thorrik was not doing a good job of hiding his doubts over the whole expedition. 'Perhaps. Or they just congregated to attack us at the pass and are now heading back to different homes.'

'They're going to the same place.'

'With respect, captain, how can you know?'

Solmundsson stared meaningfully at Thorrik. 'Because the alternative is that we're lost over Skrappa Spill with no hope of finding our destination and I'm a lunatic who's following a lunatic.'

Thorrik was about to say something, then thought better of it and simply nodded.

Solmundsson looked over at Gotrek, who was pacing a few feet away. He had no idea what the Slayer's normal mental state was, but since the death of Trachos he seemed particularly erratic. It occurred to him that he might be suffering some kind of mental collapse. 'What do you mean, she's in your head?' He walked over to him. 'Do you mean she's talking to you?'

Gotrek was twitching and tapping his head in a manner that reminded Solmundsson of the now dead Stormcast Eternal. 'I can feel her in my mind.' He cursed and spat. 'Filthy aelf, crawling around where she has no damned right to be. I heard her call my name and now I can feel her in my thoughts, rummaging like a bloody cutpurse.' Gotrek paused and stared at the deck. 'Damn her!'

He stayed like that for a few seconds, then looked up, as though surprised. 'She's gone.' He frowned. 'And I saw something.'

Solmundsson and Thorrik exchanged glances.

'What did you see?' asked Solmundsson.

'The head of a bloody great giant, as big as one of your guildhalls. And it was glowing.'

Thorrik raised an eyebrow. 'A glowing giant's head? Was it attached to a glowing giant?'

Gotrek glared at him. 'No. Floating in a lake. Surrounded by lots of little heads.'

Solmundsson was about to ask for more details. Then he shook his head, deciding he'd rather not hear any more. *It's just the damned moon,* he thought. Since the moon had come closer and the storm grown stranger, his own thoughts had started to wander. It was as though his dreams were creeping into his waking mind. As the silver rolled across the deck, he saw shapes swaying in the deluge – tall, arrow-headed toadstools that leant towards him. It was as if they knew he had seen them. He staggered towards them, horrified and fascinated at the same time, realising that all

the toadstools contained people – men, aelves and duardin, trapped forever, gasping for breath.

CHAPTER TWENTY

The grot backed away from Maleneth, blinking its grotesquely enlarged eye as the light faded. 'What was dat?' hissed the charred creature, looking to the other greenskins. It turned to the crab-shaped monster. 'Mangleback, d'ya see dat?'

For a moment, Maleneth struggled to focus on them. She had seen, quite clearly, an image of Solmundsson's ship in her mind, and she had seen the captain himself, looking at her with concern. The *Angaz-Kár* had been sailing through a silvery storm and she could still feel the sensation of its deck rocking beneath her feet. As the afterimage of the ship faded, she had a shocking thought. She had understood the one-eyed grot. It was not speaking her language as the other greenskin had done – she had understood its absurd, screeching gibberish.

'Weird,' replied the grot called Mangleback. 'Like she was burnin'.'

'How can I understand you?' Maleneth glared at the one-eyed grot. 'What have you done to me?'

The grots stared at her in shock, then burst into laughter. 'It ain't me,' said the one-eyed grot. 'Yer growin'.'

'Growing? Khaine's teeth. What do you mean, "growing"?'

The grot laughed. 'You're becoming part of da Gibbermarsh. A scryshroom. Part of da Asylum.' It pointed to Mangleback's fungal shell. ''Appens to da best of 'em. And as da Asylum sinks into ya, yer startin' to fink like we do.'

Maleneth howled, trying again to free herself from the puffball. The pain was so intense she almost lost consciousness, and she failed to move an inch.

'Get 'er out, Stinkeye,' said Mangleback. 'Scragfang don't want 'er stuck out 'ere in the marsh. 'E wants 'er safe in Slathermere.'

Stinkeye limped back over to Maleneth, and she realised how the creature had got its name. The slime oozing from its eye stank of rotten meat, and Maleneth gagged as Stinkeye's face came within inches of hers.

'Just gotta, er, tickle 'er out,' said Stinkeye. The grot took a teardrop-shaped bottle from its robes and held it up to Maleneth. 'Yer, er, lucky,' it whispered, shaking the contents. They looked to Maleneth like small black seeds, around ten of them. Stinkeye uncorked the bottle and tipped one of the seeds out into its palm. Then it placed it onto the puffball.

The fungus shivered. At first it was just a slight tremor, but in a few seconds it was shaking so violently Maleneth felt like she was being rattled in a gargant's fist. A squeaking sound came from the pulpy mass behind her, and then she was hurled forwards.

Maleneth collided with Stinkeye then slid across the road, coming to a stop in a puddle on the opposite side. The grots were still laughing as she climbed to her feet and glared at them, wiping mud from her leathers. The archers all had their arrows trained on her face, and Maleneth was still chained so there was nothing she could do but scowl as her guard shoved her back onto the road and the group continued walking.

Maleneth assumed they were making for the enormous head. Even from a couple of miles away, she could see greenskins coming and going through gates carved in its neck, gathering in groups or heading off through the marsh on roads that wound off into the glimmering lights. It was clearly a fortress of some significance, and there were flocks of flying squigs circling around its scarred brow. The gargant's eyes were long gone, leaving two ragged holes that were so crowded with bioluminescent growths that they looked like beacons, glaring through the gloom.

'Is that where the Loonking lives?' she asked, twisting her head to address Mangleback.

The creature grinned cheerfully at her. 'He will do soon.'

'What do you mean?'

'Scragfang lives in Slathermere. An soon 'e'll be Loonking. It was 'is idea ta use you as bait.'

'Scragfang?' Maleneth looked around the crowd of grots examining their long, hooked faces, trying to spot the one Mangleback was referring to.

''E ain't 'ere,' laughed Mangleback. ''E's sunk in da Weeping Brook. Once we fish 'im out ya can 'ave a cosy chat. 'E's gonna be well 'appy.'

To Maleneth's surprise, the group turned off the main road, climbed up a slope and headed away from Slathermere. They headed through a series of bogs and marshes that were even more fungus-crowded than the fields around the main road. They had been marching for hours by this point and Maleneth was exhausted. The greenskins showed no sign of flagging, despite their scrawny frames. Maleneth wondered how they were managing to scurry on with such endless energy. Then she noticed their secret. Whenever one of them started to slow, the grot called Stinkeye would reach into its robes and fish out a bag filled with wriggling grubs. The grots grimaced as they chewed the grubs, spitting out their bright blue shells with disgust, but the results were impressive. One grub was enough to send them sprinting on down the road with blank stares on their faces.

Ask for one.

Don't be absurd, thought Maleneth. *I'm already changing. I don't want to start eating their food. Have you seen their faces after they've eaten it? They look even more deranged than before.*

Well you need to do something. If you collapse they'll gut you.

I have a plan, thought Maleneth.

You have nothing. Your arm looks like something plucked from a stew.

And you're so tired you can barely stand. Get your hands on some of that food.

I do have a plan, but I'm not doing anything until I've seen the one they call Scragfang.

Why? What's the difference between one fungus-brained runt and another?

Scragfang is the one who ordered them to capture me. She felt a delicious rush of bloodlust. *And that's the one I'm going to take out of here. Scragfang is going to live a long, agonising life.*

Not if that stuff keeps growing up your arm. What do you think it will do when it reaches your brain?

Maleneth looked down at her arm and shivered in distaste. The growths had spread up to her bicep and she could feel more straining under her skin, about to pop through. She shook her head and smiled. *It doesn't matter.*

What are you talking about? You're ruined. How can you honour Khaine now?

Maleneth kept smiling. 'I'll honour him.'

The grots led her down into a boggy valley towards a winding black brook. Everything in the valley was coated in luminescent spores and they were drifting over the stream, giving the whole scene a hazy, dreamlike appearance. In fact, Maleneth had felt for several hours that she was stumbling through some confused nether region of her mind. She could still feel the place where the puffball had merged with her skull and her arm was trembling constantly as new life boiled beneath the surface. She battled to keep a grip on her senses as she approached the black brook, thinking to herself, over and again, *I have a plan.*

Most of the grots halted a few feet away from the brook, eyeing the surrounding hills warily. Some of them kept their bows trained on Maleneth, but most pointed their arrows at the toadstools that blanketed the valley. Stinkeye and Mangleback glanced at Maleneth to ensure she was still securely chained, then crawled down towards the sluggish liquid.

There was a hump in the middle of the river, like the crest of a small island just beneath the surface, and the two grots waded through the clinging liquid towards it. The creature called Mangleback was the first to reach it, and after a nod from Stinkeye, the grot used its tendrils to reach down and haul the shape out of the river.

Maleneth leant forwards, keen to see the architect of her abduction. It was a grot, as scrawny and hook-nosed as all the others. The creature gasped and kicked as Mangleback dragged it back towards the shore.

Stinkeye hurried forwards, wading through the gunk, grabbing the grot's thrashing limbs and helping Mangleback carry it to safety. Once they had deposited the creature on the shore Maleneth got her first good look at it. It was drenched and coughing furiously, but she saw how it had been altered by the swamp. The back half of its skull had formed into a bracket of hard, gnarled fungus that jutted out like a ledge from its head. Rather than leather armour or a simple jerkin, Scragfang wore black robes that were draped with bone necklaces and animal skulls. Maleneth had fought greenskins enough times to know that this was one of their sorcerer prophets. The creature slumped weakly in the arms of the other two grots as they wiped gunk from its face. Then it looked around in confusion. Its eyes cleared as they focused on Mangleback. 'We lost Lord Zogdrakk?' Its voice was a shrill creak. 'An' Boglob?'

The one called Mangleback nodded, moving its whole shell up and down. Then it loosed Scragfang and performed a ridiculous dance, turning in circles around Scragfang before halting and pointing at Maleneth. 'But we did it. You did it.'

The grot shaman wiped more muck from its eyes and squinted at Maleneth. Its eyes widened in recognition and a grin spread across its goblinoid features. 'We zoggin did.'

As Maleneth studied the idiotic creature, she felt such a wave of ecstatic hate that she could have wept. It was a glorious gift. She was going to make Khaine so proud of her.

The shaman staggered over, shaking oil from its trembling limbs. It looked hungrily at her. 'It's just as I saw. It's all comin' true.'

Scragfang walked around Maleneth, then the smile fell from its face. 'What 'ave ya zoggin done to 'er?'

'Just made 'er look a little bit more fancier,' said Mangleback. 'Ain't we, Stinkeye?'

Stinkeye nodded, and Scragfang started giggling. The whole group quickly grew hysterical, rolling across the muddy turf and kicking their short, withered legs. Then, to Maleneth's amazement, Mangleback took out a bone whistle and started to play a tune. This sent the grots off into even more violent paroxysms of laughter.

Another grot grabbed a squig and lifted it up into the air, eliciting more cheers. The squig was smaller than the others and there were tube-like protrusions jutting from its scarred hide. The grot placed its mouth to one of the tubes, pressed its fingers over the others and blew. The squig doubled in size and a droning sound filled the valley.

The grot bounded and skipped as it played the squig and the rest of the greenskins danced around it, delighted by the discordant screeches.

Maleneth stared in disbelief. Then she realised that none of the grots were looking her way. Mangleback was still scuttling in circles, peeping and shrieking with the whistle while the other grot honked through the squig, and the rest had all abandoned themselves to a frenzied jig, wailing tunelessly and clanging finger cymbals. Even Maleneth's guard joined the victory dance, letting go of her chain and rolling on the ground, tears streaming from its eyes.

Now.

Maleneth nodded but waited a moment longer, studying Scragfang's face, imprinting it on her memory. 'I'll be back for you,' she whispered. She quietly lifted her chain from her wrist, having picked the lock hours ago.

She scrambled up the slope, smiling to herself. She was almost away when one of the guards saw her and rushed over, raising its bow and opening its mouth to shout. She lashed out with her good arm, silencing him with a quick punch in the guts. Then she kicked him into a pool of yellow gloop, ducked low and raced off into the forest of toadstools.

CHAPTER TWENTY-ONE

The *Angaz-Kár* howled, ploughing through liquid mercury. Metal splashed over the hull, washing over the deck and hissing furiously. Solmundsson and the other officers were in his cabin with Gotrek, strapped into their seats, and the rest of the crew were below decks. Solmundsson gritted his teeth as the ship burst from the lake, rose briefly back into the air and then crashed down onto a plain of rusted iron, spraying sparks and filling the ship with the smell of burning. This was the jewel of his father's fleet, and Solmundsson felt every jolt like an attack on his own skin. Finally, after grinding along for several minutes, the huge vessel screamed to a halt, teetered, then crashed onto its side, sending books and charts flying across the cabin.

Solmundsson and the others sat in silence, staring at each other. Their chairs were riveted in place so they were hanging at a peculiar angle above the wall that had now become the floor. There was no sound other than the rattle of falling silver. They had flown down through the storm and escaped the wind, but the moonlight was still everywhere, painting everything in cool, cheerless light.

Gotrek gave Solmundsson an incredulous look. 'Only the Kharadron could invent a flying ship that can't land.'

Despite assuring everyone it would be fine, Solmundsson had not been entirely sure they would survive the landing, so hearing the familiar sound of Gotrek's bile was such a relief he smiled.

'We do not usually land like this,' explained First Officer Thorrik, scowling at Gotrek. 'None of our landing equipment is working. We lost half the ship over Valdrakh Pass.'

'We've achieved something few others would dare attempt,' said Solmundsson. 'We've reached the Loonking's Asylum.'

'We think,' said Thorrik.

'We followed the squigs,' said Solmundsson. 'And Ornolf heard Maleneth say they were heading to the Asylum. This should be it.' The ship shifted again, hurling more maps and furniture.

'And how will we leave?' Thorrik looked out through one of the portholes. The iron plain was just visible through the downpour. 'We can't walk from here to Barak-Urbaz. However much damage we do to the greenskins, we'll have no way to get home.'

'Nonsense,' said Solmundsson. 'Think who's onboard. The finest endrineers in Ayadah. No one understands aethermatics like they do. And this is Skrappa Spill. We can find any form of metal we need here.' He unbuckled his harness and carefully dropped down onto the slanting floor. 'There's always a way, First Officer Thorrik.'

Gotrek thudded down next to the captain and picked some silver from his beard.

Solmundsson led the way out and they emerged onto the listing deck. The *Angaz-Kár* was surrounded by fields of rust. Slabs of crumbling iron were heaped in every direction and the landscape was punctuated by towers of steam that hissed up through the cracks. Some were no bigger than a man, but others were great geysers that boiled and hissed as they reached up to the clouds. Boulders of raw metal lay scattered across the plains. Some were ragged hunks, but others were formed into geometric shapes – glinting cylinders lay next to dark, oily cubes in a bewildering profusion that resembled a vast discarded puzzle. It was early morning, by Solmundsson's reckoning, but the clouds were so dark and heavy that the plain seemed to be sunk in a perpetual, fitful dusk. He grabbed his spyglass and, to his relief, saw a line that jutted up from the plain.

'There,' he said, pointing it out as the others gathered around him on the deck.

Thorrik nodded. 'Aye, that's where the squig landed.' He looked around at the rust fields. 'But we can't leave the ship like this. The greenskins will see her from miles off. They may have already spotted us.'

Solmundsson nodded. 'We need to hide her.' He climbed through the wreckage, picking up pieces of broken machinery. 'Which of the aethermatic devices survived the attack?'

'Nothing that could mask an entire ship. Not without being reconfigured. Perhaps if we stay here for a few days, the endrineers could–'

Gotrek snorted. 'You couldn't engineer yourself out of bed. We can't just sit here playing with spanners. We're on the enemy's doorstep.'

Solmundsson nodded. 'You have a point, Slayer, but if we leave the ship on display we'll have no chance of getting into the Asylum. Subterfuge is not the Kharadron way, but the Code clearly states that in times such as this a captain may not leave his ship–'

Gotrek pointed his axe at Solmundsson. 'You read too much. The Code says this, the Code says that. I'm all for following tradition, but a book can't tell you everything about how to live.' He looked around at the savage landscape then strode off across the deck.

Solmundsson and the other officers rushed after him as the rest of the crew started clambering up onto the deck, lugging weapons and grappling with equipment.

Gotrek reached the railing nearest to the ground and vaulted over it. He briefly vanished from sight, engulfed by a cloud of rust flakes. When the rust settled, Solmundsson saw that the Slayer was knee-deep in it. It eddied around him as he grabbed a handful, letting it pour through his fingers. 'Probably not many farmers round here,' he said, wading off across the field.

Solmundsson and Thorrik dropped down from the ship, but Solmundsson waved the other officers back, telling them to gather the crew and prepare for a journey.

Gotrek halted fifty feet from the downed ship and looked around at the landscape again, peering at the peculiar jumble of metal cubes and spheres.

Solmundsson followed his gaze but could see nothing of use. There were just endless, block-strewn plains and the towers of whirling steam.

'Do you mean to grab some of this metal?' he asked, looking at a bronze cone. The thing was as big as a guildhall.

'Don't believe everything the Fyreslayers tell you,' replied Gotrek. 'I'm not a bloody god.' He hefted his axe, widened his stance and rolled his shoulders, as though preparing to fell a tree. 'Stand back.'

Solmundsson's heart sank as he realised Gotrek was about to swing at the thin air.

'Back!' snapped Gotrek.

Solmundsson and Thorrik took a few steps backwards.

Gotrek rolled his shoulders again, whispered, then swung his axe into the ground.

Solmundsson shook his head.

'It's not your fault,' said Thorrik. 'The Lord Admiral himself sanctioned this expedition. Who could have predicted that the Slayer was insane?'

Gotrek swung his axe again, even harder this time. There was a flash of sparks and a groaning sound came from beneath his feet.

Gotrek whistled tunelessly and swung his axe a third time, wielding the weapon with such force that his feet left the ground. This time there was a definite tremor, followed by a loud cracking sound.

Gotrek staggered backwards as steam shot up through the rust, spitting and hissing.

Solmundsson looked around at the geysers scattered across the landscape. He gripped Thorrik's shoulder. 'He's not mad.'

Gotrek looked over at them, his chest heaving and sweat pouring down his face. 'I'm bloody mad.'

Before Solmundsson could reply, the Slayer turned and swung his axe again. This time the tremor was so violent that they all staggered, struggling to stay on their feet. The column of steam tripled in size and a slab of iron jolted up through the rust. Heat washed over Solmundsson, so intense that he could feel it through the rubber of his suit.

'Captain,' said Thorrik, pointing out a jagged line that was appearing in the rust. It was zigzagging towards the ship. 'Look what he's doing.'

Gotrek swung again and the resultant blast of steam kicked him through the air, sending him tumbling back in the direction of the *Angaz-Kár*. The geyser he had created was now a vast column of steam, blocking the view to the south of the ship.

The ground shuddered again and Solmundsson stumbled to his knees. Then he stood and hurried after Gotrek.

The Slayer waded through the rust until he was standing near the aft of the ship. Then, before Solmundsson had guessed his intent, Gotrek attacked the ground with his axe again.

This time the first blow was enough to release a violent rush of steam.

'Wait,' gasped Solmundsson, coughing and struggling to stay on his feet.

Gotrek swung again and the column erupted into another vast geyser. The two towers of steam merged into a single seething wall that soared high up into the air and howled like a tornado.

As Gotrek pounded off to the other side of the ship, Solmundsson remained sitting in the rust, staring at the roiling wall of steam. 'He's not mad,' he muttered. 'He's a damned genius.'

Thorrik helped Solmundsson to his feet, looking dubious. 'There's a fine line between the two.'

Solmundsson shook his head as Gotrek began hacking at the ground again. 'He's cutting through iron like it's rotten wood.'

They both watched as Gotrek produced a third mountain of steam. By now half of the *Angaz-Kár* was hidden from view.

'Is it the rune he carries?' asked Thorrik. 'Is that what gives him his power?'

Solmundsson frowned. 'I thought so, when I first met him, but now I'm not so sure. Look. The rune's lifeless. There's no fire in the ur-gold. When Fyreslayers use battle runes the metal lights up. But Gotrek's is dull. The power is in *him*.'

Gotrek continued striding around the ship for the next half an hour, hacking at the ground and unleashing gouts of steam until the *Angaz-Kár* was entirely hidden. Solmundsson and Thorrik had returned to the deck to talk with the other officers, and when Gotrek had finished he climbed back up over the railings and marched over to them. He was coated in sweat, blood and rust and breathing in quick gasps. He slammed the head of his axe on the deck, rested his palms on the pommel and stared at Solmundsson. 'Happy?'

Solmundsson looked around. The iron plains were gone. All he could see from the deck now was a wall of grey. The heat from the geysers was immense, but they were not so close as to damage the ship. 'Perfect,' he said. 'Apart from one thing.'

Gotrek narrowed his eye.

Solmundsson waved at the steam. 'How do we get out?'

Gotrek muttered then thudded across the deck and squinted out into the steam. Then he looked back at the damaged ship and pointed to the aft. 'What's that?'

Solmundsson looked back and saw what Gotrek was pointing to. 'A gunhauler. They're used to defend the larger ships in the fleet. They don't carry much fuel, though – what are you thinking?' He shook his head. 'They only carry two duardin at a time. It would take an age to fly the whole crew over this wall of steam. We'd be here for hours.'

Gotrek headed over to the gunhauler. It was little more than a gun on a platform topped with a spherical endrin. Gotrek tapped the hull. 'If you show me how to fly it I can get to the Asylum.'

Solmundsson laughed. 'Alone? Into the Loonking's fortress?'

'As opposed to what? Taking your punch-drunk crew? How many of them are left?' Gotrek looked around the ship. 'Twenty? Thirty? Is that enough to take on a nation of grobi? We're here to give them a bloody nose. To show them what happens when they attack your flying castles. I can do that alone. I'll just find the ugliest, biggest greenskins I can and relieve them of their heads.'

CHAPTER TWENTY-TWO

Hillel shuffled in his chair, sipping his hazkal and trying to rid himself of a fear he could not explain. Why should he feel so anxious? He had made it. He had reached the safety of Barak-Urbaz. There was nowhere safer in all of Ayadah. Outside the khordryn he could hear all the triumphant sounds of the sky-port – aethermatic anvils and fume-belching rotary engines that shook the floor beneath his boots. The Kharadron would not be conquered. They had proven it time and again. Inside the khordryn there were dozens of travellers. Some were human, like him, but there were aelves and nomadic duardin too, all drinking and talking, all happy to have found a haven from the madness of the Bane Moon. They were gathered in the khordryn's drinking hall – a wide circular room filled with beer-laden benches and thick with clouds of pipe smoke. It was just as Hillel had always pictured it would be. He had dreamt of this moment so many times and it had lived up to all his expectations. And yet, at the back of his mind, the gnawing doubt persisted.

'I'm impressed that you got here,' said the woman opposite him. She was dressed in robes and furs and looked extremely wealthy. She smiled. 'The roads are so dangerous. And there are so many refugees looking for safety. You were lucky to get passage up here on a ship. Were you travelling on foot?'

He sipped his ale and grinned back at her. 'I travelled in style. The idiots in my village saw to that.' The woman raised an eyebrow and he continued, his tongue loosened by the potent Kharadron ale. 'They treated me like an outsider my whole life. Not one of them ever gave me the time of day. Just because I knew things they didn't. They hated that I could read and learn and speak about more things than just cattle. They hated that I knew so much about the Kharadron and places like this. They ignored me my whole life. But they had no idea. I was always one step ahead of them. In the end they gave me everything they had – horses, clothes, weapons, food, everything I needed to cross Ayadah and buy passage on a sky-ship.'

'If they hated you so much, why did they give you their possessions?'

He sipped his drink and leant back with a grin. 'Because I saw what was coming. I saw what they were too stupid to see. The Bane Moon. I saw it when they didn't. I knew what it would mean, what it would do. I heard it from the elders more times than I wanted to, and I read it in books too. When the Bane Moon comes, it's time to get out. The Bane Moon doesn't just turn milk sour, like they thought, it does the same to human blood. That light changes you, from the inside. I knew it, and I wasn't going to stay there and let the moon turn me into something I wasn't meant to be.' He glanced around the room, checking no one was close enough to hear, then leant close to her and spoke in an eager whisper. 'So I started collecting bottles.'

'Bottles?'

'Bottles. I bought them from travellers and dug them from burying grounds. I cleaned them up and made labels, painting the letters myself, just like the elders taught me. I made the bottles look like they had come from one of Sigmar's golden cities, covered in comets and hammers and all the godly symbols I could imagine. And then I waited.'

'Waited for what?'

'For the Bane Moon to start its work. To do what *I* knew it was going to do. I wasn't gonna end up like all the others. I hid inside, apart from when it was so cloudy that the Bane Light couldn't get through. Then, when everyone saw what the moon did...' He grimaced. 'How it changed them. *Then* they wanted to talk to me. Then they wanted to listen. I told them I had a cure for the moon curse. I'd filled the bottles with the green water that comes up from Munk Spring and sealed the corks with all the ear wax I'd been saving, stamping more of Sigmar's symbols on there. They looked so real.' He felt a strange pang of anger as he remembered them. 'So real. No one could have guessed they were fake. Then, when everyone came grovelling, I told 'em they could have a bottle each, but only if they gave me everything I wanted. A cart, horses, weapons and anything else I could think of. Then, before they could find out I'd tricked them, I rode out of there.' The inexplicable anger gripped him again. 'I rode out of there!' he repeated, spitting beer across the table and staring at the woman, as though she had refuted his claim.

She stared back. The smile slowly fell from her face, her features growing slack.

'I got out!' he yelled, the anger growing in him until he wanted to hurl his beer across the room. He drank it instead, as quickly as he could, glugging the liquid down, grimacing at the bitter sediment. As he drank, he finally remembered the waking dream that kept haunting him – the dream he was drinking to forget. It pressed on his thoughts, trying to break his will. He refused to acknowledge it, but it flickered across his mind all the same. In the dream, he was not the one who made the bottles – he was one of the wretched dupes who bought the fake cure. One of the idiots who did not know what the Bane Moon could do. In the dream he was trapped in the gloom and submerged in a brackish pool, his body bloated out of all recognition, his head twisted into a fungal lobe. In the dream he could not move or speak. In the dream he could do nothing but stare at the moon as it glided silently from behind the clouds.

CHAPTER TWENTY-THREE

Maleneth paused to listen as she heard howls of outrage. It had only taken the grots a minute or so to notice she was missing, but she was already heading deep into the fungal forest. She sprinted away from the glimmering lights, towards an ink-dark glade.

The greenskins charged after her then came to a halt. She could hear them cursing and wailing and arguing with each other.

Maleneth hurried on into the gloom but then slowed when she realised the voices were growing more distant as she plunged deeper into the darkness. She stopped again and looked back. Scragfang and the others were just visible in the distance. They had halted within reach of the lights that lined the road, peering anxiously into the toadstool forest she had entered.

Why don't they follow?

Because they're spineless grots, afraid of their own shadows. But as she started running again, she noticed that the darkness around her was very mobile. The creaking noises reminded her of the sound the puffball had made when it enveloped her skull. She took the tear-shaped bottle from her leathers and waved it menacingly at the shadows, rattling the seeds against the glass. She had stolen the bottle from Stinkeye when the grot used it to free her from the puffball, snatching it from the creature's belt as she crashed into it. To her delight, her threat seemed to carry some weight. The shadows edged away from her. 'Yes.' She smirked. 'You know what this is, don't you? Seeds that burn. Seeds that kill. Take one step closer and I'll share some with you.'

Her aelven eyes were quickly adjusting to the darkness, and she saw a peculiar mix of shapes – slender, arrow-shaped toadstools, plump, dome-capped mushrooms and pale, pitted puffballs. All of them were backing away from her with peculiar lurching movements. They had no legs or feet that she could see, but there were nests of gossamer-like thread spreading from their stems that hauled them over the mud.

Maleneth pressed on, waving the bottle before her like a brand, and gradually made her way up the slope, scrambling through pools of stagnant water and slipping on lichen-covered rocks.

You're going the wrong way. They brought you in here from the south. You're heading north. You need to go back to the other side of the valley and find a way out of here.

'I'm not looking for a way out.' Maleneth grabbed the moss-robed branch of a leafless tree, using its crooked limbs as a ladder and climbing higher up the slope.

What are you talking about? Is that mushroom still stuck in your brain? We have to get out of here. You're already speaking the grot tongue and your body is sprouting fungus. Meanwhile, the Slayer is on his way to the Iron Karak. And once he gets there the rune will be lost to you forever. The Kharadron do not share wealth, Witch-blade.

Maleneth ducked as a shape whistled through the darkness. A trail of fine threads latched around her arm and yanked the bottle from her grip. She cursed, then fell back down the slope, caught in the threads. She slipped and stumbled, trying to dig her heels into the mud, and then she fell several feet, landing with a splash in a small pool. On the far side there was an enormous bracket fungus – a gnarled salmon-pink disc with a gaping mouth larger than Maleneth. It was fixed to a shelf of rock and seemed unable to move, but it had cast lines of mycelium, lassoing Maleneth with a bundle of threads.

Maleneth cried out as the fungus hauled her across the pool like a fisherman, making hungry, groaning sounds.

There! By the tree stump!

Maleneth leant back, throwing all her weight against the threads, and looked around the pool. The bottle had landed on a chair-like stump that was jutting from the mud. She stopped resisting the bracket's pull and allowed herself to be catapulted through the air. As she passed the stump she snatched the bottle, opened it and cast a seed into the bracket's mouth.

The fungus immediately dropped her, letting her splash down into the pool, and then whipped its tendrils back towards its mouth, clawing frantically. It made no sound but its ridged flesh was rocked by violent spasms, and as Maleneth emerged from the pool her attacker started to shrivel, as though caught in an invisible fire. The gossamer threads turned to ash and the rest of the fungus retracted into the hillside, twitching frantically as it disappeared.

Maleneth heard movement behind her and whirled around, raising the bottle and jabbing it at the shadows. There was a rustle of dead leaves and the sound of things sliding through mud, then the grove was quiet again.

Maleneth wiped the mud from her face then remained motionless in the middle of the pool for a few moments, keeping the bottle raised. Then she hauled herself out and began climbing back up the slope.

What are you going to do about Gotrek and the rune?

'I'll try to find Gotrek when I'm finished here,' she muttered, pausing to study a moss-robed tree. She knew how hard that would be though. Gotrek rarely stayed in one place long and the realms were impossibly vast. Fury coursed through her veins as she thought of everything the grots had stolen from her.

What do you mean, finished here? What in the name of the Murder God are you talking about? What is there for us here?

Maleneth found a branch that was about the length of a knife and snapped it off. Then she took a piece of stone from the mud and sharpened the stick. 'Revenge,' she said, swinging her makeshift blade back and forth, testing its weight.

On who? That creature they fished from the river?

'Yes. Scragfang, they called it. The grot who ordered its minions to bundle me up like a dead goat and bring me down to this wretched cave. I'll leave here, but I'm not leaving without Scragfang. That creature is going to feel the wrath of Khaine. I may have failed the Murder God before, but I'll make it right. I'll show Khaine my worth.'

You've lost your mind. Why would Khaine listen to you? It doesn't matter how skilfully you torment that grot – Khaine will never look your way again. There was a mixture of rage and delight in her mistress' voice. *You're ruined. Look at your arm. You're a broken blade. You can't fight your way back into his favour now.*

Maleneth laughed as she continued climbing through the darkness. 'I would have thought that you, of all people, would know not to under-estimate me. I told you, I have a plan.' There were some beams of light shining through the mushroom caps and dead branches. The light cast silver spears through the darkness, catching on the clouds of dancing spores so that they glinted like shards of metal. Maleneth studied the light for a moment, trying to find its source, then she changed direction, clambering sideways across the slope, using roots and rocks as handholds. The light was coming from a pale, translucent toadstool about as tall as Maleneth, but it showed no signs of moving, so Maleneth climbed up to it, sat on a rock and used the light to study her arm. Bile rushed into her mouth. There was no inch of the skin that had not sprouted fungal growths. It looked like a miniature recreation of the valley that surrounded her.

'We must change to survive,' she said. 'That's where you failed – clinging to the old ways, mastering the ancient rites and performing every sacrifice, exactly as the calendar dictated, but never taking time to study the lesser races. Never learning anything new. Never looking outside your own life.'

What are you talking about? What have you ever learned? Except how to disgrace yourself in the eyes of the Murder God and ruin the flesh he gave you? You were never a great fighter, it has to be said, but look at you now. You're useless.

Maleneth took Stinkeye's bottle from her belt and dropped a seed on her arm. Pain licked across her skin as though she had plunged it into a flame, but she refused to flinch. 'You would never have thought to take this bottle.' Her voice became taut as the pain grew, but she could see immediately that the grot magic was working. The growths were shrivelling and darkening. 'If you were here you'd still be performing the same old blood rites you learned as a child, wondering why your prayers were going unanswered. Waiting for a divine intervention that would never come.'

The pain eased as the fungus crumbled to ash. Maleneth brushed it away and revealed the perfect, porcelain skin of her arm. 'Times have changed. And only those who change with them will survive. Prayers are no longer enough. Faith in the gods is no longer enough. You won't...' Maleneth's words trailed off as she realised how much she sounded like one of the Kharadron. What was happening to her? She shook her head, trying to clear her thoughts.

Filthy apostate. Those who deserve Khaine's love will receive it. Those who kill with finesse and skill will never be abandoned. Only the clumsy and the weak need fear for their lives.

'Remind me,' snapped Maleneth. 'Did Khaine come to your aid when I killed you? Or were you too clumsy and weak?'

Maleneth's mistress was finally at a loss for words.

Maleneth stood, threw back her shoulders and took a deep breath, feeling strength flood her body. She was hungry and tired, but the sight of her untainted skin had filled her with vigour. She held her wooden knife up into a shaft of light and grinned. 'Not long now, Scragfang.'

CHAPTER TWENTY-FOUR

Solmundsson struggled to hold his position on the gunhauler as it chugged over the fractured landscape. By ripping away some weapons, they had managed to make enough room for the vessel to hold him, Gotrek and First Officer Thorrik, but it was not the most secure of arrangements. They had left the *Angaz-Kár* hours ago and the moon storm had grown wilder with every mile. The landscape was still a plain of rusting slabs but the wind was whipping them up, hurling metal geysers into the air. Along with the metal pyramids and cubes scattered across its surface, there were now lumps of quicksilver rushing above the ground, spinning like stones caught in a whirlpool. Some were as small as raindrops, others as big as the *Angaz-Kár* – vast, rolling blobs that reflected the gunhauler as it passed, giving Solmundsson a chance to see how precarious his position was. He could feel the moon watching overhead. Glaring at him and driving the storm on. Every now and then, the clouds would part to reveal its horrific grin.

'Captain,' said Thorrik, pointing to the east.

Solmundsson dragged his thoughts from the moon and tried to see what Thorrik was referring to. Picking anything out clearly was hard. The moon-light turned the landscape into a glittering mass of spheres, but eventually he saw what Thorrik meant. There was an avenue of standing stones half a mile away from where they were currently flying. They stood out in sharp contrast to their surroundings. Everything else Solmundsson could see was made of metal – either the rusting slabs that formed the ground or the mercurial blobs floating above it – but the two parallel rows of standing stones were chiselled from dull black rock. Those that were nearest towered over the landscape, but each pair of stones was shorter than the previous ones until, eventually, at the far end of the colonnade, they vanished from view. 'I see it. What of it?'

'The squig,' said Thorrik, struggling to be heard over the storm.

The creature was being led down the centre of the colonnade. As it waddled past the stones it was disappearing from view, and Solmundsson realised his mistake. The stones did not get shorter as they progressed – they flanked a slope that headed beneath the ground. Grots were running alongside the squig, struggling to stay on their feet in the metal-laden wind.

He nodded and grinned at Thorrik.

Gotrek shuffled in his seat, trying to see, nearly dislodging Solmundsson in the process. 'What is it?'

'A way down,' replied Solmundsson. 'The entrance to the Asylum is buried somewhere beneath Skrappa Spill. And if our friends are heading down that slope, this may well be one of the ways to approach it. Get us down there,' he said. 'And keep us out of sight.'

Thorrik nodded and steered the gunhauler down through the banks of floating ore.

'I'm a son of the Everpeak,' said Gotrek. 'I don't mind hiding your boat, but I'm not going to skulk like a damned aelf.'

Solmundsson was beginning to get the measure of the Slayer. Arguing directly with him was pointless. Subtlety was needed. 'Then we'll make our stand at the entrance. I had hoped to see the inside of the place and maybe even the Loonking himself, but a glorious battle with his guards will suffice. We should take dozens down before they overwhelm us. We should still be able to create enough of a distraction.'

Gotrek glared at him. 'If there's one thing I can't bear it's a clever dick. I see what you're trying to do and it won't work. You two can creep around all you like, but I won't cower before grots. If there are grobi nearby, they're going to feel the sharp end of my axe.'

Solmundsson studied the violence in Gotrek's face. His hatred for greenskins surpassed anything he had ever seen before. It radiated from him like a heat haze.

'This is personal for you, isn't it?' he asked. 'You bear a grudge against them.'

'More than one, beardling.' His eye darkened. 'I've seen how they can crush the life from a people.'

Thorrik landed the gunhauler a hundred feet or so from the avenue of standing stones, dropping it down in the shadows behind a cone-shaped lump of iron. Rust clouds billowed around the three duardin as they climbed down from the ladder. The iron cone was the size of a large hill, and by heaping slabs of rusty iron over the gunhauler they did a pretty good job of hiding it. Then, as Gotrek climbed up the cone's side, peering out across the plains towards the standing stones, Thorrik grabbed Solmundsson by the arm and spoke in an urgent whisper.

'Captain. What's your plan? He can't fight his way through a whole army, even if he thinks he can. And if we do make it down that slope, what would we do then?'

Solmundsson nodded confidently. 'I have no idea.'

Thorrik's expression turned thunderous. He had served with the Lord Admiral when Solmundsson was an infant and sometimes seemed to forget that Solmundsson was his superior. 'No idea?'

'What would *you* have done?' asked Solmundsson. 'Let the Slayer head off on his own, taking that rune beyond our reach? Then return to Barak-Urbaz and tell my father to ready himself for defeat?'

'Defeat? What defeat, captain? What do you mean?'

'Since Kazak-drung returned the Moonclans are strangling us. Did you know the Zakhain fort was taken last month? And Bartakh Keep the week before that.'

Thorrik paled.

Solmundsson nodded. 'The admiralty haven't disclosed half our losses for fear of losing trade. Who'd want to invest in fleets from a city about to fall?'

Thorrik laughed grimly. 'Barak-Urbaz is not about to fall.'

'Half of our supply routes are impassable, Thorrik. And these are not random attacks. The Moonclans are cutting us off. Each night the moon grows bigger and each night they grow more ambitious. Any time now the moon will be full, and they're getting ready for it. Readying themselves for an attack on Barak-Urbaz. All the admirals have told my father the same story – there's an attack coming like nothing we've faced before. And it will happen when the moon waxes full.' He nodded at Gotrek, scrambling up the slope above them. 'But that rune could change everything. I've never seen anything so powerful. Whatever the Fyreslayers intended to make, that rune has become something else. I think it has reacted somehow with the power of the Slayer. He says he's from another world, and if that's true it might explain why the rune has been transformed.' He leant close to Thorrik. 'He has no idea of its real value. The aetheric currents I measured with the burning glass were enormous. We could combine the output of every buoyancy endrin in our fleet and still not match it. I've never seen anything like it. I can understand why Maleneth wanted to keep it to herself.'

Thorrik looked up at Gotrek. 'But how does coming here help us? Whatever he's got in his chest, we can't take on the entire grot nation.'

Solmundsson waved at the shapes drifting overhead and the leering moon. 'This is all building to a head. We have to do something. And crawling back to Barak-Urbaz with bad news would help no one. We'd probably arrive just in time to watch the place burn. Here is where we could actually make a difference. If we can get the Slayer into the Asylum the greenskins will think they've missed something terrible. They'll think we're launching a counter-attack. They'll drag back their armies in a panic. They're a cowardly breed. If they think their home is being plundered they'll rush back here as fast as their runty little legs will carry them. Meanwhile, the moon will wax full and they'll miss their chance.'

Thorrik sniffed hard and looked at Gotrek again, watching the Slayer as he bounded back down the slope of the pyramid. 'You know he's insane.'

Solmundsson gripped Thorrik's arm. 'We have a chance. Do you see? If we get him down there we have a chance.' He shook his head, thinking about the moon overhead but refusing to look at it. 'But if we head back now we have nothing.'

'We'll die in there.'

Solmundsson nodded. He placed his hand over the Solmund Company rune on his flight suit. 'But Barak-Urbaz might live.'

They stood in silence, watching Gotrek march back towards them through the downpour. Silver spray bounced off his massive shoulders, shimmering like a halo. There was no sign he had noticed the hideous moon. No sign of doubt in his eye. He looked unstoppable.

Thorrik thought for a moment, then nodded, clapping his hand over the symbol on his chest.

CHAPTER TWENTY-FIVE

Maleneth cursed as another puffball lurched towards her through the rain. She had already used half the seeds and could not risk wasting more. She lashed out with her makeshift knife and opened a gash in the puffball's side. The thing was taller than her, and as she cut it open, spores billowed from the wound. She flipped away through the swamp, her hand over her mouth as she managed to find one of the few patches of solid ground. She scrambled up a muddy slope and turned to see the puffball tumble up it towards her, still trailing spores.

You need to get out of here, you idiot.

How would I manage without your wonderful insights? she thought, leaping over the fungus, landing on the opposite side of the hollow and sprinting away. She left the shuffling predator behind, clambered up another rain-slick incline and then, as she crested the brow of the hill, nodded in satisfaction. She was still in the toadstool forest, but she was looking down over a glum, sodden track criss-crossed with rows of boot prints. It was the route the grots had been leading her along before they made the detour to the river. In one direction she could see the distant shape of Slathermere, its colossal head staring through the drizzle. In the other direction the road trailed off through tumbling, fungus-crowded hills before disappearing into the darkness.

Her mistress spoke with grudging respect. *You've found the way out. You must have stumbled across this road by accident. I don't credit you with the wit to have memorised the route.*

Maleneth shook her head. *The routes aren't constant. This place changes every time the fungi move. Memorising routes is exactly the kind of point-less exercise you would have spent your time on. I was following these.* She nodded to a trail of blue shells lying in the mud. It was the remains of the food Stinkeye had been handing out to flagging grots. She smiled as her mistress seethed in silence.

Maleneth stayed in the fungal forest, keeping back from the road and out of sight, but she began following its route back through the hills, heading towards the point where she had first seen the marsh. She was accompanied by the endless groans and prayers of the figures trapped in the toadstools, and some of them, seeing her bottle, cried out in desperation, grasping and shuddering as she rushed past. Maleneth ignored their pleas, lashing out with her knife whenever a tendril came too close.

She followed the road for nearly an hour and began to wonder if she had made a mistake.

Her mistress stirred again. *They might not be the only grots out here eating blue grubs. This might not be the same road.*

'It is.' Maleneth looked back at the gargant head, still visible in the distance, haloed by cold lights. 'That's Slathermere.' She spotted a rock jutting out of a stagnant pool and jumped lightly up onto it, looking out across the fungus colonies, squinting into the gloom.

What are you looking for? Just keep following the damned road. If you're so sure it's the right one it will lead to the cave mouth. Or the door. Whatever it is, the entrance to this place must be so big even you won't be able to miss it.

I'm not looking for the way out. Maleneth batted away flies and climbed higher up the rock. *I'm not going anywhere without Scragfang.*

The fungus has rotted your brain. You've just left Scragfang. He's back there with his friends, by the river.

I had to escape. I can't do this alone. Do you remember the burnt grot? The one they called Stinkeye? It was a sorcerer. I wouldn't have got two steps with Scragfang before Stinkeye used its potions on me. And Scragfang is a shaman too. In fact, none of that group are normal grots. Getting away from them was easy enough, but I'll need help getting Scragfang out of here. She grinned. *And there it is.*

What in Khaine's teeth are you babbling about?

Maleneth did not bother to reply. She leapt down from the rock, almost slid over in the mud, then rushed on down an avenue of muttering fungi.

She paused at the edge of the road, looking in both directions, then dashed across the track to a toadstool on the far side.

The Azyrite sorcerer recognised her as she approached him. 'You came back.' He started struggling with such violence that the toadstool quivered and spewed a cloud of spores.

Maleneth stepped back, keeping her hand over her mouth, glaring at the aelf.

The wizard stopped moving. 'Stay. I beg you. Help me.' The fungus had covered more of him since Maleneth last saw him. Only his face and one arm were still visible. Maleneth guessed that eventually even they would be gone. She looked around and saw that all the surrounding fungi were growing at an incredible rate, seeming to have doubled in size since she first saw them. 'What's happening?' She was not really expecting an answer, but the aelf replied in strangled tones.

'It's the moon. It's almost full. It's affecting the Asylum even more than the rest of Ayadah. Spreading the grot madness, gods help us.'

She laughed. 'I don't think we're in the gods' thoughts at the moment, my friend. Not down here in this... in whatever this place is.' She looked up, glimpsing stalactites hanging overhead. 'Is it a cave?'

The aelf must have been in agony but he gave no sign of it. He spoke in soft, considered tones. 'The Asylum exists outside reality. It is reached through Skrappa Spill, but it is actually something else entirely. It follows its own rules.' His eyes rolled in the toadstool's flesh as he looked up and down the road. 'The greenskins are not the lumbering morons we thought. Not all of them, at least. These moon-worshipping clans have mastered a crude form of sorcery. It's unlike anything we have studied in Azyr.' He hesitated. 'You are from Azyr, aren't you? I sensed it when you looked at me. We're kin, you and I. Is that why you came back? Have you come to save me?'

Why are you wasting your time on this wretch? If he had any power would he be trapped like this?

'Are you a sorcerer?' she asked.

'I am Cerura of Dinn-tor. And yes, I am an adept of the Eldritch Council. And I have also studied with the magisters who reside in the Towers of the Eight Winds. I have mastery over the elements and I have–'

'You're currently trapped in a toadstool,' interrupted Maleneth, annoyed by the wizard's pompous tone. 'So you do not appear to have mastery over very much.'

'The grots tricked me. One of them disguised itself as an adept of my own order. It offered me a talisman of immense power. And when I touched the thing I passed into a deep sleep. When I awoke I was here.'

Maleneth nodded. 'But is your power intact? Or would it be if you were freed from your prison? Does your magic live in your flesh? Or would you require philtres and charms?'

'My power is intact. I require no talismans.' Cerura spoke with the calm gravitas of someone who was used to being listened to. 'My power resides in my mind. If the grots had not tricked me I could have burned the skin from their bones. Or frozen the blood in their veins. But, more importantly, if you free me we will have no problem leaving the Asylum. I have the means to pass through the magicae semita.'

'The what?'

'The portal. Do you recall your passage into the Asylum? When you passed through the–'

'I was not awake when they brought me in. I saw nothing.'

'Then you do not understand the nature of our prison. There is only one way out of here. The Asylum is bound to reality at a single point. A form of Realmgate. A lesser form, it has to be said, but it behaves in the same way. I could not study it in any detail, but I have the measure of it.' He laughed bitterly. 'I have had plenty of time to think. I have gleaned the incantations that would be required to use the gate and leave.'

'Is the gate not guarded?'

'Heavily guarded. But we would have no need to approach it. I have the measure of it, friend. I have it in my mind's eye. I could use it as an aetheric fulcrum. There would be no need to actually approach it or even pass through it. Free me and I can take us both out of here. I could cast us back into Skrappa Spill.'

'You're describing very powerful magic, wizard. I've met members of your order before. None of them claimed they could hurl people from one realm to another.'

'I can do this. If the Asylum were a true realm, it would be a different matter. Passing through a Realmgate is the only way to move between true realms. Even I could not circumnavigate the usual methods if that were the case. But the Asylum is something else. It is an anomaly – a kind of simulacrum of a realm produced by unstable greenskin magic. A sub-realm, if you will. I have the ability to cast us through its gate. You will have to trust me.'

'I don't *have* to do anything.'

'It is not my power that will free us,' he said. 'I would be harnessing the power of the Asylum Gate. I would simply be doing it from a distance.'

'Simply?'

Cerura looked at her with the unshakeable confidence Maleneth had seen before in adepts of the Eldritch Council. 'Simple for *me*.'

Maleneth walked around the toadstool, tapping it with her knife. 'In which case, it should also be simple for you to free yourself from your prison. There are no greenskins watching over you. Why not turn your magic on this toadstool? Why have you remained here all this time?'

'My mind is not my own. I am crippled in here. This growth is locked around my thoughts, gripping my soul. It has robbed me of my art. If I try to pierce the aetheric veil all I see is the moon grinning back at me. Look around. I am not alone. There are other sorcerers in the same situation. Most of these captives are magic users of one kind or another. The greenskins are using us. Filling us with thoughts of their moon. Dragging visions from our pain. Cut me out and I will be able to see clearly again.'

Maleneth shook her head. 'You'd bleed to death. Your flesh is bonded with that thing. You're part of it now.'

'Then why did you come back?' Despite the grotesque absurdity of his predicament, Cerura retained his calm. 'You noticed me when you passed here before and you have returned to find me. You are here with a purpose. You must have some reason to want me free.' He looked her up and down, and his gaze fell on the bottle of seeds at her belt. 'And some way to free me.'

Maleneth nodded, pleased to see he was not a fool. 'I have a reason. I seek a way out, like you, but I have someone to find first.'

'Who?'

'The grot called Scragfang.'

'The leader?' Cerura looked towards Slathermere. 'You would have to enter the fortress.'

Maleneth nodded.

'I could do it,' said Cerura. 'I could mask our forms. We could enter unseen. But why? What business do you have with Scragfang?'

Maleneth looked at her knife. 'Khaine's business.'

CHAPTER TWENTY-SIX

Solmundsson cursed as a chunk of iron clanged against his helmet, causing him to stumble against First Officer Thorrik. The closer they got to the avenue of standing stones, the more violent the rust storm became. Gotrek seemed oblivious, striding on through the sparkling torrent, but Solmundsson could barely fight through the wind. And it was not just his muscles that were straining. Every step seemed to rob him of more sanity. He could see the moon's face constantly now, even without looking at it, and the air was so full of drifting metal that it was hard to distinguish the ground from the sky.

'Captain!' Thorrik struggled to be heard over the howling wind. 'There are grots down there. He won't get much further without being seen.'

Gotrek was approaching the beginning of the slope that led down beneath the ground. He was shrouded by dust clouds, but if the wind changed direction he would be visible for all to see. Grots were hurrying up the slope, passing the standing stones and moving out onto the plain.

'Gotrek!' cried Solmundsson, stumbling after the Slayer. 'Wait! We'll be seen! You have to...' His words trailed off as he saw how many grots were rushing up the slope. There were thousands of them. Some were marching in ragged formation, holding their spears aloft, and others were hurtling past the standing stones on squigs or giant spiders, clinging desperately to their steeds and laughing hysterically. There were also larger creatures ambling through the crowds, towering, hideous troggoths covered in warts and fungus, their long, powerful arms trailing behind them through the rust. Many of the grots were playing musical instruments and the sounds of whistles, gongs and drums echoed down the colonnade. The grots made no attempt to play in time with each other and the din was dreadful, like hundreds of instruments falling down a ravine.

Solmundsson dragged Gotrek behind another block of iron and Thorrik hurried over to join them.

'We need to get into their lair if we're going to cause a really big stir,' said Solmundsson. 'And even you couldn't fight through that many grots. Don't make your stand out here. Don't die unnoticed.'

Gotrek shrugged him off and opened his mouth to say something dismissive. Then he frowned, looking at the rows of grots marching past. 'Maybe you're right. It would be good to get down there into their lair and cause some real damage.'

Solmundsson nodded. 'There must be a way to get down that slope. We could kill some grots and take their armour. It's hard to see anything in this weather. They won't notice we're duardin.'

Gotrek stared at Solmundsson in disbelief. 'I'm not dressing up as a bloody goblin.'

Solmundsson could see that there would be no point arguing, so he looked back down at the grots, trying to think of another idea. 'We need to get you a chance to fight where it matters.'

'Then use one of your fancy machines,' said Gotrek. 'They must be useful for something. Some clever engineering. Something to hurl us past the guards so we can reach the gate. If Makaisson were here he'd...' The name seemed to dampen the fire in Gotrek's eye and he lost his thread. 'Subtlety has never been my strong point. I leave that to the aelf. She can...' His words trailed off again and he looked even more morose. Then he noticed the box at Solmundsson's belt. 'What's in there? One of your clockwork pistols? Perhaps you could draw their attention with a few well-placed shots while I make a dash for it?'

Solmundsson shook his head, holding the box protectively. 'It's the burning glass. It's not a weapon. Well, not in the way you mean.'

'It must be some bloody use. What was it you said? Powerful enough to defy physics. Able to separate element from element. You were happy to sing its praises in Barak-Urbaz. Put it to a practical use.'

Solmundsson shook his head. 'I can't shoot grots with it, if that's what you mean. It can divide matter or transform it. It can alter the physical make-up of things.'

'Then I'll just go down there and take them all on. If I hit them hard enough I'll be down that slope before they know I'm there.'

'No.' Solmundsson put his hand on Gotrek's shoulder. 'Wait. I think you're on to something. I could use the lens – I'm just trying to think how.'

Gotrek shrugged. 'Turn the grots into something. Turn them into squigs and make them eat each other.'

'It doesn't work that way. It works on metal. I could have extracted your rune if I'd had enough power, but I couldn't alter what you are. It's not a disguising machine.'

'It works on metal?' Gotrek waved his axe at their surroundings. The landscape was heaped with blocks of iron and copper and the storm was hurling rust and silvery globules all around them. 'If only there was some of that around.'

Solmundsson looked at the spheres and cubes. 'They do look malleable. The burning glass could manipulate them.' He patted a row of tins clipped to his flight suit. 'And I have enough aetheric cells to fuel a temporary trans-mutation. I couldn't achieve a genuine transmutation, but I could produce something that would last a little while. I suppose we could–'

His thought went unfinished as a thin shriek filled the air. They looked around and came face to face with a grot. The bony little wretch was looking down at them in horror from the top of an iron slab. It turned to flee, then slammed to the ground with Gotrek's axe in its back. The Slayer thudded up the slope, wrenching the axe free in time to bat away an arrow that whistled towards him from the shadows.

Solmundsson and Thorrik raced up the slope and saw half a dozen grots sprinting away from them, shrieking and cursing.

The duardin both drew pistols, filling the air with sparks as they opened fire. Three of the grots tumbled to the ground but the others vanished into the darkness.

Gotrek laughed. 'Not much chance of skulking now.' He looked back at Solmundsson. 'Whatever we're going to try, we need to try it quickly.' He tapped the box containing the burning glass. 'So, can you use this to alter one of the metal blocks?'

Solmundsson nodded.

Gotrek gave them both a feral grin. 'I've got an idea.'

CHAPTER TWENTY-SEVEN

Maleneth stepped back and raised her knife as Cerura walked towards her. He bore all the hallmarks of a powerful sorcerer. She was taking a risk by freeing him. Whatever his allegiance to Azyr, he had never met her before. He was also likely to be quite insane by this point.

Cerura stared at the smouldering remains of the toadstool that had imprisoned him, then looked at his long, elegant limbs, turning them and trying to spot any sign of fungus. 'It worked,' he whispered, emotion finally creeping into his voice. His ceremonial robes were torn and filthy, but the body underneath was whole. He patted himself down, seeming unable to quite believe what had happened. 'I've been here months. Years, perhaps. And every day a little more of me vanished into that... into that thing.' He looked hard at Maleneth, his eyes glittering with emotion. 'Sigmar preserve you. You saved me.'

Maleneth lowered her blade. She was skilled enough at lying to see that Cerura's gratitude was genuine. For a moment, she had a glimpse of how it might feel to be Gotrek. She had seen this look of devotion in the eyes of everyone the Slayer inadvertently saved. Gotrek had no desire for worshippers, but he amassed them all the same. People saw his lack of fear. His refusal to kneel, even to the gods. And they loved him for it. Gotrek was rude, ill-mannered and obstinate, but people often looked at him the way Cerura was now looking at Maleneth.

The wizard held one of his palms out into the rain and whispered something. Green flames blossomed from his hand and hovered above his skin, turning and dripping as they formed the shape of a griffin. Then Cerura whispered again and the fire vanished, filling Maleneth's vision with a bright afterimage.

'My power is undiminished. All is as it was.' He approached Maleneth, and for a dreadful moment she thought he might hug her. Instead, he dropped to one knee and bowed his head. 'I am your servant. You have given me back everything I thought lost. I will ensure you escape this realm, even if it takes my life to do it.'

She turned and looked back down the road. 'First we need to enter Slathermere and find its lord. I will not leave until Scragfang is in my grasp.'

Cerura nodded. Then he frowned, looking her up and down. 'Why did Scragfang bring you here?' He waved at the tormented faces swaying gently all around them in the darkness. 'He brings magic users here – witches and prophets. Do you have the gift of seersight? Or divination? Are you able to project your thoughts into the mind of another?'

Maleneth thought of the amulet at her neck and her ability to talk to her dead mistress, but she decided that was not what Cerura was referring to. 'I pay tribute to Khaine,' she said. 'Tributes of blood. Acts of devotion performed in the heat of battle. And he often answers my prayers, gifting me the strength to fight with greater elegance and skill.' She shrugged. 'Is that what you mean?'

'No. Not that.' He shook his head. 'You say Scragfang chose you specifically?'

'Well, he was floating in a muddy river while his underlings did the work, but they presented me to him like a fatted calf. And he was ecstatic to see me.' Fury washed through her at the memory. 'I was stolen to order.'

'I wonder why he wanted you in particular?'

'I think he had some absurd notion that my companions would come and rescue me.' She gave Cerura a suspicious look. 'Are you sure you can do this? Scragfang's followers looked like they had powers of their own.' She glanced at her bottle. 'I still have a few seeds left. Perhaps I should search for some more Azyrite scholars?'

Cerura looked at the bottle. 'How many are there?'

'Five.'

'Keep them. Most of these people have been here longer than me. Look at them. I doubt they could remember their own names, never mind where their allegiance lies. And even if they were sane enough to understand you, they would most likely flee. But you may still have need of those seeds before you leave here. It would only take one unfortunate injury or one bad fall for you to suffer another transformation. How would you heal yourself if all the seeds have been used?'

'You just told me you are all-powerful. Surely you could heal me if I started sprouting again. In fact, why would I need to use the seeds at all? Can't you drag some of these people out of their prisons?'

'Greenskin magic springs from another source entirely than my own art. A source I have no knowledge of. These particular grots seem to get their power from the moon.' He grimaced at the pale shapes scattered all around them. 'I tried for months to unearth its mysteries. As, I've no doubt, did all of these other poor souls. Nothing I do has any effect.' He looked at her bottle again. 'Where did you get those seeds?'

'From one of Scragfang's grots. The one that looks like burnt scraps.'

Cerura nodded. 'Use them sparingly.'

How is he going to get you into Slathermere if he has no power over greenskin magic? Do not waste your time on this failure. You should be looking for the way out.

Maleneth studied the sorcerer's wasted body and tattered robes, wondering if her mistress had a point. 'How will you get me into Scragfang's fortress if you can't understand his magic?'

Cerura waved at the fungal shapes lining the road. 'I can't release these poor souls, but I can harness the elements. The grots' version of nature is beyond my understanding, but true nature is my willing servant.' He reached out into the drizzle and the rain formed a silvery vortex above his palm, dancing and flashing as it turned. The column pulsed brighter and then washed over the sorcerer, enveloping him in a blanket of rain.

Maleneth was about to speak when she realised Cerura was no longer visible. There was nothing in front of her except the endless downpour. 'Where are you?' She felt a moment's alarm at the thought he might have tricked her.

'Still here,' he said, his voice coming from the same place as before. The rain shimmered and Cerura reappeared.

Maleneth nodded. 'Impressive. And what if it's not raining inside Slathermere? Might we not look a bit conspicuous?'

'Any of the elements will serve me, Maleneth. There is always something I can harness – smoke, shadow, mist. There will be a way.'

'Good.' Maleneth was not surprised by his power. She had survived longer than most of her kind because she had developed the ability to judge people at a glance. The first time she saw Cerura's stern, unyielding features she had known he was a powerful figure. Everything she had said to him since was simply to confirm what she already knew. 'Then weave your spells,' she said. 'We must move fast. Scragfang seems to think he will gain great power once the moon is full. And I think that will be any time now.'

Cerura looked at the frenzied growth surrounding the road and nodded. Then he held his hand up and cast rain over them like a net.

Maleneth smiled as she looked down and saw that she was completely hidden. She had to pat her limbs to believe they were still there. Cerura had vanished too, and a passer-by would have seen nothing but an empty road and the remains of a man-sized toadstool. She jogged quickly down the road, heading for Slathermere. Then she halted and looked back. 'Cerura?'

'Here.' His voice came from a few feet away.

'How will you follow me?'

'It is I who have woven the glamour, Maleneth, so it has no power over my eyes. I can see you with absolute clarity.'

Something about the words 'absolute clarity' troubled Maleneth. What was he implying? She touched the amulet at her throat, thinking of all the secrets it contained. She wavered for a moment, feeling a vague premonition of danger. Then, seeing she had little choice, she nodded and ran on, joining herself to the rain.

CHAPTER TWENTY-EIGHT

'Calm down.' Mangleback was circling Scragfang's throne room, showing no sign of following his own advice. 'Gettin' in a tizz won't help.'

Scragfang was hunched on his throne, feeling oppressed by the grandeur of the chamber. It had been carved from the thickest part of the gargant's skull, worked by sorcery and the toil of slaves until it resembled a natural cave, complete with stalactites and patches of lichen. Like the rest of Slathermere, it had been a gift from the Loonking – a reward for all the visions Scragfang unearthed in the Gibbermarsh. Everything he had stemmed from his loyalty to the Loonking. How could he have thought about deceiving him? 'I shoulda told 'im about da vision. He needs ta know dat da Fyreslayer's rune is the key ta melting Barak-Urbaz. When 'e finds out wot I done 'e's gonna feed me to my own squigs.'

'Rubbish.' Stinkeye was sitting on the steps beneath the throne, looking for something in his robes. 'Nuffin has gone wrong. Trust da moon.'

'Nuffin's wrong?' Scragfang lurched from his throne and began pacing around the room with Mangleback. 'Da zoggin aelf has gone wrong. She's loose in the marsh. Wanderin' about like she owns the place, deciding how she's gonna kill me.'

Stinkeye laughed. 'Fink 'ow many grots are between you an' 'er.'

Scragfang clutched his head and shook it with both hands, trying to shake out the fear. Stinkeye was right. Events were preceding exactly as his vision had shown him. They had got Maleneth to the Asylum and scouts had already brought word from the gates that Gotrek was following. The rune was probably already in the Asylum and headed his way. 'Wot if the Fyreslayer finds Maleneth before he gets to Slathermere? I told 'im to come 'ere, but why's 'e gonna bovver if 'e meets Maleneth first? He might leave without ever comin' 'ere.' He waved his blade at the source of the light that filled the chamber. There was an altar in the centre of the hall. It was a shallow iron bowl balanced on a crooked pedestal and filled with loonlight. The light was cool and soothing, rippling over the craggy walls and giving the chamber the feel of an underwater grotto. ''E's gotta be near dat light when da Bad Moon is ready. That's wot I saw.'

Stinkeye rose from the steps, his charred skin creaking as he limped over to him. 'So wot exactly did ya see in da marsh?' He gave Mangleback a suspicious look. ''E ain't never told me exactly.'

Scragfang headed over to the altar and stared into it, whispering the words that had been circling inside his head for weeks.

Splitskulls worming, dripping clagg,
Withering sprouts and mucal gag,
Lurking greylugs ooze and drag,
Scragfang, Scragfang, splitting clagg.
Bringing ruin, bringing slag,
Scragfang, Scragfang, dripping clagg.

'Wot's it mean?' asked Stinkeye. 'It makes no zoggin sense.'

Mangleback shrugged. 'Seems clear ta me. When da Bad Moon is full, Scragfang will get da Slayer in da loonlight an' take his power. But it only works if da Fyreslayer's 'ere, right in the middle of Slathermere. Dat's why I 'ad dis pool made, bringin' da light down 'ere.'

Stinkeye frowned, rummaging in his robes again. Then he nodded and looked back at Scragfang. 'Dat's all good. Da Fyreslayer will come 'ere.'

Scragfang was still worried. ''Ow can I be sure? 'Ow can I know 'e won't bump inta Maleneth first?'

Stinkeye hobbled across the room, juddering and spilling embers from his skin. He jabbed Scragfang with a crooked finger. 'You know cuz da Bad Moon showed you.'

Scragfang shook his head, staring into the altar. 'Da moon shows me tonnes of stuff, Stinkeye.' He looked up into the shadows and saw the feet that hounded him constantly. They were circling above him, their toes linked and their wings flapping furiously. 'Least, I fink it's da moon.'

Mangleback scuttled over and stood with them next to the altar, nodding eagerly. ''E's right, Scragfang. Fink wot 'appened on the sky-boat. Da moon led us straight to 'im and we gutted all dem stunties before dey knew wot was goin' on. Your dreams were true, Scragfang.' He waved one of his limbs at the throne. 'Lord of Slathermere ain't enough. Da Bad Moon wants more for ya, Scragfang. You 'is da zoggin chosen one.'

Scragfang frowned. 'Any more word of da Fyreslayer?'

Mangleback shook his head. 'But don'tcha see? 'E's 'ere, in Skrappa Spill. 'E's followed us back. Dat's all we needs ta know. It's exactly wot ya saw in the Gibbermarsh. It's all comin' true. Everyfin.'

Scragfang took a deep, juddering breath and nodded. 'Yer right.' He kept looking at the bowl of loonlight, letting it burn through his eyes. 'Yer always right, Mangleback.'

Mangleback grinned. His face was so distorted by his fungal carapace that the smile looked more like a grimace, but Scragfang found it as reassuring as ever. Mangleback had never led him wrong before.

As Scragfang stared into the light, snatches of the vision whirled around his head. He saw the Slayer's rune, radiating incredible power. He saw himself, in his throne room, approaching Gotrek, knife raised and giggling. The Fyreslayer was crippled and weighed down by slabs of fungus that were crushing the life out of him. In the vision, Scragfang was laughing as he brought his loonblade down towards Gotrek's rune. Then there was a glorious wave of destruction – an eruption of flames and toppling walls, culminating in the fall of the golden face that fronted the main building in Barak-Urbaz. He nodded, dragging his thoughts back to the throne room. ''E's zoggin tough. Are we ready?'

Mangleback grinned again, scuttling over to the throne room doors and waving for them to follow. They walked out onto a circular path that surrounded the vast atrium at the heart of Slathermere. The path spiralled around the walls in a confusing mess of loops and curls, and it was crowded with grots that were readying weapons and strapping on armour.

'That's a lot,' muttered Scragfang. He only had a vague grasp of what a hundred meant, but he was sure that he was looking at lots of hundreds of grots. He scratched at the fungus on the back of his head. 'We needs 'im ta survive, Mangleback. It's no use killin' 'im before he can reach da loonlight.'

Mangleback laughed. 'D'ya remember what happened on dat cloud boat? 'E woulda butchered all of us if we'd not scarpered. 'E's some kinda stuntie daemon.'

Scragfang winced. 'Daemon?'

'Don't worry,' said Stinkeye, his bottles rattling as he limped out of the throne room. 'Da Bad Moon's got yer back. Yer gonna be fine.'

CHAPTER TWENTY-NINE

The *Angaz-Kár* cut through the metal storm. Its endrins flashed in the moonlight as it banked majestically over Skrappa Spill. The crew were lined up along the railings, their uniforms immaculate and their cutlasses gleaming. It was half a mile from the colonnade of standing stones that led underground, but the grots saw it immediately and a great hubbub broke out. Solmundsson was still watching from behind the metal cone with Gotrek and Thorrik, but his spyglass revealed the mayhem in wonderful detail. The grot leaders hurried to consult, clearly panicked by the sight of a Kharadron ironclad coming in to land within shooting distance of where they were standing. Their monster steeds snapped and snarled at each other as the grots argued and yelled. Meanwhile, the ranks of spear-carrying troops began to mill around in confusion. Some carried on marching out into the plains, headed towards the landing ship, raising their weapons, and others scampered back down the slope, wailing in terror. Finally, the leaders managed to agree and began yelling orders. There was a great ringing of shrill horns and most of the grots formed into units again, changing direction and marching towards the *Angaz-Kár* with their leaders in the vanguard.

'It's working,' whispered Solmundsson, not quite able to believe it.

'Course it's working,' said Gotrek, striding out from behind the rock and making for the avenue of stones.

'Wait!' cried Thorrik. 'They're not all gone yet.'

'I don't want them *all* to go,' cried Gotrek over his shoulder. 'Where would the fun in that be?'

Solmundsson and Thorrik ran after him, pistols raised and cutlasses drawn, as he headed for the slope.

All the confusion had kicked up even more rust clouds, and as the three duardin approached the two lines of standing stones, Solmundsson felt like he was stumbling through a fire. The stones were hundreds of feet tall, but even they were hard to see clearly as the clouds banked around them. There were smaller shapes dashing past – grots, he presumed – but he fixed all his attention on the Slayer's back. If he lost sight of Gotrek, he would have no chance of making it down the slope into the lair.

'Ai!' howled Gotrek as a row of grots appeared in front of him, seeming to materialise from the rust clouds. One of them fired an arrow, but Gotrek batted it away with his axe and sent it clattering across the ground. Then he picked up the terrified grot and hurled it at the others, toppling them like he was playing ninepins.

Most of the grots bolted, vanishing into the miasma, but Gotrek caught another by its neck and threw it aside before running on.

Moments later they ran into another group of grots. There were far more this time, over thirty, Solmundsson guessed, and their numbers gave them courage. They screamed and charged, waving knives and spears.

Gotrek scythed the first row down and then shouldered into the rest, dealing out a flurry of axe blows.

Solmundsson and Thorrik rushed to his side, cutlasses drawn, cutting down the few grots that evaded Gotrek's axe. Then Gotrek marched on again, passing the base of one of the standing stones and heading out into the middle of the colonnade.

Grots were dashing in every direction and most of them were in such a panic that they barely registered the three duardin running down the slope.

'Look!' cried Thorrik, pointing back the way they had come. The rust clouds had cleared for a moment, revealing a glimpse of the *Angaz-Kár*. 'They've almost reached it.'

'Then we don't have long,' said Solmundsson. 'As soon as they reach the hull they'll see that it's just a facade.'

Gotrek stared at him. 'A facade?'

'I can't create an entire sky-ship. It's just like a piece of set dressing. The illusion will only hold until the grots reach it.'

'Should give me enough time, I suppose,' muttered Gotrek. Then he dashed on down the slope.

The distraction had actually worked better than Solmundsson had hoped. Most of the grots had broken ranks and rushed towards the *Angaz-Kár*. And the few groups they ran into were so terrified by the sight of Gotrek that they barely managed to wail before he hacked them down and ran on.

Eventually, they reached the far end of the slope and headed underground, leaving the moonlight behind along with the din of the grots. The path narrowed from a broad road to a ragged, damp tunnel, crowded with stalactites and stalagmites. As they ran on, leaping over rocks and cutting down grots, they began to leave the rust clouds behind. The air was no clearer though. Banks of yellow spores drifted through the gloom, clogging Solmundsson's face mask, and a dank chill washed over them that seemed to reach right into his bones.

'Damn it,' muttered Gotrek, stumbling to a halt and wiping his face with the back of his hand. 'I can't see a thing.' He coughed and spat. 'And this bloody mist is clogging my lungs.'

'Follow me,' said Solmundsson, hurrying past him. 'Our suits are designed to filter out anything toxic. I can still see.' He clipped a small aether lamp to the barrel of his gun and shone it ahead, picking out a route between moss-covered rocks and forests of sagging cobwebs.

'How did they muster an army down here?' said Thorrik, cursing as he struggled to make his way down the tunnel.

'They're like rats,' muttered Gotrek. 'They'd scurry over this kind of ground faster than you could sprint down a road.'

As if to prove his point, a group of grots turned a corner and came racing towards them. They stumbled to a halt as Solmundsson's light flashed in their eyes, then began screaming furiously, clearly unable to see who they were facing.

Gotrek roared and charged. The sound of his battle cry was enough to spur the greenskins into action. They scattered into the gloom, leaving Gotrek stumbling in circles and spitting curses. 'Cowardly filth! Come back!'

Solmundsson hurried on, pointing his light at the bend in the tunnel. 'We have to keep moving. They'll probably have discovered our ruse by now, and the tribal leaders might have heard that we're down here.'

He turned the next corner and halted. 'What in the name of Grungni is that?'

The other two stopped beside him, grunting in disgust.

Ahead of them, the tunnel opened into a large cavern. It was full of rocks and scummy pools, and they were all lit up by a glow that was not coming from Solmundsson's aether lamp. At the centre of the cave there was a gnarled, pale shape about the size of a grown man.

Solmundsson edged closer to it, holding his cutlass before him. 'A toadstool?'

'Be careful, captain,' warned Thorrik.

Solmundsson shook his head. 'I think it's something they've planted here to give them some light.' His mind began racing as he considered the possibilities. 'I wonder what the chemicals are that make it glow like that? It might be that we could extract some of them and–'

A tendril lashed out from the toadstool's stem and wrapped around Solmundsson's waist, dragging him closer.

Gotrek strode forwards and chopped the toadstool down with a single swing of his axe. Then he cursed as a torrent of milk-like liquid splashed from the severed trunk and washed across his body. 'Bugger,' he muttered, trying to wipe it off. 'Bloody stinks.'

'Captain,' said Thorrik as voices echoed down the tunnels towards them. 'We should keep moving.'

'Aye!' snapped Gotrek, pointing his axe at Solmundsson. 'Just keep away from the mushrooms.'

They circled around the edge of the cavern, keeping clear of the toppled fungus, then left by an opening on the far side. The next tunnel was even more crowded with yellow spores, and they reflected Solmundsson's light back at him with such a dazzling glare that he was almost as blinded as the Slayer. The three of them struggled on, making dozens of lefts and rights with no clear idea of where they were going. Solmundsson had the vague impression that some of the turnings were actually junctions, but there was no time to stop and explore. He could hear footsteps all around them now, echoing through the shadows and merging with the sound of dripping water until it seemed like legions of grots were approaching from every direction.

'Captain,' said Thorrik as they stumbled into a tunnel that was wider than the ones that preceded it. 'Extinguish your lamp for a moment.'

Solmundsson killed the light and could immediately see better. The spores had thinned out a little and he saw that there was a pale light shining somewhere up ahead of them. 'Another one of those toadstools?'

Gotrek shook his head. 'That's coming from something much bigger. Look at those shapes moving past it.'

Solmundsson took out his spyglass and saw that Gotrek was right – there were figures walking around the base of the light. 'How did you see that?'

Gotrek laughed grimly. 'I might only have one eye, but it's the eye of a *real* dwarf. I can see better underground than I can in your cloud town.' He looked back the way they had come. 'At least, I can now we're out of those spores.'

'Are they grots?' asked Solmundsson, looking more closely at the figures near the light. 'They look different.'

'They've got some scraps of armour on, that's all,' said Gotrek, marching off across the cave. 'Let's see what they're guarding. That looks like an entrance to me. I think we've found their lair.'

They hurried down another long tunnel towards the light. They could hear creatures moving in the tunnels all around them – the giggling of grots, the guttural snort of squigs and the skittering sound of giant spiders – but none of them came close enough to be visible. As more waves of spores drifted towards them, clouding their vision and muffling the sounds, Solmundsson had the strange sensation that he was slipping into a dream. There was something odd about the light they were approaching. It seemed to cling to his skin and dazzle his eyes, making him stumble even more than he had in the previous caves.

As they neared the light, he had the horrible feeling that he was approaching the mouth of the monster. The light was framed by what looked like long, crooked teeth, and it seemed to be exhaling the spores that filled the rest of the cave network.

'Gotrek,' he whispered. The sound of his voice was unnaturally loud in his own ears, but neither of his companions seemed to hear him, carrying on down the tunnel. Solmundsson grew so disoriented that he felt drunk, lurching and reeling between the rocks and pools. The light and the spores clouded his thoughts, making him so confused he could barely remember why they were even in the caves. All he could do was keep his gaze locked on the hulking form of the Slayer, watching his tattooed back as if it were a beacon in a storm.

Finally, Gotrek came to a halt at the entrance to another big cavern. It was much larger than any of the ones they had passed through so far, and dozens of cave mouths led into it from other tunnels. The air here was so clouded with spores, Solmundsson could see nothing beyond the light on the far side. Gotrek had been right about its size. It dominated the large cave, looming high up into the air. Solmundsson felt, more than ever, that it was a cavernous maw, preparing to devour them.

Gotrek turned to face him and Thorrik. His face was masked by spores and cobwebs and his eye looked strangely blank, as though he could no longer see them. He yelled something, shouting so loud the veins bulged at his neck, but Solmundsson could not make out his words. They sounded like they were coming from the other side of a thick wall.

'I can't hear you,' he gasped.

Gotrek continued staring blindly past them, looking back down the tunnels and shouting again. Then he shook his head, spat and made his way out into the cave.

Grots rushed at him from every direction. There were dozens of them, gripping knives and spears, and they swarmed over the Slayer, dragging him to the ground.

Solmundsson and Thorrik ran to help, but before they reached Gotrek he rose to his feet and flung off his attackers, sending them tumbling across the cave floor. He yelled again, but again the sound was oddly stifled by the spores. He cut down a few of the grots but most sprinted away from him, terrified.

Gotrek lowered his head and charged across the cave, making straight for the blazing wall of light on the far side. Thorrik hesitated, saying something, but Solmundsson grabbed him by the arm and dragged him after Gotrek.

As Solmundsson ran, trying to keep pace with the charging Slayer, he felt things writhing across the floor, slipping past his boots. He peered down through the spores and saw what looked like tentacles snaking around the rocks. Some were the size of rope, others as thick as his arm, and they were revoltingly gaudy.

The light suddenly dimmed and Solmundsson looked up again. Something had stepped out in front of the opening and was headed straight towards them. It was clearly not a grot. It towered over Gotrek as it reached him, eight or nine feet tall, and it was covered in clumps of fungus. It was dressed in crudely hammered plates of armour and was clutching a stone hammer that was bigger than Gotrek.

'Troggoth!' cried Solmundsson, raising his pistol to shoot.

His shot went wide as a grot charged into him, sending him crashing to the ground.

Thorrik thrust his cutlass through the grot and then kicked it back the way it had come, but dozens more rushed from the shadows, grinning and wielding long knives.

Solmundsson lashed out with his sabre, cutting down one grot as he fired into the face of another. He and Thorrik fought back to back as waves of the creatures scampered towards them.

Solmundsson struggled to keep track of Gotrek for a moment, then saw him tumble into view, hacking wildly at the troggoth, shearing armour and pieces of fungus as he drove it back towards the light.

The Slayer must have been feeling as disoriented as Solmundsson because the troggoth actually managed to land a blow on him, cracking its boulder hammer into Gotrek's chest. There was a flurry of sparks as the Slayer rolled backwards, leapt back onto his feet and raced at the troggoth. He slammed his axe into the creature's leg and sheared it off.

The troggoth staggered, but before it could fall over, the fungus on its thigh sprouted tendrils that spiralled down to the floor and formed into the shape of a new leg. Gotrek and the other two duardin stared in shock as the troggoth laughed, stamped its new foot to test it, then swung its club, dealing Gotrek another hammer blow to the chest.

Solmundsson was too busy fighting grots to follow what happened next, but then, after another barrage of aethershot, he and Thorrik blasted a path through the grots and ran towards the light.

Gotrek staggered back into view, his head low between his shoulders and his axe gripped in both of his boulder-like fists. The troggoth rushed at him again. This time Gotrek cut both legs from under it, and as it slammed to the ground, he leapt into the air and sliced its head off.

Catching sight of Solmundsson, Gotrek yelled, pointing his axe at the wall of light. Then he sprinted into the blaze and vanished from sight.

Solmundsson hesitated for a moment, wondering if he dared follow. He looked back across the cavern and saw hundreds of pairs of red eyes looming from the darkness. 'No choice now,' he whispered. Waving for Thorrik to follow, he ran into the light.

CHAPTER THIRTY

The journey was longer than Maleneth had expected. She had faith in Cerura's magic, so they stuck to the road and the two aelves were as fleet as any of their kind, but the marsh's strange lights made distance hard to gauge and even after an hour's run they seemed no nearer to the gargant's head. It stared blindly at them through the mist and rain, seeming to taunt Maleneth. They came across several groups of greenskins but none of the creatures noticed as the two aelves slipped past them in silence. Maleneth resisted the urge to slaughter the witless things. It would have been no real sport, and the piles of corpses might raise an alarm and prevent her reaching Scragfang. She could not resist blowing the occasional toxin at them as she passed, however, laughing to herself as she heard bodies hit the ground followed by howls of panic and confusion.

After another hour of running, she heard Cerura calling to her from back down the road. He sounded breathless and pained.

There were no grots in sight, so she felt safe in calling back to him. 'What is it? Are you injured?'

The sorcerer shimmered into view, shrugging off his coat of rain. He took a few stumbling steps towards her then dropped to his knees, his face as grey as the mist.

She rushed back to him and helped him to his feet. 'You're wounded.'

He shook his head. 'Just weak. I have not eaten or drunk for months.'

She handed him her water flask, noticing that it was nearly empty. 'Then how are you alive?'

'My prison nourished me.' Cerura looked at the fields of fungi, swaying in the rain. He grimaced. 'I dread to think how. I had no need for food or drink while I was bonded with its flesh.' He finished the flask and looked pained. 'But now my hunger returns with a vengeance. And I have a thirst such as you would not believe.'

'Use your magic. We don't have time for hunting expeditions.'

He shook his head. 'Even I cannot feed on the aethertide, Maleneth. My flesh has the same needs as any other aelf's.' He looked doubtfully at the caps and trunks that surrounded the road. 'I shall have to eat soon. And I must have more water.'

Maleneth handed him some cured meat from a pouch at her belt. As the wizard ate she looked around at the fields. 'I have no idea what any of these things are. I doubt very much that they will provide you with nourishment. They'd be more likely to kill you.' She touched her dry lips with her tongue and looked at the empty flask. 'I need to drink too, though.'

He nodded, swallowing the last of the meat, and looked up into the banks of rain. 'That should not be such a problem.' He held the empty flask up and whispered to it. Some of the rain formed into a funnel and whirled into the flask, filling it in seconds. He took a few swigs and then handed it to Maleneth.

She drank, then hesitated, looking at the flask with suspicion. 'Does this taste odd to you?'

He took the flask, sniffed it, then took another swig. 'There is an aftertaste.' He waved at their surroundings. 'But look where we are. Nothing here is going to be exactly pure.'

Maleneth spat, wishing she had put up with her thirst. 'If this place is a cave, where is the rain coming from?'

Cerura had no answer.

Maleneth fastened the flask back onto her belt. 'Come. The sooner I can get my hands on Scragfang, the sooner we can leave.'

Cerura turned his fingers in the air and robed them in rain. Then they continued running down the road. 'What were you doing when the greenskins captured you?' he asked, his voice coming from nowhere. 'I'm still intrigued as to why Scragfang brought you here.'

'I was travelling with a duardin Slayer. On a Kharadron sky-ship.' She felt a flash of rage as she remembered that she had lost her chance to claim Gotrek's rune. What would she say to her superiors in Azyr? How could she ever return home now?

'An aelf and a Fyreslayer, travelling together? With the Kharadron? Why would you demean yourself by mingling with such low company?'

'Gotrek is not a Fyreslayer. He is...' She hesitated, conscious that Cerura would think her insane if she tried to explain Gotrek. 'He is something else. He claims to be from a world beyond the Mortal Realms.'

'Is that true?'

'No... well, yes, perhaps. He's something of a mystery.' She sneered. 'Even to himself.'

'And it was this mystery that led you to become his travelling companion?'

The wizard was irritatingly close to the mark, so Maleneth decided to change the subject. 'It doesn't matter. I lost him. So he will remain a mystery. But only a fool steals a Daughter of Khaine from her prey. Scholars will have to invent new words for pain when they hear what I have done to Scragfang.'

'Grots,' said Cerura, and they both fell silent as they ran towards another group of greenskins. This one was larger than the others and racing in the same direction as they were. The grots were riding squigs, and it was one of the most absurd sights Maleneth had ever seen. The grots could barely cling to their backs as they scrambled and swerved along the road, snapping at each other and spraying lines of drool through the rain.

As Maleneth reached the greenskins, some of the squigs sensed her presence, snorting and trying to turn back towards her. The riders howled and yanked furiously at their reins, trying to keep the squigs on course, but some of the beasts refused to obey and several bolted towards her.

She drew her knife and dropped into a fighting stance, but before the squigs reached her she felt her feet lift off the ground and realised she was floating up into the rain. By the time the first squig reached her she was so high the monster could do nothing but leap and snarl as she drifted higher.

'They can smell us,' whispered Cerura in her ear. She turned to look at him, but even with his face so close she could not see through his glamour.

The sensation of gliding through the air was wonderful, and Maleneth laughed as she flew over the furious squigs and their riders. 'Can we travel like this all the way?'

She heard a smile in his reply. 'As you wish.'

Leaving the ground allowed them to ignore the road's meandering curves and head straight for Slathermere, but it was still several hours later when they reached the fields that surrounded the mouldering head. Cerura dropped them down in a patch of open ground not far from the road, and Maleneth muttered a curse as she sank knee-deep in mud. 'This whole place is a stinking bog,' she hissed, clambering up onto a rock.

She felt Cerura climb up beside her and they looked around. They could now see that four roads approached Slathermere from different directions, and most of them were busy with traffic. Grots, troggoths and squigs were rushing to and from the gargant's head, and Maleneth noticed that there were also spiders scuttling through the crowds – spiders large enough to carry a grot and, in some cases, large enough to carry several grots. There was no sunlight or moonlight, but the scene was brightly lit all the same. All the surrounding marshes were glittering with pale lights that shone from the bodies in the fungus. And Slathermere itself was coated with so much luminescent mould that it rippled as though it were covered in burning oil.

She took another drink from her flask, grimacing at the yeasty taste, then held it out for Cerura. As the wizard drank, Maleneth realised how exhausted she was. She massaged her face and sighed. Then she snatched her hand back with a gasp. 'What's this?'

Cerura said nothing for a moment, and his silence only made Maleneth more concerned. She ran her hands over her head and whispered a curse. It was covered in tough, fibrous domes. 'Damn it! This place is changing me again!' She turned to Cerura. 'Let me see myself.'

They were so far back from the road that there was little danger of them being seen, and Cerura did as she asked. As Maleneth's limbs reappeared from the rain, she saw that they were as deformed as her head. Pale domes had blossomed all down her forearms. 'Damn this place,' she muttered.

'I have been equally afflicted,' said Cerura, materialising from the rain and holding up his arms. There was fungus all over them, and through the rips in his robes, Maleneth saw growths all over his torso.

'Khaine,' she whispered, placing a tentative hand inside her doublet. Her fingers ran over rows of swellings.

Cerura leant close and held her arm, peering at it. 'They have faces.'

She snatched her arm back and examined the mushroom caps. Each one had a leering, goblinoid face, and Maleneth found it all the more disturbing because the face was familiar. 'Kazak-drung,' she whispered.

'The what?'

'The grot moon. The duardin of Barak-Urbaz call it Kazak-drung.'

Cerura was trying to remain calm, but Maleneth could see he was unnerved. 'This should not have happened. We have not so much as brushed against any fungus. And usually it takes greenskin devilry to cause this kind of transformation.'

Maleneth looked at the flask on her belt. 'It's the water. I could taste mould in it. We've poisoned ourselves.' As she spoke, the mushrooms were sprouting up her neck and nuzzling her chin. The ones on her arms were growing fast, and they were all staring at her with amused expressions. Maleneth had the dreadful feeling that when they reached a certain size they would start speaking to her. She took her knife and cut one of the caps away. It immediately re-sprouted and smiled again.

The seeds, you moron. Her mistress sounded incredulous. *You really could not survive a day if I wasn't here to hold your hand. You still have the seeds you took from Stinkeye.*

Maleneth whispered a prayer of thanks – not to her mistress, but to Khaine. She took the bottle from her belt and frowned at the contents. There were only three seeds left. 'Do you have any of these?' she asked, looking at Cerura.

He shook his head, still staring at the fungus sprouting across his body.

'Blood of Khaine,' she spat, popping one seed into her mouth and giving another to Cerura. 'I am not going to spend the rest of my days stuck in a puddle telling greenskins where to stick their squigs.'

She had barely swallowed the seed when heat radiated from her stomach and spread quickly over her skin. The mushrooms crumbled into powder and washed away in the rain, returning her skin back to its normal state.

'Thank the gods,' gasped Cerura as the fungus washed from his skin. 'And thank you.' He looked at Maleneth. 'You have saved me twice.'

'It won't happen a third time.' She tapped the bottle, causing the last seed to rattle around. 'I may have need of this before I leave here.'

Cerura nodded. Then he looked at Slathermere. 'Once we are in the fortress, I shall show you what I am capable of. You have seen but a fraction of my skills. I will repay the debt.'

Maleneth stood and wiped the muck from her face. 'You'd better.'

CHAPTER THIRTY-ONE

'By the Code,' muttered Solmundsson as something hurtled towards him. It looked like a circle of pale fire, and Solmundsson could do nothing to avoid it. As he raced into the light there was a loud grinding sound, like rocks being crushed together, and sparks danced across his vision. The noise grew so loud that Solmundsson clamped his hands over his helmet, trying to drown out the din. Thorrik was nearby, shouting something, but his words were lost under the roar. The world of colours vanished, replaced by a blinding whiteness, and Solmundsson wondered if he was dying. Was he about to enter the halls of his ancestors?

Then the noise ceased, the light vanished and Solmundsson found himself lying on his back in a muddy puddle with plump, warm raindrops pinging off the faceplate of his helmet.

'First Officer Thorrik?' he said, sitting up and looking around. Thorrik and the Slayer were still with him. The three of them were lying in a boggy hollow, surrounded by groves of misty, starlit trees. No, he realised, not trees. Toadstools. He climbed to his feet and looked around at the peculiar landscape. The surrounding fields were crowded with fungi of every imaginable size and colour – tapered, conical, domed, bulbous, spear-shaped, fleshy, gilled, gaudy and buff-coloured – all of them nodding sadly in the twilight as the rain beat down on their slimy caps.

'Where are we?' he muttered. There was no sign of the cave network they had been running through. Or the grots they had been fighting. And the drizzly, autumnal swamp resembled nothing he had ever seen before in Ayadah. Even the stars were unfamiliar. He looked harder and realised that they were not stars at all. It looked like there were rocks glinting overhead, reflecting lights that were shining up from the fields. He waded through the mud to where Thorrik was sitting, wiping his suit down and picking clods from his helmet. 'Are you hurt?' he asked.

Thorrik shook his head, then stared around in wonder at the rippling fields of mushrooms. 'It's like we've entered another world.'

Gotrek was sitting further up the slope, muttering as he tapped a tobacco pipe on a rock. 'Full of bloody mud.' He held it up and squinted into the bowl. 'Or something *like* mud.' He struggled with tinder and flints, shielding them from the rain, and finally managed to light the pipe. He shook his head. 'Your father's weed is damned good.' Then he leant back against a lichen-covered rock and began to smoke.

'Aren't you wondering where we are?' said Thorrik, stumbling and trying to extract his feet from the mud.

Gotrek had his eye closed and tilted his head back as he savoured the tobacco. 'I don't wonder about much these days. There aren't any surprises left for Gotrek Gurnisson. I've seen a *lot* of strange places.' He blew out a plume of smoke. 'But I've realised it's always worth making time for the simple pleasures.' The smoke coiled around his head, then flickered with the same pale lights that were coming from the mushroom forest. Gotrek eyed the smoke suspiciously, sucked on the pipe again and shrugged.

Solmundsson helped Thorrik from the mud and they both clambered up the rain-drenched grass to the top of the hollow. The fungal groves stretched as far as Solmundsson could see, even when he took out his spyglass, but there were also signs of civilisation – a muddy road snaking through the mist and, in the far distance, a fortress of some kind, shrouded by rain. 'We should head for that keep,' he said. 'We need to find out where we've come.'

'You brought me here,' grunted Gotrek. 'How is it you don't know where we are? I've heard so much talk about the navigation skills of you Kharadron, but as far as I can tell, you could get lost in your own larder.'

'I don't think this is Skrappa Spill,' said Solmundsson, looking around at the towering mushrooms and bloated puffballs. 'It doesn't look like any part of Ayadah that I've ever heard of.' He trudged over to a toadstool as big as a full-grown oak and reached out to touch its glistening flesh. His fingers were inches away when a mouth opened in its stem, revealing rows of long, needle-thin teeth. The toadstool growled as its mouth gaped wider, the cavernous maw growing as big as Solmundsson. He was so shocked that he remained where he was as the toadstool began moving towards him, sliding through the mud.

There was a bang and a flash of light and the toadstool toppled away from him, a charred hole in its stem.

Thorrik marched past Solmundsson, his pistol still raised, and fired until the toadstool let out a moist gargle and lay still, trailing black spores from its wounds.

Gotrek waved his pipe at the dead fungus. 'That is *slightly* unusual, to be fair.'

A rustling sound sprang up all around them as the rows of fungi started to move, shuffling towards them with a peculiar mix of lurches, lunges and spasms. Some of the stems split to reveal teeth, like the toadstool Thorrik had shot, but others revealed entire faces – grinning, goblinoid heads that strained from the flesh of the fungi, giggling and snorting.

'See!' Gotrek extinguished his pipe and waved it at Thorrik. 'Take time for the little pleasures when you can.' He stashed the pipe, gripped his axe in both hands and stomped past Thorrik and Solmundsson, whistling cheerfully as he slammed the blade into a toadstool. The fungus crumpled with an explosion of white spores that covered Gotrek so completely he looked like he had attacked a sack of flour. The Slayer did not seem to notice, swinging his axe back and forth with surprising grace for someone so squat. Caps and stems whirled through the rain as Gotrek fought, still whistling tune-lessly. The more he fought, the louder the rustling sound grew as more of the fungi sprang into life, ambling towards the Slayer.

'Make for the road!' cried Solmundsson, drawing his pistol and joining Thorrik in firing a barrage of shots. 'None of them are on the road!'

Gotrek gave no answer but began chopping in that direction with the other two stumbling behind him, firing wildly. Fighting seemed to invig-orate the Slayer rather than tire him. The rain and spores mixed together to make him as colourful as the things he was cutting, and pieces of fungus lodged in his crest of hair, twitching like fish trapped on a rock.

By the time they stumbled out onto the road, Gotrek had butchered dozens of the toadstools, but when Solmundsson looked back into the field, there was no sign of the carnage. The fungi had surged down from the surrounding hills and swamped the path cut by Gotrek. As Solmundsson had hoped, however, they seemed unable, or unwilling, to spread out onto the road.

Gotrek had a savage grin on his face, and when he saw that the toadstools had not followed him, he let out a bullish roar and leapt back into the fields, vanishing from sight as he charged off into the drizzle.

'They'll kill him,' gasped Thorrik, his hands on his knees as he fought to catch his breath.

'I don't think so,' said Solmundsson.

They both stood there in the rain, listening to the sound of Gotrek cutting through the fields. Every now and then they saw his axe, or his fiery crest of hair, then he would disappear again with another unintelligible war cry.

Solmundsson squinted through the downpour, looking down the road, trying to make out the fortress in more detail. It was speckled with lights, so he reasoned that it must be occupied, but it was not built like any keep he had seen before – it looked like it had been built to resemble a head. 'Who builds like that?' he asked.

'Grungni knows. I've never seen anything like it.' Thorrik studied the fungi that were straining towards them from the roadside. 'You don't think *they* built it, do you?'

Solmundsson laughed. Then he looked at the toadstools and his laughter stalled. Some of the fungi were watching him with eyes that showed a bright, malicious intelligence. 'Toadstools don't build things,' he said, but without much confidence.

'They don't usually have faces either,' replied Thorrik.

'Valaya's arse!' cried Gotrek, tumbling back onto the road in a shower of rubbery flesh. 'They've got some fight in 'em.' He weaved back and forth across the road, wiping spores and slime from his face with the back of his arm, readying himself for another charge.

'Wait!' Solmundsson grabbed his arm. 'Remember why we're here.'

Gotrek stared at him, panting and wiping more muck from his face.

'Can you remember why we're here?' demanded Thorrik.

'Of course I bloody can!' Gotrek glared at Thorrik. Then he looked around at the sodden hills.

A pained silence followed.

'Barak-Urbaz,' prompted Solmundsson.

'Aye!' Gotrek sniffed, grimaced, then spat some virulent-looking slime. 'Barak-Urbaz. Exactly. You've let the grobi scum fester under your feet for years, now you need the Slayer to clean up the mess. And you need me to get the job done quickly so they pull their rabble back from your city until their moon has waned.' He bared his broken teeth in a proud grin. Then he frowned, as though remembering something else, and looked at the ground.

He's thinking of the aelf, thought Solmundsson. He glanced at Thorrik, wondering if he understood, but the first officer was still glaring at Gotrek.

Gotrek frowned, squinting at the rocks overhead. 'Are we still in a cave?'

'I'm not sure where we are.' Solmundsson nodded at the distant building. 'But that looks like our best chance of finding out.'

Gotrek grimaced and broke into a violent coughing fit. A cloud of spores billowed from his mouth, sparkling and shifting colour before dissolving in the rain. Gotrek frowned, wiped his mouth, then marched off down the road. 'Don't just stand there,' he muttered.

Thorrik clenched his fists and was about to shout something at Gotrek's back when Solmundsson silenced him with a warning glare.

The three of them hurried down the road, and they had not gone far before Gotrek glanced back at them. 'Looks like we're not so far off track,' he said as he reached the brow of a hill.

'What do you mean?' asked Solmundsson as he caught up with the Slayer and looked down the road into a broad valley.

Gotrek appeared pained, and abruptly burst into another coughing fit, spitting more spores and coughing so hard he could not speak for several minutes.

'That's no mushroom,' Gotrek finally gasped, pointing out a shape a few hundred yards down the slope, looming over the caps and spotted domes.

They walked a little further down into the valley and Solmundsson saw what Gotrek meant. Someone had chiselled a boulder into the shape of a crescent moon and hung a disparate collection of skulls, fetishes, necklaces and fungus on it.

'That's grobi work,' said Gotrek. 'Even shoddier than the things you lot make.'

'Moonclan,' said Thorrik, studying the shrine with distaste.

'Then we made it.' Solmundsson grinned at him. 'This must be the Asylum. This is where the grots have been building their armies. We were right to follow that squig.'

'May as well carry on following it then,' said Gotrek, struggling to stifle another cough as he pointed his axe at a shape on the far side of the valley, travelling on the same road they were using.

'The squig.' Solmundsson patted Gotrek on the shoulder, creating another cloud of spores. 'It's the same one!'

Thorrik frowned. 'It is. How strange.'

Solmundsson glanced at him. 'What do you mean?'

'Well, it just seems strange that after everything we've been through, that same squig is still just ahead of us.'

Solmundsson took out his spyglass. 'Well, it's definitely the same one. I don't know why it's walking though. Perhaps it's exhausted? It carried the grots all the way back here from Valdrakh Pass.'

Gotrek laughed. 'Squigs don't get tired. They're not even real animals. They're just something the grobi breed out of their droppings.'

Solmundsson shook his head. 'Is that true?'

'No idea. I can't remember who told me. They don't get tired though. There must be some other reason why it's waddling along like that.'

Thorrik gave Solmundsson a sideways glance. 'Does none of this seem odd to you? That we're still on the trail of this same squig, I mean, and that we entered the grot lair so easily?'

'Easily?' Gotrek raised an eyebrow. 'I doubt you would have found it easy fighting that armoured troll. Every time I trimmed its legs they grew back again.'

Thorrik shrugged. 'We got in here without that much resistance and we've been strolling down this road like we own the place without being challenged.'

Solmundsson waved at the slime that was still clinging to Gotrek's muscles. 'I would say those toadstools gave us quite a challenge.'

'I'm talking about the greenskins. If this *is* the Asylum – if it really is their secret lair – don't you think it odd that we have been able to just fight our way in here?'

'What's your point?'

'My point is that this smells like a trap. We've trailed that squig all the way from Valdrakh Pass, and now it's ambling along the road slowly enough for us to follow even though we have no ship.' Thorrik looked at Gotrek. 'Maybe Scragfang wanted you to come here. Maybe he wants to have some kind of showdown with you.'

Gotrek thought for a moment. Then he grinned and pounded his axe in the mud. 'A greenskin warlord has brought me to his kingdom so we can go toe to toe. This is starting to look promising.'

Solmundsson shook his head. 'Seems far-fetched.' He held up a hand to silence Thorrik. 'But we should tread carefully, I agree. Just in case you're...'

His words trailed off as he realised Gotrek was sprinting down the road towards the giant squig. 'By the anvil,' he said, hurrying after the Slayer. 'How has he lived so long?'

By the time Solmundsson and Thorrik were nearing the squig, Gotrek was already on its back, dealing out blows with his axe and sending grots tumbling from the howdah.

Solmundsson and Thorrik drew pistols and began firing lumps of aether-shot into the fray, kicking back the grots that screamed and charged towards them.

There were only around a dozen grots and they made short work of them, but the squig proved more of a challenge, bounding across the road with Gotrek clinging to its back as it tried to shake him off. As the Slayer fought he was wracked by more coughing fits, trailing such a thick cloud of spores that he looked like a smoking furnace.

Finally, the squig managed to hurl Gotrek to the ground, and he cried out as he rolled heavily through the mud.

Thorrik continued firing at the giant squig as Solmundsson raced over to Gotrek and helped him up. 'Are you wounded?'

'What in the name of Grungni is this?' demanded Gotrek, reeling away from Solmundsson and clutching at his face, grabbing at his eye.

'Let me see!' cried Solmundsson, snatching Gotrek's hand away from his face. 'By the Code,' he gasped.

'What is it?'

Solmundsson shook his head, unsure how to answer. There was a thin, pale blue tube hanging from Gotrek's eye. It had squeezed out next to his tear duct and was now dangling in front of his face. 'One of your veins...' Solmundsson grimaced. 'One of your veins has come out.'

A weight slammed into Solmundsson and he flew through the air, landing in the fungus that bordered the road. Tendrils lashed out, grabbing his wrist as he tried to raise his pistol.

'A vein?' bellowed Gotrek, wading into the toadstools and hacking them down with his axe. Before they could attack again, Gotrek hauled Solmundsson back out onto the road. 'What do you mean, a vein?'

The squig thundered across the road and Gotrek threw a punch, smashing his fist into the creature's face and sending it tumbling back down the road. 'How can my vein be outside my body?'

Solmundsson was too breathless to speak, but Thorrik wandered over. 'It has a cap.'

Gotrek cursed and snapped the stem from his eye, holding it up in front of his face. It was a slender, arrow-headed toadstool.

Solmundsson and Thorrik backed away, shaking their heads.

'What are you staring at me like that for?' demanded Gotrek. 'I've pulled the bloody thing out.' Then he cursed as another tendril slid from his eye, thicker than the previous one. 'Damn it,' he muttered. 'That actually stings a bit.' As he reached up to remove the second growth, a dusty bracket fungus burst from his forearm. Gotrek stared at it. He was about to speak when another shape rose from his shoulders – another thick crust of pitted fungus that curled around his ribs, encasing his torso like a shell. He reached round and snapped it off. A large hunk of muscle and skin came away with the fungus and blood splashed down the Slayer's legs. He staggered and gritted his teeth, making a low growling sound.

The squig slammed into him and they both rolled back down the road, Gotrek landing punches and axe blows and the monster tearing at his body with its teeth and claws. Gotrek freed himself with a punch that sent the squig rolling into the forest of toadstools. The creature tried to bound back towards him, but a blanket of gossamer thread engulfed it and it was dragged down into the toadstools. There was a flurry of caps and gills and a tearing sound, then there was silence and the toadstools were still again.

'Lightweight,' muttered Gotrek. Then, when Solmundsson and Thorrik simply stared back at him, the Slayer looked down at himself and grimaced. There were fungal growths all over his body. He glared at Solmundsson. 'Why aren't you two covered in this bloody stuff?'

Solmundsson felt a crushing weight bearing down on him, and he could not bring himself to reply. If the Slayer was lost, everything was lost. All of this was for nothing.

'It's probably our aethermatic armour,' said Thorrik, tapping the helmet of his suit. 'Our suits filter out toxins. None of those spores will have reached our lungs, but you...' He shook his head and looked at Solmundsson. 'What are we going to do, captain?'

For once, Solmundsson could think of nothing to say.

Gotrek glowered at them. 'A bit of mushroom won't stop me.' He slapped an orange-coloured crust that had encased his stomach, filling the air with more spores. 'It won't stop me splitting heads.'

He stomped off down the road, heading for Slathermere. 'Stand there blubbing if you like,' he yelled over his shoulder. 'The Slayer's got work to do.'

CHAPTER THIRTY-TWO

Slathermere looked even more surreal seen close up. Maleneth and Cerura halted a few feet from a cave mouth and looked up at the grotesque architecture. Maleneth was not even sure whether 'architecture' was the right word. It was more like taxidermy. The gargant's head had been transformed by grot sorcery. It was unnaturally huge, and its skin was coated in mould that shone from within. Maleneth tried to imagine how big the gargant would have been when it still had a body, but her mind baulked at the task.

There were grots everywhere, rushing in and out of the cave mouth, and Maleneth found that she was still able to understand most of them. 'They're preparing for an attack,' she said, knowing that Cerura would be nearby. 'Scragfang must have guessed I'd come looking for him.' She halted a few feet from the opening. 'It won't be raining inside. We're going to look quite odd waltzing in there as a column of water.'

'There are other elements,' said Cerura. 'Let me have a closer look inside.'

Maleneth felt him rush past and then, a moment later, return to her side. 'It's very dark in there and full of dust. It will be an easy enough matter to go unnoticed.'

For a moment, Maleneth thought the sorcerer was suggesting they simply hide in the gloom, but then he whispered a few arcane phrases and she felt a peculiar rippling sensation pass through her limbs.

'Inside, quickly,' whispered Cerura, steering her into the darkness. The cave mouth was crowded with grots and squigs. The squigs were around the same height as their keepers, but their spherical bodies were packed with muscle and the grots were cursing as they struggled to hold them back, yanking furiously on their reins and lashing them with whips. As Maleneth crept around the cave's perimeter she realised that she was the cause of the squigs' excitement. Some of them leapt at her, their tiny coal-stud eyes rolling above their gaping mouths, but she slipped away, dodging their attacks as their grot handlers hauled them away from her.

'Into the passageway,' whispered Cerura.

Maleneth sprinted through the cave, leaping over squigs and swerving around grots, until she reached an opening on the far side and raced on into a dark tunnel. There were fewer grots here and no squigs, so it was an easy matter to run up the slope and leave the commotion behind. The way was lit by veins of glowing mould that lined the walls, and Maleneth saw how expertly the sorcerer had disguised her. She was just one of the dust clouds whipping through the fitful shadows.

'Cerura?' she whispered, reaching a junction.

'Here,' he said, close by.

'I have to find Scragfang,' she said. 'Where do you think he'll be? In the upper levels?'

'No. I think not. The Moonclans tend to hide in the deepest, darkest pits they can find. I would advise heading down that slope.'

Maleneth listened to the sounds of the fortress. There were howls and screeches coming from every direction. As well as the cries of the grots themselves, she could hear the snarling of squigs and the sound of badly played musical instruments – gongs, bells and pipes all combined into a dreadful, cacophonous din. 'It sounds like there are thousands of those wretched things in here. I need a better plan than simply grubbing around in the dark hoping to get lucky.' She turned to where she guessed Cerura was standing. 'You said you had wonderful powers at your disposal. Can't you just tell me where to find him?'

'You have to understand, every breath of air down here is crowded with evil humours. It takes a lot of effort to hold the fungus from invading our flesh. And at the same time I am having to maintain our disguise. I have completely hidden our true forms. There are very few mages who would have the skill to perform both deeds at once. If I attempt to cast my thoughts elsewhere in the fortress, I might risk revealing us.'

Nicely done, sneered Maleneth's mistress. *You've used those seeds freeing a conjuror so witless he can only perform one trick at a time.*

'No matter,' snapped Maleneth. 'I have skills of my own.' She jogged off down the slope, heading towards the grot voices.

The passageway grew warmer as it descended, and damper too, so that Maleneth began to feel her feet sticking in the mud, even though she could not see them. Other tunnels forked off in different directions but Maleneth kept on heading for the voices that echoed up towards her. Eventually, she spotted figures up ahead. They were grots, and for a moment she thought they were struggling with a large squig, but as she came closer she saw that it was actually a spider, taller than her and dragging a bloated abdomen through the muck as it lashed out with barbed legs.

She paused to watch, wondering if the spider had attacked the grots. Then they managed to lash a harness on it and she realised it was a beast of burden that had turned on its keepers. The fight went out of the creature once it was bound, and the grots steered it on down the tunnel, heading for the lower levels.

Maleneth singled out a straggler, lagging behind the rest of the group. She listened out for the creature's name and then, once it was alone, she crept closer.

'Gutcutter,' she whispered, speaking in the guttural greenskin language.

The grot glared back into the shadows. 'Oozat?'

'You're better than all of them, Gutcutter,' she continued. 'You're too powerful to be treated like this. You're destined for greatness.'

Gutcutter came hesitantly towards her, still waving a knife and scowling, a mixture of fear and intrigue in its eyes. 'Umpy? Iz dis yer idea of a joke?'

'This is not a joke. I have been watching you.'

The grot sneered, then looked shocked, then sneered again. 'Shut yer gob, Umpy. Get out 'ere and stop prattin' about. We're all meant ta be gettin' together. Scragfang's orders. 'E wants us all ready at the Moon Well.' He turned to go.

Maleneth rushed forwards and whispered right in his ear, adopting a sterner tone. 'Do *not* refuse the will of the moon.'

Gutcutter stumbled to a halt and looked around, eyes wide. 'Ow's ya doin' dat, Umpy?'

'This is not Umpy. I am the moon. And I have come to lift you from servitude.'

'Da moon?'

'I have come to put you in your proper place. You are far more cunning than your superiors. You are meant to be giving them orders, not the other way around.'

Gutcutter nodded, slowly. 'Dat is true.' As the grot adopted a smug expression, Maleneth smiled to herself. She had found exactly the right kind of disenfranchised moron.

'I have come to make you a boss,' she said.

Enlightenment dawned in the grot's eyes. 'Yes. Dat makes sense. I *should* be a zoggin boss.' The grot lowered the knife and all suspicion vanished from its face. 'Right. Wot's I gotta do?' Doubt crept back into its voice. 'Will I 'ave ta do any tests?'

Maleneth replied in her most unctuous tones, 'All you have to do is lead me to Scragfang. Then I shall explain that you should be giving orders instead of receiving them.'

The grot's eyes burned with excitement, but then it shook its head, looking anxious. 'Are ya sure? I ain't very big.'

Maleneth resisted the urge to strike him and managed to keep her voice gentle. 'You are big on the inside.'

The grot's eyes widened. 'Da *inside*. Of course. Now it all makes sense. Moon, yer exactly zoggin right.'

The creature turned a few cartwheels and made to sprint off down one of the tunnels that forked off the main passage.

'Stay close,' whispered Maleneth to Cerura.

'Of course,' he replied.

Maleneth almost lost the grot in the shadows, but now that she was so close to her prize, she was filled with a delightful vigour and bounded easily over grots and piles of rubble.

How will you find your way out?

Her mistress had a point. Slathermere was even larger than Maleneth had guessed. Gutcutter was dashing through a labyrinth of loops and bends that did not seem to follow any kind of logic. They passed crooked moon shrines and what looked like entire greenskin villages huddled in the darkness. They even skirted broad underground lakes that boiled with squigs and other grotesque creatures. Even if Maleneth had been making a map as she ran, it would have been an indecipherable mess within minutes. *I'll get him to lead me back out*, she thought.

After you've stuck a knife in his chieftain? I'm not sure he'll consider you quite such a good friend then.

He won't see anything. I'll still be hidden. And I'm not going to kill Scragfang, I'm going to capture him.

You haven't worked any of this out. You're going to make the same pig's ear of this as you do everything else.

Maleneth smiled at the panic in her mistress' voice. *I don't think I'll ever tire of making you squirm.*

Gutcutter heaved a mouldering door open and led them into a wide chamber with a roof so low Maleneth had to stoop. It appeared to have been flooded at some point, and the ground was even boggier than the rest of Slathermere. As Maleneth waded through the mud, she noticed pale blobs swimming through it and paused, dropping to one knee so she could examine them. They looked like bloated yellow tadpoles, but then one of them rolled over and she saw that it had a tiny, perfectly formed human face. The creature stared at her, opening and closing its mouth as though trying to speak, then rolled over again and swam off through the puddles.

'Blood of Khaine,' she whispered. 'What are these things?'

Gutcutter splashed to a halt and peered back at her through the half-light. 'Eh?'

'Nothing,' said Maleneth, grimacing and treading carefully through the mud, trying not to touch the pale shapes. 'Keep going.'

Once they had crossed the boggy chamber they climbed a set of slumped stone steps that were carpeted in moss. At the top of the steps, the grot shoved open a heavy door and hurried out into a huge cave. The din of many voices rushed down the steps to Maleneth, and as she reached the top she saw a cave that was crowded with hundreds of grots. The chamber was circular and the ceiling was so distant she could not make it out in any detail. The mud-packed walls were covered with crooked walkways and wonky platforms, and every one of them was crowded with greenskins. They were all talking at once – gibbering, screeching and giggling at such a volume that Maleneth winced as she stepped out from the doorway. Some of the grots were playing instruments and singing but most were readying themselves for battle, testing bows, filling quivers, pouring poisons into bottles and sharpening knives. Some of them were mounted on large spiders like the one she had seen earlier and others were careering back and forth on squigs. It was utter mayhem. She had never seen so many grots gathered in one place, and her excitement faded as she realised what an absurd risk she was taking. *Why didn't I get out when I had the chance?* Then she remembered that Scragfang had robbed her of her one chance at returning to Azyr. He had robbed her of the rune. Anger crushed her doubt.

'Where's Scragfang?' she demanded.

''E's gonna be 'ere soon.' The grot was looking warily at the shadows around Maleneth, trying to spot her. 'A mighty champion's comin' to attack 'im. An 'e wants the fight to 'appen 'ere, in da Moon Well.'

Laughter filled Maleneth's head. *Mighty champion? You?*

Maleneth shrugged. She was a little surprised to hear someone describe her in that way, but she wasn't going to accept ridicule from her dead mistress. *I escaped from Scragfang, remember. He dragged me all the way across Skrappa Spill and I got away from him. And now he's realised that I'm coming to make him pay. Scragfang probably isn't used to people who actually stand up to him. Those money-grubbing mechanics in Barak-Urbaz certainly never do.*

I wouldn't let it go to your head. An aggrieved ant would seem like a champion to these runts.

'The atmosphere in here is so toxic,' whispered Cerura in her ear. 'The power of your seeds may not work much longer. I'm doing what I can to help, but it's hard to hold back the fungus and keep us hidden at the same time.'

'Show some mettle,' she hissed, but she could hear by the pain in his voice that she did not have long.

'Where will Scragfang appear?' she asked, turning back to Gutcutter.

The grot pointed its knife at the distant eaves of the chamber. 'Up in 'is royal lair.' With that, Gutcutter scampered across the crowded cave and began climbing one of the ramshackle wooden walkways that were nailed to the walls. Maleneth raced after him, barging through the crush. The scene was so chaotic that none of the grots noticed as a pair of dust clouds slipped past them. The higher they climbed, the more of the grots Maleneth saw. They were teeming from every swaying gantry and gurney, like mites burrowing through a corpse. *There must be a thousand of them in here*, she thought, imagining what would happen if the wizard's magic did fail.

Even by your standards this was a spectacularly stupid move.

Maleneth ignored her and kept her gaze locked on Gutcutter's back as the grot fought through the crowds, bolting up ladders and vaulting piles of scrap. Within a few feet, she started to encounter problems. She was hidden, but that did not mean the grots did not notice her climbing past them. She used all her elegance and speed to snake in and out of them, but sometimes there was no way to progress without shoving grots aside. One of them cried out in confusion as she moved it out of her way. She lashed out with her knife, sending the grot tumbling in a shower of blood, but all the nearby grots noticed what happened and began calling out. As word spread she realised she might never make it to the top of the chamber. She reached into her robes and grabbed one of the vials she kept strapped close to her skin. She unstopped it and hurled it at the wall a dozen feet away from where she was climbing. A column of blue flame exploded from the glass and raced up the wall. The surrounding grots howled and scrambled away, creating a clear path for Maleneth. She continued, keeping as near to the burning oil as she dared. The grots seemed horrified by the brightness of the flames, and she made quick progress up the wall.

Finally, Maleneth reached the uppermost circle of platforms, and she thanked Khaine that she was light on her feet. Some of the walkways had broken or were no more than a plank wide, and the drop below must have been several hundred feet. One misstep would have sent her tumbling to her death. She spotted Gutcutter a few feet away and rushed over to him. 'Where now?'

''E'll be over here,' gasped Gutcutter, breathless from the climb, heading towards an antechamber that opened up off the far side of the cave. Cold, silvery light was coming from the antechamber, and Maleneth saw dozens of grots scurrying back and forth dressed in the greenskin equivalent of finery. There were moon designs stitched into their black hoods and they were gripping spears that looked like they might survive more than a single thrust. As Gutcutter led her towards the antechamber, long shadows spilled out across the walls. There were more grots in there, and they were gathered around the source of the light.

'He's there,' whispered Maleneth, her pulse quickening as she saw Scragfang hunched over a cauldron, staring into the light that spilled from its bowl.

'Did ya, er, miss us?' said someone in a thin, scratchy whisper.

Maleneth paused and turned to see one of the grots staring directly at her. It was the wizened little creature with one eye, the grot that looked like a strip of charred meat.

Stinkeye hobbled from the shadows, leaning heavily on a staff laden with bone fetishes and dried mushrooms. The creature looked from Maleneth to Cerura, clearly able to see through their disguises. It spoke in reverential tones. 'It's all just as Scragfang has foreseen. You're 'ere, exactly where you're meant ta be.'

Maleneth raised her knife and tried to lunge at Stinkeye, but her feet were rooted to the spot.

Stinkeye continued smiling and rattled the fetishes on its staff.

The dust conjured by Cerura drifted away, leaving the two aelves visible.

Maleneth gasped in disgust as she saw why she was unable to move. From the knees down, her legs had morphed into a single fungal stem, like the bole of a mushroom. She was rooted to the rock and Cerura was in the exact same fix.

'How dare you!' she gasped, gripping her knife and preparing to cut at the stem.

'Don't!' cried Cerura. 'It's your flesh now. It's part of you. Your arteries are running through it. Cut it and you'll bleed to death.'

'Do something!' howled Maleneth, glaring at him.

Cerura's face was a dreadful grey colour as he shook his head.

'Aelf spells ain't no good,' wheezed Stinkeye, spluttering a cloud of embers. 'Yer bound to Slathermere. Yer one of us.'

Gutcutter was standing a few feet away, watching the exchange with a look of abject terror.

'You!' cried Maleneth. 'Get me out of here!'

The grot turned and sprinted back the way it had come, whimpering.

The creature called Stinkeye raised its staff and croaked a few words.

Strands of fungus blossomed up from the rocky floor and engulfed Gutcutter. As the grot thrashed and wailed, trying to free itself, the fungus grew faster until, in a few seconds, Gutcutter had vanished beneath a ball of white, feathery strands. Then, with a moist popping sound, the gossamer threads solidified, forming a single pockmarked puffball with Gutcutter's eyes staring out from its centre, rolling in their sockets.

'Traitor,' whispered Stinkeye. Then the shaman limped off across the walkway, waving its staff in warning at the surrounding grots. 'Don't touch 'em. Dey ain't for killin'. They're bait.'

'Bait?' cried Maleneth. 'What are you talking about? I'm the champion who's come to kill you.'

Stinkeye stopped and looked back at her, laughing. 'Yer just da bait. Da champion is on 'is way 'ere to save you.'

'He? Save me? What in the name of Khaine are you talking about?'

'Da Fyreslayer. 'E's comin'. 'E finks 'e can rescue ya.'

'You useless morons. Do you mean Gotrek? He wouldn't come to save me. He hates me. You really thought Gotrek would follow me?' Maleneth felt sick at the absurdity of it. She was going to spend the rest of her life in this grot-filled hole as a talking mushroom because the grots thought she would lure Gotrek to them. She was going to spend eternity as a mindless slave. She was a disgrace. She let out a thin, trembling howl of rage.

Then several things happened at once. The light in Scragfang's cave flashed brighter, causing her to squint and shield her face, there was a loud smash from the bottom of the atrium, like the sound of a cave-in, and in response, there was a huge roar from the crowds of grots.

Maleneth slumped against the wall, filled with despair.

'Come back and fight, you grobi scum!'

The familiar, bludgeoning tones jolted Maleneth back into an upright position. 'It can't be him,' she breathed. 'It can't be.'

The din grew louder as something rocketed from one side of the atrium to the other, kicking up dust and smashing gantries, sending grots tumbling to their deaths. It looked like a ball had been hurled into the cave and was bouncing its way up towards her. It took a few seconds for Maleneth to realise it was a squig. The grot on its back was so encrusted with fungal plates that it was barely recognisable, but it was managing to steer by landing punches on the side of the squig's head. As the squig crashed into another walkway and sent more grots tumbling to their deaths, the rider let out a booming laugh. 'Out of the bloody way!'

'Gotrek?' whispered Maleneth, staring in disbelief as the punch-drunk squig slammed into the wall a few feet away and sent its rider somersaulting through the air.

'Now!' cried Stinkeye, turning to the distant figure of Scragfang.

Scragfang stared into the altar's iron bowl, dazzled by loonlight, weeping tears of joy. Everything was coming to pass exactly as he had foreseen. The Fyreslayer was here. He could hear him outside the throne room, bellowing curses and smashing gantries. And the Bad Moon was full. It was grinning up at him from the altar, filling him with power like nothing he had ever felt before. It was flowing through his loonblade and into his veins like the most potent shroom he had ever eaten. He was drunk on loonlight. He felt as though he could fly, and no sooner did he have that thought than his feet left the ground, letting him glide weightlessly above the rock. The final moments of the vision were playing over in his mind constantly now – his knife hovering over the Fyreslayer's chest, and then an orgy of destruction as walls toppled and the bright golden face of Barak-Urbaz melted and fell.

'I'm comin' for ya,' he said, turning from the altar and heading out of the throne room, his knife jangling in his grip.

'For Barak-Urbaz!' cried Solmundsson, blasting furiously with his pistol and sprinting up another gantry. Thorrik was still with him and there was a trail of dead grots clogging the walkways behind them. The Slayer had butchered most of them, but Solmundsson was determined to show that he and Thorrik could hold their own. 'For the Solmund Company!'

There were hundreds of grots in the atrium, but Gotrek had thrown them into such disarray that Solmundsson and Thorrik were able to blast through with relative ease. They reached a point where the gantry had been smashed, leaving a twenty-foot gap.

'We can't jump that!' cried Solmundsson, gunning down a mob of grots that came thundering towards them on a squig. Robbed of its riders, the squig went into a frenzy and began savaging everything within reach, causing even more mayhem and wrenching more walkways from the walls.

Solmundsson struggled to keep his balance as the rickety structure beneath him began to shudder and groan.

'One moment, captain,' said Thorrik, fixing a grappling hook to the muzzle of his gun and firing it over the gap.

The hook crashed through the woodwork on the far side of the gap, and when Thorrik yanked it back, it held firm. 'Hold on, captain,' he said, and Solmundsson had only a second to comply before Thorrik launched them both out across the drop.

They landed safely on the far side, crashing into a wall of grots and sending half of them cartwheeling from the ledge. They shot the rest and sprinted on up the ramp.

'I can see him!' cried Solmundsson, spotting Gotrek at the top of the atrium, charging into battle, his axe raised, sending more grots tumbling from a ledge. It was a glorious sight. There was no way they could survive this, but Solmundsson did not feel afraid. All he felt was exhilaration. They had got the Slayer deep into the enemy's keep and he was wreaking such carnage that every grot in Skrappa Spill would soon be pouring back into the Asylum in a panic, rather than attacking Barak-Urbaz as they meant to. Incredibly, despite everything that had gone wrong, they were going to achieve what they had set out to do.

They barrelled through another wave of grots, scaled more ladders, crossed another series of gantries and finally burst out onto the upper level of the atrium. There was a line of grots waiting for them, bows raised and arrows nocked.

'For Barak-Urbaz!' howled Solmundsson as he and Thorrik unleashed another barrage of aethershot.

'What are you doing here?' cried Maleneth as she saw the two Kharadron charging towards her, muzzles flashing as they ripped a channel through the grots. They yelled something in reply, but there was too much noise for her to hear. Gantries were crashing down all around her and the grots were all screaming war cries as they fought. She strained to move, but it was useless. All she could do was lash out with her knife at any grots that were stupid enough to come close.

Stinkeye had gone, heading off to join Scragfang in the antechamber, and Gotrek was still careering through the crowds. Losing his squig steed had done little to slow him down. He was fighting in a way that was erratic even for him, lurching and staggering into his opponents as though he had lost his sense of balance. *Is he drunk?* she wondered. 'Khaine's teeth,' she whispered when he finally paused to catch breath and she saw the fungal carapace that had encased him. His back was sporting a forest of toadstools and his legs were dragging trails of mycelium. The few inches of his skin that weren't hidden by bracket fungus were coated in a blue-green carpet of mould that billowed dust as he lurched back into battle.

'It's got him,' she whispered. 'The Asylum. It's in his blood.' The thought that Gotrek was doomed shocked Maleneth. Despite all her derisive comments, she had come to believe he was as indestructible as he claimed.

The Slayer slammed his axe into another wave of grots, sending them tumbling over the edge of the walkway, but he was slowing with each blow.

'He's being consumed,' said Cerura.

Fungus was bursting from Gotrek's body with every step he took. A lime-coloured puffball burst from his abdomen, replacing his stomach with a leering moon face, and clouds of black spores were spewing from his mouth. Gotrek cried out as he fought, but his words were muffled by the spores.

Captain Solmundsson punched his way towards Maleneth and reached out to help her. Then he saw her mutated legs and snatched back his hand, shaking his head.

'What in the name of Khaine is Gotrek doing here?' she cried, lashing out at another grot. She felt ridiculous saying it, but she had to ask. 'Did he come here for me?'

Solmundsson sidestepped an arrow and pummelled a grot with the butt of his pistol. Then he wiped blood from the faceplate of his helmet and nodded at Maleneth. 'He won't admit it though.'

Maleneth was filled with inexplicable rage. 'I betrayed him. Why would he ruin himself coming to help me?'

Solmundsson gunned down another attacker, dodged another blow, then staggered towards her, clearly exhausted from fighting up the gantries. Grots were circling him in their dozens, aiming arrows at him, and he was bleeding from several wounds, but he still managed a grim laugh. 'You two are hilarious.'

Maleneth sneered. 'I hate him.'

Solmundsson was about to reply when an arrow thudded into his chest. His eyes widened in shock. He staggered backwards with a grunt of pain, dropping his pistol to grab at the arrow. Then he bellowed a war cry and charged back at the grots, raising his cutlass and cutting several of them down. Another two arrows punched into him, one in his chest and one in his stomach, tearing through the rubber of his flight suit. He dropped to his knees and then crumpled onto the floor, gasping and choking. Thorrik howled and raced towards him, shielding him from more shots and firing at the grots. He sent dozens of the creatures hurtling to their deaths and dragged Solmundsson back towards the wall, propping him up against the rock. A grot rushed at him and he cut it down. 'For Barak-Urbaz!' he spat, cutting down another, then another. Solmundsson managed to lift himself up on his elbow and started firing his pistol again. A mound of grot bodies began to form around them as they blasted and lunged.

An arrow punched through Thorrik's faceplate. He continued firing as he slid to the floor, leaving a smear of blood on the rock. Then he crumpled into a heap. Solmundsson cursed and tried to help him back up. Arrows sliced into him, ripping through his suit and smashing his helmet. He fired one last shot, then fell back onto Thorrik's corpse, his pale, grimacing face visible through his wrecked mask.

Maleneth stared at them in disbelief. 'Why did you come here?'

'Finally,' said Scragfang as he glided from the throne room and into the fighting outside. Mangleback was scuttling after him, giggling wildly, and Stinkeye was there too, wheezing and limping out onto the walkway. Scragfang was only vaguely aware of the fighting. The combatants seemed like faint shadows, flickering at the edges of his moonstruck mind. His attention was locked on the Fyreslayer's rune. As Gotrek strained under the weight of the fungus, shouldering his way through the scrum towards the aelf, the mould on his skin avoided the rune, unable to sully its gleaming surface.

Scragfang's loonblade was like cold fire, flickering and freezing. It was hungry for the rune's power, straining and leaping towards it. Scragfang was finding it hard to separate the vision from reality as the two aligned. He was now living through the scenes that had first appeared to him in the Gibbermarsh. Everything was as he had predicted. The Fyreslayer was on his knees, rent out of shape by the transformations wracking his body, but he was still crawling towards the aelf, determined to reach her, bellowing incoherently as he hacked and punched.

Scragfang let the moonlight carry him over the heads of grots and raised his loonblade, readying himself for the incredible power he was about to steal.

Maleneth stared at Gotrek as he dragged himself towards her, parrying spear thrusts and arrows with less and less force as his body was consumed. His face was still visible, as was the master rune, but everything else was either covered in mould or buried under powdery growths. He gave another enraged howl and managed to stagger to his feet, grabbing a grot in one hand and using it as a club while swinging his axe with his other hand. With a few more brutal blows he managed to stagger to Maleneth's side.

'What are you doing?' she said, her stomach turning as she saw his growths in detail.

Gotrek's reply was so mangled that Maleneth could barely make out the words. 'I've come. To teach. These grobi. Some bloody respect.'

He staggered as an arrow sank into his shoulder. Then again as another one punched into his knee. The bracket fungus was so thick that it acted as armour, but it was clearly crushing the breath from his lungs. His breathing was horribly laboured. His face was as purple as the toadstools growing on his back.

'Have you done this for me?' asked Maleneth. 'Did you come here for me?'

'Don't. Be. Idiot,' gasped Gotrek, but she saw a flash of embarrassment in his eye and knew that she was right.

He looked at the stem that had replaced her legs and grimaced, shaking his head.

'You don't even have a plan, do you?' she spat, her head whirling with anger.

Gotrek beheaded another grot, then dropped to his knees as another puff-ball blossomed from his back, crushing him under its weight.

Maleneth groaned in torment, clawing at her own face. 'Damn it. I can't let this happen.' She took Stinkeye's bottle from her belt and looked at the seed rattling around inside it.

No! Whatever you're thinking, stop thinking it. Don't you dare. Don't do this, Witchblade. Even you are not that stupid.

Maleneth glared at Gotrek, her words dripping with bile. 'I *really* hate you.' Then she took the last seed and pressed it into his mouldy skin.

Gotrek stared at her in shock. Then he gasped as flames rippled over him. He stumbled away from Maleneth, throwing back his shoulders and standing upright, stretching his limbs as though waking from a long sleep. A grot leapt at him with a spear and Gotrek split the monster down the middle with a single axe blow. He grinned as he saw that the fungus was crumbling away from his muscles, dissolving into spores and drifting away. He was drenched in snot-like gunk but his limbs were back to their normal shape. 'What did you do?' he grunted, looking back at Maleneth.

She was only half listening, too busy staring down at the fungus that was rushing up to her waist, transforming her flesh in the same way Gotrek's had been transformed. 'Khaine forgive me,' she whispered as tubular growths erupted from her stomach, coiling around each other as they sprouted into toadstools. Then she fixed him with a stare. 'You haven't got long.'

'To do what?'

She nodded at the rune in his chest, but before she could speak, the fungus raced up her torso, engulfing her head. She tried to shout, but her throat was being crushed by something.

Gotrek charged back towards her and raised his axe. For a moment, she thought he meant to kill her, but then she realised he was looking for a way to cut her free.

Why doesn't he do something?

He can't, she thought. *If he cuts the fungus, he'll be cutting me.*

Maleneth's field of vision was quickly shrinking. Darkness was washing over her eyes as she felt a warm, heavy growth encasing her skull.

She could still see Gotrek, though. Dozens of grots had surrounded him, drawing back arrows and preparing to shoot. He looked at the grots, then at Maleneth. Then he looked down at the rune in his chest.

Scragfang landed a few feet away from Gotrek and the laughter stalled in his throat. Something had gone dreadfully wrong. The old fear gripped him, crushing his innards so tight he thought he might be sick. The Slayer was drenched in blood and slime but his body was intact. The growths had vanished. He was swaying slightly but still gripping his axe in one hand and the bloody remains of a grot in the other.

One of the grots loosed an arrow and it thudded into Gotrek's bicep. The Slayer did not notice. He was staring at a pair of Kharadron corpses lying near what used to be the aelf. Then he looked at the tower of fungus that had consumed Maleneth.

'Dis is wrong!' hissed Scragfang as Stinkeye and Mangleback broke through the crush and reached his side.

'Why?' Mangleback strained to see Gotrek through the rows of archers surrounding him. 'You've got 'im exactly where ya needs 'im.' He waved a tentacle at the loonblade. 'Look at yer knife! It's gone mental.'

The loonblade was bucking and sparking in Scragfang's grip, but it did nothing to stifle his growing sense of panic. Everything until this point had been in accordance with his vision, but the vision had shown Gotrek buried under mounds of iron-hard fungus, not standing proud and free, his tattooed muscles gleaming in the loonlight as wreckage landed all around him. 'Dis is all wrong,' he whispered.

'Move now!' whispered Stinkeye. 'Da moon is full! Da loonlight won't last. Ya gotta be quick.'

Mangleback and Stinkeye both shoved Scragfang forwards, but he flinched as the Fyreslayer turned to face him. There was a flame burning in Gotrek's eye. It was not a reflection of the loonlight but something else entirely, something that made Scragfang's knees buckle. The light grew brighter, blazing in Gotrek's chest and then engulfing the Fyreslayer, radiating out of him in shards as he held his axe aloft.

And then, as a dreadful heat slammed into him, Scragfang finally saw the truth. The golden face he had seen in his vision, the face he had thought was the facade of a building in Barak-Urbaz, was actually the rune in Gotrek's chest, blazing like a trapped star. And the destruction he had foreseen was not the destruction of Barak-Urbaz at all. As Slathermere began to shake, Scragfang realised that he had not brought ruin down on the Kharadron – he had brought it down on his own head.

Maleneth gasped as flames washed over her. They scorched her skin, but as she fell to the floor, she realised they had also incinerated the fungus that had encased her legs. She backed away from the mound of ash, then tripped over one of the dead Kharadron and landed heavily on the floor. The fall saved her life. A moment later a flaming support beam crashed down where she had been standing with an explosion of sparks. She lay there in the corpses for a moment, staring in disbelief at the scene unfolding before her. Gotrek was restored and blazing with inner fire as he whirled through the greenskins. The grots were no longer paying much attention to Gotrek, however, more concerned with the fact that the fortress was falling apart. The vast severed head was shaking violently and collapsing in on itself, demolishing the jury-rigged structures that lined the walls. Ladders, gantries and platforms were tumbling down the centre of the atrium, taking crowds of grots, spiders and squigs with them.

He's lost his mind, realised Maleneth, watching Gotrek attack walls and embers as though they were opponents. *He's going to bring the whole place down and kill us all, and he's not even aware of what he's doing.*

As the Slayer hurled his axe back and forth, the light from the rune arced through the crowd, igniting and tearing everything it touched. His hair looked like a crest of flames and the brazier in his axe was burning white-hot. He ripped another gantry down, sending hundreds of grots tumbling to their deaths, and leapt onto the highest platform.

Stinkeye rushed from a doorway and hurled something. Maleneth struggled to see what it was, but it flashed and glinted as it landed at Gotrek's feet. A plume of purple smoke engulfed the Slayer, and when it cleared, he was trapped in a lump of blubbery flesh. It had encased every inch of him. Stinkeye laughed and waved at someone. Mangleback scuttled into view, followed by Scragfang, and they stared at the pile of purple fungus. The gantries and walkways were still falling from the walls and the whole building was shaking, but the three shaman grinned as they began prodding at the lump with their knives.

The fungus exploded, scattering clods of pulp through the air. Gotrek reared from the mess, head thrown back and howling, his axe raised and rippling with flames. Then he brought the weapon down and smashed Stinkeye to the floor, leaving nothing more than a bloody heap.

Mangleback tried to flee but Gotrek dodged a falling beam and sliced the creature neatly in half.

Scragfang leapt forward and plunged a knife into Gotrek's chest. The blade hit the burning rune and shattered into thousands of sparkling shards.

Gotrek was still howling as he tried to grab Scragfang by the throat, but the creature bolted and sprinted into the shadows.

Gotrek cursed, then charged, smashing into a crowd of spear-wielding grots, swinging his axe round his head and shaking with fury.

As he watched Gotrek slaughtering the grots, Cerura had an idea. Some of the rune light passed near Cerura and he reached out to catch it in his fist. It poured through his veins and gave him a surge of agonising power. The pain was horrific, but rather than recoiling, Cerura dragged it deeper, inhaling it and swallowing it until he felt it radiating through his pores. He'd

sampled similar power in Azyr but never on this magnitude. It was wonderful and appalling at the same time. He could feel the fibres of his body
straining to contain it and knew he could only bear it for a few minutes at
most. He felt as though his mind had been set alight. As the power threatened to overwhelm him, he cast his mind far from the toppling fortress,
reaching out through the shadows and the rain, past the sodden roads and
steaming marshes towards a light that was burning as brightly as the one
in his head – the Asylum Gate.

'What are you doing?' gasped a ragged voice in his ear.

Maleneth's face was white with pain and drenched in blood, but she was
far from dead. She was struggling for breath and there was an arrow sunk
deep in her midriff, but she had the strength to hold a knife to Cerura's
throat. She spoke through gritted teeth. 'Were you going to leave without
me?'

'I thought you were dead.'

'Not yet, wizard.' She spat blood from her mouth and staggered to her
feet, gesturing for him to do the same while she kept the knife pressed to
his throat.

'I will not leave you,' he said. 'I swore to help you and I will.'

She held the knife up a moment longer, then nodded and lowered it. She
was so weak she would have fallen if Cerura had not caught her. 'Where is
he?' she said, looking around at the panicked crowd and the heaps of bodies.

'Gotrek?'

She rolled her eyes, nodding at the raging Slayer. 'He's not easy to lose.
I mean Scragfang.'

Cerura shook his head in disbelief. 'The place is collapsing. In a few minutes we'll be crushed. Forget about Scragfang. They're all going to die. But
I can see the Asylum Gate.' He held up his hand, showing her the power
sparking between his fingertips. 'I have achieved a mastery of the elements
I have never managed before.'

'I'm not leaving without Scragfang,' she said, scouring the crowd for a
sign of her prey and ignoring his display of sorcery. 'There!' She grinned
and yanked Cerura across the swaying platform, making for a mound of
figures lying a few feet away. 'That's the shaman.'

The grots were all too busy fleeing for their lives or tumbling to their
deaths to stop them, and they reached the bodies easily enough.

'Where is he?' spat Maleneth, picking through the remains. 'He's not here.'

'You!' gasped Scragfang. He was lying a few feet away, trapped under a
fallen beam. At the sight of Maleneth, the grot struggled furiously, trying
to reach a spear that was just out of reach.

Maleneth grinned and reclaimed her knives from Stinkeye's belt.

'Aelf!' roared Gotrek, barrelling towards them, trailing embers and broken
bodies.

Cerura took a step backwards, shocked by the intensity of the Slayer's
gaze.

'Why did you come to this fortress?' gasped Gotrek, scowling at Maleneth. He looked like he was being repeatedly hit by lightning, jerking and

convulsing. He pointed at Scragfang. 'What business do you have with that creature?'

'He shamed me before Khaine. And he's going to pay. He's going to endure years of agony and suffering. And before his body breaks he'll learn to–'

Gotrek beheaded Scragfang, sending the grot's head bouncing off into the crowd.

Maleneth stared at the corpse in shock. 'Khaine's blood.' She pointed her knife at Gotrek, trembling with rage. 'What did you do that for?'

Gotrek gripped his axe in both hands and dropped into a fighting stance. 'You're an oathbreaker. You lied to me, aelf. All the time we were in Barak-Urbaz.'

Maleneth howled and drew back her knives, preparing to lunge.

Gotrek raised his axe.

Cerura grabbed Maleneth's arm in one hand, Gotrek's in the other, and let the Asylum Gate fill his mind, whispering a prayer as the world fell away.

CHAPTER THIRTY-THREE

Maleneth looked out through a wall of crimson. The Asylum had vanished, replaced by the rusting plains of Skrappa Spill. Gotrek was there too. He was facing away from her, staring off into the distance, but his muscle-slab silhouette was unmistakable. Why was everything drenched in blood? She could taste it in her mouth and feel it pressing against her eardrums. She was drowning in it.

'Two souls?' said a soft voice.

Cerura, she thought, his voice triggering memories of everything that had taken place in Slathermere. *I'm drowning. What have you done?*

Interesting, said her mistress. **You seem to have joined me in my private hell.**

Maleneth felt a jolt of horror as she realised it was true. She was seeing the world from within the blood vial. She was trapped in the amulet. *Cerura! What have you done to me!*

Oh, the sweet irony. Trapped in a prison of your own devising. Maleneth felt her mistress' mind pressing close to hers, holding her in an obscenely intimate embrace. **What fun we'll have.**

Cerura whispered something, then light flooded Maleneth's eyes and air rushed into her lungs. She coughed and spat, trying to rid herself of the blood, but there was nothing there. She sat up with a jolt, coming face to face with Cerura's long, mournful features. He frowned. 'What is that amulet you wear? It holds a spirit.'

She scowled at him and tried to stand, but the movement sent pain flashing up her side and she would have fallen to the ground if Cerura had not caught her. He lowered her back onto the warm metal.

'You saved him,' he said, nodding at the Slayer. 'By giving him the last seed you saved him.'

Maleneth spat, causing herself another stab of pain. Then she scowled at Cerura. '*Never* remind me of that again.'

He looked puzzled, but the anger in her stare stifled his question and he changed the subject. 'One of your wounds is serious. The best I could do was remove the arrowhead and cauterise the scar. Several muscles in your stomach have been separated by the cut. If they do not heal properly you will spend the rest of your days hobbling like a crone.'

'I'm a daughter of Khaine! We do not hobble.'

'Then you'll need to rest. For several weeks. Even then the muscles might not heal properly, but that's your only chance.'

'Rest?' Maleneth found that idea almost as nauseating as hobbling. She lay back, carefully, and looked at the clouds overhead. 'The light looks different.'

'The crisis has passed. The Bad Moon is waning.'

'And what about the boar?'

'Boar?'

'The Slayer. I presume he's drunk. Trying to forget his own name.'

'Eye-wateringly sober,' said Gotrek, dropping down onto the ground beside her.

Cerura left them alone to talk.

The light had gone from Gotrek's chest and he looked sombre. The mania that had driven him to destroy Slathermere had vanished. He seemed old and tired. He tapped the rune. The skin around it was darkened by bruising and burns, and Maleneth wondered if he had been hitting it again. 'It has its hooks in me, Witchblade. There's no way I can escape it. This thing is greater than any power I've come across.'

'I thought you wanted to remove it?'

'Removing it would be cowardice. I see it now.' He stared through her. 'If I want to live with honour, if I want to be worthy of my ancestors, I have to keep it. And find a way to use it.'

She shook her head, confused.

'I have to,' he said. 'Anything else is just running away. I have to face it. Face it down. I have to conquer it. Trachos was afraid of what he was becoming, but he fought on anyway. In the end, he fought with honour. Because he still knew what was right.'

'And he died,' said Maleneth, remembering the scenes on the *Angaz-Kár*.

'Yes. Trying to save you. However much he had endured, however much he had been changed, he did the right thing.'

Maleneth looked at the scars across Gotrek's chest where the rune had burned his skin. 'Why are these things so important to you?' she asked, genuinely intrigued. 'You're one of the few people in the realms who could live any life they choose. Nothing seems able to stop you. Why do you care so much about how you behave? You could come with me to Azyr, hand over the rune and live the life of a revered hero.'

Gotrek was still staring into the middle distance. Emotions flickered across his blocky features. 'Do you know what I would see, Maleneth, if I *did* go to Azyr?'

'What do you mean? It is the Realm of Heavens. You would see all the wonders Sigmar has wrought. You would see mighty Azyrheim – the Eternal City that all the Free Cities are only a pale imitation of. And hanging overhead, like a watchful star, you would see Sigmaron – home of the God-King himself, where he has made–'

'I would see my shame.' Gotrek turned his gaze on her, his expression grim.

'What do you mean?'

'Do you know what he keeps up there, Maleneth? Next to his pretty, sparkling palaces? He keeps a corpse. He keeps the remains of my past. A pitiful, ruined lump that was once my home. Mallus, he calls it. The Old World's remains. It's the broken, pathetic mess I left behind, and he picks at it like it's carrion. I will *never* look upon it. I can face anything but that.'

Maleneth had never heard Gotrek speak like this before. His voice was quiet and taut.

They both fell silent and the quiet was weighted with meaning. Neither of them would meet the other's eye, but she knew they were grappling with the same thought. Gotrek had shared his innermost thoughts with her. He had also abandoned his plans, fought through the Asylum and nearly died to rescue her. And she, given the choice, had used the last seed to save his life rather than her own. It should have brought them closer, but it felt like a burden. Or a wound. She despised him more than anyone she had ever met. And she knew he hated her. And now they were bound. Tied together in ways she could never have predicted.

Gotrek leant closer, fixing her with his fierce gaze. Then he tapped her stomach. 'Typical bloody aelf. Swooning over nothing. I've had worse scratches from a briar.'

Maleneth closed her eyes and let her head fall back onto the ground, wondering if eternity as a toadstool might have been preferable.

Your Celestial Highnesses,

I write to you in the midst of a fever, so please forgive the disjointed nature of this missive. My stay in Barak-Urbaz has been unexpectedly prolonged. Since reaching the Kharadron sky-port, Gotrek has been drawn into a local conflict with the Moonclan tribes that hold sway over much of Ayadah. As is his wont, he abandoned the plans that drew him here and, on a whim, threw himself into an entirely unplanned venture. He joined a misguided attempt to attack the greenskins in their own stronghold, a fungus-crowded underworld by the name of the Asylum. I say misguided because the leader of our party, an infuriatingly cheerful oaf by the name of Captain Solmundsson, was killed, along with half his crew and the Stormcast Eternal Trachos. Gotrek and I managed to return to Barak-Urbaz aboard Solmundsson's sky-ship, the Angaz-Kár, but I have sustained an injury that has since become infected, leaving me bed-bound for what may be several weeks. A local chirurgeon has filled me with so many tinctures that I feel drunk half the time and insane the rest. I am so confused I can barely measure the passing of the days.

Despite the ignominious nature of our return, Gotrek has some-how emerged, yet again, triumphant. By happenstance, rather than design, his escapades in the Asylum derailed the green-skin offensive just as the moon they worship was waxing full. This threw their plans into disarray at a crucial moment. As a result, the local Kharadron fleets have been able to reclaim many of the routes they had previously lost. One of the Barak-Urbaz magnates, an admiral by the name of Solmund, is the father of our deceased captain. I fully expected him to rage at Gotrek for leading his son to his death and perhaps even attempt to punish him, but in a turn of events I should have foreseen, Lord Admiral Solmund has adopted Gotrek as a kind of surrogate son and the two are now inseparable. Gotrek seems to have undergone a kind of epiphany. He is still fixated on the idea of finding a way to live with honour, a way to meet the expectations of his long-dead fore-bears, but since our return to Barak-Urbaz, he has decided that he can best do that by aiding the Kharadron. He still has little love for most of them, but his bond with Solmund has become so strong that he spends long hours in his company, drinking and talking. Something in Gotrek has driven Solmund to rethink his purpose in life. Between them, they have become set on the idea that they can harness their respective powers for 'the good of the realms.' I have no idea what they mean by this, but between my bouts of delirium I shall endeavour to learn their plans.

I have made some progress in another area. After the battle at the Asylum, Gotrek revealed some of his reasons for wishing to avoid Azyr. It is as illogical as all of his thinking, but now that I understand him better, I should be able to find a way to influence him. I believe I am closer than ever to achieving our goal of bringing the rune to Azyrheim.

I was about to send you this report when things took a worrying turn. Despite offers from the admiral, we are staying in the Stromez Quarter, in the same small rooms we rented when we first arrived at Barak-Urbaz. This is, I confess, mainly because I enjoy tormenting the landlord, a strutting ass by the name of Brior, but it is also because I cannot bear the endless drinking songs that fill Solmund's palace. The cramped nature of the lodgings is demeaning, but it means I am able to observe Gotrek's behaviour closely. And I am deeply troubled by what I see. He thinks I sleep more than I do and takes no care to hide his comings and goings, but there is a hard look in his eye I have never seen before. He has taken to bringing Lord Admiral Solmund back to our rooms for secret talks. They spend long hours together, poring over mouldering texts from Solmund's library. As my mind slips in and out of fever dreams I catch glimpses of the two craggy-faced duardin, hunched over books and scratching notes in the margins. Gotrek is possessed by a kind of mania, and he seems to have infected Solmund with the same fervour. I am still too ill to leave my bed, but I sense Gotrek is about to embark on another of his reckless adventures. I have seen him like this before, but he has never had the backing of someone like Solmund. The Solmund Company possesses a powerful fleet and seemingly limitless resources. If Gotrek and Solmund embark on an idealistic crusade, the rune will be lost to us forever.

This may all sound like fever-induced hysteria, but I find his altered mood disturbing. In the deeps of the night, when pain drags me from my dreams, I see him pacing through the darkness, his hand over the rune, muttering about a 'worthy doom.'

Forgive my histrionics, but despite my earlier requests to leave me in peace, I now beg for aid. The Slayer is preparing to do something. And from the look in his eye, I believe it may be something disastrous, either for him or me or for the wider realm. The Gotrek I knew is fading. And something even stranger is taking his place. Contact me here as soon as you are able, I beg you.

Your most loyal and faithful votary,
Maleneth Witchblade

DEATH ON THE
ROAD TO SVARDHEIM

Darius Hinks

'Idiots.' Gotrek stomped through the dust, his axe jolting on his sunburnt shoulders.

His words shook Maleneth out of a daze. It had been hours since either of them had spoken and his sudden outburst made her realise how close to sleep she was. They had been walking for three days with no sign of civilisation. No sign of anything, for that matter. She looked around at the desolate, sun-baked fields. The earth was the colour of blood, and so riven with cracks that it reminded her of Gotrek's scarred face. There were no clouds. No vegetation. Nothing to break the monotony of the view. There were also no people. 'Who?' she said, her voice a dry croak. 'Who are idiots?'

Gotrek nodded at the pale shapes heaped all around them. The road from Gamp to Svardheim was lined with skulls. The plains had been conquered, liberated and reconquered so many times that the ground was more bone than earth. And, at some point, Khorne's cannibals had decided to decorate the road with human heads. Crows had taken the flesh and the sun had bleached the bone. Now the skulls gleamed in the heat, grinning at everyone unfortunate enough to pass by.

For once, Maleneth agreed with the Slayer. 'How did they think they could stand against the legions of Khorne with picks and shovels? They should have fled to Svardheim. At least a few of them might have kept their heads.'

Gotrek stopped and grabbed one of the flasks at his belt. Then he muttered a curse and held it upside down, spilling a single drop of liquid into the dust. He stared at the dark spot it made, looking bereft. 'No beer.'

Maleneth rolled her eyes, threw him a flask of water and wandered over to the edge of the road. The skulls were covered in patches of crimson dust and she had not realised, until now, that there were designs scored into the bone. She stooped down to examine one of them, wiping some of the dust away. To her surprise, rather than the brutal symbols of Khorne, the skulls were scored with elegant characters that she could read. 'Sigmar?' She shook her head. 'I don't understand.'

Gotrek wiped his beard and threw the flask back. 'Probably put here by your sort. Starry-eyed lightning enthusiasts.'

'Nonsense.' Maleneth dusted down more skulls, revealing the name Sigmar on each of them. 'The God-King does not demand human sacrifices.'

'He doesn't demand anything. He just hides. Skulking in the clouds, keeping his head down and waiting for someone else to sort out the mess he made. I didn't say they were sacrifices, anyway. I just said they were put here by your sort. By people so stupid they think writing names will save them.' He booted a skull down the road. 'They put these out thinking Sigmar would see their devotion.' He laughed. 'Thinking he would send help.'

Maleneth's pulse quickened as she realised they were resuming an argument she thought they had abandoned hours ago. 'The war for the realms won't be decided by mortals. It doesn't matter how big your biceps are, Gotrek. It doesn't matter how sharp your axe is. Your fate will be decided by the will of gods. You're a piece in their great game, whether you know it or not.'

'Codswallop.' He rounded on Maleneth. 'You've skulked in my shadow longer than most, aelf, so you can't be as dim-witted as I thought. But you won't last long if you persist in thinking that gods care about you. Sigmar, Khaine, or whoever it is you really whisper to in the dark when you think I'm asleep – they don't know you exist. And if they did, they wouldn't give a rat's arse about you.'

Maleneth snatched a knife from her belt and waved it at the skulls. 'Call them idiots, Gotrek, but the people who left these have more sense than you. They know that they can't be saved by muscles or iron. They know they'll only be saved by faith. Only divine power can stop divine power. Only gods can halt gods.' So many hours without rest or food had left her nerves raw and she turned her knife on Gotrek, her hand trembling. 'And don't try to kid yourself that you're not part of the struggle. If you're not fighting for Order, you're aiding the enemy. There's no middle way. There's no impartiality. You are either with us or you're against us.' Maleneth had never accused Gotrek so directly and it was a blessed relief to finally spit the words out. They had festered between them for too long.

'I'm with no one.' He leant towards her, his eye blazing. 'And no one is with me.'

'Then perhaps you should ask yourself why. You have so much power, Slayer. Power beyond anything I have encountered.' She tapped the rune embedded in his chest. 'Power that can't be explained by this Fyreslayer gold. And where do you think it came from? Do you think you caught it, like an ague? Do you think you gained it through heroic consumption of beer? Do you think you earned it by being more ill-mannered than anyone else? Of course not. So where in all the hells of Shyish do you think it came from?'

Gotrek's expression darkened but he seemed at a loss. He spat into the dust.

'It came from the gods,' she continued. 'Or one particular god. Either way, you're a pawn. A piece in the game whether you know it or not. And if you don't lend your strength to Sigmar's crusade then you might want to think about why. Maybe it's because your power comes from the forces he has sworn to defeat.'

'Chaos?' He gripped his axe in both hands and began circling her. 'You've got some bloody balls, saying that to a son of the Everpeak.'

'Then prove me wrong. Show me you're working for something other than yourself.'

The Slayer continued pacing for a while, then marched on down the road, muttering curses.

Maleneth smiled as she followed. She doubted she had done anything to change Gotrek's mind but goading him was one of her few remaining pleasures.

They walked in silence for another few hours, with Gotrek pausing only to boot the odd skull down the road. Then, finally, just as Maleneth thought she could bear the heat no longer, the light started to dim into a sullen dusk.

'Is that a campfire?' she said, spotting a glow up ahead.

'Doubt it. Too many cannibals and brigands round here. Even the local morons know not to light fires.' Gotrek gripped his axe and nodded to Maleneth's knives. 'Keep your wits about you, aelf. This journey might not be quite as tedious as I thought.'

Maleneth drew her knives and jogged down the road, peering into the dusk, trying to make out the source of the light. It was not long before she spotted the silhouette of an overturned wagon. The horses had gone and there were flames whipping across a torn canvas. 'This happened recently,' she said, slowing and glancing back at Gotrek.

He nodded as he passed her, testing the weight of his axe and scouring the surrounding plains. 'Look there,' he said, pointing his axe towards the sinking sun. 'Another road.'

Maleneth shook her head 'Just hoofprints. Fresh ones. And I think I see the riders.'

Gotrek turned back to the smouldering cart. 'I wonder if they left anything to drink in there.' He marched towards the flames, humming tunelessly.

Bodies were scattered across the road and most of them were headless, darkening the road with their blood. They were wearing white robes trimmed with gold and stitched with hammers and comets.

'Sigmar botherers.' Gotrek paused as he reached the first one, prodding the corpse with his boot. 'They should know better than to travel these plains.' He gave Maleneth a pointed glance. 'Funny. Faith doesn't seem to have done them much good. Perhaps Sigmar was too busy having his hair plaited. He always looks so pretty in those paintings. It must be hard work keeping his nails in good condition.'

Maleneth ignored him, treading carefully through the corpses, looking for survivors.

Gotrek snorted. 'What do you care, aelf? You'd have done the same to them if you thought it would impress Khaine. He is called Khaine, isn't he? Your preferred bloodthirsty deity?'

'I serve the Order of Azyr. I'm sworn to hinder Sigmar's foes and aid his followers. It is the faith of people like this that will give the God-King his victory over Chaos.'

'And then what? If the Chaos Gods really were defeated, how much would you care about Sigmar and his followers then? You'd be doing murder dances for Khaine before I could say "fickle turncoat".'

Maleneth was about to reply when she noticed a gleam of polished metal under one of the cart's broken wheels. In truth, her reasons for scouring the corpses were not entirely virtuous; she was always on the lookout for weapons or artefacts that might be valuable. As she approached the metal, she saw it shift slightly. 'Who's there?' she cried, raising her knife and backing away.

Gotrek rushed to her side, lifting his axe.

'There's someone under here.' Maleneth nodded at the wheel. 'Armed, I think. We should tread carefully in case–'

Gotrek booted the wheel and tipped the cart over. Dust and splinters flew everywhere, and someone bolted, clutching a sword.

Maleneth was about to hurl a knife, then paused and held up a warning hand to Gotrek. It was a human priestess, dressed in the same Sigmarite robes as the others. 'Wait!' cried Maleneth. 'We serve Sigmar.'

Gotrek was about to disagree but Maleneth yelled again before he could speak. 'We mean you no harm.'

The woman ran further down the road, then, when she realised no one was following her, she paused to look back. Her robes were torn and bloodstained, and the sword trembled in her hand, but she did not look badly injured. 'There's nothing left to take,' she said, glancing at the ruined cart. She stumbled, unsteady on her feet, then pointed the sword at Gotrek, frowning as she took in his tattooed muscles and tall crest of hair. 'What are you?'

Gotrek raised an eyebrow. 'A pawn.'

The priestess looked even more confused. She shook her head and turned to go.

'Wait,' called Maleneth. 'I'm Maleneth Witchblade. I'm an agent of the Order of Azyr. I have travelled here from the Celestial Realm.'

The woman's eyes widened. 'You've seen the Eternal City?'

Maleneth nodded. 'I spent many years in Azyrheim.'

The priestess took a few, hesitant steps back towards them. 'Really? Azyrheim... Is it as beautiful as the ancient hymns claim?'

Maleneth thought of the Khainite Murder Temples where she learned to kill, picturing the blood-drenched altars and statues. 'Beauty is in the eye of the beholder.'

The woman stared at her, clearly shocked. 'I am called Carmina,' she said, lowering her sword. She looked at Gotrek. 'Are you a Fyre–'

'He's Gotrek,' interrupted Maleneth. 'He comes from the World-that-Was.'

The priestess looked even more dazed. Maleneth started to wish she had let her run off. There was nothing more annoying than a doe-eyed weakling dogging your every step. She decided that they needed to be rid of her as soon as possible. 'Who did this to you?' she asked, nodding at the corpses.

Carmina's face turned an unhealthy grey as she studied the bodies. 'All dead,' she whispered, stumbling again. 'All of them.'

'Who was it, lass?' asked Gotrek. 'Khorne's Blood Tribes?'

'No... Well... Yes, they might have been followers of Khorne. Most people are in these plains. And they were well armed and provisioned. But they weren't cannibals from the Skran Hills. I think they were just thieves. Marauders.' She clamped her eyes shut. Then she rushed over to Maleneth and gripped her hand. 'You have to help me.'

Maleneth extracted her hand and wiped it clean. 'Where were you headed? Svardheim? We're going there too. You can travel with us.'

'No.' Carmina sounded almost hysterical. 'That's not what I mean. The brigands took our cases.'

'Looks like they took everything,' said Maleneth, 'but we'll get you home.'

'There was a holy relic.' The priestess grabbed Maleneth's arm again. 'The Incorruptible Fist. The cornerstone of our faith. We must retrieve it.'

Maleneth laughed. 'Retrieve it?' She looked at the tracks she'd spotted earlier. The riders had vanished into the growing dusk. 'If we chased every rogue in this desert we'd never leave.'

'The cornerstone of your faith, you say?' Gotrek gave Maleneth a wry look. 'Sounds like the sort of thing the Order of Azyr should be protecting.'

Maleneth glared at him.

He shrugged, the playful look still in his eye. 'You lecture me on the value of faith, and then when this lass tells you that her precious Sigmar tat has been stolen you're too scared to try to get it back. Scared of a few lowlifes.'

'Scared?' Maleneth knew Gotrek was playing mind games with her but it was impossible not to bite. 'Of course I'm not scared.'

Carmina's eyes lit up. 'Then you'll help? The Incorruptible Fist is the relic that we built our temples to preserve. Losing it would be a terrible blow.' She stared at the corpses, her eyes full of tears. 'Such a blow.'

Maleneth resisted the urge to hit her. 'Yes. I'll get your damned relic back.' She jabbed her finger at the Slayer. 'Because I know that serving the God-King is the *only* way to liberate the realms.'

Gotrek raised an eyebrow. 'You have more guts than I thought.' He looked at the priestess, his eye gleaming again. 'How many of these brigands are there, would you say?'

She grimaced. 'Fifteen. Maybe even twenty.'

Gotrek looked disappointed. 'Shame. Still, better than nothing.' He hefted his axe, catching firelight on the blade. 'It's been so long since I actually used this thing.'

Maleneth nodded. 'Good. If there are so few, we can make short work of them and get out of this tedious desert.' She sheathed her knives and continued down the road, waving for the priestess to follow. 'Stay near me and away from him. He doesn't always swing that axe where he's meant to.'

Gotrek grinned at the priestess. 'Don't worry, lass, I know how to swing an axe. As long as no cowering aelves get in the way.'

Maleneth led the way to the tracks Gotrek had pointed out earlier and began following them. The going was easy for the first hour or so, but after that the land tumbled into a series of ridges that had not been visible from the road. Even with the sun almost setting, the desert was fiercely hot, and the ascents soon had Maleneth gasping for breath. It did not help matters that the priestess was clinging to her shoulder, barely able to walk.

'Why did you venture out here?' asked Maleneth. 'This whole country is full of warbands and brigands. Why would you risk your lives? Why would you risk the relic for that matter?'

'What use is it if we don't show it to people? The Fist is what drives us.' Carmina looked out into the dust clouds. 'People have cowered for so long, crushed by the boot of Chaos, but they're rising now. Because they know Sigmar is coming to their aid.'

Gotrek cast Maleneth a sideways glance but she ignored him and nodded for the priestess to continue.

'If we keep the Fist hidden away in a temple it's worthless. It has to be out here, where people can see it. See proof of Sigmar's will.'

Maleneth was about to argue with Carmina's logic when Gotrek grunted and signalled for them to keep their heads down. They had reached the brow of a hill and as Maleneth edged forwards, she saw why Gotrek had warned them. Nestling in a small valley, hidden from the surrounding plains, was a ruined keep. It must once have been large enough to house a thousand soldiers but most of it had been destroyed centuries ago. The architecture was unfamiliar to Maleneth. It did not have the spires and domes of a Sigmarite Stormkeep, nor the brutal, thorn-sharp towers of a Chaos Dreadhold. She guessed, from the organic curves of its walls, that it was from the time before recorded history, the time before Chaos laid claim to the realms. The masonry was carved to resemble mythological beasts and warriors clad in strange, elaborate armour. The light was fading fast now, but she could see that one of the towers had been refortified. The walls had been repaired and there was a light flickering inside, red and angry as it spilled from the crumbling windows. It did not seem like firelight and something about it troubled Maleneth. There were a dozen or so horses tethered outside, huddled in the shattered remains of a stone outbuilding. The sound of laughter and singing drifted up towards them through the darkness.

'Sounds like there's barely twenty,' said Gotrek.

'Good,' muttered Maleneth.

'They're heavily armed,' whispered Carmina.

The priestess grew more pathetic by the second and Maleneth cursed herself for ending up in this situation. If it had not been for the argument with Gotrek, she would never have got herself drawn into such an absurd predicament. Not for the first time, Maleneth had the horrible feeling that her true feelings were more aligned with the Slayer's than she could bear to admit. She crushed the idea, refusing to accept it. Gotrek was grinning and about to speak but she talked over him. 'Before you suggest it, we're not going to just walk down there and kick the door in.'

Gotrek's grin broadened. 'Simple plans always work best. You aelves over-complicate things. What could be wrong with clobbering them, getting the relic and clearing out?'

'Firstly, I don't trust you not to behead me. Secondly, while we're stuck at the gate, fighting guards, someone else could easily get on one of those horses and take the relic, which would make the whole exercise pointless.'

'Boring, but true, I suppose. What do you suggest then? A bit of prayer?'

Maleneth looked down at the ruins and thought for a moment. 'I suggest not acting like savages. It's almost dark. We should wait until the sun's gone down. Then, you can go ahead with your elegant door-kicking plan. But you can wait until I've positioned myself at the rear of the tower by that toppled archway. Then, when you start shouting and stamping, and all eyes are on you, I'll make my way into the tower with less opposition and find the relic.'

'You mean, I do the hard work while you sneak around and get the prize?'

Maleneth shrugged.

Gotrek nodded. 'Stops you from getting under my feet, I suppose.' He looked at the priestess. 'And what about you? What's your plan?'

The woman looked terrified. Maleneth replied on her behalf. 'Carmina will stay up here, on this ridge, until we come back for her.'

Carmina nodded eagerly, holding up her sword like it was hurting her hand. 'I would only hinder you.'

Maleneth shook her head. 'How in the name of Khaine have you reached adulthood without learning to defend yourself?'

The woman shrugged awkwardly.

Maleneth sighed and looked back at the tower, trying to discern its details before the last of the light faded. There was an exterior staircase that circled the tower from the ruined arch. It was too unstable for clumsy, heavy humans but she would be able to race up it to another archway at the top of the tower. Once Gotrek started bellowing she would easily be able to descend into the tower from there.

They sat in silence until the sun was no more than a crimson line on the horizon; then Maleneth nodded at Gotrek. 'Wait until that light has gone and then attack in whatever manner you think best. Just make sure to make a lot of noise.'

Even in the half-light she could see his rows of buckled teeth, smiling back at her.

Maleneth waved Carmina back a few steps then ran down into the narrow valley, leaping easily over rocks and scrub. She had never seen a keep hidden at the bottom of a valley before, but she could see the sense of it. It would be hidden from any of the roads that crossed the plain. As she neared the ruins, she dodged around the patches of red light thrown from the windows. The sounds of revelry grew louder as she came nearer. She could not understand the language, but it was clear from the slurred words that the brigands had been drinking. Maleneth was pleased. If they were drunk this should all be over quite quickly.

She ducked even lower as a door creaked open and a man stumbled out. He was wearing a copper-coloured cuirass and helmet, and there was an axe slung over his back, but he was clearly drunk, mumbling and singing to himself. He weaved and staggered off into the night, leaving the door open.

Maleneth waited until he was out of sight then dashed over to the side of the doorway, listening carefully for sounds of any other guards. Then she stepped inside, knives raised. The passageway was lined with doors and, at the far end, it opened onto a courtyard, which was the source of the red light. Figures were moving back and forth in front of it, dancing and stumbling. Maleneth took a few steps down the corridor, identifying the door that she thought would most likely lead out to the staircase she had seen. Then she halted. There was another sound coming from the courtyard. As well as the voices of the brigands, there was a deeper, louder sound, like the breathing of a large animal. *Very* large, she realised. Each rattling breath drew another burst of laughter and jeers from the men. Maleneth cursed. 'What is that?' she whispered. She carried on past the door, keeping to the shadows as she edged closer to the opening at the far end of the corridor.

'Khaine's teeth,' she whispered as she saw what was happening in the courtyard. There was a small group of drunken men and women, all clad in the same copper-coloured armour as the man she had seen outside, and all of them were singing. It was not the scene of wild debauchery she had expected, though. The brigands were moving with purpose, dancing around a circle of objects. Maleneth barely looked at the drunks, however. Her gaze was drawn straight to something that was seated at the centre of the circle. For a moment, she thought it was a repulsive statue. It was nearly thirty feet tall and built in the likeness of a bull but with muscular arms and the head of a slavering hound. It was gripping a sword the size of an oak tree, with the blade plunged into the ground. Maleneth quickly realised that it was not a statue. There was a palpable sense of malice pouring from it and its bare, heavily muscled chest was oozing blood.

Maleneth whispered a prayer and edged back into the passageway. 'Daemon,' she gasped, the word catching in her throat. She could not take her eyes off the thing. Every inch of it was wet. Streams of blood were rushing from its flanks and the beams of light she had seen from outside were blazing from beneath the lids of its closed eyes, spilling across the drunken dancers. The circle that surrounded it, scored into the flagstones, was incredibly complex, decorated with sigils and script and divided into eight segments. An object had been placed at the outer edge of each segment – a seemingly random assortment of holy icons and religious relics. Maleneth had seen enough blood rites to realise what was happening. These people were not simple thieves. They had sourced holy artefacts with a specific purpose in mind: to drag this monster from the aether-void.

'Gotrek,' she whispered, remembering that the Slayer was about to burst into the ruins.

She hurried back down the passageway and as she left the building, she sighed with relief. The sun had not quite set. There was still a line of red on the horizon. 'I still have time,' she whispered, heading back across the valley.

'Form a queue!' bellowed Gotrek as the sound of breaking wood echoed through the darkness. 'I can't kill you all at once!'

Maleneth clutched her head as she heard the unmistakeable sound of the Slayer wading into battle. 'It's not time!' she hissed, halting and looking back at the ruins. The red light was flickering, and she could hear the sound of blades clashing. 'I hate him,' she spat, turning and heading back towards the doorway she had just left, running back down the passageway.

She reached the courtyard in time to see Gotrek barrel into view, crashing into the crowd of drunks and sending them tumbling in every direction. 'Stand and fight, you bloody cowards!' cried the Slayer. 'There must be one of you who can–' His words stalled in his mouth as he saw the daemon. 'Grungni's balls,' he muttered, stumbling to a halt and lowering his axe, looking up at the blood-slick giant. 'You're an ugly beast.'

'Gotrek!' howled Maleneth, running across the courtyard towards him. One of the brigands lashed out at her with an axe but she ducked the blow and slit his throat without breaking her stride. 'We have to get out!'

Gotrek was staring up at the daemon and Maleneth's heart sank. His eye was flashing with kill-fever. She would not get him to leave until either he or the daemon had been destroyed. She wished she could leave the oaf to his fate, but she was sworn to protect the rune in his chest.

Another attacker lunged towards her, but she parried the blow, turned on her heel and opened his throat. Most of the brigands were already dead or sprinting for the exit, but Gotrek had clearly lost interest in them. He walked slowly towards the towering figure at the centre of the courtyard, staring at it eagerly. 'Come on,' he growled. 'Let's see what you've got.'

Maleneth halted and looked up at the daemon's canine features, praying the thing would not hear Gotrek.

Red light blazed across the courtyard as the daemon opened its eyes and turned to face Gotrek. It bared a row of tusk-like teeth. 'I remember you.' Its voice was like an earth tremor. The walls juddered with each syllable. 'The Slayer who ran.'

Maleneth's sanity was straining. The daemon's voice was not a natural sound. It was not produced by vocal cords but torn from the darkness. It split the air, rattled her teeth and filled her head with visions. She wanted to howl or flee but Gotrek replied as though he were still speaking to one of the drunks.

'Ran? What are you talking about, ran?'

The daemon's reply caused Maleneth's stomach to lurch. 'When the others marched, you fled.' The daemon glared down at Gotrek. 'Fled your own world. Left them to die.'

Gotrek looked dazed for a moment. Then his brows bristled. 'Liar.' He paced closer. 'I did not flee anything. The gods tricked me. Grimnir tricked me. He said I would find my doom.'

'Gotrek!' cried Maleneth, realising what was happening. 'Don't listen! It's goading you. It wants you to–'

Gotrek charged across the courtyard, entered the circle and dived at the daemon, raising his axe as he hurtled through the air.

The moment Gotrek entered the circle of runes, the daemon roared and rose up, shattering the roof as it drew back its sword.

Gotrek's axe clashed with the daemon sword. A wave of energy slammed into Maleneth and the few remaining drunks, sending them tumbling across the flagstones as masonry crashed down around them.

Maleneth rolled clear a moment before a stone lintel crushed her.

Coarse laughter filled her head as the daemon hurled Gotrek through the air, sending the Slayer smashing through the wall and causing another section of the tower to tumble.

Maleneth dodged more falling stone and ducked under an archway.

'You can't kill it!' she cried, as Gotrek clambered back into view and ran back into the circle, drawing his axe back and leaping up for another attack.

The daemon parried, but Gotrek's blow was so fierce that it staggered under the impact, swaying and almost falling. Maleneth noticed that the daemon's smile faltered when it neared the circle's perimeter. It managed to right itself but not before Gotrek had hacked deep into its chest, spilling crimson light.

'It's not ready to be born,' she said, looking at the objects arrayed around the circle. 'It can't leave the summoning circle.'

More wall crashed down as Gotrek and the daemon fought, and Maleneth had to dodge the falling debris.

'If not for your cowardice,' said the daemon, 'your world would never have died.'

Gotrek sneered and hacked at the daemon's leg.

Again, the daemon was so concerned with not stepping outside the confines of the circle that the Slayer was able to land another blow.

Maleneth sidestepped more falling masonry and found herself next to the circle. She could feel power radiating from inside it, crackling across her skin and pounding in her skull. She was standing beside one of the objects placed around the perimeter and realised it was an ugly, badly chiselled rendition of a fist. 'That?' She laughed in disbelief as she realised that the lumpen object must be the relic Carmina sought. She grabbed and was about to hurl it in disgust when the daemon howled and grew smaller, shrinking visibly.

It looked down and fixed Maleneth with its burning glare.

'Wait,' she gasped, backing away.

'Quick thinking, aelf!' Gotrek dropped to the ground and booted another relic from the circle.

The daemon convulsed and roared as it shrank a few more feet.

Maleneth cursed herself for not seeing the answer before. The daemon was not yet born. The circle of relics was the only thing giving it purchase in reality. She dashed around the circle, scattering objects as Gotrek did the same.

The daemon jerked and juddered as it shrank, howling and barking until, finally, it was only a few feet taller than Maleneth. The light had almost totally faded from its bloody flesh and it was struggling to stand.

Gotrek strode from the dust clouds and beheaded it with a single blow of his axe. 'A Slayer does not flee.'

The head blazed like lava then blinked out of existence. The rest of the daemon slammed to the floor then did the same.

Gotrek stood over the scorched flagstones, breathing heavily and gripping his axe, staring at where the daemon had fallen. Then the tower let out a deep groan and started to lean.

'Out!' cried Maleneth, bolting for one of the archways.

Gotrek paused to pick something up from the ground, then jogged calmly after her, wiping blood and dust from his face.

A few of the brigands had survived and were hastily mounting horses and racing from the valley, but most were sprawled in the ruins.

'Keep moving,' said Maleneth as the tower slumped slowly in their direction.

They ran on, back up to the top of the slope where Carmina was waiting, cowering on the ground, her eyes wide. She was about to speak when the tower's foundations finally gave way, sending tons of rock crashing onto the ground. Maleneth shook her head, looking at Gotrek. 'That place probably stood for thousands of years. You've been here two minutes and it's rubble.'

Gotrek gave her an elaborate bow.

'You have it,' whispered Carmina, staring at Gotrek.

'He has what?' demanded Maleneth.

Gotrek held up the Incorruptible Fist and frowned at it. 'It looks like a bloody turd, lass. Are you sure this is going to inspire devotion?'

Carmina hesitantly took it from him. As soon as she held it, cool light spilled from the knuckles, lighting up her ecstatic face. 'I'm sure.'

Maleneth took a few steps backwards. 'I've seen enough magic light for one evening. What is that?'

'The power of faith,' whispered Carmina. 'When so many souls believe in something, they imbue it with power. Power that goes beyond nature.' She held the icon towards Gotrek's face, bathing his battered features in light. 'You have achieved something incredible tonight, Slayer. You have retrieved a portion of the God-King's might.'

Maleneth expected Gotrek to say something dismissive, but he looked puzzled, staring into the glare. Then he rolled his shoulders and grunted, backing away from the priestess. The light faded from the Fist and Carmina secreted it in her robes.

Gotrek pointed down to the outbuilding. 'The idiots have left you a horse. Get yourself home, lass. You'll travel quicker on that than with us. Get that relic back to your temple.' He gave her a stern look. 'And don't go wandering around in the desert with it.'

Carmina's eyes flashed in the dark as she gripped Gotrek's hand and kissed it. Then she rushed through the shadows towards the outbuilding. A moment later they watched her ride off into the night, steering the horse with the skill of an experienced rider.

Gotrek watched her for a few minutes, muttering into his beard, then he turned and began marching back towards the road.

Maleneth hesitated before following him, thinking of how he had looked into the holy light, and how he had insisted that Carmina keep the relic safe. 'You do believe,' she said rushing after him.

He glanced back, his face half-hidden in the darkness. 'In what?'

'In faith. In gods. In the power of gods.'

'What are you talking about?'

'When you saw that fist light up, you didn't know what to say.'

'Rubbish. I just know when to shut up. Not like some people I could mention.'

Maleneth smirked, pleased to know that she had been right. Helping the annoying priestess had been the correct thing to do. Even Gotrek could see it. They had helped the followers of Sigmar preserve a powerful talisman of their faith. She sensed that there would be great ramifications in the battles to come.

They reached the skull-lined road, and for the next few hours they marched in silence, each lost in their own thoughts. Maleneth was determined not to show weakness in front of the Slayer, but she was ready to sleep at the roadside when she spotted lights in the darkness, just less than half a mile from the road.

'That might be a place to sleep in safety,' she said, pointing it out to Gotrek. He laughed. 'Safety?'

'This road is under the protection of Svardheim. I know it's teeming with brigands but a building that's so visible from the road must be under the aegis of Svardheim. It looks like a monastery to me.'

Gotrek was unimpressed. 'I say we keep on until we reach the capital.'

Maleneth thought for a moment. 'I imagine they'll have ale. And food.'

Gotrek shook his head. 'You act like I only think with my belly.' He looked at the distant lights, frowning. 'Perhaps I do.' He thought for a moment, then turned off the road and struck out across the plains.

As they neared the building, Maleneth saw that she was right: it was plastered with symbols of the Sigmarite faith and the Svardheim colours were flying from its walls.

They were still a few minutes away when voices called down from the battlements, demanding to know who they were.

'I'm Maleneth Witchblade,' she yelled back. 'I serve the Order of Azyr.'

'Get back on the road,' replied a hidden speaker, sounding angry and afraid. 'You're not welcome.'

Gotrek laughed but Maleneth felt a surge of fury. 'We have just risked our lives saving one of your most precious relics. You can at least have the decency to offer us a place to sleep.'

There was a pause. 'Which relic?'

Maleneth stiffened with anger and wondered if she could pinpoint the speaker accurately enough to hurl a knife. 'The Incorruptible Fist!'

There was another pause. 'The Incorruptible Fist was stolen last night.'

'We know that, you nitwit,' cried Gotrek. '*We* found the bloody cart. We got the relic back to Carmina.'

'The Fist was stolen from our vaults last night,' the voice was trembling with anger, 'by a murdering thief called Carmina. She disguised herself as one of our order. She and her companions killed several priests as they raided the vault.'

Maleneth could not understand what she was hearing for a moment, thinking of the timid, cowering priestess they had rescued from the cart. Then she recalled how Carmina had seemed to change her demeanour as she rode off into the night, replacing her hesitant manner with a sudden confidence. 'No,' she whispered. 'It can't be.'

'The Fist is made of realmstone,' cried the voice. 'It's priceless. Carmina will have it smashed into pieces and sold to a hundred bidders. She has stolen our most treasured prize just to make herself rich. Have you seen her? She has to be stopped.'

Maleneth gripped her scalp, trembling with hate as she realised how completely she had been deceived.

Gotrek watched her for a moment, shaking his head in disbelief. Then he threw back his head and laughed, his great, booming guffaws echoing through the night.

SOULSLAYER

Darius Hinks

Your Celestial Highnesses,

Please forgive the break in correspondence. I have been traversing the wastes of Chamon, caught up in another one of the Slayer's ludicrous obsessions. I have never known anyone who can invest so much in an idea and then abandon it so easily. His much-vaunted partnership with the Solmund Company of Barak-Urbaz has already ended in disaster. For a while, he was grudgingly impressed by the Kharadron magnate Lord-Admiral Solmund, calling him sound-headed and trustworthy. The pair spent several months working on a scheme to revive an ancient duardin kingdom called the Khazalid Empire. They claimed they were going to 'drive the forces of darkness from lands that are rightfully ours' but, of course, it all came to nothing (like so many of Gotrek's endeavours). Gotrek ended up denouncing Solmund as a 'snotling-fondler and an oathbreaker.' The disagreement originated in a Kharadron drinking hall after several days of ale-fuelled 'planning.' A fight broke out, but when Gotrek sobered up, I managed to convince him to leave the sky-port rather than 'knock it on its arse.' I have yet to uncover the details of the argument but the two duardin seem equally bent on killing each other if their paths ever cross again.

Despite severing ties with the Kharadron, Gotrek has not abandoned his vague idea of 'fixing' the realms. He has decided that the only way to honour his long-dead ancestors is to behave as they would have done in the Mortal Realms. Gotrek considers this a great revelation and he is infuriatingly evangelical about his 'new' plan. But, as far as I can tell, it makes no difference. His goal is to lock horns with anyone who disagrees with him, which is what he's been doing since the first day I met him.

All of this is a long-winded way of asking you to ignore my previous requests for aid. Now that Gotrek has severed ties with the Solmund Company, I am quite capable of monitoring his progress and protecting the rune embedded in his chest (which we are all so keen to see brought safely to Azyr). At present, we are headed south-west, away from the relatively stable core of the Spiral Crux, to a gods-forsaken backwater known as the Incendiary Coast. I sense that Gotrek has a particular destination in mind but he is refusing to share it.

As I am sure you are aware, the military situation in Chamon is as mercurial as the landscape. The armies of Chaos are dominant, of course. These are still very much their lands, and the Realm of Metal teems with daemon-worshipping sorcerers and skull-taking warlords, but... the local greenskin tribes are increasingly a thorn in their side and many duardin, both mountain-bound and skyborne, still manage to carve out a life for themselves in the shadow of the Ruinous Powers. In some places, such as the aforementioned Barak-Urbaz, the duardin are even thriving.

The pleas for help in my previous missive were the result of delirium, brought on by injuries, and I apologise for their hysterical tone. I assure you, all is now well. Please refrain from sending any more agents of the order to assist me. Their arrival would only complicate matters and antagonise the Slayer (it does not take much). I will contact you as soon as I learn more about his purpose at the coast. Until then, I remain,

Your most loyal and faithful votary,
Maleneth Witchblade

CHAPTER ONE

'Gotrek has to die.' Drymuss leant closer to Maleneth. 'Everything else has failed.' The witch hunter was handsome, for a human, with broad, strong features and the relaxed air of an idle prince. His indolence was an affectation, of course. Beneath his peaked hat and his cloak, he was a knot of righteous muscle. Maleneth had killed enough people to recognise a master of the craft. Drymuss smiled, trying to look amiable, but it was the smile of a predator. She had heard his name mentioned several times before she had left Azyrheim, usually in hushed whispers. Drymuss burned first and asked questions later. The Order of Azyr only used him when subtler methods were no longer an option. He leant back against a tree stump, his face gilded by firelight as he sipped his wine, studying her with lidded eyes. 'Don't blame yourself.'

She looked past him, out across the sea. They were near the cliff's edge and, as dusk turned to night, the Amethystine Ocean blazed in defiance, resisting the dark, flaunting its grandeur like a preening bird. Its cocktail of alloys and chemicals simmered in the gloom, trying to compete with the stars that were blinking into view overhead. The colours in the waves were vibrant even at this distance and embers spilled from the breakers, drifting to the clifftop, whirling around Maleneth like errant spirits. 'I don't blame myself,' she said. 'He's not what I thought he was.'

Drymuss frowned. 'He's just like any other Fyreslayer. Bigger perhaps. And undoubtedly peculiar. But he's still just a hairy, duardin lump. Without that rune in his chest he'd be nothing. He could easily have died the day you met him in... Where was it, a Fyreslayer gaol in Aqshy? They certainly had no problem capturing him. Were they called the Unbak lodge?'

Maleneth continued watching the embers drift around the hollow, thinking back to the Fyreslayer Halls of Censure where she had first seen Gotrek.

'I thought the same as you,' she said, 'when I first met him. He was so confused he mistook me for a daemon. He thought everyone was a daemon, in fact. His head has taken so many hits his mind doesn't work as it should. And I imagine he was a boorish oaf even before that. He fights like a drunk even on the rare occasions he's sober. He takes no pride in his kills and he dedicates them to no god. He doesn't even realise he's in thrall to gods. He thinks he's their equal. No' – she laughed – 'not equal. He thinks he's superior to them. That they have no value at all.' She waved the little bottle Drymuss had given her, letting the light catch on the twin-tailed comet etched into the glass. 'He thinks gods are fools, and that the rest of us are fools too – and that he's the only one who isn't a fool.'

As Maleneth spoke, her hatred of Gotrek simmered up from her chest. She needed to be careful around a snake like Drymuss, but her anger caught her unawares and she found herself warming to her theme. 'He's so uncouth, he can't even grasp the value of faith. It's beyond his intellect. He thinks he can just crack heads with anything that gets in his way and end up on top.' She paused, as bewildered as she always was when she thought about the Slayer. 'And he's right, damn him. That's the worst thing. He *does* come out on top. Whatever the realms throw at him he blunders through, spilling beer and breaking wind while his enemies flounder. And this is the most absurd part – half his enemies end up adopting him as a saviour. It's maddening. Gotrek is the one person who doesn't value religion and everyone decides that he must be some kind of divinity himself. He's an ugly, pig-headed idiot but he's the only person I've met who actually seems able to...' She cut herself off before she said too much, taking a deep breath to calm herself.

Drymuss studied her, his eyes glinting under the brim of his hat. '*What* is he able to do, Maleneth Witchblade? What do you think he is?'

This was a dangerous moment. Maleneth could see the pistols under his cloak. He would attack her the moment he sensed her allegiance had shifted. Her aelven reflexes would give her an advantage over his sluggish, human muscles, but she only had knives and he had guns. She preferred the odds to be weighted more heavily in her favour. And they soon would be. She would not need to play this out for much longer.

'I think Gotrek's an obstacle,' she lied. 'I think the only way we'll ever get that rune to Azyr is by cutting it from his chest. That's what I've said all along. And that's why I requested help. I just need a way to kill him.'

He continued watching her closely and she sensed he was unconvinced. He nodded at the bottle he had given her. 'That will do it. We've studied your letters. And I've conducted *thorough* interviews with people who've encountered Gotrek Gurnisson. That rune he stole from us has made him resilient. Unnaturally resilient. As you pointed out, even your Khainite toxins may not be enough to stop his heart. But that tincture I've given you is no normal poison. It will ossify him, Maleneth. His flesh will harden and turn to bone but the rune will remain unharmed. We'll pluck it from his remains like a jewel from ashes. Collegiate Arcane scholars spent months refining the recipe. And I tested it myself on various unrepentant apostates. It will turn him to bone, Maleneth, you can trust me on that. And perhaps then, as he dies, he will finally understand his place, finally see how insignificant he is compared to Sigmar Heldenhammer. All you need to do is pour those few drops down his throat before he wakes up.'

The sound of Gotrek's snoring ripped through the darkness, as if on cue. The Slayer was further up the coastal path, slumped in the back of a cart tethered to a pair of ironbacks that were almost as cantankerous as he was. It was rare for the Slayer to sleep, but after three weeks of traipsing down to the coast they had found an abandoned stash of barrels filled with something that smelled like bilge water. Gotrek had described it, through grimaces, as 'tolerable', and then proceeded to drink the lot. He had been unconscious for nearly two days.

She sighed, wondering how much longer she would need to keep up her act. She was not the Sigmar-botherer Gotrek always described her as, but lying to an agent of the order set her teeth on edge. People like Drymuss excelled at rooting out untruth.

'What is it?' he said, attempting another smile. 'Are you hesitant to kill him?' He shrugged. 'It wouldn't be so strange. You've spent a long time in his company. And you've been through a lot together. From what I hear, Gotrek has saved your life on several occasions. Perhaps you feel you owe him something?' He looked into the fire. 'Or perhaps you're just afraid of him?'

He was trying to goad her. It was a common witch hunter technique. Drymuss hoped that, by making her angry, he might trick her into revealing some kind of heretical misbelief. But she was not a hedge witch trying to summon luck from chicken guts. She was a covenite sister, an assassin without equal, hardened in the Murder Temples of High Azyr. She shook her head. 'I'm not afraid, Captain Drymuss. Of anything.' She mirrored his hard smile. 'I'm a Daughter of Khaine.'

'Khaine?' Amusement flickered in his eyes. 'You mean Morathi-Khaine?'

Maleneth hesitated, confused by the name. Morathi was the High Oracle of her sisterhood. She interpreted Khaine's will. But Maleneth had never heard the two names combined like this and she sensed, from the gleam in Drymuss' eyes, that it was more than just a slip of the tongue. There must have been some kind of political change, some shift in power that she was unaware of.

'You don't know, do you?' he laughed.

She tried to mask her confusion. 'I know everything I need to know. I know how to survive and kill, and I know how to serve.'

'Serve who?' He gave her a look of exaggerated sympathy. 'The realms are changing, Maleneth. Your own people are changing. And you know nothing about it because you're traipsing through the wilderness after Gotrek, caught up in his ridiculous feuds. You're being left behind. Use the tincture. Kill him. He could wake up at any time. You said he rarely sleeps.' He raised an eyebrow. 'Or I can do it if you lack the nerve.'

Maleneth was about to argue, but then she realised she had kept Drymuss occupied long enough. She relaxed. The danger had passed. She looked over at the cart. 'You can't kill him. And I lied when I said *I* would.'

Unease flickered in his eyes as he sensed that he might not be holding all the cards. 'What are you talking about?' Drymuss frowned and looked down at his hand. He grunted, trying and failing to move his arm. 'What?' His voice sounded odd as the muscles in his throat contracted, already stiffening, already turning to bone.

Maleneth leant towards him, holding up the bottle. She turned it upside down to reveal that it was empty. 'Expertly made. I assume, from the way you knocked back that wine, that the poison was completely tasteless.'

Drymuss' eyes widened in shock but when he tried to speak, only a strangled gargle emerged.

'Consider this my resignation from the Order of Azyr,' said Maleneth, lying back to gaze up at the stars. 'I rescind my commission.' The captain's body made an odd creaking noise as it turned to bone, and Maleneth thought about how much danger she had put herself in by killing him.

You've betrayed the only people who could have given you a route back into Azyr. You claim you're going to become a powerful figure in the sisterhood. You claim you're going to take my place. But how can you return now? You're a bigger fool than I thought. The voice only existed in Maleneth's mind and it came from an amulet hanging at her neck. There was a vial of blood mounted in the amulet and the blood was a prison, containing the tormented soul of Maleneth's former mistress. *What will they do when they hear Drymuss has gone missing? They sent him here looking for you. They sent him here at your request. Why would you be such a fool as to tell the order where you are and then kill the first envoy they send? Even for you, that's absurd.*

The sounds of the dying witch hunter merged with the crackling of the fire and the crashing of waves to make a pleasantly soothing sound. 'I changed my mind,' said Maleneth, closing her eyes. 'I can't let them kill Gotrek to get that rune.'

Why in the name of the Murder God not?

'You know exactly why. You've seen everything I've seen. You've seen how people follow him. You've seen how fearless he is. How unique. How he faces down everything in the realms.' She had to drag the words from her throat. 'He's what they all think he is – some kind of damned hero. He's going to make a difference. He's already made a difference.'

Absurd, said her mistress, but the fire had gone from her words. She was only arguing through habit. They both knew the irritating truth: Gotrek had to live.

Maleneth battled the sleepiness that washed over her but it was no use. She slipped into a dream of embers and smoke.

CHAPTER TWO

'Valaya's arse.' Gotrek was laughing. 'What's this?'

Maleneth woke with a start. It was dawn and her leathers were damp with dew. The fire was out and Gotrek was silhouetted by the rising sun. 'What's what?' she groaned, stretching her stiff limbs and patting herself down to check for her weapons and poisons.

'Did you *whittle* this?' Gotrek was peering at the ossified remains of Captain Drymuss. 'Is this how you spend your time if I have a nap? Have you got a bloody *hobby*?' He tapped the pale shape with his axe and it crumbled, forming a powdery heap around his boots. 'Typical cack-handed aelf work. Neither use nor ornament.'

Maleneth sighed, trying to summon up the energy to endure another day of Gotrek. She stood, dusted herself down and looked out at the sea. It was sullen now, the colours less dazzling, but the daylight revealed peculiar shapes circling in the currents. She had noticed them several times over the last few days. There was a weird alchemy to the whole of the Incendiary Coast. Along with the metallic fish that lived in the sea, she had caught fleeting glimpses of humanoid forms. They were like the shadows of swimmers, but there were no swimmers. She was not altogether surprised by such inexplicable sights. The further they travelled away from the heartlands of the Spiral Crux, the more unpredictable the Realm of Metal became. She needed to convince the Slayer to turn around. They needed to find something approximating civilisation or they would end up in kingdoms where science and logic no longer held sway.

Gotrek was picking his way round the hollow, kicking at Drymuss' discarded bags and weapons. He showed no signs of being hungover. His tall crest of hair was crooked from where he had slept on it and his beard was matted with grease and stale beer, but the glint was back in his eye. He radiated a rude vitality that told Maleneth they would be spending another day charging down the coast looking for trouble. The Slayer alternated between bouts of despondency and periods of wild fervour. Since hatching his latest idea he had been infuriatingly excited.

'These aren't your things,' he said, picking up Drymuss' travel bag and rummaging through it. He grunted as a Sigmarite icon fell out.

'Wait,' said Maleneth, rushing over.

Gotrek held the bag away from her as he plucked out a bundle of letters.

'What's this?' He squinted at the elegant script. 'That's your writing. I'd recognise your spidery scribble anywhere.' He looked from the letters to the icon that had fallen from the bag, then to the pile of dust that had used to be Captain Drymuss. Then he turned to Maleneth, his expression darkening. 'Still trying to betray me. Even now.' Colour flushed into his cheeks and his enormous biceps flexed as he tightened his grip on his axe. 'Writing to your friends in Azyr, planning to hand me over like a fatted calf. Trying to make me a weapon for that thunderstruck farm boy, Sigmar.'

Maleneth muttered a curse and backed away.

Now do you see? You let him live and look where it's got you. He'll have your head for this.

Gotrek clanged his axe against the golden icon in his chest. 'If you want the bloody rune, come and get it.' He nodded at her knives. 'Stop farting about. Show some backbone. Stop writing asinine letters and fight me.' His mood had turned from amiable to apoplectic in an instant. He dropped the letters and stamped around the hollow, swinging his axe, his furious eye locked on Maleneth. 'Let's get it over with. Once and for all. You've been looking for a way to kill me since the day we met. Why don't you actually do something about it? Aren't you supposed to be an assassin? You don't seem very good at killing things.'

Maleneth imagined what it would be like if she really could rid herself of the Slayer. There were still poisons she had not tried. Perhaps one, transmitted on a carefully placed blade, could work. But she knew she would not try. The time for murdering Gotrek was past. She had too much invested in him now. The moment she had killed Drymuss, she had severed all ties with the Order of Azyr. Her only hope of success now lay with the angry, swearing brute who was currently looking for an excuse to remove her head. 'I killed *him*,' she said quietly.

'Eh?' Gotrek was shouting. 'Who?'

She waved at the pile of broken bones. 'Captain Drymuss. One of the most senior witch hunters in the Mortal Realms. He came here looking for you.'

'Because you bloody told him to.'

'True. But then I changed my mind.'

Gotrek halted, glaring at her. He was a mountain of muscle, broader than any duardin she had ever met and covered in brutal-looking tattoos, but he still had to look up at her, a fact that never ceased to amuse her. 'What are you talking about, witch? Changed your mind about what?'

'About you. And about Blackhammer's Master Rune. I don't think you should go to Azyr. I think it would be a mistake. And, much as I'd like to see it done, I don't think they should cut that rune from your ribs.'

Gotrek's eye was still flashing but he lowered his axe and stopped pacing. 'This is your compassionate nature coming out, I suppose?' He gave her a caustic grin, revealing crooked, ruined teeth. 'Or is it because we're such good friends?'

She sheathed her knife, sensing that the danger had passed. They were back to their usual sparring. 'I despise you, Gotrek Gurnisson, with a passion I would hitherto have thought impossible. I hate you more than I have ever hated anyone. I would not call you friend if we were the last people left walking the Mortal Realms, but...' She hesitated. It pained her to be so open with him.

'But what?'

'But you *are* different from the rest of us.' She pointed at him. 'Note that I said *different,* not *better.* And I don't know why the gods have made it so. Perhaps it's because you were not born in these realms. Perhaps it's because you're from, what did you call it? The Karaz Peak?'

'Karaz-a-Karak. The Everpeak, and don't mangle its name with your aelven tongue.'

She shrugged. 'You say you were born in another world. In another time. Perhaps that's why you overcome enemies the rest of us can't. Even Sigmar's Stormcast Eternals can't do what you do.'

Gotrek was about to yell again when he registered what she had said. He grunted, at a loss to know how to respond. He clearly had not expected compliments.

'Do you mean what you said before?' asked Maleneth. 'About honouring your ancestors?'

'Aye.' He stared at the brazier in the head of his axe, studying the glowing embers. 'It's to my shame that I didn't see it earlier. I have to be worthy of them, even here, even in these wretched hells you call the realms. *Especially* here, where so much needs to be set right.' He began swinging his axe and pacing again, but he was no longer thinking about Maleneth. She could see the gleam of excitement back in his eye. He was thinking about his plans to purge the realms of evil. 'My old oaths died with my home.' He looked out across the sea. 'I was hiding behind them. I'm here now, in your worlds, and I must do as my father would have done, and his fathers before him. I must be as true as every *dawi* who came before me. *Dreng tromm.* How else can I hope to join them? How else can I hope to remember them? What would Kazador Thunderhorn have done if he were here? He would have hunted down every *grobi* scum until his last breath. What would Gorim Ironhammer have done, faced with all these daemon-worshipping cretins? Would he have thought only about seeking his own doom? Or his own failures? No! He'd've cleaved some bloody skulls! He wouldn't have rested until either he or they were dead. Think of all my kin, from Gurni Hammerfist to Thorgrim Grudgebearer. They're all here, now, in me. Gone but not forgotten. Through me, the dawi have to right these wrongs. Because the alternative is leaving it to the bloody gods. And trust me, all Sigmar wants is to swap one brutal regime for another. You've seen what his Stormcast Eternals are capable of. They're all cracked. Imagine if they really did reclaim the realms – things would be even worse than they are now.'

Gotrek shook his head. 'All that time I was trying to find a purpose in these new worlds. And now I see that I already have a purpose. The same purpose I always had. The purpose of all dawi.' Gotrek had climbed to the lip of the hollow and was looking at his fyresteel axe, staring into the brazier. 'Grimnir tried to rob me of my doom,' he said, returning to an old grudge that Maleneth had never quite managed to grasp. 'But I'll find a new one. I'll hunt down every grobi and orruk, every cultist and warlord, every troggoth and troll. And, as I do it, I'll teach these bloody duardin how to be dwarfs.'

Gotrek was about to say more, then stopped and glared at Maleneth, annoyed at himself, perhaps, for revealing more than he intended. His cheeks darkened and he muttered to himself, stomping back down into the hollow.

Maleneth nodded. 'I don't know anything about Hammerfists and Grudge-bearers, but there's something in you that even the Dark Gods can't crush.' She looked down the coast, back the way they had come. 'Which is why I think we should head back to somewhere you can put it to use. Just because you had a disagreement with the Kharadron doesn't mean we have to banish ourselves to the wilderness. If we keep heading further away from the Spiral Crux, we'll end up turning into lumps of tin or melting into quicksilver. This place is an alchemist's furnace. What's so special about this stretch of coast-line? What are you actually looking for?'

Maleneth did not expect Gotrek to confide in her. Ever since they had left Barak-Urbaz he had been working to an agenda that he refused to explain. But she seemed to have disarmed him. He nodded as he climbed back up to their cart. 'This is where I will start showing my kin how to live up to their history.' He climbed up into the wagon and waved for her to follow. 'Back in Barak-Urbaz, Solmund showed me his maps. And he gave me an idea of the problems that hold the duardin back.' Gotrek barked a command, driving the ironbacks into motion as Maleneth leapt up and sat next to him. The ironbacks were boar-like creatures with rusty metal hides and corroded tusks. They made grunting sounds as they clanged off across the rocks, heading away from the cliff back towards the road. 'There are people in these lands who could be making a difference. There are still armies in these wilds who could stand against the greenskins and necromancers and Chaos worshippers, but they're all bogged down in turf wars.'

It was rare for the Slayer to speak so openly and clearly, so Maleneth simply nodded, cherishing the chance to glean a little of what was going on in his boulder-like skull.

'Solmund has a sound head on his shoulders...' Gotrek frowned and lost his thread. Maleneth knew the Slayer regretted his feud with the Kharadron magnate. If it weren't for the potency of Kharadron ale, they would still be friends. Gotrek scowled and shook his head. 'In some matters at least. If he had listened to me, we could have achieved something with all that power he's been hoarding in the clouds.'

'And this coast?' prompted Maleneth.

'Aye. This coast. A good example of why everything in your realms is buggered. There are dwarfs near here, or duardin as you'd say. Solmund told me about them. They call themselves Varrukh.' He tapped the rune in his chest. 'They're the same breed of savages who made this thing. Fyre-slayers. But, by all accounts, they used to do a decent job of guarding the lands from this coast all the way up to those mountains. They're sellswords, like all Slayers seem to be nowadays. They charge people for their protec-tion, but at least they gave people a chance to live in relative safety. Solmund said they live in a mountain hold near here.'

Maleneth stared at him. 'You're taking us to another Fyreslayer lodge? Do you remember what happened last time we entered one of their magma-holds? We both ended up in chains. Besides' – she gestured to the waves breaking in the bay, still visible from the road as it snaked up into the hills – 'you said they're keeping this place safe. It sounds like they're doing a good enough job without your help.'

'They *used* to keep it safe. A few months ago, everything changed. Solmund said they now spend their time cowering in their fortress while marauders and greenskins run riot. This used to be one of the few places in Ayadah where people could travel safely but now, thanks to the cowardice of these so-called Slayers, it's as bad as anywhere else.'

Maleneth shrugged. 'The whole realm's under the heel of Chaos. Just like all the other realms. I fail to see why this particular corner is of interest.'

'Because these Varrukh idiots are my kin.' Gotrek leant forwards in his seat, his muscles tensing. 'And they're bringing shame on my ancestors. I don't care if you back-stabbing aelves skulk in your hovels and kid yourself that Sigmar will sort everything out, but these Varrukh are dawi. I won't stand by while they hide under a mountain and leave everyone else to die. Where's the honour in that? They protected these lands before so they can sodding well protect them again. Even if I have to kill them to make it happen.'

'You're going to kill them so they can do their job again?'

'Yes. No. You know what I mean. I'll teach them how to live. And how to fight. And how to die properly.'

'So you're going to be a leader now, then? A great general.' She threw up her arms in praise. 'Gotrek, warrior king of the duardin! Lord of the Free Folk. Bringer of order and beer!'

He grimaced. 'You people have enough leaders. That's half the problem. They're a plague. Every one of them vying with the other to look more impressive. No, that's not Gotrek Gurnisson's way. I know that much. But I can challenge evil where I find it.'

'And you think that will make a difference? Against the endless legions of Chaos?'

'That's not the sodding point. You don't do the right thing because it makes a difference. You do the right thing because it's the right bloody thing.'

Maleneth laughed. 'Ah, the gnomic profundities of Gotrek Gurnisson. You're quite the philosopher. Someone should write a book about you.'

Gotrek muttered something, the fire fading from his eye as he looked away.

Maleneth shook her head. She was still struggling to follow his logic but at least she knew which direction they were headed now. 'If the Slayers are conspicuous by their absence, it probably means they're dead. Chaos warbands still own this continent, whatever Solmund might have told you. I imagine the Dark Gods finally noticed your duardin friends and sent their minions to scrub them out.'

Gotrek shook his head. 'Solmund said not. He said they're still mining under their mountain. His captains have seen them from their sky-ships. The Varrukh are still alive. They just don't fight any more.'

'Fyreslayers who don't fight? Unlikely. It's what they live for. That and making money. They're not like you. They don't have any burning desire to right wrongs and honour ancestors. They don't have morals. They just like killing things and getting paid for it. They're faithless mercenaries. Trust me, if they're not fighting, it's because they're dead.'

Gotrek muttered as he steered the ironbacks round another bend and revealed the next stretch of coast. The sun was rising fast and they were high enough to see for several miles.

'There you go,' he said, pointing to a smudge on the horizon. 'My point exactly. If Slayers watch over these lands that should not be happening.'

Maleneth peered through the early morning haze. There was a column of smoke drifting from the remains of a coastal village, about five miles down the road. 'Could be the work of greenskins rather than Chaos,' she said.

'Who cares who did it? If there are Slayers out here they should keep these roads safe.' Gotrek drove on, the cart picking up speed as it rattled over the crumbling road. 'And if they can't do that they should be hunting down the culprits. Evil has to be rooted out as soon as it springs up. Grobi scum, trolls, Chaos savages or treacherous *elgi,* it's all the same. Act fast. Stamp it out. Let decent people get on with their lives.'

'We should be careful,' said Maleneth. 'This attack happened in the last few hours. There was no sign of fires when we stopped last night. There may still be fighting going on down there.'

Gotrek grinned, driving the ironbacks to even more speed.

Maleneth need not have worried. As they drove towards the village, they saw no signs of fighting. There were human corpses scattered across the nearby beach and around the village's wooden stockade, but no movement other than the smoke rising from a fishing hut and carrion birds that were picking at the dead.

Gotrek stopped the cart and tethered it to a tree stump, and then the two of them continued on foot, drawing their weapons as they approached the village. The gates were hanging drunkenly from their hinges and there were more bodies strewn across the little square beyond. As Gotrek stomped in and out of huts, examining bodies and cursing under his breath, Maleneth noticed something strange.

'Gotrek!' she called.

He leant out of a shattered doorway. 'What?'

'Look at this.' She waved her knife at a corpse. It was a young warrior, slumped over a scimitar and shield. 'Why's there no blood on him?'

Gotrek walked over, frowning at the body as Maleneth turned it over with her foot. 'What do you mean?'

'There are no wounds,' she said, dropping to one knee to examine the corpse more closely.

'Well there were plenty on the bodies outside. What difference does it make? He's still dead.'

'It's just odd. The people out on the beach carry wounds, but these ones look like they've been scared to death. Look at him, there's not a scratch on him other than where the birds have been picking at his face. His eye's gone but I think a gull probably took that. I wonder if...' Her words trailed off as she lifted the man's face closer to hers. 'Wait a minute. He's still breathing.' She put her ear to his chest. 'He's alive.'

Gotrek frowned. 'He must have been knocked out during the fighting and been overlooked.' He studied the damaged buildings. 'Probably Chaos scum. Greenskins would have done more damage. And aelves would still be here, composing a poem about how sublime the battle was. Whoever did this just wanted to kill and leave.'

'He's not unconscious,' said Maleneth, slapping the man's face and trying to rouse him. 'Look, his eye's wide open. It's like he's mesmerised.'

Gotrek wandered over to another one of the bodies. 'Odd,' he said, crouching next to it. 'This lad's the same. His eyes are open but he's poleaxed.' Gotrek bent lower, until his mouth was near the warrior's ear, and grabbed the man's shoulders. 'Wake! Up!' he bellowed at the top of his voice. The warrior lay motionless in his grip and gave no sign he had heard. 'That *is* strange,' he muttered, dropping the warrior and crossing the square to another body. 'This one's the same.' Gotrek placed his hand near the woman's nostrils. 'She's breathing and her eyes are open but there's no one at home.'

They explored all the huts and found the same thing several times – people who looked like corpses at first glance but turned out, on closer examination, to be alive. 'And look at this,' said Maleneth, calling Gotrek over to a hut that had been used as a storeroom. 'Ropes, weapons, food, armour... Why has none of this been touched? If this is the work of brigands or marauders why haven't they taken anything?'

Gotrek picked through the weapons. 'Followers of the Dark Gods murder for pleasure. They wouldn't care about looting the place.'

Maleneth shook her head. 'I don't agree. What kind of army ignores a source of free supplies? At the very least they should have taken the food.' She kicked a spear. 'And the weapons seem well made.' She looked at one of the insensate survivors. 'There's something odd going on here.'

'Look at this,' said Gotrek, picking up a piece of armour and waving it at Maleneth. 'I should have bloody guessed.'

She took it from his fingers and frowned at it. It was too elegant to have been made by humans or duardin. It was a rondel – a small, circular piece of metal that shimmered as she turned it in her fingers. It was iridescent, like fish scales, and hammered to resemble a seashell.

'That's aelf work,' spat Gotrek, looking around. 'I should have known. Anything suspicious usually leads back to your kind.'

Maleneth shook her head as she examined the intricately worked armour. 'It does look aelven but I've never seen a design quite like this.'

'There's more,' said Gotrek, pointing his axe at another scrap of armour. 'And tracks. Look. They lead to the other side of the village.'

Maleneth crouched down to examine the marks in the dirt. 'Odd. See how they ripple and curve. Like the tracks a serpent would leave.'

'Snake-riding aelves,' sneered Gotrek. 'Snakes on snakes.'

Maleneth ignored him and followed the tracks to the back of the village, where she found a section of the stockade that had been utterly destroyed.

'So they came in this way,' said Gotrek, approaching the piles of wooden stakes.

'Perhaps,' said Maleneth. 'But everything is drenched.' She picked a piece of seaweed from the wreckage. 'It's almost like a wave did this.'

'Not likely.' Gotrek waved through the gap at the rocky shore outside. 'The sea's half a mile from here.'

Maleneth headed out onto the beach. The stones that crunched under her feet were mostly precious metal – gold, silver and a myriad of alloys that shimmered as they moved beneath her boots. In another realm, people would have murdered for such riches but here, in the Realm of Metal, where gold rained from the sky or grew from corpses like mould, they had found other things to kill for. The sinuous tracks wound on towards the sea, and as Maleneth followed them, she found more scraps of armour and villagers – either dead from bloody wounds or dazed like the people they had found near the huts, breathing but otherwise lifeless, staring blankly at the clouds overhead. Since finding the scrap of aelven armour, Maleneth had noticed how precise and elegant the sword strikes were. Neither humans nor duardin would fight with such lethal grace.

Why would aelves bother themselves with people like this? Her mistress sounded incredulous. *Miserable fisherfolk and tide scavengers. And it's not even as if they took anything.*

Maleneth shook her head. 'And these tracks are like nothing I've seen aelves leave before.'

Finally, with Gotrek trudging after her, she reached the sea. The liquid hissed over the stones and she kept a few paces back from the spray. While some people said the Amethystine Ocean was a body of water and others claimed it was molten metal, everyone agreed it was toxic. The tracks trailed down the beach from dozens of different directions and joined at this point, churning up the stones before heading out into the waves. As Maleneth looked out at the sea she had the peculiar sense that it was looking back at her, studying her. 'Is that more bodies?' she said. 'Floating a little way out?'

'I don't see anything,' muttered Gotrek. 'And what's that chuffin' stink?'

Maleneth sniffed. There *was* something odd on the breeze, beneath the briny tang: something bestial, like the musk of a large animal. The sense that she was being watched increased and her instincts warned her that they were in danger. She felt a sudden urge to leave. 'What does it matter?' she said. 'A few dead villagers. We should go.'

Gotrek looked even more furious than usual as he rounded on her. 'This is exactly the bloody problem.' He jabbed a finger at the piles of bodies. 'No one in these stinking realms cares about those people. They're the forgotten and the abandoned.'

Maleneth sighed as she realised she had triggered one of Gotrek's rants.

'Sigmar or Khaine,' he growled, 'it makes no difference, don't you see? It doesn't matter who these people put their faith in. Gods only care about dominating other gods. And while they stride the heavens, hurling thunderbolts, this is what happens to everyone else. Crushed and bloody slaughtered, over and over. Ground into the earth. Food for crows. Nothing changes. No one wins. We just swap one tyrant for another.'

Whatever Maleneth thought of Gotrek, she still baulked at being lectured by him. 'You have no idea what Khaine means. No idea what he can do. Besides, if not gods, who *should* we put our faith in?' She sneered. 'You?'

'Put your faith in yourself!' Gotrek's jaw was trembling with fury. 'That's what we did. The dawi didn't expect gods to save us. We listened to the wisdom of our ancestors. We took responsibility for our own futures.'

Maleneth laughed. 'And look where it got you! Your entire world was destroyed. And now you're here, a rootless exile who failed his people, trying to convince me that you know best.'

'Because I listened to a bloody god! Because I put my faith in Grimnir when I should have put my faith in mortals like these. Me and the manling could have made a difference if I hadn't been deceived by–'

Something moved further down the beach. Maleneth was so furious with Gotrek that when she heard the noise, she turned on her heel to hurl a knife.

Gotrek's hand shot out with surprising speed, grabbing her wrist and causing the knife to fall uselessly to the ground.

She hissed as valuable toxins spilled from the blade and splashed across the shards of metal.

Gotrek glowered at her. 'Not everyone needs killing.' He nodded to the figure who had made the sound. It was a man, sprawling on the beach and clutching at his wounds.

'Debatable,' muttered Maleneth as she followed Gotrek towards the stranger, picking up her knife and pretending to hurl it at the Slayer.

CHAPTER THREE

The man was around thirty years old and he looked nothing like all the other villagers they had seen. He was clad in an elaborate metal suit that glinted and clanged as he tried to rise. He stared back at them as they approached, shaking his head and mouthing blood-flecked prayers. He was powerfully built and his arms, which were uncovered, were almost as muscular as Gotrek's. As she approached him, Maleneth realised that the man's metal suit was covered in moving parts: mainsprings and cogs that clicked and whirred as he moved, trying to rise. There was a leather bag near him that had spilled mechanical devices onto the beach.

'Still alive,' grunted Gotrek.

Maleneth nodded to the terrible wounds that covered him. 'Not for long.'

The Slayer glared at her. 'Help him.'

She gave him an incredulous look.

Fury burned in Gotrek's eye and he gripped his axe, leaning against her. '*Help* him.'

Maleneth sighed, reached into one of the pockets that covered her leathers and stuffed some powder into the man's mouth before he had a chance to object.

He coughed and stared at her in disbelief, but before he could say anything, she yanked an arrow from the plates of his metal suit and pushed powder into the wound.

He gasped and lay back, his eyes widening in delight. 'The pain's gone.'

Maleneth nodded. 'You'll be fine now.'

'Gods be praised,' he breathed, grasping her hand, tears of gratitude in his eyes. 'You're not them,' he gasped. His limbs were shaking and his skin was an unpleasant shade of grey.

Maleneth snatched her hand back and wiped it on her leathers.

'Who did this to you?' demanded Gotrek.

'What do you mean?'

'Don't be tiresome,' snapped Maleneth. 'He means all this.' She waved at the bodies on the beach and the damage to the fishing village. 'Who attacked you? Were they aelves? Like me?'

The man looked confused, staring past her to the waves breaking on the shore. He shook his head, began to speak then frowned. 'I can't remember.'

'You can't remember who was trying to kill you?' Gotrek tried to speak in a gentle tone but even that verged on a bellow. 'What do you mean? How long ago did this happen?'

The man was still peering at the sea as if he had never seen it before. Then his eyes widened as something came back to him. 'Leviathans,' he whispered. He looked around at the bodies on the beach. 'The sea was alive.'

Maleneth looked back at Gotrek, who raised an eyebrow. She waved at the bodies. 'Those wounds are from aelven weapons.'

The man grimaced and shook his head again. 'No. Not aelves. Sea creatures. Krakens. Ridden by nymphs and kelpies. Things from the deep.'

'You lost a fight with mermaids?' said Gotrek.

The man looked even more confused and shook his head. 'I wasn't fighting anyone. I was just passing through.' He was still looking at the bodies. 'I don't belong here with these people. I'm from Vindicarum.' He looked at Maleneth. 'I'm Adorach.'

He said the name in a way that implied Maleneth should have heard of it. She shrugged and looked at Gotrek, who shook his head.

'Are you something to do with all this?' said Gotrek, waving his axe at the ruined village.

Adorach looked appalled. 'Of course not. I just spent the night here. I'm trying to reach Barak-Urbaz. I was leaving early so I could be past the foot-hills before dark. And then...' He frowned and massaged his brow. 'And then I don't know what.' He patted down his mechanical suit. 'Nothing broken,' he muttered, turning keys and flicking levers, causing parts of the suit to slide and click.

'Are you an engineer?' asked Gotrek, peering at his strange outfit.

'I'm Adorach. Are you sure you've never heard of me?' He looked around, reached into his bag and took something from it. He held it out to them with a theatrical flourish. It was a metal dragon that danced on the palm of his hand. The thing was only a few inches tall but it was incredibly detailed and it moved with the liquid grace of a real serpent, making a pleasing jingling sound as it coiled and uncoiled. 'Adorach the puppeteer,' said the man, looking at them expectantly.

Gotrek ignored the puppet and gestured inland, at the distant mountains. 'What about the dwarfs?'

Adorach struggled to focus on Gotrek. 'The what?'

'Grungni's beard. Did the aelves put something in your bloody ears? Duardin. Slayers. Fyreslayers. Whatever you want to call them. The warriors who are meant to protect this coast. The Varrukh. Where were they when the mermaids invaded? Where do we find them?'

'The mercenaries?' The man shook his head. 'They haven't been seen for months. They stay up in their fortress. Up on Slayer's Cauldron.'

'Slayer's Cauldron?'

'A volcano. The Fyreslayers have another name for it – Dreng-Gungron, I think.' The man was staring at the ruined village and bodies. 'Are they all...?'

Maleneth shook her head. 'You don't want to know.'

'Dreng-Gungron,' said Gotrek. 'Those are dawi words. It means Slayer's forge.'

'Yes,' said the man, still looking at the bodies. 'Slayer's Forge. I've heard it called that.'

'Where is it?'

'North-west of here. Half a day. You can't go there, though.'

'I go where I like, manling.'

'No sane person climbs that volcano. It's active, for one thing, but that's not the main problem. The Varrukh are the only ones who know the safe routes across those rocks. There's a concentration of aetheric currents up there. It's on some kind of ley line. The elements are always in flux.'

Gotrek shrugged and waved his axe at the sea. It was shimmering with dozens of different colours and forming peculiar shapes with its viscous waves. 'That's true of the whole realm. What's so different about this volcano?'

'It's the fumes. They mesmerise people. It's chymical smoke. Anyone who doesn't know the correct routes ends up deranged. People see visions and nightmares, and they either fall into a crevasse or run screaming back down into the foothills. Even the followers of the Dark Gods have never taken that peak, though they've tried enough times.'

Gotrek snorted in disdain. 'So the Slayers hide in the fog, is that what you're telling me? Is that what my people have come to?'

Adorach was rummaging in his sack, checking his belongings were intact, but he looked up at Gotrek's comment. 'No, not until recently at least. They used to spend all their time down here on the coast, locking horns with anyone they could find. They're a very warlike people. It's only recently that they've been staying up in Karag-Varr, their fortress.' He shrugged. 'If they are even up there. No one actually knows where they've gone. It could be that their fortress has finally been taken. Or perhaps the volcano finally tired of her tenants and drowned them in lava?'

Gotrek looked around at the people lying on the beach, his beard bristling. 'Well, if they are still alive they've got a lot to answer for. They broke faith with these people. They might be a pitiful excuse for dawi but they *are* dawi. And I'll not have them bringing shame on us like this.'

'Us?' said Maleneth, surprised. 'So you see yourself as one of them, now?'

He looked like he had tasted something bitter. 'We're kin. And I won't stand by while dwarfs fail to uphold their oaths.'

Adorach narrowed his eyes. 'You're going to try and climb Dreng-Gungron?'

'I don't try, manling, I do. I'll find this Karag-Varr and see what the Slayers are playing at.'

Adorach pursed his lips and looked thoughtful. He glanced at the mechanical devices in his sack. 'I could come with you.'

Maleneth gave him a suspicious look. 'You said you were headed for Barak-Urbaz. That's the opposite direction.'

'But there are ores in those foothills that are found nowhere else. I'm not fool enough to attempt the ascent, but even on the lower slopes there are treasures to be found. I may be able to find something that has long eluded me. The Fyreslayers do not welcome guests.' He nodded at Gotrek.

'But if I was travelling with one of their kinsmen I should be safe to at least approach the volcano. And we're actually very close.' He proceeded to reel off a list of directions to the fortress.

'Good,' said the Slayer, when Adorach had finished explaining the route. 'That's helpful. I'll let you travel with us to the bottom of the mountain. Then you can clear off and play with your dolls while I knock some heads together.'

'And what about this mess?' laughed Maleneth, waving at the people who were still breathing, staring blankly out at the waves.

Gotrek frowned. 'Buggered if I know. They look bewitched to me. Maybe the cowardly Slayers know something about mermaids.'

'So you're just going to leave them like this, for the tide to take them?' She laughed again. 'You talk about honour and doing the right thing, but you still seem suspiciously similar to the savage killer I met in Aqshy.'

Gotrek tugged at his beard, pacing between the prone villagers. 'Shut up and let me think.' He looked from the shapes on the beach to the smoking ruins of the village. 'That fire won't spread. We can put the living ones back in their houses.'

Maleneth continued laughing. 'Put them back in their houses? To do what, exactly? Stare at each other? Shall we tuck them up in their beds? Or stack them in a pile?'

Gotrek levelled his axe at her. 'Get on with it, Ditchmaid, or you'll be staying here with them.'

'It's Witchblade,' she muttered, but she was too amused to be angry. She could think of nothing more ridiculous than the Slayer trying to adopt the role of helpful do-gooder.

'You too,' rumbled Gotrek, turning to Adorach. The man gave no reply. His head had dropped to the ground, his eyes rolled back in their sockets. Gotrek dropped to his side, shook him, then looked up at Maleneth with a furious expression. 'He's dead!'

'Of course he's dead.' Maleneth shook her head. 'Look at those wounds. I'm an assassin, not a damned healer. I eased his pain. What more do you expect of me?'

'You told him he would live.'

She laughed. 'How much information would we have got out of him if I hadn't? He would have been too busy screaming and sobbing. Thanks to me, you now know where your Fyreslayer friends are.'

Maleneth's laughter stalled in her throat as she saw the psychotic gleam in Gotrek's eye. 'Ingrate,' she muttered, heading off to start dragging the bodies.

CHAPTER FOUR

When they had finished laying the villagers out in their huts, they made their way back up to the coastal road and climbed into the cart. Gotrek steered it into motion and they began clattering through the foothills. There were no more villages, and as the sun rose higher it revealed a land of jagged promontories and rocky coves. Gotrek still had some of the Kharadron equipment Solmund had given him and he used a blocky, ornate compass to plot their route, taking them off the road along a series of dirt tracks that headed away from the sea. To the north of them were the Grymmpeaks, a vast wall of mountains that punctured the clouds, their shoulders glittering with snow and metal.

Gotrek was in a feverish frame of mind that Maleneth found particularly irksome. He could go for weeks without speaking, but at times like this, when he was in the grips of an obsession, he rambled incessantly. As the hours rolled by, he talked about the hearth halls of his homeland, where history merged with the present, and the wisdom of elder times was relayed to eager young apprentices. As his voice rumbled on, it mingled with the grunts of the ironbacks and the crunch of the wheels across the rocks. Maleneth distracted herself by studying the slabs of sweaty muscle that covered the Slayer, trying to decide which would be the best place to jab a toxin-laced blade. An elaborate fantasy played out in her mind in which she killed the Slayer and earned the adoration of the gods. Khaine himself praised her for ridding the realms of such a tedious relic. Power and glory followed. She was just picturing the moment at which she ascended to godhood, taking Sigmar's place at the head of the Pantheon, when she noticed something in the distance.

'What's that?' she said, leaning back over the cart.

'What?' grunted the Slayer, without turning.

It was nearly midday and the hills were drenched in sunshine, but back towards the coast, on the horizon, it looked as though someone had torn a strip out of the daylight. 'I think there's a storm coming in,' she said. Clouds were scudding towards them and her sharp, aelven eyesight made out lines of silvery rain banking back and forth across the cliffs.

Gotrek gave a non-committal grunt and continued listing reasons why the young should defer to the old. Maleneth tried not to listen but fragments of his talk bludgeoned their way into her thoughts. 'People have forgotten how to listen... Too young to understand their place... It comes down to respect. When I was a beardling I did what I was bloody told... This is where the rot sets in... I once spent a year hammering at the same anvil because that's what...'

The cart's wheels were rattling over loose scree and the ironbacks made a horrendous din with their rusting hooves, but as Maleneth listened hard, she heard the rumble of distant thunder.

'Remember,' she said, talking loud enough to lift her voice over Gotrek's lecture, 'we're in Ayadah. In Karick-azam, a storm probably just meant another excuse to put your feet up by a fire and plait your beards, but this is the Realm of Metal. Storms mean trouble.'

'Karaz-a-Karak,' corrected Gotrek, looking back towards the coast. 'That weather's an hour away. Maybe more. We'll reach the Slayers before you have to worry about getting your hair wet.' Despite his dismissive tone, he studied the thunderheads intently, then turned back to the ironbacks and yanked the reins. The beasts lowed mournfully but broke into a heavy trot, splitting rocks and trampling tree stumps as they headed down into another steep-sided gulley.

Moor and scrubland soon gave way to a barren expanse of gleaming, jumbled ore. Shafts of gold and lead punctuated a blanket of jagged, black basalt. The higher they climbed, the harder it became to see. Dust and ash filled the air, pouring down across the rocks, and even from her seat in the cart Maleneth could feel heat radiating up from the ground. Horses would have found it hard to climb such rugged terrain but the ironbacks made light work of it. They were bred all along the Incendiary Coast and their claws were equipped with iron talons that hooked into the rocks as they climbed, kicking up sparks and rubble.

Maleneth muttered a curse as embers settled on her face, singeing her skin. 'Why exactly,' she said, brushing them away, 'have you pinned all your hopes on these duardin?'

Even now, as the smoke grew thicker and a sulphuric stench filled the air, Gotrek's excitement was growing rather than fading. His face was unusually animated and he was humming tunelessly to himself.

'Eh? The Fyreslayers? I'm pinning nothing on them, lass. They're a sorry excuse for dawi. But they could be the pebble that starts the landslide. I'm going to show you people the right way to sort out the mess Sigmar's handed you. There's good in these realms, as well as evil. I see that now. And I'm going to tip the balance in the right direction.'

'Good and evil!' Maleneth laughed. 'For someone so old, you sound remarkably like a child. Good and evil? Who uses those terms? They're just matters of perspective. Surely you know that. Nothing's ever black and white. Ask your mercenary friends when we reach them. Wars are about territory, wealth or power, or imposing an ideology. They're never about right and wrong.' She sneered. 'Good and evil. Really?'

Gotrek gave her a pitying look. 'You've handled too much poison. It's withered your soul. There's good and evil. And there's also right and wrong. There's courage and cowardice. There's success and failure. These things exist. You aelves try to muddy the truth with riddles but the truth is still there. Some things just *are*. It's good to help people like those villagers we just saw and it's evil to let them die.'

Pleased to see that she had punctured the Slayer's cheerful mood, Maleneth pressed harder. 'You don't even know who attacked those villagers. And you don't know why. What if the sea monsters that killed them lived along this coast before the coming of man? What if they are just fighting back to reclaim lands that were stolen from them in an earlier age? And what if the villagers don't know that? So the villagers fight for lands they consider rightfully theirs while the monsters do the same. Who's "good" in that scenario, Gotrek? And who is "evil"?'

Gotrek levelled a blocky finger at her. 'There you go! Wrong-headed gibberish. Typical aelf claptrap. People are being murdered by things that crawl from the sea. That's bad. And it needs to be put right. Don't over-bloody-think everything. Sometimes it's clear what's right and wrong. And if there are dawi living on this mountain, they need to get off their arses and do something about it.'

He paused, and Maleneth saw that the pained, haunted look had come back into his eye. 'We forgot it before and we mustn't forget it again. It's why Karak Ungor fell, and Karak Eight Peaks, and all the other holds we lost. It's why we lost everything, in the end. We were dazzled by other things. Petty things. Things that blinded us to what matters. We're the Elder Race. Heirs of Grungni. Lords of the Karaz Ankor. We've got the grit to get things done. But we lost our way.' He studied the blasted mountainside, watching the ember-jewelled smoke, his gaze distant. 'And look where it led. We have to stand for truth. Or we don't stand for anything.'

Maleneth had no idea what he was talking about but she had done enough. He would now sink into a morose silence that she found infinitely preferable to lectures on deference and tradition. She leant back in her seat, toying with one of her knives, but her peace was short-lived. As the ironbacks hauled them higher up the rocks, the smoke became so thick it was hard to breathe. Maleneth coughed and spluttered, and even Gotrek muttered into his beard.

'What's that, up ahead?' Maleneth pointed her knife at something in the smoke. There was a patch of darkness even deeper than the rest. It was as if someone had opened a doorway. 'Wait here,' she said, dropping lightly down onto the rocks as Gotrek halted the cart. She approached the darkness with difficulty, slipping on the thick carpet of ash that covered everything. As she drew near to the object she saw that it was twitching and shivering, and she dropped into a crouch, holding her knife before her as she edged closer.

'What have you found?' boomed Gotrek, thudding down from the cart behind her.

Even as she approached the shape, Maleneth found it hard to answer, and Gotrek headed off in a different direction, muttering in a surprised tone as he spotted something else in the smoke. Maleneth took a few more steps and saw that someone was sitting on one of the rocks. At first she could only see a pair of long, lithe legs clad in leather boots, but then she laughed in disbelief as she saw that it was her dead mistress, as beautiful and cruel-looking as ever, studying her with heavy-lidded eyes.

You look awful, she smirked, rising to greet Maleneth.

Maleneth snorted. 'I killed you with my own hands. I'm hardly going to believe you're walking about in Ayadah.'

If I'm dead, sneered the witch aelf, sauntering towards Maleneth, *there's no need to defend yourself.* In a single, fluid movement, she snatched a pair of knives from her belt and lashed out at Maleneth.

Maleneth tried to sidestep then gasped as blood sprayed from her shoulder. When her mistress spoke, the words came not just from the figure in front of her but from the vial of blood that spoke to her mind. It was dizzying and confusing. But years of training in the Murder Temples meant she could defend herself from any attack, however unexpected. She flipped across the rocks, somersaulting through the smoke and then rushing back at her opponent with a lunge of her own.

You're even slower than I remember, laughed her mistress, hidden somewhere in the smoke. *Is this what comes of spending your time with an oaf like Gotrek?*

Maleneth hissed as blood exploded across her back. She whirled around, knives raised, to see her mistress backing away, eyes full of triumph. 'You're in my mind,' spat Maleneth. 'The human warned us this would happen.'

Is that pain in your mind? Is this? The witch aelf lunged again.

Maleneth was faster this time. She parried and fought back with a high kick, landing her boot on her mistress' jaw and sending her toppling through the smoke. Maleneth rushed after her and drew her knives back for a killing blow.

'*Now* you decide to attack me?' boomed Gotrek, rising up from the fumes. He gripped his axe and dropped into a crouch, grinning at her.

Maleneth backed away, lowering her knives, confused. There was no sign of her mistress. 'You fool,' she whispered, shaking her head. 'I wasn't attacking you. It was her. She was here.'

Gotrek lowered his axe, looking disappointed. 'Her? Who are you talking about?'

'Nothing. No one.'

Tell him, sneered the voice in her head. *Tell him what you do to your companions. Tell him what a mistake he's making keeping you by his side.*

Are you here? thought Maleneth. *Are you on this volcano with me?*

I'll be with you until the end, Witchblade. Until I make you pay.

Gotrek glared at Maleneth. 'You've been at the bloody ale.' He looked around, trying to spot the cart. 'And I was just working up a thirst.'

'I'm not drunk, you oaf. It's the air, playing tricks on me, just as that human said it would.' She listened hard, trying to pick up the sound of her mistress' boots rushing over the rocks, but there was nothing.

'Don't breathe so much then,' grunted Gotrek, turning and climbing up the slope, waving for her to follow.

They had only been walking a few steps when Maleneth saw more shapes moving around her in the gloom. She whispered a prayer to Khaine, trying to ignore them. 'Can you see anything following us?' she said, giving Gotrek a sidelong look. The shapes had moved closer and she recognised their silhouettes. They were stooped, diseased wretches, robed in flies. Tusks jutted from their foreheads and they each had a single, bloated eye. Daemons. She had faced them in battle and knew all too well of the pox they carried. It oozed from their infected skin and dripped from their rusty blades. 'Do you see that?' she hissed, waving at the shapes.

Gotrek did not even spare the figures a glance. 'I see rocks, Witchblade. And I see smoke. Anything else is nonsense.' He looked back, his face inches from hers, his gaze iron hard. 'Nonsense.'

She nodded and, to her surprise, when she looked again at the daemons, she saw that they were fading back into smoke. Gotrek's conviction was so great, it had driven them from her thoughts.

Gotrek turned and marched on, whistling in a tuneless monotone as he picked his way through the rocks. He had only gone a few paces when a shadow rose up before him – a vast, gelatinous mound. It was as rotten as the shapes Maleneth had glimpsed earlier, but it was the size of a hill and its head was crowned with broken antlers. As it lumbered through the smoke, Maleneth felt a rush of panic. It radiated an aura of intense wrongness. It was not meant to exist on the physical plane. It was a horror spawned in the places between worlds.

'Rubbish,' muttered Gotrek as he stomped through the daemon. The disdain in his voice dispelled the illusion. The daemon rippled away into the fumes.

Maleneth stared at him in disbelief. 'You *did* see that, didn't you? You just ignored it.'

'I spent an eternity in the Realm of Chaos, lass. Everything in there's a lie.' He pounded his axe handle on the ground. 'That taught me to know what's real.' He strode on.

Other shapes lurched towards them as they climbed, but Maleneth kept her eyes locked on Gotrek's tattooed shoulder blades, refusing to acknowledge the voices that called out through the smoke, lisping and snarling and demanding that she halt. Every now and then, one of the figures would lunge at Gotrek, but each time it happened he simply muttered the word 'rubbish' and thudded on up the rocks, dispersing phantoms with his unshakeable conviction. The tide of visions grew so vast that Maleneth felt like she might scream, or drop to the ground and cover her head, but whenever she felt she was on the verge of breaking, Gotrek would dismiss the apparitions in such a scornful, deadpan voice that it gave her the ballast to keep going.

As they climbed, the ground grew hotter. Steam began hissing up through cracks in the rocks to join the thickening acrid smoke. The heat was all too real, and Maleneth had to dodge scorching geysers as she followed the Slayer. Without the sun as a guide she soon struggled to keep track of time. Gotrek's stamina was limitless, but as the going became more difficult, Maleneth began to feel weary. The slope was so steep in places that they had to haul themselves up over sheer faces and leap narrow crevasses. Heat and smoke combined to cloud Maleneth's thoughts and, where she would usually be nimble and fast, she found herself stumbling and scraping the skin from her shins.

Maleneth hated to appear weak in front of the Slayer, but he was utterly tireless and her muscles were screaming. She was about to call out for a rest when she heard him laugh in surprise. He was a dozen feet or so higher than her, standing on a narrow ledge that jutted out over a drop.

'What is it?' she called, her voice echoing oddly through the smoke.

'A liar,' spat Gotrek.

'I wish,' muttered Maleneth, climbing up towards him, 'that, just once, you could say something intelligible. You talk so much about how your people told great sagas and–'

The words faltered in her mouth as she reached the ledge and stood next to Gotrek. 'Khaine,' she whispered. She now saw the reason for the awful heat that was singeing her face and making her eyes stream. They had reached the lip of the volcanic crater. The caldera spread out below them – a lake of magma so bright that Maleneth felt like she was staring into the sun. It was not the lava that caused her to stare in wonder, however. Rising from the flames was a god.

'Is that...?' gasped Maleneth.

'Aye,' snarled Gotrek. 'Grimnir. The lying worm.'

CHAPTER FIVE

At the centre of the caldera there was an enormous fortress – a Fyreslayer magmahold, larger than any Maleneth had seen before. It had been built in the shape of Grimnir's upper body, so that the Slayer God seemed to be rising from the lava, bellowing a war cry. The whole structure was forged of polished gold and, as the lava boiled around it, spewing smoke and steam, the metal reflected the light so that the whole fortress appeared to be on fire. The hold was reached by two bridges that approached it from either side, straddling the lava and linking the fortress to the lip of the crater. The two bridges were Grimnir's shoulders, and his beard snaked down from his face into the lava. Even from half a mile away, Maleneth could see glinting metal standards raised on the battlements and bowl-shaped braziers jutting from the walls, as big as carts and filled with flames. It looked like a massive funeral pyre.

'Shoddy work,' said Gotrek, but he did not speak with his usual conviction and Maleneth could guess why. Much as she hated to admit it, the Fyreslayers' magmahold was a remarkable sight. Every part of it had been built on an absurdly large scale and the design was so cleverly wrought that it really did seem as though a deity were tearing up through the lava, howling into the inferno.

'Shoddy?' she said, still struggling to take in all the details. There were channels cut into the walls that spewed lava down Grimnir's chest, giving the impression that he was wounded, and in one of his hands he was gripping the horns of a dragon or godbeast, forcing it below the surface of the burning lake. As she peered through the smoke and embers, she made out sentries on the walls holding metal icons and, from the size of the duardin, she realised the structure was even larger than she had first thought. 'I'd say it looks impressive.'

Gotrek gave a dismissive grunt. 'From a distance. Half hidden by smoke. And look at all that gold. What a waste. These Slayers are as flashy as the sky dwarfs.'

Maleneth looked at him, noticing that his voice sounded oddly rigid, as though he were battling to suppress something. He was not looking at the battlements and walkways, or the cloud-scraping towers and stairways; his gaze was locked on Grimnir's face and his expression was even more intense than usual. He was gripping his fyresteel axe so tightly his knuckles were gleaming.

'You're a Slayer,' she said, shaking her head. 'And Grimnir is the god of Slayers. How can you hate him so much? What kind of betrayal would make you forsake your god?'

Gotrek did not speak for a moment and his expression grew even darker. Then he finally answered, still staring at the likeness of Grimnir. 'He called me his heir. He told me I would take up his mantle and hold back the tides of Chaos.' He closed his eye and let his head rock back on his massive shoulders. 'All of it lies. If I'd ignored him I could have stayed with the manling. I might have saved my world, saved my people, saved my friend. Or at least I could have tried.'

As ever, Maleneth found Gotrek's logic baffling. 'You told me that you want to pitch yourself against "servants of evil". And Grimnir gave you a chance to fight the daemons of Chaos. Surely that was exactly what you wanted – a chance to defeat the ultimate enemy?'

Gotrek rounded on her, his eye burning. 'I defeated nothing, aelf. Don't you understand? At Grimnir's word I missed the final battle of my people and what did it achieve?' He waved his axe back down the slope. 'While I was lost in their netherworlds, the Gods of Chaos claimed everywhere else. Call these realms what you like but they belong to the Ruinous Powers. My sacrifice meant nothing. Worse than nothing.' He stared back at the likeness of Grimnir. 'And now he's gone. I can never hold him to account. I can never–' He howled and reeled away from Maleneth, slamming his axe into a rock, splitting it with an explosion of embers.

Maleneth backed away. If Gotrek slipped into his berserk state he might cleave her in two without even realising. But his rage faded as quickly as it had come. 'No matter,' he said, looking for a way down to the nearest of the two bridges. 'It's better this way. I was a fool but I won't be fooled again. I'll honour my ancestors in the way I see fit and I will never listen to another god.' He spotted a path heading down to the crater and began climbing down to it. 'I'd advise you to do the same.'

Maleneth scrambled after him but she struggled to keep up. The heat was radiating through the soles of her boots and the air scorched her lungs. She had to bat embers away as she clambered down towards the heart of the volcano. It took nearly an hour to reach the bridge and by the time she stumbled onto the path, Maleneth could hide her exhaustion no longer. She collapsed onto the hot stone, gasping for breath and grabbing a flask of water from her belt. Gotrek noticed she was struggling and, to her surprise, paused to let her rest, sitting down near her on the low wall that lined the path. The entrance to the bridge was flanked by two colossal statues that looked, to Maleneth's eyes, like the wingless dragons Fyreslayer nobles rode into battle – magmadroths, they were called, and they made her uneasy as they reared over the bridge, forming an arch cast from the same metal as the fortress at the far end.

'No sentries,' said Gotrek, standing and walking past the statues onto the bridge. He was only a dozen feet from Maleneth but the heat was so fierce he rippled as he walked away from her, blurred by the infernal temperature. There was a constant wall of embers drifting up from the lake below and as Gotrek strode down the centre of the bridge, it looked like he was entering a tunnel of flames. The bridge was built on the same grand scale as everything else, broad enough that fifty Slayers could have marched down it side by side. 'Don't these people want to protect their god castle?'

Maleneth finished her drink, climbed wearily to her feet and followed him out onto the bridge. The metal was even hotter than the rocks, and was engraved with runes that glowed in the heat. She shrugged. 'Perhaps they have no need of sentries. Adorach said no one ever gets past those phantoms you just ignored. We're probably the first people to come up here for centuries.' She squinted through the smoke, trying to see the opposite end of the bridge. The air was liquid and mobile, but she realised that some of the movement was more than just heat haze. 'There *is* someone coming,' she said, drawing her knives.

Gotrek slapped the head of his axe against his palm. 'Good. Time for some answers.' He marched off into the smoke. 'Keep up, manling.'

Gotrek had often called Maleneth manling when they had first travelled together, confusing her with a long-dead friend, but he had not done it for months. She caught up with him and studied him as he walked. At first she could not see anything untoward but then she frowned in surprise. 'Look at the master rune.'

Gotrek looked down at his chest and cursed. It was glimmering with inner fire. The rune was forged to resemble a face – the same face that adorned the fortress up ahead of him. 'What's going on?' said Gotrek, tapping the rune with his axe.

Maleneth stared at the metal. It usually only lit up when the Slayer was in one of his berserk rages. She nodded at the magmahold. 'It was forged in one of these Fyreslayer keeps.'

Gotrek gave the rune a suspicious look. When they had first come to Ayadah, Gotrek had been bent on taking the rune from his body but since then he had made an uneasy peace with it. He distrusted anything so closely linked to Grimnir and tried to avoid triggering its power, but he had come to admit that it was sometimes useful. 'If it starts trying to change me I'll douse the bloody thing in lava.'

Gotrek was about to start ranting but before he could start, a loud droning sound filled the air. 'Grungni's hammer.' He grimaced. 'Is something dying?'

'They're war-horns.' Maleneth nodded to the walls of the magmahold. 'Look on the battlements.' She could see figures up on the walls of the keep, carrying curved trumpets.

Gotrek nodded and picked up his pace, swinging his axe from side to side as he stormed down the bridge.

'Gotrek,' said Maleneth, hurrying after him, dizzy from the heat. 'You look like you're about to kick the doors down.'

'So?'

'Look at the size of this place. There must be thousands of warriors in there. Even you don't want to pick a fight with an army.'

Gotrek scowled, gripping his axe tighter as the shapes in the smoke came nearer.

CHAPTER SIX

The first thing to reach them was a monster: a magmadroth, almost as large as the statues at the start of the bridge and twice as fierce. Its scales burned as hot as the lava below and it was surrounded by a thick, brimstone stink that caught in Maleneth's throat and made her cough and hawk. The creature towered over Gotrek as it stomped towards him, causing the bridge to judder and groan.

Gotrek stood his ground, glaring up at the beast's rider – a Fyreslayer carrying a brazier-topped staff and wearing an ornate, dragon-crested helmet. Dozens more Fyreslayers were gathering around the creature's legs. To Maleneth, they looked very similar to Gotrek – a little smaller perhaps, but with the same squat, muscular build – and though they all wore ornate, rune-inscribed battle helms, they still sported tall, red crests of hair almost identical to Gotrek's. Most of them looked as deranged as him, too. The Fyreslayer on the magmadroth was motionless, looking down with a proud, stern expression, but others were swinging their axes, swaying from side to side and mouthing feverish prayers. They were one command away from launching themselves at Gotrek. Maleneth counted thirty of them in the shadow of the beast but there were more approaching through the smoke.

The Slayer on the magmadroth reined in his steed and leant forwards in his elaborate, tall-backed throne. He pointed his staff at Gotrek, spilling embers from the brazier at its top. 'Leave.' His voice boomed out through the fumes, laden with authority and something else – something unnatural that made Maleneth grip her knives a little tighter.

'Be careful,' she warned, glancing at Gotrek.

He turned to her, eyebrow raised, then looked back at the Fyreslayer on the magmadroth. 'Who are you,' he bellowed, 'to give me orders?'

The Fyreslayer studied Gotrek. His face looked too severe to have ever been softened by a smile. His brow was like a mountain crag and his forked, black beard hung down to his boots. There were golden runes hammered into his muscles and they shimmered as he glared at Gotrek. He had black stripes under his eyes that looked like streaks of charcoal, and as Maleneth looked around at the other Fyreslayers, she saw that they were all wearing the same markings. She had met many Fyreslayers before, but she had never seen them paint their faces in such a way.

'I'm Korgan Forkbeard,' said the Fyreslayer, barely moving his lips, 'son of Ogvald the Grim, High Priest of the Varrukh Forge Temple and Rune-master of Karag-Varr.' He looked at Gotrek with cool dispassion. 'And you must leave this place while you can.' The other Fyreslayers grew even more restless, rolling their heads on their shoulders and barking oaths, inflamed by their leader's words.

Maleneth expected Gotrek to be equally animated but he simply nodded. 'You're a disgrace,' he said, speaking calmly, 'to your ancestors and your creed. You should hang your head in shame. I do not take orders from an oathbreaker.'

Something dangerous flickered in Korgan's eyes but he remained calm. 'Who are you, stranger?'

'Gotrek Gurnisson, son of the Everpeak and sworn enemy of the gods.' He waved his axe at the colossal face on the magmahold. 'Including yours.'

Korgan raised an eyebrow. 'A lunatic, then.' He lowered his staff. 'Leave and I'll overlook your hasty words.'

Gotrek's brow bristled. Maleneth mouthed a curse as she saw he was on the verge of one of his rages. 'Look how many there are!' she whispered.

Gotrek did not seem to hear. 'Before I came here,' he cried, starting to pace and swing his axe, 'I heard tales of your cowardice. Even the cloud-cowering Kharadron speak of it. And now, now that I meet you, I see with my own eyes what a disgrace you are. Not only do you hide up here, counting your gold, while people are being slaughtered all along the coast, but you have also forgotten how to welcome one of your own kin. What kind of *drengi* turn away a traveller seeking rest? You're a disgrace.'

The mob of Slayers howled and spat, shaking their heads like hounds on a leash, desperate to attack. Maleneth was surprised to see that Korgan still remained calm. She had never seen a Fyreslayer show such self-control. In her experience, they were always on the verge of violence. Korgan stood slowly in his throne and levelled his staff at Gotrek, dripping flames from the brazier. 'You all heard. I gave fair warning. No one but the Varrukh may enter Karag-Varr.' The magmadroth bucked and stomped beneath him, runes smouldering in its scales. 'This stranger would not leave by choice' – he drew back his staff, as if he were about to hurl it – 'so I will *make* him leave.' The runemaster thrust his staff forwards and roared an oath.

Gotrek howled incoherently and charged.

'What did I do to deserve him?' hissed Maleneth, running after him.

They were still a dozen feet from the Varrukh lines when Maleneth realised what was happening. Korgan had summoned a storm of embers and formed them into a glittering mass that was hurtling at Gotrek. The maelstrom flashed, coiled and coalesced into a dragon made of flames, fifty feet tall and with a wingspan that spread out from the bridge, shimmering in the heat haze.

'*Khazuk!*' roared Gotrek, laughing as he leapt at the dragon, swinging his axe around his head.

The fire spirit crashed into Gotrek, and the other Slayers howled war cries, sprinting at Maleneth.

Gotrek's axe flashed white as the blade bit deep into the dragon's shoulder, throwing sparks across the figures below. The dragon reeled backwards but lashed out with a claw at the same time, smacking Gotrek so hard he somersaulted through the air and landed heavily on the bridge.

The Slayer lurched back to his feet and laughed, blood rushing from one side of his face. 'I've slain beasts that make you look like a fledgling!' he shouted, then ran down the bridge again, drawing back his axe for another attack. The same light that was burning in the fyresteel blade was also shining from his eye and from the rune in his chest.

'Halt!' cried Korgan, his thunderous voice dragging the Fyreslayers to a standstill.

Maleneth had been about to hurl a poisoned blade, but as the Fyreslayers backed away from her, she stayed her hand.

Korgan was watching Gotrek rush at the dragon. He lunged back and forth, hacking at the fire spirit, and the rune in his chest sparked and blazed. Gotrek had learned to control the rune's power, to stop it possessing him, but it still burned when he was in one of his psychotic rages. As rune light flashed across his chest, it caused the brazier in his fyresteel axe to flash and spit, and even though the dragon had no true flesh, Gotrek's blows were having an impact, slicing through its dazzling scales and hacking gouts of flame from its claws. The beast reared up in anger and shock, spreading its wings.

Korgan cried out another oath and slammed his staff down on the base of his throne. The dragon vanished, leaving a cloud of cinders that whirled around Gotrek for a moment then drifted away down the bridge. Gotrek fell forwards, thrown by the sudden absence of an opponent, and slammed into the wall at the side of the bridge.

'Hold!' cried Korgan, gesturing for his warriors to back away from Maleneth.

Gotrek recovered and lurched away from the wall, trailing spit from his beard and shivering with fury. He looked around, confused, trying to find the dragon.

Korgan steered his magmadroth down the bridge towards Gotrek, staring at the rune in his chest. 'What are you?'

'Gotrek!' cried Maleneth, rushing over to him and gripping his arm.

The Slayer rounded on her, drawing back his axe, his eye flashing.

'It's me, damn you!' She backed away, warding him off with her knives. 'Witchblade.'

His grimace became even more ferocious, but then he managed to focus on her and steady his axe.

'They're not attacking,' she said, nodding at the Varrukh. 'So you don't need to butcher them.' She had no great love for the Fyreslayers, but if Gotrek took on a whole army, it could only end badly for her. 'Not yet at least.'

Korgan rode closer. For the first time, he seemed animated, leaning forwards in his saddle. He looked at Gotrek's rune and then turned to look at the huge fortress behind him. Both of them were likenesses of Grimnir's face and they were almost identical in design.

Gotrek nodded at Maleneth and lowered his axe. She breathed a sigh of relief. She had caught him in time.

'Your axe,' said Korgan, frowning. 'It cut the vulcanus spirit.'

'The what?'

'The magmic salamander. A being that did not exist. You were able to injure it.'

Gotrek scowled at him. 'What are you? Some kind of conjuror?'

'Which lodge do you belong to? Who forged that rune?'

'It was forged by Krag Blackhammer,' said Maleneth, sensing a chance to avert disaster. 'He's a runesmith of the–'

'I don't come from any of your pitiful tribes.' Gotrek clanged his axe against the rune. 'This bauble was made by a Fyreslayer but I'm not one of you. And this thing didn't used to look like your two-faced idiot god.'

'You lodgeless *wanaz*,' snarled another Fyreslayer, rushing forwards. He was dressed in a similar fashion to Korgan, with a dragon-crested helm, a loincloth and little else, but his appearance was different in every other respect. Where Korgan was lean and chiselled-looking, this duardin was so broad he was almost spherical. His bulk was muscle rather than fat, however, and as he stomped towards Gotrek, brandishing fyresteel axes, he reminded Maleneth of the ironbacks that hauled their cart. He snorted and twitched as he glared at Gotrek. His face was ruddy and freckled, and his beard was such a storm of ginger that his chin seemed to be on fire. His eyes were rolling in their sockets, reminding Maleneth of Gotrek in one of his most extreme rages. If anything, this duardin seemed even more psychotic. Like most of the Fyreslayers, every inch of his skin was networked by old scars and there was a line of stitches tattooed around his neck, giving the illusion that his head had been severed at some point and sewn back on. He slammed into Gotrek chest first and yelled in his face. 'Show! Some! Bloody! Respect!'

'Skromm!' said Korgan, raising his voice. 'Hold.'

Skromm and Gotrek scowled at each other, their faces contorted. Maleneth presumed Gotrek would behead the foolish Fyreslayer, but when Korgan repeated his command Skromm backed away, muttering into his fiery beard and breathing quickly, whispering frantic curses.

Gotrek still looked drunk on fury so Maleneth spoke up quickly. 'It's the master rune of Krag Blackhammer. It is *uniquely* powerful.'

Korgan's face remained impassive. 'What would an aelf know of Fyreslayer runes?'

Gotrek laughed. 'Or anything else for that matter.'

Korgan stroked the black, ropelike plaits of his beard, looking thoughtfully at Gotrek. 'You are an unusual person.'

Gotrek threw back his shoulders and raised his chin. 'I didn't come here to be ogled. I came here to find out why you people are hiding.'

Skromm made a low whining sound and his head jerked violently to one side. Sweat was pouring down his muscles and he was trembling, but Korgan held him in place with a warning glance.

Korgan looked back at Gotrek. 'We stay in Karag-Varr because Grimnir wills it.'

'Isn't Grimnir dead?' whispered Maleneth, giving Gotrek a sideways glance. She nodded at his rune. 'Unless he really is in that thing.'

Korgan caught her words. 'The Ancestor is not a fit subject for an aelf.'

'Grimnir wants you to hide yourselves up here?' said Gotrek, lowering his axe.

Korgan glanced back over his shoulder and Maleneth saw that more Fyreslayers were approaching, racing frantically down the bridge. They were more heavily armoured than the warriors with Korgan and they were carrying what looked like thick, metal pikes.

The runemaster seemed surprised to see them and sent one of his warriors to investigate. Then he looked back at Gotrek. 'I will not discuss these matters with a stranger. But I will allow you to enter Karag-Varr.'

'Is that what passes for a courteous invitation these days?'

Korgan tapped his staff. 'The salamander was only a glimpse of what I can throw at you, Gotrek Gurnisson. If you enter this hold, you do so on my terms.'

'And what terms are they?'

'You tell me your story.'

'Try stopping him,' muttered Maleneth.

Gotrek ignored her. 'I'll talk if you know how to listen.'

Korgan looked surprised by the answer. 'You have my word.'

'And your king?' said Gotrek. 'Do you have one? Do you speak on his behalf?'

Korgan's expression stiffened. 'Our runefather is Thurgyn-Grimnir.' Gotrek was about to speak when Korgan continued. 'But for now, I and the other lodge elders rule Karag-Varr.'

Even Maleneth knew that was odd. 'You rule in your king's stead?'

Korgan was about to say more when the other Fyreslayers reached him. The leader of the group looked suspiciously at Maleneth before rushing over to Korgan.

'Runemaster!' he gasped, short of breath from running down the bridge. 'It's back. Headed straight for the Cindergate. Even worse than last time.'

Korgan closed his eyes. His stoicism seemed to falter, but then he recovered his composure and nodded. He turned his lumbering steed and waved his warriors back down the bridge. 'Back to the hold. And quickly. We may have time to reach the Harulk barracks.'

There was a chorus of oaths and curses as the Fyreslayers turned and began running towards their fortress.

Gotrek called out as Korgan started to ride away. 'What are you running away from? Are you under attack?'

'Not an attack,' called Korgan over his shoulder. 'A storm. Follow me back to the hold. We have to get inside before it hits.'

Gotrek laughed. 'You're running from bad weather?'

Korgan nodded. 'You'll see.' With that, he picked up speed, riding his magmadroth past the other Fyreslayers and thundering down the bridge.

'We'll finish this later,' snarled Skromm, glaring at Gotrek, before running after the other duardin.

Gotrek laughed in disbelief, then began jogging after him.

CHAPTER SEVEN

Maleneth could easily have sprinted after the runemaster, but she stayed at Gotrek's side as he puffed and muttered down the bridge.

'Bloody ridiculous,' he gasped. 'Running from a bit of weather. Who ever heard of such a thing?'

Soon the gates of the magmahold rose up ahead from the smoke. The bridge was formed from Grimnir's pauldron and the gates were built into the side of his helmet so as Maleneth ran towards them, she saw the god's fierce visage glaring out at the other mountains, as though debating whether to rise from the lava and smash their peaks.

'That soddin' smell,' coughed Gotrek, pounding along at her side. 'The one from the fishing village.'

Maleneth sniffed. He was right. Even the sulphuric stink of the volcano could not entirely mask that there was another smell flooding across the bridge – a sharp, briny tang that made her feel oddly cool, despite the fierce heat rising from beneath them. 'Smells like the sea,' she said, frowning.

Gotrek grimaced. 'More like fish guts.'

'It must be the storm I spotted when we were climbing up here. I thought it was headed this way.'

Gotrek waved his axe at the gates they were approaching. They were hundreds of feet tall and the metal doors were a dozen feet thick. 'Why do they bloody care? Look at this place. What kind of storm could touch it?'

Maleneth thought of the ruined huts they had seen by the beach and the bodies scattered across the rocks. 'If they're worried, we should be worried.'

They reached the gates and ran through, joining a large crowd of Fyreslayers who had gathered in a grand square inside the walls of the hold. There was a great tumult as hundreds of duardin crowded round the magmadroth, calling out to the runemaster and all speaking at once, but Maleneth forgot about the approaching storm as she looked at the architecture. The square was lined with enormous statues. They were all Fyreslayers, with trailing beards, whirling axes and proud crests of hair, and all had been captured at the moment of attack, snarling as they lunged and hacked. Each of the Slayers was grappling with a daemon of some kind: putrid plaguebearers or flaming, goat-legged things with the heads of drooling hounds. Through some clever artifice of duardin engineering, magma from the lake had been channelled into the statues' axes so that they burned and smoked. This filled the square with lurching shadows, making it seem as if the colossal figures were moving. Maleneth stared up at them, feeling like she had wandered into a furious battle of the gods. The whole place radiated an intense feeling of violence. It was like a shrine to battle. The feeling of danger was so real, so palpable, that she had to resist the urge to draw out her knives and drop into a fighting stance.

'The Doomgron,' said Gotrek, looking up at the fierce-looking statues. His face was an angry puce colour and there was sweat dripping from his beard.

'Doomgron?'

'Aye. The final battle, according to these lava-chewing fanatics. Solmund told me about it back in the Kharadron cloud city. Fyreslayers think they'll fight alongside Grimnir one day, when he's reborn to save the realms.' Gotrek's words dripped with bile. 'There was a time when I might have thought they were right to put their faith in him.'

'Look there,' said Maleneth, pointing to the far side of the square. 'Some of the statues have fallen. Someone's been using siege engines against this place.'

Gotrek frowned. 'How would you lug siege engines up the side of a volcano?'

'Well something has hammered them. Look, there's rubble over there and half that hall has collapsed.'

Gotrek shrugged. 'Probably fell down. These modern Slayers take no pride in their work. They throw these places up in a hurry, without taking the time to make them sturdy, and then they let them slide into disrepair. They have no respect for honest labour or the proud skills of the mason or the–'

'To the barracks!' cried Korgan, calling out to them as he rode across the square. The other Fyreslayers were following him, heading past the warring statues to the largest of the buildings surrounding the square – an impressive rectangular structure with broad steps and rows of anvil-topped columns.

'They're not going to make it,' said Maleneth, pointing her knife to the main street that led off the square. There was a wall of fog hurtling down it, rolling and churning like waves and filling the air with spray. It was going to overtake the Fyreslayers before they could enter the barracks.

Gotrek tried to answer Maleneth but his words were drowned out by a deafening thunderclap. Lightning flashed, deep in the fog, and for a brief second something was visible in the spray – something serpentine that appeared to be swimming through the air. The flash of light was too brief for Maleneth to understand what she had seen, only that it was vast and heading their way.

'Slayers don't run from rain clouds.' Gotrek strode towards the wall of mist with his chin raised. 'These people have hammered too much metal into themselves. They need to get some bloody–'

His words were cut off as the mist engulfed them. Maleneth had the claustrophobic sense that she was drowning, that the sea had risen from the coast in a great deluge, swamping the mountain. The fog hit with such force that she staggered backwards, struggling to stay on her feet and gasping for air. She quickly realised that she could still breathe, and was not really under-water, but the odd sensation persisted as she looked around into the rolling banks of spray. In an instant, the furnace-like heat of the magmahold had been replaced with a damp, piercing chill that ate into her bones, causing her to shiver as she looked around for Gotrek. He was nearby but the fog was so dense she could barely make him out. He looked as confused as her, stumbling around and looking up into the mist.

'Wait,' she said. Her voice was muffled and odd, as if she really were underwater, and Gotrek did not hear. 'Gotrek!' she cried, stepping closer to him. He turned, finally hearing, but then he frowned and stared at something behind her. 'What is it?' she asked, looking round. Then she gasped in surprise.

Drifting towards them, floating through the fog, was a jellyfish. She stared as it rippled through the mist, trailing long, seaweed-like limbs. There was something dreadfully wrong about seeing such a creature hanging in the air. As she watched it, Maleneth felt a crushing sense of despair.

Finally, after all she had seen, after all she had survived, her mind was folding in on itself; her sanity was fragmenting.

CHAPTER EIGHT

'What kind of storm is this?' roared Gotrek. She could tell he was shouting because of his expression, but the words were barely audible, even though he was right next to her. The smell of the sea was now overpowering and Maleneth was breathing in short, quick gasps, still struggling to convince herself she was on dry land.

Lightning flashed again. The boom of thunder was distant and faint, but the light was even brighter than before and Maleneth cried out in shock. She was surrounded by sea creatures. Before the light failed, she saw more jellyfish, shoals of silver fish and larger shapes, winding through the darkness. One of the bigger creatures resembled a centipede, but dozens of feet long and propelled by fins rather than legs. It was coiling and looping in the gloom, thrashing around as though attacking something she could not see. 'This is what destroyed the fishing village,' she gasped, though no one could hear her.

She saw Fyreslayers – still heading in the direction of the barracks but, rather than sprinting, they were now wading slowly through the gloom, leaning forwards as though forcing their limbs through thick tar. Their shoulders had dropped and their expressions were grim, as though they had endured a terrible defeat. As Maleneth tried to head their way, she felt the same resistance. It was the same sensation she had experienced in dreams, when struggling to escape an enemy summoned from the recesses of her mind.

'Gotrek!' she howled. Something about the penetrating cold filled her with dread. The undersea phantoms were still flickering through the darkness, trailing tentacles and fins as they circled through the air. This could only be the work of a powerful sorcerer. Then she remembered Adorach's warning. 'This is just the mountain,' she cried. Somehow, the thought helped battle the misery that was threatening to overwhelm her. She managed to grab Gotrek's shoulder. She waved at a turtle that was swimming towards them. 'These things are just more hallucinations. It's the metal in the ground.'

Gotrek nodded, causing his beard to pool around his face. 'Mind tricks. We can ignore them, like all the others.' He looked around. 'Where's the dwarf with the wingless dragon?' He spotted the distant silhouette of the magmadroth and launched himself in that direction, moving with slow, stiff movements. 'Korgan!' he bellowed. 'None of this is real!'

Maleneth stumbled in Gotrek's wake, trying to ignore the visions as she had done when they were climbing the mountain. As she moved the air grew darker and more viscous. Huge shadows drifted overhead and she ducked, expecting an attack, but when she looked up she saw that it was fronds of kelp, as big as tree canopies. She had the odd sensation of travelling through an undersea forest. 'What's happening here?' she cried, reaching a wall of pale, tubular weeds that rippled as she battled through them. She drew deep, quick breaths, struggling to believe that she was still surrounded by air. The fiery golds and reds of the magmahold had vanished, replaced by a wash of shifting greens and greys, and when she looked down, she saw that the flagstones were hidden beneath waves of rippling seagrass.

She staggered out of the tube weeds and then halted as pain washed over the right-hand side of her body. She juddered as light pulsed from her arm and turned to see that a black, sinuous shape had wrapped itself around her bicep. It was a glossy, muscular eel and as its jaws locked around her wrist, the rest of its body sparked with electricity that jolted through her sinews and bones, burning her skin.

'Swords of Khaine!' she gasped, grabbing the thing with her other hand and trying to wrench it free. 'You're not real!' Pain blossomed across her other arm and stabbed up her throat, throwing her head back. She managed to stagger to a pillar and then proceeded to pound the eel against the fluted metal. Burning energy ripped through her muscles but, finally, the thing loosened its hold enough for her to hurl it into the shadows. She lurched after Gotrek, locking her eyes on his back as she had before, determined to ignore the illusions.

She had almost caught up with the Slayer when he stumbled to a halt. As Maleneth forced her way through the fog she saw that Gotrek was grappling with something. It was only as she reached him that she saw it was a squid with membranous webbing linking its tentacles. As Gotrek struggled, the creature slid over his head, smothering him.

Gotrek howled and pounded, but Maleneth was too dazed to help. If the sea creatures were able to harm Gotrek, how could they be figments of her imagination? The sense of hopelessness returned and Maleneth groaned in horror. As she watched the Slayer punching the bulbous sac that was consuming him, she saw something snaking through the darkness towards her, moving at sickening speed. She caught a glimpse of scarred grey skin and featureless black eyes, and a tooth-crowded mouth that was bigger than she was – then a shark slammed into her, bucking and turning in the air as it tried to lock its jaws around her head.

Maleneth felt like she was fighting through tar but she managed to jam a knife up into the creature's gills. Blood pooled around her and the shark became even more frenzied, thrashing and slamming into her, sending her reeling backwards. She struggled to right herself as the shark turned over her head and plunged towards her, eyes rolling.

Maleneth rolled clear and lashed out with her knife, tearing the blade through the shark's leathery skin. It twisted away, trailing clouds of blood. Then it jolted towards the ground, its head flipping away from its body as Gotrek's axe sliced it in two.

The Slayer toppled forwards through a cloud of crimson. There was no sign of the squid but his face was covered in fresh scars where barbs had tried to gain purchase in his flesh.

'They're injuring you!' cried Maleneth as he hauled her onto her feet. 'How's that possible? They're hallucinations!'

He looked around at the shapes flitting past. 'Not these.' He held up one of his arms. It was covered in angry welts. 'These things have teeth.'

'Someone must have summoned them from the sea,' she said, lifting her knives and readying herself for another attack. 'This is not natural weather. A sorcerer must have conjured this fog.'

'Aye,' said Gotrek, wading off in the direction of the Fyreslayers. 'Classic wizard work. Probably one of your sort. Remember the armour we found on the beach? Elgi.' He grimaced as a fat, barbed pufferfish floated in front of his face, staring at him with featureless eyes.

Maleneth was no longer listening to him. Her mind was teetering on the point of collapse and she had to find a way to rationalise what was happening. She scoured her memory for anything concerning sea aelves. In the libraries and temples of Azyr, she had studied documents that described many of the races that inhabited the Mortal Realms. Much of the knowledge had slipped away from her over the years, but she had a vague memory of blind aelves who dwelt in the ocean. There was a disgrace hanging over them, a failing of some kind. She knew their name, she was sure of it, but it eluded her. A hail of tiny fish drummed into her face, causing her to stagger and cough.

'Gotrek,' she called, seeing that he had almost disappeared from view, his tattooed bulk merging with the banks of fish weaving through the fog.

When she caught up with him, she saw that he had joined the other Slayers. Hundreds of the duardin warriors had formed a protective circle around Korgan's magmadroth, but the runemaster looked transformed. His proud, stoic manner had vanished. He slumped dejectedly in his throne, resting his brow against his staff as the brazier burned fitfully. He looked like he might drop from his steed at any moment. The other Fyreslayers looked like they were standing on a wind-lashed meadow. Purple seagrass was billowing all around them, the blades as tall as they were, and there were cold lights blinking through the mist, giving the scene a liquid, dreamlike quality. Behind them, where the barracks should have been, Maleneth saw the wreck of a ship, slumped on its side, its mast crumbling and trailing weeds.

'What kind of storm is this?' roared Gotrek as he reached the magmadroth and looked up at the runemaster.

Korgan stared past Gotrek, his face rigid. 'This is what happened. Skromm, this must be what happened. When the storm hit us all those other times, these things must have been carried inside it. This must be why it does so much damage.'

The stout Fyreslayer called Skromm was near the magmadroth and he seemed dramatically changed too. The mania was gone from his eyes and he looked weary, as if he could barely muster the strength to grip his axes. 'But did you remember any of this, runemaster? Until now, I mean.'

Korgan shook his head. 'But now that I see it, I *do* remember it. This is what happened before. This is why our magmic defences can't hold.' He looked up at the drifting kelp, his face ashen. 'This phantom tide is what took the runesons.'

'The who?' yelled Gotrek, looking from Korgan to Skromm. 'Who are the runesons? What are you people talking about?'

'There!' cried Skromm, pointing into the rolling gloom. 'Did you see that?'

'See what?' Korgan leant forwards in his throne, staring at the rolling shadows.

'Ghost soldiers.' Skromm looked furious again, rolling his head on his shoulders in a way Maleneth had seen Gotrek do. 'Like last time. This *is* what happened.'

Gotrek marched out into the seagrass and looked around. 'Ghost soldiers? What are you talking about?'

Maleneth followed, forcing her way through the mist. 'Gotrek, I think I might know what's happening. The armour we found *was* aelven, but it's not like any design I've seen before, with all those corals and frills.'

'Get to the point.'

She looked past him at the shoals of fish and the vast, half-glimpsed shapes circling behind them. 'There are many different kinds of aelves in the realms, including some who hide in the deeps of the sea. Cursed aelves who can control the tides and summon storms.'

Gotrek grimaced as an eel looked him in the eye. 'I could imagine your lot getting on well with fish. Cold, dead-eyed, no sense of–'

Silver shapes hurtled towards them. Everything else was caught in a dreamlike torpor so the sudden flash of silver was shocking. For a moment, Maleneth thought it was another shoal of fish, but then she saw that the shapes were rushing along the ground and they had limbs and weapons.

The Fyreslayers yelled war cries and Korgan raised his staff to wave them forwards, but they were painfully slow compared to the glittering phalanx that knifed towards them. Maleneth saw eyeless white faces and long, two-handed swords – then she was fighting for her life. A pale aelven warrior lunged at her, trailing mist and kelp, swinging at her face.

Maleneth brought her knives up in an X, barely managing to block the blow. Rather than being encumbered by the sea mist, her attacker was empowered by it, dancing around her with fluid grace. Maleneth found most opponents too clumsy to be more than an amusing diversion, but this aelf left her reeling as she tried to follow his movements. There were smooth patches of skin where the aelf's eyes should have been, but he seemed to anticipate Maleneth's every move. She ducked, weaved and parried, but, to her outrage, Maleneth realised her opponent was toying with her. More of the fleet figures dashed by, slicing into the lines of Fyreslayers, and Maleneth howled in frustration, trying and failing to land a blow. 'God of Murder!' she spat, forcing her muscles to battle the sluggish air.

'Slow, Khainite,' whispered the aelf in her ear, smiling, before whirling away in the swell.

Maleneth turned on her heel and stumbled, losing one of her knives and reaching out, trying to break her fall.

The pale aelf laughed and launched himself at her, raising his sword for the killing blow.

CHAPTER NINE

Maleneth was ready. The fall had been a feint. She flicked one of the rings on her fingers, opening its lid, and as the aelf moved in for the kill, Maleneth blew hard, sending powder into her opponent's face. He tried to sidestep but it was too late. As he reached up to touch his face, his skin came away in his fingers, sliding from his bones like well-cooked meat. He gasped, trying to hold his features in place. Maleneth stepped forwards, snatched her knife back from the seagrass and plunged it into his chest. Blood plumed. Maleneth felt a surge of energy as Khaine's spirit responded to the kill, filling her body with vigour, stoking her hunger for violence. Despair fell away, replaced by murderous passion.

As the aelf crumpled into the mist, another raced towards Maleneth but the power of the Bloody-Handed God was growing fast, hammering in her veins. She whipped around, bringing her knives up to parry a sword strike. Then she blew more powder from the ring. The aelf convulsed, clutching at his face. Maleneth lashed out with her blades, releasing another cloud of crimson. She quickly grew drunk on her kills, tearing into the aelves, moving with increasing speed and skill, matching the elegance of their blows with a graceful ballet of cuts and kicks. She forgot about the fear that the mist had planted in her mind. She thought of nothing but the cycle of power that was rushing through her. With every kill, she sent life force to the Bloody-Handed God. And with every blood sacrifice she offered, Khaine repaid her, filling her muscles with wonderful strength. Her confusion fell away leaving her with pure, brutal clarity of purpose. Through violence and blood, she worshipped her lord. Whatever she thought in calmer moments, she now remembered the truth. The Murder God would be her salvation. The High Oracle, Morathi, had prophesied Khaine's return and, as she killed the aelves, Maleneth felt the truth of it. She felt the power of her god. She whirled and turned, abandoning herself to the glory of the slaughter.

'Aelf!' bellowed Gotrek. It took a moment for Maleneth to steady her breathing and recall where she was. She kicked away the aelf she had just killed and backed away from the fighting, wiping blood from her face and looking around for the Slayer. The scene was chaotic. The Fyreslayers were surrounded by hundreds of the quick, sword-wielding aelves and they were making a poor job of defending themselves, attacking with clumsy lunges. The air was filled with drifting clouds of blood and shattered weapons. The runemaster, Korgan, was still riding his magmadroth and the creature was tearing into the aelves, slashing at them with its massive claws and locking its jaws around others. But Korgan was staring at his staff. The flames flickering in its brazier were fitful and weak, and Korgan looked perplexed.

'Where are you?' cried Maleneth, looking around for Gotrek but seeing no sign of him. More aelves were arriving all the time and the shimmering, fluid light made it hard to see anything with clarity. Some of the aelves were archers, launching volleys into the beleaguered Fyreslayers; some were sword-wielding infantry while others were mounted on huge eels that snaked above the battle, allowing their riders to hurl spears into the carnage. The eel riders wore intricately forged armour, as elegant as anything Maleneth had seen in Azyr and forged of a strange, pearlescent metal that shimmered like the inside of a conch. They were nobles, sitting proudly in their saddles as the eels whipped through the air and electricity flashed in the tips of their spears, charged by the motion of their steeds.

Maleneth fended off a blow, killed another swordsman and then leapt at one of the eel riders, knocking him from his steed and stealing his mount, hoping to gain a better vantage. She had assumed she would be able to ride it like a horse, but the moment she touched the creature she realised her mistake. Agony jolted through her as energy sparked from the eel's scales and blasted through her bones. Maleneth howled and the eel twisted, lunging at her, opening its jaws to reveal dagger-like teeth. Maleneth cursed and leapt into the air. Rather than slamming back down onto the ground, she floated, with peculiar serenity, towards the field of seagrass. The eel twisted away into the darkness, trailing arcs of electricity, and as she dropped, Maleneth shivered and cursed, weakened by the shock.

In the distance, where the shipwreck had appeared, Maleneth saw a large shape approaching. At first, she thought it was another eel, but then she saw that the creature had powerful, clawed forelimbs and a head that was almost equine, with a long, spiral tusk jutting from its brow. The noble on its back looked even more magnificent than the eel riders. He carried a curved, shell-like shield that shimmered as it caught the light, and wore an ornate helmet with a wide, coral-coloured crest. He was holding his spear aloft as his steed carried him forwards with stately calm, and Maleneth guessed that this must be the aelves' king or ruler. Other, much larger shapes were swimming out of the darkness behind him, flanked by eel riders, and she realised that the Fyreslayers were only fighting the vanguard – the full weight of the aelven forces was yet to reach them.

That's where the moron will be, said Maleneth's mistress, her words dripping venom. *He'll be headed for the biggest opponent he can find.*

'True,' said Maleneth, finally landing back on the ground. One of the aelven archers tried to take aim at her but she rolled sideways, leapt back to her feet and sent him tumbling backwards in a spray of scarlet. She raced on, heading for the approaching army, peering into the rolling shadows, trying to spot Gotrek. Arrows glided past, fletched with coral-coloured fins, and she dived for cover. It was only when she climbed back to her feet that she realised she was inside the shipwreck. Even by the standards of Chamon, there was something surreal about climbing through the ship's skeletal, mouldering hull. There was no time to examine it, however. Gotrek's unmistakable voice boomed through the pall, bellowing a duardin war cry she had heard him use before: '*Khazuk-ha!*'

Whatever you think of him, said her mistress, *even he can't take on an entire Idoneth army. There must be a thousand of these namarti wretches. And that pompous ass on the sea drake must by the king. He will be well protected.*

Maleneth stumbled to a halt. *Idoneth? Namarti? What are those names? Do you know what these things are? Why in the name of the Murder God didn't you say anything?*

Oh, so now you want my help. So now you want me to share my learning with you. I would have shared all my knowledge with you, Witchblade, if you had not betrayed me.

You were going to bathe in my blood.

And what greater sacrifice could you have made? What Daughter of Khaine would have defied her mistress in such a way? You should have given your life willingly. After all I did for you, you should have been honoured that–

There's no time for this now. What are these aelves? You called them Idoneth and namarti. What does that mean? Tell me what you know. I need to keep the Slayer alive.

There was no reply.

'Speak, damn you!' spat Maleneth, grabbing the amulet at her chest.

Gotrek's familiar battle cry boomed through the air. The noise was so loud that Maleneth almost failed to notice a movement on her left. She leapt back just in time to dodge a spear thrust as one of the eel-riding knights hurtled past.

She righted herself and clambered up a broken spar, looking out across the fighting. She easily spotted the unmistakable figure of Gotrek charging through the aelves, dealing out blows with his axe. He was surrounded by blood and fire as he vanished from sight, swamped by hordes of fast-moving warriors.

You've hung all your hopes on that idiot. If he dies, you will have no way to survive this battle. You need to do something.

Maleneth clung to the spar, thinking. Her mistress was right, but she would not achieve anything by simply standing at Gotrek's side. She leapt from the wreck, running away from Gotrek, back towards the beleaguered Fyreslayers, dodging spears and arrows as she headed towards the runemaster, Korgan. She vaulted aelves and duardin until she reached his rampaging magmadroth. The beast was like a slab of living magma, thrashing its tail and spitting lava into the oncoming aelves. Maleneth tried to approach it, but there was so much heat radiating from its scales that she could not get within more than a few feet of it.

'Korgan!' she cried.

The runemaster did not hear. He was still fixated on his staff, barking prayers at it but only managing to coax a few embers from its brazier.

'Runemaster Korgan!' howled Maleneth, climbing over dead Fyreslayers to get closer.

Korgan finally looked up. He glared at her, drawing back his staff like an axe.

'I'm not one of them!' she cried. 'I'm Gotrek's...' She hesitated, realising she had been about to say 'friend'. 'I'm Maleneth! Gotrek's travelling companion. You have to help him.'

Korgan shook his head, looking dazed. 'They're part of the storm.'

'Where are your bloody armies?' boomed Gotrek, wading through the crush towards them. He had blood splattered across his face and there were flames trailing from his axe. The rune in his chest was burning furiously.

The sight of Gotrek had a noticeable impact on Korgan. He sat up straight and tried to shrug off his stupor. 'The fyrds?' His words were slurred, as though he were emerging from a deep sleep. 'They're inside, safe from the storm.'

Gotrek waved his axe at the fighting. 'They're not safe! This is an invasion. Muster your damned armies.'

. Korgan looked around at the battle and nodded slowly, realisation dawning on his face. Of the few hundred Fyreslayers who had been standing with him, fewer than a hundred were still on their feet. Almost all of the bare-chested axe warriors had fallen. Most of the duardin left were the heavily armoured soldiers carrying magma-spewing guns.

'Call out your troops!' cried Maleneth. 'Do as he says! Or lose your home.'

Korgan took a deep breath and nodded. 'Skromm!' he cried, standing up in his throne as the magmadroth bucked beneath him. 'He's right! Summon the fyrds! Muster the Varrukh! We've been tricked. We're under attack!'

Skromm snatched a horn from his back and blew into it, producing a deafening howl. Immediately, dozens more horns rang out as other Fyreslayers responded.

Korgan steered his magmadroth back and forth, scattering warriors as he looked around at the flickering gloom, his eyes growing clearer. He raised his staff. 'To me!' The light in his brazier finally began to blaze and all the surviving Fyreslayers gathered around him as he jabbed it at the approaching aelves. Flashes of red and gold rushed from his staff. They looked like dragons made of flame and they rushed into the battle, engulfing the aelven soldiers.

The horns grew louder and other figures raced towards the battle. These were not fire spirits summoned by Korgan, but living Fyreslayers, brandishing axes and magmapikes as they poured from archways that had not been visible moments earlier. Korgan grew surer of himself by the minute, riding to the join the newcomers, bellowing commands as warriors flocked to his blazing staff.

'Yes!' roared Gotrek. 'That's the bloody way! Show them a *real* storm!' Satisfied he had done enough, the Slayer raced back into the battle. Maleneth tried to follow but, to her outrage, the newly arrived Fyreslayers made no distinction between her and the Idoneth. Gouts of molten lava hissed past as the Varrukh took aim at her. She managed to dodge the shots but soon lost sight of Gotrek.

Maleneth resisted the urge to cut down the duardin and ran back towards the aelven lines. There were now two focal points to the fighting. There was a crush around Korgan as he drove his magmadroth forwards, mustering more Fyreslayers, but also a concentration of fighting near the aelven king. 'Gotrek,' muttered Maleneth, guessing the cause of the latter. She ran along one of the ship's spars and leapt over the heads of the nearest aelves. The clinging gloom that had overtaken the magmahold was lifting. As Korgan conjured lava spirits and crowds of Fyreslayers poured from the surrounding buildings, the dream sea began to recede. The air grew warmer and the mist thinned. The aelves were shocked by the failure of their sorcery and the Fyreslayers pressed their advantage, firing barrages of lava and surging forwards with a wave of battle cries.

The weight fell from Maleneth's limbs and she found she could sprint again, racing past the floundering aelves and heading towards their king. The Idoneth were trying to regroup but the Fyreslayers were tearing into them from every direction and Maleneth used their confusion to approach the Slayer.

Gotrek was separated from the Fyreslayers by hundreds of aelves. There were eel-riding knights circling him, penning him in with spears as he tried to reach the king. Every time Gotrek hacked one down, another jabbed at him, causing him to bellow and reel. Along with the eel-riding Idoneth, there were other creatures assailing Gotrek – fish, sharks and squid were boiling around him in a frenzy, latching on to his arms and savaging his legs. Blood was drifting around the Slayer and his yells sounded deranged, but Maleneth noticed that the rune in his chest was only faintly lit. Gotrek claimed he was learning to harness the rune, to master it, but Maleneth knew better. If the rune started blazing, there was every chance Gotrek would lose control. And if that happened, there was no telling what might happen.

'Fight me, you coward!' roared Gotrek, trying repeatedly to reach the king, but the crush around him was too great.

They're holding back, said her mistress. *They're not trying to kill him. They're trapping him in that spot for some reason.*

Maleneth changed her position, trying to get a better look at the Idoneth king. He was a fantastically pompous individual, surveying Gotrek with disdain while chatting casually to another aelf who was drifting in the shadows at his side. Maleneth changed her position again but still struggled to see the king's companion clearly. He was floating above the ground and the air was whirling around him, obscuring his face. All the surrounding currents seemed to emanate from this one figure, as if he were the eye of the storm. He was holding a staff in one hand and something smaller in the other. A rune, forged from metal or perhaps carved from bone.

That's the one who summoned this phantom sea. Stop him and you'll stop all of this.

Maleneth could sense the truth in her mistress' words. When she looked at the indistinct figure, she was filled with a feeling of crushing despair, but when she looked back towards Korgan and the Fyreslayers it vanished. 'He's the sorcerer.'

Obviously, you simpleton. But not like any sorcerer you've ever encountered before. The Idoneth are corrupt. Their souls are broken. Did you read nothing in Azyr?

Maleneth was about to reply when she saw the sorcerer point his rune at Gotrek.

Gotrek immediately stumbled, lowering his axe. He opened and closed his mouth, gaping like a landed fish and clutching at his throat, swinging weakly at the aelves.

As Gotrek struggled, his face growing dark, more of the Idoneth army swam into view. Flanked by the eel riders was a shark large enough to carry two Idoneth nobles. The one at the front was clutching the reins, steering the shark towards Gotrek. The other was manning a weapon that looked like a harpoon launcher. The weapon was draped with nets.

You need to do something quick.

Gotrek fell to his knees, pawing at his throat, unaware of the shark swimming towards him. The eels and other creatures backed away, making a path for the shark, but Gotrek was oblivious, grasping at the air and shaking his head.

'Khazuk! Khazuk! Khazuk-ha!' roared Korgan, leading the Fyreslayers into battle. They crashed into the aelves like a landslide and Maleneth laughed as she saw how numerous they were. There must have been a thousand, perhaps more – and others were still flooding from the surrounding buildings. Their horns brayed as they fired magma into the Idoneth, blasting eels apart and sending the riders tumbling from their mounts. Korgan's face was as livid as his brazier and he wrenched lava from the air, hurling it at the shark, sending the creature backwards in a shower of embers and burning meat.

As the Fyreslayers attacked, the phantom sea withdrew, snatching away the Idoneth's gloomy veil and bathing them in the magmahold's furnace glow. The sorcerer fell to the ground and staggered away from the king, dropping his rune. The last vestiges of sea mist rolled away, revealing the duardin's statues in all their glory.

With his soldiers floundering, the Idoneth king rode at Gotrek, drawing back his sword to cut the Slayer down.

As the darkness faded, Gotrek drew a deep breath and looked around, coming to his senses just as the king's serpent steed bore down on him. He laughed and snatched his axe from the ground, bringing it up through the creature's neck and sending its head spinning through the air. The headless beast slammed down at his feet and Gotrek grinned at the king as he rolled clear, his armour clanging against the flagstones. 'Finally, I see your lily-white face.' He raised his axe over his head and roared. 'Come to Gotrek!'

War drums pounded as Fyreslayer berserkers rushed past Gotrek, hurling axes and shields while the Slayer charged at the kneeling king.

'Gotrek!' cried Maleneth, as she saw the Idoneth sorcerer climb to his feet and point his staff at the Slayer.

Gotrek was oblivious. He strode forwards and slammed his axe into the king, splintering his armour and filling the air with blood.

The king reeled backwards then charged at Gotrek, ignoring his wounds and swinging his sword at the Slayer's head.

The sorcerer howled an incantation and the storm returned, hitting with even more violence than before. Dark waves roared through the battle, hurling warriors into the air. Maleneth cried out as she was snatched from the ground and thrown backwards. She slammed into something and pain knifed through her skull. Then the darkness consumed her.

CHAPTER TEN

Eòrna paused at the threshold, relishing the soundless dark. Cold, black weight pressed down on her, clearing her mind and steadying her heart. Outside, beyond the chamber's ironshell walls, lay the spires and whorls of the city. Outside, there was noise and politicking and people playing mind games that crushed her spirit. She had carved a role for herself out there: saviour and hero, hunter of souls; but down here, in her private chambers, there was only the ocean. The Curaim was only an echo of the great darkness outside the city but it was still one of the largest rooms in her palace – large enough that she could see no roof or walls, large enough that she felt a rush of emotion every time she entered. In these coiling, chambered halls, she had recreated the abyssal night. In here, she could feel the boundless might of the sea. For a few moments, there was just her and the dark. She breathed it in, drinking the void. Then, slowly, a storm of blue embers began raining down towards her. It was the cold light of lanternfish, moving in brittle flurries, like snowflakes. They illuminated the ground as they reached her, picking out other shapes from the darkness. She smiled and raised her hands. Tubeworms enveloped her legs and eels shivered across the surface of her simple, namarti-style leathers. It looked like she was standing in a field of moonlit grass, but the shapes at her feet were actually the gangly, antennae-like limbs of brittle stars, heaped in their thousands across the floor of the chamber. They twitched and juddered all around her, sensing her presence. A shoal of glassfins turned slowly around her, clinking and flashing their luminous hearts. Not one of these creatures was a bond beast. Eòrna had not blinded them or broken their will. She had not cowed them with Isharann spells. They were her and she was them. Their hunger was her own.

'He has returned.' Torven's voice was unmistakable, resonant and deadpan, but it took Eòrna a moment to locate him. At first he was just a deepening of the darkness, gliding slowly towards her, but then he entered the circle of lanternfish and she saw him clearly: a pale spiral of shell, taller than she was and covered in intricate markings that resembled coral fronds. She had never seen another creature quite like Torven but he resembled the nautiluses that floated in the upper reaches of the sea, only much larger and blessed with a deep, strange intelligence. Tentacles moved around his beak as he spoke, billowing like ribbons in a breeze. 'Just a few hours before you.'

Torven had two eyes but only one was fully visible, an ink-black pool as large as her fist, protruding so far from its socket it looked barely attached. His second eye was much smaller and sunken beneath his pale skin. It was sometimes visible – a subcutaneous shadow, like a bruise, expanding and contracting in response to changes of light – but it was this second eye that had made Torven Eòrna's most valued servant. Torven could see further and clearer than any of the king's soulscryers. His deepsight was unparalleled. Everything Eòrna had achieved she owed to Torven.

She dropped the sack she was carrying and began to unfasten it. 'Who has returned?'

'King Dìolan, your highness.'

Torven's tone was unwavering. There was never a hint of emotion in his voice. She was sure he felt emotions but they were buried too deep to colour his speech. In their long years of companionship, Eòrna had at least learned to sense when he was trying to stress the importance of something. There was a barely perceptible pause between the words 'King Dìolan' and 'your highness' that made her glance at him.

'My brother has returned from where?'

'King Dìolan led several battalions against Karag-Varr.'

Eòrna's good mood slipped away from her. She felt a flash of annoyance at Torven. He knew she came here seeking respite, to escape the intrigues of court and thoughts of her brother. She tipped the contents of the sack onto the ground. A jumble of body parts slopped out, human and duardin, severed heads and broken limbs brought back from her recent hunting expedition. The air around her exploded into life. Animals snaked and twisted through the air, falling on the meat in a flurry of tentacles and teeth. Blood pooled around the corpses and Eòrna backed away. She knew Torven would be as hungry as the others and human meat was a particular favourite of his, but he continued drifting at her side, fixing her with his huge, blank eye.

'What of it?' she said, unable to hide her irritation. 'My brother is the king. He is perfectly entitled to lead his armies into battle. And he is only doing as I instructed him to do. The tighter we squeeze the Varrukh, the sooner we will draw out Gotrek. Crushing Karag-Varr is the lure. Dìolan is doing his best to follow the plan. I will go to court soon enough and let him boast of his triumph, but for now I really need to rest.'

Torven continued staring at her.

She sighed and tried to suppress her anger. She had spent weeks travelling the Myrway, she was tired and she would soon have to endure the company of her brother, but none of these things were Torven's fault. 'I can sense you wish to tell me something,' she said. 'Something about my brother's latest battle. What is it? Please speak clearly and quickly, Torven, I need to sleep.'

Torven's tentacles rippled around his beak, as they often did when he was agitated. 'The phalanx was driven back. The king was injured.'

'The idiot. How did he manage that? We've already broken the Fyreslayer king. He's mad with grief and the duardin are ready to fall. We could have finished them off before now if we weren't waiting for Gotrek to arrive.'

'Gotrek is already there.'

Eòrna was watching the feeding frenzy and it took her a moment to register what Torven had said. 'He's already there? In Karag-Varr?'

'Yes.'

Eòrna could hold back her rage no longer. She wrenched her helsabres from their scabbards and lunged at the darkness. 'And my conniving brother didn't tell me! The worm! He went without me! After I – after we – told him about Gotrek's soul.' She hacked at the air. 'And now he'll claim this whole thing was his idea. He acts so pious and then stabs me in the back. He calls me unfit to rule. Has me reduced to the rank of thrallmaster. And then he behaves like the most ill-bred namarti wretch. Where is his honour?' She looked back at Torven, breathless with anger. 'Did you say he was injured? Badly, I hope. It's no more than he deserves for capturing Gotrek without me.'

'His injuries were serious but not life threatening. And he did not capture Gotrek.'

She halted and lowered her swords, her rage subsiding a little. Whatever she thought of her brother, she did not really like the idea that he had been badly hurt. 'He didn't catch the Fyreslayer?' she asked. 'Why?'

Torven floated in silence for a moment, then answered. 'I could not see. Something happened. Gotrek is not what we thought.'

'Not what we thought? What are you talking about? His soul is not as potent as we imagined? The shock waves he created in Skrappa Spill were immense.'

'His soul *is* potent. We were correct in that regard. But when your brother tried to seize him, he...'

'He what?'

'It is hard to explain. Gotrek resisted.'

'Resisted what? The Isharann spells?'

'And the might of the entire phalanx.'

'A single Fyreslayer resisted an army?'

'Something happened to my sight, your highness. I was blinded. Something that came from Gotrek. I cannot tell you exactly what happened, only that the king was unable to capture him, even with the weight of the phalanx behind him. And when the Fyreslayer resisted I felt another shock wave, similar to the one that came from Skrappa Spill when Gotrek fought the Moonclan tribes.'

Eòrna began pacing back and forth, swinging her sabres again. 'So my idiot brother tries to take the prize without me and makes a mess of it. All the better. This plays into my hands. Everyone knows I was the one who discovered Gotrek's power.' She placed her hand on Torven's cold shell. 'Thanks to your insight, old friend. And now they'll see that only I am capable of hunting the Fyreslayer down. I have no idea how Dìolan managed to make a mess of things, but next time he attacks Karag-Varr I'll be there to make sure he does things properly.' She gave Torven a sidelong glance. 'And to show people who should really be the ruler of Dhruim-Ùrlar.'

'The king will not be attacking for a good while. His injuries will take a long time to heal. Days, perhaps weeks. The tru'heas are treating him but I can sense their concern. They are determined that the king must rest.'

'Rest?' Eòrna sneered. 'Not if I can help it. I'm going to the palace now.'

Torven did not reply. His silence was a pointed one.

'What?' asked Eòrna. 'Is there something else?'

'When Gotrek resisted your brother, I was unable to follow what was hap-pening. But the Isharann priests saw something. And whatever they saw made them very excited.'

'Something about Gotrek?'

'Perhaps. Something to do with his soul. And the rune in his chest. It was something they were keen to share with the king once he was well enough to talk. Thallacrom seemed to know the most.'

Eòrna nodded at the mention of her brother's chief soulscryer. 'Thal-lacrom will talk to me. My brother can't have completely poisoned him against me.'

'Eòrna, I am troubled,' said Torven.

Eòrna and Torven had been friends for many years. He had remained loyal to her and chose to remain in her service, even in her darkest hour, when she thought her brother might have her killed to secure his place on the throne. They had endured much together, but this was the first time he had ever described himself as troubled.

She kept her voice calm, determined not to reveal how uneasy she felt. 'My brother wants to secure his place on the throne. He has always been fixed on that goal. But when he made me a thrallmaster he was giving me a chance to live. He knows I'm a threat but he didn't try to have me murdered. What-ever he's doing now will just be to further tighten his grip on Dhruim-Ùrlar. It can't be any worse than his previous games.'

'It is more than that, Eòrna. I saw something in his face. And in the face of Thallacrom and the other priests. There is something else happening. It is not just to do with holding on to his throne. I sense a betrayal.'

'A betrayal? Of whom?'

'All of us. I can only half see it, but I am sure it is there. Your brother means to betray the Dromlech.'

'No. I can believe many things of my brother, but not that. He is devoted to preserving Dhruim-Ùrlar. He never craved power for its own sake. He craved it because he doesn't trust anyone else to do the job. He's wrong, but he's not a traitor.'

'Nevertheless, I sense a great betrayal is about to take place, unless we can stop it. Let me give you something.' Torven's tentacles rippled around his beak and a tiny shape floated from his shell.

Eòrna reached out to take it. At first, she thought it was a stone, or egg, but then, as she turned it in her fingers, she saw that it was a tiny likeness of Torven – a pale, smooth whorl of shell, no bigger than one of her knuckles. 'Why do I need this?'

'Thallacrom and the rest of the priests have ways of protecting their pri-vacy. My deepsight does not penetrate their temples. But if you take this into their inner chambers, I will see as clearly as if I were there. Then we can find out what your brother is planning.'

Eòrna nodded. 'Very well. I do not believe he would betray us, but I do like the idea of finding out what he's up to.' She secreted the shell in a pouch at her belt. 'My brother may have robbed me of my title, but he cannot deny me access to the palace. Not unless he wants outright civil war on his hands. I'll secrete this near his priests.' She looked back at the food she had brought. The bones had been stripped clean and her children were circling again. 'I wish I could stay to feed you more. I desire nothing more than to be here, resting in the darkness, but I will not sleep after what you have told me. I must brave the palace.'

She headed back towards the lobe-shaped doors of the hall. 'I'll return as soon as I can,' she said, looking back towards Torven. He was still hanging in the shadows, motionless, his fathomless eye locked on her.

'Be careful,' he said.

She nodded and left.

CHAPTER ELEVEN

Namarti flocked around Eòrna as she headed back into the upper levels of her palace. Servants fussed her, and proud warriors of the Akhelian Guard, mounted on fangmora eels, formed ranks and swam before her as she headed through the entrance halls and out into the city. The aelves of the Dromlech enclave referred to their home as a city but, in truth, Dhruim-Ùrlar was an ancient kelp forest. It sprawled for miles across the sea floor and reached hundreds of feet up into the darkness, but if a traveller were able to survive the crushing depths and swim overhead, they would see only a tangled canopy of dark green fronds. The kelps that grew in Dhruim-Ùrlar were knotted so tightly together that they hid the wonders beneath.

As Eòrna mounted her deepmare and glided down the steps of her palace, she passed through pools of turquoise light. Luminous branches spiralled around the city's buildings, and the architecture was so sinuous that, in many places, it was impossible to distinguish fortresses from flora. The ethersongs of the Chorralus spell-weavers had formed temples and townhouses from the kelp, creating a web of balconies and walkways that coiled around each other like fronds, merging seamlessly with the original forest. Some of the roads were broad and constant, but the lesser routes were unpredictable and not to be trusted. The forest had never entirely been tamed and even the oldest citizens avoided the darkways and bowers of the outer glades. Like all Idoneth cities, Dhruim-Ùrlar was not filled with water or air, but existed in a third element called the ethersea. Thanks to the powerful sorcery of the Isharann priesthood, lungs and gills worked equally well in the halls of the Dromlech. As aelven thralls walked through the shifting lights, hauling carts and carrying enormous conches, plume sharks swam over their heads, trailing tendrils like pennants. Higher still swam bell jellies the size of whales, true monsters of the deep, pulsing between the spires of Isharann temples, swelling and flashing like storm clouds.

Eòrna did not pause to study the majesty of the forest city. Anger was still trilling through her veins as she thought of her brother's treachery. She was the one who had identified the importance of Gotrek Gurnisson. And she was the one who concocted the plan to lure him to Karag-Varr. There would be other prizes; Eòrna could hunt souls more efficiently than anyone else in the enclave. But the Fyreslayer's soul would transform the thralls of

Dhruim-Ùrlar, prolonging their lives by many years. And she was damned if Dìolan was going to take the credit.

Eòrna's rage was so great that she had ridden through several groves before she realised there was something odd happening. She was travelling down the city's great east-west road, Dabbarloc-sór, a highway so wide it rarely looked busy. But today it was crowded. Her thralls were having to clear a path for her and even the side streets were packed with namarti slaves and finely dressed nobles. *What is this?* she wondered. She had been away from the city for weeks, hunting along the Incendiary Coast. Had she had forgotten a festival?

'You!' she called out to a nearby half-soul.

The slave turned his eyeless face towards her. Though they were blind, namarti could perceive the world around them with absolute clarity. 'Your highness,' gasped the slave, recognising her. All the nearby slaves that noticed the exchange were equally excited by her presence. Under normal circumstances, Eòrna would have relished the attention, but she did not have time for their adoration. 'Where's everyone going? What's the commotion? Are there envoys from another enclave visiting?'

The slave looked shocked. 'Didn't you know, your highness?'

'About what?'

'About the assemblage. The king has summoned a meeting of the high priests and royal families. But surely you were invited?'

Another snub. Eòrna wanted to howl but she simply shook her head. 'Of course I'm invited.' She tried to think of an excuse for her earlier question. 'What I mean is, where are all these slaves going? The Allmarach is huge, but it's still just one palace. It can't house the entire enclave. Why are so many people headed to the assemblage?'

The half-soul beamed. 'The priests of the Chorralus are going to relay King Dìolan's words to the palace gardens. His highness wishes to address the entire enclave.'

As the slave called out to her, more namarti recognised Eòrna and began shoving their way across the road to try and see her more clearly. 'Move!' she snapped, steering her mount on through the crowds and waving for her thralls to do the same.

King Dìolan's palace, the Allmarach, was on the opposite side of the city to Eòrna's home and even on a deepmare, the journey could take an hour. Eòrna had no idea what time her brother had specified but she was determined not to find herself shut outside with the half-souls. As she raced through the city, she spotted a familiar face, seated in the howdah of a levi-adon that had just swum onto the main thoroughfare. The huge, turtle-like creature was draped in the colours of House Deoch and the noble Eòrna had recognised was Princess Arainn Deoch. When Arainn caught sight of Eòrna, she ordered the leviadon's crew to steer it in her direction. The great beast pounded its hook-shaped fins, throwing the street into shadow as it approached.

Arainn was dressed as magnificently as ever, wearing indigo robes that billowed like clouds of ink and a crown of knotted coral. Her face was so heavily powdered that it resembled a bone mask and she was so slender she looked like she would buckle in a strong breeze. But she was the oldest and most powerful of all the nobles at court. She spawned a new fashion every time she wore a different robe and her approval was considered the greatest boon a courtier could aspire to. Before Dìolan had seized the throne, Arainn's father had been king and she was still a figurehead for the high-born who pined for the old regime. Many of her devoted followers were with her in the howdah: ancient, proud lords of Dhruim-Ùrlar, so aloof that their gazes were fixed, habitually, on a glorious horizon only they could see.

'Thrallmaster,' said Princess Arainn in a deep, musical voice. She smiled sympathetically as she said the word, emphasising Eòrna's diminished title. 'What a pleasure it is to see you.' She glanced at Eòrna's scruffy, worn leathers with an expression of mild despair, as though greeting an endearing but wayward child. 'Have you recently returned from one of your voyages?'

Eòrna refused to show how irked she was and nodded her head graciously. 'Princess. I was thinking of you just the other day. Thinking of how devoted you have been to my brother, offering him your help at every turn. You are a model subject.' She lowered her voice as the leviadon came closer. 'Whatever happens in the future, whatever becomes of our enclave, I shall always remember how loyal you were to the king.'

Princess Arainn's mouth hardened into a line. She understood the hidden barb in Eòrna's words. Dìolan was king but Arainn would have noticed how popular Eòrna had become. Perhaps even more popular than Arainn's own entourage. The half-souls adored Eòrna for her success in hunting soul-matter, and there were many of the younger members of the nobility who treated her with the same reverence. The throne of Dhruim-Ùrlar was famously difficult to retain and Princess Arainn knew all too well how easily power could shift.

'I only did what anyone else would do in my stead,' said Arainn. She kept her tone cordial but the smile did not return to her mouth. 'It is my duty to serve King Dìolan.'

The two nobles studied each other in silence for a moment, as the princess' entourage affected disinterest, keeping their regal gazes on the horizon. Eòrna shrugged. She had no energy for the subtleties of court and these weighted, brittle conversations. She looked down at the crowds. 'I've never seen a gathering like this. The entire city must be here.'

Arainn was not ready to let the matter go. 'Making you a thrallmaster was not my suggestion. The court is poorer without you. And I told your brother as much. I said it would serve him better to keep you here in Dhruim-Ùrlar.'

'Keep me here?' Eòrna looked at Arainn's beautiful, absurd robes. 'Keep me at court when there is an ocean to explore and animus to hunt?' She shook her head. 'You would be doing me a cruelty.'

Arainn regained her imperious smile. 'You always were much wilder than your brother.' Her sycophants laughed gently and muttered in agreement.

Eòrna nodded at the crowds rushing to the palace. 'What is this all about? Do you know what my brother considers important enough to drag the whole city to a halt?'

'He has returned victorious from a battle in the uplands. That's the thrust of it, I believe. He has obtained a great haul of soul-matter and he wishes to share news of the victory. It is to be a glorious affair, followed by a grand ball.'

'Victory?' said Eòrna, recalling Torven's rather different version of events. 'Are you sure?'

'Of course, child. Why else would he summon us all? He would be unlikely to call an assembral to boast of an unsuccessful raid.' She raised an eyebrow at her followers. 'And even I would not approve of balls being hosted to celebrate defeats.'

They sniffed and smirked in agreement.

Eòrna shrugged as she continued steering her deepmare above the crowds of thralls. 'I wouldn't put it past him. Since he found religion I can make no sense of his decisions. He's lost his grasp on sanity.'

'He pays tribute to the Great Illuminator. With the greatest of respect, Eòrna, there is nothing wrong with that.'

'Nothing wrong with it? I'm not so sure. He prays to a god who despises us. That's idiocy at best. If Teclis remembers us at all, he would laugh at my brother's devotion.'

Before they could say more they turned a bend in the road and saw the royal palace spread out before them. The Allmarach was the grandest structure in all of Dhruim-Ùrlar, a circle of spires that rose from the forest like a crown. Its gates were wide enough to admit hundreds of aelves at a time, but so many people were trying to crowd into the palace that a sea of thralls had gathered outside, jostling and trying to push their way forwards. The noise was immense. As well as the sound of the crowd, there was a rolling clatter of drumming coming from the palace walls and a howl of hunting horns that swelled and droned, as resonant as whale song.

Eòrna and the other nobles guided their steeds over the heads of the namarti, riding a menagerie of gaudily armoured sea creatures. Knights and princes called out to Eòrna and Arainn as they passed through the gates and through the king's coral gardens. Eòrna nodded with all the grace she could muster. She could not remember the last time she had slept and this was the last place she wanted to be, but these were the people who would one day help her to Dìolan's throne. They believed in her and she would not let them down.

'Your highness!' cried one of the nobles, riding his fangmora eel back towards her.

'Úrdach.' She smiled as a young knight reached her, pleased to see someone who viewed her with less condescension than Arainn. He had a bright, open-looking face, but Eòrna was not deceived. In his own way, Úrdach was very dangerous. He was witty and charming, which meant he was very well connected at court. He was like a sunlit stream with hidden, unexpected deeps. Luckily for Eòrna, he was unfailingly loyal to her.

'I did not see you at the battle,' he said, struggling to make himself heard over the din of the crowd. 'Were you there?'

'No,' she said, sitting proudly in her saddle, conscious that Arainn was still nearby and might overhear the exchange. 'I knew nothing of the attack.'

He grimaced. 'I thought as much. Well, you didn't miss much. It was a farce.'

She leant closer to him as they rode towards the central keep, with Arainn and the other nobles keeping pace. 'But how? The Fyreslayers are leaderless. And they have accepted the story of the curse. Even my brother should have been able to handle them.' She noticed that the plates of Úrdach's armour were damaged. 'Are you injured?'

'Only my pride. My battalion was one of the first to attack. I lost several good warriors. I'm glad you weren't there to see what a mess I made of things.'

'What went wrong?'

'Nothing, at first. Things went exactly as planned during the first waves of the attack. The king took half the phalanx with him. The thralls cut through the uplanders with ease and the priests were gathering a great harvest of souls. But then, when we found Gotrek Gurnisson, everything fell apart. He's immune to the ethersea. He saw through it. Even Thallacrom could do nothing to halt him. Gotrek marched through the waves and started cutting us down. Nothing touched him.' He shook his head. 'And he fights like a zephyr shark. Dìolan rode out to face him and even he could not touch him. Gotrek batted him away like he was the lowliest half-soul.'

Much as Eòrna would have liked to revel in her brother's defeat, she had to admit that this was peculiar. For all his faults, Dìolan was a great warrior. He had seized the throne in a bloody coup and he was generally considered one of the greatest swordsmen the Dromlech enclave had ever produced. She was about to ask Úrdach for more details when speech became impossible. Their steeds had swum through a soaring arch into the Great Hall of the Allmarach.

CHAPTER TWELVE

Arrayed across the walls, on conch-shaped balconies, were hundreds of flute and horn players, and the noise was deafening. The seats below were filled with colourfully dressed nobles and their servants, and there were more flooding in from the various archways around the perimeter. Eòrna guessed that there must be three or four thousand aelves crammed into the hall and all of them were clamouring for a view of the stage at the far end. Throngs of adoring followers swarmed around Arainn until she was obscured by a forest of gowns and gleaming armour, and more of Eòrna's friends spotted her and gathered at her side. She felt a rush of pride. There was a time when siding so visibly with her would have been considered a risk. But since becoming a thrallmaster she had led the Dromlech enclave to unprecedented seams of soul-matter – cities and coasts that were so ripe for the plucking they had prolonged the life of the Dromlech half-souls by many years. Thanks to her, their battalions had almost doubled in size. She was a hero to namarti and noble alike, and her brother would not dare lay a finger on her.

The music swelled and then died away as a group of Isharann sorcerers walked onto the stage, their gaunt faces haloed by ornate collars and their bodies swathed in ceremonial robes that billowed round them as they took their places. There was a roar of cheering and applause as King Dìolan limped onto the stage. He was surrounded by Isharann healers who were trying to help him walk, but he drove them off with angry shrugs as he stepped out from the shadows, straightening his back and lifting his chin. He was dressed for war, wearing thick, scalloped plate armour. His intricately engraved helmet was topped with a transverse crest of honey-coloured coral and the nose guard was forged in the shape of a sea serpent's head. He reached the front of the stage and stood in silence for a moment, letting the applause wash over him, his face grim and resolute. Then he held his hand up for silence.

'Children of Dhruim-Ùrlar.' His tone was low but the words reverberated through the hall and echoed out into the streets beyond. Standing just to his left was his most senior priest: Thallacrom, the spirit-navigator who guided the king's battalions through the Myrway and singled out the most potent souls in enemy armies. Thallacrom was a potent mixture of soulscryer and tidecaster, and he was also the spiritual leader of the enclave. He was a gaunt, severe-looking noble who had served the Dromlech enclave for so many generations that some claimed he was older than Dhruim-Ùrlar itself. His long, angular face was inked with runes and his left eyebrow was arched in a habitual expression of disapproval. Fierce intelligence simmered in his eyes. There were many tales told about him, including rumours that he had once served with High King Volturnos, oldest of all the Idoneth rulers. Despite his age, however, he was considered to have the sharpest mind in Dhruim-Ùrlar. As King Dìolan spoke, Thallacrom was leaning on a staff made from the tip of a narwhal tusk, his eyes closed as he whispered urgently. It would be Thallacrom's ether-magic that was amplifying King Dìolan's voice, thought Eòrna, noticing the light that was shimmering between the priest's fingers.

'We have come to a crossroads,' continued the king, surveying the crowds with a look of triumph.

'He lost the battle,' whispered Eòrna, glancing at Úrdach. 'Isn't that what you said? And he looks like he could pass out at any moment. So why does he look so pleased with himself?'

Úrdach shook his head. 'He had to be dragged back to the Myrway. He lost a lot of blood.'

There was a moment of quiet in the Great Hall as the crowds wondered what their king meant.

'For all these long centuries, we have been slaves,' continued the king. 'From the high-born Akhelians to the lowliest half-souls, we are all the same.'

Most of the nobles in the hall looked unimpressed by this comment, glancing at each other and muttering in disapproval.

'What *is* he doing?' whispered Eòrna. If her brother continued in this vein, he would alienate every Akhelian pure-soul in the hall. He would do her job for her.

'We are slaves to our past,' continued Dìolan. His face was rigid with pain and he could not quite stand straight, but he still refused any help from his servants, glaring out at the crowd. 'We are bound by the ancient curse, scavenging for the animus of lesser races when we should be masters of our own.'

A tentative cheer washed through the crowd as the nobles realised he was not really suggesting nobles were comparable with soul-withered slaves.

'We are the firstborn!' When Dìolan raised his voice, it roared through the hall, causing some of the nobles to flinch. 'When the Great Illuminator brought our ancestors into the realms he had a noble purpose in mind. We were not made to cower in our halls. We were not made to live off scraps.' He leant out from the stage, staring at the crowds, his eyes feverish. 'We were made to rule!'

The cheers were now wholehearted and Eòrna shook her head. 'What *is* he talking about?'

'Daemons crawl where we should stand. Orruks ruin where we should build. The Mortal Realms are our birthright!' He let the cheers crash over him, then gestured to one of his servants, looking pained and irritated. The servant rushed over with a conch of wine and Dìolan drank heavily. Then he stood in silence for a moment, eyes closed.

'He's going to faint,' said Eòrna, incredulous. 'In front of the entire enclave.'

The cheers died away as Dìolan remained still. Finally he nodded, threw the conch back to his slave and faced the hall again. 'But for all these years we have been shackled by the Great Hunt. Shackled by this endless search for animus.' He waved at a nearby slave. 'Shamed by our crippled offspring. But *no more!*' He glanced at the old Isharann priest, Thallacrom, who was nodding eagerly. 'In the volcanic caverns of the lesser races, I have found the answer. I have found the key that will rid us of our chains. This is a day that will be remembered through the ages. Your descendants will sing ballads about this moment. In Karag-Varr, I have discovered a soul that will finish what Teclis began all those long ages ago. A soul that carries within it a spark of divinity. The soul of a god! And with its power, finally, we will be truly born. Finally, we will be free. We will take up the mantle the Great Illuminator intended for us. Once we have harvested this soul, the Dromlech will be the first enclave in the history of all the Idoneth to escape the soul curse!'

There were several seconds of dazed silence as people looked at each other, trying to grasp what they were hearing. The king was known to be eccentric but no one had expected this.

'They'll behead him,' whispered Eòrna. 'There will be a revolution.'

But, to her amazement, some of the nobles began rising to their feet and cheering, raising weapons and howling battle cries. A roar of triumph crashed through the hall that was so loud even the king's magically enhanced words were drowned out. It was half the audience at most, but that was enough to unnerve Eòrna.

'He's lost his mind,' she said. 'What's he talking about, escaping the soul curse? It's madness. We aren't cursed, we're blessed. The Great Hunt is what we live for. It's who we are. Without that we wouldn't be Idoneth.'

When the cheers died down again, the king continued talking, explaining that Gotrek was unique. That his soul was the prize Idoneth enclaves had been seeking since prehistory. But Eòrna was barely listening. All she could think of was the ruin her brother would wreak if she did not stop him. Before this moment she had been sure that she should rule in his stead, but now it was more than that. If she did not stop her brother's madness he would destroy everything she cared about. Everything that mattered. When the king had finally finished his speech, the music began again and guards began ushering the crowds from the hall. Some of the nearby nobles were talking excitedly about the king's grand idea, talking about how glorious it would be when the Dromlech could escape their exile in the sea and become masters of the realms. But many others gathered around Eòrna, troubled by what had been said and keen to hear her response.

'He can't just tear down our traditions,' said Úrdach, looking at her. 'He can't drag us into the upper lands, to live in deserts and dust.'

'Our home is here,' agreed another noble. 'We are of the sea. And what would we be without the Great Hunt?'

Eòrna nodded but she was too furious to speak until the palace guards approached and tried to usher her from the hall. 'I will speak with my brother now,' she said, glaring at them.

Despite her royal blood, the guards looked on the verge of arguing with her, gripping their tridents nervously and glancing at each other. But then the crowd of nobles around her demanded they let her pass, appalled that mere soldiers would attempt to defy a member of the royal family. It looked for a moment as though fighting might break out, but then the soldiers saw sense and backed down, allowing Eòrna to cross the hall unhindered. She rode her deepmare quickly through the departing crowds, nodding to the people who called óut to her, both pure-souls and half-souls. When she reached the now empty stage, she dismounted. 'Wait for me here,' she said to Úrdach, who had followed her through the crowds. She handed her reins to a nearby slave and strode though a doorway.

CHAPTER THIRTEEN

The antechamber Eòrna had entered was crowded with scribes who were transcribing the king's speech onto shells. They looked up in surprise as she entered. Since the king had reduced her status to that of thrallmaster, most people were unsure how to address her, keen not to offend her but conscious that they could enrage Dìolan by using her old title of princess. One of the scribes opted for a neutral 'your highness' and the others followed suit. She ignored them and marched on into the next chamber. This room was a ballroom with a broad, vaulted dome that resembled the inside of a ribbed shell. The walls were lined with suits of armour and there was a huddle of figures at the centre of the room. Eòrna picked out Thallacrom and some of her brother's other close advisors, all clustered around the king, who had fallen to his knees. Princess Arainn was there too, with a few of her splendidly attired followers. The princess looked troubled and was whispering urgently to one of her friends. There was a pool of blood spreading around King Dìolan as he tried to shrug off the people who were trying to assist him. 'Leave me be!' he roared. 'I'm quite capable of walking.'

Dìolan lurched to his feet and began staggering on across the ballroom, trailing blood across the polished floor. Attendants and Isharann priests scurried after him holding cups and poultices, but he ignored them as he weaved drunkenly towards the door. Despite her anger, Eòrna felt a rush of pity for him. Since childhood, Dìolan had been obsessed with the idea that the Dromlech were the greatest of all the Idoneth enclaves. At times, his obsession had seemed like a talisman, lending him strength and purpose when others lost their way, but at other times it was a kind of madness. He could not rest until the Dromlech rose from the ranks of their kin. He dreamed of a past that had probably never existed and a future that could never be. And now, as he lurched across the hall, blood rushing from his armour, he looked closer than ever to destroying himself. Then Eòrna remembered what he had just said in his speech and her pity evaporated. 'You'll destroy us,' she spat.

He halted, without looking back. 'Who admitted this thrallmaster?'

The king's priests and advisors looked flustered, spouting apologies, but only one had the nerve to challenge her. Thallacrom walked slowly back across the ballroom towards her. This close, his great age was even more apparent. His skin was like silvered bark and the only colour in his face was the bruise-blue of his teeth, which he licked thoughtfully as he approached. He was so frail that he barely looked able to withstand the weight of his robes, but Eòrna knew better than to underestimate him. He was the most powerful sorcerer in any of the Isharann fanes. And his skills were not limited to a single discipline. Unlike most priests, he deployed any form of magic he chose. 'There is no need for this, your highness,' he said. His voice was firm but kind, as it had been when he had tutored her as a child.

'I'll tell you what could destroy us,' said the king, ignoring Thallacrom and limping back towards Eòrna, fury sparking in his eyes. 'Blinkered, backward traditions. People like you are so enamoured of the glorious hunt that you forget what it means. It's just a leash, Eòrna. A leash that holds us in place while our enemy moves closer. And I will stand for it no longer.'

She had never seen him look so unhinged. She had come here to try and make him see sense, but now that she saw him, she wondered if she had made a mistake. He looked feral, as if he were in the midst of battle and about to strike a killing blow. 'Our enemy?' She shook her head. 'Which particular enemy? The Mortal Realms are full of enemies.'

'You know what I mean. The great wyrm. The Serpent Who Thirsts. The Lord of Excess. Slaanesh.' He staggered back towards her. 'Do you think it is enough to hunt souls and eke a little more life into our thralls? Do you think it is enough to wait in the deeps as Chaos prepares to hunt us down? Do you think we can escape the fate that befell the uplands? Of course not. It is a matter of time. But we were not made to wait. We were made to stand. To fight. To rule.' He was spitting and twitching as he spoke, his powerful frame rocked by tremors. 'And fools like you think we can remain as we have always been, lost in the hunt, scouring beaches for sparks of life. Living off morsels.'

'Every soul I find makes us stronger,' she snapped, refusing to be cowed by him. 'Our thralls are more powerful now than at any time in our past. And it is down to me, you know it is. The half-souls in our battalions are better than–'

'They are cursed!' roared the king, looking like he might draw his sword and cut her down. 'Nothing else matters. The rest of your words are meaningless. They are a shameful failure. They are the failure that caused the Great Illuminator to drive us from his light.'

'You don't know your damned history. The gods didn't drive us from their light. Our ancestors fled. Teclis meant to destroy us. The gods despise us.'

'Perhaps,' hissed Dìolan. 'But that will change when we rise from the deeps and reclaim the realms in their name. Then they will see that we are, and always were, their most perfect weapon.'

'Rise from the deeps?' said Princess Arainn. She was standing a few feet away, looking increasingly unnerved. 'What do you mean?'

'You're raving, brother,' said Eòrna, before Dìolan could reply. 'The deeps are where we belong, not the dry, life-leeching heat of the uplands. We are the Dromlech and we are–'

'We are the Dromlech!' snapped Dìolan. 'Exactly! And we are better. Better than the Nautilar or the Dhom-hain or the Ionrach or any other enclave. We are the chosen.' He glared at Princess Arainn and then at Eòrna. 'We can do *more* than hunt from the shadows. We are destined to strike back. We will not hide, we will advance, and we will crush the followers of Slaanesh with an entire phalanx of pure-souls – aelves who live, think and fight with all the perfection the gods intended.'

'Because of this one soul?' said Eòrna. 'Because of this Fyreslayer? Can't you hear how insane you sound?'

The king took a deep breath to steady himself and glanced at Thallacrom, his eyes full of triumph. 'It is not madness.' He placed a hand on her shoulder, speaking in softer tones. 'I thank you for finding him, Eòrna, truly I do. But you had no idea. You thought it was the rune in his chest that triggered that etherstorm, but it was never that. It's *him*. He is not what we thought. He is not a normal being. His flesh is temporal but his soul is... His soul is something else. Isn't that right, Thallacrom?'

Thallacrom was watching her carefully. 'There is no need for this argument, Eòrna. You are angry because you see only fragments of the picture. When you know the full–'

'Do not lecture me!' Eòrna gripped the handles of her helsabres. 'I'm not a child any more, Thallacrom. I am–'

'You are a thrallmaster,' warned her brother. 'And you will leave me now. The healers tell me I need to rest before we can mount another attack.'

Eòrna was about to argue when she realised guards had been entering the hall while she spoke with her brother. There were now dozens of half-souls targeting her with longbows.

Her brother seemed calm and spoke to her in a kinder tone. 'You should leave, Eòrna. Events are moving fast now and they do not concern you. I do not say that out of spite. You do not believe in this cause and I will not let you hinder me. You should return to your hunts. There is a change coming and you must prepare yourself for a new way of life.'

She wanted to strike him. 'You're half-dead. And from what I hear, Gotrek has turned the Fyreslayers into something formidable. If you attack him again, you'll only make a fool of yourself.'

Her words had no effect on the king. His anger had gone. He shared another triumphant gaze with Thallacrom, nodded to Princess Arainn and then turned to leave.

'Go home, Eòrna,' said Thallacrom, giving her a kind smile. 'The matter is in hand. Wheels are in motion. And you need to rest.'

His gentle tone only made Eòrna more furious and she was about to follow him when the lines of archers interceded, stepping in front of her, bows raised and arrows nocked.

Thallacrom licked his teeth and smiled at her as he shuffled away. 'You need not worry about the king, thrallmaster. I will take care of him.'

Eòrna glared at the archers, on the verge of making a scene, then realised she would need to employ subtler methods if she wanted to uncover the details of her brother's plan. She turned and stormed from the ballroom, heading back towards the hall. When she strode back out onto the stage, Úrdach was waiting. She mounted her steed and waved for him to follow as she headed to the exit. Most of the crowd had already left, but Princess Arainn and her train of nobles had followed her back out into the hall, and some of them were looking in her direction, so Eòrna rode out into the gardens and found a quiet arbour in which to talk.

'He's plotting something with Thallacrom,' she said, after making sure they were alone.

Úrdach nodded. 'They need a better way to defeat the Fyreslayers if they're going to harvest Gotrek's soul. Or they'll risk another farcical defeat. I'm sure Thallacrom and his priests will have some ideas.'

'This must *not* happen.' Eòrna gripped Úrdach's arm. 'We have to find out what they're planning and put a stop to it. I curse the day I told my brother about Gotrek Gurnisson.' She shook her head. 'I knew he was unusual but I had no idea it would lead to this. My brother is going to destroy us.' She pulled him close. 'Do you still have access to the inner temples of the Allmarach?'

He frowned. 'They will have seen me talking to you today, and they know we are still friends. But I have never been denied admittance before. The king still trusts me, I think.'

Eòrna remembered the small crustacean Torven had given her and took it out. Its claws scuttled briefly across her palm as she studied it, as though it were eager to begin its errand. The sight of it reminded her of Torven and the memory calmed her. She took a deep breath and then handed it to Úrdach. 'Get as close as you can to the priests' chambers, then leave this creature in a hidden place. It is a spy. It will seek Dìolan out and show me what he's plotting. The plan my brother has suggested would require a ritual unlike any the Isharann have performed before. How can he think he could use Gotrek's soul to change the whole enclave? To rewrite our entire history? He must be planning something insane. Find out. Then we can make sure it fails.'

Úrdach hid the shell in his armour and kissed Eòrna's hand. 'I will not fail you, princess.'

CHAPTER FOURTEEN

Úrdach knew better than to skulk. Nothing would look more suspicious than an Akhelian noble *creeping*. He strode, straight-backed and proud through the scallop-shaped halls of the Allmarach. Namarti slaves were bustling through the rooms, preparing for the victory ball, carrying trays laden with food and wine and tuning instruments made from cowrie shells so large it took teams of aelves to carry them. He had not found time to have his armour repaired but it was clean and polished and he had draped a sash over the worst dents, so he looked presentable as he nodded to various nobles. There was a charge in the air. Everyone he passed was talking in breathless tones about King Dìolan's speech. An intoxicating mixture of fear and excitement had taken hold of Dhruim-Ùrlar.

He reached the grand ballroom, where guests were already gathering, draped in their finery and eager to discuss the day's events, but he picked up his pace, heading for an opposite door, making it clear he was there on business rather than looking for dance partners. He had almost reached the door when an unctuous voice called out to him.

'Lord Úrdach,' said Arainn, gliding across the room to his side and gripping his arm. 'Isn't it wonderful?' she said, her tone neutral.

He gave her a stiff nod, trying to hide his annoyance at the delay. 'Isn't what wonderful, Lady Arainn?'

'King Dìolan's plan. His desire to lift us up from the deeps.'

As Úrdach studied her face, he realised, to his shock, that she was afraid. It was not hard for him to guess why. Her life had been built on certainties. She knew her place at court was unassailable. But now the king was talking of changing everything and all Arainn's certainties were about to be stolen.

'It is quite incredible news,' he said, matching her flat tone.

She stared at him. 'Yes, because, if we can change the nature of the namarti...' She looked at some nearby slaves. 'If we can elevate them by shaking off their soul curse, there will be nothing that can stop us.'

Úrdach nodded.

'And then,' continued Arainn, 'we can become the aelves the Great Illuminator intended us to be. We can reclaim the *uplands*' – she grimaced at the word – 'and take our place as the pre-eminent enclave.'

'So it would seem. Now, if you would excuse me, I have business to attend to.'

Arainn did not loosen her grip on his arm. She looked at the door he had been heading towards. 'Business with King Dìolan?'

'Yes. I must take a message to his highness.'

'Perfect,' said Arainn, heading for the door. 'I need to speak with the king myself. I am keen to hear more detail concerning his wonderful idea.'

Úrdach mouthed a curse as she entered the corridor, trailed by billowing robes. The last thing he needed was someone at his side when he was trying to place Eòrna's shell.

'Arainn,' he said, hurrying after her. 'The ball will begin soon. You would be sorely missed. I imagine many people will have come here specifically to dance with you.'

She raised an eyebrow. 'I'm too old for your flattery, child. Besides, it will be an hour at least before everything is ready. And the ball will still be in full swing when the morning comes. Anyway, I will always make time for an audience with the king.'

They walked on in silence as Úrdach tried to think of a way to be rid of his unwelcome companion and Arainn waved graciously at passers-by. Then, as they crossed more chambers, they began to leave the noise of the ballroom behind and enter the regions of the palace devoted to Isharann temples. The walls were painted with images of the father of the Isharann faith, the fallen god known as Mathlann. Mathlann was shown with his mighty *fuathtar* spear held high, locked in battle with the ultimate enemy of the Idoneth, the Chaos God Slaanesh.

Úrdach had seen the murals many times but they never failed to humble him. Mathlann was a symbol of everything the Idoneth aspired to: raw, magnificent pride, like the nobility of a crashing wave. Painting after painting showed Mathlann's final battle with Slaanesh, in which he tried to save his worshippers from the predations of Chaos. His lines were perfect, his countenance divine, all of which was contrasted by the dreadful nature of his foe. Slaanesh was a sinuous mess, a lurid swirl of un-life, caressing Mathlann with razor-edged fingers and barbed, glistening tails.

It was a battle between nobility and depravity, and even in the final panel, as Slaanesh finally consumed Mathlann, it was clear that the aelven god had snatched an unexpected triumph. As Mathlann perished, his expression was victorious, causing the Serpent of Pleasure to frown, confused. The artist who had painted the mural had captured the doubt in Slaanesh's mind as the Chaos God sensed that it had missed something. In the fanes of the Isharann priesthood, Úrdach had heard many times of Mathlann's secret triumph. The aelven god of the deeps would never truly die, as long as his memory lived on in the souls of his followers. His power had been scattered, rather than diminished. Slaanesh thought it was glutting itself on a glorious meal, but it was actually crunching on an empty shell. Some of the Dromlech saw the story as a metaphor, illustrating that by keeping Mathlann's memory alive, they could embody his greatness; but others saw the tale in a very literal way, believing that Mathlann sowed his divine essence into the souls of his worshippers, making each of them, even the lowliest namarti, a vessel for his glorious power.

Priests glanced up as Úrdach and Princess Arainn passed by the shrines and altars, as did the armed guards who waited at doorways, but none of them challenged the nobles, having seen them in conversation with Dìolan many times. The princess, in particular, was almost on an even footing with the king, so highly was she regarded. Soon, they started to approach the king's private chambers. Úrdach had no desire to actually speak with his regent, and he was sure he was close enough to let the shell go now, but he could do nothing with Arainn at his side and she would be expecting him to find the king. An idea occurred to him as he spotted a seat outside one of the antechambers that led off the corridor. 'Damn it,' he muttered, coming to a halt and holding his side with a grimace.

'Are you unwell?' asked Arainn.

'Wounded. At Karag-Varr.' He tried to sound pained. 'It is nothing. We can continue.'

Frustration flickered in her eyes but she shook her head. 'No, you must rest. Look, here's a chair.' She took him by the arm and led him to the seat. 'Take time to catch your breath. I will wait.'

'No, carry on without me,' he said. 'I fear I may need to wait here for some time. And, if you do not find the king quickly he will be heading to the ball and you will miss your chance.'

'No,' she insisted, with a taut smile, 'I won't leave you.' But it was clear from the way she kept glancing down the corridor that she was desperate to carry on.

'Please,' he said. 'I will have many chances to speak with his majesty. I fight at his side in every campaign. But you may not have this opportunity again for a long while.'

She hummed tunelessly, something he had seen her do before when she was thinking. Then she nodded. 'If you're sure.' She looked around. 'I will call a slave to help you.'

'No,' he said, a little louder than he intended, then more softly, 'No, no need. I just forgot how tender my wound is. If I sit here for a while I will be fine, I assure you, and if I need a servant I can call for one.'

She nodded and made to leave, then hesitated. 'I may see you later, in the king's chambers. You know how he hates balls.' She gave him a stiff smile, then hurried on down the corridor. 'He will delay going for as long as he can.'

Úrdach remained on the seat for a while, listening to her soft footfalls fading into the distance. When he was sure she was not going to come back, he stood and peered into the antechamber behind him. It was a small room, empty apart from a statue of Mathlann in a niche, but there was a doorway on the opposite side, hung with heavy curtains.

The antechamber seemed the perfect place to leave the shell, but he wanted to see what was through the curtains first. He resisted the urge to creep and walked confidently across the room, snatching back the curtains and stepping through the doorway.

The next room was dark. Only a few veins of blue light pulsed through the walls and he struggled to see what kind of chamber it was. The sound of chanting wafted through a doorway he could not see and, as his eyes adjusted to the gloom, he realised that robed priests had gathered in the centre of the room, kneeling in prayer. A guard emerged from the shadows and approached with a stern expression. 'My lord. Forgive me. No one is to be admitted.'

Úrdach was so keen to make his presence seem beyond question that he spoke without thinking. 'I am Prince Úrdach,' he snapped. 'How dare you treat me like a common half-soul! I am here on the express orders of King Dìolan. Would you like me to tell him you attempted to bar my entry?'

The guard paled and looked to one of his comrades who had walked over at the sound of voices.

'Of course you may pass,' said the second guard quickly. 'Please forgive the mistake, prince. Lord Thallacrom has stressed at great length the importance of discretion in this matter. I'm sure you understand.'

'Of course I do,' replied Úrdach, not understanding in the slightest. 'I shall overlook your impertinence on this occasion.' Before the guards could ask him anything else, he strode on across the room. There was something odd going on. He had heard Isharann priests at prayer every day of his life, but the chant he could hear echoing through the chamber was peculiar and quite unlike anything he had encountered before. It sounded urgent and pleading, and as he walked into the next room, he had the odd sensation that the words were tugging at him, draining him of energy.

He dismissed another group of guards who tried to challenge him, speaking with even more confidence now, as he headed past another group of kneeling priests. This room was as gloomy as the previous one, but there were fragments of light blinking through the priests' fingers, as if they were holding lanternfish. They were all holding pieces of coral and their shapes were familiar in some way. Úrdach had only entered the first antechamber looking for a place to leave the shell, but he was now intrigued to know what was happening. All the guards seemed on edge, even though many of them knew him by sight, and as he passed through room after room, the chanting grew in fervour and volume.

He wandered for nearly an hour, crossing dozens of chambers, many of them filled with priests who were clutching pieces of coral, and he began to feel troubled. There was something significant about the coral but he could not place it. He reached a room so heavily guarded that he finally resorted to subterfuge, slipping down some steps and taking another door inside, creeping behind a row of statues and rushing through the entrance when the guards were looking the other way.

The next room was dominated by a long, stone table heaped with pieces of coral. A line of priests was filing into the room from one direction and exiting in another, each taking a piece of coral as they passed the table. There were no guards in this room and Úrdach approached the table with a chill of realisation, staring at the coral. 'They're pieces of the chorrileum,' he whispered, so shocked he had to reach out to the edge of the table to steady himself. The chorrileum was the resting place of the Dromlech. When they died, their souls were interred in the chorrileum by Isharann priests. Dromlech faith taught that any soul not bound to the chorrileum would be consumed by Slaanesh. It was the heart of Dhruim-Ùrlar – and here was a large section of it, dismantled and lying in pieces on a table in the Allmarach. Countless souls were being put at risk. King Dìolan must have sanctioned this, he realised, leaning heavily against the table. This must be how he intended to harness Gotrek's soul. The idea was so horrific Úrdach could barely breathe. The chorrileum was the most sacred site in the whole of Dhruim-Ùrlar. It was the king's holy duty to preserve it. 'I have to tell Eòrna,' he whispered, turning to leave.

'Wait,' said a voice from the other side of the room and a newcomer hurried through the darkness towards him.

A sudden premonition of danger jolted through Úrdach and, before the figure could reach him, he took Eòrna's shell and placed it on the table with the piles of coral.

'Prince!' whispered Thallacrom as he limped from the shadows, baring his ink-stained teeth. In the pall of the chamber he looked even more cadaverous than usual, but he seemed delighted to see Úrdach. 'You have come at an auspicious moment.'

Úrdach bowed. 'I have?'

Thallacrom nodded, studying Úrdach closely and continuing to grin. 'Let me show you.' He waved his narwhal tusk at the door through which the priests were leaving.

Úrdach could not rid himself of the sense that he was in danger but he refused to look hesitant in front of the priest, so he marched across the room with his chin raised, wondering how best to explain his presence.

'King Dìolan has tasked me with a great commission,' said the priest as they headed into a long gallery. 'Perhaps the greatest that has ever been undertaken by an Isharann fane. I and my–'

Úrdach gasped as pain flooded across his back. He whirled around to see that Thallacrom had raised the tusk and was pointing it at him. The air between the two of them shimmered, like the surface of starlit water, and the disturbance was pouring from the point of the tusk. Where it washed over Úrdach, he felt a fierce agony. The pain was so intense that he stumbled and dropped to his knees, struggling to speak. As he fell, he reached for his sword, but his arm had been transfigured by the same disturbance that had altered the air. Where his armour should have been, there was a splash of silvery ripples.

'It is unfortunate that you decided to enter these particular chambers,' said Thallacrom, letting the smile drop from his face. He walked slowly towards Úrdach, keeping the narwhal tusk raised. 'We are not ready to share our methods.'

Úrdach tried to reply but the room became a wall of ripples, as though he were viewing it from behind a waterfall. He realised he could not drag any air into his lungs. In fact, he no longer had lungs. Then the world floated away from him and he was no more.

CHAPTER FIFTEEN

Maleneth gasped for breath, clawing at her throat, her lungs burning as the darkness crushed her. Memories of violence flickered through her mind, visions of every battle she had fought, every kill she had made, every blood sacrifice she had offered – and looming behind it all was the face of Khaine, the Bloody-Handed, Lord of Murder and master of her fate. Her heart raced to know he was watching her, then horror filled her as she saw that the Murder God was studying her with a disappointed expression. He moved closer, blood and fire washing over his perfect features. 'Look at you,' he said, his voice surprisingly coarse. 'Lounging around like you've nothing better to do. Typical bloody aelf.'

As soon as Maleneth recognised Gotrek's bludgeoning voice, the world fell into place around him. The Slayer was standing over her, leaning on his axe, a look of utter disdain on his face. His tattooed muscles were draped in seaweed and spattered with blood. Something was moving in his beard, fidgeting and twitching. Gotrek frowned and picked it out, peering at it. It was a small fish that flashed silver as it moved, flapping back and forth between his thumb and forefinger. Then it was gone, dissipating into a tiny cloud of mist that floated away through the flickering light. As she watched the mist disappear, Maleneth saw that the square looked almost as it had when she had first entered the Fyreslayer keep: lined with heroic statues of daemon-battling duardin and lit by hellish light. Things were not entirely as they had been, though. Some of the statues had been damaged and were now missing weapons or limbs, and there were piles of rubble scattered across the flagstones. In some places the walls themselves had been knocked through, admitting clouds of smoke and embers from the volcano. Everywhere she looked, there were wounded Fyreslayers. Thanks to Gotrek, many hundreds had sallied forth from the buildings that bordered the square and lots of them were now dead or dying, crumpled in heaps along with the broken masonry. Other duardin were rushing between them, tending wounds and offering water. All of them bore the same dark marks across their cheeks and they carried themselves in a manner that seemed unusual for Fyreslayers. Rather than feverish and wild, they appeared sombre and grim.

'What kind of storm can tear down walls like these?' she said, looking around at the carnage in disbelief.

Gotrek had been about to walk away but her words stopped him. He frowned at her. 'Storm? What are you talking about?'

As soon as he answered her, Maleneth felt an inexplicable sense of dread, as if she were losing hold of her sanity. 'The storm that followed us from the coast.' She waved at the wreckage in the square. 'The weather that did all this.'

'Weather? What is it with people blaming everything on the weather? It wasn't mist that knocked the walls down, was it? It wasn't the mist who stuck spears in these people. Don't try and pass elgi treachery off as bad bloody weather.' His lip curled in disgust. 'If there's one thing you can bank on, one thing that never sodding changes, it's that aelves will let you down. All your talk of allegiance and forces of "Order" but look what happens when someone takes their eye off you for a moment – you ride in on fish horses and butcher the people you're supposed to be siding with.'

Maleneth gripped her head, feeling even more disturbed. Gotrek talked nonsense a lot of the time and she had learned, long ago, to ignore most of what he said. But when he spoke of aelves riding fish, it triggered a memory – glimpses of aelves in pearlescent battleplate, with pale skin and coral-coloured banners. The memories were impossible to grasp, however. As soon as she tried to bring them into focus, they slipped away. 'Were there aelves in the storm?' she asked. She had the uncomfortable feeling that their roles had been reversed. Usually Gotrek was the one trying to rouse himself from a stupor as she reminded him what had happened the night before.

Gotrek stared at her, looking even more incredulous than usual. 'Un-bloody-believable.' Then he stomped off across the flagstones. 'Where's Korgan?' he bellowed, and someone directed him to a huge, vaulted portico on the opposite side of the square where Korgan's magmadroth was just visible through the smoke.

'Wait,' groaned Maleneth, lurching to her feet. Pain knifed through her stomach and she doubled over, spitting a curse. It was an old wound, sustained when she and Gotrek had battled the Moonclan tribes. She had thought it healed but now, as she pressed a hand against her stomach, she could feel the muscles beneath her skin, twisted and ugly, still damaged. 'Curse him,' she muttered, blaming Gotrek for the injury as she stumbled after him. She must have landed heavily during the storm. It was not just her stomach that ached. All of her limbs were bruised and stiff, and she shook them as she walked, trying to get the blood flowing.

You'll need to do more than that if you want Khaine to help you.

'What do you suggest?' whispered Maleneth. 'Shall I start attacking these Fyreslayers? I'm somewhat outnumbered.' She knew her mistress was right, though. The only way she could reinvigorate herself was by making blood offerings to the Murder God.

I shouldn't worry, Gotrek has a skill for turning allies into enemies. You won't have to wait long.

'What would I do without you to point out the obvious at every turn?' sneered Maleneth.

'Aelves!' roared Gotrek as Maleneth reached him. He was glowering at

Korgan, who was still seated up on the magmadroth. 'Salad-eating elgi!' He waved at Maleneth. 'Like this little milksop.'

Maleneth could see from Korgan's expression that he was as confused as she was. 'It was a storm,' he said, but there was doubt in his voice as he looked around at the nearby Fyreslayers. 'Did you see any aelves?'

The other Fyreslayers shook their heads but looked troubled and quickly found other things to do.

Gotrek's face turned purple. 'You're all bloody cracked. There were aelves. Riding on eels and sharks. Hundreds of the sodding things. And they were attacking you. Less than ten minutes ago. Why do you keep talking about storms?'

The runemaster shook his head and looked steely again. He waved his staff at the damaged walls, causing the brazier at its head to flare. 'This is Grimnir's judgement, stranger. And now that you have entered Karag-Varr, you may find that you are as damned as we are.'

Gotrek sneered. 'Perhaps I was damned, once, but I've given it up. It's just another bloody excuse for not getting things done. What do you mean Grimnir's judgement? You're his people, aren't you? You do his bidding, whether he knows it or not. Why would he damn you?'

Near to the magmadroth there was a group of Fyreslayers dressed in similar finery to Korgan, with tall, plumed dragon helms and braziers on staves. Korgan glanced at them, as though unsure how much to say. They looked grim and said nothing. 'No one can explain the reasoning of the gods,' he said, looking defiantly at Gotrek. 'Nor should we seek to try. All we know is that Grimnir has found us wanting and turned his wrath against us. The storm you saw was just a glimpse of what he is capable of.'

Gotrek shook his head. 'Don't you people believe Grimnir died at the dawn of these realms? Didn't I hear that in one of those tuneless dirges you call songs?'

The runemaster was about to answer, but Gotrek held up his hand to stop him. 'It doesn't matter. Just tell me why you're sitting up here darkening your eyes and sulking while the elgi are free to come and go as they please, murdering every innocent soul from here to the Spiral Crux. How did servants of the Slayer God become cowards?'

'Cowards?' Korgan gripped his staff in both hands and embers billowed from its head, flashing in his staring eyes. 'You would insult the Varrukh in their own keep?'

'If I hadn't taken charge there wouldn't be any bloody Varrukh left to insult. You'd all be eel food.'

The doubt returned to Korgan's face. 'Eels,' he muttered, frowning and looking out over the piles of bodies.

Throne of Khaine, this could go on for ever. Can't you talk some sense into them?

'Is this why you've been hiding up here?' asked Maleneth, dragging Korgan's attention back from the dead. 'These storms?'

Gotrek gave a grudging nod. 'Exactly. Grimnir was liar and a cheat, in my experience, but he never shied away from a fight.'

'In your experience?' Korgan shook his head. 'What do you mean, "in your experience"?'

'Ancient history, lad. Answer the aelf's question. You're hiding up here grizzling because you think Grimnir wants you to be cowards. Tell me why you think that and I'll tell you why you're being idiots. Then we can all get back to doing something useful with our time.'

Korgan looked from the aftermath of the battle to Gotrek. 'You did something. You helped me.'

'Aye, I told you to pull your head from your arse and get your fyrds out here. And then, what a surprise, the aelves didn't find it so easy to kill you.'

Korgan shook his head. 'You turned back the storm.' He pointed his staff at the slab of metal in Gotrek's chest. 'It was something to do with your rune. It gave you the power to hold back Grimnir's storm. And it was the same when I was going to attack you on the bridge.' He tapped the magmadroth's flank and the creature dropped to its knees, causing the ground to judder and allowing Korgan to dismount and approach Gotrek, still staring at the rune. 'I think you were sent to us for some reason.' He was now speaking confidently again. 'I'll discuss it with the lodge elders. Perhaps this is significant.'

Korgan gave orders to some of the other Fyreslayers, telling them to fetch more hands to deal with the wounded. Then, when he was satisfied, he strode off down the portico, gesturing for Gotrek and Maleneth to follow him.

'Can you hear me talking?' said Gotrek, glancing at Maleneth. 'I feel like I'm talking to myself. Can *anybody* hear me?'

'I can always hear you,' replied Maleneth sadly.

Gotrek nodded. 'Then why's that strutting oaf still blathering on about storms from Grimnir?' He looked closely at Maleneth as they walked down an avenue of metal columns, each cast to resemble a duardin with a flaming beard, holding up the portico's roof. 'You do really remember that fight, don't you? You do remember all those sea aelves?'

Maleneth saw the fragmented memories again but they were already growing weaker. She saw little more than pale, aelven faces and the sinuous curl of a sea creature, shimmering through dark waters. 'I see something,' she said, 'but it is so vague I can hardly remember it.' She looked at the Slayer's craggy face. For all Gotrek's faults, he was not a liar. There was something very odd going on. 'Tell me what you saw.'

'Elgi, in their hundreds, wearing armour made from shells. And they were swimming through the air like it was water, riding on sharks and turtles. There was a battle in the square. A pretty decent scrap, too, once I forced the Fyreslayers to get off their arses. It was odd though. Fish floating in mist. Squid drifting overhead.' He glared angrily at Maleneth, as though expecting her to mock him.

'There are aelves who are linked to the sea,' she said. 'They're called Idoneth. They're mentioned by cultures in many realms, but usually only as folk tales and legends. When I was back in Azyr, I learned a little about them, but not much more than the name. They dwell in underwater cities and they're secretive – beyond that, I know nothing. They're cursed or exiled, or criminals of some kind. Whatever the reason, they keep to themselves.'

Gotrek shook his head. 'Is everyone drunk? You've already told me this.'

She frowned. 'Why would everyone forget what happened apart from you? I wonder if it's something to do with the rune.'

Gotrek looked at the metal in his chest. 'Fyreslayers are stuffed with these things. It doesn't seem to have made any difference to them.'

'Then perhaps it's because you weren't born in the realms? If it was the Idoneth, perhaps they use a kind of sorcery that you're immune to.'

Gotrek was about to answer when they reached the end of the colonnade and approached a pair of vast doors that led into the volcano. The doors were cast in burnished metal and designed to resemble the roaring mouth of a salamander. The scale was as grand as everything else in the magmahold and they both paused to study the metalwork. 'Shame,' muttered Gotrek, as the doors swung inwards with a reverberating clang. He walked over to the door frame and patted the rune-inscribed metal. 'There's skill here. And ambition. But no discipline. They haven't taken any pride in it. It's all so hurried.' He traced his finger over the metalwork. 'Look at this. It's not a bad idea. The concept is sound. But it's half finished. It's like everything here was built in a rush. If they'd spent a few more decades on these doors they could have been worth something.'

'Decades? To build a door?'

'If a job's worth doing, it's worth doing properly. The smiths who made this place clearly knew what a well-made door *should* look like, they just couldn't be bothered to put the hours in.'

'They're Fyreslayers,' said Maleneth, as they were led through the gates into a mountain hall. 'They don't like anything that gets in the way of fighting or making money. I'm amazed they bothered with doors at all. They clearly don't worry about clothes.'

Some of the surrounding Fyreslayers caught her words and muttered into their beards. 'They're so like you,' she laughed. 'Egos like eggshells. A few hard words and I could have them frothing at the mouth.'

The group came to a halt just inside the hall as more Fyreslayer priests rushed over to Korgan and began talking urgently, looking repeatedly at Gotrek and Maleneth, clearly troubled by the presence of strangers inside the mountain. Dozens of other duardin were rushing in the opposite direction, towards the doors, carrying bandages and water, calling out for help as more Fyreslayers spilled into the hall from doorways and staircases. It was a chaotic scene, but Maleneth and Gotrek stepped aside into a relatively empty space to look around at the hall. It had been carved from a natural cave, with jagged, rough-hewn walls, but it was circled by the same giant statues they had seen in the square outside, and each one held a brazier, flooding the hall with smoke and embers. The heat was even greater inside the keep and Maleneth began to feel light-headed as the temperature soared.

After a few minutes of waiting impatiently, Gotrek muttered a curse and marched across the vast chamber, barging through the crowds of shouting

Fyreslayers and heading for Korgan and the other priests. 'Who's actually in charge of this mess?' he said, glaring at their surprised faces.

Korgan's nostrils flared and he raised his chin. 'It is rare for one of the Dispossessed, such as yourself, to be admitted into Karag-Varr. You may not wander at will.' He nodded to some of the Fyreslayers with magmapikes. 'The Hearthguard will escort you to the barracks, where you may rest. You are welcome to stay for as long as you need. Let it not be said that the Varrukh do not show charity to their kin.' He glanced at the rune. 'I will seek you out once I have spoken with the lodge elders.'

'You're going to have a council meeting?' Gotrek laughed in disbelief. 'Elgi have just trounced half your army and put holes in your walls. The only council you need is a council of war. Why are you heading back into your halls when you're under attack?'

Skromm was at Korgan's side and he looked like he was about to swing at Gotrek, but the runemaster stopped him with a warning look. 'The storm will not come again for weeks,' said Korgan. 'This has happened many times before.'

Gotrek pointed his axe at Korgan. 'You know that was more than a squall. Those were aelves.' He looked at Maleneth. 'What did you call them? Idoneth?'

Maleneth nodded.

Korgan frowned. 'Idoneth? The *Vongall-varr*?' He looked at Skromm.

Skromm was still flushed and twitching with anger. He seemed to be in a state of perpetual mania. 'That might explain what happened to the runesons,' he snarled. 'If the Vongall-varr were in the storms, perhaps they poisoned them.'

Korgan shook his head. 'Now is not the time to discuss this, Skromm.'

'Is Vongall-varr your name for the Idoneth?' asked Maleneth.

Korgan looked suspiciously at her, then turned to Gotrek. 'I have to talk to the other lodge elders.' He softened his tone. 'My memory is clouded, but I sense that you did me a great service out there, Gotrek son of Gurni. And I will not forget it.'

Not again, thought Maleneth, as she sensed Korgan was on the verge of joining the long line of Gotrek's devotees. She resisted the urge to roll her eyes.

Korgan placed a hand on Gotrek's shoulder. 'Though I do not understand exactly how, I feel I am in your debt. And your talk of the Vongall-varr may help us understand the curse that has overtaken us.'

'*My* talk of the Vongall-varr,' said Maleneth, but Korgan kept his eyes on Gotrek.

'Go with Skromm,' said Korgan. 'Let him show you the hospitality of the Varrukh. I will find you this evening and we can talk more.' He glanced at the rune in Gotrek's chest. 'It feels significant to me that you have arrived here now, when we are at out lowest ebb. I am interested to hear your tale.'

To Maleneth's surprise, Gotrek nodded in an almost amiable manner. 'Hospitality sounds like a good idea.' He looked at Skromm. 'I presume, in a hold of this size, you have things like breweries and ale stores?'

Skromm glared at Gotrek, his lips curling back.

CHAPTER SIXTEEN

Skromm stomped off, leading them across the hall towards another pair of vast doors. The doors led out onto a walkway, lined with more statues, that reached across a sea of angry, hissing steam. As Maleneth stepped onto the metal structure she grimaced, feeling intense heat radiating up through the soles of her boots. 'Don't you people ever feel the heat?' she said to Skromm. He shrugged and she noticed how red his skin was. It looked like he had been roasted alive. There were golden runes hammered into each of his biceps, like smaller cousins of the one in Gotrek's chest, and they were so rounded and glossy they resembled globules of lava, boiling up through his angry flesh. 'Aye, I feel it,' he rumbled. 'Feels good. Reminds me I'm not an aelf.'

Gotrek laughed approvingly.

The walkway looped in a lazy arc through the fumes and led deep into the sweltering depths of the hold, heading down a series of broad, sweeping stairs that had been cut from the inside of the volcano. There were brands in some chambers but much of the illumination came from streams of magma that ran down channels cut into the walls. By rights, the lava should have destroyed the rooms it passed through, but the Fyreslayers had used their obscure smithing skills to contain the volcano's lifeblood. The deeper they climbed, the more Maleneth realised the scale of the place. In its own way, the keep was as impressive as the Kharadron sky-port she had left a few weeks earlier. She saw foundries and forges, where huge teams of Fyreslayers laboured over vast furnaces. There were also armouries crowded with gleaming weapons and countless shrines to Grimnir, some no more than niches in the wall, cradling a flame, and others as large as palaces, built around huge statues of the duardin war god. Most of the chambers were in the process of being emptied, however, as people rushed past them, heading to the upper levels, their expressions grim as they learned of the attack.

Finally, to Gotrek's obvious delight, they passed through busy, steam-filled kitchens and pantries crowded with hanging cuts of meat, baking ovens and blocks of cheese. Maleneth had always found duardin food so stodgy and bland as to be almost inedible, but the smell of fresh bread and cured meat reminded her that she had not eaten for a day.

Skromm ushered them into a rectangular feasting hall. A single, rune-scored table ran down the length of the hall and it was heaving with food

618 · DARIUS HINKS

that had been abandoned by the people rushing up to the square. 'Where does all this come from?' asked Maleneth. 'You have no farms? No fields even?'

Skromm patted his prodigious gut and nodded. The mania faded from his eyes and he looked calm for a moment. 'We barter for whatever we want. We deal with traders from across the realm.'

Gotrek sat down heavily at the table and began eating, reaching across the plates for a jug of ale. As Maleneth sat next to him, she noticed that none of the food was fresh. Apart from the bread, everything was dried, salted or preserved in some way. 'And when did you last do any trading?' she asked.

Skromm's face turned an even angrier shade of red as he joined Gotrek at the table and grabbed a salver of cold meat. 'We haven't left the hold for weeks. It's forbidden.' He crammed a piece of thick, buttered bread into his mouth and continued talking, spraying Gotrek and Maleneth with crumbs.

'Why?' said Maleneth.

Skromm scowled and continued shovelling food into his mouth, refusing to say more on the subject. Gotrek gave Maleneth a look that she could not read as he slid the jug of ale towards Skromm. 'Is this the best brew you've got?'

Skromm took the jug, filled a cup and started drinking. The cup was very large and it took him a while to empty it, but he persevered; then, once he was done, he slammed the empty cup back down on the table. 'No.' He poured himself another cup and, again, drank it without pausing for breath. 'This is Odger's Finest.' He wiped the froth from his beard and nodded. 'Worst beer in Ayadah. Worse even than Odger's other beers.'

He poured himself a third cup and was about to drink it when Gotrek said, 'Where I come from we brewed ale that *didn't* taste like goat's piss. Bugman's Special Brew. Durgrund's Helfire. *Real* beer. None of you Fyreslayers are capable of making anything with flavour.'

Skromm's face turned purple and for a moment he was unable to speak. He rocked back on the bench and made a peculiar whining sound, like an injured dog. Maleneth realised he was trying to stay calm. When he had finished howling, he leant closer to Gotrek and jabbed him with his finger. 'A rootless wanderer like you could never comprehend the ways of the Varrukh.'

Gotrek raised an eyebrow. 'I'm starting to get an idea.'

For a moment, Maleneth thought Gotrek was picking a fight because he was bored, something she had seen him do on many occasions, but then she noticed how cool his manner was. He was up to something. For all his oafish manners, the Slayer was capable of surprising subtlety.

'I'll show you what a *real* drink tastes like,' said Skromm, rising and marching off down the hall, looking at the various jugs that had been placed on the table. 'Here!' he said, grabbing one and bringing it back over, slamming it down in front of Gotrek, spilling froth over the side. Before Gotrek could touch it, Skromm poured himself a cup and drank, closing his eyes and sighing with pleasure. 'Try that!' he said, glaring at Gotrek with beer glistening in his beard. He filled Gotrek's cup and his own, and nodded for Gotrek to drink.

'Better,' said Gotrek when he was done, and as Maleneth ate, the two duardin drank several cups in quick succession. 'I was after something darker though, really,' said Gotrek, when they had finished the jug. 'Something more substantial.'

The furious look was gradually fading from Skromm's eye and he rocked back on the bench again, looking pensive and tugging at his wild hedge of a beard. 'Darker, yes... Maybe Olfsson's Reserve.' He shifted his impressive girth out from the table and wandered off down the hall again. Not finding what he wanted to hand, he disappeared through a doorway, muttering to himself and calling out to see if there were any servants left in the hall.

'What are you up to?' whispered Maleneth, prodding her food and grimacing.

Gotrek shrugged. 'There's only one way to learn anything about a dwarf.' He tapped the empty jug. He shrugged. 'I don't blame Korgan for wanting to keep secrets. We're strangers here. Why should he share private matters with us? He's not some witless beardling. But I have a feeling this big lad can be won over. I think he has the kind of tongue that is easily loosened.'

Skromm sounded almost cheerful as he came back into the hall carrying a tray laden with four large jugs of beer. 'It's an acquired taste,' he said, as he poured them both a thick, dark ale. His mood had lightened so much that he even offered the jug to Maleneth. She raised an eyebrow and he shrugged and lowered it again. 'Takes a few pints to really get the flavour,' he said, clanking his cup against Gotrek's.

Maleneth continued inspecting her food, happy that she understood Gotrek's plan. She had seen him employ it before. Even compared to other duardin he had an iron constitution, so when he wanted to unearth secrets, he simply drank people into a stupor. Skromm's bulky physique meant that Gotrek's ploy took a little longer than usual, however. They had been chugging ale for almost two hours before the Fyreslayer began to slur his words and drop his guard.

'If it wasn't for the bloody curse, I could have offered you some Fellmann's Neck Oil. Now there's a beer.' He looked fierce again, making his strange howling sound. 'But if we can't bloody leave Karag-Varr, we can't get any more orders to Fellmann.'

'Curse?' said Maleneth. She was lying further down the bench, trying to block out the tedious duardin talk, but that word caused her to sit up. They were the only people left in the hall and her voice echoed through the gloom.

Skromm ignored her comment but Gotrek had also noticed the word. 'You're not bloody cursed.' He clapped Skromm on the back. 'This ale has made me see you people in a better light. You're dawi. That means you're blessed. Why would you think of yourselves as cursed?'

Skromm slammed his forehead against the table, hitting the wood with such force that the plates rattled. For a moment he stayed like that, face crushed against the table, and Maleneth wondered if he had knocked himself unconscious. Then he sat up again, wiping beer from his face with a loud sniff. 'I don't think we're cursed either. But Uzkal thinks we are. And that's all that matters. Especially now he's got all the other lodge elders agreeing with him.'

Gotrek topped up Skromm's cup. 'Uzkal?'

'The auric flamekeeper!' boomed Skromm, giving Gotrek an incredulous look, as though it were absurd that Gotrek would not know who he meant. 'Uzkal said we're cursed until he can get his hands on the runesons' bodies.'

Maleneth sat up and moved closer down the bench, intrigued. 'Runesons? They're the heirs to your throne, is that right? They will rule when your runefather dies?'

'Obviously, yes,' said Skromm. 'Why do you keep stating the bleedin' obvious?' His tone turned bleak. 'Or at least, they would have been the runefather's heirs if they hadn't got themselves killed.'

Maleneth knew little of Fyreslayer religion or politics, but she knew that having no heirs would be a disaster for any ruler.

Skromm seemed too angry even to drink, glaring at his reflection in his beer, his head shaking. 'Thurgyn-Grimnir's sons are all dead. All killed in the storms. And now Uzkal has convinced everyone we're cursed.'

Gotrek gently steered Skromm's cup towards his mouth so that the Fyreslayer continued drinking. 'Why would anyone believe such an absurd notion? Kings have been losing their sons in battle since before even I was born.'

Skromm's voice was a confused mumble and his head rolled loosely on his shoulders. 'It's not because they're dead. That's not the problem. To die defending the magmahold is nothing to be ashamed of. Even Uzkal wouldn't claim that.'

'Then why do you think you're cursed?' growled Gotrek, losing his patience.

'Easier...' mumbled Skromm, trying to push his belly back from the table, 'to... show you.' He managed to get off the bench but would have fallen if Gotrek had not gripped his arm and kept him on his feet. 'This way!' barked Skromm, stumbling off with Gotrek helping him and Maleneth following. He gave them an exaggerated warning look. 'Throne room. Don't tell Korgan. He's very touchy... on the subject... of the thing.'

CHAPTER SEVENTEEN

The feast hall was empty, but as Skromm led them out into a corridor, they had to pause to let a group of pike-wielding Fyreslayers rush past. The warriors all nodded respectfully to Skromm as they went by, and Maleneth realised that, incredible as it might seem, he must be a person of some significance in the Varrukh lodge. Skromm waited until the soldiers were almost out of sight, pretended to enter a chamber on the opposite side of the corridor, then lurched off in the other direction to the soldiers, still gripping a cup of ale. He led them through a series of hallways and crossed a bridge that stretched over another smouldering chasm, then left the main routes and took them down a humbler-looking passageway. They entered it through a small, unimposing door, and the walls were far plainer than the rest of the keep. There were no runes cut into the stone and the floor was unpaved, covered in loose scree.

'This is the way to the throne room?' rumbled Gotrek, sipping at his beer and looking at the roughly carved walls.

'Servants' access,' replied Skromm with a conspiratorial look. 'All the ceremonial ways are guarded. Korgan and Uzkal don't want anyone to see...' His words trailed off and his face sagged. 'Not far,' he said, leading them down an even narrower passageway. There was no lava running through the walls and the only illumination came from braziers that hung to either side. The light was fitful and weak, but every now and then they would pass an opening in the wall and be bathed in a fiery glow from a furnace or a lava flow.

Maleneth found the atmosphere oppressive and wished she were back in the upper levels of the keep, but she could see that it was having the opposite effect on Gotrek. The deeper they went, the happier he seemed. The weight dropped from his shoulders and his habitual scowl started to soften.

'You love it down here, don't you?' she said. 'Deep under the earth in this sweaty furnace.'

He took a deep breath of the dank, sulphuric air and sighed. 'Reminds me of home.'

'Then why don't you spend more time in places like this?'

His eye glazed over and he sounded grim again. 'Reminds me of home.'

'Hold your tongues,' whispered Skromm, swaying slightly as he held up a warning finger. 'Not far now.' He led them round a few more bends and down a flight of narrow, chiselled steps. Then he extinguished the light of a brazier and plunged them into darkness.

Even Maleneth's aelven senses struggled to cope with absolute darkness, and she had to trail her hands against the walls as she followed the heavy tread of duardin boots. The rock scorched her palms but it was not long before ruddy light filtered down the corridor towards them, reaching another bend up ahead.

Skromm gestured that they should creep carefully as he led them round the bend and into the light. They had reached a metal grille, embedded in the wall, about six feet square. As Maleneth crept up to the bars, she saw that the grille looked down on another statue-lined hall. It was a circular room, centred on a large, round dais that supported a group of six thrones. All of the thrones were cast in gold and designed to resemble the gaping maws of dragons. The statues had their arms raised and their palms pressed to the domed ceiling, as though holding it aloft. There were lines of magma running through their angular muscles and the light bounced off the thrones, filling the hall with movement and shadows. The shifting illumination seemed to move in time to a sound that filled the hall – a quick, urgent mumbling, like prayers, that echoed through the shadows, giving the place an eerie, dreamlike atmosphere.

There were a few guards dotted around the circumference of the hall – Maleneth counted ten – all wearing dragon helms and gripping magmapikes, but it was the shapes on the dais that caught her eye. There were five shrouded figures lying on the flagstones in front of the thrones and a sixth slumped in the largest of the thrones. 'Corpses?' she whispered. They were so high up that she doubted the guards would hear her, but the Fyreslayers' halls had a habit of throwing one's voice in unexpected ways. 'Are they dead? Are they the dead sons?'

Skromm nodded and, incredibly, Maleneth saw tears glimmering in his eyes. She shook her head in disbelief. The duardin boasted, endlessly, about their capacity to drink cartloads of ale, but Skromm was so drunk he looked like he might start sobbing. 'The five on the floor are the runesons,' he said. 'The one on the throne is Thurgyn-Grimnir, Runefather of Karag-Varr.'

'Your king's dead?' Maleneth shook her head. 'That's not what Korgan said.'

'He's not dead,' muttered Gotrek. 'I see his beard moving.'

Maleneth peered closer at the figure on the throne. He was horribly emaciated and his dragon helm was slumped to one side as his head lolled onto his beard, but the strangest thing about him was his skin. There was barely an inch of him that was free of metal. Dozens of golden runes had been hammered into his muscles, far more than Maleneth had seen in even the most zealous Fyreslayer berserker. He almost looked like one of the metal statues that lined the hall. There were runes sunk into his chest, limbs and even his throat. It was as though he had been hammered to death by a runesmith. Gotrek was right though; as she studied him, she saw his chest rise and fall, almost imperceptibly.

'How is he still alive?' she whispered. 'He looks like a skeleton. A skeleton that's been smashed by golden trinkets.'

'Trinkets?' hissed Skromm, glaring at her and grabbing her by the arm. 'Do you know what ur-gold is, aelf?'

'Not really,' she said, nodding to the knife she was holding at his throat.

Skromm's eyes widened and he was about to shout, but then he seemed to change his mind and he loosed her arm, turning away and muttering into his beard. 'The runefather still lives,' he said eventually. 'But the rune madness has left him unable to move or even speak.'

'Rune madness?' asked Gotrek.

'Aye. Too many runes will do that to you. But no one could make him see sense. It started when his first son fell. Thurgyn came to Korgan and demanded that we fill his body with the most powerful runes. He was too furious to heed any warnings so we did as he asked.' He was speaking quickly now, utterly drunk. 'Then he lost another son, and then another, each taken by the storms. The runefather demanded more power, more runes and he would not listen to reason.' Skromm stared at the broken figure in the throne. 'No one can endure such power and keep their mind intact. But with each lost son, a little more of the runefather's mind slipped away.' Skromm turned to face them, his jowly face lit up by the glow of the statues. There was such horror in his eyes that Maleneth looked over her shoulder, half expecting to see a daemon rushing towards them. 'Then we all started to hear him. In the wreckage of the storms, as we tended to the wounded and tried to fix the walls, we heard his voice.'

'Whose voice?' asked Gotrek.

'The Slayer. Grimnir. He said that the runefather had damned us all.'

'Because he grieved for his sons?' Gotrek looked at the bodies on the dais. 'Even Grimnir wouldn't begrudge him that.'

'No, you don't understand.' Skromm nodded at the shrouded corpses. 'He didn't grieve in the proper way.' The pain of the memory seemed to be sobering the Fyreslayer up. His words still tumbled into each other but he was no longer swaying as he talked. 'When the storms come, people die, every time, but it's more than that. We're always left with warriors who are neither living nor dead, but somewhere in between. And that's what happened with the runesons. Every time the storm died, another runeson was left in a waking sleep. Their eyes were open and they were breathing, but they could not move or talk.' He tugged at his beard. 'It was terrible to see. The king tried to keep his sons alive. He tried everything he could to wake them – demanded that Korgan use every form of rune charm he could think of, but nothing would work. Thurgyn tried to pour water down his sons' throats but they would not swallow. The water just ran out of their mouths. There were many afflicted with the same terrible fate, but to see the runesons stricken like that was dreadful. When his sons finally died, the runefather refused to accept the truth. He said his sons were still under some kind of spell. Even when they began to...' He grimaced. 'Even when the bodies began to decay, he would not listen to reason. The Zhargrimm tried chanting the old sagas and telling the old legends but it all fell on deaf ears. Thurgyn banished everyone from the throne room and threatened to kill anyone who entered without his permission.'

Maleneth edged closer, trying to get a better view of the runefather. 'So he just sits there? Every day? Doing nothing?'

'He talks to his sons,' said Skromm, his voice bleak.

Maleneth realised that the murmuring sound was coming from beneath the runefather's matted beard. She shook her head and looked at Gotrek. 'There's nothing you can do for someone that spends his time talking to corpses. I've seen you do many things I didn't expect but you are not the person to comfort a grieving parent.'

Gotrek frowned. 'I still don't see why you should consider yourselves cursed. A father grieves for his dead sons. There's no great shame in that.'

'It's not grief that's the problem,' said Skromm. 'It's the breaking of tradition. The runefather never allowed his sons to be cremated. Their bodies were never taken to the pyre. Their eternal spark has not travelled to the halls of our ancestors.' His voice was stiff with emotion. 'They will never be judged. Never reborn. They will not join us at the final battle.' He lowered his voice to whisper, staring at the shrouds. 'From fire we are born, to fire we return.' He looked at Gotrek. 'Do you understand? The runefather robbed them of their place at the Doomgron. It would be a tragedy for any warrior, but for it to happen to our runesons is beyond anything.'

'But you don't believe you're cursed,' said Gotrek. 'You said in the feast hall.'

'No, I don't. I can see that this is a tragedy. Our runefather's mad. And he's robbed his sons of their future. But when Uzkal says we have to hide ourselves away in shame, I cannot believe that's right. I can't believe Grimnir would want that of us.'

Gotrek shook his head. 'Grimnir was a liar, but he wouldn't want you to cower up here like this. This is nothing to do with him. The voice you heard after the storms, telling you that you're cursed, that wasn't Grimnir. Even I know enough of your crooked religion to see that doesn't make sense. It's the bloody aelves.' He scowled at Maleneth. 'If there's treachery and deceit involved, it's always the bloody elgi. They've got you cringing like whipped hounds and you don't even remember them. Sorcery and lies, just like always.' Gotrek pointed at the runefather. 'And I'll tell you the biggest lie of all – that he's beyond saving. That's grief. Nothing more, nothing less. His heart is broken. I've seen it a dozen times and there's only one way to fix him. Did you really think a load of talking and singing was going to do anything? You people have forgotten who you are. You're warriors.'

Skromm nodded eagerly. 'Aye, that makes sense to me.' Then he slumped back against the wall and looked despondent again. 'But there's nothing to be done. Uzkal said we're cursed and no one listens if I try to argue.'

'They'd listen to their king,' rumbled Gotrek.

'But look at him. Thurgyn is a ruin.'

'And what does this Uzkal suggest you do to escape your curse?' asked Gotrek.

'He says we must contain our shame up here at the top of Dreng-Gungron until the curse is lifted, or we might spread it to others. Korgan and the other elders all agree with him. So all of our outposts have been lost. We had three other keeps: Karag-Agril, Karag-Duril and Karag-Wyr, but they have all been overrun by greenskins since we stopped marching to their aid. It's a bitter blow. They were smaller than Karag-Varr but they were still proud citadels. Still worthy shrines to Grimnir.'

Gotrek looked furious. 'So, until recently those keeps were still in your hands?'

'It's a matter of weeks since we lost them. And before that they had been ours for centuries.'

Gotrek's lip curled. 'You need a king to lead you, not a faith-drunk priest.' He looked down at Thurgyn. 'He needs to remember who he is.'

Skromm shook his head. 'Nothing will rouse him.' He moved to drink from his cup of ale but Gotrek put a hand on his arm to stop him.

'I told you,' said Gotrek. 'I've seen this before. I can remind your king who he is.'

'Really?' Skromm's eyes widened and he put his cup down. 'You think you can bring him back?'

'I don't think. I know.' Gotrek turned to Maleneth and nodded to the pouches at her belt. 'Do you have anything that can knock someone out rather than cook their insides?'

Maleneth shrugged. 'I do. But what good will that do you? Sending the runefather to sleep won't make him any less deranged.'

Gotrek nodded and leant back against the wall of the passageway. 'Don't kill the guards.'

Maleneth shook her head. 'What are you talking about? Why would I? They're not–'

With his back still pressed against the opposite wall, Gotrek slammed his boots forward into the metal grille, sending it spinning into the throne room. Dust filled the air and Maleneth backed away, covering her face and coughing. Then, as she picked rubble from her face, she heard the grille clang onto the floor below as the guards cried out in alarm.

'What in the name of Khaine did you do that for?' gasped Maleneth, but as the air cleared she saw that Gotrek was no longer hunkering in the passageway. She was alone with Skromm. 'Where is he?' she demanded.

Skromm stared at the ragged hole with a dazed expression.

Maleneth shoved past him and saw that as the Fyreslayer guards raced towards the dais, raising their magma weapons, Gotrek was clambering down one of the statues, his axe slung over his back.

'What are you doing?' she yelled, stepping carefully through the hole Gotrek had made and leaning out over the throne room, gripping the wall as she looked down at the dizzying drop.

'The guards!' roared Gotrek, as he climbed quickly down the statue. 'Deal with them!'

'He's insane,' whispered Skromm, looking at Maleneth in horror.

She nodded. Then she spat a curse and leapt out into the air, landing lightly on the statue's raised arm and hurrying down the polished metal.

'Do *not* approach the throne!' cried one of the Fyreslayer guards, raising his pike as he ran, targeting Gotrek.

Gotrek ignored him as he dropped to the floor and began stomping towards the dais at the room's centre. 'Deal with them, aelf!'

The guard triggered his weapon, hurling a dazzling arc of magma through the air.

Gotrek marched on oblivious.

'Protect the runefather!' cried the guard, and the other Fyreslayers opened fire, filling the hall with light and heat.

Maleneth paused halfway down the statue, took a handful of stones from a pouch at her belt and hurled them at the approaching guards. The stones flashed as they hit the flagstones. An acrid smell filled the throne room. The guards stumbled, crying out in surprise and lowering their pikes, reaching for their throats.

Maleneth continued climbing and by the time she reached the bottom, the guards were on their knees, their weapons dropped as they struggled to breathe, their faces turning purple. 'Don't make a fuss,' she sneered, striding past them. 'You won't die.' She heard them thudding to the floor behind her as she reached the dais. 'I don't think.'

She climbed the steps and picked her way through the shrouded bodies. 'How do you think you're going to help him?' she laughed, heading after the Slayer. 'Kind words and a hug?'

Gotrek had nearly reached the throne and he paused a few feet away to unsling his axe and grip it purposefully in both hands. 'There's only one way to help him,' he said, preparing to swing the axe at the runefather's head.

CHAPTER EIGHTEEN

'Wait!' howled Skromm, looking down from the hole, high up in the throne room wall.

Gotrek ignored him and swung his axe at the runefather, who was slumping in his throne.

Maleneth cursed, realising Gotrek was about to earn the enmity of the entire Fyreslayer lodge, but at the last moment, the runefather jerked into motion, raising a large key-shaped axe from the side of his throne. Thurgyn moved like a revenant, awkward and stiff, but he was fast enough to parry Gotrek's blow and the two axes clanged, scattering sparks around the dais. As the weapons collided, the runes in Thurgyn's skin blazed, dazzling Maleneth so that she had to back away, raising her arm in front of her eyes.

When her vision cleared, Maleneth saw that Gotrek had stumbled back from the throne and seemed dazed, rolling his head on his massive shoulders as he righted himself and glared at Thurgyn.

The runefather looked equally confused, staring around at the empty throne room. He was taller than any Fyreslayer Maleneth had ever seen, almost as tall as she was, but he was so gaunt he looked like a cadaver. He was clearly very old, with a beard like frost-covered lead, but being so emaciated made him look even older, with deep creases across his brow and around his eyes. And there were so many runes embedded in his flesh that he barely seemed able to straighten his limbs. 'Where is everyone?' he said, his voice emerging as a croak. He frowned as he looked at the guards Maleneth had drugged, his face growing rigid with anger. Then his eyes fell on the shrouded remains of his sons. His shoulders drooped and the head of his axe clattered on the flagstones. His eyes glazed over. 'Of course,' he muttered, staggering backwards, about to drop back into his throne.

'Stand and fight,' said Gotrek, speaking in a low growl as he rushed at the runefather, drawing back his fyresteel axe.

Anger flashed in Thurgyn's eyes and he steadied himself, bringing his massive axe round with surprising force. His runes lit up again, mirrored in his eyes as he pounded the axe into Gotrek's blade. There was another flash and, again, Gotrek was thrown back across the dais.

'Aye!' roared Gotrek, reeling and stumbling down a few of the circular steps. 'That's more like it, you dotard.'

'How dare you!' gasped Thurgyn, a little colour seeping into his hollow, grey cheeks. He lurched across the dais, gripping his latchkey axe in both hands and glaring at Gotrek.

'By all the hells of Shyish,' muttered Maleneth, backing away from the two duardin. 'What are you doing, Gotrek?'

Thurgyn hissed furiously and attacked, swinging his axe at Gotrek's chest.

Gotrek parried, scattering more sparks and causing Thurgyn to stumble backwards. Then he rushed across the dais and slammed his forehead into the runefather's nose. There was a crack of breaking bone and Thurgyn whirled away in a spray of crimson, dropping his axe and cursing. He would have fallen had he not managed to steady himself by gripping one of his sons' thrones.

Gotrek charged after him but Thurgyn turned with a howl, runes blazing as he wrenched the throne from the floor and smashed it into Gotrek.

The chair tore a piece of Gotrek's cheek away, spraying more blood as the Slayer fell backwards and tumbled down the steps.

Thurgyn grabbed his key-shaped axe and staggered after him, swinging at Gotrek again.

Do you think the entire duardin race is insane? asked Maleneth's mistress as Maleneth watched the fight from the top of the dais. *Or are we particularly unlucky in meeting these idiots?*

'I've never met any others that were quite this moronic,' replied Maleneth as she watched Gotrek and Thurgyn reel around the throne room, swinging and parrying and demolishing pieces of furniture. Within a few minutes, they were both drenched in blood and howling incoherently. Gotrek was utterly frenzied, and Maleneth could see he had slipped into the berserk state that meant it would be pointless trying to reason with him. But, if anything, Thurgyn was even more deranged. He seemed to be more metal than muscle and, as he punched and pounded Gotrek, his whole body was ablaze.

Do you think he might actually harm him?

Maleneth was about to laugh at the suggestion, but then she realised Thurgyn *did* seem to have the upper hand. It was as if weeks of pent-up anger were boiling up from his chest, igniting the metal in his skin.

'How dare you?' bellowed Thurgyn, repeating the question several times as he attacked Gotrek. As they fought, they overturned tables and sent braziers rattling across the flagstones, but neither seemed able to land a killing blow.

'Perhaps I should lend a hand?' wondered Maleneth, toying with one of the poison knives at her belt.

You're as dim-witted as Gotrek. What do you think will happen if you kill their runefather? They'll fry you in a lava pit. You need to stop Gotrek, not help him.

Maleneth was about to reply when a deafening braying sound filled the hall. Gotrek and Thurgyn were too enraged to notice but Maleneth cursed and whirled around, looking for the source. 'Skromm!' she hissed, spotting the Fyreslayer at the foot of a statue. He had managed to climb down and was blowing furiously into a horn that was so big he had had to climb inside its bends to reach the mouthpiece.

She sprinted from the dais, whipping her knives out as she ran.

Skromm backed away from the horn, scowling as she approached, swinging his axes. The amiable demeanour he had shown in the feast hall had vanished, replaced by the unhinged snarling she had seen when they had first met him on the bridge.

'I did not bring you here to attack the runefather!' he cried, stamping towards her.

'Tedious,' said Maleneth, dropping into a fighting stance and considering which poison would be the most effective way to drop such a large duardin.

A second noise filled the hall: this time it was the sound of grinding metal. Maleneth and Skromm turned to see one of the ceiling-high statues judder and jolt sideways. Either Gotrek or Thurgyn had struck its leg with such force that it had buckled, knocking the structure out of true. As the statue moved, its splayed hands tore cracks in the distant ceiling, causing slabs of rock to fall. A storm of masonry and metal began raining down, forcing Maleneth and Skromm to bolt for cover, taking shelter in one of the alcoves that lined the throne room. Dust and noise filled the hall, and for several seconds Maleneth and Skromm could do nothing but crouch next to each other, their fight forgotten as they wondered if they were going to be buried alive.

'Perhaps there is a curse,' muttered Skromm, staring at the apocalyptic scene.

'It's called Gotrek,' replied Maleneth.

When the dust cleared and the echoes faded, Maleneth could see no sign of Gotrek or the runefather. There were mounds of rubble scattered everywhere and small fragments of stone were still pattering down across the throne room like a hailstorm, bouncing off the flagstones and statues.

'There,' said Maleneth, when she spotted a glimmer of gold not far from the dais. 'That's one of them.'

'Why did your friend do this?' said Skromm as they began picking their way across the hall. He still showed no sign of remembering that he wanted to kill Maleneth. She toyed with the idea of killing him while he was distracted, but then decided to keep her options open. Perhaps there was still a way she could talk her way out of this.

'I gave up trying to understand his motives a long time ago,' she replied. 'It only makes me angry.'

They reached the piece of gold and saw that it was one of the runefather's runes. He was half buried under a pile of rocks but his runes were still shimmering. Thurgyn was staring up into the darkness, muttering curses.

Gotrek was a few feet away, equally buried, and as Skromm helped the runefather sit up, Maleneth did the same for Gotrek. Once the two old duardin were upright, they dusted themselves down and looked around at the rubble. Both of them looked dreadful. The dust had stuck to the blood that covered them, making them look like they had been dunked in flour. Thurgyn's nose was broken at a revoltingly unnatural angle and half of Gotrek's cheek was hanging from his face, revealing a flash of white bone. They sat there for a moment, looking around. Then, when they caught sight of each other, their faces twisted into savage smiles.

'Wait a minute,' said Maleneth, backing away. 'Look at what you've already–'

Thurgyn moved fastest, bringing the haft of his axe up from the rocks into the underside of Gotrek's jaw. The blow lifted Gotrek from his feet, sending him pinwheeling back through the clouds of dust.

Maleneth ran to stop the runefather as he stumbled after Gotrek, but the air exploded from her lungs as Skromm planted a punch in her stomach, doubling her over and leaving her gasping for breath. She turned her fall into a pirouette and landed a high kick on the side of Skromm's head, sending him flying backwards.

Thurgyn stood and lurched towards Gotrek, swinging his axe again, but he was so dazed that he staggered, almost dropping the weapon.

Gotrek lunged from the rocks with a roar, slamming his forehead into the runefather's bloody nose. There was another crunch of breaking bone and the two duardin fell, landing in a cursing, jumbled heap. They both tried to land another blow, then slumped against each other, unable to catch their breath.

Skromm clambered to his feet and reached for his axe, only to find Maleneth holding a knife to his throat and shaking her head in disapproval.

Too exhausted to move, the runefather lay on his side in the wreckage, glaring at Gotrek as rubble continued to fall on him. Slowly, his breathing eased and the mania faded from his eyes. He continued staring at Gotrek but the rage had been replaced by a profound agony. For several seconds he did not move or speak and when he did, his voice was a desolate growl. 'My sons,' he said.

Gotrek wiped some of the blood from his brow and stared at Thurgyn, his chest heaving, his face flushed. He looked surprised by the runefather's words, but then he nodded, slowly. 'I know.'

Skromm backed away from Maleneth and looked at Thurgyn with amazement. 'Runefather,' he whispered. 'You can speak. Your mind is clear.'

'It was my fault.' Thurgyn kept looking at Gotrek. 'How do I live?'

Gotrek stared at the runefather, and Maleneth was surprised by the depth of feeling in his eye. Thurgyn's pain was mirrored in Gotrek's face. The Slayer climbed wearily to his feet, brushing off more dust and rubble. Then he limped over to Thurgyn and held out a hand.

Thurgyn looked through Gotrek's hand. 'How do I live?'

Gotrek's hand was trembling but he continued to hold it out. He raised his voice, as though addressing an audience only he could see. 'We live because we have to. And because we're more than our failures.'

Thurgyn looked up, frowning.

'We're not just the things we did wrong,' said Gotrek. 'We can't let them be our epitaph.' His voice was strident and he was no longer looking at the runefather. 'No one can live in the past. We can learn from the past. And remember it. But we have to move on. It's the only honourable way.' He waved at the circle of thrones. 'While you sit here, grieving, your warriors have forgotten how to live. They have forgotten how to fight. Without you to lead them they're lost. They've let these lands be overrun. Your outposts have been taken.'

Thurgyn winced. Then he looked past Gotrek to the shrouded shapes on the dais, shaking his head. 'I robbed my children of their future.'

'You robbed them of nothing. They died with honour. And their spark is in you, in every sinew of your body. Live with pride. Fight with honour. And I promise you, you will see them again.'

Thurgyn studied Gotrek closely, as though seeing him properly for the first time. 'I'd cuff the ears of anyone else who made promises like that, but there's something about you...' The runefather shook his head. 'Who *are* you?'

'Gotrek, son of Gurni. Born beneath the mountains of a world that died. A world where good people hid in the past while evil ones claimed the present.' He fixed his gaze back on Thurgyn. 'I won't make the same mistake again.'

CHAPTER NINETEEN

Thurgyn continued looking at Gotrek with an incredulous expression as blood poured from his broken nose, staining his steel-grey beard. He was about to speak when the doors to the throne room crashed open, banging against the walls as dozens of Fyreslayers rushed into the hall gripping magmapikes and axes and howling war cries. They were led by Korgan and another Zhargrimm priest. The second priest was clearly a figure of great importance. He wore a long, scaly cloak that trailed across the floor and his battle helm was fronted by a fierce golden mask that hid his face. He held a brazier axe in one hand, but most striking of all was what he held in his other hand: a metal rune engulfed in flames. Heat haze shimmered around the metal, but the priest held it with no sign of discomfort.

'Protect the runefather!' cried Korgan, his face thunderous as he raced across the rubble.

Gotrek turned to the approaching mob, but Maleneth noticed how unsteady he was. Despite his wasted appearance, the runefather had been a match for Gotrek's strength. The Slayer looked like he might fall at any moment. She looked around for an escape route. Seeing none, she spat a curse and dashed to protect Gotrek's weaker side, raising her knives and whispering a prayer to Khaine.

'Hold!' cried Thurgyn, struggling to his feet and raising a hand.

The Fyreslayers looked like they had seen a ghost, staggering to a halt, the colour draining from their faces.

'Runefather,' breathed Korgan, shaking his head. 'You're...' He was too shocked to finish the sentence.

'I've been talking to this foreigner,' said Thurgyn, 'and he tells me my lodge is a disgrace. That it has been neglecting its duties.' Thurgyn gestured for Skromm to pick his latchkey axe from the rubble, and once he had it in his grip again, he used it as a crutch, hobbling through the wreckage, heading back towards his throne. 'I have not been myself.' He gave Korgan a fierce look. 'But that's no excuse for backsliding. Muster the fyrds, Runemaster Korgan. I want to see what state they're in.' He dropped heavily into his throne and spat on the floor, leaving a tooth on the flagstones. 'And fetch me some bloody ale. My throat's as dry as an aelf's blade.'

Korgan stared in disbelief for a moment, then joy shone in his eyes. 'Fetch the runefather a drink, by Grimnir,' he snapped, glancing at one of the other Fyreslayers. 'And some food.' Then he waved at the rubble. 'And see to this mess.'

Fyreslayers leapt into action, dashing from the hall or rushing to the piles of fallen rocks.

Thurgyn nodded in satisfaction. 'And wipe those stupid black marks off your face. We're not dead yet.'

Korgan took a deep breath. His face remained as stern as ever, but Maleneth could feel the relief radiating from him. As the hall filled with movement and noise, the two priests climbed up onto the dais, followed by Gotrek and Maleneth, and stood before the runefather. Gotrek was limping, but when Maleneth offered him her arm he glared at her and struggled on up the steps, leaning heavily on his axe.

The masked priest with the flame stared at Maleneth. 'An aelf?' His voice was a rough-edged rasp, as though he had spent his life yelling. 'What is she doing in the throne room?' He turned to Gotrek. 'And who is this?'

Gotrek's beard bristled and he was about to give an angry reply when Korgan spoke up. 'He's a friend, Uzkal. When the storm came, he helped me turn it back. He has saved many Varrukh lives today.'

Uzkal shook his head. 'He arrived today. How can he claim to be a friend of the Varrukh? And I've just been up to the square. The walls are in tatters and there are scores of dead.'

'It would have been much worse if this stranger had not aided me,' said Korgan. 'The entire hold would have fallen. He's the reason we're still alive.'

Uzkal looked at Gotrek. 'Those storms come from Grimnir. It's his judgement. This is our curse.' He waved his flaming rune at the shrouded corpses, embers spilling from his fist. 'The runesons were never taken to the Ancestor Halls. They have never been granted the stone-sleep they deserve.' He was practically howling, leaning towards Korgan as though he were about to strike him. 'Their runes have never been reclaimed! They're still lying in that cold, lifeless flesh!'

'Uzkal!' The runefather spoke to the priest in an equally furious roar, slamming his axe on the flagstones. 'Hold your damned tongue! There are outsiders present!'

Do these people only have one volume? hissed Maleneth's mistress.

They're all deaf, thought Maleneth. *They've spent too much time hammering gold.*

'Why are you talking about curses?' continued Thurgyn, glaring at the masked priest. 'And why would Grimnir send a storm against us?'

Uzkal was uncowed. 'We have earned the wrath of the Slayer God! The lodge was robbed of the runesons' fire. They have lain here, mouldering, when they should have been returned to the Ancestor Halls and reclaimed by fire. We have broken faith with Grimnir. And these storms are his response.'

'How dare you speak to the runefather like that!' howled Korgan, his eyes flashing as he rounded on Uzkal.

Thurgyn lurched to his feet, angry red veins spidering across his ashen face. 'They weren't dead!'

To Maleneth's disbelief, it looked like the lodge elders were about to attack each other. 'Wait!' she cried.

The duardin turned and looked at her in shock. Even Gotrek seemed taken aback by the rage in her voice.

'The storms are nothing to do with your dead Slayer God. There's no mystery here.' She held out the fragment of armour she had taken from the beach. 'Your enemy isn't weather, it's sorcerers. They're called the Idoneth.'

She turned to Gotrek. 'Tell them! Tell them what you saw.'

Gotrek shrugged. 'Bloody great leviathans, swimming over your walls, along with packs of eel-riding knights who made mincemeat of your warriors.'

Korgan nodded eagerly as Gotrek spoke, and though Uzkal seemed about to disagree, something about the Slayer's words must have triggered a memory. Gotrek told of mist-shrouded monsters and pale, eyeless aelves, and as he did, the masked priest seemed to deflate, shaking his head and backing away from the throne, staring at the rune in his fist.

'I see them,' muttered Uzkal. 'As you describe them, I see them in my mind – aelves mounted on serpents, armour like shells. How can I have forgotten it? Why did I not remember them until you spoke?'

'It's the nature of their sorcery,' said Korgan, looking at Maleneth. 'Isn't that right? Your people mesmerised us.'

'They're not *my* people.' Maleneth shrugged. 'They're aelves, I suppose, but they do not worship Khaine, or the Shadow Queen of Ulgu, or Sigmar of Azyr. They live beneath the sea and pray to gods of their own. And when they attack, they harness storms and waves to mask their attacks. It's not a true storm that has been battering your fortress. It's an Idoneth conjuration. And part of its power is that it leaves no mark on your memory.'

'Can it be true?' whispered Uzkal. 'Can I have been so wrong?'

'Think about it,' said Thurgyn. 'You claim these storms were a curse, sent from Grimnir. You say it's because I...' He gave a pained look at his sons' bodies. 'Because I neglected the old traditions. But how can that be? The storms began *before* my sons fell. My sons fell to these storms.'

The fury had vanished from Uzkal's voice. He sounded crushed. 'Then I am the problem. I am the one who has damned us.'

'No one's bloody damned,' snapped Gotrek. 'Too much god-bothering, that's the problem, as usual.' He waved at the runefather. 'Your king's back. A little the worse for wear but that's nothing that won't be fixed by some food, ale and rest. You still have scores of warriors and most of your hold is still intact. And it's not a bad keep. Your work's slapdash by true dawi standards, but still better than most of the hovels I've seen in these realms. And you're well prepared. I passed through your storerooms and armouries on the way down here, and you have enough weapons and equipment to fight all the hosts of the Three-Eyed King himself.' He shook his head. 'You just need to stop thinking like aelves. Stop making things complicated where they should be simple. Cremate your fallen princes. Heal your king. Then march to bloody war.' The light from Uzkal's rune flashed in his eye and gave his face an even more hellish appearance. 'Take the fight to your foes. Reclaim your keeps. Heal yourself with war. Reforge yourself with combat. Cauterise your scars. You call yourself Slayers. It's time to slay.'

Korgan and Uzkal looked from Gotrek to their runefather, watching for

his response. Thurgyn was staring intensely at Gotrek, his face battered and
blood-smeared. He looked utterly psychotic. Even more so when a brutal
grin spread across his face.

'Time to slay,' he said, all trace of confusion gone from his voice.

CHAPTER TWENTY

Korgan closed his eyes, whispering a prayer to Grimnir as the heat of the Forge Fire washed over him. It stoked the rage in his chest, causing the runes in his muscles to pulse and filling him with zeal.

He was deep in the Zharrgrim temple, the burning heart of the magmahold, where every breath scorched the lungs and even his runesmiters grimaced as they took their places, forming a circle at the centre of the vast chamber. It was an octagonal tower, open to the heavens, like a huge, ornately worked chimney stack. Embers drifted up through the distant opening to mingle with the stars, rising from a burning pit at the centre of the hall. The pit was hundreds of feet in circumference and had been designed to resemble the open jaws of an enormous, fire-breathing salamander: Vulcatrix, the Ur-Salamander, the great fire wyrm that had fought with Grimnir, merging its spirit with him as they both died.

It was the aftermath of that apocalyptic battle that had scattered ur-gold across the realms, a metal imbued with power that only the sons of Grimnir could understand. To most, it looked like simple gold, so that across the realms the Fyreslayers were seen as greedy mercenaries, obsessed with hoarding gleaming metal. But, in truth, they hungered for something greater than wealth. Every god-fuelled fragment brought the lodges closer to Grimnir, closer to the day that he would be reborn and lead them in the final war for the realms, a battle so glorious it would make the others look like brawls over spilled ale.

Korgan looked back over his shoulder to see Gotrek entering the inferno, closely followed by the auric flamekeeper, Uzkal. The runefather had insisted that Gotrek be included in the funeral rites but Uzkal had been appalled by the idea. And, Korgan had to admit, it was strange to see a lodgeless wanderer at this most secret of rituals. Uzkal had not dared to defy Thurgyn but he was watching Gotrek closely as he joined the circle. Along with Gotrek and Uzkal, there were a hundred or so Fyreslayers present, mostly Zhargrimm priests, arrayed around the circumference of the firepit. The runefather was alone, standing on a platform made from Vulcatrix's tongue. The whorl of metal was so hot that it bathed Thurgyn in heat haze. The air around him was so liquid and mobile that he looked like he was standing behind a waterfall. But Korgan could still see how grief-stricken he was. The Dron-Gungron rite was usually a stirring, proud affair, but Thurgyn was shaking his head as he looked down into the fire-pit. A dozen feet below him, on an intricately worked metal bier, were the bodies of his fallen sons, their hands closed around axes and forge keys. Korgan's runesmiters had removed the ur-gold runes from their bodies but they had been replaced with common gold. It should have been a moment to celebrate the runesons' death in battle, to celebrate their future at Grimnir's side, but the runesons had not died in battle; they had wasted away, their minds stolen by the magic of the Idoneth. Thurgyn moved towards the edge of the platform, leaning on his latchkey axe like a crutch, muttering to himself.

Korgan was filled with grief. Not for the fallen runesons, but for their father. He could not bear to see Thurgyn so tormented.

'He looks bloody awful,' grunted Gotrek, reaching Korgan's side. 'Is this going to take long? He'll fall in if he has to stand up there too long.'

Korgan looked at Gotrek in shock. Other than the formal words of the funerary rites, speech was not allowed during Dron-Gungron.

Uzkal glared at Gotrek and approached the edge of the pit, holding out his ceremonial flame. He looked around at the gathering and called out into the clouds of smoke and embers, his voice ringing through the metal of his mask. 'We have marked our foes well. We have readied our weapons and steeled our hearts. We have tested our strength. And when we enter that final battle we will burn as bright as the First Fire. We will strike as one. Our strength will be Grimnir's strength. Our fury will be Grimnir's fury. Our vengeance will be Grimnir's vengeance. And then, on the day of final judgement, when Grimnir separates the gold from the clinker, the weak from the strong, our spirits will shine. The unworthy will be left in the ashes of his wrath but we, the true-hearted Varrukh, we will stand free, marching at Grimnir's side in his hour of triumph.'

Gotrek glanced at Korgan, his eyebrow raised, and Korgan felt a rush of anger. He, more than anyone present, believed Gotrek had been sent to aid them, but he would not stand by if Gotrek tried to ruin the sanctity of the ritual.

'From fire we are born!' cried Uzkal, holding his flame aloft.

All around the hall, hidden in shadows and smoke, runesmiters began drumming, pounding hammers against anvils and making a clanging, pulse-like beat.

'To fire we return!' cried Korgan, along with all the other Fyreslayers in the hall.

'From fire we are born!' repeated Uzkal, kneeling and taking a key from beneath the magmadroth scales of his robes. It was as large as his forearm and scored with runes.

'To fire we return!' yelled the other priests, drawing out identical keys and dropping to their knees.

The hammering grew more savage and erratic, scattering embers and pounding against Korgan's eardrums. The heat and the noise were intox-icating. Kill fever surged through him. He had to battle the urge to attack the warriors nearby. His muscles tensed and his pulse hammered as he did as all the other priests had done, dropping to his knees with his forge key in his hand.

Uzkal repeated his cry, and as Korgan roared in answer, he and the other priests slammed their keys into holes in the floor of the chamber, locking them into place with a chorus of oaths.

'He's off,' muttered Gotrek.

Korgan was so caught up in the ritual that he barely registered Gotrek's words, even though he was standing at his side. No one else noticed as Gotrek pointed at the runefather. 'Is he meant to be doing that?'

With an incredible effort, Korgan drew his gaze from the fire and saw what Gotrek meant. Thurgyn was stumbling back down the platform, away from the firepit, shaking his head. 'No,' gasped Korgan, horrified. 'If he doesn't turn his key the rite will fail. The runesons will never know peace. *We* will never know peace.'

Gotrek glared at Korgan, then looked at the grief-stricken runefather. 'Sod that. I'm not having you lot moping again.' He stomped off through the smoke, heading in the direction of Thurgyn.

'No!' gasped Korgan, but the rite was now almost complete. If he moved from his position he would disrupt the ceremony.

'From fire we are born!' howled Uzkal, his eyes closed as fervour consumed him. He was oblivious to the fact that Thurgyn and Gotrek had both left their allocated positions.

'To fire we return!' came the booming reply as Korgan and all the other priests turned their keys. It was only then that Uzkal realised something was wrong. With all the keys turned, the rite should have reached its climax, but nothing happened. Uzkal opened his eyes and looked around, confused, just in time to see Gotrek reach Thurgyn and put his hand out to stop the runefather leaving the temple.

All around the hall, Zhargrimm priests looked up from their keys and saw Gotrek grip Thurgyn's shoulder. Everyone, even Uzkal, was too shocked to speak, watching the exchange in mute horror. Korgan could not believe what he was seeing. Dron-Gungron had never been disturbed like this.

The Fyreslayers at the anvils were obviously too far gone to notice what was happening. They continued hammering out their wild, clanking rhythm, filling the hall with noise and making it impossible to hear what Gotrek and Thurgyn were saying to each other.

Thurgyn yelled something at Gotrek, pointing his axe at the corpses on the bier and shaking his head. Gotrek stood in silence as the runefather raged, his runes blinking and his head shaking with passion. Then, when Thurgyn finally paused, gasping for breath, Gotrek gripped his shoulder and spoke urgently into his ear.

'What's this?' demanded Uzkal, looking at Korgan. 'What is he telling him?'

Korgan shook his head. Whatever Gotrek was saying seemed to enrage Thurgyn even more. His eyes flashed and, as Gotrek spoke, he backed away, breaking free of the Slayer's grip and shaking his head. But Gotrek persevered, following the runefather and continuing to talk. Finally, something shifted in Thurgyn's demeanour. His furious expression softened. He looked appalled by whatever Gotrek was saying. Pity filled his eyes and his anger faded away. Gotrek nodded, saying one last thing and slapping the flat of his axe against his chest.

The drummers continued pounding their anvils but everyone else watched in astonished silence as Thurgyn and Gotrek embraced. They stayed like that for a while, embers whirling around them. Then Thurgyn nodded and looked at his dead sons, his expression resolute. With Gotrek at his side, the runefather climbed wearily back up onto the platform. He hesitated briefly, then slammed his key-shaped axe into a hole at his feet and looked over at Uzkal, nodding for him to continue.

Uzkal stared back in shock, then nodded and knelt, gripping his key and looking around at all the other priests, indicating that they should do the same. When everyone was back in position, gripping their keys, he cried out one last time. 'From fire we are born!'

'To fire we return!' cried everyone in the hall as the drumming became deranged. As one, all the priests turned their keys. This time, Thurgyn did the same, and at that moment a column of lava roared up from the pit. It blasted from Vulcatrix's mouth, burning through the dead runesons and obliterating their remains before spewing up through the opening in the roof and out into the night.

Korgan, like everyone else present, struggled to hold his position as the heat doubled in ferocity. Even his hardened Fyreslayer skin blistered and tears streamed from his eyes. The eruption only lasted a few seconds but it took every ounce of Korgan's will to keep hold of his key. Then the drumming ceased and the lava tumbled back out of sight. The after-image left Korgan temporarily blind as he removed the key and staggered to his feet, swaying like a drunk. The sudden silence felt as deafening as the drumming had been. He backed away, wiping sweat and ash from his face and praying to Grimnir. All around him, people were doing the same, blinking and trying to catch their breath.

Now that the ritual was over, and his battle lust was fading, Korgan remembered what had happened when Thurgyn tried to leave the hall. As his vision returned, he spotted Gotrek heading towards the exit, marching through the thick smoke. Korgan hurried over to him, catching up with him as he stepped out into an antechamber.

'What did you say?' Korgan's voice was ragged and he coughed up a cloud of embers.

Gotrek did not halt but he glanced back. 'Eh?'

'When you spoke to the runefather. What did you say? How did you convince him to carry on?'

Gotrek laughed bitterly. 'I told him what happens to people who live in the past.' His expression darkened. 'I told him how it feels to be me.'

CHAPTER TWENTY-ONE

It took Maleneth a while to understand what had happened to Gotrek. She stared at him as he rode at the head of the Varrukh fyrds. He was travelling next to Runefather Thurgyn and the other lodge elders, standing precariously on a gilded throne, high on the back of a smouldering magmadroth, and as Maleneth studied his face, an incredible truth hit her. *He's happy.* She had seen him in various states: driven, morose, obsessed, deranged, drunk and furious, but never like this.

The Fyreslayers were advancing through rusting, dusty foothills, the dawn at their backs, sunlight flashing on their dragon helms and smoke trailing from their magmadroths. It was a magnificent sight. Nearly two thousand Fyreslayers had spilled from Karag-Varr, filled with bloodlust and pride at the return of their king. Drummers pounded, horns brayed and the Zhargrimm priests roared tributes to Grimnir, causing the warriors' runes to flash. But it was the change in Gotrek that Maleneth found most incredible. She could barely recognise him. His face was still disfigured by scars but there was a new vitality shining from him. He seemed almost youthful. He had slicked his flame-coloured hair with a fresh coat of animal fat so that the crest stood tall and proud, he had polished his axe and his lion-shaped pauldron, and Maleneth had a suspicion he had even bathed. His muscles were so scratched, weather-beaten and sunburned that she could not be entirely sure, but he definitely smelled less like an outhouse.

Maleneth was on foot, marching next to Skromm. She had not been deemed worthy of a magmadroth steed, or even a place in the command group with the lodge elders. It was only thanks to Gotrek that she had been allowed to join the fyrds at all. And she had a suspicion he had only demanded she accompany them because he thought she would find the whole expedition a chore.

After the revelations in the throne room, Maleneth had been forced to endure several days of Skromm's company. Gotrek and the lodge elders had spent long hours in the innermost halls of the keep, performing secret funerary rites for the dead runesons. Uzkal was still appalled by Maleneth's presence in Karag-Varr and had refused to admit her to the ceremonies, so she had spent her time watching an endless succession of feasts, shouting contests and training fights as the Fyreslayers celebrated the end of their 'curse' and the return of their runefather.

'What's the name of this outpost again?' asked Maleneth, peering through the rust clouds and trying to make out the shape on the far side of the next valley.

'Karag-Wyr!' cried Skromm. The Fyreslayer had not drunk any ale since the night before but he seemed even more intoxicated than at the celebration feast. As they jogged across crumbling iron he twitched and lunged constantly, lashing out at imaginary foes and spitting war cries. He seemed barely aware of his surroundings, lost in an imaginary battle. He ducked and weaved like a pit fighter, barking curses and laughing as he mimed death blows. He had lost the ability to talk and could only shout, even though Maleneth was right next to him. 'We'll see it soon!'

'I see it now,' she replied, squinting as she studied the shape that rose from the distant hills. There was so much smoke drifting from it that even she struggled to make out the details, but the outpost appeared to be built in similar style to Karag-Varr. It was smaller and, rather than Grimnir, resembled the head of a salamander, bursting from a rocky hilltop, but much of it was constructed from golden, polished metal. The smoke trailing up from behind its walls was full of garish colours – pinks and purples that made it look like the building was draped in a gaudy sash.

'You can see it from this distance?' Skromm stopped lunging to stare at her.

'Of course. I don't have your feeble duardin eyesight. You people can't see anything unless it's half a mile underground.'

'Is it ruined?' he yelled, spitting at the ground. 'Have the greenskins torn it down?'

'No. As far as I can make out, it looks intact. There's some colourful smoke but no other sign of damage. It doesn't look like the work of greenskins to me.'

'Perhaps the scouts were mistaken then? Perhaps it's still in our hands?'

Maleneth grimaced as she saw the standards that had been mounted on the walls, crudely daubed onto wooden boards. 'Only if your sigil is a serpent turning into a flame.'

'Chaos!' spat Skromm, returning to his mimed battle, hacking at the dust and snarling. 'We kept those *thagi* worms from these hills for decades. It's typical of them to crawl back in on their bellies while the runefather is looking the other way. I have to tell Runemaster Korgan. This could change our plan of attack.'

Maleneth looked at the frenzied multitude surrounding her. 'You make plans?'

Skromm halted and glared at her. He shifted his weight from foot to foot, waving his axes and shaking with anger, on the verge of attacking her. Then he decided against it and sprinted off towards the magmadroths at the head of the army.

Maleneth reluctantly followed. 'You'll need me,' she said. 'I'm the only one here who can see further than my belly.'

'Runefather!' bellowed Skromm as they neared the command group. 'It's not greenskins who have the keep! It's a Chaos warband.'

Runefather Thurgyn and the others looked down at Maleneth and Skromm, breaking away from a conversation.

'Did *she* tell you that?' demanded Uzkal, staring at Maleneth through the eyeholes of his mask.

'The aelf has good eyes,' said Gotrek. 'Whatever other faults she may have.' He leant out of his throne to get a better look at her. 'What did you see, Witchblade?'

Gotrek rarely called Maleneth by her true name and she had the odd sense that he felt protective of her. She quickly crushed the idea and decided his unusually good humour must have made him forget to insult her.

'Their sigils definitely looked Chaos in nature. A serpent turning into a flame.'

'Aye,' snarled Runefather Thurgyn. 'That one's used by many of the local warbands. They would never have dared attack Karag-Wyr under normal conditions. They know we rule these hills.' He glanced at Runemaster Korgan. 'But Korgan tells me Karag-Wyr was levelled by the thing we thought was storms. The aelves.'

'They're called Idoneth,' said Maleneth, irritated that the Fyreslayers seemed unable to grasp the idea that aelves were not a single, unified people. 'And they would not march under the banner of Chaos.'

'No one's suggesting they do,' said Runemaster Korgan, studying her with his habitually imperious expression. 'Karag-Wyr stood undefeated until your aelf kin bewitched it. But these Idoneth do not seem interested in keeping what they seize, so it looks like a warband has taken advantage of the situation.' His lip curled in distaste. 'It suits them. They're carrion crows. Living off scraps.'

Gotrek shook his head. 'Chaos cults are like a disease. They spread. If this rabble gets a foothold in these hills they'll send the call out to all their daemon-loving friends. Before you know it, this place will be a hellish netherworld.' He looked around at the corroded hills and shrugged. 'A *different* hellish netherworld.'

Runefather Thurgyn nodded. He was strapped into his throne and his face was still corpse grey, but his eyes gleamed as he looked at the horizon. 'They won't last long against the fyrds. I only wish we had a worthier foe. Look at the ill-bred wretches. Cowering behind the walls of Karag-Wyr won't save them.'

Gotrek grinned and raised his axe.

The runefather smiled back, lifting his axe in response.

Maleneth clenched her teeth.

CHAPTER TWENTY-TWO

Thurgyn waved his latchkey axe and the fyrds rumbled on, charging across the hills, throwing up rust clouds as they pounded drums and brayed on horns. Before long the Fyreslayers could spy the keep up ahead, and as the details became clearer to her, Maleneth saw what the runefather meant. There were Chaos warriors dashing from the surrounding fields, alarmed by the sight of the approaching Fyreslayers, and they looked scrawny and badly equipped. Most of them wore no more than leathers, similar to her own, and their weapons were a jumble of stolen swords and spears. The closest they came to a uniform was a swirl of yellow painted on the front of their jerkins and shields, presumably meant to be a flame, and they all had the sallow-skinned, sunken-eyed look of consumptives.

'A few hundred,' sneered Runefather Thurgyn. 'Five hundred at most. Hardly worth interrupting the feast for.'

'That's your fortress they're smearing sigils over,' said Gotrek.

'I was joking,' said Thurgyn. He patted his axe. 'It's been a long time since I used this in anger and I was hoping for something bigger to hit.'

They came to a halt at the top of a shallow incline that led down to the walls of the fortress. 'What are they doing?' asked Gotrek, leaning forwards in his throne. The cultists were gathering outside the hold and making no attempt to close the gates or man the walls. They had formed a line in front of the keep and were readying their weapons. 'They should look more scared than that,' he muttered.

'We'll soon give them something to be scared of,' said Thurgyn, looking down his lines of Fyreslayers. 'Grimnir's fire is in you!' he bellowed, straining forwards in his war throne.

His words ignited the fyrds. If they had been frenzied before, they were unhinged now, whirling in the dust and swinging their axes so furiously Maleneth was surprised they didn't butcher each other. They howled and punched their chests, shaking their fiery crests of hair and roaring at the clouds.

'Battlesmiths!' cried Thurgyn. 'Advance!'

Four figures broke away from the Fyreslayer lines, marching purposefully across the ruptured metal. Each of them carried a metal standard, forged to resemble Grimnir's face. The sight of these raised icons sent the other Fyreslayers into even greater ecstasies of battle lust, and even Maleneth felt a wave of bloodlust wash through her. The Fyreslayers' war cries were like the roar of an ocean and it lit a hunger in her chest. She gripped her knives, battling the urge to sprint forwards.

Control yourself, warned her former mistress. *This is not your fight. Don't be drawn into their madness.*

'A kill's a kill.' Maleneth was shivering with barely constrained violence. 'Khaine won't care whose fight it is.'

Look at the graceless oafs. They fight like Gotrek. They're deranged. You don't want to end up like that.

'Can you feel it?' howled Thurgyn as runes lit up across his body, shining like irons in a furnace. Maleneth could see smoke trailing from his skin. He pointed his axe at the figures gathering before the keep, his eyes blazing as brightly as the runes. 'Let! It! Burn!'

'Let it burn!' shouted the Fyreslayers, finally exploding into movement, hurling themselves down the slope after the standard bearers. The lodge elders followed the charge, their steeds thundering down the hillside as Thurgyn continued howling his battle cry. 'Let! It! Burn!'

Maleneth could no longer resist. She joined her voice to the chorus, wailing an ululating battle cry as she sprinted after them, forgetting about Fyreslayers and Gotrek as bloodlust formed a crimson tunnel in her vision, blocking out everything but the Chaos warriors. Despite her mistress' warning she abandoned herself to the battle frenzy, screaming prayers as she raced past most of the stocky Fyreslayers and sprinted out into the front lines.

The warband watched calmly as the fyrds thundered towards them. Maleneth's blood was pounding in her ears and she could think of nothing but the impending slaughter, yet even through such intense passion there was a part of her that sensed something was wrong. The warband looked too nonchalant, their weapons held loosely and their poses relaxed. Her doubts were washed away by a tide of bloodlust as Maleneth reached the enemy lines and dived at the first warrior she reached, somersaulting through the smoke and hammering knives into his chest.

The warrior tumbled backwards, blood spraying from the wounds. He crashed to the ground and Maleneth crouched over him, wrenched her blades free and flipped clear, looking around for another target.

Then she realised something was wrong. It was not blood spraying from the warrior, but liquid metal. It flashed in the morning light as it bubbled from his jerkin, then solidified, as if cooling, and vanished, leaving smooth skin where the man's chest should have been torn open. The warrior rose calmly to his feet, grabbed his greatsword from the ground and thrust it at Maleneth.

She was so surprised that she barely parried, just managing to bring up her knives in time to block the blow, and lost her footing, stumbling backwards as the warrior lunged after her.

You're fighting like a Fyreslayer. Show some skill. Remember who you are.

Maleneth did not need a lecture. She was furious at herself for moving in such a clumsy fashion. She took a step back to steady herself and prepare a more considered attack. The Fyreslayers had caught up with her and were crashing into the enemy lines, but as their flaming axes rose and fell, she saw that they were as ineffectual as her knives. The blades cut the Chaos warriors down, but rather than blood, lines of quicksilver gushed from the wounds and then the liquid metal meshed torn flesh back together, flowing like solder.

The warrior in front of Maleneth sauntered towards her, drawing back his sword for another swipe. As she studied his face properly for the first time, Maleneth saw that his eyes were featureless silver orbs, formed of the same liquid that had bled from his wounds. She saw her furious face reflected in the silver discs as he locked them on her and swung the sword.

She sidestepped, whirled behind him and slammed her knives in his back, landing the blows with such force that he thudded to the ground for a second time. Again, it was quicksilver rather than blood that rushed from the wounds and the man laughed as he rolled over to face her, metal bubbling between his teeth. 'Keep trying,' he grinned, sprawling happily on the ground. 'You'll soon grow tired.' He leered at her. 'And then I'll make you do a different dance.'

She cursed and hurled a flurry of knife strikes at him, slashing and hacking so hard that her prey vanished in a fountain of quicksilver. Even when she knew he must be dead, she kept on, knives blurring through the air. When she finally reeled back from him, his body had been torn apart and scattered across the ground. As she stood over him, panting and drenched in quicksilver, the metal pouring from his body collected in pools and began to coagulate, merging until he had re-formed entirely. She had never seen anything like it. She had fought undead creatures that were oblivious to their injuries, but she had never seen bodies that repaired themselves at will.

'What are you?' she gasped as the man lurched to his feet and faced her again.

'We are the Covenant of Fire.' His eyes were glinting as he spoke. 'We are the change that has come. We are the new beginning. We are-'

'Boring,' said Maleneth, beheading the man with a cross-handed slash. As his head fell away she kicked it as hard as she could, sending it spinning over the heads of the battling Fyreslayers.

'There's a change for you,' she said as the headless man dropped to his knees.

CHAPTER TWENTY-THREE

Maleneth was about to rush back into the main crush of the battle when she saw something infuriating. There was quicksilver bubbling from her dead opponent's neck and it was solidifying, forming into a shape. 'Blades of Khaine,' she hissed as the shape became a head made of liquid metal with blurred, half-formed features.

Maleneth kicked the man back into the crowds of Fyreslayers and then gave up on him, marching through the fighting and looking for the Slayer. 'Gotrek!' she cried, dodging sword strikes and lashing out with her knives, opening wounds that were already healing as she moved on. 'Where are you?'

Her bloodlust was fading and the charge of the Fyreslayers had whipped up rust clouds, making it hard to see more than a few feet in any direction. The enemy were massively outnumbered so Maleneth was mostly surrounded by throngs of Fyreslayers who were lashing out wildly with their axes, irrespective of whether they could actually find a foe to attack. There was no sign of Gotrek but, a hundred paces or so from where she was standing, she could see the hulking, fortress-like silhouette of one of the magmadroths. She sprinted towards it.

'They're heading for the standard!' cried Thurgyn as Maleneth reached his magmadroth. The runefather looked magnificent, like a burning idol, flames rippling down his muscles as he dealt out brutal, frenzied axe blows. Maleneth had never seen a Fyreslayer so consumed by rune-power. It was like watching Gotrek at his most incensed. The Varrukh near Thurgyn were equally wild, inspired by his wrath, hacking at the humans with their axes and firing volleys of magma, but it was all pointless: each time a Chaos warrior fell, he simply rose again, his body re-forming with a ripple of quicksilver.

'Protect the banner!' cried Runemaster Korgan, riding to Thurgyn's side and waving the Fyreslayers towards one of the standard bearers.

'Where's Gotrek?' she called out.

Korgan shook his head and continued directing Fyreslayers to the standard, but someone else answered Maleneth from the heart of the fighting. 'Near the gates,' cried Skromm, bludgeoning his way through the crush, a wild grin on his face.

Maleneth felt another surge of bloodlust. Skromm was revelling in the slaughter, heedless of anything except the joy of battle. His opponents rose as quickly as he cut them down but he did not mind. In fact, he seemed to delight in the idea of a foe he could kill more than once. All around Skromm there were crowds of Fyreslayers who were behaving the same way. Their eyes were rolling like feeding sharks and their war cries were hoarse and wild. Maleneth wrenched her gaze from the bloodshed and ran towards the gates. Chaos warriors sauntered past her as she ran, dealing out lazy sword strikes and laughing. Some were fighting even while they were still re-forming, their limbs and features bubbling back into place as they lunged and stabbed.

Maleneth weaved between combatants, dealing out knife strikes as she ran, then spotted Gotrek near the wall of the keep. He had picked up a warrior and was using him as a club, swinging him into his comrades, causing his head to explode and re-form. The garish smoke Maleneth had spotted from the hillside was still pouring from the fortress and it was pooling around Gotrek as he fought. 'Die when I kill you!' roared Gotrek, smashing the man into another warrior, creating a shower of quicksilver. He still had his fyresteel axe, but had clearly decided the warrior was a better weapon. 'Does nobody know how to do anything properly in these bloody realms?'

'This is a bad joke,' spat Maleneth, reaching the Slayer's side with a flurry of knife strikes. 'They must be daemons.'

Gotrek paused to stare at her, the man juddering and re-forming in his grip. 'These mewling things aren't daemons. They're manlings.'

Maleneth dodged a sword strike and kicked her attacker back into the crowd. 'Men don't bleed metal. And they don't get up when you kill them.'

'We're not killing them.' Gotrek hurled his groaning weapon into the mob and backed away from the fighting for a moment, wiping sweat from his face. 'They're not undead. They're lackeys of the Chaos Gods. Servants of Tzeentch. Look at that flame symbol. They're devious, book-reading types. This is wizardry.' He looked around at the battle. 'And where there's wizardry, there's a wizard.' He nodded at the gates to the keep. They were open, but there was a mob of Chaos cultists blocking the way into the courtyard beyond. 'Somewhere in there, but I can't get through those smirking idiots.' He slammed his forehead into the face of a man who was trying to rise from the ground, creating another fountain of quicksilver. 'I need to draw them out.' He looked out across the carnage, to the smoke-shrouded silhouettes of the magmadroths. Thurgyn was visible even from this distance, blazing and hacking through the crush.

Gotrek grinned. 'He's a true son of Karak Ankor, that one. Look at him. He's got real dawi blood in him.' Then he frowned. 'What are they mucking about over there for? Why aren't they attacking the gates like we discussed?'

'They're defending a standard. The cultists keep targeting them.'

Gotrek frowned. 'The standards? Why?'

Maleneth shrugged. 'Fyreslayers are obsessed with them. I think they react with the runes in their bodies.' Maleneth parried another sword slash and kicked her opponent in the face, not even bothering to use her knives any more. She shrugged. 'And if I know that, I suppose these cult-ists might. Maybe they think they can defeat the Fyreslayers by destroying their standards?'

'Not a bad tactic,' grunted Gotrek. 'If they trash all the standards, the Fyreslayers will probably start whingeing about curses again.' He punched a cultist, snapping the man's neck at a revolting angle and sending him reeling back into the crowd.

'We could do this all day and not get anywhere,' said Maleneth.

Gotrek nodded. 'We need to stop farting about with monkeys and find the organ grinder.'

Maleneth stared at him. 'I know all of those words but I have no idea what you're talking about.'

'We need to get through that gate,' he said, looking at the cultists blocking his way. 'Got it,' he muttered, spotting something in the crowds of Fyre-slayers. Without any more explanation, he stomped off through the battle, landing punches and headbutts as he went.

Maleneth ran after him, but the colourful smoke was getting thicker by the minute and it lined her throat, greasy and tacky, causing her to cough as she battled through the scrum. 'Where are you going?' she called out, her voice a rough croak. 'You said attack the gates but you're heading away from them.'

Gotrek did not reply, heading for the thick of the fighting and shoving his way through the Fyreslayers. Maleneth felt a rush of alarm when she realised he was making directly for one of the metal standards they had just been discussing.

He's going to do something stupid, said the voice from Maleneth's amulet.

'Helpful, as always,' muttered Maleneth, picking up her pace. Struggling figures blocked her way and, try as she might, she could not catch up with Gotrek before he reached the Fyreslayer standard.

Even in their frenzied state, the Fyreslayers recognised Gotrek, cheering as he approached and forming a path for him. He nodded back at them, stomped towards the battlesmith holding the banner and punched him, hard, in the face.

'Gotrek!' cried Maleneth as the battlesmith tumbled to the ground.

Gotrek caught the banner as it slipped from the duardin's grip and then marched off with it, making for a patch of raised ground.

All the nearby Fyreslayers howled in alarm but they were too confused to try to stop Gotrek, calling out to him furiously and staggering back from their opponents.

Gotrek reached the top of the incline and held the likeness of Grimnir's face above his head. 'Come and get it!' he roared, waving the standard back and forth so that it blinked in the smoke.

The figures at the gate surged forwards, running towards Gotrek, their blank eyes fixed on the banner. Gotrek waited until they were only thirty paces from where he stood, then turned and threw the banner into the rust field, away from the keep. As cultists and Fyreslayers bolted after it,

Gotrek walked calmly back down the slope, heading in the opposite direction towards the now unguarded gates. He grinned as he marched past Maleneth, unslinging his axe from his back as he headed towards the keep. 'Simple plans. Always best.' There were a couple of cultists still waiting by the gates but Gotrek floored them with a single swipe and headed into the keep with Maleneth close behind him.

Inside, the smoke was even thicker and it reeked. Maleneth struggled not to gag as she followed Gotrek through the fumes. The colours were more violent too, an eye-watering clash of pink and blue that boiled around her as she tried to make out the scene. Her eyes were streaming and that, combined with the smoke, made it almost impossible to see what was happening.

Gotrek seemed to have less difficulty, marching on into the courtyard. Maleneth tensed as towering figures loomed into view, but then she realised they were Fyreslayer statues, similar to the ones in Karag-Varr. 'Keep up!' boomed Gotrek's voice from somewhere up ahead.

As they approached the centre of the courtyard Maleneth saw another large shadow, but she could tell immediately that it was not a statue. It looked more like a hill, right at the heart of the keep, and it was the source of the dreadful stench. There was also an intense heat radiating from it that washed over her face and snatched her breath.

'On my oath,' said Gotrek. 'That's ripe.'

They both grimaced as they reached the mound and saw what it was. It was a pyre of Fyreslayers, all of them burning, drenched in pink-and-blue fire, their remains so charred they would have been unrecognisable if not for their crested dragon helms and golden runes.

'This must be the whole garrison,' said Maleneth. There were hundreds of Fyreslayer corpses in the mound, thrown unceremoniously on top of each other.

Gotrek muttered a curse as he stared at the blackened remains. 'Grungni,' he whispered. Over the time she had spent in his company, Maleneth had come to understand the Slayer a little. He liked to masquerade as an anvil-browed brute, as a cold-hearted killer, but she knew the truth. Sights like this caused him pain. 'So many...' he muttered, shaking his head.

'Look,' said Maleneth, pointing one of her knives to the top of the pyre. A metal scaffold had been erected over the fire, suspending a cauldron as big as an outhouse. The burning bodies were heating the cauldron, causing it to bubble and spit, and, hunched over it with its back to them, standing on a platform, was a slender figure. It was holding a book in one hand and a dagger in the other.

Gotrek scowled and spat on the ground.

Maleneth waved some of the fumes away, trying to see the figure more clearly. It was a woman, but there was something odd about her head. It took her a moment to realise that the woman was looking back at them, even though her body was facing in the opposite direction. The sorceress had rotated her head one hundred and eighty degrees. She had large, lemon-yellow eyes that stared out from a feathered, blue face. As she locked her hideous gaze on Gotrek, she let out a screech like scraping blades.

CHAPTER TWENTY-FOUR

Maleneth staggered backwards as the sound lashed against her, and even Gotrek grimaced, shaking his head. As the sorceress screamed, the cauldron's fumes danced in time to her voice, forming slender tendrils that looped and coiled in the air before hurtling towards the ground. When the smoke touched the flagstones it transformed, becoming columns of quicksilver, identical to the liquid that had spilled from the cultists' wounds.

'Watch yourself, aelf,' growled Gotrek. '*This* is the organ grinder.'

'The what?' Maleneth was about to demand an explanation when she realised that the silver columns were taking on humanoid shapes. The quicksilver rippled and flowed, forming arms and legs and smooth, featureless faces. The metal figures were large – seven or eight feet tall and powerfully muscled. They swayed for a moment, as though unused to standing, then sprinted at Gotrek and Maleneth. As they ran, their arms reflowed, changing shape again, becoming long, curved blades.

Gotrek roared as the first of the automata reached him, bringing his fyresteel axe round in a low swipe that cleaved the creature in two. It collapsed, becoming liquid again, splashing quicksilver across the ground. Then another one of the metal figures reached the Slayer, swinging its bladed arms down towards his head. Gotrek parried the blow then cursed as he saw that the first automaton was already re-forming, pooling back together and solidifying, rising from the ground like a metal sapling.

Maleneth raced to Gotrek's side as a third automaton reached him, thrusting its bladed arms at his neck. She parried and kicked the creature in the chest, sending it stumbling back the way it had come.

The sorceress was still producing a birdlike shriek and more automata were springing up from the flagstones as prismatic smoke rushed from the cauldron. There was a clamour of voices outside the gates as Fyreslayers tried to enter the keep but were blocked by cultists who had returned to the entrance.

Gotrek and Maleneth fought desperately as a crowd of the metal figures formed around them, attacking in silence, their muscles shimmering in the firelight. Gotrek barrelled into them, trying to approach the pyre, but it was no use. However savagely he fought, he remained mired in a tangle of gleaming limbs. 'Damn it, aelf!' he roared, his face flushing a furious purple. 'Can't you do something? I need to get up on that platform.'

Maleneth looked at the pouches fixed to her belt. She carried poisons that could stop hearts and scorch flesh, but how could she kill an enemy made of metal? 'They're not alive!' she yelled back, fending off more blows. 'How can I kill walking statues?'

Every moment you spend with that lout drains you of intelligence, said her former mistress. *You were never bright but now you're as dim as he is. What would you do if you needed to force a blade through thick armour?*

Maleneth frowned as she parried another attack, barely preventing one of the automata from beheading Gotrek. *I'd coat the blade in narúna oil.*

Well done, idiot girl. And why would you do that?

Because it corrodes metal. Maleneth was irritated that she had not thought of it herself. Narúna oil was incredibly corrosive but she had never thought of it as a weapon in its own right. 'Wait,' she said to Gotrek, sidestepping another blow and grasping a pouch from her belt. 'There is something. But I'm not sure if it will work.'

'Do it quickly,' grunted Gotrek, staggering back towards her as more of the silver figures crashed into him, lunging and stabbing.

Maleneth smeared the oil across her knives and leapt past Gotrek, cutting and hacking at the automata. Steam hissed from the metal figures and a black patina washed over their burnished skin. The oil burned like acid and Maleneth grinned as she clambered on through a crowd of toppling, crumbling bodies.

There were still more figures rising from the ground but Maleneth had managed to cut an opening for Gotrek and he crashed forwards with a howl, charging towards the pyre. There was no ladder up to the platform and the Slayer hesitated for a moment, staring at the burning bodies. Then he roared a curse and leapt into the fire, clambering through the garish flames.

The sorceress' scream rose in pitch and Gotrek halted, halfway up the pyre, bellowing in pain and leaning backwards. It looked, for a moment, as if he were going to fall, but then he lurched forwards and hurled his axe. The weapon trailed embers and landed neatly between the sorceress' eyes.

The scream ended as the sorceress dropped into her own cauldron. Then there was a boom as the cauldron exploded, hurling smoke, fire and corpses through the air. Gotrek landed heavily near Maleneth in a shower of embers and ash. There was a series of splashes as the metal golems melted to the ground, turning to gleaming pools, and Maleneth found herself alone with Gotrek in the smoke. She remained in a fighting pose for a moment, expecting an attack, but when none came she rushed over to the Slayer and turned him over. She hissed and snatched her hand back as his skin burned her palm. He was badly blistered and, suddenly, she realised he might be dead. A dreadful chill rushed through her. She slapped his face. 'Gotrek!'

He grinned savagely, crumbling the layer of ash that covered his face. 'Nicely done,' he croaked, struggling for breath. He slapped her shoulder so hard she stumbled. 'Knew you'd come in useful eventually.'

There was another crashing sound as the cauldron's scaffolding gave way, dropping it onto the pyre and hurling more flames. 'Come on,' said Maleneth, giving Gotrek her hand and helping him to his feet. Together, they limped away from the wreckage, heading for the wall. As they leant against each other, dusting themselves down and gasping for breath, Maleneth considered how many times she had done this. She had escaped disaster so often with Gotrek that it was beginning to feel like all she had ever done. Annoying as he was, he was starting to eclipse the life she had led before she met him. It was not a pleasant realisation. Suddenly, she felt a presentiment of danger – not from the enemies that constantly assailed Gotrek, but from something worse: her reliance on him. She was starting to *depend* on him. Without ever intending to, she was investing everything in him. Since her youth in the Murder Temples she had relied on faith and her ability to wield a knife. But now, for the first time in her life, she felt as if she needed someone else.

You're going down a dangerous path, said her former mistress, reading her thoughts and sounding even bitterer than usual. *Take it from me, you can't trust anyone else.*

Maleneth reached the wall of the keep and slumped against the metal, looking at Gotrek with a growing sense of claustrophobia. He was a few paces away from her, doubled over, coughing sooty phlegm down his beard. She recalled the emotion she had felt when she had thought he was dead. It had been suspiciously close to panic. Panic! When had Maleneth Witch-blade ever panicked? *I'm losing myself,* she thought. *Losing myself in him. And it's making me weak.* Perhaps it was the heady fumes that were still hanging in the air, clogging her lungs and muddying her thoughts, but she suddenly felt as though she had to do something drastic. She had to change the direction she was headed in.

Gotrek seemed to sense she was staring at him. 'Are you hurt?' he said, looking up at her and wiping muck from his face. His features were as savage as ever but she saw genuine concern in his face.

She could not bring herself to reply, her sense of claustrophobia growing worse. *What is this? Are we friends now? Do we* care *about each other*? The idea appalled her. She had never cared about *anyone*. Other than herself, of course. She felt as though she had abandoned a piece of essential armour.

There was a clamour of anguished voices as the Fyreslayers flooded into the courtyard. The axe-wielding berserkers ran through the smoke, heading for the toppling pyre, followed by the pike-wielding guards and then the hulking, ground-shaking bulk of the magmadroths, who had to stoop to fit through the gateway into the keep. There was no sign of any cultists. Gotrek must have been right, decided Maleneth. With the sorceress dead, the Chaos worshippers had become as feeble as they looked.

As the crowds of Fyreslayers continued pouring into the keep, the sound of their pain and outrage grew. It went beyond simple grief. When they reached the charred remains, they picked runes from the ashes, staring at the inert metal as though they cared about it as much as their dead kin.

'They're just pieces of gold,' said Gotrek, following the direction of her gaze. He shook his head sadly. 'It's the curse of my people. Look at them. Howling over lumps of metal in a land where it springs from every mountainside.'

Again, Gotrek was speaking to her as a confidant, as a friend, and again it gave her a chilling sense of foreboding. She could not explain exactly how, but she felt that she had made an unforgivable error. She wondered if, even now, she could escape the Slayer's pull, but she knew she could not. The fight for the realms hinged on him, she was sure of it. The fight against Chaos, next to which all other concerns were insignificant, was bound up in Gotrek Gurnisson. She shivered and backed away from him, but before she had gone very far, she saw that the Fyreslayer elders were approaching. Thurgyn, Korgan and Uzkal were riding their magmadroths through the grieving mob, heading straight towards Gotrek. Maleneth prepared herself for another nauseating wave of gratitude and hero worship, but then she saw the Fyreslayers' expressions. They looked furious. Uzkal's face was hidden but she could see from his pose that he was rigid with anger, and Thurgyn looked livid.

'You can trust the Slayer to clear up your messes,' said Gotrek cheerfully, oblivious to the glares being directed at him.

'How dare you,' snarled Thurgyn when he was close enough to address Gotrek.

Gotrek laughed when he saw how angry they were. 'What are you talking about? How dare I what?'

The runefather gestured for one of his warriors to approach. The Fyreslayer was carrying a mangled lump of metal and, after a moment's confusion, Maleneth realised it was the icon of Grimnir that Gotrek had used to draw the cultists away from the gate. It had buckled where it had hit the ground, and the cultists had obviously managed to attack it before the sorceress died. It was distorted and cleaved in several places, rent out of shape by sword strikes. The Fyreslayer carrying it looked even more furious than his king, and Maleneth struggled not to laugh.

'I don't think they liked you pushing their flag-waver over,' she whispered, leaning over to him.

'You struck a battlesmith of the Varrukh lodge!' bellowed Thurgyn, veins snaking around his sunken eye sockets. 'And you attacked a likeness of the Slayer God.' He pointed his latchkey axe at the standard. 'You defiled Grimnir's memory!'

Gotrek seemed too shocked to reply. Then he shook his head and pointed at the pile of burned corpses. 'They did this to your people and you're whingeing about dents in your little sign. Is this some kind of bloody joke?'

Thurgyn studied the toppled pyre and then looked back at Gotrek, his words taut. 'You have aided us, again, Gotrek Gurnisson, but I will not stand for this. You will not treat our holy icons like scrap metal. This standard is a record of every battle and–'

'It's a lump of metal.' Gotrek's voice was dangerously quiet.

'Gotrek,' whispered Maleneth. 'They were on your side a minute ago. Apologise for hitting their damned banner.'

'Apologise?' He stared at her as though she were speaking a different language.

'It's a thing people do,' she said.

Gotrek ignored her and locked his glare back on Thurgyn. 'This is exactly where you people go wrong. Honour the past, by all means, but don't get bloody stuck in it.' He nodded at the icon. 'If that thing helps, all well and good, but if it doesn't, use it another way.'

'Blasphemy,' snarled Thurgyn, looking even more outraged.

'You people tie yourself in knots,' cried Gotrek. He waved at the runes in Thurgyn's body and the sigils on his throne. 'What do you think all this stuff is for?' Thurgyn started to reply but Gotrek shouted over him. 'They're tools. They're ways to win. Means to an end. Do you see? And it's the winning that matters, not the bloody tools. You need to think about the victory, not the trinkets that get you the victory.' He looked around at the crowd. 'Am I talking another language? Does anybody here understand me? If Grimnir's ghost really is up there somewhere, watching over you, what do you think he wants you to do?' Thurgyn tried again to speak but Gotrek boomed on. 'He wants you to slay! He wants you to drive out the bloody idiots. He wants you to put an end to people who are so dim they think it's clever to bargain with daemons.' He pointed his axe at the icon, spit flying through his crooked teeth as he addressed the whole Fyreslayer army. 'You brought that thing here to help you win. And what did it do? It helped you bloody win!'

Thurgyn looked even angrier, as did Korgan and every other Fyreslayer that Maleneth could see. There was a stunned silence as the normally frenetic duardin all stared at Gotrek in disbelief. Then, one by one, they all gripped their weapons and began stomping across the smoke-filled courtyard.

'Every time...' muttered Maleneth. She drew her knives and prepared to fight. 'Only you could make enemies of an army you just saved.'

'Wait,' said a voice. Maleneth thought, at first, that it had come from the runefather, but as Thurgyn looked back at Uzkal she realised it was the masked priest. 'Runefather,' said Uzkal. 'I'm starting to see what is happening here. I think I have been wrong about this stranger.'

'Finally!' cried Gotrek. 'Someone who understands what I'm saying.'

The Fyreslayers all turned to their priest. 'We've been labouring under a delusion,' said Uzkal, riding his magmadroth out in front of the army. 'For all these weeks we believed that Grimnir had abandoned us. That he had cursed us. We endured hardships beyond count.' He glanced at Runefather Thurgyn. 'And the loss of our runesons. But we endured our trials with stoicism and faith. We held fast to the old ways. And now, now that we have finally returned the runesons to the Sacred Fire, look at what has happened.' He raised the burning rune he was gripping in his fist, waving it at the keep. 'We have driven out our enemies. We have reclaimed what is ours.' He stood in his throne and the fire burned brighter in his fist. 'This is a sign! As sure as any I have seen. Grimnir has judged us! And he has deemed us worthy!'

An awed murmur rippled through the crowd and the Fyreslayers nodded at each other, exhilarated by Uzkal's words. 'And this stranger,' said the priest, waving the flame at Gotrek, 'was the messenger who brought us Grimnir's word.' His voice grew even more impassioned. 'He is a prophet of the Slayer God!'

All across the courtyard, the Fyreslayers turned to stare in wonder at Gotrek. Even Thurgyn's eyes strained with revelation. Then he howled and gripped his axe in both hands, lifting it over his head. 'Let it burn!' he roared, shaking his head from side to side.

'Let it burn!' howled the fyrds, shaking their weapons and spilling embers from their axes.

As the cheering grew in volume, Maleneth turned to look at Gotrek. He was shaking his head, an incredulous expression on his face as he muttered something. She did not need to hear the word to know what it was.

'Morons.'

CHAPTER TWENTY-FIVE

Eòrna ran through fields of brittle stars. She ignored the ink-dark beauty of the Curaim, dashing through the chamber so fast that lanternfish scattered before her, flashing and blinking as they rolled up into the blackness. She felt none of the calm her inner sanctum usually granted her. Her brother's speech at the Allmarach had horrified her. And with every moment that passed, her fears grew. Her brother was insane and he was the king. That was a potent combination. He was not some remote corner of the nobility; he was regent of Dhruim-Ùrlar and he had the backing of the Isharann fanes. He might actually be able to realise his lunatic ambitions. She had to find Torven quickly. He would know what to do.

She passed through seemingly boundless chambers, knowing the hidden paths and where she would find Torven. The Galdach Hall was at the very centre of the Curaim and, unlike most of the city, it radiated a fierce heat. Eòrna entered it at a sprint, leaving the brittle stars behind and bounding up slopes of jagged, volcanic rock. It was brighter in this chamber and the light radiated from the walls of a vast, crooked tower that rose from the rocks. It was a natural chimney, a spiralling vent formed from cooled magma that roared constantly, filling the chamber with noise and spewing columns of hot water that would have dwarfed most mountains. The water boiled and flashed as it rose, reaching so high its top was not visible. Somewhere, many hundreds of feet above Eòrna's head, it emerged from the roofs of Dhruim-Ùrlar and spilled out into the abyssal plain. The chimney appeared to be molten but the movement was an illusion created by thousands of crabs that crawled constantly over its pitted surface. The crabs scattered as Eòrna pounded up the rocks, heading for Torven's cave. Her priests had bound the chamber with complex Isharann spells, making it safe for her to enter, but she still winced at the heat, so alien to the deeps of Dhruim-Ùrlar.

Torven was waiting at the cave entrance and he glided back into the shadows as she climbed up towards him, heading back into his lair. She climbed in after him and followed his spiral-shaped shell as it floated down a tunnel, past several openings and grottos, into a central, roughly circular cave. The cave was filled with undulating light that spilled from an opening in the far wall. The opening was oval and as tall as Eòrna, and it looked onto the jet of heated water that was howling up the thermal vent.

'You were right!' she cried, rushing over to him. 'It *is* a betrayal! He means to end the Great Hunt! He wants us to live like uplanders.' She reeled around the cave, scattering fish as she waved her hands. 'He wants us to abandon Dhruim-Ùrlar and live in dust and sunlight like humans. And he thinks that will make us masters of the realms. It's madness.' She shook her head, remembering her childhood. 'He was always obsessed with this idea of appeasing Teclis. Where's the sense in it? How can we live our lives trying to please a god who always despised us? Betrayal is exactly what this is, betrayal of our entire way of life.'

'It's more than that,' replied Torven, his tone as neutral as ever. 'There is a greater treachery.'

Eòrna stared into Torven's lightless eye. 'What could be a greater treachery than stealing our way of life?' She gripped her helsabres. 'And what will happen to the namarti? If they are freed from the curse, that would make them our equals. They could challenge our right to rule.' She laughed bitterly. 'Dìolan thinks they will adore him for this, but they will probably put his head on a spike and take the throne for themselves. He's going to tear down everything that holds society together. Life needs order and structure. He's going to replace it with anarchy.'

'All true,' said Torven, 'but this is not the betrayal I sensed. What did you do with the shell I gave you?'

'I gave it to Úrdach and he swore to take it to Dìolan's chambers. He should have no difficulties. Everyone's drunk on Dìolan's madness.' She laughed incredulously. 'They're preparing a celebratory ball.'

'Good. I thought you might have been forced to bring it back here.' Torven rotated slowly until his eye was facing the light-filled window. 'Let us see what it uncovers.'

The window flashed brighter, forcing Eòrna to shield her eyes. Then the light died, plunging the cave into darkness. The only illumination was a weak glow from the lanternfish outside. Torven became a cool shadow at Eòrna's side, but she could tell he was staring at the window. She had seen him use his deepsight many times but it never failed to impress her. It was quite unlike the etherstorms of the Isharann priests. The priests conjured power from the elemental fury of the sea, but Torven's power emanated from somewhere in the chambers of his shell. She heard the familiar sound of his thoughts: dull, echoing clangs that reverberated through the shell's spirals, as though its structure were being reconfigured.

Then a new light poured in through the window – a cool, silvery blue that rippled across the opening, fragmenting the darkness like moonlight on a pool. Eòrna forgot her rage for a moment, spellbound. The shapes eddied and churned as clunking sounds continued to reverberate through Torven's shell. Then an image started to form in the opening.

'Dìolan's apartments,' said Eòrna, recognising the grand, gilded stateroom, lined with columns.

'Yes,' replied Torven. 'Úrdach was successful.'

'Who's that at the far end?' Eòrna leant closer to the window. 'Is it my brother?'

The image in the window drifted down the long chamber, heading towards a group of figures who had gathered around a table. Eòrna quickly recognised Dìolan and Thallacrom and several of her brother's close advisors. 'I can't hear what they're saying.'

'Thallacrom has warded your brother's apartments with sorcery. Even with a physical presence in the room I am struggling to see clearly.'

Eòrna could see how tenuous his glimpse on the scene was. Her brother and the others looked like they were beneath the surface of a river, their features rolling and tumbling as she tried to focus on them. 'Then this is useless. How will we know what they're discussing?'

Torven's emissary glided closer to Dìolan, and Eòrna saw that her brother was holding something. It looked like a piece of shell, or coral. As the scene shifted again, she realised that the table was covered with a great heap of similar objects. They all burned with an inner fire that flashed on the faces of her brother's counsellors and generals.

'No,' she breathed, as she recognised the shapes. 'It can't be. Has he cut those from the chorrileum?' Nausea washed through her as she realised she was right. To see pieces of the chorrileum butchered and broken was worse than seeing the corpses of her fellow nobles. Each piece contained the soul of one of her kin. 'What in the name of the gods is he doing?'

'*This* is the treachery,' said Torven. 'This is the great betrayal I felt. It makes sense now. You heard his speech – he means to harness Gotrek's soul and use it to break the curse. And this is how he will do it.'

'By sundering the souls of our ancestors?'

'There is only one reason he would do such a thing,' replied Torven. 'The king means to summon an Eidolon of unusual power. A great spirit of the Fallen God. And he has harvested the souls of his own people to do it.'

'But why?' cried Eòrna. The Isharann had summoned Eidolons before. They were divine manifestations, formed in the likeness of the god Mathlann and fuelled by the souls in the chorrileum. Such beings had been conjured many times in Dhruim-Ùrlar's history, but it had never required anything as horrific as this.

'He does not mean to summon any ordinary Eidolon. Gotrek carries the spark of divinity in him. Only the power of a god can crush the power of a god. Your brother means to create something greater than the Eidolons you have summoned before. Something so significant he is prepared to sacrifice all those souls.'

'But he's damning them all! They will go to the Dark Prince. They will go to Slaanesh.'

Torven drifted away from the window as more of the dull hammering sounds chimed through his shell. 'I have heard of such a thing. Your kin in the Faobhar enclave attempted it during the Palladium Wars. There was a manifestation they called the Apogaion Eidolon. Your own libraries contain references to it. It is said it was so great it could level mountains and crush entire armies. Your brother seems to have found a way to subdue Gotrek Gurnisson.'

'But he must have begun planning this before his disastrous battle. He can't have begun something on this scale in the last few hours.'

Torven thought for a moment. 'Then this must always have been his plan. When you told him that we had found a potent soul, one capable of strengthening the namarti, he was lying to you. He had already hatched a plan to use Gotrek's soul in another, more profound way – as a way to break the curse.'

'It's not a curse!' hissed Eòrna. 'And I'm not the only one who thinks that.' She paced around the cave. 'We have to tell people what he's doing. There will be riots. Even his most ardent supporters will be appalled.' Suddenly, she realised what an opportunity this was. 'He's gone too far. Everyone will agree. It's all very well to speak of curing the half-souls and rising from the sea to conquer the realms, but what will people say when they realise he's sundering the souls of their parents to do it? They'll bay for his blood.' She turned and began rushing from the cave. 'I have to tell people.'

'And what will your brother say?' Torven's tone was still deadpan. 'Will he admit his crime and reveal the pieces of broken coral?'

Eòrna stopped and glared at him. 'No, of course not, but I will–'

'You will what? Fight your way into the king's apartments, slay all of his soldiers and take the evidence? Or will you stand at the palace gates, telling anyone who will listen that their beloved king is damning their ancestors to an eternity of torment? Railing like a lunatic. Do you think people will listen to the embittered, exiled sister, or the triumphant king who is about to make them lords of the realms?'

Eòrna drew one of her sabres and slashed at the darkness. 'They have to know.'

'And once your accusations have fallen on deaf ears, do you think your brother will continue to tolerate your presence in Dhruim-Ùrlar? Or do you think he will be forced to finally deal with his most credible challenger?'

Eòrna sighed and slid her sword back in its scabbard. She shook her head and walked back over to the window, watching her brother with a mixture of horror and grudging respect. 'There's nothing he will not do. His faith in himself is so absolute. Dìolan is no monster. I know what it would mean to him, breaking those souls from their sanctuary. But he won't let it stop him.' She turned to Torven. 'Very well, you've made your point. I'm impulsive. I know I am. It would be a mistake to let my brother know we have learned his plans. So let me suggest an alternative. He is desperate to launch another attack on Karag-Varr. He means to drag half the enclave to the uplands. It will be a glorious host and he will no doubt seize his prize. But while he's up there, hurling battalions at Gotrek, his palace will be empty and barely guarded. His friends and allies will be up on that volcano with him, desperate to earn a place in his new order. What if I bide my time, wait until the palace has emptied, then steal into my brother's chambers and take some of the chorrileum that he has stolen?'

Torven thought for a moment, his shell clanging and hissing. 'That *would* be the right time to act. But taking the pieces of coral would only give your brother an easy excuse to kill you. He would pass the blame on to you and say *you* were responsible for stealing the souls while he was leading his battalions into battle. No, it would be better to take some nobles into the palace with you. Even if King Dìolan fields a huge army, there will be many nobles left behind – people who are too old, or simply unskilled in the art of war. And among them will be many prominent political figures. If you led those nobles into the palace under some pretext, you could act surprised when you stumble across the king's treachery. You could even play the part of a caring sister who tries to find an innocent explanation for Dìolan's crime. You will seal his fate at the same time as appearing to be his most loyal supporter.'

Eòrna laughed. 'Gods, that's devious. I pray I never have your intellect working against me.' She patted his shell as she watched Dìolan and Thalla-crom sorting through the pieces of coral. 'I almost feel sorry for him.'

CHAPTER TWENTY-SIX

King Dìolan woke in the darkness with a start. When the Isharann priests had summoned Dhruim-Ùrlar into being, they had granted it a cycle of light and dark, recreating a semblance of night and day, driven by ancestral instincts they could barely explain. The corals that formed the city's spires grew less luminous as the evenings wore on, becoming completely lightless at night.

When Dìolan lurched from his bed, his window looked out on almost pitch darkness. Only the faint glimmer of a lanternfish illuminated the ornamental gardens that surrounded his palace. He leant heavily on the sill, pain knifing through his innards and his mind filled with the echoes of his dream.

It had been Gotrek, again, who dragged him from his rest. The tru'heas healers had told him, repeatedly, that only rest would heal his wounds, but every time he tried to sleep he saw the Fyreslayer striding towards him, hacking through the ethertide, rune light blazing from his chest. It was a memory that should have filled him with elation. This was the great prize he had sought all his life. The fulcrum he would use to set the Dromlech on their true path. But the thought of Gotrek was troubling rather than pleasing. It pained him far more than his wounds, all the more so because he could not explain why. The Fyreslayer's ugly, battered face haunted him, bringing with it inexplicable doubts and making him feel that his mind was no longer his own.

'Your highness,' said Thallacrom. The priest was sitting in a tall chair on the far side of the king's bedchamber. He had not left Dìolan's side since they had returned from Karag-Varr and he slept in the same chair every night, ready to fetch water or medicine. He stood slowly, massaging his skeletal face and yawning as he crossed the room, pulling his robes tight against the chill. 'Do you need something? Is the pain bothering you? I can call the servants. What do you need?'

'Just this,' muttered Dìolan, taking a cup of wine from a table and drinking. The wine was heavy and strong and it eased the pain almost instantly. Wine was the only thing that stopped him feeling that he was losing his mind. He sat at the table and Thallacrom sat opposite, pouring himself a cup of wine. The two nobles had known each other so long that Thallacrom felt able to forgo formalities. They drank without speaking for a while, Thallacrom studying the king as the faint light of the lanternfish washed over his face.

'It was more than the pain that woke you,' said Thallacrom, when he finally broke the silence.

Dìolan nodded.

'You seemed troubled at the ball.'

'I despise those things.'

'It was more than that.' Thallacrom leant across the table. 'We always knew this would be hard. But we are so close now.'

Dìolan drank more wine, still trying to rid himself of Gotrek's face.

'What are you thinking?' asked Thallacrom.

'What if there was another way?' replied Dìolan. 'Another way to harness Gotrek's soul. A way that did not require...' He thought of the broken pieces of the chorrileum, the sundered souls of his ancestors, lying on the table in the rooms below where he was now sitting. 'A way that did not require such sacrifice.'

'Do you regret what we have done?' Thallacrom's expression was neutral. Dìolan had the annoying sense that his childhood tutor was testing him.

'Regret?' he replied, hearing the anger in his own voice. 'I regret every day we remain in Dhruim-Ùrlar while the slaves of Chaos rule the uplands. I regret that our entire race is content to cower under the sea. I regret that even High King Volturnos, supposedly the greatest of us, must hunt in the shadows while others rule the realms.' He put his cup down on the table with a clank of coral against stone. 'I have many regrets, Thallacrom. They weigh heavily on me.'

Thallacrom gave a slight nod. 'But you wish we had not removed souls from the chorrileum.'

'The Dromlech enclave have summoned Eidolons before and this has never been required. It is an abomination, Thallacrom, and you know it. We are damning our ancestors.' He shook his head. 'If any of the other priests had suggested this, I would have had them locked away.'

'The idea to free us of the soul curse was yours, your highness. I only pointed out that Gotrek was a way to do it. And there is no other way to perform the ritual. Gotrek's spirit is unlike anything we have hunted before. It is unique. Even I cannot say exactly why, but there is something in him that is not of the Mortal Realms. An echo of the divine. When your sister drew our attention to him–'

'Do not remind me of Eòrna,' muttered Dìolan.

Thallacrom held up his hands. 'She's only a problem because you refuse to deal with her. Labelling her thrallmaster and sending her on errands does not stop her being a threat. The half-souls adore her. They think she is their champion.'

Dìolan shook his head and poured more wine. 'I'm the one who is about to heal their souls and it's my damned sister they flock to.'

'So let me *deal* with her.' Thallacrom's eyes were gleaming. 'Your place on the throne will never be secure while she roams free, poisoning people against you with every word she utters. It is not just the half-souls who adore her – many of your courtiers would prefer to see her on the throne of Dhruim-Ùrlar. And while we work so hard to free the Dromlech, she consorts with that bizarre menagerie in her palace, giving credence to peculiar, alien notions. It is not right for someone in her position. It would be a simple matter for me to-'

'No,' snapped Dìolan. Whenever his advisors spoke to him like this, presuming to tell him how foolish he was for letting his sister live, he felt the same flush of outrage. They were not fit to decide the fate of people like Eòrna. If his sister were on the throne, they would no doubt be insisting she have him killed. 'We need to strike soon,' he said, changing the subject. 'I can't stay in this room forever. It makes me question things I know are right. I believe in this more than you can imagine, Thallacrom. I have seen this coming since I was knee-high. The Mortal Realms cannot be left to the likes of humans and duardin. They have failed. And they will always fail. It was their ancestors who let the realms fall into the hands of the Ruinous Powers. And nothing they have done since has ever changed the situation.

'I hear people talk of Sigmar's Stormcast Eternals, sent from the Celestial Heavens to redeem us all. As if *we* are going to be saved by the bumbling of the lesser races. And look at what a pathetic mess they make. They butcher a few Chaos warlords, throw up an ugly building or two and say they have reclaimed the realms. And then, as soon as the Great Enemy notices them, they're wiped from the map. And so it goes on, over and over. Sigmar sends his clumsy hordes, they make a hash of things and then they're driven out. It's like a terrible joke.'

He rose from his seat and began pacing around the bedchamber. 'While we, the elder race who actually have the skill and wisdom to drive Chaos from the realms, do nothing.' He glanced at a small shrine in the corner of his room. It contained a statue of the aelven god Teclis and he had treasured it since childhood. 'Is it any wonder the Great Illuminator despaired of us? We, who were born to lead, have spent all these long ages hiding in the shadows, obscuring ourselves with mists and deceits.' He jabbed a finger at the window. 'My sister thinks we're destined to be hunters and nothing more, but that's not what Teclis intended. He didn't mean us to pick at carrion, he meant us to rule. To drive out the corruption of Chaos.'

He knew Thallacrom had heard this speech from him many times, but it felt good to say the words. It drove out the doubts that had robbed him of sleep. 'It can be done. And it will be done. But not by those plodding brutes from Azyr, with their clumsy hammers and ramshackle cities. It will be done by us. The true children of Teclis. The firstborn. We are the light bringers. We are the *only* ones who can drive away the darkness.'

He grabbed a history book from his shelves and waved it at Thallacrom, about to continue his impassioned speech, when an agonising cough rattled through his chest. It was so violent and unexpected that he dropped the book and fell against the wall, struggling to breathe. 'Damn it,' he wheezed, seeing crimson spots on the front of his tunic. 'Can none of you priests do anything? Can none of you rid me of this weakness?'

Thallacrom rushed over and tried to take his arm, but Dìolan grabbed him by the shoulders and spoke urgently into his face. 'We have to move soon. We have to begin. I cannot stay here, waiting like this. Waiting to die.

We must take Gotrek's soul and use it. We must begin the ritual. Or I will...'
He shook his head. All his life he had been filled with a furious belief in the
pre-eminence of his people. The politics of court meant nothing to him. But
he knew that the Dromlech were the only ones who could truly save the
Mortal Realms. And now, on the very cusp of beginning his great revolution,
he was powerless to act, hindered by the fragility of his mortal flesh.

Thallacrom studied him. 'There must be another way. A way to accelerate your healing.' He looked out into the darkness, frowning. 'Perhaps
there is something.'

'What?' demanded Dìolan.

'There are more ways than one to heal someone. The tru'heas are skilled,
but their arts are slow to take effect. So perhaps we should try using the
fruit of our labours. Perhaps it is time for you to see what all this sacrifice
has achieved.'

'The Eidolon?' Dìolan shook his head. 'Has it already risen? I thought we
were a long way from that.'

'The Eidolon is little more than a beginning. A fraction of the great storm it
will become. But even now, half-born, it is suffused with power. By sundering souls in the way we have, we are creating something unlike any Eidolon
we have ever summoned before.' He studied his narwhal tusk, as if he were
reading something in the grain. 'I wonder... If we brought you to the Eidolon
now, I could attempt a smaller version of the rite that will rid us of the soul
curse. I could pass some of its power into you.'

'And it would heal me?' Dìolan gripped one of the bedposts, leaning
eagerly towards the old priest.

'It would certainly grant you strength, and perhaps that strength would
act as a cure. And, at the same time, it would allow me to see if our plan is
going to work – if harvesting souls in this way really has made the Eidolon
especially powerful. I have been wondering how to be sure. We need to
gauge its strength. Otherwise, there's no way of knowing if we can really
use Gotrek's soul in the way I claimed. There's no use killing Gotrek if we
are unable to do anything with his spirit afterwards.'

Thallacrom continued talking, explaining how he would use the Eidolon
to extract Gotrek's soul from his body and feed it to the chorrileum, but
Dìolan was not really listening. He was just excited by the idea that he could
finally act, that he could finally do something. 'Take me to it,' he demanded,
managing to stand, despite the pain in his chest.

'Can you walk?'

'Of course,' snapped Dìolan, rising from the bed and grabbing some
clothes. 'I was sleepy, that was all.' As he said the words, he realised it was
true. Now that he was properly awake he found his strength returning. He
stifled a cough, threw a cloak around himself and headed for the door,
snatching a sword as he went. 'Quickly. I cannot wait any longer. Heal me
tonight and tomorrow we will begin. Karag-Varr must fall.'

CHAPTER TWENTY-SEVEN

The streets of Dhruim-Ùrlar flowed and danced, moving around Dìolan as he rode through the half-light. His steed was white, a regal-looking deepmare he had ridden into battle many times. The reptilian creature seemed to sense his every wish, responding to such slight movements that he felt as though it were an extension of his body, gliding effortlessly past the spired temples and sprawling manses that bordered his estates.

At this hour, most of the Dromlech were asleep, or at least indoors, and the streets were empty and quiet. Thallacrom was riding at his side and there was a small group of guards following in their wake on fangmora eels. No army had ever invaded Dhruim-Ùrlar, or, for that matter, even learned of its existence, but there were still dangers to be found. Occasionally, schools of barb-sharks emerged from the kelp forests, hungry and venomous. On rare occasions, medusa squid had even been known to loom over the city, colossal, ink-dark leviathans that could tear down buildings and devour hundreds of aelves before being driven back onto the abyssal plain. Besides which, an Idoneth regent could never be complacent when crossing his kingdom. The crown of Dhruim-Ùrlar was won rather than inherited, and there was always someone eager to vie for such a valuable prize.

'How far?' asked Dìolan. Since leaving the Allmarach he had been feeling awful. He was sitting erect in his saddle, refusing to display weakness, but he was not sure how long he could maintain the act.

'Only an hour's ride, highness,' replied Thallacrom. The priest was hunching forwards in his saddle, gripping his stave, robes billowing around him as they glided through clouds of silt. 'The Eidolon is being born very close to the chorrileum.'

Kelp fronds brushed against Dìolan's armour as they left the city's main streets, riding into a winding maze of dappled leaves and darting fish. A stranger to the city would quickly have become lost. The paths through the kelp forest were in constant motion, seemingly impossible to follow, but each had a name and a personality that was known to the deepmares. However much the routes shifted and writhed, the creatures could follow, swimming confidently round convoluted bends and through dark, lonely glades.

After what seemed to Dìolan a very long time, lights began glimmering up ahead, blinking through the boughs like stars that had fallen to the sea floor. Dìolan felt a rush of emotion. The light came from the chorrileum: the resting place of fallen Dromlech aelves, a sacred haven where souls were warded from the predations of Chaos. Since times forgotten, the Dromlech had trusted their spirits to these lights, confident they were safe. And now, at Dìolan's command, souls were being cut away, used like kindling on a fire. The emotion Dìolan felt was not guilt, or doubt, but a burning determination. This great sacrifice, ordered by him, had to be made worthwhile. Such an appalling act of brutality could only be forgivable if it achieved the great transformation he had always dreamed of – the ascension of the Dromlech and the end of the Idoneth curse. No more would they battle to keep their half-souls alive with life force stolen from lesser beings. Soon, they would live free.

His pulse quickened as he pictured a mighty host of Idoneth, led by Dromlech nobles as they crossed the uplands in broad daylight, making no attempt at subterfuge as they scoured Chaos from the realms, showing Teclis once and for all that in the Idoneth he had achieved perfection. Dìolan knew what his fellow Akhelian nobles thought of him. They assumed he wanted power for power's sake, as all his predecessors had done. But they were wrong. Dìolan no longer cared for the throne or all the other badges of office. None of this was for personal gain or glory. He did not even care if his name was recorded as the architect of this great plan. He just cared that there was now hope for the forces of Order and sanity, a chance to drive back the madness of the Chaos Gods. The Dromlech were the realms' last chance. And he had sworn to unshackle them.

They reached a high path, looking down over the hollow that contained the chorrileum. Dìolan paused to survey the glorious sight. It looked like a coral reef, several miles wide, translucent and pale and lit from within by cool, pulsing light. There was no sign of the stolen souls. Thallacrom's adepts had been careful not to damage any of the places that were visible to passers-by

'Not far now,' said Thallacrom, steering his deepmare away from the chorrileum and heading back into the kelp groves. They had not ridden far when another light flashed through the gloom, slicing through the fronds that lined the path.

Dìolan urged his steed forwards, his strength waning. He prayed, silently, to Teclis, that this healing would work. He barely had enough strength left to stay in his saddle, never mind lead an attack on Karag-Varr.

They reached the slopes above another sunken clearing. This hollow was smaller than the chorrileum but still hundreds of feet wide. It was a tiered amphitheatre with arches of coral woven around it, forming a vast, cage-like dome of yellow polyps that were all entwined, like thousands of interlocking fingers. Every finger of coral radiated light, and the space beneath the amphitheatre was even brighter than the chorrileum. There were warriors of the Akhelian Guard dotted around the perimeter, standing proudly to attention and facing out at the surrounding kelp forest. The nearest one saluted as Dìolan and the others glided down a colonnaded slope that led into the amphitheatre. At the centre of the space, drifting above a dais, was a shell,

similar in shape to a conch but the size of a small house. It was made of
the same colourful, translucent material as the surrounding coral and there
was a light at its heart, flashing with an arterial pulse.

Dìolan dismounted and walked up some steps onto the circular dais,
Thallacrom following a few paces behind.

'Is that him?' he said, looking up at the imposing shape, feeling the need
to speak in hushed tones, as if he had entered a shrine. At the centre of the
shell, silhouetted by its light, there was a figure. It was no larger than a child
and hard to see in detail, but Dìolan thought he could discern glimpses of
scalloped armour and flowing hair. It was standing still, head bowed, hands
clasped in front of its chest, as though in prayer.

Thallacrom rarely displayed emotions but his voice was rigid with pride.
'He is like no Eidolon we have summoned before. Like nothing we have
even dreamt of.'

Dìolan circled the shell, looking at the figure inside. He had seen Eidolons before, in the heat of battle, but never had a chance to study one so
closely. He could feel waves of energy buffeting him as he stepped closer.
'What do I do?' he asked, bathing himself in the sacred light.

'The Eidolon's cocoon is charged with etheric power,' said Thallacrom in
hushed tones. 'It is the spiritual force of every soul we have severed. Under
normal circumstances, some power would pass from the souls in the chorrileum to the Eidolon. But with this ritual, we have freed all the power of
the souls. They are unshackled. Their purpose is to give birth to the Eidolon
but, at the moment, I can see no harm in you tapping into it.'

'Tapping into it?' Dìolan hesitated, glancing back at the ancient priest.
'The severed souls will pass into me, rather than the Eidolon?'

'No. Not exactly. A part of their essence will pass *through* you, as lightning passes through the boughs of a tree.'

Dìolan frowned. 'When lightning strikes a tree, things rarely end well
for the tree.'

'Do you trust me?'

'Of course.' It was true. Dìolan had never doubted Thallacrom. In truth,
after the defeat at Karag-Varr, the priest could not have been blamed if
he had sided with Eòrna. Dìolan had been so weak from his injuries it
had seemed like he might die. And if Thallacrom had turned against him,
the other Isharann priests would have followed suit. But Thallacrom had
stayed loyal.

'It's a simple rite,' said Thallacrom, taking a string of shells from his belt.
They were inscribed with tiny runes and clicked musically against each
other as he shuffled them along the thread, looking for something specific. He stepped closer, peering at the tiny shell held between his bony
fingers, light washing over the intricate tattoos that covered his face. The
light made him look even more skeletal, highlighting the angular bones
and sunken eye sockets. 'You must simply hold your hand against the surface of the cocoon,' he said, still squinting at the runes scored into the shell.
'I will recite a short incantation. You must keep your hand in place until I
say you can remove it.'

'And will that be difficult? Holding my hand in place, I mean.' Dìolan was not afraid, he simply wanted to be prepared.

Thallacrom licked his lips, revealing a flash of blue teeth. 'There will be no physical pain. But when your mind comes into contact with the souls we have removed from the chorrileum, you may feel an urge to withdraw from them. You must resist the urge. If you break contact before I complete the rite...'

'What?'

'If I do not complete the incantation, there may be unexpected results. I cannot say what, exactly, but the rite would fail and there would be no healing.'

'Has anyone tried this before?'

There was a slight pause before Thallacrom replied. 'Not that I know of.'

Dìolan nodded, looking back up at the cocoon and the figure standing inside it. 'Tell me when.'

Thallacrom held the tiny shell to his eye. 'When I begin speaking, press your hand to the cocoon. It should not take more than a minute or so.' He paused to clear his throat, then proceeded, speaking in the ancient language of the Isharann priesthood.

Dìolan immediately pressed his hand against the cocoon – or, at least, he tried to. His palm passed straight through the surface and he realised it was not solid. It felt more like thick smoke. He glanced at Thallacrom to see if he was doing the right thing, but the priest was too engrossed to notice, so Dìolan held his hand where it was, feeling the strange, viscous light moving across his skin. The sensation was odd, but not unpleasant, and Dìolan could not see why it should be hard for him to keep his hand in place. Thallacrom's words droned on and, after just a few moments, Dìolan felt a pleasing warmth passing through his hand and through his veins, pouring into his body and making his head feel light. It was similar to the sensation one felt after drinking wine but it quickly grew in force. Dìolan did not feel any pain or doubt. There was something very natural about the sensation, even though he had never experienced it before. It felt so normal that it took him a moment to realise that his feet were hovering a few inches from the ground.

What have you done?

At first, Dìolan thought Thallacrom had spoken, but then he realised the priest was still absorbed in his incantation. The voice had come from somewhere else.

What have you done to us? The voice was hoarse with grief and terror, and Dìolan realised it was coming from in front of him, inside the cocoon.

He has cut us! cried another voice, female and bordering on a scream.

He has betrayed us! howled another.

The voices were passing into Dìolan with the waves of light that had seemed so pleasing only a moment earlier. One voice summoned another, and then another, until there was a whole chorus of tormented voices crying out, denouncing Dìolan as a traitor. There was such pain in their words that he wanted to clamp his hands over his ears. But he knew that would not help. The words were in his head. He could only silence them by with-drawing his hand. And, although the voices tortured him, he could feel that Thallacrom's rite was working: his body was filling with a strength and vigour that surpassed anything he had felt before. He felt invincible, as though he could tear down a palace wall.

We are not safe! screeched a voice even louder than the others. *You have damned us! Murderer! The Dark Prince will take us! Fix what you have broken!*

Yes! replied a clamour of panicked voices. *Quickly! Return what you have taken! It is not too late! You can save us! Dìolan! Return our souls to the chor-rileum! It is not too late!*

It was agonising to hear their cries. As the screams grew louder and more desperate, Dìolan's resolve started to falter. He could remove his hand and grab Thallacrom. He could order him to abandon the idea of summoning the Eidolon. It *wasn't* too late.

The light pulsed brighter and he felt a hand lock around his, holding it firmly in place. Dìolan tried to pull away, assuming that one of his accus-ers had managed to take hold of him, given purchase in the physical realm by their hatred. But as he stared into the light, he realised his mistake. The person gripping his arm was not one of his ancestors. It had the face of a god. A magnificence that no mortal being could hope to match. The Eido-lon's eyes burned into him, fierce and tempestuous, and the waves of energy flooding through Dìolan suddenly became too powerful to endure.

Dìolan howled, trying to snatch back his hand, but rather than letting go the Eidolon gripped harder and opened its mouth to speak. No words emerged, but the roar of a storm jolted through Dìolan, causing him to shake and clamp his eyes shut. The sound swelled, growing so loud he thought his skull would crack. And then it was over. The Eidolon loosened its grip, the sounds ceased, and Dìolan tumbled backwards from the cocoon, kick-ing up a cloud of silt as he landed heavily on the ground.

Thallacrom hobbled over as fast as he could, gripping his staff as he knelt down beside Dìolan, looking troubled. 'I had not finished,' he said. 'You should not have let go.'

'I was thrown back,' said Dìolan, his voice cracking. 'I did not let go.'

'Thrown?'

'The Eidolon.' Dìolan stood, then smiled as he realised he was full of strength. He backed away from Thallacrom and drew his sword, trying a few lunges and finding that his weakness was gone, replaced by such fierce vitality that he laughed out loud. 'You did it,' he cried, pacing around the clearing, swiping and slashing. He leapt onto a rock and stretched his limbs, arching his back as though emerging from a long sleep. 'It worked.'

The priest was still watching him with the same troubled expression. Then he looked back up at the cocoon. The light had faded a little but the silhou-ette of the Eidolon was still visible. It was watching Dìolan. 'The rite was not complete,' he said, speaking quietly. 'I did not sever the link between you and the Eidolon.'

'What does it matter? I am healed. More than healed. I haven't felt this strong for years.' Dìolan dropped down from the rock and grabbed Thallacrom by the shoulder. 'Be pleased. It worked.'

Thallacrom shook his head. 'I have no idea what this means.'

Dìolan laughed. 'It means we are ready for war. It means I can crush those savages in Karag-Varr and we can drag Gotrek Gurnisson back here.' He waved his sword at the cocoon. 'So that the Idoneth can be born again. Born as we should have been.'

Thallacrom shrugged and seemed mollified. He peered at Dìolan. 'I suppose, if there were any ill effects, you would not seem so hale.'

'Exactly!' Dìolan was about to say more, when he noticed how faint Thallacrom seemed. The darkness behind the old priest deepened and erupted into motion, making Thallacrom look oddly insubstantial, as though he were not truly there. It took Dìolan a moment to realise that he was looking at the surface of the sea. It was impossible, of course, all these fathoms down, but he could see waves, breaking and crashing against the hull of a ship. The ship was of a peculiar design that he did not recognise. It bore symbols of the Sigmarite faith, but it was not like any ship he had seen before. As he looked at the ship, he felt an inexplicable surge of rage. The waves swelled, seeming to grow in response to his anger, lashing against the ship.

'What is it?' asked Thallacrom. As soon as the priest spoke, he regained his solidity and the scene behind him vanished, revealing the dome of coral and the drifting fronds of the kelp forest beyond. 'What are you looking at?'

The doubt was back in Thallacrom's eyes and Dìolan could imagine what the priest would say if he learned Dìolan was hallucinating. The attack on Karag-Varr would be delayed again. 'Nothing,' he said. He massaged his face, rubbing his palms into his eye sockets. 'I'm just dazed from being so close to the Eidolon.' He smiled again and left the dais, climbing back up onto his deepmare. 'Thallacrom. We have waited long enough. Let us begin.'

CHAPTER TWENTY-EIGHT

Gotrek patted the orruk chieftain on the head, causing its bestial features to quiver. 'I knew we'd see eye to eye eventually,' he said. The orruk did not reply.

Gotrek's words were met with a roar of approval. Cheers and laughter reverberated around the cavernous feast hall of Karag-Varr. Gotrek had insisted on bringing the orruk's head to the victory feast and he had propped it up on top of a serving bowl so that its sagging, blood-spattered face was level with his. The Slayer bared his teeth in a lopsided grin that Maleneth was horribly familiar with. It was the smile that meant he had finally consumed enough ale to become drunk.

After the battle at Karag-Wyr, the Fyreslayers had marched on the other two keeps they had lost. Karag-Agril and Karag-Duril had both proved less of a challenge, however. Rather than cultists and sorcery, the Fyreslayers had found greenskin tribes, and the subsequent battles had seemed more like a glorious celebration than war. The greenskins had numbered in the thousands but that had not mattered. The Fyreslayers delighted in their favourite pastime: killing orruks. And, after adopting Gotrek as a revered prophet, the Varrukh revelled in every one of his facile pronouncements.

The illness that had plagued Thurgyn fell away as he fought at Gotrek's side, and despite Gotrek's oft-stated hatred of Fyreslayers, it seemed to Maleneth that he had finally found a people who were just like him. Their delight in combat and carnage was identical and, as the battles raged on, Maleneth had found it harder to distinguish Gotrek from Korgan, Skromm or any of the other duardin. The fighting had been messy and undignified. After the first few encounters she had withdrawn, unable to revel in the kills – such a crude, leering fight was beneath the Lord of Murder and she watched the final parts of the battle from a distance, muttering curses as the Fyreslayers rallied around Gotrek, following his every move and attempting to imitate his archaic manner of speech.

What am I doing here? she thought, as drunks milled around her, belching and roaring drinking songs or spewing smoke from tobacco pipes. The feast had been going on for so many hours Maleneth felt like she had never been anywhere else, other than this reeking, noisy hall. Platters of meat, bread and cheese were carried constantly to the table but, by this point, the Fyreslayers were so drunk that the food was being used mostly as ammunition, hurled through the air as the duardin re-enacted key moments of the battles with legs of meat or teetering, beer-drenched pies. Skromm was sitting to her left but he had not moved for the last hour. He had slumped forwards and his face was lying in his plate of food. Only the occasional snort gave any indication that he had not drowned in meat broth.

Gotrek had been seated in a place of honour, at Thurgyn's side. The two had been inseparable since the runesons' funeral. The runefather had shrugged off his illness and grief, and clearly held Gotrek responsible. Gotrek, meanwhile, had been so impressed by Thurgyn's rune-fuelled violence that he had adopted the runefather as a worthy battle-brother. In the fights with the greenskins, they had fought side by side, Thurgyn's runes blazing as he matched Gotrek blow for blow, his strength growing with every fight. Now Thurgyn had his arm slung over Gotrek's massive shoulders and they were plotting like old friends, jabbing at a beer-sodden map of the Spiral Crux. They had spent the last hour discussing an ancient duardin kingdom called the Khazalid Empire. One of the Fyreslayer bards had mentioned it in a booming, interminable ballad and Gotrek had demanded to hear more. When Thurgyn revealed that the ruined capital, Karaz-a-Zaruk, lay to the north of Karag-Varr, Gotrek looked like a miser who had discovered a lost coin. Maleneth forced herself to try and follow the tedious conversation. The Khazalid Empire was one of Gotrek's obsessions and she had a suspicion she would be hearing more about Karaz-a-Zaruk. The ancient, abandoned capital of a duardin empire was exactly the kind of thing to entice him into another fool's errand. For a while, the two old warriors were engrossed in the map, but as they grew drunker, it went forgotten, buried under plates of food as their conversation devolved into bawdy jokes and slurred singing.

'Entering the keep through the sewers was a genius idea!' laughed Thurgyn, slapping Gotrek on the back. 'I'll never forget the look on their faces when we charged from those drains.'

'Aye,' slurred Gotrek. 'It reminded me of the time I worked as a sewerjack under Nuln, hunting ratmen with Felix.' He laughed incredulously. 'Turned out they were in cahoots with the bloody secret police.'

Maleneth was sure that no one in the hall had the faintest idea what Gotrek was talking about, but they all paused to listen as he began relaying another one of his rambling, fantastical anecdotes, punctuating the story with wild lunges of his axe and rattling burps. Maleneth had heard the tale countless times and knew how Gotrek would spit and curse when he came to the part concerning a skaven called Thanquol.

The sounds of merriment died away as the Varrukh listened to Gotrek, staring in wonder as he warmed to his theme, climbing up onto the table and trampling through their feast as he acted out his story. As Maleneth studied their rapt faces, she felt the same chill she had felt in Karag-Wyr. The same crushing sense of being dragged in Gotrek's wake. *I will not become like them,* she thought. *I will not worship him. I will not be subsumed by him. I'm not going to become a footnote in his story.*

What choice do you have? Her former mistress was clearly amused by Maleneth's predicament. ***You murdered a damned witch hunter. The order***

will already know about it. They'll be devising especially creative ways to execute you. The Slayer is your only chance of staying alive. If you're not Gotrek's footnote, you're just another dead aelf.

There was a cheer as Gotrek illustrated part of his story by kicking the orruk chieftain's head down the length of the table.

No, thought Maleneth. *That's not true. I still have options. How would the order know it was me who killed Drymuss? He was travelling alone through the Spiral Crux. Chamon is as dangerous as any other realm. There's nothing to say I'm the one who killed him.*

Apart from the fact that he came looking for you, a renowned poisoner, and was then poisoned.

He was killed by a tincture he was carrying on his person. Any band of wandering brigands could have done that to him.

The order aren't stupid. Of course they'll know it was you. Besides, even if they didn't, it makes no difference. If you leave the Slayer, you leave the rune. And if you abandon the rune, you're dead anyway. Do you think the order will tolerate failure? Do you think they will be sympathetic to your change of heart? Your commission was to get Blackhammer's Master Rune to Azyr. Or failing that, get Gotrek to Azyr. Fail to do one of those things and they will want you dead.

Khaine will preserve me. Think of the kills I have made in his name. Think of the tributes I have offered him. I do not need to stay with this drunken boor, acting like another doe-eyed lackey, pretending to be like his beloved Felix.

He's important, you said. He's the one who can make a difference. Her mistress sounded as scornful as ever, but Maleneth sensed that she, too, was unsure of the right path.

He is important, she thought. *But look at him. He has this entire Fyreslayer lodge in the palm of his hand. They've known him a matter of days and they'd fight to the death for him. If Gotrek really is destined to achieve some great victory against Chaos, he doesn't need my help to get there.*

Then what will you do? You can't return to Azyr without that rune. That was your only chance. Your crimes will not have been forgotten.

'I will pray to Khaine,' she whispered, suddenly full of conviction. She gripped the knives at her belt, realising that everything was far simpler than she had imagined. The Slayer was such a garish distraction that he had blinded her to the obvious truth. *I will pray with steel and blood, just as I've always done. And I will lead my own life.*

She paused, waiting to hear her mistress' reply, but none came. She stood and pushed her huge, heavy chair back from the table.

Gotrek was still staggering through the plates of food, relaying his ridiculous story of rat-filled sewers and a treacherous human called von Haldstadt. 'The manling,' he said, over and over, ending almost every sentence with a mention of the human who had accompanied him before Maleneth. The human who died because of his devotion to Gotrek.

'No,' whispered Maleneth, growing angrier and more determined by the moment. She left the table and shoved her way through the crush of drunk, stumbling Fyreslayers.

The entire Varrukh lodge seemed to have crowded into the hall and it took her several unpleasant minutes to shove her way through the singing, beer-slick mob until she could reach the anvil-shaped doors. She paused at the threshold and looked back. To her surprise, Gotrek paused his anecdote and stumbled to a halt, looking directly at her through the fug of pipe smoke. His expression darkened. For a moment she thought he had guessed her intentions and was about to call out to her. But then he let out a deep, rattling belch and resumed staggering around the table, continuing his ratmen story.

She watched him for a moment then shook her head in despair and headed through the door. It led out into a series of vast, pillared corridors, cut deep in the walls of the volcano and veined with so much magma that her skin burned as she strode through the darkness, crossing hallways and sprinting up long, winding stairs. Gotrek's infuriating, boastful tale was echoing round her head as she climbed up through the gloom.

The keep looked like it was abandoned, with only the distant, echoing cheers from the feast revealing the truth. It felt odd to pass through such grand halls with no sign of guards or servants. Maleneth paused to look at a shrine to Grimnir, built around a colossal, golden statue of the Slayer God. It looked like a shrine to Gotrek. In fact, the whole place could have been a shrine to Gotrek.

Maleneth spat a curse and hurried on, heading up a final flight of steps and emerging from the tunnels into the slightly less oppressive atmosphere of the square. It was evening. She guessed there would probably be stars somewhere overhead but a shroud of smoke made it impossible to know either way. There were a few sentries up on the walls, looking sullen and aggrieved, no doubt because they were missing out on the celebrations below, but otherwise Maleneth was alone. She considered calling out and asking someone to let her out of the magmahold, but she held her tongue. She did not like the idea of asking for permission to leave, and the guards might well refuse in any case. The Fyreslayers had treated her with suspicion since she had arrived and rarely did anything she asked unless Gotrek was there to glare at them. Besides, she was an assassin. A lethal daughter of the Murder Temples. She did not need anyone's permission to leave a place.

Maleneth kept to the shadows around the edge of the square as she headed towards the entrance gates through which she and Gotrek had originally entered the keep. When she desired, she could move with a silence that heavy-footed Fyreslayers could barely comprehend. She padded through the gloom, pulling her hood down low as she reached a doorway just off to the side of the gates. She had spent several days in the magmahold, bored, when the Fyreslayers were performing funerary rites for their fallen runesons, and she had used the time wisely, leaving Skromm behind whenever she could to explore the fortress and learn some of its secrets. She slipped through the small, easy-to-miss doorway and ran silently up a spiral staircase that led to the walls above the gate. When she reached the top she hesitated, peering out onto the battlements. The nearest sentry was a hundred paces from her and looking in the opposite direction, leaning heavily on a magmapike.

Are you sure? Her mistress did not even attempt to sound sardonic this time. *If Gotrek is significant, shouldn't we stay with him?*

No, admitted Maleneth, *I'm not sure.* But now that she had acted she was determined to keep going. Determined to break free. She had a dreadful feeling that it was now or never. *I will not become his prop. I will not become a name in his drunken anecdotes. I have a fate of my own.* She slipped from the shadows and crossed the wall, reaching the opposite side of the battlements. As she looked out over the edge, she was dazzled by the light of the lava-filled caldera. She was at the top of one of the fortress' enormous shoulders, clinging to a piece of Grimnir's ornate, mountain-sized armour. Her eyes streamed as she looked down to the bridge that spanned the lava. She was looking for a piece of guttering that she had identified when she was exploring the fortress. It was only a slender tube of metal, not strong enough to hold the weight of a duardin or a full-grown man, but she was light enough to crawl down on it and make a leap to a ledge further below. From there she would be able to drop down onto the bridge. The only problem was, she could not seem to find the piece of guttering. 'Where is it?' she muttered, wiping away more tears and squinting into the glare.

The harder she looked, the more blurred her vision became. She could not explain it. Then, as she rubbed furiously at her eyes, she noticed something else: the heat was dropping. At first, she thought it was just the breeze, snatching away some of the volcanic heat, but then she realised there was also an odd smell – a damp, briny stink that was horribly familiar.

'Idoneth,' whispered Maleneth, backing away from the edge. She still had no clear memory of the last attack on Karag-Varr, but she knew it had been preceded by this smell. And this mist. Sure enough, as she backed away from the battlements, she saw tendrils of fog snaking over the metalwork, stretching towards her and pooling at her feet.

She clawed at her memory, trying to remember any details of what had happened before, but there was nothing – just Gotrek's vague talk of sea monsters and snake-riding archers. 'Blood of Khaine,' she whispered, remembering that most of the Varrukh lodge were currently inebriated, down in their feast hall. 'This is going to be a massacre. Even Gotrek's drunk. I need to warn them. They need to lock the gates to the keep.'

I thought you were abandoning Gotrek to his fate? I thought you were done with him?

Maleneth laughed bitterly and waved at the fog pouring over the walls. 'What would you have me do? Rush out there and take on the Idoneth all by myself? I'm skilled but I'm not fighting an entire army.' She rushed along the wall, looking for one of the sentries as the mist overtook her, covering the battlements and streaming down into the square.

'You!' she cried, as a figure loomed out of the mist up ahead. 'Sound the alarm!' It was only as she came closer that she realised the dark shape could not be one of the Varrukh. It was drifting in the air, at about head height, coiling and uncoiling like a snake. She snatched her knives from her belt, approaching cautiously. The mist parted to reveal a long, slender shark, its brutal, arrow-shaped head covered in old scars. The creature was seven feet long and it rolled in the air as it saw her, fixing her with glossy black eyes. There was crimson mist around its mouth and one of the Varrukh sentries was lying on the ground beneath it, grasping feebly at a ragged mess that used to be his throat.

The shark studied Maleneth with cool indifference, then darted forwards, slicing through the blood.

Maleneth tried to sidestep the shark but the mist clung to her limbs, weighing her down as if she were moving through water. The shark hit her like a toppling wall. She staggered back, turning side-on and trying to raise her knives as pain exploded across her shoulder. Another cloud of red filled the air as the shark rolled and savaged her arm.

She gasped, hammering a knife into the shark's eye. The shark bucked and rolled away, but she did not give it time to recover. She lunged after it, forcing her body through the heavy air, taking a stiletto from her belt and jamming it into the shark's other eye. The poisoned blade took immediate effect and the shark's face shrivelled and blackened, as though held against flames. The creature looped and then bolted away from her, vanishing into the blood-tinged mist.

Maleneth dropped down next to the wounded Fyreslayer and grabbed him by the shoulders, yelling into his slack-jawed face. 'I need to sound the alarm! How do I alert everyone?'

The sentry lolled weakly in her grip, his face horribly pale as blood billowed around him. 'The war-horn,' he managed to groan. 'Further down the wall.'

She dropped him to the flagstones and ran on through the mist, heading in the direction he had suggested. She had a peculiar sensation of déjà vu as she struggled to run. There was something dreamlike about fighting through such sluggish air. As she fought her way down the wall, her honed senses warned her that she was being followed. There were several shadows in the mist, keeping pace with her, and they were up high in the air, gliding silently in packs. 'More sharks,' she spat, infuriated by the absurdity of the situation. As the sharks swam closer, she began to make out their sleek silhouettes in more detail. They were at least as large as the one she had just blinded, perhaps larger, and she could already make out six heading towards her.

She halted, seeing a shape up ahead on the wall, then realised it was a group of Fyreslayer sentries. They were huddling together, back to back with their magmapikes raised. They tensed as they saw her approaching, then relaxed as they recognised her.

'This is no ordinary storm,' said the karl in charge as she reached them. 'This is aelf magic.'

'I know,' snorted Maleneth. 'I'm the one who explained that to your elders. We have to warn everyone. They're all drunk. They need to bar the doors to your buildings and stay down in the holds.'

The karl was about to reply when a silver-flighted arrow cut through the mist, landing neatly between his eyes. He fell in silence, his magmapike clattering to the ground.

The Fyreslayers howled battle cries as aelven archers sprinted towards them. Arrows filled the air and the Varrukh fired their pikes, spewing lava at their foes. Some of the archers fell from their saddles, torn apart by the magma, but more were riding into view, loosing arrows with a speed that even Maleneth found impressive. She left the sentries and ran on along the wall. The din of fighting grew louder as more of the Varrukh rushed to join their comrades, spitting molten death at their fleet, shimmering attackers.

There it is, said Maleneth's dead mistress as a sentry tower loomed up ahead with a curved battle horn fixed to its roof.

Maleneth had already seen the spur of metal and ran along the wall towards it. There was another mauled Fyreslayer corpse by the door. The body was floating, drifting a few feet up from the floor, turning slowly in a cloud of blood. Maleneth leapt over it and ran through an open doorway into the tower. It consisted of a single, empty chamber and a spiral staircase that led up to the roof. As she ran into the room, Maleneth came face to face with the dead guard's killer. It was an aelf with bone-white skin. The warrior's top half was naked but his legs were encased in scalloped, shimmering armour. He was gripping a two-handed sword, curved and serrated like a shark's tooth. The aelf had smooth hollows where his eyes should have been, but his blindness did not hinder him. He swiped at Maleneth with the sword, aiming for her throat.

She parried with her knives, but the effort sent another stab of pain through her shoulder and she staggered back out onto the wall.

The aelf followed her into the mist, thrusting his blade at her stomach.

Maleneth arched her back and the sword sliced through empty air. Then she turned on her heel and brought her knives down towards the aelf's extended arm. The air robbed her of speed. The warrior dodged her attack, pirouetting and landing in a crouch facing her, looking infuriatingly confident.

Maleneth backed away and swapped one of her knives for a smaller blade clasped at her belt. The aelf watched her with calm disinterest as he stood erect and prepared to swing his sword, the blade of which was as long as Maleneth was tall. She hurled the knife at his face.

The aelf sneered, swinging his sword and easily knocking the blade away. Rather than clattering to the floor, Maleneth's knife exploded. The blade was made of glass and the air rippled as it broke, releasing the toxins that had been trapped inside.

The aelf did not register the gas until he strode towards Maleneth, passing straight through it. Then he stumbled, a shocked expression on his face as his skin began to melt. He reached out for Maleneth but his legs collapsed beneath him, the bones bubbling beneath melting muscles.

Maleneth did not pause to watch him die. There was a time to savour her offerings to Khaine, but this was not it. She ran past the dissolving aelf, back into the tower and up the steps. She stepped out onto the roof with care, crouching low and looking around for Idoneth. There was no one there. The true attack had yet to begin. Her opponent must have been a scout. She could see the Varrukh sentries down on the wall, still firing magma into the mist. They were making a good show of it. Another one of them had fallen but they were surrounded by the charred remains of aelves and sea creatures. There were more Idoneth gliding over the battlements, arriving in larger numbers and riding the mist like surf, but they were all fixated on the group of duardin. No one was looking her way.

She rushed over to the brass horn. The thing was the size of a small building, covered in loops and curves and scored with intricate runes. There was almost certainly a correct way to play it but Maleneth simply found the mouthpiece and blew as hard as she could. The sound it emitted was disappointing. The fog muffled the note so that it sounded like a distant echo. It was so faint that Maleneth was sure it would not have travelled more than a few feet. She tried again, blowing hard enough to make her head spin, but it made no difference – all that emerged was a muted drone.

Maleneth cursed, slapping her palm against the mass of metal tubing. She thought again of the drunken mob in the feast hall. 'This is a disaster. They'll be butchered and they'll be too drunk to even notice.' She imagined the Slayer's disdain if he could see her struggling to use the horn. *Feeble bloody aelf,* he'd say, before shoving her aside and showing her how to use the thing properly. Anger rushed through her, tearing from her throat as an outraged howl. The howl reverberated through the horn and produced a long, proud note. Maleneth laughed and backed away, staring at the convoluted instrument in disbelief. 'How typical of Fyreslayers, making an instrument you have to yell at.'

She looked down into the mist that was filling the square. *But they're all drunk,* she thought. *And they're singing. Will they have heard that?*

Another droning sound cut through the fog. At first, Maleneth thought it might be the call of a leviathan, summoned by the Idoneth. But then an identical note pealed out from another direction and she realised it was another war-horn, answering hers. Sentries all around the walls of the magmahold were signalling the alarm. Unlike Maleneth, they held their notes, creating a proud, thundering chorus.

That should be loud enough even for Gotrek's thick skull.

'Perhaps,' muttered Maleneth. 'But I'd better make sure.' She ran back out of the tower, headed away from the embattled sentries and ran in the opposite direction along the wall, heading for a ladder that led back down into the square. As she descended, she sensed movement all around her as shapes knifed through the mist. She paused and looked around. The magmahold looked like a sinking ship, with ocean waves pouring over its gunwales. The mist crashed down over metal and stone, filling the air with spray and spume. But it was not the scale of the storm that surprised Maleneth, it was the size of the army that was riding it. Along with a myriad of sea creatures there was a host of aelves. Most were riding armoured, oversized eels, but others sat atop larger monsters. She saw turtles the size of siege engines, with harpoons and howdahs fixed to their backs. And there were sharks too, with whorls of armour fixed to their flanks and crowds of warriors riding them. In the distance was a much larger shape that she could not make out yet. 'So many,' she breathed as the vanguard flooded into the square.

This isn't an army, said her mistress. *It's a nation.*

Maleneth had to agree. She had accompanied Gotrek through countless warzones as they had crossed the Mortal Realms, but she could not recall seeing an invasion on this scale. She climbed quickly down the rest of the ladder and leapt the last dozen feet, rolling as she landed on the flagstones and running back towards the doors she had emerged from when she was planning on fleeing the magmahold.

The horns rose in pitch and more sentries emerged from guardhouses, hurling axes and firing magma. She ran past them towards the gates that led down into the lower levels of the keep. To her relief, she saw that a group of guards had already begun heaving them shut. The cloying air was slowing them down, but they were gradually swinging the slabs of metal towards each other. She rushed to help, slapping her hands against the doors and throwing her weight against them. Some of the Fyreslayers gave her suspicious looks but none of them refused her aid, and with a rumble of cogs and hinges, the doors began to close.

Don't get yourself trapped out here! Make sure you're on the other side when these doors shut.

Maleneth nodded. The Fyreslayers, to their credit, were clearly not concerned with their own safety. They were going to trap themselves outside to preserve the sanctity of the magmahold. Maleneth had no such intention. She had not come all this way to die for a Fyreslayer castle, however grand it was. The doors were only a few feet from slamming shut and she readied herself to slip through the gap.

'Let the Slayer at 'em!' slurred a familiar voice as the doors suddenly jolted back towards her, pushed from the other side.

CHAPTER TWENTY-NINE

Maleneth and the Fyreslayers were hurled back into the square as the doors flew open, and a crowd rushed out into the mist. Gotrek weaved into view, swinging his axe wildly, his face flushed with drink and his eye rolling. Korgan was at his side, along with Skromm and a mob of howling, red-faced Fyreslayers. Behind them, rushing up from the depths of the magmahold, came hundreds more of the Varrukh, all baying for blood as they followed Gotrek out into the square. They were all hopelessly drunk, bumping into each other and blinking as they struggled to focus. Behind them, she could see the runefather and his pike-wielding honour guard, jeering and bellowing and tripping over each other as they raced down a hallway.

'Khaine preserve us,' whispered Maleneth as the Fyreslayers spilled into the square. The crowds from the feast hall had been joined by the rest of the Varrukh. The whole lodge was abandoning the safety of their vaults, rushing from the tunnels with a roar of oaths and battle cries.

The horns rose to an even higher pitch as the musicians saw the rabble stumbling out to meet the aelven host. Maleneth had to roll clear to avoid being trampled as the Fyreslayers ran past her. The stink of alcohol was even stronger than the smell of the sea.

'Gotrek!' she howled, jumping to her feet and running over to him.

He had paused to survey the approaching host and turned to face her. It took him a moment to bring her into focus, but when he realised who she was, he grinned. 'The aelf!' He threw his arms around her and crushed her in a fierce, breath-stealing embrace. 'I take back everything I just said about you.' He let go of her, gripped his axe and pointed it at the lines of aelves hurtling towards him. 'For Karaz-a-Karak!' he howled.

Behind him, hundreds of ragged voices echoed his cry. 'Karaz-a-Karak!' they roared, creating such a din that the very air seemed to shake. Maleneth stared at the Fyreslayers in amazement. They were rallying behind the Slayer like he was their runefather, calling out words they did not understand, and they were preparing to fight an army while so drunk they could barely stand. Never, in all her years of travelling with Gotrek, had she been so sure that she was in the wrong place, with people she could never understand.

'Khazuk!' grinned Gotrek, sprinting forwards into the lines of approaching aelves.

'Khazuk-ha!' roared the Fyreslayers, thundering after him.

Maleneth was jostled and shoved and carried forwards by the mob. All around her, the Varrukh were howling and twitching, waving axes and pikes as they raced after Gotrek. They were more like incensed pit fighters than an army and none of them could charge in a straight line, weaving and staggering as they spilled from the gates. Despite her revulsion, Maleneth's blood surged. It was madness. The ale-stewed Varrukh were lunging towards thousands of elegantly armoured aelves, riding shockingly fast steeds and cloaked in powerful sorcery. It was going to be a massacre. And still, Maleneth felt vigour flooding her muscles. Massacres were what she lived for. 'For the Bloody-Handed God!' she howled, leaping after Gotrek with Khaine's fury crashing in her pulse.

Gotrek was the first to meet the enemy. A noble had ridden ahead of the aelven lines, riding a fast-moving eel. He was wearing pearlescent battle-plate, with a scalloped shield on his arm and a serrated falchion in his other hand. His face was hidden inside a crested helm, but his posture screamed arrogance and disdain. As he reached Gotrek, he stooped from his saddle, slashing his sword at Gotrek's face with such elegance and speed that even Maleneth would have struggled to dodge it.

Gotrek was horribly drunk. As he reached the aelf, he tripped, struggling not to drop his axe. Maleneth could barely bring herself to watch. But then, something incredible happened. Gotrek's gait was so erratic that the aelven noble missed his mark, slicing through the air as Gotrek staggered sideways. Then with the grace of the hopelessly drunk, Gotrek righted himself and, with a fluid lurch, brought his axe up through the eel's neck. The blow was more accidental than skilful, but it neatly severed the eel's head.

The noble fell from his saddle as his steed dropped from the air. Then he vanished from view as the Varrukh lines crashed over him, howling and baying.

Across the square, sleek, silver-clad elegance collided with beer-stained, tattooed savagery. The battle cries ceased, replaced with the brutal crunch of weapons cutting bones and armour. Maleneth grinned as she hacked through the fighting, but a part of her mind remained calm enough to observe something incredible. As the Fyreslayers reeled and lurched, clumsy with drink, it actually seemed to help them. The elegant precision of the aelves was thrown by the unpredictable nature of their foe. The Fyreslayers could barely see straight, but that only made them more brutal. They fought like lunatics, convulsing and spitting, fighting with their heads and teeth as much as their weapons. Maleneth had never seen anything so brutal. Even greenskins had a style of combat that could be measured and countered, but the drunk Fyreslayers fought without reason, never making the same move twice.

The aelves tried to form battle lines and phalanxes, tried to give the fight some semblance of order, but it was like trying to corral a landslide. Everywhere Maleneth looked, crests of fiery hair were smashing through the Idoneth ranks. It was a slaughter, as she had predicted, but not a one-sided one. The Idoneth were being dragged from their steeds and hacked to pieces by Fyreslayers too deranged to realise they were mortally wounded. She saw a howling berserker, arrows embedded in his neck and chest, clamber up the fins of a turtle, flinging aelves from its howdah and staggering so clumsily away that no one could land a blow on him. By the time the Fyre-slayer dropped to his knees, overcome by blood loss, the turtle was riderless and out of control, crashing through the lines of eel-riding nobles that surrounded it.

'Karaz-a-Karak!' thundered Gotrek, and Maleneth realised he was some-where nearby. She lashed out with her knives, cutting down another aelf, then stepped back from the violence, trying to catch her breath and locate Gotrek. The Slayer had climbed up onto the shell of the giant turtle Maleneth had seen earlier. The monster was now dead and lying at the heart of the square, crowds of combatants crashing against it as the fighting ebbed and flowed. Gotrek was staggering, looking drunker by the moment, waving his flaming axe as aelves sprinted up the sides of the shell, trying to land sword strikes on him. She fought through the crowd and clambered up onto the turtle's back, joining Gotrek with a storm of knife strikes.

'This is it!' roared Gotrek, staring wildly at her, his face drenched in blood. 'This is how to celebrate victory! Bloodshed and wrath! And another victory!'

Maleneth howled another prayer to Khaine and took her usual place at Gotrek's weaker side. She could see the runefather and the other lodge elders close by. Their magmadroths were stomping through the aelves, vomiting lava, adding clouds of black smoke to the sea mist. Thurgyn looked reborn. He was swaying in his saddle, laughing and singing as he fought, as drunk as all the other Fyreslayers and delighting in the mayhem. There was no trace of the illness and grief that had weighed on him for so long. Every now and then he looked over at Gotrek, dealing out death from the back of the turtle, and with every glance at the Slayer, Thurgyn seemed to grow in stature and wrath, smashing his latchkey axe back and forth and flinging butchered aelves through the air.

Wave after wave of Idoneth attacked, banking and diving on their mon-strous steeds. But their clever tactics were useless. They were killing dozens of Fyreslayers but it gained them nothing and they were falling in equal numbers. It was a brutal mess. Smoke, blood and mist whirled around the square as warriors rose and fell, howling as they died. In the distance, she saw the large shape she had seen at the start of the battle. It was a truly enormous leviathan, as big as one of the statues that lined the square. There were dozens of Idoneth on its back as it coiled through the mist, tearing whole sections of the magmahold apart, hurling rubble onto the crowds below. Maleneth breathed deep, savouring the iron tang of blood. No one could survive this, but she found she was at peace with the idea. Khaine's hunger screamed through her muscles. She leapt into the scrum, laughing and howling.

CHAPTER THIRTY

'A strange choice of meeting place,' said Princess Arainn as she approached Eòrna. The princess was accompanied by her usual throng of self-absorbed nobles and they nodded in agreement, looking around at the towering walls of kelp that lined the road.

Eòrna studied the princess and her acolytes as they walked towards her, fascinated by them. For her whole life, Eòrna had been a restless wanderer, using the ancient routes of the Myrway to cross oceans and continents, always seeking stranger, more potent souls to claim. Her brother had made her a thrallmaster as a way to remove her from court but, in truth, it was the perfect role for her. Searching out new shores and races was what she lived for. And it was only now, after travelling for so long, and so far, that she could see how peculiar the Dromlech nobles truly were. Arainn and the other aristocrats were consumed by their petty games. They fell in and out of favour constantly and that ebb and flow of power was all they could think about. Arainn and her followers had not left the city for so long that they wore the most outlandish, impractical outfits. With no need to dress for war, they had turned themselves into walking ornaments, as luminous and contorted as the coral reefs that surrounded Dhruim-Ùrlar. Eòrna craved the isolation of the deeps as much as any of the Dromlech but, as she nodded her head in greeting, it occurred to her that there was a kind of madness to these people: they had forgotten that there was a world above the sea.

'You must forgive me my eccentricities,' she replied, smiling at the princess. 'There is something I wish you to see.' Eòrna knew that her eccentricities would need no forgiving. There was nothing Princess Arainn and her coterie liked more than royal intrigue. They could sniff scandal like sharks on the trail of blood.

Arainn looked around at the narrow avenue. Since Dìolan had set off for Karag-Varr even the city's largest thoroughfares had emptied, but this winding, narrow route was particularly lonely. If it had not been for Torven's deepsight, Eòrna would never have found it and even now, as she studied the kelp fronds that surrounded it, she could tell it was moving, shifting into another position. In a day or two it would lead to a completely different destination and would be no use to her.

'Where does this path lead?' asked the princess. 'It is unfamiliar to me.'

Eòrna smiled, doing her best to play the part of an elegant courtier. 'Let me keep you in suspense a little longer. Another ten minutes' walk and you will recognise where you are.'

Arainn studied her with half-lidded eyes. For a worrying moment, Eòrna thought the princess might refuse to follow. For all her pride and affectation, Arainn was fiercely clever. As a child, Eòrna had been terrified of her. There was every chance that she might guess Eòrna was luring her into something dangerous. Curiosity got the better of the princess, however, and she smiled back. 'Then lead on, thrallmaster. With the Allmarach left empty, there is very little to entertain us at the moment. Until your brother returns with that duardin's head, things shall be very tedious.'

Eòrna gestured for her thralls to lead the way and the group walked on down the path, with Princess Arainn taking Eòrna's arm.

'Have you thought any more about what my brother said in his speech?' asked Eòrna.

There was a pause as the princess considered the question. 'I tried to speak with him about it, before he left.' Her tone was neutral. 'But he was too busy planning his attack on the Fyreslayers. He did not even appear at the ball, which I consider a poor show as it was a ball *he* was hosting.'

The princess had answered without answering, something she was expert at. Eòrna could understand her reasons. To speak openly against the king of Dhruim-Ùrlar was dangerous, even for a scion of the old regime. But Eòrna needed to push her. Whatever she thought of these peculiar old relics, they were her only chance of stopping her brother. Arainn, in particular, was the fulcrum on which Dromlech society pivoted. If she failed to win the princess over to her cause, there would be no way to make a stand against Dìolan. Eòrna glanced back at the other nobles. They were so drenched in robes that they looked like waves of silt, fluttering down the path. 'And how do you feel about a life in the uplands, marching to war with our Idoneth kin, prising the realms from Chaos?'

Arainn gave her a warning glance. 'You have known me a long time, child. Did you really call me out here in the hope I would start denouncing your brother? The king's plan is bold and surprising, and I am intrigued to see how it progresses. But for now, I have little else to say on the subject. When he returns to the city I shall insist he makes time to speak with me, and perhaps after that, when I know more, we can have the heated debate you so clearly desire.'

Eòrna battled her frustration and simply smiled. They had almost reached the end of the path and the princess would soon have something else to consider. The path widened as it turned a corner and led up to a pair of tall, beautifully wrought gates. They were built in the shape of a vast kraken, with the creature's boiling, writhing limbs making up the bars of the gate. It was ancient and crumbling, but when new it must have been startlingly lifelike. There was blue light drifting through it from the other side and recognition flickered in Princess Arainn's eyes.

'The chorrileum?' She approached the serpentine gates, shaking her head, and then gasped, staring at the kraken in shock. 'The Briondal Gate.' She stroked the dusty, pitted coral. 'I have not seen this place since... since my father was alive.' For a moment, her regal facade slipped. Naked emotion flashed across her face, transforming her. 'So long ago. So much has changed.' Her face grew rigid again but her voice was husky with grief. 'It is a peculiar thing to have outlived one's generation. Wonderful and tragic at the same time. So many people have left me since I last stood here.'

Eòrna's pulse quickened. Perhaps her years playing politics at court had not been entirely wasted. Things were proceeding exactly as she had hoped. This was just how she had predicted the princess would react.

'Our kin never leave us,' said Eòrna. She nodded through the gates to the rippling lights beyond. 'Not while we preserve the chorrileum. While it endures, our past will always be with us.'

The princess nodded and whispered a prayer. Eòrna had never seen such a visible display of emotion from her. 'What made you think to show me this?' She sounded genuinely moved. 'I appreciate it more than you can imagine, but I'm afraid it will not change my position on your politics.' She leant close to Eòrna and whispered in her ear. 'Do you understand why I have lived so long, child? Do you know why I have retained my place at court, even after my father was killed, when so many others were exiled or executed? Because I keep my opinions to myself. I side with everyone and no one. I am above the debate. It's not that I don't sympathise with you, Eòrna. But only a fool reveals their hand in Dhruim-Ùrlar. The people I knew and loved, the people who used to pass through these gates with me – they died because they lent their voice to a cause, because they chose a side.'

Eòrna nodded.

Arainn seemed on the verge of saying more, then shook her head and decided against it. She took a long, lingering look at the gates, then turned to leave.

'There is one more thing to see,' said Eòrna. 'Inside the chorrileum.'

Arainn stroked the gate with a wistful look on her face. 'I fail to see how you could surpass this. The Briondal Gate is famously reclusive. Lead on, child. I am intrigued.'

Eòrna's thralls opened the gates and the group of nobles swept through, heading into the resting place of their ancestors. During her years of travelling, Eòrna had heard tales of the chorrileums maintained by other enclaves. They were all unique, no two taking the same shape. She had heard that some were underwater lakes – silvery pools that existed in deeps of the ocean, with shores and tides, even though they were surrounded by water. Others were no more than a gemstone in the hilt of a falchion or a crumbling statue of Mathlann, the Fallen God. But, whatever shape they took, Eòrna could not believe any of the other chorrileums were as beautiful as the one in Dhruim-Ùrlar. The souls of the Dromlech dead resided in a drifting forest: clouds of barbed, transparent spheres, each the size of an aelven skull and formed of glittering gossamer. The spheres floated in clusters or swayed in vast, interlinked chains and they were all luminous, flashing brighter when disturbed by currents or passers-by. Passers-by were rare in the chorrileum, however. It was the most sacred of all the holy places in Dhruim-Ùrlar. A priceless treasure, containing not just the souls of the Dromlech ancestors but also the souls of lesser races that had been captured and would eventually be used to prolong the life of namarti half-souls such as Eòrna's thralls. Entry to this sacred glade was only permitted to the soul wardens of the Isharann and nobles who had been granted permission to visit the ghosts of their fallen kin.

Eòrna, Arainn and the rest of the nobles advanced slowly, taking in the grandeur of the scene. Eòrna always felt a peculiar mixture of emotions when she saw the chorrileum. To see the numberless dead was humbling and, in some ways, terrible; but it was also inspiring to see so much wisdom and experience, preserved for the good of the enclave. As the barbed spheres glided above them, spilling their light and throwing shadows, voices drifted through the air. The chorrileum was filled with a gentle chorus: whispered prayers and hymns that ebbed and flowed with the swaying of the spheres. It was the music of the dead; they were singing in praise of their haven and sending prayers of strength and hope to the living. Eòrna could easily have been overwhelmed by the beauty of it, but she kept her purpose in mind, conscious she might not have long.

Under normal circumstances, guards would have challenged them the moment they entered, but the path was deserted. Once again, Torven had proved himself to be invaluable. It was he who had told Eòrna that the Briondal Gate still existed, even though most people thought it long gone. Torven had pointed out that the forgotten gate rarely approached the chorrileum and was unlikely to be guarded. As soon as he mentioned it, Eòrna had grasped at the idea, remembering that the princess had often mentioned the gate, citing it as a treasured memory from her youth. The path would not be deserted for long, however – they would be discovered eventually – so Eòrna nodded to her thralls, giving them a subtle signal. They vanished from view, disappearing beneath the drifting lights.

Arainn and the members of her entourage were too absorbed in admiring the chorrileum to notice the thralls leaving. Eòrna gave them a while to enjoy the sanctity and peace, and then gently took Arainn's arm. 'Come, this is not what I wanted you to see. There is something else. Something further inside.'

Arainn nodded and allowed Eòrna to lead the group at a quicker pace, following the tortuous loops of the path. They continued in silence for another ten minutes and Eòrna resisted the urge to cry out when she saw her destination up ahead. They had almost made it. She turned left at a fork in the path and led the nobles up a gentle incline.

'This is familiar, too,' said Princess Arainn, frowning and looking around at the lights. 'I have been here before. I remember–'

'Halt!' cried a stern voice as a group of guards rushed into view. They were clad in the ceremonial armour worn by all guardians of the chorrileum and were armed with helsabres identical to Eòrna's. She counted twelve of them as they ran down the path, drawing their swords.

'Put your weapons away,' said Arainn in an outraged tone, glaring at the soldiers in disbelief. 'How dare you? You know perfectly well who I am.'

'Your highness,' said the leader, looking deeply uncomfortable. 'Of course I know you. I... Well... Under any normal circumstances I would be honoured

to escort you through the chorrileum, but I must insist that you leave immediately.' He glanced at Eòrna. 'All of you.'

Veins of colour spidered across Arainn's bone-white cheeks. 'I have *never*
been spoken to like this. I shall see you put in–'

Her words were cut off by a flight of arrows that whistled from beneath the
floating spheres. While the princess was talking, Eòrna had given another
signal to her hidden thralls, and their carefully aimed arrows sank neatly
through the eye slits of the guards' helmets. The guards clattered to the
ground, every one of them dead.

Arainn stared at the corpses in shock. Then the princess noticed that
Eòrna did not look surprised and her eyes widened. 'What have you done?'
Her voice was trembling with rage.

'I have saved us,' said Eòrna, as her archers emerged from their hiding
places and gathered on the path.

Arainn's companions were all wide-eyed with horror, mouthing silent
curses and shaking their heads, but the princess strode towards Eòrna, her
expression thunderous. 'You have damned yourself.' She paced back and
forth, shaking her head. 'But you will not take me down with you. I will not
join you in this madness. Whatever you're planning, I am *not* part of it.'

'You already are,' said Eòrna, 'whether you like it or not. You were seen
coming here, with me and my thralls. You know we are not permitted to
enter the chorrileum without the permission of the soul wardens.' She gestured at the corpses on the path. 'And who will believe that you weren't
part of this?'

'Why?' gasped the princess, aghast. 'Why would you do this to me? You
know I would never be involved in any kind of...' She grimaced, as though
tasting something bitter. 'In any kind of insurrection.'

'Do you know why this place is familiar?' asked Eòrna.

'What?' Arainn spat the word. She was transformed. Eòrna had never
seen her like this. All her elegance and pride had fallen away. She looked
like a cornered animal, ready to lash out. She looked up the path. 'What
do you mean?'

'Your ancestors,' said Eòrna. 'Your friends. Your lovers. They are all here.
Or, at least they were.'

Arainn looked like she might scream. 'What in the name of the gods are
you talking about?'

'Take a look.'

Arainn looked at the other nobles. Her face was contorting and twitching. Eòrna could guess what she was thinking. Should she order the other
nobles to attack? That might give some credence to her claim that she was
not working with Eòrna. Or should she simply flee and deny she was ever
here? But the princess' eyes kept returning to the path ahead, and the place
where she used to visit her ancestors. Eòrna could see the recognition in
her eyes. She had sowed enough doubt that the princess could not leave
without taking a few steps more.

'You will pay for this,' hissed the princess as she strode up the path.
The moment she reached the brow of the hill she stopped. She stepped

backwards, shaking her head and staring at what lay on the other side of the slope. Then she collapsed in silence, folding to the ground.

Her companions cried out in dismay and ran towards her. When they reached the top of the slope they gasped and some of them fell to their knees as others gathered around the fallen princess, helping her to sit.

Eòrna followed slowly. She had already seen what her brother had inflicted on the chorrileum, but only dimly, in Torven's cave. She braced herself, but even so, when she reached the brow of the hill, she struggled not to do as the princess had done and topple to the ground. Screened from the larger paths, a broad swathe of the chorrileum had been butchered. The luminous spheres had been cut from their tendrils and were now lying on the ground, grey and lifeless, like heaps of flayed skin. Eòrna shook her head and tears sprang to her eyes. The vision in Torven's cave had not revealed the extent of the destruction, nor conveyed the horror of it. Thousands of souls had been cut from their place of rest. Nausea rushed through Eòrna as she forced herself to take in the magnitude of her brother's treachery.

She realised that Princess Arainn was looking up at her, dazed. 'You... you are shocked by this... Why did you bring me here if you did not know about it?'

'I knew.' Eòrna sat down next to Arainn on the ground. 'But I had not seen it with my own eyes. I did not know how many he had taken.'

The princess' voice was hollow. 'Did he really do this? Your brother? Did Dìolan do this to his own people?'

Eòrna nodded. Even now, after everything she had learned, it pained her to admit that this was his doing. 'This is how he will harness Gotrek Gurnisson's soul. Thallacrom is going to use the souls as fuel for a rite. He has summoned an Eidolon of unusual power, and when he feeds Gotrek's soul to it, it will change everything about us. It will transform us beyond recognition. But to create the Eidolon, Thallacrom had to commit this appalling crime. And this is not all of it.' She gestured to the lights bobbing in the distance. 'There are many parts of the chorrileum that look like this now.'

'Fuel?' Arainn shook her head. 'There is no way to repair this. No way to retrieve what he has taken. It is inconceivable. He has robbed us of our past. He has betrayed our families.'

For a long time they sat there, unable to speak. Then Arainn took Eòrna's hand, and squeezed it, her eyes still glistening with tears. 'I am with you, child,' she said, her voice hoarse. 'Tell me what you need.'

Eòrna nodded. This was what she had hoped for. It should have felt like a triumph, but surrounded by such desecration, the most she could feel was relief.

CHAPTER THIRTY-ONE

'It's like clutching at smoke!' King Dìolan's deepmare bucked and struggled beneath him as he tried to advance. His battalions were doing exactly as he had ordered: the Akhelian Guard were diving in from the east and west, their eels cutting into the Fyreslayer flanks as the namarti half-souls met them head-on, charging at the Varrukh in fast-moving lines. But his carefully planned tactics were useless. The Fyreslayers were a shambles. They moved in such nonsensical, unpredictable surges that the namarti kept floundering, unsure which way to advance, and the Akhelian Guard found themselves attacking flanks that no longer existed, faltering and slowing as they charged into empty spaces. The Fyreslayers were too outnumbered to drive the aelves back, but the battle was deadlocked. Neither side could gain any ground. And the resultant slaughter was dreadful to see.

'Why don't they care?' said Thallacrom, reining in his steed at the king's side. The priest was looking at the massacre in disbelief. 'Look how many warriors they're losing. Why are they all laughing?'

'They're drunk,' said Dìolan.

'Drunk?' Thallacrom stared in disbelief.

Dìolan sat stiffly in his saddle as aelven warriors surged past him. Cold hate burned in his chest. 'After all I've done. All we've sacrificed. I am faced with this… this *mess.*' He thought of the chorrileum. Of the spirits he had severed. The great crime he had committed. In the light of everything he had done, the senseless behaviour of the Fyreslayers seemed like a personal insult.

He maintained his composure and turned to one of his guards. 'Release the kharibdyss. Let these fools see the power we have at our disposal.'

Orders were yelled and Dìolan smiled as he heard the distant sounds of the kharibdyss thrashing against its restraints. It was a true monster that had grown far beyond the natural size of its kind, feeding on other monsters in the deepest, most hidden trenches of the ocean. Dìolan turned to Thallacrom. 'Tidecaster. Show them the fury of the storm.'

Thallacrom nodded in approval, gripping his stave. 'Highness.' He steered his fangmora eel on, across the advancing lines of namarti until he had almost reached the bewildering chaos of the front lines. Then he held the staff aloft and called into the whirling banks of mist, beginning an incantation. The miasma turned around him like the hub of a great wheel, and a tempest whipped up from the ground.

Dìolan's rage eased as he watched the display. Thallacrom's might as a tide-caster was unsurpassed. The ethertide roared over the walls of Karag-Varr, ripping metal and stone from the battlements and shaking statues from pedestals. The currents drove the namarti infantry onwards and they started to regroup, regaining some semblance of order. But when the waves hit the Fyreslayers, it had the opposite effect, driving them back, hitting them like a physical sea. Dìolan rode forwards and raised his sword. 'Show the drunken scum who we are.'

He had not ridden far when the battle was snatched away from him, replaced by a vision of a raging sea. It was not the furious etherstorm summoned by Thallacrom, but a real sea that had nothing to do with the battle for Karag-Varr. As Dìolan watched the waves, they smashed the strange ship he had seen days earlier, when he was still in Dhruim-Ùrlar. As the vessel collapsed, its Sigmarite banners snatched up into the tornado, he felt a rush of dizzying power and triumph.

WE ARE ONE.

The voice hit Dìolan like a wave.

Then the sea vanished and Dìolan was back in Karag-Varr, watching Thallacrom destroy the Fyreslayer lines. Dìolan shook his head and rode towards Thallacrom, trying to rid himself of the peculiar vision. He had been plagued by them since his encounter with the Eidolon but he had told no one. He would accept no more delays.

As Dìolan approached Thallacrom, a Fyreslayer cleaved his way through the lines of namarti, making straight for him. He was carrying a flaming axe in both hands and there were runes blazing in his biceps. Unlike most of the Fyreslayers, who were squat but lean, this warrior had a sagging gut and was as broad as a barrel. He also had a circle of stitches tattooed around his neck, as though daring someone to try and behead him. The namarti tried to stop him reaching their king, but the Fyreslayer was running in such an unstable manner that they could not land a blow on him. Swords and arrows swiped past him as he stumbled, hacking as he ran.

Dìolan was transfixed, unable to comprehend a society that could produce such an appalling person. The Fyreslayer's beard was an explosion of greasy, wiry hair, matted with blood and pieces of food. His crest had been slicked with beer and animal fat, and half his teeth were missing. His nose had been broken so many times it looked like the angular rune on his helmet. But it was his demeanour that truly sickened Dìolan. War was a sacred endeavour, to be revered and respected. But the fat Fyreslayer was laughing and singing as he fought. He beheaded a namarti thrall, punched a second in the groin, then swaggered forwards. The ranks of namarti swords-men formed a line to meet him but the Fyreslayer was not as inebriated as he looked. At the last moment, he changed direction, rolled into an open space and leapt at Dìolan, howling as he swung his axes.

Dìolan parried but the Fyreslayer's weight threw him from his saddle and they both crashed into the mounds of dead. The Fyreslayer's filthy beard engulfed his features, and a reek of stale beer filled Dìolan's nostrils as his attacker roared incoherently into his face.

Then the Fyreslayer vanished, replaced by a savage storm and the prow of a ship, looming over him. Wonderful strength rushed through Dìolan and he rose to his feet, gripping the howling Fyreslayer by the neck as he stood, tightening his grip.

There was a dry crunching sound as Dìolan crushed his attacker's throat. The battle rushed back into view and he saw the Fyreslayer's face, just an inch from his, grinning maniacally. It took Dìolan a moment to realise the Fyreslayer was dead, his feet hanging above the ground and his head lolling at an unnatural angle. Dìolan hurled the corpse away and looked around, sword raised, expecting another attack. There were only namarti thralls nearby. They had formed a circle around him and were holding back the mobs of Fyreslayers. He had no time to try and understand what was happening to him. He had formed a bond with the Eidolon but it was aiding him rather than hindering him so he did not question it any further. He looked around for his steed and saw that the deepmare was a few feet away, tearing into a group of Fyreslayers, gouging them with the horn that jutted from its brow. He rushed to aid the creature, felling the last of the Fyreslayers, then leapt into her saddle and looked out across the battlefield.

Dìolan had expected to see a scene of victory. When he had last looked, Thallacrom had been in the process of summoning a storm to crush their enemies. But the storm had vanished. Thallacrom was still in the same spot, surrounded by eel-riding nobles, but the old priest was now bathed in flames. It was no ordinary fire. As Dìolan rode closer, he saw that the flames had limbs, tails and talons, and they were savaging Thallacrom. They looked like wingless dragons and were wrapping themselves around Thallacrom as he howled and waved his stave, trying to fend them off.

'No,' whispered Dìolan. 'This will not happen.' If Thallacrom were to die, all of this would have been for nothing. The sorcery that was giving the Eidolon life came from Thallacrom. If he died, the Eidolon would be extinguished.

Dìolan followed the lines of fire to their source: a Fyreslayer who was wearing a scaled cloak and an ornate triple-crested helmet with a mask that completely covered his face. In one hand he was gripping a brazier axe, but the flames came from a rune he was clutching in his other hand. Dìolan rode with all the speed and fury he could muster, whispering curses as he soared over the battlefield. As he rode, he saw the storm-lashed sea again, but this time it was overlaid on top of the battle for Karag-Varr, merging into a seamless torrent of waves and surging battle lines.

I AM WITH YOU.

The voice of the Eidolon gave Dìolan such a surge of strength that he stood in his saddle, holding his sword aloft as the deepmare hurtled towards the masked Fyreslayer. As he raised the sword, the waves from his vision became waves in Karag-Varr. The sorcery that Thallacrom wielded was now pouring from Dìolan and, using nothing more than his will, he directed it at the Fyreslayer.

There was a thunderclap as the etherstorm collided with the masked Fyreslayer. A column of water rose from the battle and a tremor rippled across the square, causing aelves and Fyreslayers alike to stumble and fall.

The glare was so bright that, for a few seconds, Dìolan rode blind, trusting to the instincts of the deepmare. When his vision cleared, he allowed himself a small smile. The masked Fyreslayer was dead, cast onto the ground by the force of the blast, his body broken and his rune knocked from his grip, lying inert a few feet away. The surrounding Fyreslayers were already leaping back to their feet, too drunk to register the loss of their priest, smashing back into the lines of aelves, but Dìolan sensed that the battle was now turning in his favour. The power of the Eidolon was inside him. He carried the spirits of the Dromlech. He could wield his fallen ancestors like a weapon. The memory of the chorrileum reminded him of Thallacrom and he turned his steed away from the enemy lines, searching for the priest. Thallacrom was not visible but then Dìolan saw other Isharann priests congregating at the feet of a statue, near the fortress wall, and he guessed that was where he would find him.

'What did you do?' gasped Thallacrom, trying to sit as he saw his king riding towards him. 'You are not Isharann. How was that possible? How did you harness the ethersea?'

Dìolan dropped from his steed and rushed to Thallacrom, helping him stand. 'The Eidolon is in me, Thallacrom. It is speaking to me. It acted through me.'

Thallacrom stared at him in disbelief. 'Yes,' he murmured. 'I feel it. You are bonded somehow.' He gripped Dìolan's shoulders. 'This is incredible. You can use the force of the Eidolon against them. Their antics won't save them from that.'

Dìolan shook his head. 'I don't know how. I'm not Isharann like you. I'm not a tidecaster. I don't know how to control such power.'

Thallacrom thought for a moment, as the fighting raged around them. 'Perhaps you don't need to.'

'What do you mean?'

'Perhaps we're going about this all wrong. We are spending so many lives trying to take this fortress. I'm sure we will succeed eventually, but what will be left of us when we do? Half the citizens of Dhruim-Ùrlar will have died. How can we conquer the uplands if we sacrifice our whole army trying to capture Gotrek Gurnisson?'

'But we need Gotrek. Sacrificing him and taking his soul is the only way to escape the curse. Isn't that right?'

'True. But do we need to conquer the whole Fyreslayer army to do that?' He leant close to Dìolan, struggling to be heard over the din of the battle. 'The power of the Eidolon is in you. And I can harness it. If we can get you close to Gotrek, I can use the might of the Eidolon to snatch Gotrek away and anchor him in Dhruim-Ùrlar. We wouldn't need to conquer the whole keep. We could simply use the Eidolon's power to take the Fyreslayer. Then, once we have sacrificed him, and we have an army of pure-soul nobles' – his eyes flashed – 'we will be unstoppable.'

'But the Eidolon is not yet fully born. Is it safe to drain its power like that?'

'It might set us back a few days, maybe more. But if we fail to capture Gotrek Gurnisson then the Eidolon is no use anyway.'

Dìolan could still see glimpses of the phantom sea, superimposed over the battle. Everything was liquid and mobile. Even Thallacrom's face was hard to make out clearly. But he could hear the conviction in the priest's voice. He did not profess to understand all of what Thallacrom said, but he trusted him completely. He looked around, trying to focus on his surroundings. They were encircled by a battalion of his finest guards fighting with silent grace, holding back the Fyreslayer berserkers who were trying to reach Dìolan and Thallacrom. 'Very well,' he said. 'If we take these guards we can cut a path to Gotrek. My plan was to turn them on the Fyreslayer king, to behead their army, but we can use them to reach Gotrek instead. The duardin are so deranged I doubt they'll even notice us moving towards a specific target. And, from what I have seen of Gotrek, even if he *does* notice, he would relish a chance to get near us.' He looked at Thallacrom's pained expression. 'You must stay here though. We can't risk losing you. Without you, the whole thing will have been for nothing.'

Thallacrom shook his head. 'I need to be with you when you reach Gotrek. I must be nearby to perform the rite.'

Dìolan leapt back into his saddle and reached down for Thallacrom, hauling him up onto the deepmare. 'Akhelians!' he cried, causing the Idoneth nobles to regroup and gather round him, their steeds writhing and sparking. 'The fate of the Dromlech is in our hands! And the fate of the very realms. I have to cross this battlefield. And whatever the Fyreslayers throw at us, I must not be stopped.'

'For Dhruim-Ùrlar!' cried the warriors, raising their volt-spears and casting shards of electricity through the mist.

'For Dhruim-Ùrlar!' roared Dìolan. Then he kicked the deepmare into motion, sending it hurtling back into the fray.

The guards formed a spearhead around him, not caring who they cast aside. One of them raised a conch and let out a long note of triumph, and Dìolan's blood surged in response. He lashed out with his falchion as he rode, but he refused to be overwhelmed by the fervour that was consuming him. He was determined that, in every strike and thrust, he would illustrate the difference between the Dromlech and the savagery of the lesser races.

He spotted Gotrek fighting near the gates that led out of the square, but even then he remained calm, ordering his guards in that direction with a cool, clear command. Gotrek was halfway up some steps that led to the battlements, roaring like an animal as he kicked and chopped at namarti thralls. There was a mound of aelven bodies around him and a crowd of Fyreslayers was rushing to join him, howling battle cries in their crude, duardin tongue.

Reaching Gotrek meant charging into the thickest crush of bodies, and as they reached the centre of the square, Dìolan's guards became mired in a thicket of axes and swords. There were now so many corpses that the combatants were stumbling over their fallen comrades and even the Varrukh berserkers were starting to show signs of exhaustion.

As Dìolan struggled to fight through the impasse, he saw mounds of fallen aelves, their armour ruptured and limbs shattered, blood pouring from

their wounds, dark and shocking against their pale skin. In all the Dromlech campaigns he had never heard of such appalling carnage. And many
of the dead were pure-souls. Those precious, noble individuals who were
gifted so rarely to Idoneth mothers. 'This has to work,' he whispered.

'It will,' gasped Thallacrom in his ear. He sounded like he was struggling
to breathe but there was no trace of doubt in his voice. 'Just get to Gotrek.
As soon as we drag him back to Dhruim-Ùrlar this can all cease. I will
summon the ethertide. I will carry our battalions home. Just reach Gotrek.'

Dìolan stared at the piles of dead, resolve tightening in his stomach. He
yanked the reins and left his guards behind, gliding away from the crush
and racing towards the wall where Gotrek was butchering thralls.

The deepmare rolled to the left, almost throwing its riders from the saddle.
Heat washed over Dìolan's face as magma tore through the air, missing
him by inches thanks to the instincts of the creature. He raised his shield
just in time to deflect a second barrage. The deepmare screamed in pain,
struggling to right itself. Then it thrashed its tails and turned to face a row
of Fyreslayers. They looked as drunk as the berserkers but, rather than axes,
they were gripping pikes that were trailing smoke.

'Your people had their chance!' cried Dìolan, pointing his falchion at
them. 'And you failed the realms!'

The Fyreslayers showed no sign they could understand him and prepared to fire again.

Thallacrom wheezed an incantation and jabbed his narwhal tusk at them.
A column of spume rose from the mounds of dead, lifting the Fyreslayers
off their feet and hurling them backwards. They fired as they fell, but the
magma spewed uselessly up into the clouds of smoke.

Dìolan rode at them with a curse, and as they thudded back onto the
corpses, he sent the Fyreslayers to their ancestors, removing their heads in
a flurry of perfectly placed cuts. Then he yanked the reins again and turned
back to face Gotrek, pressing on through the battle.

Fyreslayers staggered towards him as he rode on, shouting and hurling
axes at him. Gotrek was only moments away but Dìolan's steed was badly
wounded. The Fyreslayers had burned holes through her flank and she
was gulping and listing as she swam on, struggling to move with any
speed.

'You have to reach him!' said Thallacrom, but the more Dìolan yanked
the reins, the more his deepmare struggled.

A deafening boom shook the square, like a seismic tremor, and pieces of
wall whistled down, smashing into buildings and warriors. The air was so
thick with mist that it took a moment for Dìolan to locate the source of the
explosion. The kharibdyss was tearing across the square – an enormous,
five-headed serpent that lashed through the battle, devouring aelves and
Fyreslayers in a frenzy, gouging a path into the crowd. 'Thallacrom!' cried
Dìolan. 'It's attacking our own troops. What's happening?'

Thallacrom stared at the frenzied monster. 'It's because my strength is
fading, highness. And if I use the little I have left to subdue the kharibdyss,
I'll be too weak to seize Gotrek Gurnisson.'

Dìolan scowled as he watched the leviathan wreaking havoc. 'There'll be nothing left of us if that creature isn't called to heel.'

'Then move quickly. Reach Gotrek and I can end this. All we need is him.' The Slayer was still adding to his pile of dead aelves, creating almost as many corpses as the kharibdyss.

Dìolan tried to ride on, dealing out more sword strikes as he steered through the battle, but the deepmare gave a last, tormented howl and crashed to the ground, hurling Dìolan and Thallacrom from the saddle.

Fyreslayers rushed to attack but Dìolan drove them back with a storm of sword strikes, crying out in frustration as he saw that he was surrounded. He called out for support but none of his soldiers were anywhere near him.

Thallacrom fought at his side, using the tusk like a spear, still trying to save the vestiges of his power, but he looked worried. 'We can't cut through the whole army on foot.'

A cold horror threatened to overwhelm Dìolan but he drove it down. 'I will not fail,' he gasped, lunging and hacking at the Fyreslayers. 'I cannot fail!' He led Thallacrom up onto the corpse of the deepmare so they could look over the heads of the Fyreslayers. There were dozens of duardin between them and Gotrek and there was no way he could fight through all of them, but then he spotted Thurgyn, much closer by, and had an idea. The runefather was wounded and on foot, and there were very few Fyreslayers near him. 'Gotrek roused the runefather from his grief, is that right?'

Thallacrom smiled, seeing Thurgyn and guessing Dìolan's plan. 'They have become close friends.'

There was another thunderous boom as the kharibdyss crashed past them, writhing and hurling warriors through the air.

When the monster had passed, Dìolan nodded at Thallacrom. 'Let's see if we can get Gotrek's attention.'

Maleneth leapt clear as a section of wall crashed down towards her, sending metal and rock clattering across the ground. 'What in the name of Khaine is that thing?' she gasped, staggering clear of the rubble.

Gotrek was above her, balancing on a flight of steps as they tore loose from the wall. He swayed precariously for a moment then, as the steps gave way, dived into the battle, roaring and laughing. Bodies flew in every direction as Gotrek laid about himself, hacking and punching towards Maleneth. When he reached her, he paused for breath, grinning at the aelves who were scattered around him, limping and bleeding and grabbing weapons from the ground. 'We've got them on the run, lass,' he growled, juggling his axe from one hand to the other, as happy as she had ever seen him.

Maleneth looked around at the battle. There were mounds of dead in every direction, both aelf and Fyreslayer. 'This doesn't look like victory to me,' she said.

'Rubbish!' Gotrek headbutted a nearby aelf and slammed his axe into another. 'We're slaughtering them.'

'Slaughtering aelves.' Maleneth shook her head, despatching another warrior with her knife. Her bloodlust began to fade. 'Slaughtering warriors we could have fought alongside, against the armies of Chaos.'

Gotrek frowned at her. Then he noticed something and shoved past her, climbing up on the rubble. 'No you bloody don't,' he muttered, his face turning pale.

'What is it?' demanded Maleneth, leaping up by his side. Not far from where they were standing, there was a clearing in the battle, a path of corpses produced by the passing of the kharibdyss. Standing alone, fighting for his life, was Thurgyn. The runefather had become separated from his Hearth-guard and the king of the Idoneth was raining sword blows down on him. Thurgyn was clutching a wound in his side and struggling to wield his latchkey axe with one hand. He was cursing the aelven king as he fought, bellowing at him, but his strength was fading, his blows becoming weaker with every strike.

The aelven king paused and looked directly at Gotrek, giving him a cold smile. Then he sliced his sword through Thurgyn's neck. The runefather's head whirled through the air, leaving his headless corpse to topple.

'No!' howled Gotrek, leaping from the pile of rubble and careering through the battle, making straight for the Idoneth king. Maleneth struggled to keep up as he ploughed forwards, roaring at Thurgyn's killer. 'You will pay for that!' he cried, his voice cracking. 'By the Everpeak, I swear it!'

Maleneth had no doubt that Gotrek was right. The Slayer was now more like an animal than a duardin, ripping and clubbing his way through the aelves. Then she noticed something troubling. As Gotrek raced towards the Idoneth king, the aelf was waiting quite calmly for him. Rather than pre-paring to defend himself, he was leaning nonchalantly on his sword hilt, watching Gotrek with amused disdain as Thurgyn's blood pooled around his feet. Then Maleneth noticed the frail, stooped figure at his side. The sor-cerer was pointing a rune at Gotrek and speaking quickly. And as he spoke, the storm was swelling, turning overhead and snatching corpses from the ground as it rushed towards the Slayer.

'Wait!' she cried, but there was no way to make Gotrek hear. He continued barrelling through the crowd and had almost reached the Idoneth king.

Maleneth howled at him, filled with dread as the storm grew wilder, plunging the battle into darkness and sending warriors slamming into each other.

'Gotrek!' she cried again as the Slayer reached the king, but at that moment the storm grew so furious she was lifted from her feet, caught in a huge wave. She rolled and flailed and came face to face with a leviathan. The giant sea serpent was rushing towards her, its five cavernous maws opening wide.

CHAPTER THIRTY-TWO

Maleneth lay in the darkness, swaying gently back and forth. She had not been bred to enjoy idleness or to appreciate luxury but she was exhausted, and her body was so battered that she sank gratefully into the cushions and stretched her tired limbs, whispering a prayer to Khaine, thanking him for this unusual moment of respite. But as she lay there, savouring the peace, a sense of foreboding washed over her. Why was the floor moving? She shrugged off the feeling of calm. It was a lie. It had to be. She opened her eyes but it made no difference. She was in complete darkness. She could not remember her cell in Karag-Varr ever being so dark before. There was always an infernal glow, leaking through the walls and under the door. Veins of lava ran through the entire magmahold. The thought of lava made her realise something else: rather than furnace-like, the air was cool and damp. She thought back over the day, trying to remember what she had done before retiring to her room. She remembered the victory feast and her decision to desert Gotrek… And then everything came back: the Idoneth invasion and the subsequent carnage, and then, with a gasp, she remembered trying to save Gotrek, sprinting after him as he attacked the Idoneth king.

'Not dead then,' rumbled the Slayer.

The dark was too profound for her to make out his bulky frame, but his words came from close by. There was an odd rattle to his voice and she realised that he had been injured too.

'Not dead,' she agreed, wincing as she sat up. 'And, for some reason, I can remember the Idoneth this time. I can remember the battle. I wonder why?' As she moved, she realised she was not lying on cushions but a mesh of shiny black strands. The whole floor was made up of segmented worms. They were cool and coated in a tacky substance, and some of them were attached to her skin, making sucking sounds. 'Leeches!' she hissed, picking them off. Fresh blood rushed from her skin where the worms had been attached.

'Where are we?' she asked, though, in truth, she was not sure she wanted to know. There was a dreadful smell in the room and it was different to the stench that usually surrounded Gotrek. It smelled like burned hair.

Gotrek shifted position, shuffling through the leeches towards her. There was a faint glow coming from the rune in his chest and she began to make out his face. He looked furious and Maleneth instantly recognised the stony look in his eye. He was in one of his black moods. Long, plump leeches were dangling from his chest and arms, feeding eagerly, but he did not seem to care.

'Where are we?' she repeated, looking around in horror. There were so many writhing worms that it looked like she was in a vat of bubbling oil.

Gotrek replied in a flat tone. 'Eaten.'

'Eaten?' She looked at the leeches. 'What are you talking about?'

He ignored her, muttering something unintelligible to the dark.

'Gotrek!' she snapped. 'What in the name of the gods do you mean, *eaten*?'

He shrugged. 'Last thing I saw was a big sea snake with too many heads. Big as a townhouse. I was about to crack one of its skulls when everything went dark.' He nodded at the undulating floor. 'This must be its guts. It must have eaten the leeches too.'

Maleneth had travelled through every imaginable kind of hell with the Slayer, she had seen things she would not have thought possible outside of nightmares, but to hear him blithely announce that they had been eaten was enough to make her want to scream. She resisted the urge and tried to match his unruffled tone. 'So now you're just sitting here, waiting to be digested, is that it?'

He said nothing for a moment. Then his lips curled back in a dreadful snarl. 'I'll tear him apart,' he muttered. 'On my oath, I'll make him pay.'

Maleneth could easily guess who he was talking about. She had seen the Idoneth noble who cut Thurgyn down. And she had seen the look in Gotrek's eye when it happened. 'And how exactly do you plan to avenge the rune-father,' she demanded, 'if you're digested?'

There was a long silence.

'Damn you!' she spat, picking worms from her boots. 'You said you escaped the Realm of Chaos and the destruction of an entire world – surely you can cut your way out of a fish?'

'You try.'

She patted her belt and found, to her horror, that her knives were gone. Then she realised Gotrek's axe was also missing. 'Damn it,' she muttered. Then she shrugged. 'No matter. I'll get us out of here. It won't be the first time I've got us out of a mess.' She stood up. It was only when she was on her feet that she realised how many injuries she had sustained trying to reach Gotrek. She was nauseatingly light-headed and every inch of her seemed to be bruised or bleeding. She refused to let Gotrek know she was struggling, though, and walked carefully past him, looking for a wall. She felt the ground curve upwards and realised they were in a spherical chamber, around thirty paces wide. She raised her foot, about to stamp on the floor.

'Wait,' sighed Gotrek. 'Don't.'

'What are you talking about?'

'Don't crush them. I've already tried.' He shifted position and light flickered in his chest, illuminating the side of his face. He looked awful – as much of a monster as anything the Idoneth could summon. He had been cut and burned so many times it looked like he had been chiselled from rotten wood. Lots of the wounds were old but there were fresh burns across his cheek and blood bubbling from his nostrils. The muscles in his jaw were twitching and his face was an unhealthy grey. He looked like he might struggle to stand. He fixed her with his one good eye. 'If you try hitting those leeches you'll get a shock.'

'There's not much that surprises me any more.'

'No, an actual shock. I tried. The blast threw me ten feet. When I came to, my teeth were clattering and I smelled like a burned hog.'

'Oh, it's *you* that stinks of burned hair. Makes a change from the stale beer.' She knelt down and peered at the mass of coiling worms. 'What are they?'

'Just don't bloody hit them.'

She glared at him in disbelief. 'So that's it then? Gotrek, son of Gurni, Thane of the Evertop Mountain and slayer of sewer rats, finally accepts defeat, overcome by worms and digested by a fish. I'm honoured to witness the "worthy doom" you talked about so much. If you'd told me you aspired to be fish food I could have helped you long ago.'

'I'm thinking,' growled Gotrek. 'Or, at least I *was* until you woke up and started prattling.'

Maleneth's anger was growing by the moment. She was furious with herself more than Gotrek. She'd had a chance to get away from him and she had missed it. And now she was trapped with him, again, as he sank into another interminable sulk. 'Thinking isn't really your strong point, though, is it? If you think I'm going to sit here listening to stories about your glory days in Nulndorf you're wrong.' She swung her fist back. 'I'm getting out of here.'

'No!' roared Gotrek, lurching towards her, but it was too late. There was a flash of blue light as Maleneth hit the leech-covered wall, then jarring pain, rattling through her arms and chest, kicking her backwards across the room.

When she came to a moment later, the room was dark again, even though her whole body seemed to be burning. It felt like her skin had been dipped in acid and her heart was doing something deeply troubling: racing and stalling with such violence that she felt like it would break her ribs. The smell of burning was now almost unbearable and she could feel more worms sliding onto her arms and latching on to her skin.

'*Still* not dead,' said Gotrek, sounding grudgingly impressed.

'Still not dead,' she replied, but her voice now had the same wheezing rattle as his. *Getting closer though,* she thought, picking off more worms. She expected Gotrek to jeer at her for ignoring his warning but he said something she did not expect, speaking in a tone she could not place.

'Where would you have gone?'

She lifted herself up onto her elbows, gasping at the pain. 'If I'd managed to get out of here?'

'No, when you left the victory feast in Karag-Varr – when you decided to leave me.'

She sat there in the darkness, unable to see him. Was he angry at her? Did he care that she was going to abandon him? 'I didn't think you realised. You seemed engrossed in your rat story.'

'Skaven.'

'Skaven.' She sat up and immediately regretted it. Her heartbeat became even more erratic and a fierce pain knifed between her temples. 'Damn it,' she muttered. She was about to die. The idea appalled her: not because she was afraid of death, but because she hated the idea of being killed by something Gotrek had survived. She tried not to let her pain show as she wracked her brain for a way to heal herself. There were various vials and pouches attached to her leathers, but none of them contained medicine – only poisons, toxins and hallucinogens. Her heart drummed wildly, stopped, then fluttered weakly. The pain in her head became even more intense and she struggled to stay focused on the moment; she felt like she was slipping back into a dream.

'Maleneth?' said Gotrek, but she could barely hear him.

Do something, you idiot, hissed her former mistress, jolting Maleneth back from the brink of unconsciousness. *I will not have this stomach as my eternal resting place.*

'Corr's Bane,' groaned Maleneth, grabbing a bottle from her belt. It contained a poison, intended to gradually stop a victim's heart, but she had a vague memory that, diluted, it could be used to simply steady a heart. She was not sure if she was remembering correctly but with death only moments away, the risk seemed worth taking. She took a flask of water, poured a drop of the poison into it, then drank. Nothing happened. Her heart continued skipping and the pain in her head increased. 'I will not die!' she cried, staggering to her feet and punching her breastbone. She could not say whether it was the punch or the poison, but her heart skipped one last time and then regained a steady beat. The pain eased and the sleepiness left her.

Rather than relief, Maleneth felt another surge of anger. 'I don't know where I would have gone,' she yelled, speaking to where she thought Gotrek was. 'Other than I had to get away from you.'

'What stopped you?'

'The damned Idoneth. I got as far as the walls before they attacked.' She carefully moved some of the leeches and sat next to the Slayer, gasping for breath. She thought about his question. In truth, she had not really considered where she would go if she escaped from Karag-Varr. 'I suppose I would have sought out some of my own kind.'

'Sigmar worshippers?'

'No. The Order of Azyr are probably after my blood. Thanks to you. Because you refused to come to Azyr and hand that rune over, I will be considered tainted goods.'

Because you killed that witch hunter, you mean, said her former mistress, but Maleneth ignored her.

'It would not be wise for me to show my face in a Sigmarite citadel or one of the Free Cities,' she continued. 'No, by my own kind I meant Khainites – aelves sworn to serve the Murder God. Covenite sisters. I could join a war coven.' She shrugged. 'Or perhaps it's time for me to make my pilgrimage to the First Temple, to Hagg-Nar, where the High Oracle, Morathi, founded the sisterhood.'

'And what would you do then?'

'I would take my place in the temple, serving Khaine. I would offer him blood tributes and serve the temple. I would perform–'

'You would perform,' interrupted Gotrek. 'Sounds about right. A performing monkey, prancing for the organ grinder, like those twits in Karag-Wyr.'

'I would serve my god,' hissed Maleneth. 'With all the skill and strength I could muster.' She tried to recall the mantras she had learned as a youth, in the Azyrite Murder Temples. 'In mine hand is the power and the might,' she said, surprised at how hard it was to remember the words. 'None may withstand me. By the will of Khaine I will bathe in the blood of my enemies.'

'You will serve your god,' said Gotrek. 'And then, when the killing is done, you will die.'

Maleneth could hear the bitterness in his voice. 'Yes,' she replied. 'When the time comes, I will die. And when I do, I'll know I served Khaine well. And that will be enough.' As she said the words, she heard the lie. She thought of how she had felt just a few moments earlier, when her heart was about to fail. To her annoyance, she realised that she did not believe what she was saying. When death was about to take her she had not felt peace, nor pride, just rage.

'You don't sound very convinced,' said Gotrek.

'Well, who relishes death? Do you?'

He paused, considering her question. 'I did. I sought it for so long it was all I could think of. I thought it was the only way to atone. After what I did to those...' His words trailed off. 'But I was wrong. A worthy death is not enough. A worthy *life* is what matters. I've been wrong so many times. I've fallen for the same lies as you. But it's not too late. I don't know if it's fate or luck, but I've got another chance. A chance to do something worthwhile.' His voice had sunk even lower. 'I have the rights of it now. I'm an old fool, but I've learned one thing: I can't tell myself that someone else will sort everything out. It's people like us who will fix things. Not a glorious deity in the clouds, not some thunder-cracked savage in Azyr – it's us. You can spill guts for Khaine all you like, Maleneth, but I promise you this, when you die, the realms will be in the same mess they were when you were born. Unless we do something about it.'

'Your arrogance is staggering,' she laughed. 'Do you really believe that you can bring order to the realms when the gods can't? It's insane. I admit, you have a power, a force I don't understand, but you're not divine. You're not so different from any other mortal. You still need to understand your place. The only thing that matters is faith and devotion. Paying tribute to the higher powers.'

'No. That's *not* what matters. Not even bloody close. What matters is not giving up. What matters is finding truth in madness and holding to it, fighting for it even when there's no chance of winning. Determination, courage, honour, loyalty and friendship.' He turned to face her, embers flashing in his eye. 'Yes, bloody friendship. It matters. It counts.'

Maleneth realised that, incredibly, he *was* angry with her for deserting him. She felt such a confusing mixture of contempt and pride that it made her even more furious. 'Survival,' she hissed. 'That's all that counts in the end.'

'*No one* survives. That's the whole bloody point. In the end we die. Every one of us. We're here for a moment and then we're gone.' Gotrek spread his fingers and looked at his palms. 'But in that moment we have power. Not the gods, you and me. We can change things. And anyone who claims otherwise is a coward.'

Maleneth was shaking with anger. 'I am no coward, Gotrek Gurnisson. I just know what matters – what's important.'

'*You* are important.' Gotrek gave her a look of withering scorn. 'And you don't even know it. You think you're an adjunct to a god. A bloody appendage. But you don't have to be what priests tell you to be. You're not just a piece of Khaine. Don't you see? You have your own thoughts. Your own strength. Your own mind. Your own past. You don't have to be a slave for whichever god lays claim to you.'

'Belief is not slavery!' Her palms itched for her knives. 'You're just too primitive to understand anything beyond beer, food and battle. And if you want me to give you a lesson in–'

A grinding sound interrupted her, like plates of metal being dragged against each other. Then they both cursed as light washed over them. After so long in darkness, the light was painful and they backed away, shielding their faces.

'The fish is opening its mouth,' said Gotrek. He stood slowly, wincing and muttering as leeches dropped from his muscles. 'This is our chance.'

CHAPTER THIRTY-THREE

'Ready yourself,' said Gotrek as the light grew brighter. 'We can charge up the fish's gullet and get back to Karag-Varr. Then I can find that murderous elgi king and split his–'

'You are in Dhruim-Ùrlar,' said a heavily accented voice.

As Maleneth's vision adjusted to the glare, she saw a row of slender figures standing on the far side of the room, behind what looked like a wall of blades.

'What devilry is this?' snarled Gotrek, grimacing and stumbling through the worms.

'This is King Dìolan of Dhruim-Ùrlar,' said the voice. 'Monarch of the Dromlech enclave and Sovereign Warden of the Falloch Trench.'

Maleneth could now see clearly. There were a dozen aelves standing on the other side of the blades. The one who had addressed them was a severe-looking priest who, unusually for an aelf, looked old. Aelves of any kind were long-lived, their lives often spanning centuries, but the priest looked like a living fossil. The skin on his face was stretched so tightly it revealed every contour of his skull and the hands resting on his stave were as pale and gnarled as driftwood. Maleneth recognised him from the battle. He was the sorcerer who had summoned the magical tides into Karag-Varr. He radiated power and authority, and studied Gotrek like he was something unpleasant he had found in a meal. 'I do not know where you think you are,' he continued, 'but you are in the dungeon halls of the Wrach Cavern, beneath the streets of the Dromlech capital, Dhruim-Ùrlar.'

Gotrek balled his hands into fists. He was not paying any attention to the priest, his furious gaze locked on the tall, powerfully built aelf next to him. 'King, eh?' He sneered at Dìolan's heavy plate armour and beautifully engraved helmet. 'Is that why you thought you had the right to kill Thurgyn?'

Dìolan studied Gotrek down the length of his nose but gave no reply.

'He was their runefather,' growled Gotrek. 'And my friend. I swore an oath to avenge him, so it's convenient for you to show up here dressed in all those pretty shells. Saves me the effort of hunting you down.' He walked carefully towards the wall of blades and leant back, preparing to punch it.

'You might want to reconsider,' said Thallacrom, glancing at the twisting shapes on floor. 'Iomrall leeches may be small, but they carry an impressive charge. Lethal, when they are agitated.' He gestured to the row of blades that separated the aelves from their captives. 'And their collective power is currently being channelled through this coral.' He looked at Gotrek with a peculiar eagerness. 'You are a unique specimen. A unique soul. It is possible that you would be strong enough to break a few of these spines, but you would release a huge current. There is no way you could survive it.' He glanced at Maleneth. 'Either of you.'

Gotrek tensed, muscles rippling across his massive back and his beard bristling. Maleneth knew how much Gotrek hated being ordered not do something. It was usually the best way to guarantee he would try anyway. 'Gotrek,' she said. 'That last explosion. I... My heart...'

He did not turn to look at her but he nodded. 'Aye. Me too.' Maleneth noticed how awkwardly he was holding himself. His breathing was coming in hitched gasps. She had never seen him like this. He was clearly in pain and muscle spasms kept rippling across his face. He looked like he might keel over.

Rather than falling, Gotrek edged closer to the blades, until his face was inches from the aelves on the other side. 'Let me out now,' he said calmly, glaring up at Thallacrom, 'and I'll only kill your king. Make me wait, and I'll butcher all of you.'

Thallacrom and Dìolan glanced at each other with amused expressions. 'How did you come to be like this?' asked Thallacrom. 'Your strength, I mean. It is not natural, however potent that rune may be. Which realm do you come from? What is your story?'

Gotrek sneered. 'I'll tell you my story, aelf – once I've done killing your king I'm going to kill you. Then I'm going to start the real work that you people have left undone. I'm going to hunt down every murderer, necromancer and daemon that ever crawled from under a rock. I'm going to put things right or I'm going to die trying.'

Thallacrom looked amused again, but King Dìolan nodded, looking serious. 'That is true, after a fashion, Gotrek Gurnisson. Your soul is unique. And when we take it from you in a few days it will be the catalyst that births a miracle. Your death is going to be the spark that lights a great fire. A fire that will sweep across this realm and the realms that lie beyond it. A fire that will drive back the forces you profess to despise. I believe we were destined to meet, Gotrek. Providence brought us together. You will play a key part in the final victory of Order and reason.'

The sound of Dìolan's voice caused Gotrek to twitch but he managed to control himself. 'You're going to take my soul?' He laughed. 'I'd like to see you bloody try.'

Thallacrom shook his head. 'You will see very little of the rite. The soul-rending will require your death. You may still be breathing when we take you apart, I suppose. I have seen that happen with tough specimens such as yourself. But the rite will not truly begin until your heart stops.'

Gotrek looked on the verge of throwing a punch, but Maleneth gripped his arm.

'They're probably lying,' he growled, but he looked down at the shapes writhing under his feet and Maleneth could see he was not convinced.

'And how do you plan to get us out of here,' said Gotrek, 'without me tearing your head off?'

'We are not taking you anywhere yet,' said Thallacrom. 'His highness merely wanted to see you and be sure you are intact. The rite will not begin for several days. Our preparations are not yet complete.'

'What kind of preparations?' demanded Maleneth.

'Nothing you would understand, Khainite. We have summoned an Eidolon of Mathlann but it is not yet fully formed.'

Maleneth had no idea what the priest meant but she knew of Mathlann. It was an obscure deity, but she had heard it mentioned in Azyr, in relation to storms and the sea.

'By the time we return for you, I doubt you will be able to stand,' said Thallacrom, glancing at the floor. 'The iomrall are always hungry. And as they feed they release toxins that keeps their meals docile.'

Maleneth looked at the shapes with distaste. So that was why she felt so exhausted. The aelves were turning to go, so she called out. 'Wait. You don't understand what you're doing. I'm an agent of the Holy Order of Azyr. You must release me immediately or risk the wrath of Sigmar's armies.'

Most of the aelves continued walking away, including the king, but Thallacrom paused and looked back at her in surprise. 'Sigmar? That name carries no weight here. Does it where you come from? Here, it is a byword for failure and defeat. Sigmar is a spent force. But *you* on the other hand are an interesting specimen. I did not intend to bring you to Dhruim-Ùrlar. It was an accident. You must have been touching Gotrek when I ensnared him. But I prevented the guards from killing you. Your soul is almost as unusual as his.' He peered at her. 'It is almost as though you are two souls in one. Quite unlike anything I have encountered before.'

He means me, laughed Maleneth's former mistress. *So I have saved your life. Oh, the irony. I have saved the life of my murderer.*

'So we have decided to harness your spirit along with Gotrek's,' continued Thallacrom. 'By removing your soul at the same time as his, we will have an even greater chance of success.'

Perhaps not entirely saved, then.

'Success at what?' she demanded. 'What good is our life force to you?'

'We have hunted too long,' said Thallacrom, looking off into the distance. 'It is time to rule. So we lured Gotrek to Karag-Varr.'

'You lured me?' Gotrek shook his head. 'What are you talking about?'

Thallacrom smiled, his face full of arrogance and pride. 'We tormented the Fyreslayer king until his mind was broken. We made the Varrukh believe they were cursed. They are quite the zealots so it was easy enough to do.'

'But how was that a lure for me?'

'We have been studying you since your battle with the Moonclan tribes. We knew you would be troubled by the plight of your fellow Fyreslayers and would want to lend them aid. Then, once we had you where we wanted you, it was an easy matter to bring you down here.'

Gotrek's lip curled. 'You did all of that to ensnare *me*?' He glared at the row of blades again, fists clenched.

'You won't hit them,' said Thallacrom. 'You're not the fool you pretend to be. I can see through your disguise. You play the part of a savage but there is wisdom in you. If things had been different, I would have enjoyed talking with you, Gotrek Gurnisson.' He shrugged. 'But fate has decreed otherwise.' He was on the verge of saying more, but then he shrugged and headed off after the other aelves. A moment later, the light failed and they were plunged back into darkness again, with only the faint glow from Gotrek's chest to reveal the movement of the leeches, tumbling and sliding towards the two prisoners.

CHAPTER THIRTY-FOUR

Maleneth coughed, waving away a cloud of smoke. She had spent the last few hours experimenting with poisons, trying to find something that would kill the leeches without causing an explosion. Finally, she had found a way to burn them. She dug out a tiny, thick vial of liquid and, by pouring small amounts of it across the floor of the cell, she managed to scorch a path clear of the creatures. She only had a small amount of the liquid but it was incredibly potent. Most of the creatures wriggled away, sensing the danger, and those that didn't died harmlessly, melting rather than exploding. Over many painstaking hours, she had almost cleared a route to a sunken area she had noticed in one of the walls. Gotrek had been no help whatsoever, hunkering in the far corner of the room, covered in leeches and muttering to himself. Since Thallacrom had told him he was the reason for the attacks on Karag-Varr, the Slayer's mood had grown even darker.

'It's madness,' said Maleneth, pouring another drop of liquid from the vial and creating more smoke. 'If we try to hunt down the king, we'll just be putting ourselves in more danger. Think how heavily guarded he'll be. He's most likely in a fortress or a palace. He's probably got half his army around him. Do you remember how many Idoneth warriors attacked Karag-Varr? There were thousands of them.'

'Doesn't matter,' muttered Gotrek. 'I swore an oath. I know that means nothing to an aelf, but it means everything to me. I said I'd avenge Thurgyn and I will, however many elgi get in my way.' He clenched and unclenched his fists. 'And now it turns out they only killed Thurgyn to get their hands on me.'

Maleneth stopped clearing the path and turned to face him. 'You're deluded. Even more than usual. It doesn't matter why they killed him. It doesn't matter whose fault it is. Look at yourself. You're wounded. And not just a little. I've never seen you look like this. I don't care what you think, there's no way you could take on the entire Idoneth army.'

'There's nothing wrong with me,' grunted Gotrek, standing up and throwing punches at the air. He turned an even more troubling shade of grey and stumbled before managing to steady himself. None of his wounds were healing. There was still blood running from his nostrils and several deep-looking cuts in his chest and arms. He swallowed hard, grimacing, and Maleneth thought he might vomit. 'I keep my word, aelf.' He slapped the likeness of Grimnir that was glaring out of his chest. 'Or I'd be no better than the damned gods.'

She shook her head, returning to her work. 'You talk about making a difference in the realms and then you tie yourself up in these petty vendettas. You talk big and act small.'

'Petty vendettas?' Gotrek stumbled towards her, as unsteady as if he were still drunk. 'It's a matter of honour, you thagi witch. Thurgyn was their rune-father. And he faced down a grief that would have crushed anyone else. He was going to lead those Fyreslayers back to war. They were going to reclaim that whole stretch of coast. And more besides, I'd wager. And now, thanks to these fish aelves, that's all in tatters. I won't stand by and let that happen.'

She laughed. 'Thurgyn only died because you're stomping around the realms making a name for yourself. You just said so yourself. Can't you see what a mess you're making?'

'I didn't make the bloody mess. It was elgi, as always, with their poison and treachery, twisting things until they're broken and full of spite. If people like Thurgyn can be murdered without anyone caring then your realms really are doomed. It's not a petty vendetta, it's making a stand. It's knowing the difference between what's right and what's wrong.'

Gotrek looked like he might attack her, so Maleneth quickly changed the subject. 'Look at this,' she said, gesturing at the shape she had revealed on the wall. 'I think it might be an old door.'

Gotrek continued glaring at her for a while, then looked at the smouldering path she had made on the floor, noticing what she was doing for the first time. 'What witchcraft is this?' he rumbled, crouching to look at the burned remains of the leeches.

'Not witchcraft,' she replied. 'Common sense. When we were fighting in Karag-Varr, I noticed something. When those magmadroth creatures bleed, the blood melts whatever it lands on. It's like a mixture of blood and lava.' She tapped the vial. 'So I kept a few drops. I thought it might come in handy.' She stoppered it, very carefully even though it was now empty, and placed it back in a pouch at her belt. 'While you've been boasting about your oaths and your honour, I've been finding us a way out of here.' She nodded at the depression in the wall. It was covered in cold, wet lichen and looked like it had not been opened for centuries, but now she was close to it, Maleneth was sure it was a door.

Gotrek was about to say something dismissive, but then looked at the wall and frowned. 'Does look a bit like a door, I suppose.'

She raised an eyebrow. 'Think big. Think about getting out of this place. That's my advice.' She turned back to the door and tried to prise it open with her fingertips. She felt a rush of excitement when it shifted slightly, but then it would go no further, however hard she tried.

'Let the Slayer at it, lass,' said Gotrek, shoving past her and gripping the door. He locked his blocky fingers around the edges and pulled. His muscles swelled and his veins bulged but the door did not move much further than when Maleneth had tried.

'We don't have long,' said Maleneth, looking behind them. The lava blood was cooling and the leeches were sliding back into place. 'They'll be all around the door again soon and we won't be able to open it without triggering another blast.'

'Give me a minute,' he muttered. 'I was just getting the feel of it.' He put one of his legs back, bracing himself for another attempt.

'Careful,' she whispered. 'Don't fling it open so hard it hits some of the grubs.'

He looked back at her over his shoulder, giving her a withering glare, then pulled at the door again. This time he made a low growling sound and the rune in his chest pulsed brighter. Maleneth knew how much he hated tapping into the rune's power, but despite his offhand manner, he obviously realised how urgent it was that they escape from the cell. The leeches were slowly killing them.

This time, the door made a deep, groaning sound as its hinges started to work. Gotrek made an almost identical noise as he leant back, his muscles straining and his body pouring with sweat despite the chill. Then, with a sudden lurch, the door flew open.

Maleneth felt a rush of elation as she saw darkness through the opening.

Her happiness was short-lived as she realised the darkness was a wall of leeches. The door led into some kind of cupboard or storeroom that was heaped ceiling-high with the creatures. 'Don't let them fall,' she gasped as the leeches started to tumble slowly into the cell. 'They'll explode.'

Gotrek and Maleneth grimaced as they stepped forwards, arms outstretched, and embraced the glistening tide of black shapes. There were thousands of the things, and as Maleneth tried to ease their descent, they slowly engulfed her, rolling over her face and head, sliding under her leathers and wriggling in her ears. She wanted to howl, but even that might be enough to disturb them, so she moaned in disgust as they rolled over her, filling the cell.

'You bloody–' began Gotrek but his words were muffled as the leeches filled his mouth.

As the Slayer vanished from view, submerged beneath the worms, the light from his rune was extinguished and Maleneth was plunged back into darkness. There were so many of them pouring down on her that their weight shoved her backwards. She was already so surrounded by the creatures that she did not fall, but instead tilted slowly, face to the ceiling, held up by the thick, writhing mass. She felt them starting to feed all over her body, fixing their mouths to her skin and draining her blood.

You'll suffocate, said her former mistress, sounding panicked. *Crawl back the way you came. There might not be as many there. You need to get your head above them.*

She was right. The pile of grubs was so tightly packed that Maleneth could hardly breathe. She was keeping her mouth tightly shut but leeches were already wriggling around her nostrils, trying to find their way in. Very carefully, she began to twist her torso, trying to face away from the door. It was no use. She could only move a few inches and, as she did so, leeches tumbled into the space she had made and locked her in place.

She wanted to call out to Gotrek, but the moment she opened her mouth, the leeches would rush in. She had felt dazed since she first woke up in the cell but now her head was swimming in a revolting fashion, as if it were floating away from her neck. She prayed furiously to Khaine. *Do not abandon me. I have offered you so much. And I will offer you so much more!*

There was no response. And she could not even say what kind of response she would have expected. The cold, wet leeches tightened around her, squirming and fidgeting in her hair and across her face. She moaned as one attached itself to her eyeball.

Then the whole mass of them began to move, sliding away from the wall and carrying her with them. Her feet were off the ground and it felt like she was floating in a living pool. The movement was slow and stately, and as her oxygen-starved brain grew more confused, Maleneth felt as though she were disembodied: a spirit, carried though the darkness towards another state of being.

To her surprise, the darkness began to fade, replaced by blue-green light that filtered down from somewhere overhead. 'Be careful,' said a voice. 'No sudden movements.'

The light flashed brighter and Maleneth found herself surrounded by a baying mob. They were covenite sisters like her, gathered around an arena. She was back in the Murder Temple, back in Azyr. Her knives were back in her hands and she was preparing to lunge at her opponent, an aelf with cruel, exquisite features who was leaning closer, her face just inches from Maleneth's. 'Remove them one by one,' said the aelf. 'Do not rush.'

As the aelf spoke, Maleneth felt leeches being removed delicately from her skin – and as soon as she remembered the leeches, the memory of the arena fell away and she saw where she really was. She was lying outside the cell, beyond where the row of blades had been. The blades had vanished and there was a group of Idoneth around her, kneeling at her side as they carefully picked off the leeches. The creatures had filled the cell with a glistening mass, but with the bars of the cage removed they had begun sliding out of the cavern, freeing Maleneth. The Slayer was also out, lying a few feet away, grimacing as he endured the attention of the aelves who were stooping over him. She could see by the murderous look in his eye how much he wanted to lash out, and the effort of restraining himself was causing him to growl and mutter.

'You've had a lucky escape,' said the aelf Maleneth had seen first. She was clearly a noble, her features cold and magisterial, but she was not dressed in the heavy, ornate armour Maleneth had seen on the other Idoneth highborn. She wore scarred, battered leathers, similar to Maleneth's own clothes. There was a pair of falchions at her belt and Maleneth's first thought was how easy it would be to snatch them and behead their owner, once the leeches were all removed. The aelf noticed the direction of Maleneth's gaze and smiled. 'This one is not dead, at least. How is the Fyreslayer?'

'Fyreslayer?' snorted Gotrek. 'I'm a true Slayer, lass.'

'Lass?' The aelf frowned. 'My name is Eòrna. I am a thrallmaster of the Dromlech enclave. I have no doubt that you are both considering how best to kill me, but you should know this: I came here to rescue you. And I am your only chance of escape.'

Gotrek glared at her, flexing and closing his hands.

Eòrna nodded. 'And if that is not enough to convince you, you should also be aware that my thralls are all archers of unsurpassed skill.' She leant back from Maleneth and nodded to the passageway that led away from the cell. It was crowded with pale, aelven archers who all had arrows nocked to their bows. Maleneth felt a rush of indignation as she saw that they were all targeting Gotrek. 'I understand you are very hardy,' continued Eòrna, looking at Gotrek. 'But would you survive with a dozen arrows lodged in your neck?'

Gotrek bared his teeth but said nothing.

'You're one of the Idoneth,' said Maleneth, wishing she had her knives. 'Why would you help us escape?'

Eòrna nodded. 'We do not have long, so I will have to keep my answer brief. I am sister to King Dìolan, the ruler of the Dromlech and of Dhruim-Ùrlar. My brother–'

'Dhruim-Ùrlar?' grunted Gotrek.

'This city,' replied Eòrna, clearly frustrated by the delay. 'As I was saying–'

'City?' Gotrek frowned and peered down the passageway, then looked back at the cell. The mound of leeches was still tumbling slowly out of the room. 'We're not in a stomach?'

Eòrna stared at Gotrek. For a moment she seemed thrown by his question. She frowned and looked at Maleneth. 'Is he...?'

Maleneth shook her head. 'Don't ask.' She turned to Gotrek and waved at the shapes carved into the walls, reliefs showing aelven figures riding sea creatures and surrounded by vast waves. 'Does this look like the inside of a fish? We're in a city. An aelven city. She just told you. We haven't been eaten, Gotrek, we've been captured.'

Gotrek looked around at the passageway, seeming unconvinced, but he remained quiet as Eòrna continued. 'My brother means to use your souls in a great work of sorcery. If he succeeds in killing you and harnessing your spirits, he will fundamentally change the Dromlech. He is misguided and dangerous, and I mean to stop him – by sending you back to Karag-Varr, robbing him of the chance to kill you.'

'How?' asked Maleneth. 'How will you send us back to the magmahold?' She looked around. 'Where is this city?'

'We're beneath the Amethystine Ocean. Under normal circumstances, I could have used the Myrway to take you home, but you're bound to this place by Isharann magic. The only way to send you home is to extinguish the power that summoned you here. It's called an Eidolon. I'm going to take you to it right now so that you can destroy it.' Desperation flashed in her eyes. 'But we must be quick. The Eidolon is still relatively weak and I believe Gotrek will be able to destroy it. But once it has fully emerged, it will have the power of a god.'

Maleneth was still feeling dazed and weak. She leant against the wall and carefully picked a leech from her boot. 'Why not just kill this "Eidolon" yourself? Why bother freeing us?'

'It's incredibly powerful,' replied Eòrna. 'Even with all of my soldiers, I doubt I could vanquish it, but...' She looked at Gotrek. 'But I believe you would be able to do it. You have a divine power in you that is equal even to the Eidolon. I believe you can drive it back into the aether. And the moment you do, you will return to Karag-Varr.'

Gotrek shook his head. 'I'm not going anywhere. Not until I find your brother and avenge Thurgyn.'

Eòrna's face went rigid and Maleneth had the impression that she was thinking fast. 'That works perfectly,' said the thrallmaster. 'My brother is visiting the Eidolon in a few hours. Your best chance of finding him, in such a vast city as this, is to come with me to the Eidolon.'

Gotrek studied her, his expression grim, then he nodded. 'Good. Lead me to him and I'll consider letting you live.'

Eòrna clenched her jaw, biting back a comment, then nodded and turned to her archers. 'The Briondal Gate, quickly.'

The archers turned and ran back down the passageway. Eòrna was still flanked by a dozen or so pale-skinned aelves who were carrying swords, but Maleneth was confident that, with the archers running in the opposite direction, it would be an easy matter for her and the Slayer to overcome the Idoneth. Even unarmed, Gotrek was lethal, and she still had a wealth of poisons secreted in her leathers and at her belt. Eòrna was watching Maleneth and guessed her thoughts. 'I am your only chance of getting home,' she said. Gotrek was about to say something but Eòrna spoke first. 'And of reaching my brother. Dhruim-Ùrlar is no ordinary city. It is not only vast, but also in constant flux. Streets change course unexpectedly and routes that were safe the day before can quickly become impassable. Without me, you would be lost almost instantly.'

Gotrek and Maleneth glanced at each other. 'How can we trust you?' said Maleneth.

'You can't, of course,' laughed Eòrna, as though the idea were absurd. 'But I have just rescued you. Why would I do that if I wished you dead? A few minutes ago you were buried under bloodsucking leeches. If you hadn't suffocated, the leeches would have eventually drained the life from you. If I wished you ill I could easily have left you to die.'

Gotrek looked at Maleneth. 'You're an aelf. What do you think?'

Maleneth could not remember Gotrek ever deferring to her opinion before. Or anyone's opinion, for that matter. She was too shocked to answer for a moment. Then she shrugged. 'It's true. She didn't need to come here if she wanted us to die.'

Eòrna nodded. 'I want you out of Dhruim-Ùrlar. Killing you would be too much of a risk. My brother might find a way to use your departing souls. I need you to survive. And to leave.' She nodded to her guards and turned to run after the disappearing archers. 'So we have to move now.'

Eòrna did not look back to check if they were with her, and Gotrek and Maleneth paused to look at each other before they followed. They were both covered in blood, soot and filth and they were gasping for breath. Maleneth's head was still spinning from blood loss and she could tell from the way Gotrek was swaying that he felt as bad. He still had a leech dangling from his ear, like a grotesque piece of jewellery. They both looked like they had fallen from the back of a corpse cart. A faint smile played around Gotrek's mouth as he studied Maleneth's tattered leathers and blood-matted hair. To Maleneth's surprise, his smile made her laugh.

'I hate you,' she said.

'It's mutual,' he growled. Then he limped off down the passageway. 'There's always so much bloody running,' he muttered as Maleneth rushed after him.

CHAPTER THIRTY-FIVE

Maleneth had no idea what an Idoneth city usually looked like, but she was surprised at how deserted Dhruim-Ùrlar was. When they emerged from the building, they were on what looked, to Maleneth, like a broad forest path. Hundreds of feet above her head there was a dense canopy of leaves that drifted and rippled as though suspended in water. Maleneth looked around and saw that everything seemed to be swaying and billowing, as though caught in a current. She took a deep breath, half expecting her lungs to fill with brine, but the air was normal, if a little damp, and she had no problem breathing. It was a peculiar sensation and Maleneth decided that whatever she was breathing, it was not normal air.

Eòrna and her soldiers were already sprinting off down the road, keeping to the shadows, but Maleneth and Gotrek took a moment to look around, taking in the peculiar scene. Maleneth had never seen a city like it. It was almost impossible to distinguish plant life from architecture. As she studied the shapes lining the road, Maleneth began to make out balconies, windows and spires, all wrought in an intricate and distinctly aelven style, but seemingly grown rather than built. She saw balustrades and buttresses but they were made of coral and shell and knotted kelp. There was a profusion of pale colours everywhere she looked and the whole place shone with a light that pulsed, blood-like, through the boughs of the city. It threw rippling shadows, hiding as much as it illuminated, but Maleneth saw fish and other creatures, banking in shoals through the gloom.

'This is weird,' said Gotrek, 'even for aelves.'

Maleneth could not disagree. There was something dreamlike about everything and the cold air ate into her bones, as though it had never been warmed by sunlight. 'We need to keep moving,' she said, nodding at the quickly disappearing aelves and staggering after them. 'She was right. This place looks like a labyrinth. We could wander here for decades if we get lost.'

'Especially as there's not a soul about,' said Gotrek, peering down a tunnel-like alleyway as they ran past it. 'Are aelven cities usually empty?'

Maleneth shook her head. She remembered Eòrna's expression when Gotrek had told her he intended to hunt down the king. She had clearly been keeping something from them. Maleneth had no desire to help Gotrek with his king-hunting so she kept her thoughts to herself, but she had a suspicion that whatever Eòrna was hiding might explain the empty streets.

After a while, Eòrna noticed how slowly Gotrek and Maleneth were moving and paused to wait for them, signalling for her soldiers to do the same. The archers scattered into the shadows, crouching in doorways and clumps of seaweed, arrows nocked as they watched the street. 'We have to move faster,' said Eòrna as they caught up with her. 'We have to reach the Eidolon before your escape is discovered.'

'Discovered by who?' said Gotrek, waving at the empty streets and the lightless windows looking down at them.

Eòrna did not acknowledge his question. 'The Briondal Gate is not far from here. Can you run any faster?'

'Course I can bloody run faster,' snapped Gotrek. 'You're the one who stopped to talk.'

Eòrna looked at Gotrek with a murderous light in her eyes, but she nodded and waved them on, her soldiers falling into step around her. They reached the end of the wide street and ran into a broad, circular plaza. It was surrounded by tortuous, meandering architecture, and Maleneth had the impression that it had only recently been deserted. There were objects scattered across the ground and unattended market stalls with their wares still on display.

'This way,' whispered Eòrna, pointing at one of the streets that led off the plaza and running in that direction. The group hurried after her, but before they had reached the far side of the plaza, one of the archers gasped and tumbled to the ground, clutching at his neck as blood fanned through his fingers. As he came to a halt, Maleneth saw an arrow jutting from his neck. He tried to rise, coughing up blood, but two more arrows thudded into him, landing in his chest and knocking him off his feet. He hit the ground heavily and lay still.

Maleneth dived for cover behind one of the market stalls and Gotrek followed, hunkering down next to her. Eòrna and the other aelves moved so fast they seemed to vanish, slipping quickly into the shadows. There was a moment of tense silence. From where Maleneth was crouching, she could see the dead aelf. The arrows that had felled him were the same as the ones in his quiver. 'More Idoneth,' she whispered.

There was a sound behind them and they both whirled around to find Eòrna had joined them. She and a pair of her soldiers were crouching low behind the stall. Eòrna nodded to one of the other aelves and he put a large bag on the ground. As he unfastened it Maleneth saw a flash of gold, and warmth washed over her, as if the bag contained a campfire.

Gotrek grinned as he drew his axe, Zangrom-Thaz, from the sack. The brazier at its head was fuming and spitting embers in a way that seemed utterly out of place in the dank air of the Idoneth city. 'You're giving this back to me?'

Eòrna looked unnerved and Maleneth could understand why. Gotrek in possession of an axe was not a comforting sight. 'My intention was to keep it from you until the last minute,' said Eòrna, 'but it seems that we will be forced to fight our way to the Eidolon.'

Gotrek seemed to grow as he gripped the axe, testing it with a few experimental slashes. 'It's better than I remember,' he snarled, glaring into the embers.

Maleneth looked in the bag and found, to her delight, that her knives were there too. She snatched her weapons with as much relish as Gotrek, spinning them in her hands and slicing at the air. They were undamaged and looked even sharper than the last time she had seen them.

'Proceed with care,' said Eòrna. 'There are archers at the foot of that building opposite. Only five or six but they could easily–'

Gotrek let out a bone-rattling howl and lifted the market stall from the ground, spilling bottles and jugs as he tore it free, creating a horrendous din. He had slung his axe at his back and he proceeded to charge across the plaza, bellowing as he ran, gripping the collapsing stall in both hands, holding it before him like a massive shield.

Eòrna and the other Idoneth stared in disbelief as arrows whistled towards the Slayer, thudding harmlessly into the stall. Gotrek reached the opposite side of the plaza and hurled the whole structure at the archers, who tried to flee at his approach. Then he took his axe from his back and launched himself at them, trailing sparks and curses as he began to kill.

Maleneth had seen Gotrek in action too many times to be surprised by his deranged attack. She ignored the screams and sounds of splitting bones, and rounded on Eòrna. 'Tell me the truth.'

Eòrna was staring at the carnage with an astonished expression, too dazed to register Maleneth's words. Then, as Gotrek picked the stall back up and smashed it into the aelves, she turned to Maleneth. 'What? What do you mean?'

'You were lying when you told him this was the best way to hunt down your brother, I saw it in your eyes.'

Eòrna's face was rigid and Maleneth saw, again, the fury she was struggling to hide, the desperation.

'Tell me.' Maleneth nodded at Gotrek, who was now swinging the stall around his head and howling, even though the aelves were dead. 'Or I'll tell him he's being lied to.'

Eòrna's mouth turned into a hard line. She clearly was not used to being given orders. Maleneth could respect that. In truth, there was something about Eòrna's furious determination that had impressed her.

'Look,' said Maleneth, softening her tone. 'I have no desire to follow Gotrek on a suicide mission to hunt down your king. I want to get out of here. And I'd prefer to do it while I'm still alive.' She leant closer to Eòrna, keeping her voice low. 'Gotrek is not as stupid as he looks. And if he realises you're tricking him, it will end very badly for you. But if you tell me what you're trying to do, I can help. I know how to handle him.'

On the other side of the plaza, Gotrek was slowly coming to his senses, dropping the remains of the stall and looking around at the mess he had made. Any minute now, he was going to head back over to Eòrna and Maleneth. 'I'll tell him this is a lie,' said Maleneth, 'unless you let me in on your plan.'

Eòrna studied Maleneth for a moment. Then she nodded. 'It's true. We're not heading towards King Dìolan. He won't be on his way to the Eidolon. He'll be at his palace, the Allmarach, over a mile from here.'

'How can you be so sure of that?'

Pride flashed in Eòrna's eyes. 'Because, at this very moment, my ally Princess Arainn is launching an attack on the Allmarach and Dìolan is fighting for his life. The time for change has come and the oldest families of Dhruim-Ùrlar are–'

Maleneth held up a hand. 'You're murdering your brother to take the throne. It makes perfect sense.' Eòrna shook her head and was about to argue, but Maleneth spoke over her. 'Spare me the details of your local politics. I'm sure you have perfectly good reasons and, to be honest, I don't care. Gotrek's heading back over. Tell me what I need to do to get us out of here.'

Eòrna tensed as she saw that Maleneth was right – Gotrek was stomping back over towards them, picking pieces of the market stall from his plaited beard. 'Gotrek has to destroy the Eidolon. It's the anchor that's tying you to Dhruim-Ùrlar. Once it's destroyed, the ether-magic that brought you here will be dispelled. You will return to Karag-Varr.'

Maleneth shook her head. 'Gotrek won't do it. He won't do anything that could send him home before he's killed your king. He's sworn one of his damned oaths.'

Eòrna nodded quickly, glancing at the approaching figure of the Slayer and speaking in an urgent whisper. 'The Eidolon is a violent spirit – an avatar of the etherstorm, formed from the souls of our ancestors. At the moment it is unborn, in a dormant state. If I can get you close to it, I can release it. I can bring it to life. At which point it will launch itself at anyone who is not one of the Dromlech.'

Maleneth nodded, understanding. 'You're going to make it attack Gotrek.'

'Exactly.'

'And how do you know he can defeat it?'

'I can't know that for sure. But from what I have learned about him, Gotrek is uniquely powerful. The Eidolon is a fragment of the divine, the spirit of a god, drawn from Idoneth souls. For most people it would be impossible to defeat, but your companion also has a spark of the divine in him. I believe he might be able to defeat it.' She shrugged. 'Besides, it's that or he dies.' She looked around at the city. 'And everything I cherish will be lost.'

'It's a kind of god?' Maleneth laughed. 'And you want Gotrek to fight it? I think this could work.'

Maleneth nodded at Eòrna then hurried across the plaza to the Slayer. 'The king is on his way to the Eidolon. He'll be there any minute. We have to be quick or you'll miss your chance,' she said.

Gotrek scowled and slapped his axe against his palm. 'Elgi have betrayed dawi more times than I can count.'

Maleneth continued across the plaza and Gotrek followed, glaring back at Eòrna as he went. 'But this one will pay for what he has done. Thurgyn *will* be avenged.'

CHAPTER THIRTY-SIX

Eòrna and the other aelves raced ahead of Maleneth, turning down so many twisted streets that Maleneth gave up trying to understand which direction they were heading in. Gotrek was lumbering after her, slowed by his wounds but still full of bile and determination.

'Not far now,' called Eòrna over her shoulder as she led them through a set of ancient-looking gates built in the shape of a kraken.

Maleneth found the architecture of Dhruim-Ùrlar baffling. There was much in it that was familiar, echoes of shapes she had seen in other aelven structures, but it was all so knotted with coral that she could not discern the purpose of the buildings. After passing through the gate, however, she sensed that she had entered a region of spiritual significance. The light shone brighter and she felt a charge in the air, as though many eyes were watching her. She saw shrines to various deities and decided that this must be a place of remembrance.

Eòrna rushed on through the maze of streets, leaving the shrines behind and hurrying down a broad path towards a dome of yellow coral. 'The Eidolon is in the amphitheatre,' she said, pausing to wait for Gotrek to catch them up. When they had all grouped together again, she nodded and continued at a slower pace, jogging towards an opening in the side of the dome.

Gotrek managed to keep up, and the group entered the dome together before pausing to look around. The amphitheatre was circled with tiered seating, and beyond the glow of the lemon-coloured dome was a dark forest of kelp, drifting and rustling against the cage. As Maleneth's eyes adjusted to the glare she saw a shape drifting at the centre of the amphitheatre – a shell, floating above a dais. Again, she felt a rush of spiritual power, as though her mind had brushed against something ineffable. She whispered a prayer to Khaine as she followed Eòrna and the others towards the shell. It was burning with the same inner glow as the dome, and the light silhouetted a figure at its heart. It was aelven in shape, but larger and even more elegantly proportioned. The figure was so striking that it took Maleneth a moment to realise that the amphitheatre was filled with noise. She heard waves crashing and rain pouring from thunderheads as lightning crackled overhead. Maleneth looked around, half expecting to see actual waves hurtling towards her, but there was no water beneath the dome; the sounds were emanating from the motionless shell above the dais.

'Quickly,' said Eòrna, waving them towards the dais, but as they approached it Maleneth slowed down, unnerved by the sounds coming from the shell. It was a furious din and she held her knives ready as she reached the steps of the dais.

'It's just bloody noise,' said Gotrek, marching past her, but even he seemed hesitant, holding his axe tight as he looked up at the figure in the shell.

Eòrna followed, drawing her swords.

The sound of the storm swelled and Maleneth was reminded of what had happened at Karag-Varr. She wondered why she had put so much trust in Eòrna.

'Many of you did not believe me,' cried an unfamiliar voice, coming from behind them. 'But here is the proof. Now you see Eòrna's treachery for yourself.'

Maleneth and the others whirled around to see a group of Idoneth gathering behind them on the path into the amphitheatre. King Dìolan was there, on his three-tailed steed, and the person who had spoken was the old sorcerer, Thallacrom, but there were countless other nobles who were unfamiliar to her. Some were as ancient-looking as Thallacrom and draped in fine robes and convoluted crowns. Arrayed around them was an army of blind, pale-skinned warriors. They were emerging from the kelp forest in their hundreds, arriving from every direction.

'Arainn,' gasped Eòrna, staring in horror at one of the nobles riding near the king, seated in a howdah on the back of a huge turtle. 'She betrayed me.' Arainn stared defiantly back at Eòrna with an almost imperceptible shake of her head. 'How could she, after what I showed her?' whispered Eòrna.

'Let me guess,' sneered Maleneth, as the lines of grim-faced warriors continued to swell. 'These people are all your close friends and they've come to wish us well.'

Eòrna was still staring at Arainn. 'Eòrna!' snapped Maleneth, grabbing her by the arm. 'What do we do?' Eòrna licked her lips, looking around at the vast army that was still spilling into the amphitheatre. Her guards numbered no more than a few dozen. For a moment, Eòrna looked panicked, but then her eyes hardened. She nodded. 'We do as we planned.' She looked at the ranks of warriors gathering around them. 'There is no chance for us now. We have been betrayed. But we will still stop my brother. We will still send Gotrek home.'

'Send us *both* home, you mean?' said Maleneth as the army advanced towards them.

Eòrna glanced at her. 'Make sure you hold on to Gotrek when the Eidolon dies. If you don't, you will remain here.' There were tears glinting in Eòrna's eyes but she spoke calmly as she turned to her guards. 'Charge the front lines. Move fast. Fight like you have never fought before. I can rouse the Eidolon but you will have to buy me time.' She looked at each of them in turn, her voice shaking. 'Our lives mean nothing now. We fight for something greater. Everything hinges on this moment.' The guards looked shocked but they raised their swords in salute, pressing the hilts to the runes on their brows. 'If we fail,' continued Eòrna, 'we fail every one of our ancestors. If

Dìolan keeps Gotrek Gurnisson here he will use him to destroy everything that we are.' The guards mouthed prayers then turned to face the army, adjusting their weapons and armour.

Maleneth looked around for Gotrek and cursed. He was already limping towards the Idoneth army, scything his axe through the air, his eye locked on Dìolan. There was blood rushing from his various wounds and he seemed unable to walk in a straight line. 'What in the name of the gods are you doing?' she called out to him.

'Fulfilling my oath,' he snarled, carrying on across the plaza. 'While I still bloody can.' He levelled his axe at Dìolan. 'That aelf dies today.'

'Don't be an idiot,' she yelled. 'It's an army, Gotrek. And you can barely walk.'

He ignored her and continued forward as Eòrna's guards sprinted past him, raising their swords in silence as they ran to their deaths.

'Is everyone insane?' muttered Maleneth as the clatter of fighting rang out through the noise of the storm. Eòrna's guards had formed into a spearhead. They were fighting with speed and determination, slicing into the army, breaking up the well-ordered ranks, but they would be dead within minutes.

Maleneth shook her head in disbelief as Gotrek followed in their wake, dealing out a flurry of axe blows and crashing into the aelves. 'For the runefather!' he cried. 'And Karag-Varr!'

For once, Maleneth was unsure how to act. 'I can't leave here if I'm not *touching* him?' She watched in dismay as Gotrek bellowed and smashed his way towards Dìolan, sinking deep into the Idoneth lines. 'How in the name of Khaine am I supposed to do that?'

The sound of the storm swelled in volume, becoming so loud that everyone in the amphitheatre hesitated. Even Gotrek paused to look around for the source of the noise.

Maleneth stumbled and clamped her hands over her ears. It was only then that she realised Eòrna was not at her side. She whirled around and saw that the aelf had climbed to the top of the dais and swung her sword at the shell. A crack had snaked across its surface and the light inside was blazing brighter.

'Stop her!' cried Dìolan, his voice barely audible over the howling of the storm. Dozens of his soldiers continued fighting Gotrek and Eòrna's guards, but those in other parts of the amphitheatre charged towards the dais.

'What are you–' began Maleneth, rushing up to Eòrna, but before she could finish, the shell detonated. Waves crashed into Maleneth, hurling her back down the steps. She rolled painfully to a halt just as a crowd of sword-wielding Idoneth raced towards her. Before they could reach her, spectral waves pounded into them, scattering them across the ground and sending their swords spinning through the air. The waves boiled and turned around the dais, forming a whirlpool hundreds of feet wide. It rolled through Dìolan's army, hurling warriors around like leaves in a breeze. A chorus of howls merged with the noise of the waves as aelves crashed into each other. The scene quickly descended into chaos. There was no way for anyone to fight as the amphitheatre became a lightning-charged tempest. Dìolan's steed bucked and snaked beneath him, and the king howled orders that no one could hear.

Maleneth managed to cling to one of the railings that led up to the dais as warriors and weapons whirled around her. Gotrek was nowhere to be seen but Eòrna was nearby, hanging on to the same railing as Maleneth.

'How exactly does this help?' cried Maleneth, dragging herself closer to Eòrna.

Eòrna was watching the carnage unfold, her face rigid with horror. Then she focused on Maleneth. 'Gotrek has to kill the Eidolon!' she cried, waving at the broken shell. As the storm grew even more violent, the figure at its heart was moving, climbing from the shell, wreathed in banks of mist and rain.

Maleneth felt a rush of dread as the thing loomed over the dais. 'Gotrek's not interested in killing that,' she managed to say.

Eòrna dragged herself closer to Maleneth as she replied. 'But the Eidolon will be interested in him. He's not an aelf. It will not tolerate his presence.'

Maleneth was about to ask how the Eidolon would feel about her, when it became impossible to speak. The storm howled as the Eidolon glided out across the dais, carried on banks of rain and crashing waves. It looked like an aelven noble clad in beautiful armour, but as it moved it broke apart and re-formed, like the waves that surrounded it, rising and falling and merging with the storm. To Maleneth's shame, she felt a rush of fear. For the first time in her life, she understood the contempt that the sea felt for the races who dwelt on dry land. She felt a hatred older than the realms themselves: an ancient, bitter loathing that made her gasp in panic. The Eidolon held a spear aloft as it rushed towards her, howling words, singing the vengeful song of the sea.

Eòrna huddled next to Maleneth, shaking her head and gasping prayers, but to Maleneth's relief the Eidolon moved past them, crashing down the steps in a cloud of spume and mist. Some of the Idoneth tried to kneel and humble themselves before the Eidolon but they were simply washed away, howling and tumbling across the amphitheatre as the god spirit crashed over them. It was moving with a clear purpose and Maleneth saw that Eòrna was right: it was heading for Gotrek. As the aelves were washed away by the deluge, Gotrek was left in an open space, bracing himself against the storm and gripping his axe as he glared up at the Eidolon. He howled as he saw that Dìolan was now beyond his reach, retreating with hundreds of soldiers around him. 'You will not rob me of vengeance!' he roared, pointing his axe at the approaching spirit.

The Eidolon answered with a howl like the end of the world. The noise was so loud that Maleneth felt as though her skull were about to shatter.

Gotrek charged into the tempest and the Eidolon rushed to meet him. In one of its hands it was gripping a hook, and as it reached Gotrek it slammed the weapon into his chest, through the centre of Blackhammer's Master Rune.

The din vanished. Silence filled the amphitheatre. Maleneth watched in amazement as the world froze around her. Gotrek was staring in shock at the hook that had punctured the rune, while all around him Idoneth were hanging in the air or lying motionless on the ground, trapped in a fragment of time, their hands outstretched or held over wounds.

Maleneth tried to speak but she was as statue-like as everyone else. Even the Eidolon was motionless, looming over Gotrek, shrouded in the unmoving majesty of the storm, its spear held aloft. Then, at the point where the hook was embedded in Gotrek's rune, flames began to sprout, rippling across the metal and washing over Gotrek's chest. The fire was unnaturally bright, bringing tears to Maleneth's eyes as it spilled over Gotrek's muscles, engulfing him like armour. The flames kindled in Gotrek's crest of hair, turning it into a blade of fire that rose from his skull, spitting and flashing. The Slayer grew larger as the flames engulfed him, pouring down the haft of his axe and igniting the blade.

Time began again with a thunderclap. Sounds erupted from every direction as people jolted back into motion. The storm exploded into life, hurling aelves and ripping coral from the walls. Gotrek and the Eidolon had become a single point of light, rising up from the ground, dazzling turquoise spirals meshed with a column of ruddy flame. Gotrek was visible in the maelstrom but Maleneth could barely recognise him. He was transformed. It was more than just his crest of flames. His face was altered. He features were less haggard and brutalised. He looked both younger and older. With the hook still embedded in his chest and his feet hanging dozens of feet above the ground, he swung his axe, carving the air with fire and hurling its magma-like blade at the Eidolon's neck.

The Eidolon parried, blocking the blow with its spear, and Maleneth felt a surge of confusing emotions as they fought. The Eidolon was terrifying but it was also beautiful. She felt like kneeling in adoration. It was a beguiling mixture of nobility and savagery. Its face was proud and magisterial, and its limbs were wreathed in the wildness of the sea. As it cast Gotrek down to the ground, Maleneth had to battle the urge to cheer. This was the power of divinity and the might of the ocean, all bound into a single, glorious vision.

Gotrek tumbled across the ground, trailing fire and embers and struggling to rise, but Maleneth was powerless to help him. The Eidolon surged forwards, engulfing the Slayer in waves of mist and spume. For a moment, it looked like Gotrek would be crushed. Then, just as the waves broke over him, he whirled around and leapt at the Eidolon, his face locked in a snarl, his axe a plume of flames as it slammed into the Eidolon's neck.

The storm gave another deafening howl, then collapsed, splashing across the ground. As the waves toppled, so did the Eidolon. It fell, headless, into the storm, exploding into millions of eddying waves.

Gotrek dropped to the ground with a crunch of breaking bones that was audible even from where Maleneth was hunkering on the dais. As the Eidolon vanished, so did the Slayer's fire, and as he landed, he was Gotrek once more. If anything, he looked even older and more disfigured as he struggled to his feet, one of his arms hanging limply at his side and blood pouring from a fresh cut on his brow. As the noise of the storm faded, everyone in the amphitheatre stared at Gotrek. He swayed, punch-drunk and muttering, then raised his axe with his one good arm, pointing it at the distant figure of Dìolan. He cried out, trying to say something, but his mouth was so swollen and bloody that his speech was mangled. Then he began hobbling towards the aelves, spitting blood and teeth.

Maleneth grabbed Eòrna. 'The Eidolon is dead.' She looked back at the shell. It was dark and lifeless. 'He vanquished it. Will we leave now?' She glared at the thrallmaster. 'If you lied to me I will–'

'I didn't lie,' said Eòrna. Like everyone else, she was looking at Gotrek with an expression of disbelief. 'Thallacrom dragged Gotrek here with the power of the Eidolon. You need to reach your friend if you don't want to remain here.'

Maleneth nodded and climbed to her feet, feeling as though she had just survived a shipwreck. Her head was still filled with echoes of the storm and her leathers were sodden. She paused, halfway down the steps. 'Your king will kill you for this. Is that right?'

Eòrna made no effort to stand. She looked exhausted but there was a gleam of triumph in her eyes. 'Yes. I will be executed.'

Maleneth was conscious that she needed to reach Gotrek before he vanished, but something about Eòrna's fatalism bothered her. 'Don't you care?'

'I have saved us,' said Eòrna. 'We can remain as we were. Hidden from the likes of you. Our traditions preserved. We will not be dragged into your wars.'

As Eòrna spoke, Maleneth realised that this was the counterpoint to Gotrek's creed. This was the antithesis of everything the Slayer believed. Rather than trying to save the realms, Eòrna simply wanted to save her way of life. She wanted to avoid the muddled wars of the lesser races. Maleneth might once have understood but now, as she studied Eòrna, she felt revulsion. This was just another form of cowardice.

Eòrna frowned, still looking over at Gotrek. 'He should already be changing. He should be fading.'

Maleneth felt a rush of panic as she saw how far away Gotrek was. He was dozens of feet from her, surrounded by Dìolan's dazed-looking soldiers. 'I need to get over there.'

'No.' Eòrna stood and grabbed her arm. 'Wait. Something's wrong.' They both looked over at Gotrek. He had reached the first lines of Idoneth soldiers; as they scrambled to their feet, grabbing weapons, he knocked them aside, swinging his axe with one hand as he limped towards Dìolan. 'He's not changing,' said Eòrna. 'I don't understand. It was the Eidolon that was anchoring him here. When Thallacrom dragged you both down...' Her words trailed off and she looked around at the crowds. 'It's him,' she breathed, pointing out the sorcerer who was standing not far from the dais, surrounded by guards and pointing his narwhal tusk at Gotrek. 'He's holding Gotrek here somehow.'

There was a clatter of weapons from the other side of the amphitheatre. Dìolan's soldiers had recovered from their shock and were massing around Gotrek, surrounding him in gleaming lines. The Slayer was batting them aside, cursing and shouting, but even from here Maleneth could see that the rune in his chest was dark and lustreless. The Eidolon's hook had changed it. Gotrek stumbled on, shouldering through the aelves, but his wounds were starting to tell. He was slowing. And the slower he went, the fewer swords he managed to parry. Cuts were opening across every inch of him and his shouts were growing hoarse. 'They're killing him,' whispered Maleneth. Rather than grief or pity, the idea summoned a feeling of horror in her.

'Why doesn't he use the power of the rune?' demanded Eòrna.

Maleneth shook her head. 'It's lifeless. And even if it weren't he could never have taken on a whole army.' She rounded on Eòrna, waving a knife in her face. 'You told me he just needed to defeat the Eidolon. Why is he still here?'

Eòrna pointed her sword at Thallacrom, who was reciting an incantation. 'It's the priest,' she said again. 'He's holding him here. We have to kill Thallacrom.'

Maleneth nodded. 'Killing is my particular area of expertise.' She thought for a moment. 'He's a damned sorcerer though.'

There was another bellow from the other side of the amphitheatre as waves of soldiers swarmed around Gotrek and he staggered to a halt, still a dozen feet away from King Dìolan. Dìolan looked vaguely amused as his soldiers rained blows down on the Slayer, filling the air with his blood.

'Damn it,' gasped Maleneth. 'He's not meant to die.' Some of the nearby soldiers had noticed her and were running in her direction. Time was running out. She grabbed Eòrna by the shoulder. 'If I can get within twenty feet of Thallacrom I can kill him. Can you make sure he doesn't notice me coming?'

Eòrna nodded.

The two aelves grasped each other's hands. Then Eòrna sprinted towards Thallacrom while Maleneth ran in a wide loop, approaching the sorcerer from behind. As Maleneth drew closer, she saw that Eòrna was not quite right. From her new vantage point she could see a vague shimmer of power lancing out of the narwhal tusk. Rather than targeting Gotrek, though, Thallacrom was dragging energy from Dìolan, hauling power from the king and casting it at Gotrek. The details were irrelevant, however. Thallacrom had to die. Gotrek was now on his knees, furious and savage as ever, but clearly on the verge of death. Hundreds of warriors were pressing to get close to him and there were arrows jutting from his muscles. He sounded deranged, pausing between blows to level his axe at Dìolan, but unable to get any closer.

Deftly, Maleneth took a pouch from her belt. There was a small leaf inside it. Very carefully, keeping the leaf contained, she dragged it along the blade of her knife, smearing sap along the metal before dropping the pouch.

To her left, a few dozen feet away, Eòrna leapt at Thallacrom's guards. Maleneth nodded in appreciation as she saw how Eòrna sliced through them, whirling and diving in an impressive display of acrobatics. *She would have done well in the Murder Temples,* she thought.

Better than you, at least, sneered her mistress.

As the guards struggled to slow Eòrna's advance, Thallacrom looked furious. 'Stop her, you idiots!' he snarled, keeping his attention fixed on Gotrek. 'What are you doing?'

Eòrna grinned as she ran on, and Maleneth sensed that she was revelling in the chance to attack the priest.

Maleneth was almost close enough to hurl her knife when she remembered what Eòrna had said. 'I have to be holding him when he leaves,' she gasped, looking at the distant figure of Gotrek. 'I'll never reach him.'

Her dead mistress struggled to hide her panic. *Then let him die. Flee. Live to fight again, you fool.*

Maleneth stumbled to a halt, still watching Gotrek. He was surrounded by piles of aelven dead but he was dying. She could barely comprehend it. He was so weak he could barely swing his axe. He was on the verge of falling backwards, and when he did it would all be over. 'He has to live,' she whispered, filled with horror as she turned back to Thallacrom. 'He matters. He means something. I can't let him die.'

You hate him!

I hate *him,* agreed Maleneth, feeling numb. Then she threw the knife.

Thallacrom staggered forwards with a bark of surprise. He looked around, confused, to see who had shoved him. Then he noticed the knife tip jutting out of his chest. His eyes widened in disbelief, then he collapsed, his flesh sliding from his bones and slopping to the ground. Within seconds, there was nothing left of him but a smouldering puddle.

Eòrna was still fighting with his guards but she paused to howl in triumph. Maleneth rushed to her side, and between them they cut down the remaining guards. Then they both looked back over at Gotrek.

For a horrible moment, Maleneth thought the Eidolon had returned. The air around Gotrek was turning and sparking, forming a tornado. Soldiers were thrown clear as he rose from the ground, limp and blood-sodden, but still hurling curses and pointing his axe at Dìolan. As he rose, the Slayer began to fade, just as Eòrna had promised, his flesh becoming as translucent as the storm.

Idoneth soldiers began rushing at Maleneth. Robbed of Gotrek, Dìolan's army turned its attention to her. Hundreds of warriors surged in her direction, their faces full of wrath.

Eòrna leant against Maleneth, gasping for breath. She looked almost as bad as Gotrek, covered in cuts and gripping her arm to her side. She grabbed Maleneth's shoulder. 'Thank you.'

Maleneth could not speak, still dazed by what she had done. The entire Idoneth army was racing towards her. She was completely surrounded. She was going to die. She was going to die for Gotrek.

You absurd child! screamed her mistress. *You've killed us both!*

Ridiculous as it was, Maleneth and Eòrna dropped into battle stances, back to back and preparing to fight, whispering prayers to their respective gods.

Just before the Idoneth reached her, Maleneth looked up and saw Gotrek. The storm had almost taken him. He was breaking apart, his body fragmenting in the wind, but she could still see how furious he was. He was pointing at her, howling and cursing. He was outraged that she had robbed him of his chance to reach Dìolan, but there was also another emotion in his face. Behind the rage there was something even more powerful, a terrible sorrow. She realised that, rather than trying to reach Dìolan, he was now trying to reach her, trying to save her.

Then he was gone. The storm vanished, leaving no trace of the Slayer.

Maleneth turned to face the army, baring her teeth in a brutal smile, her pulse quickening in anticipation of the coming bloodshed. Arrows thudded into her, puncturing muscles and shattering bones, but her bloodlust was so great she barely noticed. As the front lines reached her she leapt forwards to meet them, stabbing and lunging, howling Gotrek's name as Idoneth blades sliced into her body, spilling her blood into the cold, unnatural air.

CHAPTER THIRTY-SEVEN

'There he is,' muttered Korgan, filled with relief when he saw Gotrek's unmistakable silhouette. It was dusk and the Slayer was sitting at the edge of an outcrop, looking out at the ocean. Korgan climbed down from his magmadroth and ordered his Hearthguard to remain with her as he headed off along the edge of the promontory, picking his way between slabs of rusting iron.

'You are not well enough to be out here, Gotrek,' he said as he approached the Slayer. He said the words mainly so as not to surprise Gotrek. The Slayer's axe was lying not far away and Korgan knew perfectly well what would happen if Gotrek mistook him for an enemy.

Gotrek did not acknowledge him, continuing to watch the colourful waves as they boomed against the cliff wall. Despite the Slayer's silence, Korgan felt safe to approach and sit next to him on the cliff's edge. Gotrek still looked terrible. It was nearly a week since he had reappeared in Karag-Varr, tumbling into the square from the storm clouds that had been hammering the mountain since Thurgyn died. And in that week every healer in the magmahold had done their best to treat Gotrek's wounds, but he still looked like he had been mauled by something, or several somethings. His left arm was broken, there was a deep gash across his forehead, and his one good eye was so bruised he was almost blind. Even the rune in his chest seemed altered – dark and inert where it had previously gleamed. Since he had returned, Gotrek had been uncharacteristically calm, accepting the attentions of the healers and eating the food he was served, but he had not spoken a single word. So Korgan was surprised when, after a few minutes, the Slayer addressed him in gravelly tones. 'I should have listened to you.'

Korgan was so taken aback at hearing Gotrek speak that it took him a moment to answer. 'You should have listened to me when?'

Gotrek continued looking out at the starlit sea. It was cold, this far from the mountains, but he showed no sign of feeling the wind that was whistling through the rocks. 'You were the first one I met. On the bridge into your hold. You told me I should leave while I still could.'

'Ah.' They sat in silence for a while, listening to the waves. Then Korgan said, 'Can you tell me what happened? After you left us. After the storm killed the runefather.'

Gotrek scowled. 'Don't start that storm rubbish again. Thurgyn was killed by aelves. There was a battle.'

'I understand…' Korgan hesitated, guessing that he was probably about to enrage Gotrek even further. 'But none of us can remember it. We remember your words and those of your Khainite companion. We remember your talk of aelves who rode the storm. But we don't actually remember them.' He shook his head. 'I've tried, repeatedly, to summon a memory of it, but I can't.'

Gotrek glowered, but then he shook his head and the heat faded from his eye. 'What does it matter?' He looked back out at the sea. 'It makes no difference. I don't think they'll attack you again. It was me they were after and I'm leaving. All these trials you've faced, all these losses you suffered, it was all because they wanted me. For all my fine talk of fixing the realms, I've made things bloody worse. That's why I'm going. I need to get away from you people.' He nodded to a redoubt, further down the coast. Even at this late hour, there were signs of building work as Fyreslayers and humans worked to repair the walls and create new defences. 'You're back on your feet now. You've reclaimed your outposts and watchtowers. You're rebuilding.' He frowned. 'Do you have a new runefather yet?'

Korgan struggled to hide his pride. 'The lodge elders chose me.'

Gotrek nodded. 'You have good dawi steel in your spine. I saw it the first day I met you. You'll do well, lad.'

If anyone else had called Korgan 'lad' he would have been outraged, but from a relic like Gotrek, it seemed reasonable. 'The healers tell me you are not fit to go anywhere, yet. Those wounds are more serious than you realise.'

Gotrek muttered. 'A few scratches never stopped me before. Especially scratches I got from aelves dressed in seashells.'

'But where will you go?'

Gotrek shrugged. 'Away. I think the sodding aelf was right. I'm more trouble than I'm worth.'

Korgan shook his head and nodded at the lights in the distance where the redoubt was being rebuilt. 'None of this would be happening if you hadn't come to us. We used to defend coastal villages from greenskins. Sometimes we'd even strike at the Great Enemy if we saw a chance, ambushing Chaos caravans or outposts. But all we were really doing was surviving, getting by. Now we're doing more than that. We're extending our reach. Karag-Wyr and the other holds are just the beginning. You showed us what we're capable of. And it's all because you saved Thurgyn-Grimnir.' He looked Gotrek in the eye. 'You lit a spark in him. And in the rest of us. You showed us that we can do *more* than survive. We can fight back.'

Gotrek nodded. 'You're dawi. Of course you'll fight back. It's what you were built for.'

'But you didn't answer my question,' said Korgan. 'What happened to you after Thurgyn was killed?'

'I tried to avenge him.' Gotrek spat on the ground. 'I *would* have avenged him. But that thagi witch Maleneth stopped me.' The Slayer clenched his fists. 'She stopped me' – he held up his finger and thumb – 'when I was *this* close.'

'So Maleneth was working with the other aelves?'

'No! Of course she wasn't working with them. She was trying to save me.' He lurched to his feet, glaring at the sky. 'As if *I* need bloody saving!'

The thought of Maleneth seemed to madden Gotrek more than anything else. Korgan decided to remain quiet as Gotrek strode along the cliff's edge, yelling and tugging at his beard as he cursed the aelf.

'What happened to her?' asked Korgan when Gotrek had fallen quiet and sat down next to him again.

'Dead.' Gotrek's voice was hollow. 'Bloody dead. Just like I told her she would be.'

Korgan was struggling to tell if Gotrek was furious because Maleneth had betrayed him or because she was dead. He took out a small, wax-sealed scroll. 'She wrote this,' he said. 'The day before you were taken. Just before the victory feast. She wanted it sent to an address in Barak-Urbaz.'

Gotrek took the letter and stared at it, hatred burning in his eyes. Then he hurled it into the darkness without breaking the seal. 'Still writing to her friends in Azyr,' he muttered. 'Still spying on me.'

Korgan had searched for Gotrek hoping to help him, but he realised his presence was making the Slayer's mood worse. 'Of course you may leave whenever you wish,' he said. 'I just wanted to thank you for everything you have given us. You do not realise the change you have made. The Varrukh are reborn. We are making plans that would have been laughed at before you came. Because of you, the lodge elders are even considering sending an expedition to Karak-a-Zaruk.'

'Karak-a-Zaruk?' Gotrek was looking in the direction he had thrown the letter, as though he regretted not keeping it. 'Is that another one of your holds?'

'No. A ruin. I believe you discussed it with Thurgyn after the battle of Karag-Wyr. Do you remember? It's swarming with skaven now, but it was once the capital of a duardin kingdom, our ancestors' kingdom, the Khazalid Empire.'

'Oh, aye.' Gotrek nodded. 'I've heard of it.' His tone remained bitter. 'A glorious, realm-spanning dawi empire. The sky dwarfs of Barak-Urbaz were banging on about it. I admit, the idea caught my attention. It sounded so much like my own...' He shook his head. 'But if it was everything you people claim, Chaos could never have taken these lands.' He glanced at Korgan. 'Why did this great dawi kingdom fall? Let me guess, were they obsessed with hoarding wealth? Or blinded by hubris and too proud to realise the danger? Or did they stop listening to the wisdom of their elders?'

Korgan shrugged, recalling the sagas and legends of the Khazalid Empire. 'It wasn't any of those things. The empire stood firm. It lasted for many centuries. It would probably still be here now if the Maker hadn't left the realm. He left the duardin to fend for themselves. It was only then that the empire fell.'

Gotrek had been gazing out to sea again but he stiffened and turned to Korgan. 'Grungni?'

'Yes. According to the old sagas, at least. He guided and ruled them, granting them wisdom and performing great feats of engineering. Under his gaze the Khazalid Empire thrived. But then he left and the empire fell. Then came the Age of Chaos and all the terrible things that followed. Our lands were taken from us and the duardin race was sundered. According to the legends, Fyreslayers and Kharadron and all the other races of duardin are remnants of that one, single kingdom.'

Gotrek was staring at Korgan. He spoke quietly. 'Where did the Maker go?'

'Who would claim to know the movements of the gods? But the Sigmarites claim he's with them. They say Grungni dwells in the Celestial Realm, working as a weaponsmith for Sigmar.'

Korgan realised that Gotrek's mood had suddenly shifted. Rather than despondent, he now looked incensed. 'You're telling me that dawi once ruled these lands, and kept them safe, and Grungni abandoned them?'

'I didn't say abandoned.'

'Abandoned,' growled Gotrek, rage sparking in his bloodshot eye. 'I'll bloody say it.' He slapped the lifeless piece of metal in his chest. 'This is what gods do. Do you see? They play with mortals. Use them like toys. Then they cast them aside when something else catches their eye. All this mess. All these deaths. It's on their heads. They sprawl in the heavens, feathering nests while everyone else burns. I've seen it with my own eyes, everywhere I go. Cannibals burning innocent people. Sorcerers welcoming daemons with open arms. The bloody skaven, left to run free, squatting in your old capital, filling it with their filth.' He snatched his axe from the ground, filling the air with embers. 'Well, not any more. This Slayer has had enough. Let Grungni hide up there with his feet on the hearth. Let him be Sigmar's bloody lapdog. I don't need him. I don't need any of them.' He pointed his axe at Korgan. 'Where is it?'

Korgan had fought unspeakable horrors in his life, but faced with a raging Gotrek he struggled to keep his voice level. 'Where's what?'

'The capital. The seat of this old empire. Karak-a-Zaruk. Where is it?'

There was such wrath in Gotrek's eye that Korgan's pulse hammered. 'It lies to the north, somewhere past the Grymmpeaks. No one knows exactly where. And it would be a long journey. Are you well enough?'

'Oh, I'm well enough.' Gotrek glared at his axe, firelight glinting in his eye. 'I'm not done yet, lad. Not by a bloody long shot.'

Gotrek's fervour was so infectious that Korgan felt like howling a battle cry, but he tried to think logically. He shook his head. 'Rebuilding a kingdom means more than reclaiming an old ruin. We could sacrifice thousands of lives trying to drive out the skaven, but what would be left of us? We'd be a spent force. We'd die trying to right an ancient wrong.' He could feel Gotrek glaring at him and he almost backed down, but then he thought about his new role as runefather and held his nerve. 'I will not sacrifice my lodge needlessly.'

'Needlessly?' snarled Gotrek, rising to his feet and glowering at Korgan, his voice trembling.

Korgan stood and backed away from Gotrek, gripping his latchkey axe. As they stared at each other Korgan cursed himself for coming to find Gotrek.

He should have left him to brood alone. Now one of them was going to die. And he doubted it would be Gotrek.

Gotrek readied his weapon, his muscles shaking and glistening with sweat. Then he lowered his axe and stared into the distance. 'It's my fault she died.'

It took Korgan a moment to realise that Gotrek's rage had vanished, leaving him as quickly as it came. He lowered his weapon but kept hold of it just in case. Gotrek's mood changes were unpredictable, even for a Fyreslayer. 'The Khainite?'

'Aye.' Gotrek's expression was bleak. He looked as old as the cliffs, like a piece of blasted, volcanic rock. 'We could have escaped. One of the fish aelves wanted us gone. Maleneth died because I wouldn't listen. Because I couldn't think straight. I couldn't let go.' He looked up at Korgan. 'And here I am, trying to do it again. Trying to lead you to your death. Trying to ease my grief with your blood. I'm bound by my past. I can't shake it off. Everywhere I go. Everything I do. I can't escape it.'

Korgan shook his head. 'I don't know what happened with you and the Khainite, but I know this – she was no pushover. She made her own choices. And you've told me things that give me hope for the future of the realms. *Hope*. Who could have ever expected that? After all these years.' He thought for a moment, then continued. 'You said something at the victory feast. You said you want to drive evil from the realms. And that it was possible. That's not living in the past. That's not trying to right old wrongs. That's making a stand. And I'd stand with you, Gotrek Gurnisson. We all would. And who knows, perhaps then, if we gathered enough allies, if we won enough victories, perhaps there *would* be a way to rebuild the things we've lost.'

Gotrek stared at him, emotions flickering across his face: grief, rage, hope and pain all warring in his eye. Then his gaze cleared and he looked resolute again. 'No. I'd be your bloody death knell. Just like all the others. I won't do it.'

Korgan was going to disagree but Gotrek held up a hand to silence him. 'You're a true dawi, Korgan-Grimnir. You'll make a good runefather and I'm proud to have met you. You've made me realise I was wrong about many things.' He brandished his axe. 'But if you try to stop me, you won't live to regret it.'

Korgan shook his head but he had the sense not to argue. 'Good luck, Gotrek Gurnisson.' They clasped each other's arms.

Then Gotrek slung his axe over his shoulder and marched off down the coast. Korgan stood at the edge of the precipice, watching him go. There was another storm whipping in from the sea, lashing against the cliffs and stirring up the waves. It moaned and howled around Gotrek as he disappeared into the darkness, as though unwilling to lay its fingers on him. Then he was gone.

Korgan whispered a prayer for him, then turned away, heading back towards the hulking silhouette of his magmadroth. He had not gone far when he spotted something pale lying on the rocks. As he picked it up he realised it was the letter Maleneth had written just before she was killed. He opened the scroll and started to read.

Your Celestial Highnesses,

I hope this missive will reach you, but my current hosts are unpredictable, to say the least. I have bribed a servant to deliver it to an agent in Barak-Urbaz but, in truth, he's as likely to leave it under an empty ale cup or accidentally set it alight. The Slayer and I are residing in a Fyreslayer magmahold by the name of Karag-Varr, in the southernmost reaches of the Grymmpeaks. The Fyreslayers are an unruly rabble and we arrived to find them in a state of disarray. To add to the confusion, the hold has been attacked, several times, by Idoneth aelves for reasons that are beyond me. What interest could aelves have in such a place? I know very little of the Idoneth but, as far as I can tell, they have no desire to take the Fyreslayers' lands or goods, so I can only presume the attacks stem from a vendetta of some kind.

When we arrived at the magmahold, the Fyreslayers were in the grips of a religious mania but Gotrek employed his usual tactic of shouting until people lose the will to argue. As a result of his browbeating, the Fyreslayers are now in the process of reclaiming their territories. His behaviour since we left Barak-Urbaz, and the impact he has had on the Fyreslayers, has confirmed a suspicion I have been grappling with for a long time. Great as Blackhammer's Master Rune is, Gotrek is greater. We thought that the rune was a weapon that could help us reclaim the realms, but I now see that Gotrek himself is the realms' greatest hope. He is an appalling specimen, in almost every respect; my opinion remains unchanged in that regard. But he is also unstoppable. Nothing we have encountered has held him back or even slowed him down. And, in recent weeks, he has set aside his various personal obsessions and remained fixed on his idea of setting the realms to rights. I may have ridiculed his ambitions in the past, but the more time I spend with him, the harder it is to mock him. I think he actually has the strength and resolve to make a difference. I can imagine your snorts of derision as you read this, and I can understand your cynicism, but let me say this: until you spend time in the company of Gotrek Gurnisson, you can have no idea of what he is capable of. I have decided that, whatever fate has in store for him, I must do my best to keep him alive and to hold him to this course he has set himself.

Since leaving Azyrheim, I have come to fully understand the scale of the challenge that lies ahead. The worshippers of Chaos are legion. Sigmar's Stormhosts are like a spear hurled at an ocean. There are many reasons for despair, but in Gotrek I see a reason for hope. And I have decided that the best way to utilise his power is to keep him here, on the front lines, where the wars of reclamation are taking place, rather than ensnare him in the halls of Azyr. I realise this is a deviation from our plan, but I urge you to keep faith in me and refrain from sending other agents to intervene. I recently heard a rumour that Captain Drymuss had been killed, not far from here, while attempting to track me down. Drymuss was a valuable agent and, as I'm sure you know, he was also a great personal friend of mine. I would not want you to sacrifice any more members of the order on my behalf. If I need your help, I will contact you, but until then, I assure you, I am perfectly capable of looking after myself and I remain,

Your most loyal and faithful votary,
Maleneth Witchblade

THE CROWN OF
KARAK-KHAZHAR

Darius Hinks

Sephyrum was burning. In some quarters of the city the heat was so intense it had warped the buildings, teasing shapes from the flames. Spires grew knotted limbs that stretched through the inferno. Domes sprouted pink and blue growths that opened like petals. Towers that once stood proud were now as twisted and grotesque as the corpses on their steps.

As Ulvgrid picked her way through the streets, she could not avoid the dead. They were everywhere: hanging from windows and stacked in market squares. They had been betrayed, all of them. These people were believers. When the Stormhosts came, preaching the word of the God-King, they saw their salvation. And instead they got this. This was where their faith had led them. She could still hear the sounds of fighting somewhere beyond the river, on the other side of the city, but Sephyrum had fallen. All that remained of its garrison were pitiful, blackened corpses. Even the ground itself seemed to be under attack. In several places the streets had buckled, spewing toxic geysers of quicksilver. The fighting Ulvgrid could hear was that of desperate survivors, battling to reach the Auratum Gate, looking for a way out. But Ulvgrid had seen the Auratum Gate. There were so many bodies it was impossible to crawl through them. There was no escape.

She paused near some of the dead, spotting a group of duardin lying among the humans. Members of the Ironpeak Clan. Her people. Some were even Ironbreakers like her, wearing the same heavy suits of master-worked armour. If she looked close enough, she might even be able to put names to the dead. Anger surged through her and she whispered a curse. Some of the bodies had been hacked and gored, or filled with arrows, but others had died in a more peculiar way, touched by the streams of alchemical metal. Their flesh had undergone a metamorphosis, transformed into lumps of mangled silver. The quicksilver was a form of liquid changestone and Ulvgrid was careful to avoid it as she moved on, jogging through the smoke, gripping her hammer and raising her shield, hiding in the banks of smoke that filled the street. Somewhere above the fumes there was probably daylight, but since the city had fallen she had stopped measuring time in days. She would have struggled even to say how long it was since the enemy came. At least a week. Two? Perhaps longer. How long had she been scouring these corpse-crowded ruins for a way out?

She paused to drink, taking off her gromril helmet and lifting a flask to her mouth. The water was ash-clogged and greasy but she forced it down, determined to stay focused. Determined not to give up. And she had more than just grit to keep her going now. She had a plan. A hope of getting out. She only had to hold her nerve for a little longer. And then, once she was far away, there would be time for grief and rage.

She ducked into an archway, crouching low. Her squat duardin stature enabled her to take cover behind the plinth as a crowd of soldiers rushed down the street towards her. It was the cultists. She knew it even before they emerged from the smoke. She could hear their thin, cawing laughter. Then they were running past her and she had to stifle the urge to howl a curse. They danced on the dead, kicking the bodies and sneering at them. They looked like characters from an obscene play, with blue, tattooed skin and long, curved beaks in place of mouths. Some of the cultists were human but others, like these, were so corrupted by their devotion to Chaos that it had warped their flesh, tugging swooping horns from their brows and replacing their feet with ridged, blood-encrusted hooves. Ulvgrid found it hard to remain where she was. Every part of her being screamed at her to attack them. To avenge the fallen. They were a sickening mixture of human, bird and goat, but even more disturbing was the way their flesh boiled and simmered, in constant flux, as though not yet settled on a permanent form. The quicksilver had no effect on them, however. They splashed through the metal without a thought. It was a weapon that only harmed the innocent people of Sephyrum, she realised.

Ulvgrid took deep, steadying breaths until they had passed, then she emerged from behind the pillar and sprinted down another street. For a worrying moment she thought she had taken a wrong turn. Then she saw the remains of a guildhall up ahead and knew she was still on the right track. The building belonged to the Ironpeak Clan, and her father had helped build it. It pained her to see it. The anvil-topped columns had buckled and slumped, ripping away sections of wall and causing some of the roof to collapse. A statue of Grungni that once looked out over the entrance had fallen, lying face down in the street.

Ulvgrid waited at the side of the road, staring into the smoke and listening intently. There were screams and cries coming from every direction and the distant crackle of blackpowder weapons, but none of it was nearby. She dashed across the street and in through the blasted façade of the guildhall. It was even gloomier inside. As Ulvgrid reached the central meeting hall, she paused to look around. Everything had been warped by the intense heat. Tiered seating reared over her, tortured into bristling spines by the flames that had ripped through the building. Embers were still rising through the floor, but the flames had ebbed away, having consumed everything they could. The twisted seats gave the place a threatening look and there were blackened remains heaped near one of the exits. Ulvgrid rushed past the bodies, circled carefully around one of the pools of quicksilver and left the meeting hall, heading on through a series of smaller rooms until she reached a storeroom at the rear of the building. After checking again that she was not being watched, she lifted a hatch and hurried down some steps.

The steps were long and narrow, heading into the city's ancient sewers, and she heard the echoing sound of water flowing beneath the city. At the bottom of the steps she paused, looking up at a huge, barrel-vaulted ceiling. Some of the torches had been lit, and as she studied the architecture, she had to battle another surge of rage. Like the guildhall above, her ancestors had built the sewers to be a thing of wonder, a tribute to duardin empires of old. Thick, sturdy columns punctuated the shadows, carved with skilfully wrought runes and relief work. Here was a reminder of what her people were capable of. What they stood for, what they believed in, before they were swayed by the false promises of the Sigmarites.

The sound of laughter echoed through the shadows, interrupting her thoughts, and she hurried on, dropping into the water and wading off into the darkness. Ten minutes later she halted before a large, circular door and knocked with her hammer, striking the metal with a complex series of taps. After a minute or so there was a rumble of hinges and the door swung inwards, revealing a ragged-looking human with greasy hair. The woman's eyes were sunken and wild and she grinned as she leant towards her. 'I knew you'd come back, Mirza,' she said, wrapping her spindly arms around Ulvgrid's powerful, armoured bulk.

'I'm not Mirza,' said Ulvgrid, even though she knew it was pointless to argue.

The woman gave her a sage look and winked. Then she whispered in her ear. 'You saved them, Mirza. The others told me what you did. That you got them out before the fighting started. They'll be fine now. All safe.' The woman's mouth twitched as she spoke and she was blinking furiously. Ulvgrid sensed that she was just sane enough to hear the lie in her own words. 'Isn't that right?' she said urgently, squeezing Ulvgrid's shoulders tighter.

Ulvgrid nodded. She was uncomfortable lying, even to someone who was so obviously insane, but she would be trapped at the door otherwise.

The woman looked relieved and let go of her, nodding her head violently. 'All safe,' she said, repeating the words over and over as she stumbled away from Ulvgrid.

Ulvgrid watched her go, then slammed the door and headed after her. She had half expected the place to have been discovered by now. It could only be a matter of time. She hurried down a smaller tunnel, following the muttering woman. The sounds of laughter and cheering grew gradually louder, echoing weirdly across the old stonework, and after a few minutes the woman opened another doorway and light spilled down the tunnel.

When Ulvgrid reached the opening she paused at the threshold, looking down over a large, circular room with a domed ceiling. It was part of the sewer network, but the waste had been redirected, creating a dry, if filthy, chamber. Dozens of gaunt, wide-eyed survivors were sitting in a circle, leaning against the walls, clutching cups of ale and howling. The centre of the chamber was lower than the rest, creating a pit. The pit was twenty paces or so in diameter and the pipes that encircled it were being used as seating by the drinkers. They were a desperate, ragtag bunch. There were wounded survivors from the local Freeguild regiments, their uniforms in tatters and their cuirasses dark with blood. And there were duardin too. A few were from the Ironpeak Clan and she was careful to avoid their gaze, but there were also foreigners, travellers from the other side of the Muspel-zharr Mountains. Despite their different origins, the crowd were united by one thing: they were all deranged by grief, red-faced and spitting as they leant forwards from the seats on the pipes, howling at the figures in the pit.

Ulvgrid had seen Gotrek Gurnisson fight before. She had spent several days doing just as these people were doing – drinking and betting, trying to become so consumed by the bouts that she forgot the horrors outside; forgot how much had been lost. It was madness. They all knew it. But what did it matter? They had lost everything they ever loved. They were going to die. Madness seemed a blessing. Until now. Now she had hope.

Gotrek was fighting a trio of mercenaries. Humans, from Vindicarum, by the looks of them. Their muscles were covered in tattoos that proclaimed their Sigmarite faith. Two of them were wielding glaives that were taller than they were, and the third was carrying a sword and net of chains. They hissed prayers as they fought. The two with the polearms were trying to corner Gotrek, jabbing their blades at him while the third paced back and forth, looking for an opportunity to hurl his net. As Ulvgrid looked at Gotrek, she forgot her purpose, shocked again by his appearance. He was larger than any Fyreslayer she had ever seen, stout, but almost as broad as an orruk chieftain. His muscles heaved and rolled as he moved, covered in sweat and filth. He was gripping a massive fyresteel axe that was clearly a powerful relic, a brazier burning at its head, spitting embers as Gotrek switched the rune-etched blade back and forth, glaring at his opponents. Even through the muck, she could see the knotted tattoos that covered his skin. Some of the runes were familiar but others were unlike any she had seen on other Fyreslayers. Indeed, she had heard Gotrek deny that he even was a Fyre-slayer, claiming not to worship Grimnir despite there being a metal likeness of the god embedded in his chest. It was none of these things that stopped Ulvgrid in her tracks, however; it was Gotrek's face. His tanned, weathered skin was covered in the most horrific scars, and one side of his face looked like it had been splashed with acid. The skin was shiny and knotted. He had lost one of his eyes at some point and the one that remained burned with such intense emotion that she found it hard to meet his gaze. There was a potent mixture of rage and pain in his eye that she found almost as dis-turbing as the scenes she had witnessed in the city above.

Gotrek sneered with disdain as one of the mercenaries lunged, thrusting his glaive. Gotrek sidestepped the blow and hammered his axe down through the shaft of the weapon, splitting it in two and causing his attacker to stumble backwards, clutching his arm.

The man with the sword hurled his net, but Gotrek moved with a speed that belied his muscular bulk, leaping across the pit, avoiding the net and slamming his forehead into the face of the second glaive-carrier. The man's nose exploded, spraying blood as he fell back, clutching his face and howling. Gotrek reached down and yanked the net towards him. The man tumbled through the air and Gotrek caught him by the throat, punching him twice in the face and hurling him up into the seats.

The crowd exploded into life, jumping to their feet and howling in either outrage or delight, depending on how they had betted. The scene was even more debauched than the last time Ulvgrid had come. Some of the spectators were baying for blood, demanding that Gotrek kill his defeated rivals. But Gotrek seemed oblivious to all of it. With the fight over, the light faded from his eye and he trudged back across the pit, sitting heavily on one of the pipes and grabbing a large cup of ale. As far as Ulvgrid could tell, he drank constantly but never became drunk. He grimaced as he did so, as though the ale were poison, but he continued glugging it down, emptying the cup and then refilling it from a barrel that no one else dared approach.

As Ulvgrid stared at him she felt a pain she could not quite explain. He reminded her of the façade of the guildhall: a broken ruin, twisted by violence and savagery, but seamed with echoes of something else – a dignity that set him apart from his surroundings. His tall crest of hair was matted with blood and there were fragments of bone in his beard, but somehow, despite all of this, he radiated a rough-hewn nobility.

She snatched her gaze from him and made her way through the crowd. The fights were organised by a low life called Pharasalus, and as the mercenaries lay groaning in their own blood, people crowded around the man, waving slips of parchment and demanding their winnings. He saw Ulvgrid approaching and nodded but, for a few moments, he was too busy to speak to her. Where Gotrek had a rough exterior that seemed to hide something greater, Pharasalus was the opposite. His appearance was absurdly magnificent. *One man's misfortune is another man's chance at glory,* thought Ulvgrid as she watched him holding court. He was a wretched individual, but down here, as the city burned above him, Pharasalus had dressed himself as a king.

When the crowd dispersed and people returned to their drinks, Pharasalus sauntered over to her. He was garbed in rich, colourful robes that swamped his bony street-rat body, and he was fiddling with a jewel-studded flintlock pistol, which he waved at a corner of the chamber, gesturing for her to move away from the mob. He nodded with regal flamboyance at the people he passed, then he stooped and spoke quietly to Ulvgrid. 'Well? What did you find?'

She hesitated. The man was a charlatan. Was she really going to do this? Then she reminded herself that the Ironpeak Clan was gone. Nothing mattered any more. The best she could hope for now was to survive. And her only chance of doing that was Pharasalus. 'They've left a single guard,' she said, 'but it's a–'

'A single guard?' exclaimed Pharasalus, his eyes gleaming. 'This will be easier than I expected. The idiots. Who conquers a city and then leaves its treasures unguarded? Morons, that's who. The Ironpeak estates are magnificent. Any fool could see they're worth investigating.'

'They haven't conquered the city yet,' she muttered. 'There's still fighting at the Auratum Gate. And there are a few Stormcast Eternals holding out in Sigendil Palace. Once that's over I'm sure the cultists will make time to divide up the spoils. Besides, I didn't say the estate is unguarded.'

'One man, you said. That means much the same thing.'

She shook her head. 'Not a man. I don't know exactly what it is. It's got hooves and horns, but it stands upright like a man.'

He shrugged. 'I've seen creatures like that. Beastmen.' He pointed his gun at Gotrek. 'The Fyreslayer makes mincemeat of 'em.'

'No, this thing's different.' She grimaced as she remembered the creature. 'It's *much* bigger. Its spear was taller than you are.'

Pharasalus shrugged and nodded to Gotrek, who was readying himself for another fight by swigging down more ale. 'He's like nothing I've ever seen. Haven't you been watching him? He's got beer where he should have brains, but he could still take down an army.' He sneered. 'I'll grind him down eventually. And when he's finally broken, I'll still be able to make use of him. When that day comes, I'll know to bet against him. Even in death he'll be a good little earner for me. But he's not done yet. There's a few more fights left in him. And I'm quite sure he can deal with one guard.'

Ulvgrid barely knew Gotrek, but Pharasalus' attitude sickened her. Bleeding a Fyreslayer dry for profit was grotesque. He was right about Gotrek's strength, though. 'Very well, manling,' she said. 'But we'd better move fast. Once the fighting at the Auratum Gate is done the cultists will be free to start looking around. And you're right. They can't have failed to notice that the Ironpeak estate is impressive. That will be one of the first places they come back to.'

'Agreed. We should leave now.' He frowned at her. 'And you're sure you know the exact location of the crown?'

She hesitated.

'Don't be coy now,' he smirked. 'Your Warden King is dead.' He waved dismissively at the duardin slumped on the pipes with blank, haunted expressions on their faces. 'And that's what's left of your clan. What use is a crown now?' He spoke even more quietly. 'But *I* can make use of it. And if you secure me that prize, I can show you a way out of this hellhole. I'll get you out of Sephyrum alive.'

She nodded. 'I know how to reach the crown. I served the Warden King for years. It was my job to guard the thrindrongol vaults. I can lead you to the right one and I know how to open it.'

'Good.' Pharasalus looked over at Gotrek and unease flickered in his eyes. 'Then I will talk to the Fyreslayer.'

'How do you know he will be willing to help?'

'Help?' Pharasalus laughed. 'He's not the helpful sort. But gods does he love to fight. More than anyone I've ever met. He's only interested in pitting himself against something bigger and nastier than the last thing. He's sulking about something. He told me all about it when he was even drunker than usual. Someone died. Someone he cared about. And it was all his fault. So now he's trying to make himself feel better by swinging that axe at people. If I tell him about your giant beastman, he'll be desperate to take him on. And, to be honest, after that, I don't care what he does.' He nodded at the pit. 'I'm through with all this. I've made enough to tide me over, but if I can get myself the crown, I'll be so wealthy this will all seem like small change. And then I can buy my way out of this wretched realm.' His eyes glinted. 'I can buy a route to Azyr.'

'Azyr?' Ulvgrid had heard the same stories as everyone else. Tales of a heavenly kingdom, filled with beautiful cities that were free of Chaos and war. A place where people lived in peace and prosperity. A place that sounded far too perfect to be true. 'How do you know it's even real?'

'Of course it's real. I've spoken to the Sigmarite priests and even some of the Stormcast Eternals. They've been there. Some of them were born there. Azyr's real and when I have the crown I will find a way to buy passage.' He sneered at the pitiful crowd. 'I'm not doing this any more. I won't live like this. Waiting for the axe to fall. I'm getting out. So the Fyreslayer can do as he pleases once he's dealt with that guard. He could raid the vault if he likes. So could you for that matter. All I want is the crown.'

Ulvgrid could hear the hunger in his voice. The crown was ancient and priceless, but its true value was more esoteric. The band that ran round its base was forged of chamonite, a material that was prized by alchemists above all others. Pharasalus would be able to name his price for an object of such power. She felt another rush of shame as she pictured him cradling it. But then she reminded herself why she was doing this. The Ironpeak Clan was no more. Its grandeur was a memory. And she refused to die in this city. She refused to be a victim. Determination tightened in her guts. She would escape this mess, whatever the cost. She nodded, clenching her jaw. 'Let's go.'

The flames were spreading again. While Ulvgrid had been in the sewers, fires that seemed to be dying had reignited and several streets were now impassable: dazzling infernos with prismatic flames that boiled and danced over the buildings. As she led Pharasalus and Gotrek through the smoke, she realised that the sounds of battle were closer than before. The people who tried to reach the gate must have been driven back and were now being hunted down by the cultists. Along with the clang of blades and the bark of guns, she could hear the shrill, birdlike laughter of beastmen.

Ulvgrid turned a corner and halted, muttering a curse. The road she had intended to take had ruptured, vomiting quicksilver into the air and turning the surrounding buildings into huge, mirrored works of art. There was no way to get past the lethal flood. 'We'll have to circle round,' she said, heading for a side street and gesturing for the others to follow.

This street was clear of quicksilver but it was narrow, and so thick with smoke she struggled to see clearly. Ulvgrid hesitated, then shook her head and marched on. She had grown up in Sephyrum and knew these streets well: the ramshackle inns and dosshouses of the city's poor quarter. Sephyrum had always seemed secure; inviolable. Now it was a slaughterhouse, and the walls that had protected it for so long had become a prison.

A choked scream echoed through the smoke. She halted, horrified, as she saw a woman slumped in a doorway. Part of the wall had fallen and she was trapped under the rubble as a pool of quicksilver spread slowly towards her.

Her face was white with pain and terror as she watched the liquid coming closer. 'I can't move,' she gasped, reaching out to Ulvgrid.

Ulvgrid whispered another curse and hurried over to help. She was conscious of how close the cultists sounded. A delay could ruin everything and she was already having to take the long way round. She grabbed the stone lintel that was pinning the woman to the floor but, however hard she pulled, it would not move. The woman's eyes filled with terror as she saw Gotrek stomping towards her through the smoke, glowering and blood-smeared.

'No time!' hissed Pharasalus as he saw what Ulvgrid was doing. He rushed over, grabbed Ulvgrid by the shoulder and hauled her away from the woman, shoving Ulvgrid on down the narrow street. 'We have to be quick. If we don't keep–'

His words faltered as he realised Gotrek had turned his savage scowl in his direction.

'We have to go,' insisted Pharasalus, but Gotrek ignored him, heading over to the woman. He lifted the lintel with ease and threw it into the street. The woman stared at him, wide-eyed as he crouched at her side and examined her leg. 'Not broken,' he growled. It was the first time Ulvgrid had heard him speak and there was something shocking about hearing intelligible words coming from such a brutal-looking face.

Gotrek reached out a hand to help the woman up, but she screamed and bolted, scrambling off into the ruins. As Gotrek watched her go, emotion flickered in his eye. Was it anger? Or pain? Ulvgrid could not tell. Perhaps both. Then he nodded and his face regained its habitual scowl. He rose to his feet and headed back over to them. She thought he might speak again but he just waited in silence, staring into the smoke.

Pharasalus smirked at him. 'Feel better now? Now you've helped her live a few more minutes.' He laughed bitterly. 'Probably would have lasted longer if you'd left her under that stone.' He shook his head and gestured for Ulvgrid to keep moving.

Ulvgrid paused, looking at Gotrek. 'Thank you,' she said.

He looked up in surprise, staring at her, then he fixed his gaze back on the rolling smoke.

Ulvgrid had an inexplicable desire to make him speak again, to draw him out somehow, but Pharasalus glared at her so she headed on down the street. It led past more burned-out buildings and, finally, onto a market square. She paused under an archway, peering out at the smoke-shrouded stalls and awnings, looking for movement. Pharasalus did the same, crouching at her side and pointing his pistol at the drifting fumes, but when Gotrek reached the end of the street he did not wait, stomping out into the marketplace with his axe slung over his shoulder, looking absurdly nonchalant.

'Wait,' she hissed, but Gotrek was already halfway across the marketplace. There was no sign of attackers so she cautiously headed out after him, making her way through the overturned stalls, holding her shield before her, waiting to hear the horrible laughter of the beastmen. No attack came and Gotrek paused when they reached the opposite side of the square, waiting for Ulvgrid to lead the way.

She pointed her hammer down another narrow street. The houses leant forwards at such a drunken angle that their upper levels almost touched each other, forming a kind of tunnel. 'We keep going that way for another mile,' she said, 'until we come to the edge of the Ironpeak estate.'

Pharasalus nodded, hurrying on through the smoke, his pistol raised. But Gotrek hesitated. He was looking at a doorway. It was one of the city's older structures, built by Ulvgrid's ancestors. The door was tall and imposing and framed by a grand portico. Runes had been chiselled into the columns and Gotrek leant closer to study them.

'We have to go,' she said, but she spoke without conviction, intrigued by Gotrek's behaviour.

'Did your people make this?' he said, tracing a finger over the runes, his voice low.

'The Ironpeak Clan, yes. My ancestors built most of Sephyrum. You can find the odd hovel that was thrown up by manlings, but they tend to fall down after a few decades. Anything old in this city was made by duardin hands. This was a guildhall.'

Gotrek nodded in approval, seeming pleased by her words. He looked up at the doors, studying the carvings. 'Decent work.'

'Sigmar's teeth,' hissed Pharasalus, looking back and noticing they had stopped. He tried to shout and whisper at the same time. 'Keep moving.' He glared at Gotrek. 'Use what little brains you have. This isn't the time for admiring doors.'

Gotrek ignored him and, for reasons she could not fully explain, it irritated Ulvgrid that he allowed Pharasalus to speak to him with such derision. 'Why are you with him?' she asked.

Gotrek looked at her. She could feel him studying her the same way he studied the door, staring at her through the eyeholes of her helmet.

'You're better than him,' she said. 'I can see it.' She shrugged. 'I don't know what you've done in the past. Pharasalus said you let someone down. That you failed them. But I can see that you're no savage. I saw what you did for that woman. So why do you let the manling speak to you like you're worthless? What hold does he have over you?'

'What hold does he have over you?' Gotrek's voice was like iron dragged through gravel and his eye was blank. She thought, at first, that he was simply mimicking her words, too brain damaged to understand them. Then she realised he was pitching her own question back at her. 'Why would you give him the crown of your people?' he said. 'Why would you hand it over like a worthless trinket?'

She knew nothing about Gotrek. She did not even know which Fyreslayer lodge he belonged to. But his question cut into her. 'I have no people any more,' she snapped. 'We put our faith in Sigmar's Stormhosts and that mistake cost us everything. The Crown of Karak-Khazhar *is* worthless. A worthless old relic.'

'A worthless old relic?' He laughed. It was a horrible sound. 'That's me.' He frowned. 'Karak-Khazhar? Is that the name of your kingdom?'

'No. We're the Ironpeak Clan. Karak-Khazhar was one of the elder kingdoms. The kingdoms of our most distant ancestors. Our crown is a relic from the time before Chaos came. The time when the realms were still untainted. Some say that is why it's so powerful.' She hesitated, battling emotion. 'The crown is what binds us together.'

He gave another scornful laugh. 'And you're giving it away.' He left the door and continued on up the street. As he went, Ulvgrid studied the map of scars that covered his muscles. She had never seen anyone who looked like they had endured so much violence. Every time he spoke it filled her with a desire to know more about him, about why he would demean himself by working with a wretch like Pharasalus. Her home was burning around her ears and the Ironpeak Clan was scattered and broken. She was about to hand over the most prized relic of her people because it was now worthless. She had so many terrible things to care about. And yet, instead of thinking about that, she found herself obsessing about this grizzled old Fyreslayer. For some reason, it pained her to see him trudging after Pharasalus, acting like a whipped cur. She wanted to shake him out of his bleak mood.

'My mother taught me a saying,' she said as they walked on. 'When I was very young, I was complaining about an old toy. Moaning about how scruffy it was, being ungrateful for what I had been given, and she said, "The cloak is new, only the holes are old." Have you heard that one?'

He laughed, shaking his head, and she sensed she had surprised him again. 'I have. Or something very similar. Where I come from, the saying was different: "The axe is new, only the dents are old."' As he walked on, she saw his expression lighten for a moment as he remembered something. 'The axe is new,' he muttered. Then the hard look came back into his eye and he glanced at her. 'Why do you care who I serve? Or who I failed?'

'I don't know,' she said, and it was the truth. She could not explain it even to herself. There were many other terrible things she could be thinking about. Perhaps that was it. Perhaps thinking about Gotrek was a way to avoid thinking about everything else. She was about to ask him where he came from when he halted, his muscles tensing as he gripped his axe in both fists and stared into the smoke. 'Do you see that?' he said.

She followed the direction of his gaze. He was looking above the street, where the upper storeys of the buildings leant close together. Some of the smoke was acting oddly as it drifted over the roofs, shimmering with blues and pinks and turning in a different direction to the rest of the fumes.

Pharasalus hurried back over to them. 'What is it?' he demanded, looking up at the shadows in the smoke.

'Get back,' said Gotrek quietly as more of the colourful shadows appeared and started drifting down through the smoke towards them. Pharasalus did as Gotrek said, hunkering behind a cart, gripping his pistol, but Ulvgrid stayed at Gotrek's side. He did not seem to notice her as he stepped towards the approaching shapes, swiping his axe idly back and forth and humming a tuneless dirge.

Ulvgrid stared at the patches of colour, confused. There were three of them and they were moving in an odd way, drifting and sinuous, like fish in a current. 'What are they?' she whispered. 'Birds? Or are they–'

Her words were drowned out by a scream so piercing it made her gasp.

She stumbled, almost dropping her hammer, and slumped against the wall of an inn, groaning at the pain in her head.

The first of the shapes burst into view, trailing painfully bright colours as it hurtled at Gotrek. Ulvgrid was so tormented by the scream that her eyes were streaming and her tears fragmented the shape, making it hard to see clearly.

The shape slammed into Gotrek, filling the air with blue contrails as it flapped what looked like wings. It was nothing like a bird though. More like a triangular slab of blue flesh peppered with eyes. The eyes were pus-yellow and they rolled ecstatically as the shape wrapped around Gotrek, smothering him like a blanket.

Ulvgrid was paralysed with fear and she could hear Pharasalus gasping prayers, but Gotrek simply wrenched the thing off and slammed his axe into it. It screamed louder as his axe tore it in two. Rather than blood, colour exploded from its flesh, colours so bright and strange that Ulvgrid felt nauseous as she tried to look at them. As the first monster dissolved into ripples of blue and pink, the second one dived at Gotrek. He stood his ground, cutting it down in silence, a look of mild distaste on his face. He destroyed the third with the same brutal dispassion and then, finally, the dreadful screaming ceased.

Ulvgrid lurched away from the wall, staring at the remains in shock, watching as they boiled and disintegrated, melting away into the air. She was about to ask Gotrek what they were when she noticed movement in the corner of her eye. Another of the creatures was rushing through the air, approaching fast, but Gotrek had not seen it. It was silent and hurtling at him from behind. Terror knotted in her stomach but she strode forwards to meet it, howling an oath and raising her shield.

The monster screamed as it hit her shield. The impact jarred through her shoulder but she held her ground, driving the thing back, leaning into it. Gotrek whirled around, but before he could rush over, Ulvgrid stepped back and pounded her hammer into the monster. It had nothing she could describe as a face, so she swung at the spot where it had most eyes. It tumbled away, crumpling in a heap on the ground and thrashing over the cobblestones. It tried to rise but she hit it again, bringing her hammer down with such force that colours exploded all around her.

Gotrek reached her side and roared wordlessly. He heaved his axe into the monster, splitting it down the middle and creating another gaudy explosion. Pieces of blue flesh tumbled across the ground, flapping like stranded fish. Then they dissolved, forming clouds of prismatic dust that whirled away into the darkness.

Ulvgrid and Gotrek stood side by side, breathing heavily, watching as the last traces of blue skin whipped away from them. The memory of the screams echoed around Ulvgrid's skull and she shook her head, trying to rid herself of the pain.

Gotrek laughed and clapped her on the back, his hand landing with such force that she stumbled forwards. Then, without a word, he turned and continued walking down the street.

Pharasalus rushed over, pointing his pistol at the tendrils of colour that were still drifting through the air. His face was ashen. 'What was that?' he hissed.

Ulvgrid hurried after Gotrek. 'What were those things?' she demanded.

Gotrek glanced at her, his lip curling in distaste. 'Daemons.'

She cursed, glancing back down the street. The traces of colour yet lingered in the shadows.

Gotrek was still looking at her. 'You did well to stand your ground.'

She felt an absurd rush of pride as she realised she had impressed him. Why did she care? He was a savage who wanted nothing from life but to kill things. No, she thought. That was not true. She remembered how he'd looked when she made him remember his past. There was a complexity to this Fyreslayer. A subtlety that Pharasalus had overlooked. She considered saying something to this effect, but dismissed the notion as ridiculous and marched on.

'We're here,' she said, as they reached the end of the street. It joined another that ran along the edge of a large garden. The garden was bordered by tall, iron railings and she waved her hammer at a distant pair of gates. 'It's unlocked and it still seems to be unguarded.'

'Unguarded?' Gotrek glared at Pharasalus. 'You told me there was a bloody great monster.'

'There *is* a monster,' said Ulvgrid. 'Inside the grounds, guarding the doors to the main house. If it's still in the same place, at least.'

Gotrek muttered into his beard. Then he nodded and stomped off down the road, following the railings towards the gates, swinging his axe from side to side. There were fires raging in every direction and every few seconds screams echoed through the smoke, but Gotrek made no attempt at subterfuge.

'We should keep to the shadows,' she said, catching up with him.

He gave a dismissive grunt. 'The Slayer doesn't skulk.'

Pharasalus was hurrying ahead of them towards the gates, eyes bright with avarice, but Ulvgrid stayed at Gotrek's side. 'What will you do with your treasure?' she asked. 'Are you headed for Azyr too?'

He halted and glared at her with such ferocity that she backed away. Then he shook his head and carried on. 'I will not be going to Azyr. And I don't want any of your bloody treasure.' He waved his axe at Pharasalus. 'And if you had any pride you wouldn't be letting him anywhere near it.'

'What difference does it make?' she said. 'It's in the hands of the cultists now anyway. What could be worse than that? There's nothing I can do. At least Pharasalus is better than they are.'

Gotrek let out a bark of laughter. 'He's not.'

She knew it was true. Pharasalus would not care whom he sold the crown to or how it was used. He was a murderer and a war profiteer, and before the city fell she would never have dreamt of striking a deal with him. 'There's nothing I can do,' she said.

Gotrek muttered into his beard but she could not make out his words. Then they reached the gate and Pharasalus was there waiting, pistol raised as he peered into the shadowy gardens. Compared to the rest of the city, the gardens looked relatively intact. The fires had not managed to cross the lawns and the distant stands of trees were not burning.

'Where's the beastman?' said Pharasalus.

'A beastman?' growled Gotrek. 'You promised me something worth fighting.'

'It's not the same as the others,' said Ulvgrid quickly as she realised Gotrek was about to leave. 'It's huge. And its skin is covered in glowing runes. It's not a normal creature. It's more like those things.' She waved her hammer back the way they had come. 'More like the things you called daemons. It had more horns than head.'

Gotrek still looked dubious but he no longer seemed to be on the verge of leaving. 'You'd better be right.'

She realised how tenuous the situation was. If Gotrek left, there was no way she could get Pharasalus to the crown before the cultists returned. And if she failed to get him the crown, she would never get out of Sephyrum. The thought hardened her resolve. She would *not* die here. 'Follow me,' she snapped, leaving the path and heading off across the lawns. 'Keep to the shadows. Approach the house without being seen.'

'You mean creep about?' said Gotrek with a scornful laugh. Then he marched off down the path.

'He's insane,' said Ulvgrid, watching him in disbelief.

'He's a moron,' said Pharasalus, heading after Gotrek. 'And he's drowned what little sense he had with ale. But he'll have no trouble dealing with the guard. However big. Besides, there's no time to sneak about. Speed's the only chance we've got.'

The trio rushed through the grounds of the estate and, as they left the fires behind, a little daylight managed to break through the smoke, picking out the statues that lined the way. Each statue represented a Warden King of the Ironpeak Clan. Ulvgrid looked at the ground as she walked past them, feeling their cold, dusty eyes boring into her. Gotrek glanced back and, even though she was wearing her helmet, seemed to sense her discomfort, shaking his head in disapproval. He was about to say something, but Pharasalus spoke first. 'Is that it?' he said, his voice taut with excitement. 'Is that the house?'

Ulvgrid looked up and saw a broad, hulking building looming out of the shadows. It was a magnificent sight. This building had been the royal seat of the Warden Kings for centuries and it was one of the few parts of the city that was yet to be despoiled. The clan had fought, and died, at the city gates, far from here, so their home was as it had always been – a mighty slab of stone, lined with fierce statues and surrounded by ornamental gardens. 'Aye,' she said. 'This is it. We can only reach the vaults through the main entrance and the guard was waiting just inside.'

'Finally,' muttered Gotrek, picking up his pace. There was no mistaking the front entrance. It had been built to resemble the snarling face of a duardin warrior and the doors were imposing slabs of iron covered in circles of angular runes. He jogged up the wide, sweeping steps and paused before the doors, testing the weight of his axe and looking positively excited.

'Wait,' said Ulvgrid, rushing to catch up with him. 'The guard... It's not like the other creatures.'

He looked at her in confusion. Then he laughed. 'Are you *worried* about me?'

She felt ridiculous. 'I just want you to be clear what you're facing.'

'I'm clear.' He marched up to the row of doors. One of them was wide open and she saw the polished floors inside, stretching off across the grand entrance hall. 'I just hope your friend is still inside.'

Ulvgrid looked back at the gardens. Pharasalus was still quite far from the steps, strolling in a pompous, leisurely manner, his gun trained on the lawns as he walked down the path.

'I still don't understand why you're helping him,' she said, looking back at Gotrek.

The Slayer paused, halfway to the doors. 'He provides me with distractions. Which stops me having to think.' He narrowed his eye. 'I can bear anything but bloody thinking.'

'But the city is full of monsters.' She waved her hammer at the golden haze that surrounded the estate. 'You can take your pick of opponents.'

He scowled at her, looking even more furious, and she sensed she had touched a nerve. 'I will,' he muttered. 'Now the battle is lost, I'll start hunting. This just seemed like a good place to start.'

'Now that the battle is lost? What do you mean?' Ulvgrid found his words infuriating and confusing. He radiated power and nonchalance, but nothing he said made any sense. There was something maddeningly obtuse about him. 'Why would you fight now if not before? Why wait until the battle is lost?'

He looked even angrier and colour flushed his cheeks. 'I refuse to fight Sigmar's wars for him.' His words were strained.

She felt a rush of anger. 'But you could have, couldn't you? Whatever you are. Whatever mistakes you might have made in the past. You could have made a difference here.' She forgot her fear of him and strode closer, pointing her hammer at his face, her voice raised. 'You chose not to do anything when you could have helped. It's true, isn't it? You could have done something.'

'I don't fight for the God-King.'

She was furious now. 'What about innocent people? Could you have fought for them?'

A worrying blank look filled his eye and he gripped his axe, stepping towards her.

'What's this?' laughed Pharasalus as he reached the top of the steps and saw Gotrek and Ulvgrid squaring up to each other. 'A lover's quarrel? I thought you cave-dwelling types all liked each other?'

Ulvgrid and Gotrek answered as one as they turned to face him.

'*Cave-dwelling?*'

He shrugged. 'Or whatever you call them.' He looked through the doors then waved Gotrek on. 'Come on. Get on with it. I don't have time for your bickering.'

Gotrek closed his eye and took a long, slow breath. Then he nodded and stepped inside the house with the other two following close behind.

There were no torches lit inside but daylight was falling from windows in the ceiling, creating glittering columns of dust. There were a few bodies sprawled on the polished floor – guards, clad in armour that was identical to Ulvgrid's – but there was no sign of movement. Gotrek marched out across the centre of the hall, blinking in and out of view as he passed through the columns of daylight. 'Which way?' he demanded when he reached the centre of the hall. His voice echoed around the vast, empty space.

Ulvgrid hesitated. 'The guard was in this chamber when I fled.' She looked around but there was no chance they could have missed such a large beast. 'It could be anywhere now.'

Gotrek glared at her.

'Which way are the vaults?' asked Pharasalus impatiently. He caught Gotrek's furious expression and shrugged. 'That's the most likely place it will be anyway. That's what it was sent here to watch.'

Gotrek muttered in agreement, so Ulvgrid pointed her hammer to one of the doorways on the far side of the hall and they all marched on, keeping their weapons ready. The doorway led onto a series of grand staterooms and corridors. The larger part of the building was sunk into the side of a hill, with many of the rooms underground, and as they left the entrance hall behind, the light faded. Ulvgrid had no trouble seeing in the half-light and she guessed it was the same for Gotrek. Pharasalus, however, stumbled to a halt, muttering curses. Then he took a torch down from a sconce on the wall and lit it, throwing ruddy light across the flagstones.

Finally, they reached the innermost recesses of the house, where corridors were narrower and the doors were mostly bolted and barred. Ulvgrid was leading now, confident of her route, and every now and then she looked back at the other two. Pharasalus had a look of smug condescension on his face and she sensed he was already picturing himself in Azyr, beginning a life of luxury and plenty, but Gotrek seemed distracted, muttering to himself as he stomped down the corridors. He was looking at the relief work that covered the walls: bold, angular carvings that showed the duardin ancestor gods and the heroes of the Ironpeak Clan, building and mining deep beneath the Muspelzharr Mountains. 'Decent work,' he mouthed as he brushed his fingers across the masonry. There was a look of grudging respect in his eye that pained Ulvgrid. She understood what Gotrek was feeling. It was not just the quality of the carvings that was impressive, it was the story they told. The Ironpeak Clan had endured for centuries, overcoming foes and hardships that would have crushed a lesser people. Even when the other duardin clans had been destroyed by the legions of Chaos, her ancestors had fought on. And it was all here, brought to life by the light of Pharasalus' torch. So much had been lost.

Gotrek looked at her, about to say something when a sound caused them all to halt. It was the heavy, rasping breath of a large beast, and it was coming through a doorway that was a dozen feet further down the corridor. The door was an impressive slab of metal, but it had been torn from its hinges and was lying face down on the flagstones.

Gotrek's eye flashed with excitement as he looked from the broken door to Ulvgrid. 'Finally,' he said with a savage grin. 'Is that your friend?'

She nodded, keeping her voice low. 'And that's the treasure vault. We're exactly where we need to be.'

Pharasalus closed his eyes and whispered a prayer of thanks. Then he nodded at the doorway. 'Get me my crown, Fyreslayer.'

A muscle twitched beneath Gotrek's eye and his nostrils flared. Ulvgrid thought he was about to shout at Pharasalus, but he simply nodded and ran on down the final stretch of the corridor, passing several doorways and heading into the next room with Ulvgrid and Pharasalus following close behind.

'Grungni's beard,' gasped Ulvgrid as she saw the state of the vault. The floor had split open, just a few feet from where they were standing, creating a wide fissure filled with quicksilver. The liquid had burst up with almost volcanic force, throwing the floor into a jumble of cracked planes and angles. There were a few dead guards lying gleaming on the floor, their bodies transmuted into metal statues, and some of the cupboards and cabinets had collapsed, either turned to metal or simply rent in two by the movement of the floor.

'How do we get across?' demanded Pharasalus, sounding panicked. The river of quicksilver was too wide to leap across and it barred their entry into the main part of the treasure vault.

'There,' said Ulvgrid, pointing her hammer. A stone column had been dislodged and had fallen, creating a bridge over the liquid. It was not touching the metal, so it was still made of stone, though in several places it had cracked. 'I think that would take our weight.' She was not entirely convinced by her own plan, however. The column was very slender and looked like it might crumble at any moment.

'Where's the bloody beast?' demanded Gotrek, looking around at the wrecked chamber. There was no sign of a guard.

He scowled at Ulvgrid, then marched over to the fallen column. She tensed as she watched him reach it and step out onto the crumbling stone. It creaked and shifted but it held as he walked carefully across it, gripping his axe in both hands for balance as he crossed the shimmering expanse of quicksilver. When he reached the other side he began shoving chests and tables around, as though he might find a monster hiding under the furniture.

'If it holds him, it will hold us,' muttered Pharasalus, rushing over to the bridge. He began edging across and Ulvgrid followed. Once they were all on the other side, they stood looking at the wreckage. The cultists had clearly spent some time examining their loot. Chests had been smashed and overturned and there were priceless relics everywhere: books, weapons and jewellery lay heaped in mounds. It seemed like nothing had been taken.

'I wonder if they even care about these things,' said Ulvgrid, stooping to pick up a ceremonial axe. It was centuries old, cast in the shape of a roaring dragon, and she knew every detail of its history. She knew its name and the name of the warrior who used to carry it. She studied the intricate metalwork, remembering the times she had seen the weapon used in battle, then she laid it carefully back down in the wreckage.

'Where's the crown?' demanded Pharasalus.

'Over here,' she replied, leading him to a seemingly plain stretch of wall. The stone was covered in relief work and one of the images showed the Maker God, Grungni, hammering at an anvil with such force that lightning was erupting from the blows, spreading across the wall in a fan. Ulvgrid hesitated. This was her last chance to leave the crown in peace. Perhaps the cultists would never find it? But what difference did it make? They would eventually tear this place down or melt it into quicksilver and the crown of Karak-Khazhar would be lost forever. She took a bundle of keys from her armour and slotted the largest one into the wall. It fitted neatly into a hole at the point where Grungni's hammer was smashing lightning from the anvil. She turned it with a click that resonated through the chamber. Then Grungni fell away from her as a large section of wall dropped into the floor, rumbling and spilling dust and revealing a hexagonal doorway.

Pharasalus gasped as he stepped through into the next room. It was only ten paces square and it was completely empty apart from a single plinth at its centre. Through some clever duardin artifice, the chamber had been designed in such a way that a column of daylight shone down from somewhere overhead, picking the plinth out of the darkness and glinting on the crown that was sitting on it. Ulvgrid had seen it many times before, but she still felt a rush of pride. It had been made using techniques that were lost to modern duardin. Even the finest silversmiths and jewellers had no idea how the thing had been created. It was a knot of metal bars, forged in such a way that as one studied it from different angles, it seemed to shift and take on different shapes.

'Are there any traps?' breathed Pharasalus, licking his lips eagerly as he approached the pedestal. 'Am I safe to take it?'

'No traps,' she replied, feeling numb. 'No thief could ever get this far.'

'Until now,' he said, grinning at her.

'Until now.'

He lifted the crown and held it up, turning it in his hands so that the light flashed across the bands of metal, scattering beams across the walls. 'Beautiful,' he whispered. For a horrible moment, Ulvgrid thought he was going to wear it, but then he secreted it in a bag he had slung over his shoulder and hurried from the room.

As Ulvgrid followed him out, she caught sight of Gotrek. He was on the far side of the room, axe drawn back, preparing to swing at a door. 'Wait!' she cried.

'Maybe your beast is in another room,' he grunted, swinging the axe.

There was an explosion of sparks and Gotrek staggered back from the door, shaking his head. 'Bugger,' he muttered, as he saw that the door was unmarked.

'It's gromril,' she said, hurrying over to him. 'You'd need a battering ram to knock that down. Besides' – she held up the keys – 'there are easier ways to open it.'

He muttered into his beard, then nodded at the door. 'Open the bloody thing then.'

'Why?'

He waved his axe at the treasure chamber. 'Your beast friend isn't here, is he? Maybe he's in one of the other rooms.'

Ulvgrid shook her head. 'The door's still locked. The cultists can't have gone any further than this room.'

Gotrek scowled and was about to say something when a loud crashing sound filled the chamber. They both whirled around, weapons raised, looking back towards the entrance.

'Thank you for your help,' said Pharasalus, smiling cheerfully at them. He was standing on the other side of the pool of quicksilver. He had shoved the fallen column into the liquid and, as Ulvgrid watched in horror, it sank beneath the surface. There was now no bridge. No way back to the exit.

Gotrek barked a curse and rushed across the chamber, heading for the pool of liquid metal.

'No!' cried Ulvgrid, racing after him. 'Don't let it touch you!'

Gotrek snarled but came to a halt at the edge of the metal pool. He levelled his axe at Pharasalus. 'You get back here or I'll have your bloody head.'

Pharasalus shrugged apologetically and nodded at the expanse of liquid metal. 'Not possible, I'm afraid.'

Gotrek began pacing back and forth at the edge of the pool, shaking his head and spitting.

Pharasalus laughed. 'I'm sure the cultists can help you out of here when they get back.'

Ulvgrid was shaking with rage. 'I led you to the crown. You swore you'd get me out of this city!'

'And you told me this place was guarded by a monster. Looks like neither of us was telling the truth.' He leant out over the metal and whispered theatrically. 'I'll let you in on a secret – I never had any intention of taking you to Azyr with me. I'm a survivor, Ulvgrid. And that means ditching dead weight like you. In fact, I didn't even intend to...' His words trailed off as a large shadow washed over him.

'You were right,' laughed Gotrek as a figure emerged from the corridor behind Pharasalus. 'I take it all back. He *is* a big lad.'

Pharasalus cried out in alarm and backed towards the pool of liquid metal, snatching his pistol from his bag. Ulvgrid could have told him he was wasting his time loading the thing. The monster approaching him was ten or eleven feet tall and even more heavy-set than Gotrek, layered with great slabs of muscle. She realised she was wrong about it: this thing was not a beastman. It had a tangled crown of horns and thick, blood-clotted hooves, but it was so large and muscular the ground shuddered as it stomped towards Pharasalus. A long tail snaked behind it and, rather than the lunatic stare of a beastman, its eyes were filled with an expression of cool malice. It was naked apart from a filthy loincloth, but every inch of its skin was covered in runes: angry, open wounds that shimmered, as though there was a furnace burning beneath the monster's skin. It was carrying a spiked shield and a long, barbed spear that it pointed at Pharasalus as it approached. It looked at him with disdain; then, as it caught sight of Gotrek on the far side of the pool, it smiled, hunger flashing in its inhuman eyes.

There was a loud report as Pharasalus fired his pistol. The shot hit the creature in the centre of the chest, causing it to rock back on its hooves. But it showed no sign of pain, keeping its gaze locked on Gotrek as it walked towards the pool.

Pharasalus cursed and began reloading his pistol.

As the monster reached him, it paused and casually skewered him with its spear, never taking its eyes off Gotrek.

Pharasalus cried out in shock as he saw the monster's spear jutting from his chest. He shook his head, a confused expression on his face. He looked at Ulvgrid, frowning, as though about to ask something, then the monster yanked the spear free and Pharasalus toppled to the ground in a shower of crimson.

'Come on then, pretty boy,' Gotrek said, grinning as the monster waded through the quicksilver. As with the other cultists Ulvgrid had seen, the monster seemed unaffected by the liquid changestone, walking calmly towards Gotrek. The two brutish warriors stood facing each other for a moment, wearing identical expressions, both clearly relishing the prospect of fighting each other.

'What in the name of Everpeak are you?' muttered Gotrek, looking the huge creature up and down.

To his obvious surprise, it replied, speaking in low, gravelly tones. 'Myrmidon,' it said. The creature seemed to struggle to form the word, but there was a cool intelligence in its eyes. 'What are you?'

Gotrek's grin broadened. 'A Slayer.' Then he howled and rushed forwards, swinging his axe.

The creature moved with surprising speed, dropping into a crouch and bringing up its massive, disc-shaped shield.

Embers billowed from Gotrek's axe as its blade clanged against the shield.

The Myrmidon laughed in surprise as Gotrek's blow caused it to stagger backwards. Then it turned in a quick, fluid motion and thrust its spear at Gotrek's face. The creature was not as primitive as Ulvgrid expected. It moved with the practised grace of a gladiator and Gotrek was hard-pressed to parry, bringing his axe up just in time to stop the spear.

Gotrek knocked the spear tip aside and leant forwards, howling in the monster's face. It was then that Ulvgrid realised Gotrek was the more terrifying of the two. There was something dreadful about the blank look in his eye. He looked deranged. Like a predator, intoxicated by the scent of blood. He dived at the monster, slamming head first into its chest, and the two of them rolled away through the mounds of armour and treasure, landing furious blows on each other.

Ulvgrid followed, hammer raised, trying to spot a chance to help, but they were so frenzied that she dared not risk attacking for fear of hitting Gotrek, or of being hit by him for that matter. The two brutes careered across the chamber, lunging and parrying, thrusting and blocking, but they were too well matched. Neither could land a blow. They slammed into columns, shedding masonry and kicking up clouds of dust, and Gotrek hurled a barrage of curses at the Myrmidon, howling and laughing as he slammed his axe repeatedly against its shield.

Ulvgrid looked back at the exit. Pharasalus was dead, lying in an awkward heap at the edge of the pool. And even if he were alive, there was no way he could have helped them across. As Gotrek and the Myrmidon whirled around the chamber, punching and hacking at each other, she noticed that there was another column, identical to the one they had used as a bridge. This one was still standing, still attached to the ceiling. Perhaps, if she could topple it, they could use it to span the pool? She dashed over to it and tapped it with her hammer. It was sturdy enough and seemed undamaged, but she was an Ironbreaker.

'Gotrek?' she said, but the Slayer was too busy to hear. He and the Myrmidon were fighting near the pool. Neither of them had managed to land a blow but neither showed any signs of flagging. They were fighting in silence now, their faces rigid with concentration. They had the measure of each other and they were looking for weaknesses, probing and testing with every lunge.

Ulvgrid turned back to the column and decided she had no option. Even if Gotrek managed to kill the Myrmidon they would still need a way out. She took a step back, braced herself, then swung her hammer.

The column made a sound like a thunderclap and a crack rushed up its centre.

The Myrmidon hesitated, surprised by the sound, and failed to parry one of Gotrek's blows. The Slayer's axe thudded into its chest with such force that they tumbled to the ground.

Ulvgrid staggered back from the column as pieces of masonry rained down, clanging against her armour. The ceiling let out a low, mournful groan and sagged as the column started to tear free.

'On my oath,' muttered Gotrek.

Ulvgrid whirled around, presuming Gotrek had seen the teetering column, but he wasn't looking at her. He was staring at the Myrmidon. The monster was rising from the ground, radiating a light that was coming from its own body. Gotrek's axe blow had triggered a peculiar reaction in its skin. The runes carved into its muscles were now burning furiously, spilling beams of dazzling, infernal light as the Myrmidon rose to its full, impressive height and grinned at Gotrek. Rather than being weakened by the wound in its chest, it seemed to be invigorated, flexing its muscles and stretching its arms, arching its back as though it had just woken from a satisfying sleep. Then, moving too fast for Ulvgrid's eyes to follow, it rocked forwards and hurled its spear at Gotrek.

Gotrek tried to dodge, but he was too slow and the tip thudded into his shoulder, kicking him off his feet and sending him tumbling back into a pile of ingots. The metal bars toppled down over him as he cursed and grasped at the spear, struggling to wrench it free as the Myrmidon thudded towards him.

The monster reached Gotrek and did what he had failed to do, ripping the spear free with contemptuous ease and drawing it back for another thrust.

Gotrek tried to get clear, but he was buried under dozens of ingots and his movements were painfully slow.

Ulvgrid cursed and slammed her hammer into the column. It broke free with another deafening crack and fell towards the Myrmidon.

The monster turned and raised its shield just in time. The column exploded over the metal disc, showering Gotrek and the Myrmidon in rubble. As the dust cleared, the Myrmidon looked at Ulvgrid with a scornful smile.

There was a clattering sound as pieces of metal tumbled across the floor. The monster's smile stiffened as an axe blade flashed through its neck. Then its head slid sideways from its shoulders and thudded to the floor, quickly followed by the rest of its bulk. As the Myrmidon collapsed, Gotrek lowered his axe and peered at the monster's runes, as though waiting for it to leap back to its feet and attack him.

The headless Myrmidon remained where it was. Ulvgrid half expected flames to spill from its neck, but blood rushed out instead, creating an angry cloud of steam as it met the pool of quicksilver. Gotrek held up a warning hand as Ulvgrid approached. 'Give it a second, lass. It might decide to grow another one.'

She nodded, then flinched, raising her shield as the ceiling let out another groan, hurling more rubble across the floor. 'The whole place is coming down,' she gasped, looking for another way out.

'Aye,' laughed Gotrek. 'I noticed you took a dislike to that pillar.'

She stared at him. They were stuck in a room that was about to collapse around their ears, and even if they survived that, they would be trapped until an entire army of cultists arrived. There was also a thick stream of blood rushing from Gotrek's shoulder. But, for the first time since she'd met him, he looked cheerful. 'Why are you smiling?' she gasped, as pieces of stone crashed down around them.

He tapped his axe against her armour. 'You're a proper *dawi*.' He took a deep breath, as though breathing clear mountain air rather than whirling dust. 'Does me good to see it.'

'We're going to die in here,' she said quietly. 'Doesn't that mean anything to you?'

'Die?' He laughed. 'I've never quite got the hang of that.' He grabbed the Myrmidon's corpse and hurled it across the pool, backing away as metal splashed across the floor. The monster was just large enough to rise above the surface.

There was another booming sound as the wall nearest to them bulged and shook. 'I wouldn't hang around in here too long,' said Gotrek, running across the corpse to the other side and pausing to wait at the exit, looking back at her.

The wall came free with a scream of tearing rock and Ulvgrid sprinted across the corpse, just reaching the other side of the pool as the whole chamber toppled behind her. Together, they bolted back through the corridors and halls, followed by clouds of dust and the din of collapsing walls, and a few minutes later they were back outside. There was still no sign of the cultists so they paused for a moment at the top of the steps to catch their breath, coughing and spluttering, their lungs full of dust.

Ulvgrid leant against the doors, doubled over and gasping, then noticed that Gotrek was watching her. 'What is it?' she snapped, unnerved by the intensity of his stare.

He wiped the spit from his beard and held out a hand. As she took it she felt the ferocity of his grip, even through her armour. 'The cloak is new,' he said.

'Only the holes are old,' she replied, finishing the adage. 'Why are you saying that?'

'The Ironpeak Clan is still strong,' he said.

She laughed. 'The Ironpeak Clan is dead. It died in the first wave of the attack.'

Gotrek took something from his shoulder and Ulvgrid realised it was Pharasalus' bag. He lifted out the Crown of Karak-Khazhar and handed it to her.

She stared at it, confused, as sunlight flashed across the bars of knotted metal. 'What do you expect me to do with this?'

'Wear the bloody thing.' He shrugged. 'Or choose someone else to wear it. Just don't give it away.'

Her pulse quickened as she realised what he was suggesting. For a moment she was too overcome to speak. She was on the verge of laughing again, but she bit it back. His expression was too serious. 'I don't understand what you want of me.'

'I don't want anything of you, lass. But your people do. That crown is what binds your clan together. You told me yourself. So keep it safe. And find your kin.' He waved his axe at the flames beyond the grounds of the estate. 'Lead them. Get them out of here.'

'Impossible,' she muttered, but she could not hide the sense of excitement that was rising in her. Somehow, when Gotrek spoke of the impossible, it seemed possible.

He seemed to read her thoughts and amusement flickered in his eye.

'Would you help me?' she asked, her words hesitant.

He bared his teeth in a terrifying snarl. It took her a moment to realise he was grinning.

THE DEAD HOURS

David Guymer

Nieder Pedsen had been watching the drunk since before the doors had shut them all in for the night. The drunk's hobnailed boots hung from the spectrewood stool, the iron toecaps swinging like gibbeted knights across the stretcher beam. The pale wood had been carved to resemble a human bone. Nieder was not learned enough in anatomy to know which bone, only that it looked sufficiently realistic to him. Back in the days that his thrice-great grandfather had walked as a living man, the denizens of Skeltmorr had made such objects from the real thing. The local craft shops had been famous for the things they could do with bone. But times changed. It was the way of the living to change with them.

Oblivious, the drunk snored on. His broad, bullied face lay in a puddle of ale. The table was strewn with the restless corpses of supper: empty flagons, dirty platters, intestinal loops of fried cabbage. Dried yolks clagged his orange-dyed beard and his snores rattled the cutlery. The aelf, fortunately, had left her drunken companion an hour previously. Hamnil had won the snap of the wishbone on that score, and had followed her. He was not back yet. But Nieder wasn't worried. Hamnil was careful and thorough. Nieder didn't expect to see him before Hysh-rise ushered out the dead hours.

He wasn't concerned so much as disappointed.

His gaze slid to where the duardin's axe lay on the floor under the dangling right boot. The fire bound to its uncanny metals scraped greedily at the bare stones. It had already taken off the straw, and frightened the gheist-roaches deeper into the folds of the oubliette dimensions that existed beneath the skirting boards. Black Mals had wanted to put his foot down where the axe was concerned, but there had been something in the duardin's swagger as he had come in, caked in bone dust and strange gore, shouting for ale, food and lodging – and in that particular order – that had made the old man bite his tongue and bide his time.

Nieder wasn't a worldly man, but he reckoned himself to be about as large as men came anywhere in the Princedoms. Traders passing through Skeltmorr were few these days, and tended to come in well-armed groups with big men as bodyguards. And Nieder had even been called on to subdue the occasional flesheater that wandered into the Bone Drake Inn with strange ideas in its head.

He eyed the drunk. And his axe.

Neither looked as though they would be dealt with easily.

'What are you waiting for?' Black Mals' voice rasped like a hair shirt over ghoulflesh. His eyes were large and sunken. His skin was papery. His head was crowned with a lank string of nuisance hair. Some said it was for the colour of his hair that he had earned his name. Others, and that was Hamnil and Nieder included, suspected it was because if you cut him then that would be the colour he would bleed.

'The size of him, though...'

'He's not grown any since closing time. And nor will you. Not even if you wait until the Nadir swallows the Drake with all of us still here inside.'

'We should send for Hamnil.'

'Hamnil will be preparing the aelf for the Tithekeeper. He'll be busy all night.'

'*You* could lend a hand, old man.'

Black Mals polished the countertop with a spirit-soaked rag, as though it were the skull of a particularly loathed ancestor for display above the privy shed.

'He'll wake if I have to pull him to the door,' Nieder said.

'Kill him here, then. But keep it clean. That axe of his has taken off the sawdust and I don't want a mess to deal with before serving the breakfast crowd.'

Nieder frowned, then nodded to himself and eased out of his corner.

He rolled his shoulder, limbering up the stiff joint, and pulled the wooden maul from the loop strap on his belt. He weighed it in his hand. Eyeing up the duardin's broad skull. Picking his spot. Hands of the Bone King, the duardin was even more massive up close than he had appeared from the corner. His feet may not have touched the floor, but the breadth of him was sprawled across the full width of the table.

'Enough tiptoeing.'

Nieder started.

Black Mals scowled and went on. 'Club him and be done with it.'

Nieder turned back to the table.

He found one bloodshot, madly inhuman eye glaring back up. 'Club who?' its owner slurred.

Nieder made a choking sound.

This, he promptly learned, was due to a fist the size of a corpsing shovel squeezing tight around his throat. The duardin hauled Nieder over the table and through the culinary wreckage. Nieder put up a fight, but it was like resisting a horse. The duardin drew him in until Nieder was at his eye's level. Stale beer dribbled like saliva from the creased skin of his ruined face. His beard was a drowned mess of congealed fats and mustard stains. His eyepatch sat askew, revealing a scarred hollow underneath, and his breath was so potent that being close to it was like being held face down in a barrel of ale.

Nieder remembered the maul in his hand. He struck the duardin over the head with it.

The stranger grunted. His one eye crossed. He staggered half a step, a dent in his stark crest of orange hair, but without ever loosening his grip on Nieder's throat.

Tingling in his face and in his fingers, Nieder lifted his maul for a second attempt.

Nieder was close to twice the duardin's height, but when the drunkard shoved him off he tumbled the half-dozen yards to the bar and slammed into it with a knucklebone rattle of blunt knives and broken crockery. He lay there on his side, too winded and dazed to even try and crawl away.

'Who were you calling *old man*?' said Black Mals, his ancient wheeze from beyond the countertop punctuated by the *bolt-snap* of a breech-loading rifle. 'It'll be your bones for the Tithekeeper if you don't take better care.'

The duardin stumbled as though the act of propelling Nieder so hard had upset his balance. One windmilling fist caught his table's corner and, like any wobbling drunk groping after something solid to hold on to, he pulled it hard towards him and hauled it off the floor like a huge, two-hundred-pound shield. The handful of unbroken plates and tankards still on it crashed to the floor. It just happened to be the exact moment that Black Mals took his shot.

The blast obliterated half of the table.

The duardin glowered over the jagged edge of the lower half, wood splinters and metal shrapnel sticking to the cooking fats that coated his jaw like glue. He hurled the table to one side, clear across the wide taproom, and advanced unsteadily on the bar.

Black Mals cursed. The rifle rattled in arthritic claws as he fought to clear the breech and reload.

A brief scuffle. A scream. A muffled thud.

The sound of an antique rifle stock being buried in an old man's skull.

Then a gurgle.

Blood trickled over the counter's edge and pattered the back of Nieder's neck.

Nieder wriggled determinedly along the ground towards the duardin's greataxe. There would be some collateral harm. The Tithekeeper would just have to take the duardin in two pieces instead of one.

A heavy-bottomed boot pressed on his shoulder, driving his cheek and brow into the bare stone and leaving his fingers worming impotently shy of the axe's haft.

The duardin cleared the gravel from his throat.

'I would have it known, manling, that Gotrek son of Gurni is not in the habit of brawling with the common townsfolk. His axe thirsts after redder meat. But, as has been made plain to him on one occasion too many, the rules of this time continue to escape him.' The duardin leant over his propped thigh. Nieder groaned under the added weight. 'I freely admit to making it up as I go, and shan't deny enjoying myself on occasion.'

'I–'

'Shush, manling.' Gotrek gave his head a shake, and looked blearily around the empty tavern. 'I appear to be missing a companion of mine.' He raised one bloody haunch of a hand to about the flat top of his crest of hair. 'Poisonous-looking thing. All skin and bones. About yay big.'

'I'll never– *Arrrgh!*'

Gotrek reached across to retrieve his greataxe, the duardin's full and enormous weight crushing down on Nieder's shoulder and chest.

'Forgive me, manling. You were saying something.'

The fire bound to the two monstrous blades licked at the duardin's face like a skin hound delighted at the return of its master. The grease stuck to his face popped and sizzled, but made no clear mark on his skin. Nor even his hair. The golden rune that was embedded in his wide chest appeared to brighten with the near touch of its sister flame, muttering and scowling in a voice like beaten metal and molten rock. Half heard. Wholly felt.

'Hamnil.' Nieder kicked himself inwardly, but didn't stop himself from saying it again, louder. 'Hamnil took her.'

'What does he want with my aelf? Why would anyone *take* an aelf?'

Nieder's eyes slid to the door.

Gotrek followed his look. 'All right then.' He took his weight from Nieder's back.

Nieder gasped, clawing his way back towards the bar and freedom, only then to cry out again as the duardin picked him up by the ankle and dragged him towards the door.

The duardin butted open the heavy doors and hauled him over the door jamb. A pair of lightless moons hung from the sky above like skulls mounted on posts. Behind, the grey brick façade of the Bone Drake loomed into horned shadow. The night was starless and bitter.

Gotrek let go of Nieder's ankle. He looked up and down the deserted street. Not a gheist or rasp moved. Every door was locked, every window shuttered.

'Which of these hovels has my aelf in it? Grungni alone amongst your pantheon of false gods and pretenders knows how many times I have sought to be rid of her. And she of me. But to have her snatched from my side in the dead of night by some backwater potboys with a grisly trade on the side...' The duardin seemed to harden in the dark, muscles creaking like cooling metal. 'It would sit *ill* with me. And she swore she'd guide me on to Thanator's Manse, and still owes me for the night's board.'

'She'll have been taken to the Tithekeeper.'

'Who, or what, is that?'

'The town champion. He gathers the tribute we owe and delivers it.'

'Where?'

Nieder shook his head. 'Only the Tithekeeper truly knows. Beyond the Marrow Hills and across the Sunken Sea, to a dread regent of the Undying King. He rules from a seat of bone and in exchange for the yearly tithe sends his fleshless legions elsewhere. We emptied our crypts, handed over our reliquaries, dismembered every crook in our gaols. But it wasn't enough. We took to disposing of travellers. There was a time when Skeltmorr saw a lot of travellers.'

'Few of them come back a second time these days, I'd wager. Does the aelfling live?'

'These are the dead hours. Not even the Tithekeeper would labour through Nagash's time. She will be drugged and bound, ready for the Tithekeeper come morning.' He bit his lip as if to keep himself from saying more, then blurted out. 'It was Black Mals who told me to kill you there in the tavern. I only meant to hand you over to the Tithekeeper with the aelf.'

The duardin startled him with a huge laugh. The broken lengths of old, fire-damaged chain bolted to his wrists rattled like wraiths bound in spirit iron. 'I have lost count of all the things that have sought my death, and long ago ceased taking such attempts personally, or mourning their failures.' Gotrek leant in close, threatening to smother Nieder again with his odour. 'And where did you mean to drag this corpse of mine when the shameful deed was done?'

Nieder stammered. Playing for time. Selling out Hamnil was one thing. Crossing the Tithekeeper was an altogether darker step to take.

Even now, he knew who he feared most.

A shutter banged open from across the street. Gotrek lifted his one-eyed gaze. Nieder looked up. A white-haired woman in a cryptsilk gown leant from her window. She looked across the street, silent as the night, her expression too distant to make out.

'Back to your bed, old mother,' Gotrek growled. 'Unless you're the Tithekeeper I've heard so much of then my quarrel is not with you.'

The woman disappeared back inside. The shutters banged closed.

'Nosy wench,' said Gotrek.

'I can't betray the Tithekeeper,' Nieder hissed, low enough that the words would carry no further than the duardin's ears. 'The Bone King will come looking for his missing tithe and then the whole town will die.'

'Maybe they will. Maybe your Tithekeeper's been lying through his teeth and they won't.' The duardin shrugged. 'Where's my aelf?'

From across the street a door creaked open. It was the old woman. She emerged into the street, her white gown fluttering in the thin breeze like the death shroud of a ghost. Unheard and barely seen, several more doors breathed wide and exhaled their occupants into the night.

None of them moved. They watched.

'Go back to your homes. This is no business of y–'

Gotrek grunted sharply, and Nieder's gaze travelled up to see an arrow sticking out from the side of the duardin's thick neck.

The Wislass sisters, both women widowed within a year of one another by the Tithekeeper, stood at their windowsill with shortbows in hand. The first shot had been the elder's. The youngest was still straining against her bowstring with the arrow nocked. Gotrek bared his bloody gums but made no attempt to step out of the way. If anything his drunken stagger only squared his shoulders to make an even larger target of himself.

The widow took her invitation and loosed. The arrow flew an inch clear of Gotrek's shoulder and skidded off down the dirt road.

The duardin grunted in disappointment.

'Take him to the Tithekeeper,' said the old woman from across the street, and started deliberately forwards. She pulled a long knife from the sleeve of her gown. The rest of the townsfolk followed a step behind, drawing in from every shopfront and porch step.

'I'm beginning to like this town,' said Gotrek. 'Tell me again what it's called.'

The old woman flashed her knife across the duardin's arm. He bent lazily into the blow and took it across the snarling beast maw emblazoned on his shoulder plate. He produced a crooked grin of ale-brown teeth, and with an explosion of neck strength head-butted the old woman in the chest. She flew back as though kicked by a gargant, skidding the last few yards to rest by her front door.

'Hammer of Sigmar!' Nieder made a clumsy hash of a twelve-pointed star across his chest.

'You can't just cry to whichever god suits,' Gotrek roared, blood splattering his monstrous face. 'Pick one and pray like hell that you picked right, like the rest of us do.'

Cackling mercilessly, Gotrek ducked the swing of a butcher's cleaver, broke the arm that wielded it, then hoisted the man by the belt and hurled him headlong into a dozen others, scattering them all like pins. Cockspur, the skinner, leapt on Gotrek from his blind side and rammed a knife into the muscle of his neck. Gotrek simply shrugged him off and raised his axe. Nieder sprang up with a shout. Gotrek flung back an elbow without bothering to turn, parting him from his cudgel and dropping him to the floor with a face full of broken pieces. Unstoppable, the duardin's axe clove the skinner from neck to hip. The man screamed for longer than a dead man ought, fire gouting from his open mouth as the weapon's power devoured him from the inside out. The duardin shouldered the crisped meat aside and swung his axe to meet the war-scythe that crashed into the cheek of the blade.

Nieder gawped over his broken jaw at the sight of the Tithekeeper roused to battle.

He was a strong man, beneath his dark robes, broad and tall, his features concealed behind a ghoulish sack mask. It was an old tradition, to separate the man from the grisly task, but in practice there was no one who did not know who he was or bless him for the service he gave.

Gotrek shoved back with a savage grunt. The Tithekeeper rode the push and spun, his war-scythe flickering. Gotrek sidestepped at the last, and a blow that would have claimed any other mortal's head whispered across the metal plate of his shoulder. Gotrek countered with a crude punch of his axe butt. The Tithekeeper parried it. Sparks flew where the weapons met.

The Tithekeeper was Skeltmorr's greatest fighter. He needed to be. He was the one who undertook the perilous trek to the place of tribute. He was the one it fell to, to take action when, despite the best efforts of the entire town, the sum of the tribute again fell short. Once, years ago, Nieder had thought that he had had what it took to be the Tithekeeper. The champion had put him on his back with a single move.

Now, he watched as Gotrek and the Tithekeeper traded blows, daring to blink only as the champion's charred body hit the ground and his head rolled towards the tannery.

Gotrek spat on his beaten rival, and after another few seconds had dispatched everything else in the street that was not yet smouldering and still of a mind to fight. The Wislass sisters launched a further flurry of arrows, a few of which were shallowly buried in Gotrek's chest, while the duardin moved on from slaughtering the living to set about tearing down the front wall of the women's house. The happy crackle of flames took up roost in the half-timber frame and quickly spread, smoke pouring into the street.

The duardin stepped out from the spreading inferno, unburnt. Nieder peeled himself up off the ground. He stood before Gotrek with his head bowed, as he would before his god or his king. Talking felt like chewing on a lit coal, but he did it anyway.

'I'll take you to your friend.'

The belfry at the top of the mound wasn't the largest building in Skeltmorr. That burden of honour rested on the Bone Drake. Or it had. The inn's timber skeleton was still burning. But the old church was considerably older. It had been erected on the site by the followers of Sigmar, long before there had been a town on these hills, a brotherly gift of devotion to the faithful of the God-King's dearest friend and ally. The bell had not tolled in generations and would not, so the legend went, until Nagash sought penance from his spurned brother and had forgiveness granted. Hummocks of turned earth dotted the climb towards its gates, regular as soldiers, as though a regiment of Graveswatch had been turned to crumbly ash-grey soil by the decree of the Bone King.

'What is this unhallowed ground?' Gotrek breathed, gripping tightly to his axe.

'Where we buried our dead.'

The duardin shook his head but spoke no more aloud. Nieder led him along the winding path to the church's threshold. Articulated columns of rough-hewn black stone framed its pallid gateway. Old and faded runes marked the bleached wood, Sigmarite spells to ward off the predations of skull-faced gods.

'Shoddy stonework,' said Gotrek.

'It's older than the hills.'

'So am I.'

Nieder had no answer.

'Is it locked?' said Gotrek.

'Always. And warded against–'

'Good,' said Gotrek, and kicked it down.

He stomped through. The stark light of his axe-metal sent claws of shadow deep into the crumbling masonry of the inside. A pair of smaller doors, mottled by wood mould and hanging from their hinges like rotten teeth, led to small rooms long fallen to disuse. At the end of a short corridor was a well of stairs leading up to the belfry and down to the cellar where the priests of old had stored beer and communed with the dead. Dusty hummocks of what looked like mouldering coats lay across the far end of the corridor around the mouth of the well.

'Down it is,' said Gotrek.

Nieder looked across. 'Why not up?'

The duardin gave a laugh. 'I wouldn't care to test my weight on that floor above us, and I've been looking to meet my doom since your god cheated death for the first time. Trust a dwarf. It will be down.'

Nieder said nothing, hanging deliberately back as Gotrek forged ahead.

One of the skin heaps stirred.

The Bone Kings of Nagash demanded endless tribute. Of blood. Of bone. Even of souls. But most of the human body, they shunned. Skin. Hair. Teeth. Materials that generations of Tithekeepers and a people hardened to despise waste had learned to make use of.

Nieder smiled through the pain of his face as the first skin hound rose up off the ground and sank its collection of human teeth into Gotrek's calf. The duardin bellowed in surprise as he fought to shake the thing loose, his efforts inadvertently rousing the rest of the pack from their torpor. There were nine in all. Each doggerel beast was a unique creation, a mangle of spliced parts put together in the most horrifically slight approximation of the canine they had been named for.

Gotrek succeeded in yanking the first creature's bloody jaws from his leg, just as the rest of the pack attacked. With the first hound held at arm's length, he tore open the leathery chest of the second with a blow from his axe. Stuffed innards of human hair went up like dried kindling, the golem beast bouncing off the near wall and scrabbling for footing, gummy jaws clapping even as it collapsed into flame.

Six more buried him in skin.

The ninth and last circled. It padded towards Nieder. Its head, sculpted into a canine snout, remained chillingly human. Its eyes, one brown and one blue, glimmered with lost intelligence, the faint wetness of an innocent on the brink of tears.

'No,' Nieder mumbled, struggling to speak clearly through his broken mouth. He held up an open hand as if to show the golem he was unarmed. He had lost his club in the street and had not thought at the time to pick it up. 'I brought him for you. I'm not with him.' The last words came out of him as a yelp as the skin hound lunged.

He dodged across the corridor. The skin hound hit the wall and rebounded, its tough hide rippling over soft-stuffed insides as it came back around. Nieder threw a punch. His fist walloped the side of its head and snapped it around, doing no damage whatsoever. Dead jaws champing, the skin hound snapped for his face as it bore him to the ground. Nieder got a hand under its throat and pushed it back, squeezing a last long-dead breath from its mouth and gagging on the stench. It heaved its weight against him and gnashed its teeth. Nieder beat against the side of its head with his other fist. It was like punching a bag of straw.

Suddenly the weight pushing down on him was no more. In its place came heat and a shower of stinking ash that had him coughing, then retching. He shook it off himself, and then sat up. In disbelief he looked around at the sight of eight skin hounds lying strewn and smouldering over the floor.

The ninth slid to the ground, its head mashed to a rag-doll flatness between Gotrek's fist and the wall. The duardin turned to glance at the skin hound with which Nieder had, prior to his intervention, been wrestling.

'Well fought, manling.'

Nieder tried to throw back something insulting, but the pain in his jaw turned the words to a hot-tempered gurgle that he spat, mixed with blood, onto the neck of his boot.

The duardin nodded as though agreeing with the sentiment, and then headed off for the stairs. Nieder picked himself up and followed.

There was another dead body at the bottom. This one was human, sprawled face down, half over the final two steps and half in the doorway that stood open at the bottom. Gotrek stepped over him and proceeded inside. Nieder crouched by the body. It was his junior partner, Hamnil. There was a slender knife stuck neatly between his shoulder blades. Nieder folded his fist around the delicate throwing handle and pulled it out in a spurt of blood.

'Well, well,' came Gotrek's rough voice from inside. 'I should have known you wouldn't need all that much saving.'

Leaving Hamnil where he lay, Nieder got up, knife in hand, and followed the duardin inside.

He had been inside the Tithekeeper's preparation room before. Many times. Though he had spent as little time there as he could get away with, and had never seen it properly as he did now. Ceramic urns marked with the dead hieroglyphic characters of the Bone Kings were stacked up high against the walls, filled, he supposed, with bone and neatly packed phylacteries of souls. Human skins, stretched taut over wooden frames, faced the tiny windows, there to cure in the weak Shyishan sun, though it was firelight that flickered in the ancient panes now. At the centre of the basement chamber was a table. The belfry's original priesthood had probably had a more innocent use for the drain that lay beneath it.

The aelf woman sitting cross-legged upon the table glanced up as Gotrek and Nieder entered, as though distracted from the important task of scraping blood from her fingernails.

'You took your time, Gotrek.'

'Well, if you wander off in the middle of the night and get yourself kidnapped...'

'Tears of Khaine, Gotrek, how much more of that rat poison did you drink after I left? I did not *wander off*.' She shook her head in mock despair. 'I went to take a look around. The appraising looks. The strange comments these people would make to one another when they were happy no *human* could still hear them. Only this one decided to follow me out.' She nodded to the corpse by the door. As though recognising Nieder's presence for the first time, she held out her hand and smiled the most insincere smile he had ever seen. 'Be a darling and give me that knife you found, would you?'

Nieder hung his head and meekly handed it back.

'I don't recall any of this,' Gotrek huffed.

'Sweet thing,' the aelf said to Nieder. 'Any friend of Gotrek's is a friend of mine.' She turned to the duardin and scowled. 'Somehow I do not have it in me any more to be surprised.'

'You don't have any more sharp objects hidden away under all that do you?' said Gotrek.

'A lady needs to have some secrets.'

Gotrek snorted.

'He's dead,' Nieder mumbled, looking across to where Hamnil lay in the doorway.

'Yes,' said the aelf. 'Pity. But he made two unfortunate life choices. The first was attempting to tie up and drug a Shadowblade of Khaine. The second was failing to tell me anything at all about this Bone King and his legion when I asked.'

'Oh well,' said Gotrek. 'We've done our good deed for the week the way I see it.'

The aelf shrugged, sitting upright on the cutting table and licking the throwing knife clean with every sign of delight before stabbing it back into its concealed sheath.

Gotrek made an ugly face. 'You make me sick, you know that? Like a vampire bloody kitten.'

The aelf laughed, as beautiful as broken glass, and turned to examine the urns stacked against the wall. 'What do you propose we do with these?'

'Can you read what's written on them?' said Gotrek.

'The dead languages of darkest Shyish were not a part of the temple's curriculum.'

'Then here's what I propose...'

Before Nieder could realise what the duardin intended, Gotrek had cracked open the closest urn with the flat butt of his axe. Bits of bone and pottery spilled across the chamber floor, following the shallow decline towards the blood drain. He broke another. Then another. Moving with a grim and set intent until the entire floor was carpeted in broken pottery. Nieder watched it happen. Saying nothing. Doing nothing. Wondering how many urns the bodies left in the Bone Drake and in the street outside of it would fill. How many more would need to be found before the Bone Kings came over the Marrow Hills and crossed the Sunken Sea in search of their tribute.

'Another grateful town saved,' said Gotrek, clapping the dust and grime of evil deeds well done from his enormous hands. He bared his big, blunt teeth at Nieder. 'I wonder if there's anywhere left in this town that does breakfast.'

ABOUT THE AUTHORS

David Guymer's work for Black Library includes the
Warhammer Age of Sigmar novels *Kragnos: Avatar of
Destruction, Hamilcar: Champion of the Gods* and *The Court
of the Blind King,* and the audio dramas *Realmslayer* and
Realmslayer: Blood of the Old World. He is also the author
of the Gotrek & Felix novels *Slayer, Kinslayer* and *City of the
Damned.* For The Horus Heresy he has written the Primarchs
novels *Ferrus Manus: Gorgon of Medusa* and *Lion El'Jonson:
Lord of the First.* For Warhammer 40,000 he has written
Angron: The Red Angel and *The Eye of Medusa,* amongst others.
He is a freelance writer and occasional scientist based in the
East Riding, and was a finalist in the 2014 David Gemmell
Awards for his novel *Headtaker.*

Darius Hinks is the author of the Warhammer 40,000 novels
Leviathan, Blackstone Fortress, Blackstone Fortress: Ascension
and the accompanying audio drama *The Beast Inside.* He also
wrote three novels in the Mephiston series: *Blood of Sanguinius,
Revenant Crusade* and *City of Light,* as well as the Space Marine
Battles novella *Sanctus.* His work for Age of Sigmar includes
Dominion, Hammers of Sigmar, Warqueen and the Gotrek
Gurnisson novels *Ghoulslayer, Gitslayer* and *Soulslayer.* For
Warhammer, he wrote *Warrior Priest,* which won the David
Gemmell Morningstar Award for best newcomer, as well as
the Orion trilogy, *Sigvald* and several novellas.

Robbie MacNiven is a Highlands-born History graduate from
the University of Edinburgh. He has written the Warhammer
Age of Sigmar novel *Scourge of Fate* and the Gotrek Gurnisson
novella *The Bone Desert,* as well as the Warhammer 40,000
novels *Oaths of Damnation, Blood of Iax, The Last Hunt,
Carcharodons: Red Tithe, Carcharodons: Outer Dark* and
Legacy of Russ. His short stories include 'Redblade', 'A Song for
the Lost' and 'Blood and Iron'. His hobbies include re-enacting,
football and obsessing over Warhammer 40,000.

YOUR NEXT READ

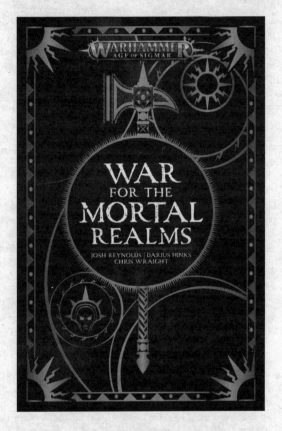

WAR FOR THE MORTAL REALMS
by Josh Reynolds, Darius Hinks & Chris Wraight

For the first time, the tumultuous saga of the Mortal Realms is told in a single volume, featuring the novella *The Gates of Azyr* by Chris Wraight, and the novels *Soul Wars* by Josh Reynolds and *Dominion* by Darius Hinks.

THE HOLLOW KING
by John French

Cado Ezechiar, a cursed Soulblight vampire, seeks salvation for those he failed at the fall of his kingdom. His quest for vengeance leads him to Aventhis, a city caught in a tangled web of war and deceit that Cado must successfully navigate, or lose everything.

YOUR
NEXT READ

BAD LOON RISING
by Andy Clark

Zograt was once a puny runt of a grot, but thanks to his brilliant cunning, the blessing of the Bad Moon, and a loyal troggoth, he's now ready to prove himself the greatest Loonboss ever.